Henry James: Selected Fiction

Henry James
SELECTED FICTION

Edited, with an introduction and notes, by

Leon Edel

A Dutton *Paperback*

NEW YORK

E. P. DUTTON

This paperback edition of
"Henry James: Selected Fiction"
First published 1964 by E. P. Dutton & Co., Inc.

Published simultaneously in Canada by Clarke, Irwin and Company Limited, Toronto and Vancouver.

SBN 0-525-47140-5

ACKNOWLEDGMENTS

Grateful acknowledgment is made to the following publishers for permission to reprint selections from works in copyright: Oxford University Press, Inc., New York, *for* the excerpts from *The Notebooks of Henry James,* edited by F. O. Matthiessen and Kenneth B. Murdock; copyright 1947 by Oxford University Press, Inc., used by permission of the publishers; Charles Scribner's Sons, New York, *for* "The Beast in the Jungle" reprinted from *The Better Sort* by Henry James; copyright 1903 by Charles Scribner's Sons, 1931 by Henry James, used by permission of the publishers; *for* "The Jolly Corner" reprinted from "The New York Edition" of *The Novels and Tales of Henry James,* Volume XVII; copyright 1909 by Charles Scribner's Sons, 1937 by Henry James, used by permission of the publishers; *for* Preface selection from Volume XI and "The Pupil" reprinted from "The New York Edition" of *The Novels and Tales of Henry James,* Volume XI; copyright 1908 by Charles Scribner's Sons, 1936 by Henry James, used by permission of the publishers; *for* Preface selection from Volume XII and "The Aspern Papers" reprinted from "The New York Edition" of *The Novels and Tales of Henry James,* Volume XII; copyright 1908 by Charles Scribner's Sons, 1936 by Henry James, used by permission of the publishers; *for* Preface selection from Volume XVII reprinted from "The New York Edition" of *The Novels and Tales of Henry James,* Volume XVII; copyright 1909 by Charles Scribner's Sons, 1937 by Henry James, used by permission of the publishers; *for* Preface selection from Volume XVIII and "Daisy Miller" reprinted from "The New York Edition" of *The Novels and Tales of Henry James,* Volume XVIII; copyright 1909 by Charles Scribner's Sons, 1937 by Henry James, used by permission of the publishers.

HENRY JAMES, brother of William James, the philosopher, was born in New York on April 15, 1843. He was educated at Harvard University and in England, France and Switzerland. The first literary work to win him international renown was *Daisy Miller* (1879). As his style matured, James produced such masterworks as *The Portrait of a Lady* (1881), *The Wings of the Dove* (1902), *The Ambassadors* (1903) and *The Golden Bowl* (1904). He settled at "Lamb House" in Rye, England in 1896 and became naturalized as a British subject in 1915. James was awarded the Order of Merit in 1916 and died in London on February 28, 1916.

CONTENTS

INTRODUCTION

THIS GROUP of stories and a short novel by Henry James are selected from three decades of his writing. The first story is of 1879, when he was thirty-six; the last is of 1909, when he was sixty-six. Arranged chronologically—and read in that order—the works here given show the artist's progression from a narrative of crystal simplicity to one of rich and elaborate complexity; his growth from maturity to greater maturity, from the creation of a formal, varnished beauty to a beauty deep and intricate.

The stories exemplify also different types of fiction written by Henry James: there is an "international" tale, a ghostly tale, a story about the "sense of the past," tales dealing with the anxieties of "poor sensitive gentlemen," a story of childhood and a short novel whose setting—like that of the ghostly tale—is the American scene, New York, the city of James's birth. Running through all the tales, no matter how we classify them, are those themes which we have come to regard as essentially "Jamesian." An American girl in Europe is faced with a "social rumpus" that goes on entirely over her head ("Daisy Miller"); a curiosity-mad "publishing scoundrel" seeks to pluck secrets out of a reluctant past ("The Aspern Papers"); a boy suffers from the mendacity of his parents ("The Pupil"); a man is haunted by his sense of a special fate reserved for him ("The Beast in the Jungle"); a man is haunted by the image of what he might have been ("The Jolly Corner").

A Henry James story, however, cannot with justice be reduced to such bare statement. The Old World and the New, for instance, is the larger theme of "Daisy Miller," and Past and Present is the larger theme of "The Aspern

Papers." But Past and Present are also the Old and the New, and so in a sense Henry James is dealing with the same inner substance in both these tales, even though the stories themselves are poles apart. And there is, in each tale, a deep moral value. The man who sets out to obtain the Aspern papers from the immortal Juliana is meddling with the Past; the American social set in Rome, which attempts to rearrange Daisy Miller's life, is meddling—with the Present, with innocence.

Similarly we can find golden threads that link "Daisy" with "The Beast in the Jungle." What both these tales have in common are men who have no understanding of women. We see the little drama of Daisy develop through the eyes of the expatriate American, Frederick Winterbourne; and he, as his frosty name suggests, is a very stuffy gentleman, who never can quite make up his mind whether Daisy is an outrageous flirt or a young innocent. "The Beast in the Jungle," on its side, is set in the very consciousness of a gentleman whose name is John Marcher, only a little less frosty, but just as chilly as Winterbourne. Marcher is totally incapable of entering into the feelings of his devoted friend, May Bartram. Thus in the one story a Daisy is withered by a wintry man and in the other a mature woman, whose name stands for springtime and sunshine, is chilled by a man whose name identifies him with the month of March. Winterbourne and Marcher!—in the whole of James's fiction they stand as arch-examples of men who see life only in the flickering light of their own troubled egoes. At the end of each story, the one has failed to understand Daisy and the other May, and both are face to face with their failures, in a cemetery, by the graves of the women they should have loved.

In noting the similarities between these stories we must, however, not lose sight of their profound differences. A difference of time separates them, twenty-five years, a profound change in style, in manner, in method. The earlier James—the one who became famous on both sides of the

Atlantic with this little story of Daisy—was addicted largely to the recording of external action, allowing the characters to develop before us through the things they say and do. The later James, no less addicted to the theory of self-revelation of his characters, shows us the thoughts that govern their actions; a spirit of painful reverie hangs over "The Beast in the Jungle" as James probes Marcher's anxieties and fears. Marcher, in a curious way, is like a character in Dostoievsky, although he functions at the opposite emotional pole from the personages of the Russian master.

II

Henry James's continual growth and development throughout his life makes the study of his work much more difficult than that of other novelists. We have to read more of him before we can generalize and we have to take into consideration individual works in each of the different phases of his creativity. We can, after reading certain representative works of Dickens, speak of "a Dickens novel." By the same token we can speak easily of "a Mark Twain novel" or even "a Robert Louis Stevenson novel"—to choose writers of fiction who were, like James, more productive than most. But can we really speak of "a Henry James novel"? Do we mean for instance *Washington Square* or *What Maisie Knew? The Portrait of a Lady* or *The Awkward Age? Roderick Hudson* or *The Sacred Fount?* A writer addicted to changes of subject and mood and to constant variations in technique could not expect his audience to be consistently loyal. Henry James won and lost more publics than most writers do during a lifetime—except during the phase when he exploited the theme of Americans abroad and Europeans in America. If James's readers had had their wish, he would have gone on creating Daisy Millers and Francie Dossons, Christopher Newmans and Pandora Days all his life. But he grew tired of the "international theme" and he was artist enough to seek out new subjects, new experiments. The central problem in his creative life—and what artist doesn't face it at some time or other?—was how to reconcile his artistic inclination with what was wanted in the literary marketplace. A professional to his finger-tips, he tried to combine art with potboiling. This required considerable sleight of hand. In his case art nearly always won. The process was frustrating, inevitably, as James's tales of unhappy writers show.

It was frustrating, but it also had its rewards. For, in his constant experimentation, James arrived at those important innovations in form which earned him the title of "Master" among his peers—if he can be said to have had a peer where techniques were concerned. There are few novelists writing today who have not, directly or indirectly, absorbed some of James's methods of storytelling. His most important innovation was to free the novel, and the short story, of the traditionally ubiquitous and often garrulous narrator who used to interpose his own personality and preachments between the story and the reader.

A confirmed realist, Henry James once accused Trollope of a "betrayal of a sacred office" because in his fiction the English novelist on occasions inserted asides reassuring the reader that after all the book was only "making believe." Henry James never could be accused of make-believe. If the novelist was a historian, as James insisted he was, a recorder of social history, manners, the life of his time, it was his duty to render this life with care and fidelity and truth. And if it was thus rendered, it could not be make-believe; it was as real as anything painted by a painter. In his search for viable forms to frame reality and sustain it, Henry James not only cut the strings of the balloon of fiction and sent it soaring away from himself, but he frequently stowed the reader into the basket before doing so. His art was so cunning that many readers, even today, take the journey in the belief they are upon the ground with the author rather than in the air with the story.

III

This scrupulous care in maintaining what James came to call "the point of view" is to be found in nearly all of James's fiction. I have said that Winterbourne gives us our view of Daisy, and makes us participate in his bewilderment. So, in "The Aspern Papers" James uses the first-person narrative to tell the story of the great Juliana and her valuable hoard of documents and arrives at a sustained effect since we read in the light of the narrator's own passion for the past as well as the candor with which he reveals his lack of scruple. The use of the point of view is particularly striking in "The Pupil," where we have two mirrors turned upon the situation: James gives us "little Morgan's troubled vision" of his family "as reflected in the vision, also troubled enough, of his devoted friend."

In "The Jolly Corner" and in "The Beast in the Jungle" we are inside the minds of the two troubled gentlemen, Spencer Brydon, whose vigil in the old house of his childhood on lower Fifth Avenue leads him to confront himself *as he might have been;* and Marcher, who gets his revelation of the great emptiness of his life—but too late. In these tales, tales sustained in mood and revelatory of inner tensions, James is foreshadowing the "internal monologue" of our time. By this method, the novelist comes closest to infusing a quality of poetry into his fiction. He is rendering the very "atmosphere of the mind."

The one story in this collection which is written in the conventional manner of nineteenth-century fiction, and where we are constantly aware of the novelist himself as narrator, is *Washington Square.* This short novel first was serialized in *Harper's* during 1880 with illustrations by George Du Maurier. It deals with the New York of Henry James's childhood. It had its origin in a story told James by his actress friend, the celebrated Fanny Kemble, who mentioned that her brother had jilted an English heiress, a dull girl with $20,000 a year. To receive a usable idea of this sort meant, with Henry James, a complete imaginative reworking of theme; and the Fanny Kemble anecdote emerged as a slender but vivid story, moved from the Old World into the New, into old New York, and turned into the drama of Catherine Sloper and her martinet father, in their house on the Square, the romantic aunt and the predatory suitor. The story has a certain Jane Austenish quality given the narrow and well-defined limits of scene, action and drama; but it is much closer to Balzac, who was invariably Henry James's model when he tried to "do" minutely such a scene. One thinks of *Eugénie Grandet* as having been in Henry James's mind as a model, but as is the case with all "influence" and all sources, where a great imaginative mind is concerned, these are but points of departure for the operation of an individual creativity. The model and the source become mere ingredients and before the work is completed have been totally absorbed. Technically *Washington Square* is superior to Balzac's love story of a girl for her cousin. The Jamesian drama moves in a straight line, the focus is entirely on Catherine and her dilemma. The Balzac work shifts in focus and lacks the sustained unity of its American successor.

The novel has been criticized for giving but a scant picture of old New York. It has been argued that the story could just as easily have been set in some other country. The fact remains that James has caught the quality of those outwardly "quiet lives" that were lived in the old elegant houses in "uptown" Manhattan of the early century: and they are American lives. We can detect also marked tenderness for the scene as exemplified in one passage James inserted in the novel, a rare passage indeed for any fiction of his. He calls it a "topographical parenthesis" but it comes much closer to being autobiography than topography—or fiction. "I know not," James writes of Washington Square, "whether it is owing to the tenderness of early associations but this portion of New York appears to many persons the most delectable." There is little doubt whose "early associations" are being invoked, for he goes on to say:

"It was here, as you might have been informed on good authority, that you had come into a world which appeared to offer a variety of sources of interest; it was here that your grandmother lived, in venerable solitude, and dispensed a hospitality which commended itself alike to the infant imagination and the infant palate; it was here that you took your first walks abroad, following the nurserymaid with unequal step and sniffing up the strange odour of the ailanthus-trees which at the time formed the principal umbrage of the Square, and diffused an aroma that you were not yet critical enough to dislike as it deserved; it was here, finally, that your first school, kept by a broad-bosomed, broad-based old lady with a ferule, who was always having tea in a blue cup, with a saucer that didn't match, enlarged the circle both of your observations and your sensations."

We know that Henry James could have written "I" in the above paragraph every time that he wrote "you." For he has set down here a passage of his own life and revealed to us at the same time how retentive the memory of that small boy in the New York of the late 1840's and early 1850's was. He remembered that the saucer didn't match the cup; the ferule probably was easier to remember, being an instrument that sometimes can be menacing; and the odour of the ailanthus, recalled by James later as unpleasant, gives to this passage a quality—in its attention to the senses—almost Proustian. James's excuse for this barely concealed introduction of moments from his own childhood was that "it was here . . . that my heroine spent many years of her life." If Henry James was not born right on the Square, as this passage suggests, he came into this world at 21 Washington Place, a few doors from it, where New York University stands today. His maternal grandmother lived on the Square and in his memoirs we can easily find the teacher with the ferule.

Late in life Henry James came to consider *Washington*

Square a "meagre" work, perhaps because it contains none of his technical devices. He excluded it from the selective edition of his novels and tales. Posterity has disagreed with his judgment and the story has come to be regarded as an American classic, not only because it catches an atmosphere long gone but because, for all its easy-going narrative, it is a tight little drama—as the play *The Heiress* derived from it, proved. Much Jamesian dialogue was bodily incorporated into that drama from the novel and with little change, so artfully did he address it always to the ear.

IV

In these tales, then, within the lively and witty narrative, the even-surfaced tone, the evocation of the spirit of near and faraway places, the creation of a mood, Henry James tells us that in our world there are persons who show no respect for the sanctity of the individual, who freely meddle in the lives of other individuals, who are blind to the tender vessels of feeling that are children and adolescents, and who use them cruelly as pawns in the clumsy game of their own muddled lives; persons who live in a tiptoe world of fear, an agony of anxiety and wasted passion because of nightmares residing in their own minds; and persons who, in the house of life, wander in mortal terror lest they may encounter—themselves! These are not moral preachings. Henry James never sits in judgment; nor does he hold up to the reader any given course of conduct. He sets forth his "observation and testimony" in the form of fundamental propositions drawn from his own life and his insight into the lives of others. He seeks, in his stories, not to set down some moral law, as certain critics insist, but to arrive at concretions of feeling and experience. He did recognize, however, that there was "one point at which the moral sense and the artistic sense lie very near together; that is in the light of the very obvious truth that the deepest quality of a work of art will always be the quality of the mind of the producer."

At every point in the work of Henry James we are made aware of the fine intelligence that insists upon our observing the maximum that is to be seen, whether it is people, or their setting, or a problem in conduct, or the atmosphere of a place, or, indeed, a whole fragment of social history. If "Daisy Miller" deals with the relationship between Daisy and Winterbourne, it at the same time tells us a great deal about the life and the standards of expatriate Americans just as *Washington Square* tells us how wealthy New Yorkers of the mid-nineteenth century took the measure of their lives. The quality of mind of the author may be felt in every tale, and it is seen best when it probes the delicate relations between persons, as in the case of Morgan Moreen and his tutor, or Marcher and May Bartram.

This story ("The Beast in the Jungle") has by degrees come to be regarded as among the greatest of Henry James's tales. By use of symbols and names—symbols of unashamed simplicity—he gives to his story a series of muted overtones that act as a kind of musical score, *pianissimo,* for the tale. In using the months to name his characters—March and May—in having the two meet in a country house named Weatherend, suggesting temporal changes and the seasons, James establishes at once the "tone of time" that is so important for this tale. The surface of its story, with its tense, slow rhythm, gives the effect of long, wasted, futile years within which the symbolic beast is crouched for the spring. We follow Marcher's spiritual adventure through this time-jungle, to the moment when the lurking beast finally rises for its final leap—the Beast that symbolizes the fear of himself, the fear to do, the blinding fear that shuts his eyes to his own passion and to the ultimate moral truth that in this world love belongs only to those who can give it to others; and that those who cannot give it are incapable of recognizing it when they receive it, because of the blindness of their own egotism. The story is one of the profoundest of our time as it is, psychologically, one of the truest.

One day during the summer of 1888 Henry James wrote to Robert Louis Stevenson: "I want to leave a multitude of pictures of my time, projecting my small circular frame upon as many different spots as possible and going in for number as well as quality, so that the number may constitute a total having a certain value as observation and testimony." The stories in this book, taken as a whole, do have this value. They must be read, however, not so much as prose narratives but as if they were plays, on the stage, in which the reader, as the playgoer, is asked to follow closely what goes on. James always demanded attentive reading; and, read attentively, he rewards the reader with stories that are not merely accounts of things that happened, but which are perfect works of art. He is recognized today as an American writer who brought the novel, on our side of the water, to a precocious maturity and by the same token altered the whole course of the English novel's history as an art form. He passed, in his fiction, from the novel of outward detail to an ultimately disfurnished novel in which only enough scenery is on the stage to serve the needs of his actors. In the same process, he transferred analysis of character and motives into the mind. If England can boast that in the nineteenth century it had a George Eliot who gave the novel a finer purity of design and made of it a more exalted literary form, if France can boast that with Flaubert the novel attained a great architecture and acquired tools it had never before possessed, America can say that after them came Henry James to set in order the whole House of Fiction.

V

Henry James left a large body of comment on the art of fiction. Toward the end of his life he recorded, in a series of remarkable prefaces, the "story" of his stories—not only their genesis, but the ruling theories that had guided him. Although the novelist destroyed most of his personal papers, there has survived a series of his notebooks and these, edited by the late F. O. Matthiessen and by Kenneth B. Murdock, were published in 1947.

In order to give the readers of this volume a picture of the growth of a Jamesian story, it has been thought apposite to append to each tale that portion of the preface in the New York Edition referring to it, together with—where such notes survived—the notebook entries made when the idea of the story first came to James. In this way it is possible to see the planting of the first seed, its growth, and finally the author's own recollections and comment upon the finished work. Where necessary, I have added such relevant editorial notes as might clarify certain allusions and bridge the gaps between the original note and the final preface.

James's historic essay "The Art of Fiction" written in 1884 and published in a volume of essays, *Partial Portraits,* in 1888, has been included here not only because it is his finest statement, in compact form, about the art he practiced, but because it in turn illuminates the working notes and the prefaces. The essay remains, after almost three quarters of a century, a great manifesto on a great art and the basic truths it contains apply to fiction in our time as in Henry James's.

James was an inveterate reviser of his writings. While not all critics agree on his late revisions of his early works, scholars who have carefully compared the different texts are unanimous in pointing out that most of the changes usually clarify and heighten the artistic surface of James's prose. In the light of this, the texts of the stories here selected are printed from the definitive versions.

LEON EDEL

New York University
March 1953

A SELECTED BIBLIOGRAPHY OF HENRY JAMES

Selected Separate Works: NOVELS—*Roderick Hudson,* 1876; *The American,* 1877; *The Portrait of a Lady,* 1881; *The Bostonians,* 1886; *The Princess Casamassima,* 1886; *The Tragic Muse,* 1890; *The Spoils of Poynton,* 1897; *What Maisie Knew,* 1897; *The Awkward Age,* 1899; *The Sacred Fount,* 1901; *The Wings of the Dove,* 1902; *The Ambassadors,* 1903; *The Golden Bowl,* 1904; *The Ivory Tower,* 1917; *The Sense of the Past,* 1917.

Selected Separate Works: STORIES & SHORT NOVELS (*Dates are those of first book publication*)—"Madame de Mauves," 1875; "The Madonna of the Future," 1875; "A Passionate Pilgrim," 1875; *The Europeans,* 1878; "Daisy Miller," 1879; "Four Meetings," 1879; "An International Episode," 1879; "A Bundle of Letters," 1880; "The Pension Beaurepas," 1881; *Washington Square,* 1881; "The Point of View," 1883; "The Siege of London," 1883; "Lady Barbarina," 1884; "A New England Winter," 1884; "The Author of Beltraffio," 1885; "A Day of Days," 1885; "A Light Man," 1885; "A Most Extraordinary Case," 1885; "Pandora," 1885; "The Aspern Papers," 1888; "Louisa Pallant," 1888; *The Reverberator,* 1888; "The Liar," 1889; "A London Life," 1889; "The Patagonia," 1889; "Brooksmith," 1892; "The Lesson of the Master," 1892; "The Marriages," 1892; "The Pupil," 1892; "Sir Edmund Orme," 1892; "The Chaperon," 1893; "Greville Fane," 1893; "Owen Wingrave," 1893; "The Private Life," 1893; "The Real Thing," 1893; "The Altar of the Dead," 1895; "The Coxon Fund," 1895; "The Death of the Lion," 1895; "The Middle Years," 1895; "The Figure in the Carpet," 1896; "Glasses," 1896; "The Next Time," 1896; *In the Cage,* 1898; "The Turn of the Screw," 1898;

"The Abasement of the Northmores," 1900; "Europe," 1900; "The Great Good Place," 1900; "Miss Gunton of Poughkeepsie," 1900; "Paste," 1900; "The Real Right Thing," 1900; "The Tree of Knowledge," 1900; "The Beast in the Jungle," 1903; "The Beldonald Holbein," 1903; "The Birthplace," 1903; "Broken Wings," 1903; "Flickerbridge," 1903; "Mrs. Medwin," 1903; "The Story in It," 1903; "The Two Faces," 1903; "Fordham Castle," 1909; "The Friends of the Friends," 1909; "The Jolly Corner," 1909; *Julia Bride,* 1909; "The Bench of Desolation," 1910; "A Round of Visits," 1910.

Selected Separate Works: NON-FICTION PROSE—*French Poets and Novelists,* 1878; *Hawthorne,* 1879; *Partial Portraits,* 1888; *Essays in London and Elsewhere,* 1893; *The Question of Our Speech/The Lesson of Balzac,* 1905; *Views and Reviews,* 1908; *A Small Boy and Others,* 1913 (autobiography); *Notes on Novelists with Some Other Notes,* 1914; *Notes of a Son and Brother,* 1914 (autobiography); *The Middle Years,* 1917 (autobiography).

Collected Editions: *The Novels and Tales of Henry James,* New York, 1907-1909 (the New York Edition for which James revised the texts and provided prefaces—24 volumes); *The Novels and Stories of Henry James,* London, 1921-1923, edited by Percy Lubbock (35 volumes); *The Complete Plays of Henry James,* Philadelphia, 1949, edited by Leon Edel; *Eight Uncollected Tales of Henry James,* New Brunswick, 1950, edited by Edna Kenton.

Selections and Edited Texts: *The Letters of Henry James,* New York, 1920, edited by Percy Lubbock; *The Art of the Novel: Critical Prefaces,* New York, 1934, edited by R. P. Blackmur; *Henry James: Representative Selections,* Cincinnati, 1941, edited by Lyon P. Richardson; *The Great Short Novels of Henry James,* New York, 1944, edited by Philip Rahv; *The Short Stories of Henry James,* New York, 1945, edited by Clifton Fadiman; *The American Scene,* New York, 1946, edited by W. H. Auden; *Henry James: Stories of Artists and Writers,* New York, 1946, edited by F. O. Matthiessen; *The American Novels and Stories of Henry James,* New York, 1947, edited by F. O. Matthiessen; *The Notebooks of Henry James,* New York, 1947, edited by F. O. Matthiessen and Kenneth B. Murdock; *The Art of Fiction and Other Essays,* New York, 1948, edited by Morris Roberts; *The Ghostly Tales of Henry James,* New Brunswick, 1948, edited by Leon Edel; *The Scenic Art: Notes on Acting and the Drama,* 1872-1901, New Brunswick, 1948, edited by Allan Wade; *The American,* New York, 1949, edited by Joseph Warren Beach; *The Aspern Papers/The Europeans,* New York, 1950, edited by Joseph M. Bottkol; *Selected Short Stories,* New York, 1950, edited by Quentin Anderson; *The Portrait of a Lady,* New York, 1951, edited by Fred B. Millett; *The Portable Henry James,* New York, 1951, edited by Morton Dauwen Zabel; *The Golden Bowl,* New York, 1952, edited by R. P. Blackmur; *The Sacred Fount,* New York, 1953, edited by Leon Edel.

Biography and Criticism: Leon Edel, *Henry James: The Untried Years, 1843-1870,* Philadelphia, 1953 (the first portion of a full biography of Henry James); Joseph Warren Beach, *The Method of Henry James,* New Haven, 1918; Van Wyck Brooks, *The Pilgrimage of Henry James,* New York, 1925; Henry Seidel Canby, *Turn West, Turn East,* New York, 1951; Frederick W. Dupee, *Henry James,* New York, 1951; Leon Edel, *The Prefaces of Henry James,* Paris, 1931; Cornelia P. Kelly, *The Early Development of Henry James,* Urbana, 1930; F. R. Leavis, "Henry James," in *The Great Tradition,* New York, 1949; F. O. Matthiessen, *Henry James: The Major Phase,* New York, 1944; Morris Roberts, *Henry James's Criticism,* Cambridge, Mass., 1929; Elizabeth Stevenson, *The Crooked Corridor: A Study of Henry James,* New York, 1949; Rebecca West, *Henry James,* London, 1916; *The Little Review,* Henry James Number, Vol. V, No. 4 (August 1918), pp. 1-64, prepared by Ezra Pound; *The Hound and Horn,* "Homage to Henry James," Vol. VII, No. 3 (April-June 1934), pp. 361-562, edited by Lincoln Kirstein; *The New Republic,* Memorial Issue on William and Henry James, Vol. CVIII, issue of February 15, 1943; *The Kenyon Review,* Henry James Number, Vol. V, No. 4 (Autumn 1943), pp. 481-617, edited by Robert Penn Warren; *The Question of Henry James,* New York, 1945, edited by Frederick W. Dupee.

Henry James: Selected Fiction

DAISY MILLER
1879

I

AT THE LITTLE TOWN of Vevey, in Switzerland, there is a particularly comfortable hotel; there are indeed many hotels, since the entertainment of tourists is the business of the place, which, as many travellers will remember, is seated upon the edge of a remarkably blue lake—a lake that it behoves every tourist to visit. The shore of the lake presents an unbroken array of establishments of this order, of every category, from the "grand hotel" of the newest fashion, with a chalk-white front, a hundred balconies, and a dozen flags flying from its roof, to the small Swiss pension of an elder day, with its name inscribed in German-looking lettering upon a pink or yellow wall and an awkward summer-house in the angle of the garden. One of the hotels at Vevey, however, is famous, even classical, being distinguished from many of its upstart neighbours by an air both of luxury and of maturity. In this region, through the month of June, American travellers are extremely numerous; it may be said indeed that Vevey assumes at that time some of the characteristics of an American watering-place. There are sights and sounds that evoke a vision, an echo, of Newport and Saratoga. There is a flitting hither and thither of "stylish" young girls, a rustling of muslin flounces, a rattle of dance-music in the morning hours, a sound of high-pitched voices at all times. You receive an impression of these things at the excellent inn of the "Trois Couronnes," and are transported in fancy to the Ocean House or to Congress Hall. But at the "Trois Couronnes," it must be added, there are other features much at variance with these suggestions: neat German waiters who look like secretaries of legation; Russian princesses sitting in the garden; little Polish boys walking about, held by the hand, with their governors; a view of the snowy crest of the Dent du Midi and the picturesque towers of the Castle of Chillon.

I hardly know whether it was the analogies or the differences that were uppermost in the mind of a young American, who, two or three years ago, sat in the garden of the "Trois Couronnes," looking about him rather idly at some of the graceful objects I have mentioned. It was a beautiful summer morning, and in whatever fashion the young American looked at things they must have seemed to him charming. He had come from Geneva the day before, by the little steamer, to see his aunt, who was staying at the hotel—Geneva having been for a long time his place of residence. But his aunt had a headache—his aunt had almost always a headache—and she was now shut up in her room smelling camphor, so that he was at liberty to wander about. He was some seven-and-twenty years of age; when his friends spoke of him they usually said that he was at Geneva "studying." When his enemies spoke of him they said—but after all he had no enemies: he was extremely amiable and generally liked. What I should say is simply that when certain persons spoke of him they conveyed that the reason of his spending so much time at Geneva was that he was extremely devoted to a lady who lived there—a foreign lady, a person older than himself. Very few Americans—truly I think none—had ever seen this lady, about whom there were some singular stories. But Winterbourne had an old attachment for the little capital of Calvinism; he had been put to school there as a boy and had afterwards even gone, on trial—trial of the grey old "Academy" on the steep and stony hillside—to college there; circumstances which had led to his forming a great many youthful friendships. Many of these he had kept, and they were a source of great satisfaction to him.

After knocking at his aunt's door and learning that she was indisposed he had taken a walk about the town and then he had come in to his breakfast. He had now finished that repast, but was enjoying a small cup of coffee which had been served him on a little table in the garden by one of the waiters who looked like *attachés*. At last he finished his coffee and lit a cigarette. Presently a small boy came walking along the path—an urchin of nine or ten. The child, who was diminutive for his years, had an aged expression of countenance, a pale complexion and sharp little features. He was dressed in knickerbockers and had red stockings that displayed his poor little spindle-shanks; he also wore a brilliant red cravat. He carried in his hand a long alpenstock, the sharp point of which he thrust into everything he approached—the flower-beds, the garden-benches, the trains of the ladies' dresses. In front of Winterbourne he paused, looking at him with a pair of bright and penetrating little eyes.

"Will you give me a lump of sugar?" he asked in a small sharp hard voice—a voice immature and yet somehow not young.

Winterbourne glanced at the light table near him, on which his coffee-service rested, and saw that several morsels of sugar remained. "Yes, you may take one," he answered; "but I don't think too much sugar good for little boys."

This little boy stepped forward and carefully selected three of the coveted fragments, two of which he buried in the pocket of his knickerbockers, depositing the other as promptly in another place. He poked his alpenstock, lance-fashion, into Winterbourne's bench and tried to crack the lump of sugar with his teeth.

"Oh blazes; it's har-r-d!" he exclaimed, divesting vowel and consonants, pertinently enough, of any taint of softness.

Winterbourne had immediately gathered that he might have the honour of claiming him as a countryman. "Take care you don't hurt your teeth," he said paternally.

"I haven't got any teeth to hurt. They've all come out. I've only got seven teeth. Mother counted them last night, and one came out right afterwards. She said she'd slap me if any more came out. I can't help it. It's this old Europe. It's the climate that makes them come out. In America they didn't come out. It's these hotels."

Winterbourne was much amused. "If you eat three lumps of sugar your mother will certainly slap you," he ventured.

"She's got to give me some candy then," rejoined his young interlocutor. "I can't get any candy here—any American candy. American candy's the best candy."

"And are American little boys the best little boys?" Winterbourne asked.

"I don't know. *I'm* an American boy," said the child.

"I see you're one of the best!" the young man laughed.

"Are you an American man?" pursued this vivacious infant. And then on his friend's affirmative reply, "American men are the best," he declared with assurance.

His companion thanked him for the compliment, and the child, who had now got astride of his alpenstock, stood looking about him while he attacked another lump of sugar. Winterbourne wondered if he himself had been like this in his infancy, for he had been brought to Europe at about the same age.

"Here comes my sister!" cried his young compatriot. "She's an American girl, you bet!"

Winterbourne looked along the path and saw a beautiful young lady advancing. "American girls are the best girls," he thereupon cheerfully remarked to his visitor.

"My sister ain't the best!" the child promptly returned "She's always blowing at me."

"I imagine that's your fault, not hers," said Winterbourne. The young lady meanwhile had drawn near. She was dressed in white muslin, with a hundred frills and flounces and knots of pale-coloured ribbon. Bareheaded, she balanced in her hand a large parasol with a deep border of embroidery; and she was strikingly, admirably pretty. "How pretty they are!" thought our friend, who straightened himself in his seat as if he were ready to rise.

The young lady paused in front of his bench, near the parapet of the garden, which overlooked the lake. The small boy had now converted his alpenstock into a vaulting-pole, by the aid of which he was springing about in the gravel and kicking it up not a little. "Why, Randolph," she freely began, "what *are* you doing?"

"I'm going up the Alps!" cried Randolph. "This is the way!" And he gave another extravagant jump, scattering the pebbles about Winterbourne's ears.

"That's the way they come down," said Winterbourne.

"He's an American man!" proclaimed Randolph in his harsh little voice.

The young lady gave no heed to this circumstance, but looked straight at her brother. "Well, I guess you'd better be quiet," she simply observed.

It seemed to Winterbourne that he had been in a manner presented. He got up and stepped slowly toward the charming creature, throwing away his cigarette. "This little boy and I have made acquaintance," he said with great civility. In Geneva, as he had been perfectly aware, a young man wasn't at liberty to speak to a young unmarried lady save under certain rarely-occurring conditions; but here at Vevey what conditions could be better than these?—a pretty American girl coming to stand in front of you in a garden with all the confidence in life. This pretty American girl, whatever that might prove, on hearing

Winterbourne's observation simply glanced at him; she then turned her head and looked over the parapet, at the lake and the opposite mountains. He wondered whether he had gone too far, but decided that he must gallantly advance rather than retreat. While he was thinking of something else to say the young lady turned again to the little boy, whom she addressed quite as if they were alone together. "I should like to know where you got that pole."

"I bought it!" Randolph shouted.

"You don't mean to say you're going to take it to Italy!"

"Yes, I'm going to take it t' Italy!" the child rang out.

She glanced over the front of her dress and smoothed out a knot or two of ribbon. Then she gave her sweet eyes to the prospect again. "Well, I guess you'd better leave it somewhere," she dropped after a moment.

"Are you going to Italy?" Winterbourne now decided very respectfully to enquire.

She glanced at him with lovely remoteness. "Yes, sir," she then replied. And she said nothing more.

"And are you—a—thinking of the Simplon?" he pursued with a slight drop of assurance.

"I don't know," she said. "I suppose it's some mountain. Randolph, what mountain are we thinking of?"

"Thinking of?"—the boy stared.

"Why going right over."

"Going to where?" he demanded.

"Why right down to Italy"—Winterbourne felt vague emulations.

"I don't know," said Randolph. "I don't want to go t' Italy. I want to go to America."

"Oh Italy's a beautiful place!" the young man laughed.

"Can you get candy there?" Randolph asked of all the echoes.

"I hope not," said his sister. "I guess you've had enough candy, and mother thinks so too."

"I haven't had any for ever so long—for a hundred weeks!" cried the boy, still jumping about.

The young lady inspected her flounces and smoothed her ribbons again; and Winterbourne presently risked an observation on the beauty of the view. He was ceasing to be in doubt, for he had begun to perceive that she was really not in the least embarrassed. She might be cold, she might be austere, she might even be prim; for that was apparently—he had already so generalised—what the most "distant" American girls did: they came and planted themselves straight in front of you to show how rigidly unapproachable they were. There hadn't been the slightest flush in her fresh fairness however; so that she was clearly neither offended nor fluttered. Only she was composed—he had seen that before too—of charming little parts that didn't match and that made no *ensemble;* and if she looked another way when he spoke to her, and seemed not particularly to hear him, this was simply her habit, her manner, the result of her having no idea whatever of "form" (with such a tell-tale appendage as Randolph where in the world would she have got it?) in any such connexion. As he talked a little more and pointed out some of the objects of interest in the view, with which she appeared wholly unacquainted, she gradually, none the less, gave him more of the benefit of her attention; and then he saw that act unqualified by the faintest shadow of reserve. It wasn't however what would have been called a "bold" front that she presented, for her expression was as decently limpid as the very cleanest water. Her eyes were the very prettiest conceivable, and indeed Winterbourne hadn't for a long time seen anything prettier than his fair countrywoman's various features—her complexion, her nose, her ears, her teeth. He took a great interest generally in that range of effects and was addicted to noting and, as it were, recording them; so that in regard to this young lady's face he made several observations. It wasn't at all insipid, yet at the same time wasn't pointedly—what point, on earth, could she ever make?—expressive; and though it offered such a collection of small finenesses and neatnesses he mentally accused it—very forgivingly—of a want of finish. He thought nothing more likely than that its wearer would have had her own experience of the action of her charms, as she would certainly have acquired a resulting confidence; but even should she depend on this for her main amusement her bright sweet superficial little visage gave out neither mockery nor irony. Before long it became clear that, however these things might be, she was much disposed to conversation. She remarked to Winterbourne that they were going to Rome for the winter—she and her mother and Randolph. She asked him if he was a "real American"; she wouldn't have taken him for one; he seemed more like a German—this flower was gathered as from a large field of comparison—especially when he spoke. Winterbourne, laughing, answered that he had met Germans who spoke like Americans, but not, so far as he remembered, any American with the resemblance she noted. Then he asked her if she mightn't be more at ease should she occupy the bench he had just quitted. She answered that she liked hanging round, but she none the less resignedly, after a little, dropped to the bench. She told him she was from New York State—"if you know where that is"; but our friend really quickened this current by catching hold of her small slippery brother and making him stand a few minutes by his side.

"Tell me your honest name, my boy." So he artfully proceeded.

In response to which the child was indeed unvarnished truth. "Randolph C. Miller. And I'll tell you hers." With which he levelled his alpenstock at his sister.

"You had better wait till you're asked!" said this young lady quite at her leisure.

"I should like very much to know *your* name," Winterbourne made free to reply.

"Her name's Daisy Miller!" cried the urchin. "But that ain't her real name; that ain't her name on her cards."

"It's a pity you haven't got one of my cards!" Miss Miller quite as naturally remarked.

"Her real name's Annie P. Miller," the boy went on.

It seemed, all amazingly, to do her good. "Ask him *his* now"—and she indicated their friend.

But to this point Randolph seemed perfectly indifferent; he continued to supply information with regard to his own family. "My father's name is Ezra B. Miller. My father ain't in Europe—he's in a better place than Europe." Winterbourne for a moment supposed this the manner in which the child had been taught to intimate that Mr. Miller had been removed to the sphere of celestial rewards. But Randolph immediately added: "My father's in Schenectady. He's got a big business. My father's rich, you bet."

"Well!" ejaculated Miss Miller, lowering her parasol and looking at the embroidered border. Winterbourne presently released the child, who departed, dragging his alpenstock along the path. "He don't like Europe," said the girl as with an artless instinct for historic truth. "He wants to go back."

"To Schenectady, you mean?"

"Yes, he wants to go right home. He hasn't got any boys here. There's one boy here, but he always goes round with a teacher. They won't let him play."

"And your brother hasn't any teacher?" Winterbourne enquired.

It tapped, at a touch, the spring of confidence. "Mother thought of getting him one—to travel round with us. There was a lady told her of a very good teacher; an American lady—perhaps you know her—Mrs. Sanders. I think she came from Boston. She told her of this teacher, and we thought of getting him to travel round with us. But Randolph said he didn't want a teacher travelling round with us. He said he wouldn't have lessons when he was in the cars. And we *are* in the cars about half the time.

There was an English lady we met in the cars—I think her name was Miss Featherstone; perhaps you know her. She wanted to know why I didn't give Randolph lessons—give him 'instruction,' she called it. I guess he could give me more instruction than I could give him. He's very smart."

"Yes," said Winterbourne; "he seems very smart."

"Mother's going to get a teacher for him as soon as we get t' Italy. Can you get good teachers in Italy?"

"Very good, I should think," Winterbourne hastened to reply.

"Or else she's going to find some school. He ought to learn some more. He's only nine. He's going to college." And in this way Miss Miller continued to converse upon the affairs of her family and upon other topics. She sat there with her extremely pretty hands, ornamented with very brilliant rings, folded in her lap, and with her pretty eyes now resting upon those of Winterbourne, now wandering over the garden, the people who passed before her and the beautiful view. She addressed her new acquaintance as if she had known him a long time. He found it very pleasant. It was many years since he had heard a young girl talk so much. It might have been said of this wandering maiden who had come and sat down beside him upon a bench that she chattered. She was very quiet, she sat in a charming tranquil attitude; but her lips and her eyes were constantly moving. She had a soft slender agreeable voice, and her tone was distinctly sociable. She gave Winterbourne a report of her movements and intentions, and those of her mother and brother, in Europe, and enumerated in particular the various hotels at which they had stopped. "That English lady in the cars," she said —"Miss Featherstone—asked me if we didn't all live in hotels in America. I told her I had never been in so many hotels in my life as since I came to Europe. I've never seen so many—it's nothing but hotels." But Miss Miller made this remark with no querulous accent; she appeared to be in the best humour with everything. She declared that the hotels were very good when once you got used to their ways and that Europe was perfectly entrancing. She wasn't disappointed—not a bit. Perhaps it was because she had heard so much about it before. She had ever so many intimate friends who had been there ever so many times, and that way she had got thoroughly posted. And then she had had ever so many dresses and things from Paris. Whenever she put on a Paris dress she felt as if she were in Europe.

"It was a kind of a wishing-cap," Winterbourne smiled.

"Yes," said Miss Miller at once and without examining this analogy; "it always made me wish I was here. But I needn't have done that for dresses. I'm sure they send all the pretty ones to America; you see the most frightful things here. The only thing I don't like," she proceeded, "is the society. There ain't any society—or if there is I don't know where it keeps itself. Do you? I suppose there's some society somewhere, but I haven't seen anything of it. I'm very fond of society and I've always had plenty of it. I don't mean only in Schenectady, but in New York. I used to go to New York every winter. In New York I had lots of society. Last winter I had seventeen dinners given me, and three of them were by gentlemen," added Daisy Miller. "I've more friends in New York than in Schenectady—more gentlemen friends; and more young lady friends too," she resumed in a moment. She paused again for an instant; she was looking at Winterbourne with all her prettiness in her frank gay eyes and in her clear rather uniform smile. "I've always had," she said, "a great deal of gentlemen's society."

Poor Winterbourne was amused and perplexed—above all he was charmed. He had never yet heard a young girl express herself in just this fashion; never at least save in cases where to say such things was to have at the same time some rather complicated consciousness about them. And yet was he to accuse Miss Daisy Miller of an actual or a potential *arrière-pensée,* as they said at Geneva? He felt he had lived at Geneva so long as to have got morally muddled; he had lost the right sense for the young American tone. Never indeed since he had grown old enough to appreciate things had he encountered a young compatriot of so "strong" a type as this. Certainly she was very charming, but how extraordinarily communicative and how tremendously easy! Was she simply a pretty girl from New York State—were they all like that, the pretty girls who had had a good deal of gentlemen's society? Or was she also a designing, an audacious, in short an expert young person? Yes, his instinct for such a question had ceased to serve him, and his reason could but mislead. Miss Daisy Miller looked extremely innocent. Some people had told him that after all American girls *were* exceedingly innocent, and others had told him that after all they weren't. He must on the whole take Miss Daisy Miller for a flirt—a pretty American flirt. He had never as yet had relations with representatives of that class. He had known here in Europe two or three women—persons older than Miss Daisy Miller and provided, for respectability's sake, with husbands—who were great coquettes; dangerous terrible women with whom one's light commerce might indeed take a serious turn. But this charming apparition wasn't a coquette in that sense; she was very unsophisticated; she was only a pretty American flirt. Winterbourne was almost grateful for having found the formula that applied to Miss Daisy Miller. He leaned back in his seat; he remarked to himself that she had the finest little nose he had ever seen; he wondered what were the regular conditions and limitations of one's intercourse with a pretty American flirt. It presently became apparent that he was on the way to learn.

"Have you been to that old castle?" the girl soon asked, pointing with her parasol to the far-shining walls of the Château de Chillon.

"Yes, formerly, more than once," said Winterbourne. "You too, I suppose, have seen it?"

"No, we haven't been there. I want to go there dreadfully. Of course I mean to go there. I wouldn't go away from here without having seen that old castle."

"It's a very pretty excursion," the young man returned, "and very easy to make. You can drive, you know, or you can go by the little steamer."

"You can go in the cars," said Miss Miller.

"Yes, you can go in the cars," Winterbourne assented.

"Our courier says they take you right up to the castle," she continued. "We were going last week, but mother gave out. She suffers dreadfully from dyspepsia. She said she couldn't any more go—!" But this sketch of Mrs. Miller's plea remained unfinished. "Randolph wouldn't go either; he says he don't think much of old castles. But I guess we'll go this week if we can get Randolph."

"Your brother isn't interested in ancient monuments?" Winterbourne indulgently asked.

He now drew her, as he guessed she would herself have said, every time. "Why no, he says he don't care much about old castles. He's only nine. He wants to stay at the hotel. Mother's afraid to leave him alone, and the courier won't stay with him; so we haven't been to many places. But it will be too bad if we don't go up there." And Miss Miller pointed again at the Château de Chillon.

"I should think it might be arranged," Winterbourne was thus emboldened to reply. "Couldn't you get some one to stay—for the afternoon—with Randolph?"

Miss Miller looked at him a moment, and then with all serenity, "I wish *you'd* stay with him!" she said.

He pretended to consider it. "I'd much rather go to Chillon with you."

"With me?" she asked without a shadow of emotion.

She didn't rise blushing, as a young person at Geneva would have done; and yet, conscious that he had gone very far, he thought it possible she had drawn back. "And with your mother," he answered very respectfully.

But it seemed that both his audacity and his respect

were lost on Miss Daisy Miller. "I guess mother wouldn't go—for *you,*" she smiled. "And she ain't much *bent* on going, anyway. She don't like to ride round in the afternoon." After which she familiarly proceeded: "But did you really mean what you said just now—that you'd like to go up there?"

"Most earnestly I meant it," Winterbourne declared.

"Then we may arrange it. If mother will stay with Randolph I guess Eugenio will."

"Eugenio?" the young man echoed.

"Eugenio's our courier. He doesn't like to stay with Randolph—he's the most fastidious man I ever saw. But he's a splendid courier. I guess he'll stay at home with Randolph if mother does, and then we can go to the castle."

Winterbourne reflected for an instant as lucidly as possible: "we" could only mean Miss Miller and himself. This prospect seemed almost too good to believe; he felt as if he ought to kiss the young lady's hand. Possibly he would have done so,—and quite spoiled his chance; but at this moment another person—presumably Eugenio—appeared. A tall handsome man, with superb whiskers and wearing a velvet morning-coat and a voluminous watch-guard, approached the young lady, looking sharply at her companion. "Oh Eugenio!" she said with the friendliest accent.

Eugenio had eyed Winterbourne from head to foot; he now bowed gravely to Miss Miller. "I have the honour to inform Mademoiselle that luncheon's on table."

Mademoiselle slowly rose. "See here, Eugenio, I'm going to that old castle anyway."

"To the Château de Chillon, Mademoiselle?" the courier enquired. "Mademoiselle has made arrangements?" he added in a tone that struck Winterbourne as impertinent.

Eugenio's tone apparently threw, even to Miss Miller's own apprehension, a slightly ironical light on her position. She turned to Winterbourne with the slightest blush. "You won't back out?"

"I shall not be happy till we go!" he protested.

"And you're staying in this hotel?" she went on. "And you're really American?"

The courier still stood there with an effect of offence for the young man so far as the latter saw in it a tacit reflexion on Miss Miller's behaviour and an insinuation that she "picked up" acquaintances. "I shall have the honour of presenting to you a person who'll tell you all about me," he said, smiling, and referring to his aunt.

"Oh well, we'll go some day," she beautifully answered; with which she gave him a smile and turned away. She put up her parasol and walked back to the inn beside Eugenio. Winterbourne stood watching her, and as she moved away, drawing her muslin furbelows over the walk, he spoke to himself of her natural elegance.

II

HE HAD, however, engaged to do more than proved feasible in promising to present his aunt, Mrs. Costello, to Miss Daisy Miller. As soon as that lady had got better of her headache he waited on her in her apartment and, after a show of the proper solicitude about her health, asked if she had noticed in the hotel an American family—a mamma, a daughter and an obstreperous little boy.

"An obstreperous little boy and a preposterous big courier?" said Mrs. Costello. "Oh yes, I've noticed them. Seen them, heard them and kept out of their way." Mrs. Costello was a widow of fortune, a person of much distinction and who frequently intimated that if she hadn't been so dreadfully liable to sick-headaches she would probably have left a deeper impress on her time. She had a long pale face, a high nose and a great deal of very striking white hair, which she wore in large puffs and over the top of her head. She had two sons married in New York and another who was now in Europe. This young man was amusing himself at Homburg and, though guided by his taste, was rarely observed to visit any particular city at the moment selected by his mother for her appearance there. Her nephew, who had come to Vevey expressly to see her, was therefore more attentive than, as she said, her very own. He had imbibed at Geneva the idea that one must be irreproachable in all such forms. Mrs. Costello hadn't seen him for many years and was now greatly pleased with him, manifesting her approbation by initiating him into many of the secrets of that social sway which, as he could see she would like him to think, she exerted from her stronghold in Forty-Second Street. She admitted that she was very exclusive, but if he had been better acquainted with New York he would see that one had to be. And her picture of the minutely hierarchical constitution of the society of that city, which she presented to him in many different lights, was, to Winterbourne's imagination, almost oppressively striking.

He at once recognised from her tone that Miss Daisy Miller's place in the social scale was low. "I'm afraid you don't approve of them," he pursued in reference to his new friends.

"They're horribly common"—it was perfectly simple. "They're the sort of Americans that one does one's duty by just ignoring."

"Ah you just ignore them?"—the young man took it in.

"I can't *not,* my dear Frederick. I wouldn't if I hadn't to, but I have to."

"The little girl's very pretty," he went on in a moment.

"Of course she's very pretty. But she's of the last crudity."

"I see what you mean of course," he allowed after another pause.

"She has that charming look they all have," his aunt resumed. "I can't think where they pick it up; and she dresses in perfection—no, you don't know how well she dresses. I can't think where they get their taste."

"But, my dear aunt, she's not, after all, a Comanche savage."

"She is a young lady," said Mrs. Costello, "who has an intimacy with her mamma's courier!"

"An 'intimacy' with him?" Ah there it was!

"There's no other name for such a relation. But the skinny little mother's just as bad! They treat the courier as a familiar friend—as a gentleman and a scholar. I shouldn't wonder if he dines with them. Very likely they've never seen a man with such good manners, such fine clothes, so *like* a gentleman—or a scholar. He probably corresponds to the young lady's idea of a count. He sits with them in the garden of an evening. I think he smokes in their faces."

Winterbourne listened with interest to these disclosures; they helped him to make up his mind about Miss Daisy. Evidently she was rather wild. "Well," he said, "I'm not a courier and I didn't smoke in her face, and yet she was very charming to me."

"You had better have mentioned at first," Mrs. Costello returned with dignity, "that you had made her valuable acquaintance."

"We simply met in the garden and talked a bit."

"By appointment—no? Ah that's still to come! Pray what did you say?"

"I said I should take the liberty of introducing her to my admirable aunt."

"Your admirable aunt's a thousand times obliged to you."

"It was to guarantee my respectability."

"And pray who's to guarantee hers?"

"Ah you're cruel!" said the young man. "She's a very innocent girl."

"You don't say that as if you believed it," Mrs. Costello returned.

"She's completely uneducated," Winterbourne acknowledged, "but she's wonderfully pretty, and in short she's very nice. To prove I believe it I'm going to take her to the Château de Chillon."

Mrs. Costello made a wondrous face. "You two are going off there together? I should say it proved just the contrary. How long had you known her, may I ask, when this interesting project was formed? You haven't been twenty-four hours in the house."

"I had known her half an hour!" Winterbourne smiled.

"Then she's just what I supposed."

"And what do you suppose?"

"Why that she's a horror."

Our youth was silent for some moments. "You really think then," he presently began, and with a desire for trustworthy information, "you really think that—" But he paused again while his aunt waited.

"Think what, sir?"

"That she's the sort of young lady who expects a man sooner or later to—well, we'll call it carry her off?"

"I haven't the least idea what such young ladies expect a man to do. But I really consider you had better not meddle with little American girls who are uneducated, as you mildly put it. You've lived too long out of the country. You'll be sure to make some great mistake. You're too innocent."

"My dear aunt, not so much as that comes to!" he protested with a laugh and a curl of his moustache.

"You're too guilty then!"

He continued all thoughtfully to finger the ornament in question. "You won't let the poor girl know you then?" he asked at last.

"Is it literally true that she's going to the Château de Chillon with you?"

"I've no doubt she fully intends it."

"Then, my dear Frederick," said Mrs. Costello, "I must decline the honour of her acquaintance. I'm an old woman, but I'm not too old—thank heaven—to be honestly shocked!"

"But don't they all do these things—the little American girls at home?" Winterbourne enquired.

Mrs. Costello stared a moment. "I should like to see my granddaughters do them!" she then grimly returned.

This seemed to throw some light on the matter, for Winterbourne remembered to have heard his pretty cousins in New York, the daughters of this lady's two daughters, called "tremendous flirts." If therefore Miss Daisy Miller exceeded the liberal licence allowed to these young women it was probable she did go even by the American allowance rather far. Winterbourne was impatient to see her again, and it vexed, it even a little humiliated him, that he shouldn't by instinct appreciate her justly.

Though so impatient to see her again he hardly knew what ground he should give for his aunt's refusal to become acquainted with her; but he discovered promptly enough that with Miss Daisy Miller there was no great need of walking on tiptoe. He found her that evening in the garden, wandering about in the warm starlight after the manner of an indolent sylph and swinging to and fro the largest fan he had ever beheld. It was ten o'clock. He had dined with his aunt, had been sitting with her since dinner, and had just taken leave of her till the morrow. His young friend frankly rejoiced to renew their intercourse; she pronounced it the stupidest evening she had ever passed.

"Have you been all alone?" he asked with no intention of an epigram and no effect of her perceiving one.

"I've been walking round with mother. But mother gets tired walking round," Miss Miller explained.

"Has she gone to bed?"

"No, she doesn't like to go to bed. She doesn't sleep scarcely any—not three hours. She says she doesn't know how she lives. She's dreadfully nervous. I guess she sleeps more than she thinks. She's gone somewhere after Randolph; she wants to try to get him to go to bed. He doesn't like to go to bed."

The soft impartiality of her *constatations,* as Winterbourne would have termed them, was a thing by itself—exquisite little fatalist as they seemed to make her. "Let us hope she'll persuade him," he encouragingly said.

"Well, she'll talk to him all she can—but he doesn't like her to talk to him": with which Miss Daisy opened and closed her fan. "She's going to try to get Eugenio to talk to him. But Randolph ain't afraid of Eugenio. Eugenio's a splendid courier, but he can't make much impression on Randolph! I don't believe he'll go to bed before eleven."

Her detachment from any invidious judgement of this was, to her companion's sense, inimitable; and it appeared that Randolph's vigil was in fact triumphantly prolonged, for Winterbourne attended her in her stroll for some time without meeting her mother. "I've been looking round for that lady you want to introduce me to," she resumed—"I guess she's your aunt." Then on his admitting the fact and expressing some curiosity as to how she had learned it, she said she had heard all about Mrs. Costello from the chambermaid. She was very quiet and very *comme il faut;* she wore white puffs; she spoke to no one and she never dined at the common table. Every two days she had a headache. "I think that's a lovely description, headache and all!" said Miss Daisy, chattering along in her thin gay voice. "I want to know her ever so much. I know just what *your* aunt would be; I know I'd like her. She'd be very exclusive. I like a lady to be exclusive; I'm dying to be exclusive myself. Well, I guess we *are* exclusive, mother and I. We don't speak to any one—or they don't speak to us. I suppose it's about the same thing. Anyway, I shall be ever so glad to meet your aunt."

Winterbourne was embarrassed—he could but trump up some evasion. "She'd be most happy, but I'm afraid those tiresome headaches are always to be reckoned with."

The girl looked at him through the fine dusk.

"Well, I suppose she doesn't have a headache every day."

He had to make the best of it. "She tells me she wonderfully does." He didn't know what else to say.

Miss Miller stopped and stood looking at him. Her prettiness was still visible in the darkness; she kept flapping to and fro her enormous fan. "She doesn't want to know me!" she then lightly broke out. "Why don't you say so? You needn't be afraid. *I'm* not afraid!" And she quite crowed for the fun of it.

Winterbourne distinguished however a wee false note in this: he was touched, shocked, mortified by it. "My dear young lady, she knows no one. She goes through life immured. It's her wretched health."

The young girl walked on a few steps in the glee of the thing. "You needn't be afraid," she repeated. "Why should she want to know me?" Then she paused again; she was close to the parapet of the garden, and in front of her was the starlit lake. There was a vague sheen on its surface, and in the distance were dimly-seen mountain forms. Daisy Miller looked out at these great lights and shades and again proclaimed a gay indifference—"Gracious! she *is* exclusive!" Winterbourne wondered if she were seriously wounded and for a moment almost wished her sense of injury might be such as to make it becoming in him to reassure and comfort her. He had a pleasant sense that she would be all accessible to a respectful tenderness at that moment. He felt quite ready to sacrifice his aunt—conversationally; to acknowledge she was a proud rude woman and to make the point that they needn't mind her. But before he had time to commit himself to this questionable mixture of gallantry and impiety, the young lady, resuming her walk, gave an exclamation in quite another tone. "Well, here's mother! I guess she *hasn't* got Randolph to go to bed." The figure of a lady appeared, at a distance, very indistinct in the darkness; it advanced with a slow and wavering step and then suddenly seemed to pause.

"Are you sure it's your mother? Can you make her out in this thick dusk?" Winterbourne asked.

"Well," the girl laughed, "I guess I know my own mother! And when she has got on my shawl too. She's always wearing my things."

The lady in question, ceasing now to approach, hovered vaguely about the spot at which she had checked her steps.

"I'm afraid your mother doesn't see you," said Winterbourne. "Or perhaps," he added—thinking, with Miss Miller, the joke permissible—"perhaps she feels guilty about your shawl."

"Oh it's a fearful old thing!" his companion placidly answered. "I told her she could wear it if she didn't mind looking like a fright. She won't come here because she sees you."

"Ah then," said Winterbourne, "I had better leave you."

"Oh no—come on!" the girl insisted.

"I'm afraid your mother doesn't approve of my walking with you."

She gave him, he thought, the oddest glance. "It isn't for me; it's for you—that is it's for *her*. Well, I don't know who it's for! But mother doesn't like any of my gentlemen friends. She's right down timid. She always makes a fuss if I introduce a gentleman. But I *do* introduce them—almost always. If I didn't introduce my gentlemen friends to mother," Miss Miller added, in her small flat monotone, "I shouldn't think I was natural."

"Well, to introduce me," Winterbourne remarked, "you must know my name." And he proceeded to pronounce it.

"Oh my—I can't say all that!" cried his companion, much amused. But by this time they had come up to Mrs. Miller, who, as they drew near, walked to the parapet of the garden and leaned on it, looking intently at the lake and presenting her back to them. "Mother!" said the girl in a tone of decision—upon which the elder lady turned round. "Mr. Frederick Forsyth Winterbourne," said the latter's young friend, repeating his lesson of a moment before and introducing him very frankly and prettily. "Common" she might be, as Mrs. Costello had pronounced her; yet what provision was made by that epithet for her queer little native grace?

Her mother was a small spare light person, with a wandering eye, a scarce perceptible nose, and, as to make up for it, an unmistakeable forehead, decorated—but too far back, as Winterbourne mentally described it—with thin much-frizzled hair. Like her daughter Mrs. Miller was dressed with extreme elegance; she had enormous diamonds in her ears. So far as the young man could observe, she gave him no greeting—she certainly wasn't looking at him. Daisy was near her, pulling her shawl straight. "What are you doing, poking round here?" this young lady enquired—yet by no means with the harshness of accent her choice of words might have implied.

"Well, I don't know"—and the new-comer turned to the lake again.

"I shouldn't think you'd want that shawl!" Daisy familiarly proceeded.

"Well—I do!" her mother answered with a sound that partook for Winterbourne of an odd strain between mirth and woe.

"Did you get Randolph to go to bed?" Daisy asked.

"No, I couldn't induce him"—and Mrs. Miller seemed to confess to the same mild fatalism as her daughter. "He wants to talk to the waiter. He *likes* to talk to that waiter."

"I was just telling Mr. Winterbourne," the girl went on; and to the young man's ear her tone might have indicated that she had been uttering his name all her life.

"Oh yes!" he concurred—"I've the pleasure of knowing your son."

Randolph's mamma was silent; she kept her attention on the lake. But at last a sigh broke from her. "Well, I don't see how he lives!"

"Anyhow, it isn't so bad as it was at Dover," Daisy at least opined.

"And what occurred at Dover?" Winterbourne desired to know.

"He wouldn't go to bed at all. I guess he sat up all night —in the public parlour. He wasn't in bed at twelve o'clock: it seemed as if he couldn't budge."

"It was half-past twelve when I gave up," Mrs. Miller recorded with passionless accuracy.

It was of great interest to Winterbourne. "Does he sleep much during the day?"

"I guess he doesn't sleep *very* much," Daisy rejoined.

"I wish he just *would!*" said her mother. "It seems as if he *must* make it up somehow."

"Well, I guess it's we that make it up. I think he's real tiresome," Daisy pursued.

After which, for some moments, there was silence. "Well, Daisy Miller," the elder lady then unexpectedly broke out, "I shouldn't think you'd want to talk against your own brother!"

"Well, he *is* tiresome, mother," said the girl, but with no sharpness of insistence.

"Well, he's only nine," Mrs. Miller lucidly urged.

"Well, he wouldn't go up to that castle, anyway," her daughter replied as for accommodation. "I'm going up there with Mr. Winterbourne."

To this announcement, very placidly made, Daisy's parent offered no response. Winterbourne took for granted on this that she opposed such a course; but he said to himself at the same time that she was a simple easily-managed person and that a few deferential protestations would modify her attitude. "Yes," he therefore interposed, "your daughter has kindly allowed me the honour of being her guide."

Mrs. Miller's wandering eyes attached themselves with an appealing air to her other companion, who, however, strolled a few steps further, gently humming to herself. "I presume you'll go in the cars," she then quite colourlessly remarked.

"Yes, or in the boat," said Winterbourne.

"Well, of course I don't know," Mrs. Miller returned. "I've never been up to that castle."

"It is a pity you shouldn't go," he observed, beginning to feel reassured as to her opposition. And yet he was quite prepared to find that as a matter of course she meant to accompany her daughter.

It was on this view accordingly that light was projected for him. "We've been thinking ever so much about going, but it seems as if we couldn't. Of course Daisy—she wants to go round everywhere. But there's a lady here—I don't know her name—she says she shouldn't think we'd want to go to see castles *here;* she should think we'd want to wait till we got t' Italy. It seems as if there would be so many there," continued Mrs. Miller with an air of increasing confidence. "Of course we only want to see the principal ones. We visited several in England," she presently added.

"Ah yes, in England there are beautiful castles," said Winterbourne. "But Chillon here is very well worth seeing."

"Well, if Daisy feels up to it—" said Mrs. Miller in a tone that seemed to break under the burden of such conceptions. "It seems as if there's nothing she won't undertake."

"Oh I'm pretty sure she'll enjoy it!" Winterbourne declared. And he desired more and more to make it a certainty that he was to have the privilege of a *tête-à-tête* with the young lady who was still strolling along in front of them and softly vocalising. "You're not disposed, madam," he enquired, "to make the so interesting excursion yourself?"

So addressed Daisy's mother looked at him an instant with a certain scared obliquity and then walked forward in silence. Then, "I guess she had better go alone," she said simply.

It gave him occasion to note that this was a very different type of maternity from that of the vigilant matrons who massed themselves in the forefront of social intercourse in the dark old city at the other end of the lake. But his meditations were interrupted by hearing his name very distinctly pronounced by Mrs. Miller's unprotected daughter. "Mr. Winterbourne!" she piped from a considerable distance.

"Mademoiselle!" said the young man.

"Don't you want to take me out in a boat?"

"At present?" he asked.

"Why of course!" she gaily returned.

"Well, Annie Miller!" exclaimed her mother.

"I beg you, madam, to let her go," he hereupon eagerly pleaded; so instantly had he been struck with the romantic side of this chance to guide through the summer starlight a skiff freighted with a fresh and beautiful young girl.

"I shouldn't think she'd want to," said her mother. "I should think she'd rather go indoors."

"I'm sure Mr. Winterbourne wants to *take* me," Daisy declared. "He's so awfully devoted!"

"I'll row you over to Chillon under the stars."

"I don't believe it!" Daisy laughed.

"Well!" the elder lady again gasped, as in rebuke of this freedom.

"You haven't spoken to me for half an hour," her daughter went on.

"I've been having some very pleasant conversation with your mother," Winterbourne replied.

"Oh pshaw! I want you to take me out in a boat!" Daisy went on as if nothing else had been said. They had all stopped and she had turned round and was looking at her friend. Her face wore a charming smile, her pretty eyes gleamed in the darkness, she swung her great fan about. No, he felt, it was impossible to be prettier than that.

"There are half a dozen boats moored at that landing-place," and he pointed to a range of steps that descended from the garden to the lake. "If you'll do me the honour to accept my arm we'll go and select one of them."

She stood there smiling; she threw back her head; she laughed as for the drollery of this. "I like a gentleman to be formal!"

"I assure you it's a formal offer."

"I was bound I'd make you say something," Daisy agreeably mocked.

"You see it's not very difficult," said Winterbourne. "But I'm afraid you're chaffing me."

"I think not, sir," Mrs. Miller shyly pleaded.

"Do then let me give you a row," he persisted to Daisy.

"It's quite lovely, the way you say that!" she cried in reward.

"It will be still more lovely to do it."

"Yes, it would be lovely!" But she made no movement to accompany him; she only remained an elegant image of free light irony.

"I guess you'd better find out what time it is," her mother impartially contributed.

"It's eleven o'clock, Madam," said a voice with a foreign accent out of the neighbouring darkness; and Winterbourne, turning, recognised the florid personage he had already seen in attendance. He had apparently just approached.

"Oh Eugenio," said Daisy, "I'm going out with Mr. Winterbourne in a boat!"

Eugenio bowed. "At this hour of the night, Mademoiselle?"

"I'm going with Mr. Winterbourne," she repeated with her shining smile. "I'm going this very minute."

"Do tell her she can't, Eugenio," Mrs. Miller said to the courier.

"I think you had better not go out in a boat, Mademoiselle," the man declared.

Winterbourne wished to goodness this pretty girl were not on such familiar terms with her courier; but he said nothing, and she meanwhile added to his ground. "I suppose you don't think it's proper! My!" she wailed; "Eugenio doesn't think anything's proper."

"I'm nevertheless quite at your service," Winterbourne hastened to remark.

"Does Mademoiselle propose to go alone?" Eugenio asked of Mrs. Miller.

"Oh no, with this gentleman!" cried Daisy's mamma for reassurance.

"I *meant* alone with the gentleman." The courier looked for a moment at Winterbourne—the latter seemed to make out in his face a vague presumptuous intelligence as at the expense of their companions—and then solemnly and with a bow, "As Mademoiselle pleases!" he said.

But Daisy broke off at this. "Oh I hoped you'd make a fuss! I don't care to go now."

"Ah but I myself shall make a fuss if you don't go," Winterbourne declared with spirit.

"That's all I want—a little fuss!" With which she began to laugh again.

"Mr. Randolph has retired for the night!" the courier hereupon importantly announced.

"Oh Daisy, now we can go then!" cried Mrs. Miller.

Her daughter turned away from their friend, all lighted with her odd perversity. "Good-night—I hope you're disappointed or disgusted or something!"

He looked at her gravely, taking her by the hand she offered. "I'm puzzled, if you want to know!" he answered.

"Well, I hope it won't keep you awake!" she said very smartly; and, under the escort of the privileged Eugenio, the two ladies passed toward the house.

Winterbourne's eyes followed them; he was indeed quite mystified. He lingered beside the lake a quarter of an hour, baffled by the question of the girl's sudden familiarities and caprices. But the only very definite conclusion he came to was that he should enjoy deucedly "going off" with her somewhere.

Two days later he went off with her to the Castle of Chillon. He waited for her in the large hall of the hotel, where the couriers, the servants, the foreign tourists were lounging about and staring. It wasn't the place he would have chosen for a tryst, but she had placidly appointed it. She came tripping downstairs, buttoning her long gloves, squeezing her folded parasol against her pretty figure, dressed exactly in the way that consorted best, to his fancy, with their adventure. He was a man of imagination and, as our ancestors used to say, of sensibility; as he took in her charming air and caught from the great staircase her impatient confiding step the note of some small sweet strain of romance, not intense but clear and sweet, seemed to sound for their start. He could have believed he was *really* going "off" with her. He led her out through all the idle people assembled—they all looked at her straight and hard: she had begun to chatter as soon as she joined him. His preference had been that they should be conveyed to Chillon in a carriage, but she expressed a lively wish to go in the little steamer—there would be such a lovely breeze upon the water and they should see such lots of people. The sail wasn't long, but Winterbourne's companion found time for many characteristic remarks and other demonstrations, not a few of which were, from the extremity f their candour, slightly disconcerting. To the young man himself their small excursion showed so for delightfully irregular and incongruously intimate that, even allowing for her habitual sense of freedom, he had some expectation of seeing her appear to find in it the same savour. But it must be confessed that he was in this particular rather disappointed. Miss Miller was highly animated, she was in the brightest spirits; but she was clearly not at all in a nervous flutter—as she should have been to match *his* tension; she avoided neither his eyes nor those of any one else; she neither coloured from an awkward consciousness when she looked at him nor when she saw that people were looking at herself. People continued to look at her a great deal, and Winterbourne could at least take pleasure in his pretty companion's distinguished air. He had been privately afraid she would talk loud, laugh overmuch, and even perhaps desire to move extravagantly about the boat. But he quite forgot his fears; he sat smiling with his eyes on her face while, without stirring from her place, she delivered herself of a great number of original reflexions. It was the most charming innocent prattle he had ever heard, for, by his own experience hitherto, when young persons were so ingenuous they were less articulate and when they were so confident were more sophisticated. If he had assented to the idea that she was "common," at any rate, *was* she proving so, after all, or was he simply getting used to her commonness? Her discourse was for the most part of what immediately and superficially surrounded them, but there were moments when it threw out a longer look or took a sudden straight plunge.

"What on *earth* are you so solemn about?" she suddenly demanded, fixing her agreeable eyes on her friend's.

"*Am* I solemn?" he asked. "I had an idea I was grinning from ear to ear."

"You look as if you were taking me to a prayer-meeting or a funeral. If that's a grin your ears are very near together."

"Should you like me to dance a hornpipe on the deck?"

"Pray do, and I'll carry round your hat. It will pay the expenses of our journey."

"I never was better pleased in my life," Winterbourne returned.

She looked at him a moment, then let it renew her amusement. "I like to make you say those things. You're a queer mixture!"

In the castle, after they had landed, nothing could exceed the light independence of her humour. She tripped about the vaulted chambers, rustled her skirts in the corkscrew staircases, flirted back with a pretty little cry and a shudder from the edge of the oubliettes and turned a singularly well-shaped ear to everything Winterbourne told her about the place. But he saw she cared little for mediæval history and that the grim ghosts of Chillon loomed but faintly before her. They had the good fortune to have been able to wander without other society than that of their guide; and Winterbourne arranged with this companion that they shouldn't be hurried—that they should linger and pause wherever they chose. He interpreted the bargain generously—Winterbourne on his side had been generous—and ended by leaving them quite to themselves. Miss Miller's observations were marked by no logical consistency; for anything she wanted to say she was sure to find a pretext. She found a great many, in the tortuous passages and rugged embrasures of the place, for asking her young man sudden questions about himself, his family, his previous history, his tastes, his habits, his designs, and for supplying information on corresponding points in her own situation. Of her own tastes, habits and designs the charming creature was prepared to give the most definite and indeed the most favourable account.

"Well, I hope you know enough!" she exclaimed after Winterbourne had sketched for her something of the story of the unhappy Bonnivard. "I never saw a man that knew so much!" The history of Bonnivard had evidently, as they say, gone into one ear and out of the other. But this easy erudition struck her none the less as wonderful, and she was soon quite sure she wished Winterbourne would travel with them and "go round" with them: they too in that case might learn something about something. "Don't you want to come and teach Randolph?" she asked; "I guess he'd improve with a gentleman teacher." Winterbourne was certain that nothing could possibly please him so much, but that he had unfortunately other occupations. "Other occupations? I don't believe a speck of it!" she protested. "What do you mean now? You're not in business." The young man allowed that he was not in business, but he had engagements which even within a day or two would necessitate his return to Geneva. "Oh bother!" she panted, "I don't believe it!" and she began to talk about something else. But a few moments later, when he was pointing out to her the interesting design of an antique fireplace, she broke out irrelevantly: "You don't mean to say you're going back to Geneva?"

"It is a melancholy fact that I shall have to report myself there to-morrow."

She met it with a vivacity that could only flatter him. "Well, Mr. Winterbourne, I think you're horrid!"

"Oh don't say such dreadful things!" he quite sincerely pleaded—"just at the last."

"The last?" the girl cried; "I call it the very first! I've half a mind to leave you here and go straight back to the hotel alone." And for the next ten minutes she did nothing but call him horrid. Poor Winterbourne was fairly bewildered; no young lady had as yet done him the honour to be so agitated by the mention of his personal plans. His companion, after this, ceased to pay any attention to the curiosities of Chillon or the beauties of the lake; she opened fire on the special charmer in Geneva whom she appeared to have instantly taken it for granted that he was hurrying back to see. How did Miss Daisy Miller know of that agent of his fate in Geneva? Winterbourne, who denied the existence of such a person, was quite unable to discover; and he was divided between amazement at the rapidity of her induction and amusement at the directness of her criticism. She struck him afresh, in all this, as an extraordinary mixture of innocence and crudity. "Does she never allow you more than three days at a time?" Miss Miller wished ironically to know. "Doesn't she give you a vacation in summer? there's no one so hard-worked but they can get leave to go off somewhere at this season. I suppose if you stay another day she'll come right after you in the boat. Do wait over till Friday and I'll go down to the landing to see her arrive!" He began at last even to feel he had been wrong to be disappointed in the temper in which his young lady had embarked. If he had missed the personal accent, the personal accent was now making its appearance. It sounded very distinctly, toward the end, in her telling him she'd stop "teasing" him if he'd promise her solemnly to come down to Rome that winter.

"That's not a difficult promise to make," he hastened to acknowledge. "My aunt has taken an apartment in Rome from January and has already asked me to come and see her."

"I don't want you to come for your aunt," said Daisy; "I want you just to come for me." And this was the only allusion he was ever to hear her make again to his invidious kinswoman. He promised her that at any rate he would certainly come, and after this she forbore from teasing. Winterbourne took a carriage and they drove back to Vevey in the dusk; the girl at his side, her animation a little spent, was now quite distractingly passive.

In the evening he mentioned to Mrs. Costello that he had spent the afternoon at Chillon with Miss Daisy Miller.

"The Americans—of the courier?" asked this lady.

"Ah happily the courier stayed at home."

"She went with you all alone?"

"All alone."

Mrs. Costello sniffed a little at her smelling-bottle. "And that," she exclaimed, "is the little abomination you wanted me to know!"

III

WINTERBOURNE, who had returned to Geneva the day after his excursion to Chillon, went to Rome toward the end of January. His aunt had been established there a considerable time and he had received from her a couple of characteristic letters. "Those people you were so devoted to last summer at Vevey have turned up here, courier and all," she wrote. "They seem to have made several acquaintances, but the courier continues to be the most *intime*. The young lady, however, is also very intimate with various third-rate Italians, with whom she rackets about in a way that makes much talk. Bring me that pretty novel of Cherbuliez's—'Paule Méré'—and don't come later than the 23d."

Our friend would in the natural course of events, on arriving in Rome, have presently ascertained Mrs. Miller's address at the American banker's and gone to pay his compliments to Miss Daisy. "After what happened at Vevey I certainly think I may call upon them," he said to Mrs. Costello.

"If after what happens—at Vevey and everywhere—you desire to keep up the acquaintance, you're very welcome. Of course you're not squeamish—a man may know every one. Men are welcome to the privilege!"

"Pray what is it then that 'happens'—here for instance?" Winterbourne asked.

"Well, the girl tears about alone with her unmistakeably low foreigners. As to what happens further you must apply elsewhere for information. She has picked up half a dozen of the regular Roman fortune-hunters of the inferior sort and she takes them about to such houses as she may put *her* nose into. When she comes to a party—such a party as she can come to—she brings with her a gentleman with a good deal of manner and a wonderful moustache."

"And where's the mother?"

"I haven't the least idea. They're very dreadful people."

Winterbourne thought them over in these new lights. "They're very ignorant—very innocent only, and utterly uncivilised. Depend on it they're not 'bad.' "

"They're hopelessly vulgar," said Mrs. Costello. "Whether or no being hopelessly vulgar is being 'bad' is a question for the metaphysicians. They're bad enough to blush for, at any rate; and for this short life that's quite enough."

The news that his little friend the child of nature of the Swiss lakeside was now surrounded by half a dozen wonderful moustaches checked Winterbourne's impulse to go straightway to see her. He had perhaps not definitely flattered himself that he had made an ineffaceable impression upon her heart, but he was annoyed at hearing of a state of affairs so little in harmony with an image that had lately flitted in and out of his own meditations; the image of a very pretty girl looking out of an old Roman window and asking herself urgently when Mr. Winterbourne would arrive. If, however, he determined to wait a little before reminding this young lady of his claim to her faithful remembrance, he called with more promptitude on two or three other friends. One of these friends was an American lady who had spent several winters at Geneva, where she had placed her children at school. She was a very accomplished woman and she lived in Via Gregoriana. Winterbourne found her in a little crimson drawing-room on a third floor; the room was filled with southern sunshine. He hadn't been there ten minutes when the servant, appearing in the doorway, announced complacently "Madame Mila!" This announcement was presently followed by the entrance of little Randolph Miller, who stopped in the middle of the room and stood staring at Winterbourne. An instant later his pretty sister crossed the threshold; and then, after a considerable interval, the parent of the pair slowly advanced.

"I guess I know you!" Randolph broke ground without delay.

"I'm sure you know a great many things"—and his old friend clutched him all interestedly by the arm. "How's your education coming on?"

Daisy was engaged in some pretty babble with her hostess, but when she heard Winterbourne's voice she quickly turned her head with a "Well, I declare!" which he met smiling. "I told you I should come, you know."

"Well, I didn't believe it," she answered.

"I'm much obliged to you for that," laughed the young man.

"You might have come to see me then," Daisy went on as if they had parted the week before.

"I arrived only yesterday."

"I don't believe any such thing!" the girl declared afresh.

Winterbourne turned with a protesting smile to her mother, but this lady evaded his glance and, seating herself, fixed her eyes on her son. "We've got a bigger place than this," Randolph hereupon broke out. "It's all gold on the walls."

Mrs. Miller, more of a fatalist apparently than ever, turned uneasily in her chair. "I told you if I was to bring you you'd say something!" she stated as for the benefit of such of the company as might hear it.

"I told *you!*" Randolph retorted. "I tell *you,* sir!" he added jocosely, giving Winterbourne a thump on the knee. "It *is* bigger too!"

As Daisy's conversation with her hostess still occupied her Winterbourne judged it becoming to address a few words to her mother—such as "I hope you've been well since we parted at Vevey."

Mrs. Miller now certainly looked at him—at his chin. "Not very well, sir," she answered.

"She's got the dyspepsia," said Randolph. "I've got it too. Father's got it bad. But I've got it worst!"

This proclamation, instead of embarrassing Mrs. Miller, seemed to soothe her by reconstituting the environment to which she was most accustomed. "I suffer from the liver," she amiably whined to Winterbourne. "I think it's this climate; it's less bracing than Schenectady, especially in the winter season. I don't know whether you know we reside at Schenectady. I was saying to Daisy that I certainly hadn't found any one like Dr. Davis and I didn't believe I *would*. Oh up in Schenectady, he stands first; they think everything of Dr. Davis. He has so much to do, and yet there was nothing he wouldn't do for *me*. He said he never saw anything like my dyspepsia, but he was bound to get at it. I'm sure there was nothing he wouldn't try, and I didn't care what he did to me if he only brought me relief. He was just going to try something new, and I just longed for it, when we came right off. Mr. Miller felt as if he wanted Daisy to see Europe for herself. But I couldn't help writing the other day that I supposed it was all right for Daisy, but that I didn't know as I *could* get on much longer without Dr. Davis. At Schenectady he stands at the very top; and there's a great deal of sickness there too. It affects my sleep."

Winterbourne had a good deal of pathological gossip with Dr. Davis's patient, during which Daisy chattered unremittingly to her own companion. The young man asked Mrs. Miller how she was pleased with Rome. "Well, I must say I'm disappointed," she confessed. "We had heard so much about it—I suppose we had heard too much. But we couldn't help that. We had been led to expect something different."

Winterbourne, however, abounded in reassurance. "Ah wait a little, and you'll grow very fond of it."

"I hate it worse and worse every day!" cried Randolph.

"You're like the infant Hannibal," his friend laughed.

"No I ain't—like any infant!" Randolph declared at a venture.

"Well, that's so—and you never *were!*" his mother concurred. "But we've seen places," she resumed, "that I'd put a long way ahead of Rome." And in reply to Winterbourne's interrogation, "There's Zürich—up there in the mountains," she instanced; "I think Zürich's real lovely, and we hadn't heard half so much about it."

"The best place we've seen's the *City of Richmond!*" said Randolph.

"He means the ship," Mrs. Miller explained. "We crossed in that ship. Randolph had a good time on the *City of Richmond.*"

"It's the best place *I've* struck," the child repeated. "Only it was turned the wrong way."

"Well, we've got to turn the right way sometime," said Mrs. Miller with strained but weak optimism. Winterbourne expressed the hope that her daughter at least appreciated the so various interest of Rome, and she declared with some spirit that Daisy was quite carried away. "It's on account of the society—the society's splendid. She goes round everywhere; she has made a great number of acquaintances. Of course she goes round more than I do. I must say they've all been very sweet—they've taken her right in. And then she knows a great many gentlemen. Oh she thinks there's nothing like Rome. Of course it's a great deal pleasanter for a young lady if she knows plenty of gentlemen."

By this time Daisy had turned her attention again to Winterbourne, but in quite the same free form. "I've been telling Mrs. Walker how mean you were!"

"And what's the evidence you've offered?" he asked, a trifle disconcerted, for all his superior gallantry, by her inadequate measure of the zeal of an admirer who on his way down to Rome had stopped neither at Bologna nor at Florence, simply because of a certain sweet appeal to his fond fancy, not to say to his finest curiosity. He remembered how a cynical compatriot had once told him that American women—the pretty ones, and this gave a largeness to the axiom—were at once the most exacting in the world and the least endowed with a sense of indebtedness.

"Why you were awfully mean up at Vevey," Daisy said. "You wouldn't do most anything. You wouldn't stay there when I asked you."

"Dearest young lady," cried Winterbourne, with generous passion, "have I come all the way to Rome only to be riddled by your silver shafts?"

"Just hear him say that!"—and she gave an affectionate twist to a bow on her hostess's dress. "Did you ever hear anything so quaint?"

"So 'quaint,' my dear?" echoed Mrs. Walker more critically—quite in the tone of a partisan of Winterbourne.

"Well, I don't know"—and the girl continued to finger her ribbons. "Mrs. Walker, I want to tell you something."

"Say, mother-r," broke in Randolph with his rough ends to his words, "I tell you you've got to go. Eugenio'll raise something!"

"I'm not afraid of Eugenio," said Daisy with a toss of her head. "Look here, Mrs. Walker," she went on, "you know I'm coming to your party."

"I'm delighted to hear it."

"I've got a lovely dress."

"I'm very sure of that."

"But I want to ask a favour—permission to bring a friend."

"I shall be happy to see any of your friends," said Mrs. Walker, who turned with a smile to Mrs. Miller.

"Oh they're not my friends," cried that lady, squirming in shy repudiation. "It seems as if they didn't take to *me*—I never spoke to one of them!"

"It's an intimate friend of mine, Mr. Giovanelli," Daisy pursued without a tremor in her young clearness or a shadow on her shining bloom.

Mrs. Walker had a pause and gave a rapid glance at Winterbourne. "I shall be glad to see Mr. Giovanelli," she then returned.

"He's just the finest kind of Italian," Daisy pursued with the prettiest serenity. "He's a great friend of mine and the handsomest man in the world—except Mr. Winterbourne! He knows plenty of Italians, but he wants to know some Americans. It seems as if he was crazy about Americans. He's tremendously bright. He's perfectly lovely!"

It was settled that this paragon should be brought to Mrs. Walker's party, and then Mrs. Miller prepared to take her leave. "I guess we'll go right back to the hotel," she remarked with a confessed failure of the larger imagination.

"You may go back to the hotel, mother," Daisy replied, "but I'm just going to walk round."

"She's going to go it with Mr. Giovanelli," Randolph unscrupulously commented.

"I'm going to go it on the Pincio," Daisy peaceably smiled, while the way that she "condoned" these things almost melted Winterbourne's heart.

"Alone, my dear—at this hour?" Mrs. Walker asked. The afternoon was drawing to a close—it was the hour for the throng of carriages and of contemplative pedestrians. "I don't consider it's safe, Daisy," her hostess firmly asserted.

"Neither do I then," Mrs. Miller thus borrowed confidence to add. "You'll catch the fever as sure as you live. Remember what Dr. Davis told you!"

"Give her some of that medicine before she starts in," Randolph suggested.

The company had risen to its feet; Daisy, still showing her pretty teeth, bent over and kissed her hostess. "Mrs. Walker, you're too perfect," she simply said. "I'm not going alone; I'm going to meet a friend."

"Your friend won't keep you from catching the fever

even if it *is* his own second nature," Mrs. Miller observed.

"Is it Mr. Giovanelli that's the dangerous attraction?" Mrs. Walker asked without mercy.

Winterbourne was watching the challenged girl; at this question his attention quickened. She stood there smiling and smoothing her bonnet-ribbons; she glanced at Winterbourne. Then, while she glanced and smiled, she brought out all affirmatively and without a shade of hesitation: "Mr. Giovanelli—the beautiful Giovanelli."

"My dear young friend"—and, taking her hand, Mrs. Walker turned to pleading—"don't prowl off to the Pincio at this hour to meet a beautiful Italian."

"Well, he speaks first-rate English," Mrs. Miller incoherently mentioned.

"Gracious me," Daisy piped up, "I don't want to do anything that's going to affect my health—or my character either! There's an easy way to settle it." Her eyes continued to play over Winterbourne. "The Pincio's only a hundred yards off, and if Mr. Winterbourne were as polite as he pretends he'd offer to walk right in with me!"

Winterbourne's politeness hastened to proclaim itself, and the girl gave him gracious leave to accompany her. They passed downstairs before her mother, and at the door he saw Mrs. Miller's carriage drawn up, with the ornamental courier whose acquaintance he had made at Vevey seated within. "Good-bye, Eugenio," cried Daisy; "I'm going to take a walk!" The distance from Via Gregoriana to the beautiful garden at the other end of the Pincian Hill is in fact rapidly traversed. As the day was splendid, however, and the concourse of vehicles, walkers and loungers numerous, the young Americans found their progress much delayed. This fact was highly agreeable to Winterbourne, in spite of his consciousness of his singular situation. The slow-moving, idly-gazing Roman crowd bestowed much attention on the extremely pretty young woman of English race who passed through it, with some difficulty, on his arm; and he wondered what on earth had been in Daisy's mind when she proposed to exhibit herself unattended to its appreciation. His own mission, to her sense, was apparently to consign her to the hands of Mr. Giovanelli; but, at once annoyed and gratified, he resolved that he would do no such thing.

"Why haven't you been to see me?" she meanwhile asked. "You can't get out of that."

"I've had the honour of telling you that I've only just stepped out of the train."

"You must have stayed in the train a good while after it stopped!" she derisively cried. "I suppose you were asleep. You've had time to go to see Mrs. Walker."

"I knew Mrs. Walker—" Winterbourne began to explain.

"I know where you knew her. You knew her at Geneva. She told me so. Well, you knew me at Vevey. That's just as good. So you ought to have come." She asked him no other question than this; she began to prattle about her own affairs. "We've got splendid rooms at the hotel; Eugenio says they're the best rooms in Rome. We're going to stay all winter—if we don't die of the fever; and I guess we'll stay then! It's a great deal nicer than I thought; I thought it would be fearfully quiet—in fact I was sure it would be deadly pokey. I foresaw we should be going round all the time with one of those dreadful old men who explain about the pictures and things. But we only had about a week of that, and now I'm enjoying myself. I know ever so many people, and they're all so charming. The society's extremely select. There are all kinds—English and Germans and Italians. I think I like the English best. I like their style of conversation. But there are some lovely Americans. I never saw anything so hospitable. There's something or other every day. There's not much dancing—but I must say I never thought dancing was everything. I was always fond of conversation. I guess I'll have plenty at Mrs. Walker's—her rooms are so small." When they had passed the gate of the Pincian Gardens

Miss Miller began to wonder where Mr. Giovanelli might be. "We had better go straight to that place in front, where you look at the view."

Winterbourne at this took a stand. "I certainly shan't help you to find him."

"Then I shall find him without you," Daisy said with spirit.

"You certainly won't leave me!" he protested.

She burst into her familiar little laugh. "Are you afraid you'll get lost—or run over? But there's Giovanelli leaning against that tree. He's staring at the women in the carriages: did you ever see anything so cool?"

Winterbourne descried hereupon at some distance a little figure that stood with folded arms and nursing its cane. It had a handsome face, a hat artfully poised, a glass in one eye and a nosegay in its buttonhole. Daisy's friend looked at it a moment and then said: "Do you mean to speak to that thing?"

"Do I mean to speak to him? Why you don't suppose I mean to communicate by signs!"

"Pray understand then," the young man returned, "that I intend to remain with you."

Daisy stopped and looked at him without a sign of troubled consciousness, with nothing in her face but her charming eyes, her charming teeth and her happy dimples. "Well, she's a cool one!" he thought.

"I don't like the way you say that," she declared. "It's too imperious."

"I beg your pardon if I say it wrong. The main point's to give you an idea of my meaning."

The girl looked at him more gravely, but with eyes that were prettier than ever. "I've never allowed a gentleman to dictate to me or to interfere with anything I do."

"I think that's just where your mistake has come in," he retorted. "You should sometimes listen to a gentleman—the right one."

At this she began to laugh again. "I do nothing but listen to gentlemen! Tell me if Mr. Giovanelli is the right one."

The gentleman with the nosegay in his bosom had now made out our two friends and was approaching Miss Miller with obsequious rapidity. He bowed to Winterbourne as well as to the latter's compatriot; he seemed to shine, in his coxcombical way, with the desire to please and the fact of his own intelligent joy, though Winterbourne thought him not a bad-looking fellow. But he nevertheless said to Daisy: "No, he's not the right one."

She had clearly a natural turn for free introductions; she mentioned with the easiest grace the name of each of her companions to the other. She strolled forward with one of them on either hand; Mr. Giovanelli, who spoke English very cleverly—Winterbourne afterwards learned that he had practised the idiom upon a great many American heiresses—addressed her a great deal of very polite nonsense. He had the best possible manners, and the young American, who said nothing, reflected on that depth of Italian subtlety, so strangely opposed to Anglo-Saxon simplicity, which enables people to show a smoother surface in proportion as they're more acutely displeased. Giovanelli of course had counted upon something more intimate—he had not bargained for a party of three; but he kept his temper in a manner that suggested far-stretching intentions. Winterbourne flattered himself he had taken his measure. "He's anything but a gentleman," said the young American; "he isn't even a very plausible imitation of one. He's a music-master or a penny-a-liner or a third-rate artist. He's awfully on his good behaviour, but damn his fine eyes!" Mr. Giovanelli had indeed great advantages; but it was deeply disgusting to Daisy's other friend that something in her shouldn't have instinctively discriminated against such a type. Giovanelli chattered and jested and made himself agreeable according to his honest Roman lights. It was true that if he was an imitation the imitation was studied. "Nevertheless," Winterbourne said to himself, "a nice girl ought to know!" And then he came back to the dreadful question of whether this *was* in fact a nice girl. Would a nice girl—even allowing for her being a little American flirt—make a rendezvous with a presumably low-lived foreigner? The rendezvous in this case indeed had been in broad daylight and in the most crowded corner of Rome; but wasn't it possible to regard the choice of these very circumstances as a proof more of vulgarity than of anything else? Singular though it may seem, Winterbourne was vexed that the girl, in joining her *amoroso,* shouldn't appear more impatient of his own company, and he was vexed precisely because of his inclination. It was impossible to regard her as a wholly unspotted flower—she lacked a certain indispensable fineness; and it would therefore much simplify the situation to be able to treat her as the subject of one of the visitations known to romancers as "lawless passions." That she should seem to wish to get rid of him would have helped him to think more lightly of her, just as to be able to think more lightly of her would have made her less perplexing. Daisy at any rate continued on this occasion to present herself as an inscrutable combination of audacity and innocence.

She had been walking some quarter of an hour, attended by her two cavaliers and responding in a tone of very childish gaiety, as it after all struck one of them, to the pretty speeches of the other, when a carriage that had detached itself from the revolving train drew up beside the path. At the same moment Winterbourne noticed that his friend Mrs. Walker—the lady whose house he had lately left—was seated in the vehicle and was beckoning to him. Leaving Miss Miller's side, he hastened to obey her summons—and all to find her flushed, excited, scandalised. "It's really too dreadful"—she earnestly appealed to him. "That crazy girl mustn't do this sort of thing. She mustn't walk here with you two men. Fifty people have remarked her."

Winterbourne—suddenly and rather oddly rubbed the

wrong way by this—raised his grave eyebrows. "I think it's a pity to make too much fuss about it."

"It's a pity to let the girl ruin herself!"

"She's very innocent," he reasoned in his own troubled interest.

"She's very reckless," cried Mrs. Walker, "and goodness knows how far—left to itself—it may go. Did you ever," she proceeded to enquire, "see anything so blatantly imbecile as the mother? After you had all left me just now I couldn't sit still for thinking of it. It seemed too pitiful not even to attempt to save them. I ordered the carriage and put on my bonnet and came here as quickly as possible. Thank heaven I've found you!"

"What do you propose to do with us?" Winterbourne uncomfortably smiled.

"To ask her to get in, to drive her about here for half an hour—so that the world may see she's not running absolutely wild—and then take her safely home."

"I don't think it's a very happy thought," he said after reflexion, "but you're at liberty to try."

Mrs. Walker accordingly tried. The young man went in pursuit of their young lady who had simply nodded and smiled, from her distance, at her recent patroness in the carriage and then had gone her way with her own companion. On learning, in the event, that Mrs. Walker had followed her, she retraced her steps, however, with a perfect good grace and with Mr. Giovanelli at her side. She professed herself "enchanted" to have a chance to present this gentleman to her good friend, and immediately achieved the introduction; declaring with it, and as if it were of as little importance, that she had never in her life seen anything so lovely as that lady's carriage-rug.

"I'm glad you admire it," said her poor pursuer, smiling sweetly. "Will you get in and let me put it over you?"

"Oh no, thank you!"—Daisy knew her mind. "I'll admire it ever so much more as I see you driving round with it."

"Do get in and drive round *with* me," Mrs. Walker pleaded.

"That would be charming, but it's so fascinating just as I am!"—with which the girl radiantly took in the gentlemen on either side of her.

"It may be fascinating, dear child, but it's not the custom here," urged the lady of the victoria, leaning forward in this vehicle with her hands devoutly clasped.

"Well, it ought to be then!" Daisy imperturbably laughed. "If I didn't walk I'd expire."

"You should walk with your mother, dear," cried Mrs. Walker with a loss of patience.

"With my mother dear?" the girl amusedly echoed. Winterbourne saw she scented interference. "My mother never walked ten steps in her life. And then, you know," she blandly added, "I'm more than five years old."

"You're old enough to be more reasonable. You're old enough, dear Miss Miller, to be talked about."

Daisy wondered to extravagance. "Talked about? What do you mean?"

"Come into my carriage and I'll tell you."

Daisy turned shining eyes again from one of the gentlemen beside her to the other. Mr. Giovanelli was bowing to and fro, rubbing down his gloves and laughing irresponsibly; Winterbourne thought the scene the most unpleasant possible. "I don't think I want to know what you mean," the girl presently said. "I don't think I should like it."

Winterbourne only wished Mrs. Walker would tuck up her carriage-rug and drive away; but this lady, as she afterwards told him, didn't feel she could "rest there." "Should you prefer being thought a very reckless girl?" she accordingly asked.

"Gracious me!" exclaimed Daisy. She looked again at Mr. Giovanelli, then she turned to her other companion. There was a small pink flush in her cheek; she was tremendously pretty. "Does Mr. Winterbourne think," she put to him with a wonderful bright intensity of appeal, "that—to save my reputation—I ought to get into the carriage?"

It really embarrassed him; for an instant he cast about—so strange was it to hear her speak that way of her "reputation." But he himself in fact had to speak in accordance with gallantry. The finest gallantry here was surely just to tell her the truth; and the truth, for our young man, as the few indications I have been able to give have made him known to the reader, was that his charming friend should listen to the voice of civilised society. He took in again her exquisite prettiness and then said the more distinctly: "I think you should get into the carriage."

Daisy gave the rein to her amusement: "I never heard anything so stiff! If this is improper, Mrs. Walker," she pursued, "then I'm *all* improper, and you had better give me right up. Good-bye; I hope you'll have a lovely ride!" —and with Mr. Giovanelli, who made a triumphantly obsequious salute, she turned away.

Mrs. Walker sat looking after her, and there were tears in Mrs. Walker's eyes. "Get in here, sir," she said to Winterbourne, indicating the place beside her. The young man answered that he felt bound to accompany Miss Miller; whereupon the lady of the victoria declared that if he refused her this favour she would never speak to him again. She was evidently wound up. He accordingly hastened to overtake Daisy and her more faithful ally, and, offering her his hand, told her that Mrs. Walker had made a stringent claim on his presence. He had expected her to answer with something rather free, something still more significant of the perversity from which the voice of society, through the lips of their distressed friend, had so earnestly endeavoured to dissuade her. But she only let her hand slip, as she scarce looked at him, through his slightly awkward grasp; while Mr. Giovanelli, to make it worse, bade him farewell with too emphatic a flourish of the hat.

Winterbourne was not in the best possible humour as he

took his seat beside the author of his sacrifice. "That was not clever of you," he said candidly, as the vehicle mingled again with the throng of carriages.

"In such a case," his companion answered, "I don't want to be clever—I only want to be *true!*"

"Well, your truth has only offended the strange little creature—it has only put her off."

"It has happened very well"—Mrs. Walker accepted her work. "If she's so perfectly determined to compromise herself the sooner one knows it the better—one can act accordingly."

"I suspect she meant no great harm, you know," Winterbourne maturely opined.

"So I thought a month ago. But she has been going too far."

"What has she been doing?"

"Everything that's not done here. Flirting with any man she can pick up; sitting in corners with mysterious Italians; dancing all the evening with the same partners; receiving visits at eleven o'clock at night. Her mother melts away when the visitors come."

"But her brother," laughed Winterbourne, "sits up till two in the morning."

"He must be edified by what he sees. I'm told that at their hotel everyone's talking about her and that a smile goes round among the servants when a gentleman comes and asks for Miss Miller."

"Ah we needn't mind the servants!" Winterbourne compassionately signified. "The poor girl's only fault," he presently added, "is her complete lack of education."

"She's naturally indelicate," Mrs. Walker, on her side, reasoned. "Take that example this morning. How long had you known her at Vevey?"

"A couple of days."

"Imagine then the taste of her making it a personal matter that you should have left the place!"

He agreed that taste wasn't the strong point of the

Millers—after which he was silent for some moments; but only at last to add: "I suspect, Mrs. Walker, that you and I have lived too long at Geneva!" And he further noted that he should be glad to learn with what particular design she had made him enter her carriage.

"I wanted to enjoin on you the importance of your ceasing your relations with Miss Miller; that of your not appearing to flirt with her; that of your giving her no further opportunity to expose herself; that of your in short letting her alone."

"I'm afraid I can't do anything quite so enlightened as *that,*" he returned. "I like her awfully, you know."

"All the more reason you shouldn't help her to make a scandal."

"Well, there shall be nothing scandalous in my attentions to her," he was willing to promise.

"There certainly will be in the way she takes them. But I've said what I had on my conscience," Mrs. Walker pursued. "If you wish to rejoin the young lady I'll put you down. Here, by the way, you have a chance."

The carriage was engaged in that part of the Pincian drive which overhangs the wall of Rome and overlooks the beautiful Villa Borghese. It is bordered by a large parapet, near which are several seats. One of these, at a distance, was occupied by a gentleman and a lady, toward whom Mrs. Walker gave a toss of her head. At the same moment these persons rose and walked to the parapet. Winterbourne had asked the coachman to stop; he now descended from the carriage. His companion looked at him a moment in silence and then, while he raised his hat, drove majestically away. He stood where he had alighted; he had turned his eyes toward Daisy and her cavalier. They evidently saw no one; they were too deeply occupied with each other. When they reached the low garden-wall they remained a little looking off at the great flat-topped pine-clusters of Villa Borghese; then the girl's attendant admirer seated himself familiarly on the broad ledge of the wall. The western sun in the opposite sky sent out a brilliant shaft through a couple of cloud-bars; whereupon the gallant Giovanelli took her parasol out of her hands and opened it. She came a little nearer and he held the parasol over her; then, still holding it, he let it so rest on her shoulder that both of their heads were hidden from Winterbourne. This young man stayed but a moment longer; then he began to walk. But he walked—not toward the couple united beneath the parasol, rather toward the residence of his aunt Mrs. Costello.

IV

HE FLATTERED himself on the following day that there was no smiling among the servants when he at least asked for Mrs. Miller at her hotel. This lady and her daughter, however, were not at home; and on the next day after, repeating his visit, Winterbourne again was met by a denial. Mrs. Walker's party took place on the evening of the third day, and in spite of the final reserves that had marked his last interview with that social critic our young man was among the guests. Mrs. Walker was one of those pilgrims from the younger world who, while in contact with the elder, make a point, in their own phrase, of studying European society; and she had on this occasion collected several specimens of diversely-born humanity to serve, as might be, for text-books. When Winterbourne arrived the little person he desired most to find wasn't there; but in a few moments he saw Mrs. Miller come in alone, very shyly and ruefully. This lady's hair, above the dead waste of her temples, was more frizzled than ever. As she approached their hostess Winterbourne also drew near.

"You see I've come all alone," said Daisy's unsupported parent. "I'm so frightened I don't know what to do; it's the first time I've ever been to a party alone—especially in this country. I wanted to bring Randolph or Eugenio or some one, but Daisy just pushed me off by myself. I ain't used to going round alone."

"And doesn't your daughter intend to favour us with her society?" Mrs. Walker impressively enquired.

"Well, Daisy's all dressed," Mrs. Miller testified with that accent of the dispassionate, if not of the philosophic, historian with which she always recorded the current incidents of her daughter's career. "She got dressed on purpose before dinner. But she has a friend of hers there; that gentleman—the handsomest of the Italians—that she wanted to bring. They've got going at the piano—it seems as if they couldn't leave off. Mr. Giovanelli does sing splendidly. But I guess they'll come before very long," Mrs. Miller hopefully concluded.

"I'm sorry she should come—in that particular way," Mrs. Walker permitted herself to observe.

"Well, I told her there was no use in her getting dressed before dinner if she was going to wait three hours," returned Daisy's mamma. "I didn't see the use of her putting on such a dress as that to sit round with Mr. Giovanelli."

"This is most horrible!" said Mrs. Walker, turning away and addressing herself to Winterbourne. *"Elle s'affiche, la malheureuse.* It's her revenge for my having ventured to remonstrate with her. When she comes I shan't speak to her."

Daisy came after eleven o'clock, but she wasn't, on such an occasion, a young lady to wait to be spoken to. She rustled forward in radiant loveliness, smiling and chattering, carrying a large bouquet and attended by Mr. Giovanelli. Every one stopped talking and turned and looked at her while she floated up to Mrs. Walker. "I'm afraid you thought I never was coming, so I sent mother off to tell you. I wanted to make Mr. Giovanelli practise some things before he came; you know he sings beautifully, and I want you to ask him to sing. This is Mr. Giovanelli; you know I introduced him to you; he's got the most lovely voice and he knows the most charming set of songs. I made him go over them this evening on purpose; we had the greatest time at the hotel." Of all this Daisy delivered herself with the sweetest brightest loudest confidence, looking now at her hostess and now at all the room, while she gave a series of little pats, round her very white shoulders, to the edges of her dress. "Is there anyone I know?" she as undiscourageably asked.

"I think every one knows you!" said Mrs. Walker as with a grand intention; and she gave a very cursory greeting to Mr. Giovanelli. This gentleman bore himself gallantly; he smiled and bowed and showed his white teeth, he curled his moustaches and rolled his eyes and performed all the proper functions of a handsome Italian at an evening party. He sang, very prettily, half a dozen songs, though Mrs. Walker afterwards declared that she had been quite unable to find out who asked him. It was apparently not Daisy who had set him in motion—this young lady being seated a distance from the piano and though she had publicly, as it were, professed herself his musical patroness or guarantor, giving herself to gay and audible discourse while he warbled.

"It's a pity these rooms are so small; we can't dance," she remarked to Winterbourne as if she had seen him five minutes before.

"I'm not sorry we can't dance," he candidly returned "I'm incapable of a step."

"Of course you're incapable of a step," the girl assented. "I should think your legs *would* be stiff cooped in there so much of the time in that victoria."

"Well, they were very restless there three days ago," he amicably laughed; "all they really wanted was to dance attendance on you."

"Oh my other friend—my friend in need—stuck to me; he seems more at one with his limbs than you are—I'll say that for him. But did you ever hear anything so cool," Daisy demanded, "as Mrs. Walker's wanting me to get into her carriage and drop poor Mr. Giovanelli, and under the pretext that it was proper? People have different ideas! It would have been most unkind; he had been talking about that walk for ten days."

"He shouldn't have talked about it at all," Winterbourne decided to make answer on this: "he would never have proposed to a young lady of this country to walk about the streets of Rome with him."

"About the streets?" she cried with her pretty stare. "Where then would he have proposed to her to walk? The Pincio ain't the streets either, I guess; and I besides, thank goodness, am not a young lady of this country. The young ladies of this country have a dreadfully pokey time of it, by what I can discover; I don't see why I should change my habits for *such* stupids."

"I'm afraid your habits are those of a ruthless flirt," said Winterbourne with studied severity.

"Of course they are!"—and she hoped, evidently, by the manner of it, to take his breath away. "I'm a fearful frightful flirt! Did you ever hear of a nice girl that wasn't? But I suppose you'll tell me now I'm not a nice girl."

He remained grave indeed under the shock of her cynical profession. "You're a very nice girl, but I wish you'd flirt with me, and me only."

"Ah thank you, thank you very much: you're the last man I should think of flirting with. As I've had the pleasure of informing you, you're too stiff."

"You say that too often," he resentfully remarked.

Daisy gave a delighted laugh. "If I could have the sweet hope of making you angry I'd say it again."

"Don't do that—when I'm angry I'm stiffer than ever. But if you won't flirt with me do cease at least to flirt with your friend at the piano. They don't," he declared as in full sympathy with "them," "understand that sort of thing here."

"I thought they understood nothing else!" Daisy cried with startling world-knowledge.

"Not in young unmarried women."

"It seems to me much more proper in young unmarried than in old married ones," she retorted.

"Well," said Winterbourne, "when you deal with natives you must go by the custom of the country. American flirting is a purely American silliness; it has—in its ineptitude of innocence—no place in *this* system. So when you show yourself in public with Mr. Giovanelli and without your mother—"

"Gracious, poor mother!"—and she made it beautifully unspeakable.

Winterbourne had a touched sense for this, but it didn't alter his attitude. "Though *you* may be flirting Mr. Giovanelli isn't—he means something else."

"He isn't preaching at any rate," she returned. "And if you want very much to know, we're neither of us flirting—not a little speck. We're too good friends for that. We're real intimate friends."

He was to continue to find her thus at moments inimitable. "Ah," he then judged, "if you're in love with each other it's another affair altogether!"

She had allowed him up to this point to speak so frankly that he had no thought of shocking her by the force of his logic; yet she now none the less immediately rose, blushing visibly and leaving him mentally to exclaim that the name of little American flirts was incoherence. "Mr. Giovanelli at least," she answered, sparing but a single small queer glance for it, a queerer small glance, he felt, than he had ever yet had from her—"Mr. Giovanelli never says to me such very disagreeable things."

It had an effect on him—he stood staring. The subject of their contention had finished singing; he left the piano, and his recognition of what—a little awkwardly—didn't take place in celebration of this might nevertheless have been an acclaimed operatic tenor's series of repeated ducks before the curtain. So he bowed himself over to Daisy. "Won't you come to the other room and have some tea?" he asked—offering Mrs. Walker's slightly thin refreshment as he might have done all the kingdoms of the earth.

Daisy at last turned on Winterbourne a more natural and calculable light. He was but the more muddled by it, however, since so inconsequent a smile made nothing clear—it seemed at the most to prove in her a sweetness and softness that reverted instinctively to the pardon of offenses. "It has never occurred to Mr. Winterbourne to offer me any tea," she said with her finest little intention of torment and triumph.

"I've offered you excellent advice," the young man permitted himself to growl.

"I prefer weak tea!" cried Daisy, and she went off with the brilliant Giovanelli. She sat with him in the adjoining room, in the embrasure of the window, for the rest of the evening. There was an interesting performance at the piano, but neither of these conversers gave heed to it. When Daisy came to take leave of Mrs. Walker this lady conscientiously repaired the weakness of which she had been guilty at the moment of the girl's arrival—she turned her back straight on Miss Miller and left her to depart with what grace she might. Winterbourne happened to be near the door; he saw it all. Daisy turned very pale and looked at her mother, but Mrs. Miller was humbly unconscious of any rupture of any law or of any deviation from any custom. She appeared indeed to have felt an incongruous impulse to draw attention to her own striking conformity. "Good-night, Mrs. Walker," she said; "we've had a beautiful evening. You see if I let Daisy come to parties without me; I don't want her to go away without me." Daisy turned away, looking with a small white prettiness, a blighted grace, at the circle near the door: Winterbourne saw that for the first moment she was too much shocked and puzzled even for indignation. He on his side was greatly touched.

"That was very cruel," he promptly remarked to Mrs. Walker.

But this lady's face was also as a stone. "She never enters my drawing-room again."

Since Winterbourne then, hereupon, was not to meet her in Mrs. Walker's drawing-room he went as often as possible to Mrs. Miller's hotel. The ladies were rarely at home, but when he found them the devoted Giovanelli was always present. Very often the glossy little Roman, serene in success, but not unduly presumptuous, occupied with Daisy alone the florid salon enjoyed by Eugenio's care, Mrs. Miller being apparently ever of the opinion that discretion is the better part of solicitude. Winterbourne noted, at first with surprise, that Daisy on these occasions was neither embarrassed nor annoyed by his own entrance; but he presently began to feel that she had no more surprises for him and that he really liked, after all, not making out what she was "up to." She showed no displeasure for the interruption of her *tête-à-tête* with Giovanelli; she could chatter as freshly and freely with two gentlemen as with one, and this easy flow had ever the same anomaly for her earlier friend that it was so free without availing itself of its freedom. Winterbourne reflected that if she was seriously interested in the Italian it was odd she shouldn't take more trouble to preserve the sanctity of their interviews, and he liked her the better for her innocent-looking indifference and her inexhaustible gaiety. He could hardly have said why, but she struck him as a young person not formed for a troublesome jealousy. Smile at such a betrayal though the reader may, it was a fact with regard to the women who had hitherto interested him that, given certain contingencies, Winterbourne could see himself afraid—literally afraid—of these ladies. It pleased him to believe that even were twenty other things different and Daisy should love him and he should know it and like it, he would still never be afraid of Daisy. It must be added that this conviction was not altogether flattering to her: it represented that she was nothing every way if not light.

But she was evidently very much interested in Giova nelli. She looked at him whenever he spoke; she was perpetually telling him to do this and to do that; she was constantly chaffing and abusing him. She appeared completely to have forgotten that her other friend had said anything to displease her at Mrs. Walker's entertainment. One Sunday afternoon, having gone to Saint Peter's with his aunt,

Winterbourne became aware that the young woman held in horror by that lady was strolling about the great church under escort of her coxcomb of the Corso. It amused him, after a debate, to point out the exemplary pair—even at the cost, as it proved, of Mrs. Costello's saying when she had taken them in through her eye-glass: "That's what makes you so pensive in these days, eh?"

"I hadn't the least idea I was pensive," he pleaded.

"You're very much preoccupied; you're always thinking of something."

"And what is it," he asked, "that you accuse me of thinking of?"

"Of that young lady's, Miss Baker's, Miss Chandler's—what's her name?—Miss Miller's intrigue with that little barber's block."

"Do you call it an intrigue," he asked—"an affair that goes on with such peculiar publicity?"

"That's their folly," said Mrs. Costello, "it's not their merit."

"No," he insisted with a hint perhaps of the preoccupation to which his aunt had alluded—"I don't believe there's anything to be called an intrigue."

"Well"—and Mrs. Costello dropped her glass—"I've heard a dozen people speak of it: they say she's quite carried away by him."

"They're certainly as thick as thieves," our embarrassed young man allowed.

Mrs. Costello came back to them, however, after a little; and Winterbourne recognised in this a further illustration—than that supplied by his own condition—of the spell projected by the case. "He's certainly very handsome. One easily sees how it is. She thinks him the most elegant man in the world, the finest gentleman possible. She has never seen anything like him—he's better even than the courier. It was the courier probably who introduced him, and if he succeeds in marrying the young lady the courier will come in for a magnificent commission."

"I don't believe she thinks of marrying him," Winterbourne reasoned, "and I don't believe he hopes to marry her."

"You may be very sure she thinks of nothing at all. She romps on from day to day, from hour to hour, as they did in the Golden Age. I can imagine nothing more vulgar," said Mrs. Costello, whose figure of speech scarcely went on all fours. "And at the same time," she added, "depend upon it she may tell you any moment that she is 'engaged.' "

"I think that's more than Giovanelli really expects," said Winterbourne.

"And who is Giovanelli?"

"The shiny—but, to do him justice, not greasy—little Roman. I've asked questions about him and learned something. He's apparently a perfectly respectable little man. I believe he's in a small way a *cavaliere avvocato.* But he doesn't move in what are called the first circles. I think it really not absolutely impossible the courier introduced him. He's evidently immensely charmed with Miss Miller. If she thinks him the finest gentleman in the world, he, on his side, has never found himself in personal contact with such splendour, such opulence, such personal daintiness, as this young lady's. And then she must seem to him wonderfully pretty and interesting. Yes, he can't really hope to pull it off. That must appear to him too impossible a piece of luck. He has nothing but his handsome face to offer, and there's a substantial, a possibly explosive Mr. Miller in that mysterious land of dollars and six-shooters. Giovanelli's but too conscious that he hasn't a title to offer. If he were only a count or a *marchese!* What on earth can he make of the way they've taken him up?"

"He accounts for it by his handsome face and thinks Miss Miller a young lady *qui se passe ses fantaisies!"*

"It's very true," Winterbourne pursued, "that Daisy and her mamma haven't yet risen to that stage of—what shall I call it?—of culture, at which the idea of catching a count or a *marchese* begins. I believe them intellectually incapable of that conception."

"Ah but the *cavaliere avvocato* doesn't believe them!" cried Mrs. Costello.

Of the observation excited by Daisy's "intrigue" Winterbourne gathered that day at Saint Peter's sufficient evidence. A dozen of the American colonists in Rome came to talk with his relative, who sat on a small portable stool at the base of one of the great pilasters. The vesper-service was going forward in splendid chants and organ-tones in the adjacent choir, and meanwhile, between Mrs. Costello and her friends, much was said about poor little Miss Miller's going really "too far." Winterbourne was not pleased with what he heard; but when, coming out upon the great steps of the church, he saw Daisy, who had emerged before him, get into an open cab with her accomplice and roll away through the cynical streets of Rome, the measure of her course struck him as simply there to take. He felt very sorry for her—not exactly that he believed she had completely lost her wits, but because it was painful to see so much that was pretty and undefended and natural sink so low in human estimation. He made an attempt after this to give a hint to Mrs. Miller. He met one day in the Corso a friend—a tourist like himself—who had just come out of the Doria Palace, where he had been walking through the beautiful gallery. His friend "went on" for some moments about the great portrait of Innocent X, by Velasquez, suspended in one of the cabinets of the palace, and then said: "And in the same cabinet, by the way, I enjoyed sight of an image of a different kind; that little American who's so much more a work of nature than of art and whom you pointed out to me last week." In answer to Winterbourne's enquiries his friend narrated that the little American—prettier now than ever—was seated with a companion in the secluded nook in which the papal presence is enshrined.

"All alone?" the young man heard himself disingenuously ask.

"Alone with a little Italian who sports in his buttonhole a stack of flowers. The girl's a charming beauty, but I thought I understood from you the other day that she's a young lady *du meilleur monde*."

"So she is!" said Winterbourne; and having assured himself that his informant had seen the interesting pair but ten minutes before, he jumped into a cab and went to call on Mrs. Miller. She was at home, but she apologised for receiving him in Daisy's absence.

"She's gone out somewhere with Mr. Giovanelli. She's always going round with Mr. Giovanelli."

"I've noticed they're intimate indeed," Winterbourne concurred.

"Oh it seems as if they couldn't live without each other!" said Mrs. Miller. "Well, he's a real gentleman anyhow. I guess I have the joke on Daisy—that she *must* be engaged!"

"And how does your daughter *take* the joke?"

"Oh she just says she ain't. But she might as *well* be!" this philosophic parent resumed. "She goes on as if she was. But I've made Mr. Giovanelli promise to tell me if Daisy don't. I'd want to write to Mr. Miller about it—wouldn't you?"

Winterbourne replied that he certainly should; and the state of mind of Daisy's mamma struck him as so unprecedented in the annals of parental vigilance that he recoiled before the attempt to educate at a single interview either her conscience or her wit.

After this Daisy was never at home and he ceased to meet her at the houses of their common acquaintance, because, as he perceived, these shrewd people had quite made up their minds as to the length she must have gone. They ceased to invite her, intimating that they wished to make, and make strongly, for the benefit of observant Europeans, the point that though Miss Daisy Miller was a pretty American girl all right, her behaviour wasn't pretty at all—was in fact regarded by her compatriots as quite monstrous. Winterbourne wondered how she felt about all the cold shoulders that were turned upon her, and sometimes found himself suspecting with impatience that she simply didn't feel and didn't know. He set her down as hopelessly childish and shallow, as such mere giddiness and ignorance incarnate as was powerless either to heed or to suffer. Then at other moments he couldn't doubt that she carried about in her elegant and irresponsible little organism a defiant, passionate, perfectly observant consciousness of the impression she produced. He asked himself whether the defiance would come from the consciousness of innocence or from her being essentially a young person of the reckless class. Then it had to be admitted, he felt, that holding fast to a belief in her "innocence" was more and more but a matter of gallantry too fine-spun for use. As I have already had occasion to relate, he was reduced without pleasure to this chopping of logic and vexed at his poor fallibility, his want of instinctive certitude as to how far her extravagance was generic and national and how far it was crudely personal. Whatever it was he had helplessly missed her, and now it was too late. She was "carried away" by Mr. Giovanelli.

A few days after his brief interview with her mother he came across her at that supreme seat of flowering desolation known as the Palace of the Caesars. The early Roman spring had filled the air with bloom and perfume, and the rugged surface of the Palatine was muffled with tender verdure. Daisy moved at her ease over the great mounds of ruin that are embanked with mossy marble and paved with monumental inscriptions. It seemed to him he had never known Rome so lovely as just then. He looked off at the enchanting harmony of line and colour that remotely encircles the city—he inhaled the softly humid odours and felt the freshness of the year and the antiquity of the place reaffirm themselves in deep interfusion. It struck him also that Daisy had never showed to the eye for so utterly charming; but this had been his conviction on every occasion of their meeting. Giovanelli was of course at her side, and Giovanelli too glowed as never before with something of the glory of his race.

"Well," she broke out upon the friend it would have been such mockery to designate as the latter's rival, "I should think you'd be quite lonesome!"

"Lonesome?" Winterbourne resignedly echoed.

"You're always going round by yourself. Can't you get any one to walk with you?"

"I'm not so fortunate," he answered, "as your gallant companion."

Giovanelli had from the first treated him with distinguished politeness; he listened with a deferential air to his remarks; he laughed punctiliously at his pleasantries; he attached such importance as he could find terms for to Miss Miller's cold compatriot. He carried himself in no degree like a jealous wooer; he had obviously a great deal of tact; he had no objection to any one's expecting a little humility of him. It even struck Winterbourne that he almost yearned at times for some private communication in the interest of his character for common sense; a chance to remark to him as another intelligent man that, bless him, *he* knew how extraordinary was their young lady and didn't flatter himself with confident—at least *too* confident and too delusive—hopes of matrimony and dollars. On this occasion he strolled away from his charming charge to pluck a sprig of almond-blossom which he carefully arranged in his button-hole.

"I know why you say that," Daisy meanwhile observed. "Because you think I go round too much with *him!*" And she nodded at her discreet attendant.

"Every one thinks so—if you care to know," was all Winterbourne found to reply.

"Of course I care to know!"—she made this point with much expression. "But I don't believe a word of it. They're only pretending to be shocked. They don't really care a straw what I do. Besides, I don't go round so much."

"I think you'll find they do care. They'll show it—disagreeably," he took on himself to state.

Daisy weighed the importance of that idea. "How—disagreeably?"

"Haven't you noticed anything?" he compassionately asked.

"I've noticed *you*. But I noticed you've no more 'give' than a ramrod the first time ever I saw you."

You'll find at least that I've more 'give' than several others," he patiently smiled.

"How shall I find it?"

"By going to see the others."

"What will they do to me?"

"They'll show you the cold shoulder. Do you know what that means?"

Daisy was looking at him intently; she began to colour. "Do you mean as Mrs. Walker did the other night?"

"Exactly as Mrs. Walker did the other night."

She looked away at Giovanelli, still titivating with his almond-blossom. Then with her attention again on the important subject: "I shouldn't think you'd let people be so unkind!"

"How can I help it?"

"I should think you'd want to say something."

"I do want to say something"—and Winterbourne paused a moment. "I want to say that your mother tells me she believes you engaged."

"Well, I guess she does," said Daisy very simply.

The young man began to laugh. "And does Randolph believe it?"

"I guess Randolph doesn't believe anything." This testimony to Randolph's scepticism excited Winterbourne to further mirth, and he noticed that Giovanelli was coming back to them. Daisy, observing it as well, addressed herself again to her countryman. "Since you've mentioned it," she said, "I *am* engaged." He looked at her hard—he had stopped laughing. "You don't believe it!" she added.

He asked himself, and it was for a moment like testing a heart-beat; after which, "Yes, I believe it!" he said.

"Oh no, you don't," she answered. "But *if* you possibly do," she still more perversely pursued—"well, I ain't!"

Miss Miller and her constant guide were on their way to the gate of the enclosure, so that Winterbourne, who had but lately entered, presently took leave of them. A week later on he went to dine at a beautiful villa on the Cælian Hill, and, on arriving, dismissed his hired vehicle. The evening was perfect and he promised himself the satisfaction of walking home beneath the Arch of Constantine and past the vaguely-lighted monuments of the Forum. Above was a moon half-developed, whose radiance was not brilliant but veiled in a thin cloud-curtain that seemed to diffuse and equalise it. When on his return from the villa at eleven o'clock he approached the dusky circle of the Colosseum the sense of the romantic in him easily suggested that the interior, in such an atmosphere, would well repay a glance. He turned aside and walked to one of the empty arches, near which, as he observed, an open carriage—one of the little Roman street-cabs—was stationed. Then he passed in among the cavernous shadows of the great structure and emerged upon the clear and silent arena. The place had never seemed to him more impressive. One half of the gigantic circus was in deep shade while the other slept in the luminous dusk. As he stood there he began to murmur Byron's famous lines out of "Manfred"; but before he had finished his quotation he remembered that if nocturnal meditation thereabouts was the fruit of a rich literary culture it was none the less deprecated by medical science. The air of other ages surrounded one; but the air of other ages, coldly analysed, was no better than a villainous miasma. Winterbourne sought, however, toward the middle of the arena, a further reach of vision, intending the next moment a hasty retreat. The great cross in the centre was almost obscured; only as he drew near did he make it out distinctly. He thus also distinguished two persons stationed on the low steps that formed its base. One of these was a woman seated; her companion hovered before her.

Presently the sound of the woman's voice came to him distinctly in the warm night-air. "Well, he looks at us as one of the old lions or tigers may have looked at the Christian martyrs!" These words were winged with their accent, so that they fluttered and settled about him in the darkness like vague white doves. It was Miss Daisy Miller who had released them for flight.

"Let us hope he's not very hungry"—the bland Giovanelli fell in with her humour. "He'll have to take *me* first; you'll serve for dessert."

Winterbourne felt himself pulled up with final horror now—and, it must be added, with final relief. It was as if a sudden clearance had taken place in the ambiguity of the poor girl's appearances and the whole riddle of her contradictions had grown easy to read. She was a young lady about the *shades* of whose perversity a foolish puzzled gentleman need no longer trouble his head or his heart. That once questionable quantity *had* no shades—it was a mere black little blot. He stood there looking at her, looking at her companion too, and not reflecting that though he saw them vaguely he himself must have been more brightly presented. He felt angry at all his shiftings of view—he felt ashamed of all his tender little scruples and all his witless little mercies. He was about to advance again, and then again checked himself; not from the fear of doing her injustice, but from a sense of the danger of showing undue exhilaration for this disburdenment of cautious criticism. He turned away toward the entrance of the place; but as he did so he heard Daisy speak again.

"Why it was Mr. Winterbourne! He saw me and he cuts me dead!"

What a clever little reprobate she was, he was amply able to reflect at this, and how smartly she feigned, how promptly she sought to play off on him, a surprised and injured innocence! But nothing would induce him to cut her either "dead" or to within any measurable distance even of the famous "inch" of her life. He came forward again and went toward the great cross. Daisy had got up and Giovanelli lifted his hat. Winterbourne had now begun to think simply of the madness, on the ground of exposure and infection, of a frail young creature's lounging away such hours in a nest of malaria. What if she *were* the most plausible of little reprobates? That was no reason for her dying of the *perniciosa*. "How long have you been 'fooling round' here?" he asked with conscious roughness.

Daisy, lovely in the sinister silver radiance, appraised him a moment, roughness and all. "Well, I guess all the evening." She answered with spirit and, he could see even then, with exaggeration. "I never saw anything so quaint."

"I'm afraid," he returned, "you'll not think a bad attack of Roman fever very quaint. This is the way people catch it. I wonder," he added to Giovanelli, "that you, a native Roman, should countenance such extraordinary rashness."

"Ah," said this seasoned subject, "for myself I have no fear."

"Neither have I—for you!" Winterbourne retorted in French. "I'm speaking for this young lady."

Giovanelli raised his well-shaped eyebrows and showed his shining teeth, but took his critic's rebuke with docility. "I assured Mademoiselle it was a grave indiscretion, but when was Mademoiselle ever prudent?"

"I never was sick, and I don't mean to be!" Mademoiselle declared. "I don't look like much, but I'm healthy! I was bound to see the Colosseum by moonlight—I wouldn't have wanted to go home without *that;* and we've had the most beautiful time, haven't we, Mr. Giovanelli? If there has been any danger Eugenio can give me some pills. Eugenio has got some splendid pills."

"*I* should advise you then," said Winterbourne, "to drive home as fast as possible and take one!"

Giovanelli smiled as for the striking happy thought. "What you say is very wise. I'll go and make sure the carriage is at hand." And he went forward rapidly.

Daisy followed with Winterbourne. He tried to deny himself the small fine anguish of looking at her, but his eyes themselves refused to spare him, and she seemed moreover not in the least embarrassed. He spoke no word; Daisy chattered over the beauty of the place: "Well, I *have* seen the Colosseum by moonlight—that's one thing I can rave about!" Then noticing her companion's silence she asked him why he was so stiff—it had always been her great word. He made no answer, but he felt his laugh an immense negation of stiffness. They passed under one of the dark archways; Giovanelli was in front with the carriage. Here Daisy stopped a moment, looking at her compatriot. "*Did* you believe I was engaged the other day?"

"It doesn't matter now what I believed the other day!" he replied with infinite point.

It was a wonder how she didn't wince for it. "Well, what do you believe now?"

"I believe it makes very little difference whether you're engaged or not!"

He felt her lighted eyes fairly penetrate the thick gloom of the vaulted passage—as if to seek some access to him she hadn't yet compassed. But Giovanelli, with a graceful inconsequence, was at present all for retreat. "Quick, quick; if we get in by midnight we're quite safe!"

Daisy took her seat in the carriage and the fortunate Italian placed himself beside her. "Don't forget Eugenio's pills!" said Winterbourne as he lifted his hat.

"I don't care," she unexpectedly cried out for this, "whether I have Roman fever or not!" On which the cab-driver cracked his whip and they rolled across the desultory patches of antique pavement.

Winterbourne—to do him justice, as it were—mentioned

to no one that he had encountered Miss Miller at midnight in the Colosseum with a gentleman; in spite of which deep discretion, however, the fact of the scandalous adventure was known a couple of days later, with a dozen vivid details, to every member of the little American circle, and was commented accordingly. Winterbourne judged thus that the people about the hotel had been thoroughly empowered to testify, and that after Daisy's return there would have been an exchange of jokes between the porter and the cab-driver. But the young man became aware at the same moment of how thoroughly it had ceased to ruffle him that the little American flirt should be "talked about" by low-minded menials. These sources of current criticism a day or two later abounded still further: the little American flirt was alarmingly ill and the doctors now in possession of the scene. Winterbourne, when the rumour came to him, immediately went to the hotel for more news. He found that two or three charitable friends had preceded him and that they were being entertained in Mrs. Miller's salon by the all-efficient Randolph.

"It's going round at night that way, you bet—that's what has made her so sick. She's always going round at night. I shouldn't think she'd want to—it's so plaguey dark over here. You can't see anything over here without the moon's right up. In America they don't go round by the moon!" Mrs. Miller meanwhile wholly surrendered to her genius for unapparent uses; her salon knew her less than ever, and she was presumably now at least giving her daughter the advantage of her society. It was clear that Daisy was dangerously ill.

Winterbourne constantly attended for news from the sick-room, which reached him, however, but with worrying indirectness, though he once had speech, for a moment, of the poor girl's physician and once saw Mrs. Miller, who, sharply alarmed, struck him as thereby more happily inspired than he could have conceived and indeed as the most noiseless and light-handed of nurses. She invoked a good deal the remote shade of Dr. Davis, but Winterbourne paid her the compliment of taking her after all for less monstrous a goose. To this indulgence indeed something she further said perhaps even more insidiously disposed him. "Daisy spoke of you the other day quite pleasantly. Half the time she doesn't know what she's saying, but that time I think she did. She gave me a message—she told me to tell you. She wanted you to know she never was engaged to that handsome Italian who was always round. I'm sure I'm very glad; Mr. Giovanelli hasn't been near us since she was taken ill. I thought he was so much of a gentleman, but I don't call that very polite! A lady told me he was afraid I hadn't approved of his being round with her so much evenings. Of course it ain't as if their evenings were as pleasant as ours—since *we* don't seem to feel that way about the poison. I guess I *don't* see the point now; but I suppose he knows I'm a lady and I'd scorn to raise a fuss. Anyway, she wants you to realise she ain't engaged. I don't know why she makes so much of it, but she said to me three times 'Mind you tell Mr. Winterbourne.' And then she told me to ask if you remembered the time you went up to that castle in Switzerland. But I said I wouldn't give any such messages as *that*. Only if she ain't engaged I guess I'm glad to realise it too."

But, as Winterbourne had originally judged, the truth on this question had small actual relevance. A week after this the poor girl died; it had been indeed a terrible case of the *perniciosa*. A grave was found for her in the little Protestant cemetery, by an angle of the wall of imperial Rome, beneath the cypresses and the thick spring-flowers. Winterbourne stood there beside it with a number of other mourners; a number larger than the scandal excited by the young lady's career might have made probable. Near him stood Giovanelli, who came nearer still before Winterbourne turned away. Giovanelli, in decorous mourning, showed but a whiter face; his button-hole lacked its nosegay and he had visibly something urgent—and even to distress—to say, which he scarce knew how to "place." He decided at last to confide it with a pale convulsion to Winterbourne. "She was the most beautiful young lady I ever saw, and the most amiable." To which he added in a moment: "Also—naturally!—the most innocent."

Winterbourne sounded him with hard dry eyes, but presently repeated his words, "The most innocent?"

"The most innocent!"

It came somehow so much too late that our friend could only glare at its having come at all. "Why the devil," he asked, "did you take her to that fatal place?"

Giovanelli raised his neat shoulders and eyebrows to within suspicion of a shrug. "For myself I had no fear; and *she*—she did what she liked."

Winterbourne's eyes attached themselves to the ground. "She did what she liked!"

It determined on the part of poor Giovanelli a further pious, a further candid, confidence. "If she had lived I should have got nothing. She never would have married me."

It had been spoken as if to attest, in all sincerity, his disinterestedness, but Winterbourne scarce knew what welcome to give it. He said, however, with a grace inferior to his friend's: "I dare say not."

The latter was even by this not discouraged. "For a moment I hoped so. But no. I'm convinced."

Winterbourne took it in; he stood staring at the raw protuberance among the April daisies. When he turned round again his fellow mourner had stepped back.

He almost immediately left Rome, but the following summer he again met his aunt Mrs. Costello at Vevey. Mrs. Costello extracted from the charming old hotel there a value that the Miller family hadn't mastered the secret of. In the interval Winterbourne had often thought of the most interesting member of the trio—of her mystifying manners and her queer adventure. One day he spoke of her to his aunt—said it was on his conscience he had done her injustice.

"I'm sure I don't know"—that lady showed caution. "How did your injustice affect her?"

"She sent me a message before her death which I didn't understand at the time. But I've understood it since. She would have appreciated one's esteem."

"She took an odd way to gain it! But do you mean by what you say," Mrs. Costello asked, "that she would have reciprocated one's affection?"

As he made no answer to this she after a little looked round at him—he hadn't been directly within sight; but the effect of that wasn't to make her repeat her question. He spoke, however, after a while. "You were right in that remark that you made last summer. I was booked to make a mistake. I've lived too long in foreign parts." And this time she herself said nothing.

Nevertheless he soon went back to live at Geneva, whence there continue to come the most contradictory accounts of his motives of sojourn: a report that he's "studying" hard—an intimation that he's much interested in a very clever foreign lady.

JAMES'S PREFACE TO *DAISY MILLER*

1909

It was in Rome during the autumn of 1877; a friend then living there but settled now in a South less weighted with appeals and memories happened to mention—which she might perfectly not have done—some simple and uninformed American lady of the previous winter, whose young daughter, a child of nature and of freedom, accompanying her from hotel to hotel, had "picked up" by the wayside, with the best conscience in the world, a good-looking Roman, of vague identity, astonished at his luck, yet (so far as might be, by the pair) all innocently, all serenely exhibited and introduced: this at least till the occurrence of some small social check, some interrupting incident, of no great gravity or dignity, and which I forget. I had never heard, save on this showing, of the amiable but not otherwise eminent ladies, who weren't in fact named, I think, and whose case had merely served to point a familiar moral; and it must have been just their want of salience that left a margin for the small pencil-mark inveterately signifying, in such connexions, "Dramatise, dramatise!" The result of my recognising a few months later the sense of my pencil-mark was the short chronicle of "Daisy Miller," which I indited in London the following spring and then addressed, with no conditions attached, as I remember, to the editor of a magazine that had its seat of publication at Philadelphia and had lately appeared to appreciate my contributions. That gentleman however (an historian of some repute) promptly returned me my missive, and with an absence of comment that struck me at the time as rather grim—as, given the circumstances, requiring indeed some explanation: till a friend to whom I appealed for light, giving him the thing to read, declared it could only have passed with the Philadelphian critic for "an outrage on American girlhood." This was verily a light, and of bewildering intensity; though I was presently to read into the matter a further helpful inference. To the fault of being outrageous this little composition added that of being essentially and pre-eminently a *nouvelle;* a signal example in fact of that type, foredoomed at the best, in more cases than not, to editorial disfavour. If accordingly I was afterwards to be cradled, almost blissfully, in the conception that "Daisy" at least, among my productions, might approach "success," such success for example, on her eventual appearance, as the state of being promptly pirated in Boston—a sweet tribute I hadn't yet received and was never again to know—the irony of things yet claimed its rights, I couldn't but long continue to feel, in the circumstance that quite a special reprobation had waited on the first appearance in the world of the ultimately most prosperous child of my invention. So doubly discredited, at all events, this bantling met indulgence, with no great delay, in the eyes of my admirable friend the late Leslie Stephen and was published in two numbers of "The Cornhill Magazine" (1878).

It qualified itself in that publication and afterwards as "a Study"; for reasons which I confess I fail to recapture unless they may have taken account simply of a certain flatness in my poor little heroine's literal denomination. Flatness indeed, one must have felt, was the very sum of her story; so that perhaps after all the attached epithet was meant but as a deprecation, addressed to the reader, of any great critical hope of stirring scenes. It provided for mere concentration, and on an object scant and superficially vulgar—from which, however, a sufficiently brooding tenderness might eventually extract a shy incongruous charm. I suppress at all events here the appended qualification—in view of the simple truth, which ought from the first to have been apparent to me, that my little exhibition is made to no degree whatever in critical but, quite inordinately and extravagantly, in poetical terms. It comes back to me that I was at a certain hour long afterwards to have reflected, in this connexion, on the characteristic free play of the whirligig of time. It was in Italy again—in Venice and in the prized society of an interesting friend, now dead, with whom I happened to wait, on the Grand Canal, at the animated water-steps of one of the hotels. The considerable little terrace there was so disposed as to make a salient stage for certain demonstrations on the part of two young girls, children *they,* if ever, of nature and of freedom, whose use of those resources, in the general public eye, and under our own as we sat in the gondola, drew from the lips of a second companion, sociably afloat with us, the remark that there before us, with no sign absent, were a couple of attesting Daisy Millers. Then it was that, in my charming hostess's prompt protest, the whirligig, as I have called it, at once betrayed itself. "How can you liken *those* creatures to a figure of which the only fault is touchingly to have transmuted so sorry a type and to have, by a poetic artifice, not only led our judgement of it astray, but made *any* judgement quite impossible?" With which this gentle lady and admirable critic turned on the author himself. "You *know* you quite falsified, by the turn you gave it, the thing you had begun with having in mind, the thing you had had, to satiety, the chance of 'observing': your pretty perversion of it, or your unprincipled mystification of our sense of it, does it really too much honour—in spite of which, none the less, as anything charming or touching always to that extent justifies itself, we after a fashion forgive and understand you. But why *waste* your romance? There are cases, too many, in which you've done it again; in which, provoked by a spirit of observation at first no doubt sufficiently sincere, and with the measured and felt truth fairly twitching your sleeve, you have yielded to your incurable prejudice in favour of grace—to whatever it is in you that makes so inordinately for form and prettiness and pathos; not to say sometimes for misplaced drolling. Is it that you've after all too much imagination? Those awful young women capering at the hotel-door, *they* are the real little Daisy Millers that were; whereas yours in the tale is such a one, more's the pity, as—for pitch of the ingenuous, for quality of the artless—couldn't possibly have been at all." My answer to all which bristled of course with more professions than I can or need report here; the chief of them inevitably to the effect that my supposedly typical little figure was of course pure poetry, and had never been anything else; since this is what helpful imagination, in however slight a dose, ever directly makes for. As for the original grossness of readers, I dare say I added, that was another matter—but one which at any rate had then quite ceased to signify.

EDITOR'S NOTE

Henry James destroyed many of his notebooks and no entry survives to indicate the original source of "Daisy Miller." Nor is it possible to identify the Roman and Venetian friends to whom he alludes in his preface, unless, indeed, in Venice, he is speaking of Katherine Bronson, the hostess of Robert Browning and of himself on various occasions, or Mrs. Daniel Curtis, at whose Palazzo Barbaro he found the inspiration for the Venetian scenes in *The Wings of the Dove.*

The editor who rejected "Daisy Miller" as an "outrage" on American girlhood was John Foster Kirk, the historian and editor of *Lippincott's* from 1870 to 1886. The story accordingly appeared first in England, in the *Cornhill Magazine,* and was, as James observed, promptly "pirated," in those lax days of copyright, in Boston, in Litell's *Living Age* (July 6, and July 27, 1878) with the signature, Henry James Jr. appearing only at the end of the second instalment and with no credit to the author in the table of contents.[1] What James did not know was that it had been pirated equally by the *Home Journal* (now *Town and Country*) in New York, in its issues of July 31, August 7 and 14. Published finally in the Harper Half-Hour Series, the story made Henry James famous on both sides of the Atlantic. In England to this day the term "a Daisy Miller" is used to describe a certain type of young innocent from America.

The novelist does not discuss the story in detail in the portion of the preface here given since, in an earlier preface, to *The Reverberator,* he dealt fully with the whole subject of his treatment of the "international" theme—the American abroad. What had struck him about New Yorkers or Bostonians in Europe at that period, he says, was their "state of innocence," their being "unaware of life"—that is "as the old European order expressed life." This was a subject suited to his own experience. "Conscious of so few things in the world," he wrote, "these unprecedented creatures . . . were least of all conscious of deficiencies and dangers; so that, the grace of youth and innocence and freshness aiding, their negatives were converted and became in certain relations lively positives and values." And that, in essence, is what "Daisy Miller" became.

[1] I am indebted to Mr. Dan H. Laurence of New York University for this bibliographical information.

WASHINGTON SQUARE
1881

I

DURING a portion of the first half of the present century, and more particularly during the latter part of it, there flourished and practised in the city of New York a physician who enjoyed perhaps an exceptional share of the consideration which, in the United States, has always been bestowed upon distinguished members of the medical profession. This profession in America has constantly been held in honor, and more successfully than elsewhere has put forward a claim to the epithet of "liberal." In a country in which, to play a social part, you must either earn your income or make believe that you earn it, the healing art has appeared in a high degree to combine two recognized sources of credit. It belongs to the realm of the practical, which in the United States is a great recommendation; and it is touched by the light of science—a merit appreciated in a community in which the love of knowledge has not always been accompanied by leisure and opportunity.

It was an element in Doctor Sloper's reputation that his learning and his skill were very evenly balanced; he was what you might call a scholarly doctor, and yet there was nothing abstract in his remedies—he always ordered you to take something. Though he was felt to be extremely thorough, he was not uncomfortably theoretic; and if he sometimes explained matters rather more minutely than might seem of use to the patient, he never went so far (like some practitioners one had heard of) as to trust to the explanation alone, but always left behind him an inscrutable prescription. There were some doctors that left the prescription without offering any explanation at all; and he did not belong to that class either, which was after all the most vulgar. It will be seen that I am describing a clever man; and this is really the reason why Doctor Sloper had become a local celebrity.

At the time at which we are chiefly concerned with him he was some fifty years of age, and his popularity was at its height. He was very witty, and he passed in the best society of New York for a man of the world—which, indeed, he was, in a very sufficient degree. I hasten to add, to anticipate possible misconception, that he was not the least of a charlatan. He was a thoroughly honest man—honest in a degree of which he had perhaps lacked the opportunity to give the complete measure; and, putting aside the great good-nature of the circle in which he practised, which was rather fond of boasting that it possessed the "brightest" doctor in the country, he daily justified his claim to the talents attributed to him by the popular voice. He was an observer, even a philosopher, and to be bright was so natural to him, and (as the popular voice said) came so easily, that he never aimed at mere effect, and had none of the little tricks and pretensions of second-rate reputations. It must be confessed that fortune had favored him, and that he had found the path to prosperity very soft to his tread. He had married, at the age of twenty-seven, for love, a very charming girl, Miss Catherine Harrington of New York, who, in addition to her charms, had brought him a solid dowry. Mrs. Sloper was amiable, graceful, accomplished, elegant, and in 1820 she had been one of the pretty girls of the small but promising capital which clustered about the Battery and overlooked the Bay, and of which the uppermost boundary was indicated by the grassy waysides of Canal Street. Even at the age of twenty-seven Austin Sloper had made his mark sufficiently to mitigate the anomaly of his having been chosen among a dozen suitors by a young woman of high fashion, who had ten thousand dollars of income and the most charming eyes in the island of Manhattan. These eyes, and some of their accompaniments, were for about five years a source of extreme satisfaction to the young physician, who was both a devoted and a very happy husband.

The fact of his having married a rich woman made no difference in the line he had traced for himself, and he cultivated his profession with as definite a purpose as if he still had no other resources than his fraction of the modest patrimony which, on his father's death, he had shared with his brothers and sisters. This purpose had not been preponderantly to make money—it had been rather to learn something and to do something. To learn something interesting, and to do something useful—this was, roughly speaking, the programme he had sketched, and of which the accident of his wife having an income appeared to him in no degree to modify the validity. He was fond of his practice, and of exercising a skill of which he was agreeably conscious, and it was so patent a truth that if he were not a doctor there was nothing else he could be, that a doctor he persisted in being, in the best possible conditions. Of course his easy domestic situation saved him a good deal of drudgery, and his wife's affiliation to the "best people" brought him a good many of those patients whose symptoms are, if not more interesting in themselves than those of the lower orders, at least more consistently displayed. He desired experience, and in the course of twenty years he got a great deal. It must be added that it came to him in some forms which, whatever might have been their intrinsic value, made it the reverse of welcome. His first child, a little boy of extraordinary promise, as the Doctor, who was not addicted to easy enthusiasm, firmly believed, died at three years of age, in spite of everything that the mother's tenderness and the father's science could invent to save him. Two years later Mrs. Sloper gave birth to a second infant—an infant of a sex which rendered the poor child, to the Doctor's sense, an inadequate substitute for his lamented first-born, of whom he had promised himself to make an admirable man. The little girl was a disappointment; but this was not the worst. A week after her birth the young mother, who, as the phrase is, had been doing well, suddenly betrayed alarming symptoms, and before another week had elapsed Austin Sloper was a widower.

For a man whose trade was to keep people alive he had certainly done poorly in his own family; and a bright doctor who within three years loses his wife and his little boy should perhaps be prepared to see either his skill or his affection impugned. Our friend, however, escaped criticism; that is, he escaped all criticism but his own, which was much the most competent and most formidable. He walked under the weight of this very private censure for the rest of his days, and bore forever the scars of a castigation to which the strongest hand he knew had treated him on the night that followed his wife's death. The world, which, as I have said, appreciated him, pitied him too much to be ironical; his misfortune made him more interesting, and even helped him to be the fashion. It was observed that even medical families cannot escape the more insidious forms of disease, and that, after all, Doctor Sloper had lost other patients besides the two I have mentioned; which constituted an honorable precedent. His little girl remained to him; and though she was not what he had desired, he proposed to himself to make the best of her. He had on hand a stock of unexpended authority, by which the child, in its early years, profited largely. She had been named, as a matter of course, after her poor mother, and even in her most diminutive babyhood the Doctor never called her anything but Catherine. She grew up a very robust and healthy child, and her father, as he looked at her, often said to himself that, such as she was, he at least need have no fear of losing her. I say "such as she was," because, to tell the truth— But this is a truth of which I will defer the telling.

II

WHEN the child was about ten years old, he invited his sister, Mrs. Penniman, to come and stay with him. The Miss Slopers had been but two in number, and both of them had married early in life. The younger, Mrs. Almond by name, was the wife of a prosperous merchant and the mother of a blooming family. She bloomed herself, indeed, and was a comely, comfortable, reasonable woman, and a favorite with her clever brother, who, in the matter of women, even when they were nearly related to him, was a man of distinct preferences. He preferred Mrs. Almond to his sister Lavinia, who had married a poor clergyman, of a sickly constitution and a flowery style of eloquence, and then, at the age of thirty-three, had been left a widow—without children, without fortune—with nothing but the memory of Mr. Penniman's flowers of speech, a certain vague aroma of which hovered about her own conversation. Nevertheless, he had offered her a home under his own roof, which Lavinia accepted with the alacrity of a woman who had spent the ten years of her married life in the town of Poughkeepsie. The Doctor had not proposed to Mrs. Penniman to come and live with him indefinitely; he had suggested that she should make an asylum of his house while she looked about for unfurnished lodgings. It is uncertain whether Mrs. Penniman ever instituted a search for unfurnished lodgings, but it is beyond dispute that she never found them. She settled herself with her brother and never went away, and, when Catherine was twenty years old, her Aunt Lavinia was still one of the most striking features of her immediate *entourage*. Mrs. Penniman's own account of the matter was that she had remained to take charge of her niece's education. She had given this account, at least, to every one but the Doctor, who never asked for explanations which he could entertain himself any day with inventing. Mrs. Penniman, moreover, though she had a good deal of a certain sort of artificial assurance, shrunk, for indefinable reasons, from presenting herself to her brother as a fountain of instruction. She had not a high sense of humor, but she had enough to prevent her from making this mistake; and her brother, on his side, had enough to excuse her, in her situation, for laying him under contribution during a considerable part of a lifetime. He therefore assented tacitly to the proposition which Mrs. Penniman had tacitly laid down, that it was of importance that the poor motherless girl should have a brilliant woman near her. His assent could only be tacit, for he had never been dazzled by his sister's intellectual lustre. Save when he fell in love with Catherine Harrington, he had never been dazzled, indeed, by any feminine characteristics whatever; and though he was to a certain extent what is called a ladies' doctor, his private opinion of the more complicated sex was not exalted. He regarded its complications as more curious than edifying, and he had an idea of the beauty of *reason,* which was, on the whole, meagrely gratified by what he observed in his female patients. His wife had been a reasonable woman, but she was a bright exception; among several things that he was sure of, this was perhaps the principal. Such a conviction, of course, did little either to mitigate or to abbreviate his widowhood; and it set a limit to his recognition, at the best, of Catherine's possibilities and of Mrs. Penniman's ministrations. He nevertheless, at the end of six months, accepted his sister's permanent presence as an accomplished fact, and as Catherine grew older, perceived that there were in effect good reasons why she should have a companion of her own imperfect sex. He was extremely polite to Lavinia, scrupulously, formally polite; and she had never seen him in anger but once in her life, when he lost his temper in a theological discussion with her late husband. With her he never discussed theology, nor, indeed, discussed anything; he contented himself with making known, very distinctly, in the form of a lucid ultimatum, his wishes with regard to Catherine.

Once, when the girl was about twelve years old, he had said to her—

"Try and make a clever woman of her, Lavinia; I should like her to be a clever woman."

Mrs. Penniman, at this, looked thoughtful a moment "My dear Austin," she then inquired, "do you think it is better to be clever than to be good?"

"Good for what?" asked the Doctor. "You are good for nothing unless you are clever."

From this assertion Mrs. Penniman saw no reason to dissent; she possibly reflected that her own great use in the world was owing to her aptitude for many things.

"Of course I wish Catherine to be good," the Doctor said next day; "but she won't be any the less virtuous for not being a fool. I am not afraid of her being wicked; she will never have the salt of malice in her character. She is 'as good as good bread,' as the French say; but six years hence I don't want to have to compare her to good bread-and-butter."

"Are you afraid she will be insipid? My dear brother, it is I who supply the butter; so you needn't fear!" said Mrs. Penniman, who had taken in hand the child's "accomplishments," overlooking her at the piano, where Catherine displayed a certain talent, and going with her to the dancing-class, where it must be confessed that she made but a modest figure.

Mrs. Penniman was a tall, thin, fair, rather faded woman, with a perfectly amiable disposition, a high standard of gentility. a taste for light literature, and a certain foolish indirectness and obliquity of character. She was romantic; she was sentimental; she had a passion for little secrets and mysteries—a very innocent passion, for her secrets had hitherto always been as unpractical as addled eggs. She was not absolutely veracious; but this defect was of no great consequence, for she had never had anything to conceal. She would have liked to have a lover, and to correspond with him under an assumed name, in letters left at a shop. I am bound to say that her imagination never carried the intimacy further than this. Mrs. Penniman had never had a lover, but her brother, who was very shrewd, understood her turn of mind. "When Catherine is about seventeen," he said to himself, "Lavinia will try and persuade her that some young man with a mustache is in love with her. It will be quite untrue; no young man, with a mustache or without, will ever be in love with Catherine. But Lavinia will take it up, and talk to her about it; perhaps, even, if her taste for clandestine operations doesn't prevail with her, she will talk to me about it. Catherine won't see it, and won't believe it, fortunately for her peace of mind; poor Catherine isn't romantic."

She was a healthy, well-grown child, without a trace of her mother's beauty. She was not ugly; she had simply a plain, dull, gentle countenance. The most that had ever been said for her was that she had a "nice" face; and, though she was an heiress, no one had ever thought of regarding her as a belle. Her father's opinion of her moral purity was abundantly justified; she was excellently, imperturbably good; affectionate, docile, obedient, and much addicted to speaking the truth. In her younger years she was a good deal of a romp, and, though it is an awkward confession to make about one's heroine, I must add that she was something of a glutton. She never, that I know of, stole raisins out of the pantry; but she devoted her pocket-money to the purchase of creamcakes. As regards this, however, a critical attitude would be inconsistent with a candid reference to the early annals of any biographer. Catherine was decidedly not clever; she was not quick with her book, nor, indeed, with anything else. She was not abnormally deficient, and she mustered learning enough to acquit herself respectably in conversation with her contemporaries —among whom it must be avowed, however, that she occupied a secondary place. It is well known that in New York it is possible for a young girl to occupy a primary one. Catherine, who was extremely modest, had no desire to shine, and on most social occasions, as they are called, you would have found her lurking in the background. She was extremely fond of her father, and very much afraid of him; she thought him the cleverest and handsomest and most celebrated of men. The poor girl found her account so completely in the exercise of her affections that the little tremor of fear that mixed itself with her filial passion gave the thing an extra relish rather than blunted its edge. Her deepest desire was to please him, and her conception of happiness was to know that she had succeeded in pleasing him. She had never succeeded beyond a certain point. Though, on the whole, he was very kind to her, she was perfectly aware of this, and to go beyond the point in question seemed to her really something to live for. What she could not know, of course, was that she disappointed him, though on three or four occasions the Doctor had been almost frank about it. She grew up peacefully and prosperously; but at the age of eighteen Mrs. Penniman had not made a clever woman of her. Doctor Sloper would have liked to be proud of his daughter; but there was nothing to be proud of in poor Catherine. There was nothing, of course, to be ashamed of; but this was not enough for the Doctor, who was a proud man, and would have enjoyed being able to think of his daughter as an unusual girl. There would have been a fitness in her being pretty and graceful, intelligent and distinguished—for her mother had been the most charming woman of her little day—and as regards her father, of course he knew his own value. He had moments of irritation at having produced a commonplace child, and he even went so far at times as to take a certain satisfaction in the thought that his wife had not lived to find her out. He was naturally slow in making this discovery himself, and it was not till Catherine had become a young lady grown that he regarded the matter as settled. He gave her the benefit of a great many doubts; he was in no haste to conclude. Mrs. Penniman frequently assured him that his daughter had a delightful nature; but he knew how to interpret this assurance. It meant, to his sense, that Catherine was not wise enough to discover that her aunt was a goose—a limitation of mind that could not fail to be agreeable to Mrs. Penniman. Both she and her brother, however, exaggerated the young girl's limitations; for Catherine, though she was very fond of her aunt, and conscious of the gratitude she owed her, regarded her without a particle of that gentle dread which gave its stamp to her admiration of her father. To her mind there was nothing of the infinite about Mrs. Penniman; Catherine saw her all at once, as it were, and was not dazzled by the apparition; whereas her father's great faculties seemed, as they stretched away, to lose themselves in a sort of luminous vagueness, which indicated, not that they stopped, but that Catherine's own mind ceased to follow them.

It must not be supposed that Doctor Sloper visited his disappointment upon the poor girl, or ever let her suspect that she had played him a trick. On the contrary, for fear of being unjust to her, he did his duty with exemplary zeal, and recognized that she was a faithful and affectionate child. Besides, he was a philosopher: he smoked a good many cigars over his disappointment, and in the fullness of time he got used to it. He satisfied himself that he had expected nothing, though, indeed, with a certain oddity of reasoning. "I expect nothing," he said to himself; "so that, if she gives me a surprise, it will be all clear gain. If she doesn't, it will be no loss." This was about the time Catherine had reached her eighteenth year; so that it will be seen her father had not been precipitate. At this time she seemed not only incapable of giving surprises; it was almost a question whether she could have received one—she was so quiet and irresponsive. People who expressed themselves roughly called her stolid. But she was irresponsive because she was shy, uncomfortably, painfully shy. This was not always understood, and she sometimes produced an impression of insensibility. In reality, she was the softest creature in the world.

III

As a child she had promised to be tall; but when she was sixteen she ceased to grow, and her stature, like most other points in her composition, was not unusual. She was strong, however, and properly made, and, fortunately, her health was excellent. It has been noted that the Doctor was a philosopher, but I would not have answered for his philosophy if the poor girl had proved a sickly and suffering person. Her appearance of health constituted her principal claim to beauty; and her clear, fresh complexion, in which white and red were very equally distributed, was, indeed, an excellent thing to see. Her eye was small and quiet, her features were rather thick, her tresses brown and smooth. A dull, plain girl she was called by rigorous critics—a quiet, lady-like girl, by those of the more imaginative sort; but by neither class was she very elaborately discussed. When it had been duly impressed upon her that she was a young lady—it was a good while before she could believe it—she suddenly developed a lively taste for dress: a lively taste is quite the expression to use. I feel as if I ought to write it very small, her judgment in this matter was by no means infallible; it was liable to confusions and embarrassments. Her great indulgence of it was really the desire of a rather inarticulate nature to manifest itself; she sought to be eloquent in her garments, and to make up for her diffidence of speech by a fine frankness of costume. But if she expressed herself in her clothes, it is certain that people were not to blame for not thinking her a witty person. It must be added that, though she had the expectation of a fortune—Doctor Sloper for a long time had been making twenty thousand dollars a year by his profession, and laying aside the half of it—the amount of money at her disposal was not greater than the allowance made to many poorer girls. In those days, in New York, there were still a few altar-fires flickering in the temple of Republican simplicity, and Doctor Sloper would have been glad to see his daughter present herself, with a classic grace, as a priestess of this mild faith. It made him fairly grimace, in private, to think that a child of his should be both ugly and overdressed. For himself, he was fond of the good things of life, and he made a considerable use of them; but he had a dread of vulgarity, and even a theory that it was increasing in the society that surrounded him. Moreover, the standard of luxury in the United States thirty years ago was carried by no means so high as at present, and Catherine's clever father took the old-fashioned view of the education of young persons. He had no particular theory on the subject; it had scarcely as yet become a necessity of self-defence to have a collection of theories. It simply appeared to him proper and reasonable that a well-bred young woman should not carry half her fortune on her back. Catherine's back was a broad one, and would have carried a good deal; but to the weight of the paternal displeasure she never ventured to expose it, and our heroine was twenty years old before she treated herself, for evening wear, to a red satin gown trimmed with gold fringe; though this was an article which, for many years, she had coveted in secret. It made her look, when she sported it, like a woman of thirty; but oddly enough, in spite of her taste for fine clothes, she had not a grain of coquetry, and her anxiety when she put them on was as to whether they, and not she, would look well. It is a point on which history has not been explicit, but the assumption is warrantable; it was in the royal raiment just mentioned that she presented herself at a little entertainment given by her aunt, Mrs. Almond. The girl was at this time in her twenty-first year, and Mrs. Almond's party was the beginning of something very important.

Some three or four years before this, Doctor Sloper had

moved his household gods up town, as they say in New York. He had been living ever since his marriage in an edifice of red brick, with granite copings and an enormous fan-light over the door, standing in a street within five minutes' walk of the City Hall, which saw its best days (from the social point of view) about 1820. After this, the tide of fashion began to set steadily northward, as, indeed, in New York, thanks to the narrow channel in which it flows, it is obliged to do, and the great hum of traffic rolled farther to the right and left of Broadway. By the time the Doctor changed his residence, the murmur of trade had become a mighty uproar, which was music in the ears of all good citizens interested in the commercial development, as they delighted to call it, of their fortunate isle. Doctor Sloper's interest in this phenomenon was only indirect—though, seeing that, as the years went on, half his patients came to be overworked men of business, it might have been more immediate—and when most of his neighbors' dwellings (also ornamented with granite copings and large fan-lights) had been converted into offices, warehouses, and shipping agencies, and otherwise applied to the base uses of commerce, he determined to look out for a quieter home. The ideal of quiet and of genteel retirement, in 1835, was found in Washington Square, where the Doctor built himself a handsome, modern, wide-fronted house, with a big balcony before the drawing-room windows, and a flight of white marble steps ascending to a portal which was also faced with white marble. This structure, and many of its neighbors, which it exactly resembled, were supposed, forty years ago, to embody the last results of architectural science, and they remain to this day very solid and honorable dwellings. In front of them was the square, containing a considerable quantity of inexpensive vegetation, enclosed by a wooden paling, which increased its rural and accessible appearance; and round the corner was the more august precinct of the Fifth Avenue, taking its origin at this point with a spacious and confident air which already marked it for high destinies. I know not whether it is owing to the tenderness of early associations, but this portion of New York appears to many persons the most delectable. It has a kind of established repose which is not of frequent occurrence in other quarters of the long, shrill city; it has a riper, richer, more honorable look than any of the upper ramifications of the great longitudinal thoroughfare—the look of having had something of a social history. It was here, as you might have been informed on good authority, that you had come into a world which appeared to offer a variety of sources of interest; it was here that your grandmother lived, in venerable solitude, and dispensed a hospitality which commended itself alike to the infant imagination and the infant palate; it was here that you took your first walks abroad, following the nursery-maid with unequal step, and sniffing up the strange odor of the ailanthus-trees which at that time formed the principal umbrage of the Square, and diffused an aroma that you were not yet critical enough to dislike as it deserved; it was here, finally, that your first school, kept by a broad-bosomed, broad-based old lady with a ferule, who was always having tea in a blue cup, with a saucer that didn't match, enlarged the circle both of your observations and your sensations. It was here, at any rate, that my heroine spent many years of her life; which is my excuse for this topographical parenthesis.

Mrs. Almond lived much farther up town, in an embryonic street, with a high number—a region where the extension of the city began to assume a theoretic air, where poplars grew beside the pavement (when there was one), and mingled their shade with the steep roofs of desultory Dutch houses, and where pigs and chickens disported themselves in the gutter. These elements of rural picturesqueness have now wholly departed from New York street scenery; but they were to be found within the memory of middle-aged persons in quarters which now would blush to be reminded of them. Catherine had a great many cousins, and with her Aunt Almond's children, who ended by being nine in number, she lived on terms of considerable intimacy. When she was younger they had been rather afraid of her; she was believed, as the phrase is, to be highly educated, and a person who lived in the intimacy of their Aunt Penniman had something of reflected grandeur. Mrs. Penniman, among the little Almonds, was an object of more admiration than sympathy. Her manners were strange and formidable, and her mourning robes—she dressed in black for twenty years after her husband's death, and then suddenly appeared, one morning, with pink roses in her cap—were complicated in odd, unexpected places with buckles, bugles, and pins, which discouraged familiarity. She took children too hard, both for good and for evil, and had an oppressive air of expecting subtle things of them; so that going to see her was a good deal like being taken to church and made to sit in a front pew. It was discovered after a while, however, that Aunt Penniman was but an accident in Catherine's existence, and not a part of its essence, and that when the girl came to spend a Saturday with her cousins, she was available for "follow-my-master," and even for leap-frog. On this basis an understanding was easily arrived at, and for several years Catherine fraternized with her young kinsmen. I say young kinsmen, because seven of the little Almonds were boys, and Catherine had a preference for those games which are most conveniently played in trousers. By degrees, however, the little Almonds' trousers began to lengthen, and the wearers to disperse and settle themselves in life. The elder children were older than Catherine, and the boys were sent to college or placed in counting-rooms. Of the girls, one married very punctually, and the other as punctually became engaged. It was to celebrate this latter event that Mrs. Almond gave the little party I have mentioned. Her daughter was to marry a stout young stock-broker, a boy of twenty: it was thought a very good thing.

IV

Mrs. Penniman, with more buckles and bangles than ever, came, of course, to the entertainment, accompanied by her niece; the Doctor, too, had promised to look in later in the evening. There was to be a good deal of dancing, and before it had gone very far Marian Almond came up to Catherine, in company with a tall young man. She introduced the young man as a person who had a great desire to make our heroine's acquaintance, and as a cousin of Arthur Townsend, her own intended.

Marian Almond was a pretty little person of seventeen, with a very small figure and a very big sash, to the elegance of whose manners matrimony had nothing to add. She already had all the airs of a hostess, receiving the company, shaking her fan, saying that with so many people to attend to she should have no time to dance. She made a long speech about Mr. Townsend's cousin, to whom she administered a tap with her fan before turning away to other cares. Catherine had not understood all that she said; her attention was given to enjoying Marian's ease of manner and flow of ideas, and to looking at the young man, who was remarkably handsome. She had succeeded, however, as she often failed to do when people were presented to her, in catching his name, which appeared to be the same as that of Marian's little stock-broker. Catherine was always agitated by an introduction; it seemed a difficult moment, and she wondered that some people—her new acquaintance at this moment, for instance—should mind it so little. She wondered what she ought to say, and what would be the consequences of her saying nothing.

The consequences at present were very agreeable. Mr. Townsend, leaving her no time for embarrassment, began to talk to her with an easy smile, as if he had known her for a year.

"What a delightful party! What a charming house! What an interesting family! What a pretty girl your cousin is!"

These observations, in themselves of no great profundity, Mr. Townsend seemed to offer for what they were worth, and as a contribution to an acquaintance. He looked straight into Catherine's eyes. She answered nothing; she only listened, and looked at him; and he, as if he expected no particular reply, went on to say many other things in the same comfortable and natural manner. Catherine, though she felt tongue-tied, was conscious of no embarrassment; it seemed proper that he should talk, and that she should simply look at him. What made it natural was that he was so handsome, or, rather, as she phrased it to herself, so beautiful. The music had been silent for a while, but it suddenly began again; and then he asked her, with a deeper, intenser smile, if she would do him the honor of dancing with him. Even to this inquiry she gave no audible assent; she simply let him put his arm round her waist—as she did so, it occurred to her more vividly than it had ever done before that this was a singular place for a gentleman's arm to be—and in a moment he was guiding her round the room in the harmonious rotation of the polka. When they paused, she felt that she was red; and then, for some moments, she stopped looking at him. She fanned herself, and looked at the flowers that were painted on her fan. He asked her if she would begin again, and she hesitated to answer, still looking at the flowers.

"Does it make you dizzy?" he asked, in a tone of great kindness.

Then Catherine looked up at him; he was certainly beautiful, and not at all red. "Yes," she said; she hardly knew why, for dancing had never made her dizzy.

"Ah, well, in that case," said Mr. Townsend, "we will sit still and talk. I will find a good place to sit."

He found a good place—a charming place; a little sofa that seemed meant only for two persons. The rooms by this time were very full; the dancers increased in number, and people stood close in front of them, turning their backs, so that Catherine and her companion seemed secluded and unobserved. "*We* will talk," the young man had said; but he still did all the talking. Catherine leaned back in her place, with her eyes fixed upon him, smiling, and thinking him very clever. He had features like young men in pictures; Catherine had never seen such features—so delicate, so chiselled and finished—among the young New Yorkers whom she passed in the streets and met at dancing-parties. He was tall and slim, but he looked extremely strong. Catherine thought he looked like a statue. But a statue would not talk like that, and, above all, would not have eyes of so rare a color. He had never been at Mrs. Almond's before; he felt very much like a stranger; and it was very kind of Catherine to take pity on him. He was Arthur Townsend's cousin—not very near; several times removed—and Arthur had brought him to present him to the family. In fact, he was a great stranger in New York. It was his native place; but he had not been there for many years. He had been knocking about the world, and living in queer corners; he had only come back a month or two before. New York was very pleasant, only he felt lonely.

"You see, people forget you," he said, smiling at Catherine with his delightful gaze, while he leaned forward obliquely, turning toward her, with his elbows on his knees.

It seemed to Catherine that no one who had once seen him would ever forget him; but though she made this reflection she kept it to herself, almost as you would keep something precious.

They sat there for some time. He was very amusing. He asked her about the people that were near them; he tried to guess who some of them were, and he made the most laughable mistakes. He criticised them very freely, in a positive, off-hand way. Catherine had never heard any one—especially any young man—talk just like that. It was the way a young man might talk in a novel; or, better still, in a play, on the stage, close before the foot-lights, looking at the audience, and with every one looking at him, so that you wondered at his presence of mind. And yet Mr. Townsend was not like an actor; he seemed so sincere, so natural. This was very interesting; but in the midst of it Marian Almond came pushing through the crowd, with a little ironical cry, when she found these young people still together, which made every one turn round, and cost Catherine a conscious blush. Marian broke up their talk, and told Mr. Townsend—whom she treated as if she were already married, and he had become her cousin—to run away to her mother, who had been wishing for the last half hour to introduce him to Mr. Almond.

"We shall meet again," he said to Catherine as he left her, and Catherine thought it a very original speech.

Her cousin took her by the arm, and made her walk about. "I needn't ask you what you think of Morris," the young girl exclaimed.

"Is that his name?"

"I don't ask you what you think of his name, but what you think of himself," said Marian.

"Oh, nothing particular," Catherine answered, dissembling for the first time in her life.

"I have half a mind to tell him that!" cried Marian. "It will do him good; he's so terribly conceited."

"Conceited?" said Catherine, staring.

"So Arthur says, and Arthur knows about him."

"Oh, don't tell him!" Catherine murmured, imploringly.

"Don't tell him he's conceited! I have told him so a dozen times."

At this profession of audacity Catherine looked down at her little companion in amazement. She supposed it was because Marian was going to be married that she took so much on herself; but she wondered too, whether, when she herself should become engaged, such exploits would be expected of her.

Half an hour later she saw her Aunt Penniman sitting in the embrasure of a window, with her head a little on one side, and her gold eye-glass raised to her eyes, which were wandering about the room. In front of her was a gentleman, bending forward a little, with his back turned to Catherine. She knew his back immediately, though she had never seen it; for when he left her, at Marian's instigation, he had retreated in the best order, without turning round. Morris Townsend—the name had already become very familiar to her, as if some one had been repeating it in her ear for the last half hour—Morris Townsend was giving his impressions of the company to her aunt, as he had done to herself; he was saying clever things, and Mrs. Penniman was smiling, as if she approved of them. As soon as Catherine had perceived this she moved away; she would not have liked him to turn round and see her. But it gave her pleasure—the whole thing. That he should talk with Mrs. Penniman, with whom she lived and whom she saw and talked with every day—that seemed to keep him near her, and to make him even easier to contemplate than if she herself had been the object of his civilities; and that Aunt Lavinia should like him, should not be shocked or startled by what he said, this also appeared to the girl a personal gain; for Aunt Lavinia's standard was extremely high, planted as it was over the grave of her late husband, in which, as she had convinced every one, the very genius of conversation was buried. One of the Almond boys, as Catherine called them, invited our heroine to dance a quadrille, and for a quarter of an hour her feet at least were occupied. This time she was not dizzy; her head was very clear. Just when the dance was over, she found herself in the crowd face to face with her father. Doctor Sloper had usually a little smile, never a very big one, and with this little smile playing in his clear eyes and on his neatly shaved lips, he looked at his daughter's crimson gown.

"Is it possible that this magnificent person is my child?" he said.

You would have surprised him if you had told him so; but it is a literal fact that he almost never addressed his daughter save in the ironical form. Whenever he addressed her he gave her pleasure; but she had to cut her pleasure out of the piece, as it were. There were portions left over, light remnants and snippets of irony, which she never knew what to do with, which seemed too delicate for her own use; and yet Catherine, lamenting the limitations of her understanding, felt that they were too valuable to waste, and had a belief that if they passed over her head they yet contributed to the general sum of human wisdom.

"I am not magnificent," she said, mildly, wishing that she had put on another dress.

"You are sumptuous, opulent, expensive," her father rejoined. "You look as if you had eighty thousand a year."

"Well, so long as I haven't—" said Catherine, illogically. Her conception of her prospective wealth was as yet very indefinite.

"So long as you haven't you shouldn't look as if you had. Have you enjoyed your party?"

Catherine hesitated a moment; and then, looking away, "I am rather tired," she murmured. I have said that this entertainment was the beginning of something important for Catherine. For the second time in her life she made an indirect answer; and the beginning of a period of dissimulation is certainly a significant date. Catherine was not so easily tired as that.

Nevertheless, in the carriage, as they drove home, she was as quiet as if fatigue had been her portion. Doctor Sloper's manner of addressing his sister Lavinia had a good deal of resemblance to the tone he had adopted toward Catherine.

"Who was the young man that was making love to you?" he presently asked.

"Oh, my good brother!" murmured Mrs. Penniman, in deprecation.

"He seemed uncommonly tender. Whenever I looked at you for half an hour, he had the most devoted air."

"The devotion was not to me," said Mrs. Penniman. "It was to Catherine; he talked to me of her."

Catherine had been listening with all her ears. "Oh, Aunt Penniman!" she exclaimed, faintly.

"He is very handsome; he is very clever; he expressed himself with a great deal—a great deal of felicity," her aunt went on.

"He is in love with this regal creature, then?" the Doctor inquired, humorously.

"Oh, father!" cried the girl, still more faintly, devoutly thankful the carriage was dark.

"I don't know that; but he admired her dress."

Catherine did not say to herself in the dark, "My dress only?" Mrs. Penniman's announcement struck her by its richness, not by its meagreness.

"You see," said her father, "he thinks you have eighty thousand a year."

"I don't believe he thinks of that," said Mrs. Penniman; "he is too refined."

"He must be tremendously refined not to think of that!"

"Well, he is!" Catherine exclaimed, before she knew it.

"I thought you had gone to sleep," her father answered. "The hour has come!" he added to himself. "Lavinia is going to get up a romance for Catherine. It's a shame to play such tricks on the girl. What is the gentleman's name?" he went on, aloud.

"I didn't catch it, and I didn't like to ask him. He asked to be introduced to me," said Mrs. Penniman, with a certain grandeur; "but you know how indistinctly Jefferson speaks." Jefferson was Mr. Almond. "Catherine, dear, what was the gentleman's name?"

For a minute, if it had not been for the rumbling of the carriage, you might have heard a pin drop.

"I don't know, Aunt Lavinia," said Catherine, very softly. And, with all his irony, her father believed her.

V

HE LEARNED what he had asked some three of four days later, after Morris Townsend, with his cousin, had called in Washington Square. Mrs. Penniman did not tell her brother, on the drive home, that she had intimated to this agreeable young man, whose name she did not know, that, with her niece, she should be very glad to see him; but she was greatly pleased, and even a little flattered, when, late on a Sunday afternoon, the two gentlemen made their appearance. His coming with Arthur Townsend made it more natural and easy; the latter young man was on the point of becoming connected with the family, and Mrs. Penniman had remarked to Catherine that, as he was going to marry Marian, it would be polite in him to call. These events came to pass late in the autumn, and Catherine and her aunt had been sitting together in the closing dusk, by the fire-light, in the high back parlor.

Arthur Townsend fell to Catherine's portion, while his companion placed himself on the sofa beside Mrs. Penniman. Catherine had hitherto not been a harsh critic; she was easy to please—she liked to talk with young men. But Marian's betrothed, this evening, made her feel vaguely fastidious; he sat looking at the fire and rubbing his knees with his hands. As for Catherine, she scarcely even pretended to keep up the conversation; her attention had fixed itself on the other side of the room; she was listening to what went on between the other Mr. Townsend and her aunt. Every now and then he looked over at Catherine herself and smiled, as if to show that what he said was for her benefit too. Catherine would have liked to change her place, to go and sit near them, where she might see and hear him better. But she was afraid of seeming bold—of looking eager; and, besides, it would not have been polite to Marian's little suitor. She wondered why the other gentleman had picked out her aunt—how he came to have so much to say to Mrs. Penniman, to whom, usually, young men were not especially devoted. She was not at all jealous of Aunt Lavinia, but she was a little envious, and, above all, she wondered; for Morris Townsend was an object on which she found that her imagination could exercise itself indefinitely. His cousin had been describing a house that he had taken in view of his union with Marian, and the domestic conveniences he meant to introduce into it; how Marian wanted a larger one, and Mrs. Almond recommended a smaller one, and how he himself was convinced that he had got the neatest house in New York.

"It doesn't matter," he said; "it's only for three or four years. At the end of three or four years we'll move. That's the way to live in New York—to move every three or four years. Then you always get the last thing. It's because the city's growing so quick—you've got to keep up with it. It's going straight up town—that's where New York's going. If I wasn't afraid Marian would be lonely, I'd go up there—right up to the top—and wait for it. Only have to wait ten years—they'll all come up after you. But Marian says she wants some neighbors—she doesn't want to be a pioneer. She says that if she's got to be the first settler she had better go out to Minnesota. I guess we'll move up little by little; when we get tired of one street we'll go higher. So you see we'll always have a new house; it's a great advantage to have a new house; you get all the latest improvements. They invent everything all over again about every five years, and it's a great thing to keep up with the new things. I always try and keep up with the new things of every kind. Don't you think that's a good motto for a young couple—to keep 'going higher'? What's the name of that piece of poetry—what do they call it?—*Excelsior!*"

Catherine bestowed on her junior visitor only just enough attention to feel that this was not the way Mr. Morris Townsend had talked the other night, or that he was talking now to her fortunate aunt. But suddenly his aspiring kinsman became more interesting. He seemed to have become conscious that she was affected by his companion's presence, and he thought it proper to explain it.

"My cousin asked me to bring him, or I shouldn't have taken the liberty. He seemed to want very much to come; you know he's awfully sociable. I told him I wanted to ask you first, but he said Mrs. Penniman had invited him. He isn't particular what he says when he wants to come somewhere. But Mrs. Penniman seems to think it's all right."

"We are very glad to see him," said Catherine. And she wished to talk more about him, but she hardly knew what to say. "I never saw him before," she went on, presently.

Arthur Townsend stared.

"Why, he told me he talked with you for over half an hour the other night."

"I mean before the other night. That was the first time."

"Oh, he has been away from New York—he has been all round the world. He doesn't know many people here, but he's very sociable, and he wants to know every one."

"Every one?" said Catherine.

"Well, I mean all the good ones. All the pretty young ladies—like Mrs. Penniman!" And Arthur Townsend gave a private laugh.

"My aunt likes him very much," said Catherine.

"Most people like him—he's so brilliant."

"He's more like a foreigner," Catherine suggested.

"Well, I never knew a foreigner," said young Townsend, in a tone which seemed to indicate that his ignorance had been optional.

"Neither have I," Catherine confessed, with more humility. "They say they are generally brilliant," she added, vaguely.

"Well, the people of this city are clever enough for me.

I know some of them that think they are too clever for me; but they ain't."

"I suppose you can't be too clever," said Catherine, still with humility.

"I don't know. I know some people that call my cousin too clever."

Catherine listened to this statement with extreme interest, and a feeling that if Morris Townsend had a fault it would naturally be that one. But she did not commit herself, and in a moment she asked, "Now that he has come back, will he stay here always?"

"Ah!" said Arthur, "if he can get something to do."

"Something to do?"

"Some place or other; some business."

"Hasn't he got any?" said Catherine, who had never heard of a young man—of the upper class—in this situation.

"No; he's looking round. But he can't find anything."

"I am very sorry," Catherine permitted herself to observe.

"Oh, he doesn't mind," said young Townsend. "He takes it easy—he isn't in a hurry. He is very particular."

Catherine thought he naturally would be, and gave herself up for some moments to the contemplation of this idea, in several of its bearings.

"Won't his father take him into his business—his office?" she at last inquired.

"He hasn't got any father—he has only got a sister. Your sister can't help you much."

It seemed to Catherine that if she were his sister she would disprove this axiom. "Is she—is she pleasant?" she asked in a moment.

"I don't know—I believe she's very respectable," said young Townsend. And then he looked across to his cousin and began to laugh. "I say, we are talking about you," he added.

Morris Townsend paused in his conversation with Mrs.

Penniman, and stared, with a little smile. Then he got up, as if he were going.

"As far as you are concerned, I can't return the compliment," he said to Catherine's companion. "But as regards Miss Sloper, it's another affair."

Catherine thought this little speech wonderfully well turned; but she was embarrassed by it, and she also got up. Morris Townsend stood looking at her and smiling; he put out his hand for farewell. He was going, without having said anything to her; but even on these terms she was glad to have seen him.

"I will tell her what you have said—when you go!" said Mrs. Penniman, with a little significant laugh.

Catherine blushed, for she felt almost as if they were making sport of her. What in the world could this beautiful young man have said? He looked at her still, in spite of her blush, but very kindly and respectfully.

"I have had no talk with you," he said, "and that was what I came for. But it will be a good reason for coming another time; a little pretext—if I am obliged to give one. I am not afraid of what your aunt will say when I go."

With this the two young men took their departure; after which Catherine, with her blush still lingering, directed a serious and interrogative eye to Mrs. Penniman. She was incapable of elaborate artifice, and she resorted to no jocular device—to no affectation of the belief that she had been maligned—to learn what she desired.

"What did you say you would tell me?" she asked.

Mrs. Penniman came up to her, smiling and nodding a little, looked at her all over, and gave a twist to the knot of ribbon in her neck. "It's a great secret, my dear child; but he is coming a-courting!"

Catherine was serious still. "Is that what he told you?"

"He didn't say so exactly; but he left me to guess it. I'm a good guesser."

"Do you mean a-courting me?"

"Not me, certainly, miss; though I must say he is a hundred times more polite to a person who has no longer extreme youth to recommend her than most of the young men. He is thinking of some one else." And Mrs. Penniman gave her niece a delicate little kiss. "You must be very gracious to him."

Catherine stared—she was bewildered. "I don't understand you," she said; "he doesn't know me."

"Oh yes, he does; more than you think. I have told him all about you."

"Oh, Aunt Penniman!" murmured Catherine, as if this had been a breach of trust. "He is a perfect stranger—we don't know him." There was infinite modesty in the poor girl's "we."

Aunt Penniman, however, took no account of it; she spoke even with a touch of acrimony. "My dear Catherine, you know very well that you admire him."

"Oh, Aunt Penniman!" Catherine could only murmur again. It might very well be that she admired him—though this did not seem to her a thing to talk about. But that this brilliant stranger—this sudden apparition, who had barely heard the sound of her voice—took that sort of interest in her that was expressed by the romantic phrase of which Mrs. Penniman had just made use—this could only be a figment of the restless brain of Aunt Lavinia, whom every one knew to be a woman of powerful imagination.

VI

Mrs. Penniman even took for granted at times that other people had as much imagination as herself; so that when, half an hour later, her brother came in, she addressed him quite on this principle.

"He has just been here, Austin; it's such a pity you missed him."

"Whom in the world have I missed?" asked the Doctor.

"Mr. Morris Townsend; he has made us such a delightful visit."

"And who in the world is Mr. Morris Townsend?"

"Aunt Penniman means the gentleman—the gentleman whose name I couldn't remember," said Catherine.

"The gentleman at Elizabeth's party who was so struck with Catherine," Mrs. Penniman added.

"Oh, his name is Morris Townsend, is it? And did he come here to propose to you?"

"Oh, father!" murmured the girl for an answer, turning away to the window, where the dusk had deepened to darkness.

"I hope he won't do that without your permission," said Mrs. Penniman, very graciously.

"After all, my dear, he seems to have yours," her brother answered.

Lavinia simpered, as if this might not be quite enough, and Catherine, with her forehead touching the window-panes, listened to this exchange of epigrams as reservedly as if they had not each been a pin-prick in her own destiny.

"The next time he comes," the Doctor added, "you had better call me. He might like to see me."

Morris Townsend came again some five days afterward; but Doctor Sloper was not called, as he was absent from home at the time. Catherine was with her aunt when the young man's name was brought in, and Mrs. Penniman, effacing herself and protesting, made a great point of her niece's going into the drawing-room alone.

"This time it's for you—for you only," she said. "Before, when he talked to me, it was only preliminary—it was to gain my confidence. Literally, my dear, I should not have the *courage* to show myself to-day."

And this was perfectly true. Mrs. Penniman was not a brave woman, and Morris Townsend had struck her as a young man of great force of character, and of remarkable powers of satire—a keen, resolute, brilliant nature, with which one must exercise a great deal of tact. She said to herself that he was "imperious," and she liked the word and the idea. She was not the least jealous of her niece, and she had been perfectly happy with Mr. Penniman, but in the bottom of her heart she permitted herself the observation, "That's the sort of husband I should have had!" He was certainly much more imperious—she ended by calling it imperial—than Mr. Penniman.

So Catherine saw Mr. Townsend alone, and her aunt did not come in even at the end of the visit. The visit was a long one; he sat there, in the front parlor, in the biggest arm-chair, for more than an hour. He seemed more at home this time—more familiar; lounging a little in the chair, slapping a cushion that was near him with his stick, and looking round the room a good deal, and at the objects it contained, as well as at Catherine; whom, however, he also contemplated freely. There was a smile of respectful devotion in his handsome eyes which seemed to Catherine almost solemnly beautiful; it made her think of a young knight in a poem. His talk, however, was not particularly knightly; it was light and easy and friendly; it took a practical turn, and he asked a number of questions about herself—what were her tastes—if she liked this and that—what were her habits. He said to her, with his charming smile, "Tell me about yourself; give me a little sketch." Catherine had very little to tell, and she had no talent for sketching; but before he went she had confided to him that she had a secret passion for the theatre, which had been but scantily gratified, and a taste for operatic music—that of Bellini and Donizetti, in especial (it must be remembered, in extenuation of this primitive young woman, that she held these opinions in an age of general darkness)—which she rarely had an occasion to hear, except on the hand-organ. She confessed that she was not particularly fond of literature. Morris Townsend agreed with her that books were tiresome things; only, as he said, you had to read a good many before you found it out. He had been to places that people had written books about, and they were not a bit like the descriptions. To see for yourself—that was the great thing; he always tried to see for himself. He had seen all the principal actors—he had been to all the best theatres in London and Paris. But the actors were always like the authors—they always exaggerated. He liked everything to be natural. Suddenly he stopped, looking at Catherine with his smile.

"That's what I like you for; you are so natural. Excuse me," he added; "you see I am natural myself."

And before she had time to think whether she excused him or not—which afterward, at leisure, she became conscious that she did—he began to talk about music, and to say that it was his greatest pleasure in life. He had heard all the great singers in Paris and London—Pasta and Rubini and Lablache—and when you had done that, you could say that you knew what singing was.

"I sing a little myself," he said; "some day I will show you. Not to-day, but some other time."

And then he got up to go. He had omitted, by accident, to say that he would sing to her if she would play to him. He thought of this after he got into the street; but he might have spared his compunction, for Catherine had not noticed the lapse. She was thinking only that "some other time" had a delightful sound; it seemed to spread itself over the future.

This was all the more reason, however, though she was ashamed and uncomfortable, why she should tell her father that Mr. Morris Townsend had called again. She announced the fact abruptly, almost violently, as soon as the Doctor came into the house; and having done so—it was her duty—she took measures to leave the room. But she could not leave it fast enough; her father stopped her just as she reached the door.

"Well, my dear, did he propose to you to-day?" the Doctor asked.

This was just what she had been afraid he would say; and yet she had no answer ready. Of course she would have liked to take it as a joke—as her father must have meant it; and yet she would have liked also, in denying it, to be a little positive, a little sharp, so that he would perhaps not ask the question again. She didn't like it—it made her unhappy. But Catherine could never be sharp; and for a moment she only stood, with her hand on the door-knob, looking at her satiric parent, and giving a little laugh.

"Decidedly," said the Doctor to himself, "my daughter is not brilliant!"

But he had no sooner made this reflection than Catherine found something; she had decided, on the whole, to take the thing as a joke.

"Perhaps he will do it the next time," she exclaimed, with a repetition of her laugh; and she quickly got out of the room.

The Doctor stood staring; he wondered whether his daughter were serious. Catherine went straight to her own room, and by the time she reached it she bethought herself that there was something else—something better—she might have said. She almost wished, now, that her father would ask his question again, so that she might reply, "Oh yes, Mr. Morris Townsend proposed to me, and I refused him."

The Doctor, however, began to put his questions elsewhere; it naturally having occurred to him that he ought to inform himself properly about this handsome young man, who had formed the habit of running in and out of his house. He addressed himself to the elder of his sisters, Mrs. Almond—not going to her for the purpose; there was no such hurry as that; but having made a note of the matter for the first opportunity. The Doctor was never eager, never impatient or nervous; but he made notes of everything, and he regularly consulted his notes. Among them the information he obtained from Mrs. Almond about Morris Townsend took its place.

"Lavinia has already been to ask me," she said. "Lavinia is most excited; I don't understand it. It's not, after all, Lavinia that the young man is supposed to have designs upon. She is very peculiar."

"Ah, my dear," the Doctor replied, "she has not lived with me these twelve years without my finding it out."

"She has got such an artificial mind," said Mrs. Almond, who always enjoyed an opportunity to discuss Lavinia's peculiarities with her brother. "She didn't want me to tell you that she had asked me about Mr. Townsend; but I told her I would. She always wants to conceal everything."

"And yet at moments no one blurts things out with such crudity. She is like a revolving lighthouse—pitch darkness alternating with a dazzling brilliancy! But what did you tell her?" the Doctor asked.

"What I tell you—that I know very little of him."

"Lavinia must have been disappointed at that," said the Doctor; "she would prefer him to have been guilty of some romantic crime. However, we must make the best of people. They tell me our gentleman is the cousin of the little boy to whom you are about to intrust the future of your little girl."

"Arthur is not a little boy; he is a very old man; you and

I will never be so old! He is a distant relation of Lavinia's *protégé*. The name is the same, but I am given to understand that there are Townsends and Townsends. So Arthur's mother tells me; she talked about 'branches'—younger branches, elder branches, inferior branches—as if it were a royal house. Arthur, it appears, is of the reigning line, but poor Lavinia's young man is not. Beyond this, Arthur's mother knows very little about him; she has only a vague story that he has been 'wild.' But I know his sister a little, and she is a very nice woman. Her name is Mrs. Montgomery; she is a widow, with a little property and five children. She lives in the Second Avenue."

"What does Mrs. Montgomery say about him?"

"That he has talents by which he might distinguish himself."

"Only he is lazy, eh?"

"She doesn't say so."

"That's family pride," said the Doctor. "What is his profession?"

"He hasn't got any; he is looking for something. I believe he was once in the Navy."

"Once? What is his age?"

"I suppose he is upward of thirty. He must have gone into the Navy very young. I think Arthur told me that he inherited a small property—which was perhaps the cause of his leaving the Navy—and that he spent it all in a few years. He travelled all over the world, lived abroad, amused himself. I believe it was a kind of system, a theory he had. He has lately come back to America with the intention, as he tells Arthur, of beginning life in earnest."

"Is he in earnest about Catherine, then?"

"I don't see why you should be incredulous," said Mrs. Almond. "It seems to me that you have never done Catherine justice. You must remember that she has the prospect of thirty thousand a year."

The Doctor looked at his sister a moment, and then, with

lightest touch of bitterness, "You at least appreciate her," he said.

Mrs. Almond blushed.

"I don't mean that is her only merit; I simply mean that it is a great one. A great many young men think so; and you appear to me never to have been properly aware of that. You have always had a little way of alluding to her as an unmarriageable girl."

"My allusions are as kind as yours, Elizabeth," said the Doctor, frankly. "How many suitors has Catherine had, with all her expectations—how much attention has she ever received? Catherine is not unmarriageable, but she is absolutely unattractive. What other reason is there for Lavinia being so charmed with the idea that there is a lover in the house? There has never been one before, and Lavinia, with her sensitive, sympathetic nature, is not used to the idea. It affects her imagination. I must do the young men of New York the justice to say that they strike me as very disinterested. They prefer pretty girls—lively girls—girls like your own. Catherine is neither pretty nor lively."

"Catherine does very well; she has a style of her own—which is more than my poor Marian has, who has no style at all," said Mrs. Almond. "The reason Catherine has received so little attention, is that she seems to all the young men to be older than themselves. She is so large, and she dresses so richly. They are rather afraid of her, I think; she looks as if she had been married already, and you know they don't like married women. And if our young men appear disinterested," the Doctor's wiser sister went on, "it is because they marry, as a general thing, so young—before twenty-five, at the age of innocence and sincerity—before the age of calculation. If they only waited a little, Catherine would fare better."

"As a calculation? Thank you very much," said the Doctor.

"Wait till some intelligent man of forty comes along, and

he will be delighted with Catherine," Mrs. Almond continued.

"Mr. Townsend is not old enough, then? His motives may be pure."

"It is very possible that his motives are pure; I should be very sorry to take the contrary for granted. Lavinia is sure of it; and, as he is a very prepossessing youth, you might give him the benefit of the doubt."

Doctor Sloper reflected a moment.

"What are his present means of subsistence?"

"I have no idea. He lives, as I say, with his sister."

"A widow, with five children? Do you mean he lives *upon* her?"

Mrs. Almond got up, and with a certain impatience, "Had you not better ask Mrs. Montgomery herself?" she inquired.

"Perhaps I may come to that," said the Doctor. "Did you say the Second Avenue?" He made a note of the Second Avenue.

VII

HE WAS, however, by no means so much in earnest as this might seem to indicate; and, indeed, he was more than anything else amused with the whole situation. He was not in the least in a state of tension or of vigilance with regard to Catherine's prospects; he was even on his guard against the ridicule that might attach itself to the spectacle of a house thrown into agitation by its daughter and heiress receiving attentions unprecedented in its annals. More than this, he went so far as to promise himself some entertainment from the little drama—if drama it was—of which Mrs. Penniman desired to represent the ingenious Mr. Townsend as the hero. He had no intention, as yet, of regulating the *dénouement*. He was perfectly willing, as Elizabeth had suggested, to give the young man the benefit of every doubt. There was no great danger in it; for Catherine, at the age of twenty-two, was, after all, a rather mature blossom, such as could be plucked from the stem only by a vigorous jerk. The fact that Morris Townsend was poor, was not of necessity against him; the Doctor had never made up his mind that his daughter should marry a rich man. The fortune she would inherit struck him as a very sufficient provision for two reasonable persons, and if a penniless swain who could give a good account of himself should enter the lists, he should be judged quite upon his personal merits. There were other things besides. The Doctor thought it very vulgar to be precipitate in accusing people of mercenary motives, inasmuch as his door had as yet not been in the least besieged by fortune-hunters; and, lastly, he was very curious to see whether Catherine might really be loved for her moral worth. He smiled as he reflected that poor Mr. Townsend had been only twice to the house, and he said to Mrs. Penniman that the next time he should come she must ask him to dinner.

He came very soon again, and Mrs. Penniman had of course great pleasure in executing this mission. Morris Townsend accepted her invitation with equal good grace, and the dinner took place a few days later. The Doctor had said to himself, justly enough, that they must not have the young man alone; this would partake too much of the nature of encouragement. So two or three other persons were invited; but Morris Townsend, though he was by no means the ostensible, was the real occasion of the feast. There is every reason to suppose that he desired to make a good impression; and if he fell short of this result, it was not for want of a good deal of intelligent effort. The Doctor talked to him very little during dinner; but he observed him attentively, and after the ladies had gone out he pushed him the wine and asked him several questions. Morris was not a young man who needed to be pressed, and he found quite enough encouragement in the superior quality of the claret. The Doctor's wine was admirable, and it may be communicated to the reader that while he sipped it Morris reflected that a cellarful of good liquor—there was evidently a cellarful here—would be a most attractive idiosyncrasy in a father-in-law. The Doctor was struck with his appreciative guest; he saw that he was not a commonplace young man. "He has ability," said Catherine's father, "decided ability; he has a very good head if he chooses to use it. And he is uncommonly well turned out; quite the sort of figure that pleases the ladies; but I don't think I like him." The Doctor, however, kept his reflections to himself, and talked to his visitors about foreign lands, concerning which Morris offered him more information than he was ready, as he mentally phrased it, to swallow. Doctor Sloper had travelled but little, and he took the liberty of not believing everything that his talkative guest narrated. He prided himself on being something of a physiognomist; and while the young man, chatting with easy assurance, puffed his cigar and filled his glass again, the Doctor sat with his eyes quietly fixed on his bright, expressive face. "He has the assurance of the devil himself!" said Morris's host; "I don't think I ever saw such assurance. And his powers of invention are most remarkable. He is very knowing; they were not so knowing as that in my time. And a good head, did I say? I should think so—after a bottle of Madeira, and a bottle and a half of claret!"

After dinner Morris Townsend went and stood before Catherine, who was standing before the fire in her red satin gown.

"He doesn't like me—he doesn't like me at all," said the young man.

"Who doesn't like you?" asked Catherine.

"Your father; extraordinary man!"

"I don't see how you know," said Catherine, blushing.

"I feel; I am very quick to feel."

"Perhaps you are mistaken."

"Ah, well! you ask him, and you will see."

"I would rather not ask him, if there is any danger of his saying what you think."

Morris looked at her with an air of mock melancholy.

"It wouldn't give you any pleasure to contradict him?"

"I never contradict him," said Catherine.

"Will you hear me abused without opening your lips in my defence?"

"My father won't abuse you. He doesn't know you enough."

Morris Townsend gave a loud laugh, and Catherine began to blush again.

"I shall never mention you," she said, to take refuge from her confusion.

"That is very well; but it is not quite what I should have liked you to say. I should have liked you to say, 'If my father doesn't think well of you, what does it matter?' "

"Ah, but it would matter; I couldn't say that!" the girl exclaimed.

He looked at her for a moment, smiling a little; and the Doctor, if he had been watching him just then, would have seen a gleam of fine impatience in the sociable softness of his eye. But there was no impatience in his rejoinder—none, at least, save what was expressed in a little appealing sigh. "Ah, well! then I must not give up the hope of bringing him round."

He expressed it more frankly to Mrs. Penniman later in the evening. But before that he sang two or three songs at Catherine's timid request; not that he flattered himself that this would help to bring her father round. He had a sweet, light tenor voice, and, when he had finished, every one made some exclamation—every one, that is, save Catherine, who remained intensely silent. Mrs. Penniman declared that his manner of singing was "most artistic," and Doctor Sloper said it was "very taking—very taking, indeed"; speaking loudly and distinctly, but with a certain dryness.

"He doesn't like me—he doesn't like me at all," said Morris Townsend, addressing the aunt in the same manner as he had done the niece. "He thinks I am all wrong."

Unlike her niece, Mrs. Penniman asked for no explanation. She only smiled very sweetly, as if she understood everything; and, unlike Catherine too, she made no attempt to contradict him. "Pray, what does it matter?" she murmured, softly.

"Ah, you say the right thing!" said Morris, greatly to the gratification of Mrs. Penniman, who prided herself on always saying the right thing.

The Doctor, the next time he saw his sister Elizabeth, let her know that he had made the acquaintance of Lavinia's *protégé*.

"Physically," he said, "he's uncommonly well set up. As an anatomist, it is really a pleasure to me to see such a beautiful structure; although, if people were all like him, I suppose there would be very little need for doctors."

"Don't you see anything in people but their bones?" Mrs. Almond rejoined. "What do you think of him as a father?"

"As a father? Thank Heaven, I am not his father!"

"No; but you are Catherine's. Lavinia tells me she is in love."

"She must get over it. He is not a gentleman."

"Ah, take care! Remember that he is a branch of the Townsends."

"He is not what I call a gentleman; he has not the soul of one. He is extremely insinuating; but it's a vulgar nature. I saw through it in a minute. He is altogether too familiar;—I hate familiarity. He is a plausible coxcomb."

"Ah, well," said Mrs. Almond, "if you make up your mind so easily, it's a great advantage."

"I don't make up my mind easily. What I tell you is the result of thirty years of observation; and in order to be able to form that judgment in a single evening, I have had to spend a lifetime in study."

"Very possibly you are right. But the thing is for Catherine to see it."

"I will present her with a pair of spectacles!" said the Doctor.

VIII

IF IT WERE true that she was in love, she was certainly very quiet about it; but the Doctor was of course prepared to admit that her quietness might mean volumes. She had told Morris Townsend that she would not mention him to her father, and she saw no reason to retract this vow of discretion. It was no more than decently civil, of course, that, after having dined in Washington Square, Morris should call there again; and it was no more than natural that, having been kindly received on this occasion, he should continue to present himself. He had had plenty of leisure on his hands; and thirty years ago, in New York, a young man of leisure had reason to be thankful for aids to self-oblivion. Catherine said nothing to her father about these visits, though they had rapidly become the most important, the most absorbing thing in her life. The girl was very happy. She knew not as yet what would come of it; but the present had suddenly grown rich and solemn. If she had been told she was in love, she would have been a good deal surprised; for she had an idea that love was an eager and exacting passion, and her own heart was filled in these days with the impulse of self-effacement and sacrifice. Whenever Morris Townsend had left the house, her imagination projected itself, with all its strength, into the idea of his soon coming back; but if she had been told at such a moment that he would not return for a year, or even that he would never return, she would not have complained nor rebelled, but would have humbly accepted the decree, and sought for consolation in thinking over the times she had already seen him, the words he had spoken, the sound of his voice, of his tread, the expression of his face. Love demands certain things as a right; but Catherine had no sense of her rights; she had only a consciousness of immense and unexpected favors. Her very gratitude for these things had hushed itself; for it seemed to her that there would be something of impudence in making a festival of her secret. Her father suspected Morris Townsend's visits, and noted her reserve. She seemed to beg pardon for it; she looked at him constantly in silence, as if she meant to say that she said nothing because she was afraid of irritating him. But the poor girl's dumb eloquence irritated him more than anything else would have done, and he caught himself murmuring more than once that it was a grievous pity his only child was a simpleton. His murmurs, however, were inaudible; and for a while he said nothing to any one. He would have liked to know exactly how often young Townsend came; but he had determined to ask no questions of the girl herself—to say nothing more to her that would show that he watched her. The Doctor had a great idea of being largely just: he wished to leave his daughter her liberty, and interfere only when the danger should be proved. It was not in his manner to obtain information by indirect methods, and it never even occurred to him to question the servants. As for Lavinia, he hated to talk to her about the matter; she annoyed him with her mock romanticism. But he had to come to this. Mrs. Penniman's convictions as regards the relations of her niece and the clever young visitor, who saved appearances by coming ostensibly for both the ladies—Mrs. Penniman's convictions had passed into a riper and richer phase. There was to be no crudity in Mrs. Penniman's treatment of the situation; she had become as uncommunicative as Catherine herself. She was tasting of the sweets of concealment; she had taken up the line of mystery. "She would be enchanted to be able to prove to herself that she is persecuted," said the Doctor; and when at last he questioned her, he was sure she would contrive to extract from his words a pretext for this belief.

"Be so good as to let me know what is going on in the

house," he said to her, in a tone which, under the circumstances, he himself deemed genial.

"Going on, Austin?" Mrs. Penniman exclaimed. "Why, I am sure I don't know. I believe that last night the old gray cat had kittens."

"At her age?" said the Doctor. "The idea is startling—almost shocking. Be so good as to see that they are all drowned. But what else has happened?"

"Ah, the dear little kittens!" cried Mrs. Penniman. "I wouldn't have them drowned for the world!"

Her brother puffed his cigar a few moments in silence. "Your sympathy with kittens, Lavinia," he presently resumed, "arises from a feline element in your own character."

"Cats are very graceful, and very clean," said Mrs. Penniman, smiling.

"And very stealthy. You are the embodiment both of grace and of neatness; but you are wanting in frankness."

"You certainly are not, dear brother."

"I don't pretend to be graceful, though I try to be neat. Why haven't you let me know that Mr. Morris Townsend is coming to the house four times a week?"

Mrs. Penniman lifted her eyebrows. "Four times a week!"

"Three times, then, or five times, if you prefer it. I am away all day, and I see nothing. But when such things happen, you should let me know."

Mrs. Penniman, with her eyebrows still raised, reflected intently. "Dear Austin," she said at last, "I am incapable of betraying a confidence. I would rather suffer anything."

"Never fear; you shall not suffer. To whose confidence is it you allude? Has Catherine made you take a vow of eternal secrecy?"

"By no means. Catherine has not told me as much as she might. She has not been very trustful."

"It is the young man, then, who has made you his confidante? Allow me to say that it is extremely indiscreet of you to form secret alliances with young men; you don't know where they may lead you."

"I don't know what you mean by an alliance," said Mrs. Penniman. "I take a great interest in Mr. Townsend; I won't conceal that. But that's all."

"Under the circumstances, that is quite enough. What is the source of your interest in Mr. Townsend?"

"Why," said Mrs. Penniman, musing, and then breaking into her smile, "that he is so interesting!"

The Doctor felt that he had need of his patience. "And what makes him interesting?—his good looks?"

"His misfortunes, Austin."

"Ah, he has had misfortunes? That, of course, is always interesting. Are you at liberty to mention a few of Mr. Townsend's?"

"I don't know that he would like it," said Mrs. Penniman. "He has told me a great deal about himself—he has told me, in fact, his whole history. But I don't think I ought to repeat those things. He would tell them to you, I am sure, if he thought you would listen to him kindly. With kindness you may do anything with him."

The Doctor gave a laugh. "I shall request him very kindly, then, to leave Catherine alone."

"Ah!" said Mrs. Penniman, shaking her forefinger at her brother, with her little finger turned out, "Catherine has probably said something to him kinder than that!"

"Said that she loved him?—do you mean that?"

Mrs. Penniman fixed her eyes on the floor. "As I tell you, Austin, she doesn't confide in me."

"You have an opinion, I suppose, all the same. It is that I ask you for; though I don't conceal from you that I shall not regard it as conclusive."

Mrs. Penniman's gaze continued to rest on the carpet; but at last she lifted it, and then her brother thought it very expressive. "I think Catherine is very happy; that is all I can say."

"Townsend is trying to marry her—is that what you mean?"

"He is greatly interested in her."

"He finds her such an attractive girl?"

"Catherine has a lovely nature, Austin," said Mrs. Penniman, "and Mr. Townsend has had the intelligence to discover that."

"With a little help from you, I suppose. My dear Lavinia," cried the Doctor, "you are an admirable aunt!"

"So Mr. Townsend says," observed Lavinia, smiling.

"Do you think he is sincere?" asked her brother.

"In saying that?"

"No; that's of course. But in his admiration for Catherine?"

"Deeply sincere. He has said to me the most appreciative, the most charming things about her. He would say them to you, if he were sure you would listen to him—gently."

"I doubt whether I can undertake it. He appears to require a great deal of gentleness."

"He is a sympathetic, sensitive nature," said Mrs. Penniman.

Her brother puffed his cigar again in silence. "These delicate qualities have survived his vicissitudes, eh? All this while you haven't told me about his misfortunes."

"It is a long story," said Mrs. Penniman, "and I regard it as a sacred trust. But I suppose there is no objection to my saying that he has been wild—he frankly confesses that. But he has paid for it."

"That's what has impoverished him, eh?"

"I don't mean simply in money. He is very much alone in the world."

"Do you mean that he has behaved so badly that his friends have given him up?"

"He has had false friends, who have deceived and betrayed him."

"He seems to have some good ones too. He has a devoted sister, and half a dozen nephews and nieces."

Mrs. Penniman was silent a minute. "The nephews and nieces are children, and the sister is not a very attractive person."

"I hope he doesn't abuse her to you," said the Doctor; "for I am told he lives upon her."

"Lives upon her?"

"Lives with her, and does nothing for himself; it is about the same thing."

"He is looking for a position most earnestly," said Mrs. Penniman. "He hopes every day to find one."

"Precisely. He is looking for it here—over there in the front parlor. The position of husband of a weak-minded woman with a large fortune would suit him to perfection!"

Mrs. Penniman was truly amiable, but she now gave signs of temper. She rose with much animation, and stood for a moment looking at her brother. "My dear Austin," she remarked, "if you regard Catherine as a weak-minded woman you are particularly mistaken!" And with this she moved majestically away.

IX

IT WAS a regular custom with the family in Washington Square to go and spend Sunday evening at Mrs. Almond's. On the Sunday after the conversation I have just narrated this custom was not intermitted; and on this occasion, toward the middle of the evening, Doctor Sloper found reason to withdraw to the library with his brother-in-law, to talk over a matter of business. He was absent some twenty minutes, and when he came back into the circle, which was enlivened by the presence of several friends of the family, he saw that Morris Townsend had come in, and had lost as little time as possible in seating himself on a small sofa beside Catherine. In the large room, where several different groups had been formed, and the hum of voices and of laughter was loud, these two young persons might confabulate, as the Doctor phrased it to himself, without attracting attention. He saw in a moment, however, that his daughter was painfully conscious of his own observation. She sat motionless, with her eyes bent down, staring at her open fan, deeply flushed, shrinking together as if to minimize the indiscretion of which she confessed herself guilty.

The Doctor almost pitied her. Poor Catherine was not defiant; she had no genius for bravado, and as she felt that her father viewed her companion's attentions with an unsympathizing eye, there was nothing but discomfort for her in the accident of seeming to challenge him. The Doctor felt, indeed, so sorry for her that he turned away, to spare her the sense of being watched; and he was so intelligent a man that, in his thoughts, he rendered a sort of poetic justice to her situation.

"It must be deucedly pleasant for a plain, inanimate girl like that to have a beautiful young fellow come and sit down beside her, and whisper to her that he is her slave—if that is what this one whispers. No wonder she likes it, and that she thinks me a cruel tyrant; which of course she does, though she is afraid—she hasn't the animation necessary—to admit it to herself. Poor old Catherine!" mused the Doctor; "I verily believe she is capable of defending me when Townsend abuses me!"

And the force of this reflection, for the moment, was such in making him feel the natural opposition between his point of view and that of an infatuated child, that he said to himself that he was perhaps after all taking things too hard, and crying out before he was hurt. He must not condemn Morris Townsend unheard. He had a great aversion to taking things too hard; he thought that half the discomfort and many of the disappointments of life come from it; and for an instant he asked himself whether, possibly, he did not appear ridiculous to this intelligent young man, whose private perception of incongruities he suspected of being keen. At the end of a quarter of an hour Catherine had got rid of him, and Townsend was now standing before the fireplace in conversation with Mrs. Almond.

"We will try him again," said the Doctor. And he crossed the room and joined his sister and her companion, making her a sign that she should leave the young man to him. She presently did so, while Morris looked at him, smiling, without a sign of evasiveness in his affable eye.

"He's amazingly conceited!" thought the Doctor; and then he said, aloud, "I am told you are looking out for a position."

"Oh, a position is more than I should presume to call it," Morris Townsend answered. "That sounds so fine. I should like some quiet work—something to turn an honest penny."

"What sort of thing should you prefer?"

"Do you mean what am I fit for? Very little, I am afraid.

I have nothing but my good right arm, as they say in the melodramas."

"You are too modest," said the Doctor. "In addition to your good right arm you have your subtle brain. I know nothing of you but what I see; but I see by your physiognomy that you are extremely intelligent."

"Ah," Townsend murmured, "I don't know what to answer when you say that. You advise me, then, not to despair?"

And he looked at his interlocutor as if the question might have a double meaning. The Doctor caught the look and weighed it a moment before he replied. "I should be very sorry to admit that a robust and well-disposed young man need ever despair. If he doesn't succeed in one thing, he can try another. Only, I should add, he should choose his line with discretion."

"Ah, yes, with discretion," Morris Townsend repeated, sympathetically. "Well, I have been indiscreet, formerly; but I think I have got over it. I am very steady now." And he stood a moment, looking down at his remarkably neat shoes. Then at last, "Were you kindly intending to propose something for my advantage?" he inquired, looking up and smiling.

"D—n his impudence!" the Doctor exclaimed, privately. But in a moment he reflected that he himself had, after all, touched first upon this delicate point, and that his words might have been construed as an offer of assistance. "I have no particular proposal to make," he presently said; "but it occurred to me to let you know that I have you in my mind. Sometimes one hears of opportunities. For instance, should you object to leaving New York—to going to a distance?"

"I am afraid I shouldn't be able to manage that. I must seek my fortune here or nowhere. You see," added Morris Townsend, "I have ties—I have responsibilities here. I have a sister, a widow, from whom I have been separated for a long time, and to whom I am almost everything. I shouldn't like to say to her that I must leave her. She rather depends upon me, you see."

"Ah, that's very proper; family feeling is very proper," said Doctor Sloper. "I often think there is not enough of it in our city. I think I have heard of your sister."

"It is possible, but I rather doubt it; she lives so very quietly."

"As quietly, you mean," the Doctor went on, with a short laugh, "as a lady may do who has several young children."

"Ah, my little nephews and nieces—that's the very point! I am helping to bring them up," said Morris Townsend. "I am a kind of amateur tutor; I give them lessons."

"That's very proper, as I say; but it is hardly a career."

"It won't make my fortune," the young man confessed.

"You must not be too much bent on a fortune," said the Doctor. "But I assure you I will keep you in mind; I won't lose sight of you."

"If my situation becomes desperate I shall perhaps take the liberty of reminding you," Morris rejoined, raising his voice a little, with a brighter smile, as his interlocutor turned away.

Before he left the house the Doctor had a few words with Mrs. Almond.

"I should like to see his sister," he said. "What do you call her—Mrs. Montgomery? I should like to have a little talk with her."

"I will try and manage it," Mrs. Almond responded. "I will take the first opportunity of inviting her, and you shall come and meet her; unless, indeed," Mrs. Almond added, "she first takes it into her head to be sick and to send for you."

"Ah no, not that; she must have trouble enough without that. But it would have its advantages, for then I should see the children. I should like very much to see the children."

"You are very thorough. Do you want to catechise them about their uncle?"

"Precisely. Their uncle tells me he has charge of their education, that he saves their mother the expense of school-bills. I should like to ask them a few questions in the commoner branches."

"He certainly has not the cut of a school-master," Mrs. Almond said to herself a short time afterward, as she saw Morris Townsend in a corner bending over her niece, who was seated.

And there was, indeed, nothing in the young man's discourse at this moment that savored of the pedagogue.

"Will you meet me somewhere to-morrow or next day?" he said, in a low tone, to Catherine.

"Meet you?" she asked, lifting her frightened eyes.

"I have something particular to say to you—very particular."

"Can't you come to the house? Can't you say it there?"

Townsend shook his head gloomily. "I can't enter your doors again."

"Oh, Mr. Townsend!" murmured Catherine. She trembled as she wondered what had happened—whether her father had forbidden it.

"I can't, in self-respect," said the young man. "Your father has insulted me."

"Insulted you?"

"He has taunted me with my poverty."

"Oh, you are mistaken—you misunderstood him!" Catherine spoke with energy, getting up from her chair.

"Perhaps I am too proud—too sensitive. But would you have me otherwise?" he asked, tenderly.

"Where my father is concerned, you must not be sure. He is full of goodness," said Catherine.

"He laughed at me for having no position. I took it quietly; but only because he belongs to you."

"I don't know," said Catherine—"I don't know what he thinks. I am sure he means to be kind. You must not be too proud."

"I will be proud only of you," Morris answered. "Will you meet me in the Square in the afternoon?"

A great blush on Catherine's part had been the answer to the declaration I have just quoted. She turned away, heedless of his question.

"Will you meet me?" he repeated. "It is very quiet there—no one need see us—toward dusk."

"It is you who are unkind, it is you who laugh, when you say such things as that."

"My dear girl!" the young man murmured.

"You know how little there is in me to be proud of. I am ugly and stupid."

Morris greeted this remark with an ardent murmur, in which she recognized nothing articulate but an assurance that she was his own dearest.

But she went on. "I am not even—I am not even—" And she paused a moment.

"You are not what?"

"I am not even brave."

"Ah, then, if you are afraid, what shall we do?"

She hesitated awhile; then at last—"You must come to the house," she said; "I am not afraid of that."

"I would rather it were in the Square," the young man urged. "You know how empty it is, often. No one will see us."

"I don't care who sees us. But leave me now."

He left her resignedly; he had got what he wanted. Fortunately he was ignorant that half an hour later, going home with her father, and feeling him near, the poor girl, in spite of her sudden declaration of courage, began to tremble again. Her father said nothing; but she had an idea his eyes were fixed upon her in the darkness. Mrs. Penniman also was silent; Morris Townsend had told her that her niece preferred, unromantically, an interview in a chintz-covered parlor to a sentimental tryst beside a fountain sheeted with dead leaves, and she was lost in wonderment at the oddity—almost the perversity—of the choice.

X

CATHERINE received the young man the next day on the ground she had chosen—amidst the chaste upholstery of a New York drawing-room furnished in the fashion of fifty years ago. Morris had swallowed his pride, and made the effort necessary to cross the threshold of her too derisive parent—an act of magnanimity which could not fail to render him doubly interesting.

"We must settle something—we must take a line," he declared, passing his hand through his hair and giving a glance at the long, narrow mirror which adorned the space between the two windows, and which had at its base a little gilded bracket covered by a thin slab of white marble, supporting in its turn a backgammon-board folded together in the shape of two volumes—two shining folios inscribed, in greenish-gilt letters, *History of England*. If Morris had been pleased to describe the master of the house as a heartless scoffer, it is because he thought him too much on his guard, and this was the easiest way to express his own dissatisfaction—a dissatisfaction which he had made a point of concealing from the Doctor. It will probably seem to the reader, however, that the Doctor's vigilance was by no means excessive, and that these two young people had an open field. Their intimacy was now considerable, and it may appear that, for a shrinking and retiring person, our heroine had been liberal of her favors. The young man, within a few days, had made her listen to things for which she had not supposed that she was prepared; having a lively foreboding of difficulties, he proceeded to gain as much ground as possible in the present. He remembered that fortune favors the brave, and even if he had forgotten it, Mrs.

Penniman would have remembered it for him. Mrs. Penniman delighted of all things in a drama, and she flattered herself that a drama would now be enacted. Combining as she did the zeal of the prompter with the impatience of the spectator, she had long since done her utmost to pull up the curtain. She, too, expected to figure in the performance—to be the confidante, the Chorus, to speak the epilogue. It may even be said that there were times when she lost sight altogether of the modest heroine of the play in the contemplation of certain great scenes which would naturally occur between the hero and herself.

What Morris had told Catherine at last was simply that he loved her, or rather adored her. Virtually, he had made known as much already—his visits had been a series of eloquent intimations of it. But now he had affirmed it in lover's vows, and, as a memorable sign of it, he had passed his arm round the girl's waist and taken a kiss. This happy certitude had come sooner than Catherine expected, and she had regarded it, very naturally, as a priceless treasure. It may even be doubted whether she had ever definitely expected to possess it; she had not been waiting for it, and she had never said to herself that at a given moment it must come. As I have tried to explain, she was not eager and exacting; she took what was given her from day to day; and if the delightful custom of her lover's visits, which yielded her a happiness in which confidence and timidity were strangely blended, had suddenly come to an end, she would not only not have spoken of herself as one of the forsaken, but she would not have thought of herself as one of the disappointed. After Morris had kissed her, the last time he was with her, as a ripe assurance of his devotion, she begged him to go away, to leave her alone, to let her think. Morris went away, taking another kiss first. But Catherine's meditations had lacked a certain coherence. She felt his kisses on her lips and on her cheeks for a long time afterward; the sensation was rather an obstacle than an aid to reflection. She would have liked to see her situation all clearly before her, to make up her mind what she should do if, as she feared, her father should tell her that he disapproved of Morris Townsend. But all that she could see with any vividness was that it was terribly strange that any one should disapprove of him; that there must in that case be some mistake, some mystery, which in a little while would be set at rest. She put off deciding and choosing; before the vision of a conflict with her father she dropped her eyes and sat motionless, holding her breath and waiting. It made her heart beat; it was intensely painful. When Morris kissed her and said these things—that also made her heart beat; but this was worse, and it frightened her. Nevertheless, to-day, when the young man spoke of settling something, taking a line, she felt that it was the truth, and she answered very simply and without hesitating.

"We must do our duty," she said; "we must speak to my father. I will do it to-night; you must do it to-morrow."

"It is very good of you to do it first," Morris answered. "The young man—the happy lover—generally does that. But just as you please."

It pleased Catherine to think that she should be brave for his sake, and in her satisfaction she even gave a little smile. "Women have more tact," she said; "they ought to do it first. They are more conciliating; they can persuade better."

"You will need all your powers of persuasion. But, after all," Morris added, "you are irresistible."

"Please don't speak that way—and promise me this: To-morrow, when you talk with father, you will be very gentle and respectful."

"As much so as possible," Morris promised. "It won't be much use, but I shall try. I certainly would rather have you easily than have to fight for you."

"Don't talk about fighting; we shall not fight."

"Ah, we must be prepared," Morris rejoined; "you especially, because for you it must come hardest. Do you know the first thing your father will say to you?"

"No, Morris; please tell me."

"He will tell you I am mercenary."

"Mercenary!"

"It's a big word, but it means a low thing. It means that I am after your money."

"Oh!" murmured Catherine, softly.

The exclamation was so deprecating and touching that Morris indulged in another little demonstration of affection. "But he will be sure to say it," he added.

"It will be easy to be prepared for that," Catherine said. "I shall simply say that he is mistaken—that other men may be that way, but that you are not."

"You must make a great point of that, for it will be his own great point."

Catherine looked at her lover a minute, and then she said, "I shall persuade him. But I am glad we shall be rich," she added.

Morris turned away, looking into the crown of his hat. "No, it's a misfortune," he said at last. "It is from that our difficulty will come."

"Well, if it is the worst misfortune, we are not so unhappy. Many people would not think it so bad. I will persuade him, and after that we shall be very glad we have money."

Morris Townsend listened to this robust logic in silence. "I will leave my defence to you; it's a charge that a man has to stoop to defend himself from."

Catherine on her side was silent for awhile; she was looking at him while he looked, with a good deal of fixedness, cut of the window. "Morris," she said, abruptly, "are you very sure you love me?"

He turned round, and in a moment he was bending over her. "My own dearest, can you doubt it?"

"I have only known it five days," she said; "but now it seems to me as if I could never do without it."

"You will never be called upon to try." And he gave a little tender, reassuring laugh. Then, in a moment, he added, "There is something you must tell me, too." She had closed her eyes after the last words she uttered, and kept them closed; and at this she nodded her head, without opening them. "You must tell me," he went on, "that if your father is dead against me, if he absolutely forbids our marriage, you will still be faithful."

Catherine opened her eyes, gazing at him, and she could give no better promise than what he read there.

"You will cleave to me?" said Morris. "You know you are your own mistress—you are of age."

"Ah, Morris!" she murmured, for all answer; or rather not for all, for she put her hand into his own. He kept it awhile, and presently he kissed her again. This is all that need be recorded of their conversation; but Mrs. Penniman, if she had been present, would probably have admitted that it was as well it had not taken place beside the fountain in Washington Square.

XI

CATHERINE listened for her father when he came in that evening, and she heard him go to his study. She sat quiet, though her heart was beating fast, for nearly half an hour; then she went and knocked at his door—a ceremony without which she never crossed the threshold of this apartment. On entering it now, she found him in his chair beside the fire, entertaining himself with a cigar and the evening paper.

"I have something to say to you," she began very gently; and she sat down in the first place that offered.

"I shall be very happy to hear it, my dear," said her father. He waited—waited, looking at her—while she stared, in a long silence, at the fire. He was curious and impatient, for he was sure she was going to speak of Morris Townsend; but he let her take her own time, for he was determined to be very mild.

"I am engaged to be married!" Catherine announced at last, still staring at the fire.

The Doctor was startled; the accomplished fact was more than he had expected; but he betrayed no surprise. "You do right to tell me," he simply said. "And who is the happy mortal whom you have honored with your choice?"

"Mr. Morris Townsend." And as she pronounced her lover's name Catherine looked at him. What she saw was her father's still gray eye and his clear-cut, definite smile. She contemplated these objects for a moment, and then she looked back at the fire; it was much warmer.

"When was this arrangement made?" the Doctor asked.

"This afternoon—two hours ago."

"Was Mr. Townsend here?"

"Yes, father; in the front parlor." She was very glad that she was not obliged to tell him that the ceremony of their betrothal had taken place out there under the bare ailanthus-trees.

"Is it serious?" said the Doctor.

"Very serious, father."

Her father was silent a moment. "Mr. Townsend ought to have told me."

"He means to tell you to-morrow."

"After I know all about it from you? He ought to have told me before. Does he think I didn't care, because I left you so much liberty?"

"Oh no," said Catherine; "he knew you would care. And we have been so much obliged to you for—for the liberty."

The Doctor gave a short laugh. "You might have made a better use of it, Catherine."

"Please don't say that, father!" the girl urged, softly, fixing her dull and gentle eyes upon him.

He puffed his cigar awhile, meditatively. "You have gone very fast," he said, at last.

"Yes," Catherine answered, simply; "I think we have."

Her father glanced at her an instant, removing his eyes from the fire. "I don't wonder Mr. Townsend likes you; you are so simple and so good."

"I don't know why it is; but he *does* like me. I am sure of that."

"And are you very fond of Mr. Townsend?"

"I like him very much, of course, or I shouldn't consent to marry him."

"But you have known him a very short time, my dear."

"Oh," said Catherine, with some eagerness, "it doesn't take long to like a person—when once you begin."

"You must have begun very quickly. Was it the first time you saw him—that night at your aunt's party?"

"I don't know, father," the girl answered. "I can't tell you about that."

"Of course; that's your own affair. You will have observed that I have acted on that principle. I have not interfered; I have left you your liberty; I have remembered that you are no longer a little girl—that you have arrived at years of discretion."

"I feel very old—and very wise," said Catherine, smiling faintly.

"I am afraid that before long you will feel older and wiser yet. I don't like your engagement."

"Ah!" Catherine exclaimed, softly, getting up from her chair.

"No, my dear. I am sorry to give you pain; but I don't like it. You should have consulted me before you settled it. I have been too easy with you, and I feel as if you had taken advantage of my indulgence. Most decidedly you should have spoken to me first."

Catherine hesitated a moment, and then—"It was because I was afraid you wouldn't like it," she confessed.

"Ah, there it is! You had a bad conscience."

"No, I have not a bad conscience, father!" the girl cried out, with considerable energy. "Please don't accuse me of anything so dreadful!" These words, in fact, represented to her imagination something very terrible indeed, something base and cruel, which she associated with malefactors and prisoners. "It was because I was afraid—afraid—" she went on.

"If you were afraid, it was because you had been foolish."

"I was afraid you didn't like Mr. Townsend."

"You were quite right. I don't like him."

"Dear father, you don't know him," said Catherine, in a voice so timidly argumentative that it might have touched him.

"Very true; I don't know him intimately. But I know him enough; I have my impression of him. You don't know him either."

She stood before the fire with her hands lightly clasped in front of her; and her father, leaning back in his chair and looking up at her, made this remark with a placidity that might have been irritating.

I doubt, however, whether Catherine was irritated, though she broke into a vehement protest. "I don't know him?" she cried. "Why, I know him—better than I have ever known any one!"

"You know a part of him—what he has chosen to show you. But you don't know the rest."

"The rest? What is the rest?"

"Whatever it may be, there is sure to be plenty of it."

"I know what you mean," said Catherine, remembering how Morris had forewarned her. "You mean that he is mercenary."

Her father looked up at her still, with his cold, quiet, reasonable eye. "If I meant it, my dear, I should say it! But there is an error I wish particularly to avoid—that of rendering Mr. Townsend more interesting to you by saying hard things about him."

"I won't think them hard if they are true," said Catherine.

"If you don't, you will be a remarkably sensible young woman!"

"They will be your reasons, at any rate, and you will want me to hear your reasons."

The Doctor smiled a little. "Very true. You have a perfect right to ask for them." And he puffed his cigar a few moments. "Very well, then; without accusing Mr. Townsend of being in love only with your fortune—and with the fortune that you justly expect—I will say that there is every reason to suppose that these good things have entered into his calculation more largely than a tender solicitude for your happiness strictly requires. There is, of course, nothing impossible in an intelligent young man entertaining a disinterested affection for you. You are an honest, amiable girl, and an intelligent young man might easily find it out. But the principal thing that we know about this young man—who is, indeed, very intelligent—leads us to suppose that, however much he may value your personal merits, he values your money more. The principal thing we know about him is that he has led a life of dissipation, and has spent a fortune of his own in doing so. That is enough for me, my dear. I wish you to marry a young man with other antecedents—a young man who could give positive guarantees. If Morris Townsend has spent his own fortune in amusing himself, there is every reason to believe that he would spend yours."

The Doctor delivered himself of these remarks slowly, deliberately, with occasional pauses and prolongations of accent, which made no great allowance for poor Catherine's suspense as to his conclusion. She sat down at last, with her head bent and her eyes still fixed upon him; and strangely enough—I hardly know how to tell it—even while she felt that what he said went so terribly against her, she admired his neatness and nobleness of expression. There was something hopeless and oppressive in having to argue with her father; but she too, on her side, must try to be clear. He was so quiet; he was not at all angry; and she, too, must be quiet. But her very effort to be quiet made her tremble.

"That is not the principal thing we know about him," she said; and there was a touch of her tremor in her voice. "There are other things—many other things. He has very high abilities—he wants so much to do something. He is kind, and generous, and true," said poor Catherine, who had not suspected hitherto the resources of her eloquence. "And his fortune—his fortune that he spent—was very small."

"All the more reason he shouldn't have spent it," cried the Doctor, getting up with a laugh. Then, as Catherine, who had also risen to her feet again, stood there in her rather angular earnestness, wishing so much and expressing so little, he drew her toward him and kissed her. "You won't think me cruel?" he said, holding her a moment.

This question was not reassuring; it seemed to Catherine, on the contrary, to suggest possibilities which made her feel sick. But she answered coherently enough, "No, dear father; because if you knew how I feel—and you must know, you know everything—you would be so kind, so gentle."

"Yes, I think I know how you feel," the Doctor said. "I will be very kind—be sure of that. And I will see Mr. Townsend to-morrow. Meanwhile, and for the present, be so good as to mention to no one that you are engaged."

XII

ON THE MORROW, in the afternoon, he stayed at home, awaiting Mr. Townsend's call—a proceeding by which it appeared to him (justly perhaps, for he was a very busy man) that he paid Catherine's suitor great honor, and gave both these young people so much the less to complain of. Morris presented himself with a countenance sufficiently serene—he appeared to have forgotten the "insult" for which he had solicited Catherine's sympathy two evenings before—and Doctor Sloper lost no time in letting him know that he had been prepared for his visit.

"Catherine told me yesterday what has been going on between you," he said. "You must allow me to say that it would have been becoming of you to give me notice of your intentions before they had gone so far."

"I should have done so," Morris answered, "if you had not had so much the appearance of leaving your daughter at liberty. She seems to me quite her own mistress."

"Literally, she is. But she has not emancipated herself morally quite so far, I trust, as to choose a husband without consulting me. I have left her at liberty, but I have not been in the least indifferent. The truth is, that your little affair has come to a head with a rapidity that surprises me. It was only the other day that Catherine made your acquaintance."

"It was not long ago, certainly," said Morris, with great gravity. "I admit that we have not been slow to—to arrive at an understanding. But that was very natural, from the moment we were sure of ourselves—and of each other. My interest in Miss Sloper began the first time I saw her."

"Did it not by chance precede your first meeting?" the Doctor asked.

Morris looked at him an instant. "I certainly had already heard that she was a charming girl."

"A charming girl—that's what you think her?"

"Assuredly. Otherwise I should not be sitting here."

The Doctor meditated a moment. "My dear young man," he said at last, "you must be very susceptible. As Catherine's father I have, I trust, a just and tender appreciation of her many good qualities; but I don't mind telling you that I have never thought of her as a charming girl, and never expected any one else to do so."

Morris Townsend received this statement with a smile that was not wholly devoid of deference. "I don't know what I might think of her if I were her father. I can't put myself in that place. I speak from my own point of view."

"You speak very well," said the Doctor; "but that is not all that is necessary. I told Catherine yesterday that I disapproved of her engagement."

"She let me know as much, and I was very sorry to hear it. I am greatly disappointed." And Morris sat in silence awhile, looking at the floor.

"Did you really expect I would say I was delighted, and throw my daughter into your arms?"

"Oh no; I had an idea you didn't like me."

"What gave you the idea?"

"The fact that I am poor."

"That has a harsh sound," said the Doctor, "but it is about the truth—speaking of you strictly as a son-in-law. Your absence of means, of a profession, of visible resources or prospects, places you in a category from which it would be imprudent for me to select a husband for my daughter, who is a weak young woman with a large fortune. In any other capacity I am perfectly prepared to like you. As a son-in-law, I abominate you."

Morris Townsend listened respectfully. "I don't think Miss Sloper is a weak woman," he presently said.

"Of course you must defend her—it's the least you can do. But I have known my child twenty years, and you have known her six weeks. Even if she were not weak, however, you would still be a penniless man."

"Ah, yes; that is *my* weakness! And therefore, you mean, I am mercenary—I only want your daughter's money."

"I don't say that. I am not obliged to say it; and to say it, save under stress of compulsion, would be very bad taste. I say simply that you belong to the wrong category."

"But your daughter doesn't marry a category," Townsend urged, with his handsome smile. "She marries an individual—an individual whom she is so good as to say she loves."

"An individual who offers so little in return."

"Is it possible to offer more than the most tender affection and a life-long devotion?" the young man demanded.

"It depends how we take it. It is possible to offer a few other things besides, and not only is it possible, but it is the custom. A life-long devotion is measured after the fact; and meanwhile it is usual in these cases to give a few material securities. What are yours? A very handsome face and figure, and a very good manner. They are excellent as far as they go, but they don't go far enough."

"There is one thing you should add to them," said Morris—"the word of a gentleman."

"The word of a gentleman that you will always love Catherine? You must be a fine gentleman to be sure of that."

"The word of a gentleman that I am not mercenary; that my affection for Miss Sloper is as pure and disinterested a sentiment as was ever lodged in a human breast. I care no more for her fortune than for the ashes in that grate."

"I take note—I take note," said the Doctor. "But, having done so, I turn to our category again. Even with that solemn vow on your lips, you take your place in it. There is nothing against you but an accident, if you will; but, with my thirty years' medical practice, I have seen that accidents may have far-reaching consequences."

Morris smoothed his hat—it was already remarkably glossy—and continued to display a self-control which, as the Doctor was obliged to admit, was extremely creditable to him. But his disappointment was evidently keen.

"Is there nothing I can do to make you believe in me?"

"If there were, I should be sorry to suggest it, for—don't you see?—I don't want to believe in you," said the Doctor, smiling.

"I would go and dig in the fields."

"That would be foolish."

"I will take the first work that offers to-morrow."

"Do so by all means—but for your own sake, not for mine."

"I see; you think I am an idler!" Morris exclaimed, a little too much in the tone of a man who has made a discovery. But he saw his error immediately, and blushed.

"It doesn't matter what I think, when once I have told you I don't think of you as a son-in-law."

But Morris persisted: "You think I would squander her money?"

The Doctor smiled. "It doesn't matter, as I say; but I plead guilty to that."

"That's because I spent my own, I suppose," said Morris. "I frankly confess that. I have been wild; I have been foolish. I will tell you every crazy thing I ever did, if you like. There were some great follies among the number—I have never concealed that. But I have sown my wild-oats. Isn't there some proverb about a reformed rake? I was not a rake, but I assure you I have reformed. It is better to have amused one's self for awhile and have done with it. Your daughter would never care for a milksop; and I will take the liberty of saying that you would like one quite as little. Besides, between my money and hers there is a great difference. I spent my own; it was because it was my own that I spent it. And I made no debts; when it was gone I stopped. I don't owe a penny in the world."

"Allow me to inquire what you are living on now—though *I* admit," the Doctor added, "that the question, on my part, is inconsistent."

"I am living on the remnants of my property," said Morris Townsend.

"Thank you," the Doctor gravely replied.

Yes, certainly, Morris's self-control was laudable. "Even admitting I attach an undue importance to Miss Sloper's fortune," he went on, "would not that be in itself an assurance that I would take good care of it?"

"That you should take too much care would be quite as bad as that you should take too little. Catherine might suffer as much by your economy as by your extravagance."

"I think you are very unjust!" The young man made this declaration decently, civilly, without violence.

"It is your privilege to think so, and I surrender my reputation to you! I certainly don't flatter myself, I gratify you."

"Don't you care a little to gratify your daughter? Do you enjoy the idea of making her miserable?"

"I am perfectly resigned to her thinking me a tyrant for a twelvemonth."

"For a twelvemonth!" exclaimed Morris, with a laugh.

"For a lifetime, then. She may as well be miserable in that way as in the other."

Here at last Morris lost his temper. "Ah, you are not polite, sir!" he cried.

"You push me to it—you argue too much."

"I have a great deal at stake."

"Well, whatever it is," said the Doctor, "you have lost it."

"Are you sure of that?" asked Morris; "are you sure your daughter will give me up?"

"I mean, of course, you have lost it as far as I am concerned. As for Catherine's giving you up—no, I am not sure of it. But as I shall strongly recommend it, as I have a great fund of respect and affection in my daughter's mind to draw upon, and as she has the sentiment of duty developed in a very high degree, I think it extremely possible."

Morris Townsend began to smooth his hat again. "I, too, have a fund of affection to draw upon," he observed, at last.

The Doctor at this point showed his own first symptoms of irritation. "Do you mean to defy me?"

"Call it what you please, sir. I mean not to give your daughter up."

The Doctor shook his head. "I haven't the least fear of your pining away your life. You are made to enjoy it."

Morris gave a laugh. "Your opposition to my marriage is all the more cruel, then. Do you intend to forbid your daughter to see me again?"

"She is past the age at which people are forbidden, and I am not a father in an old-fashioned novel. But I shall strongly urge her to break with you."

"I don't think she will," said Morris Townsend.

"Perhaps not; but I shall have done what I could."

"She has gone too far—" Morris went on.

"To retreat? Then let her stop where she is."

"Too far to stop, I mean."

The Doctor looked at him a moment; Morris had his hand on the door. "There is a great deal of impertinence in your saying it."

"I will say no more, sir," Morris answered; and, making his bow, he left the room.

XIII

IT MAY BE thought the Doctor was too positive, and Mrs. Almond intimated as much. But, as he said, he had his impression; it seemed to him sufficient, and he had no wish to modify it. He had passed his life in estimating people (it was part of the medical trade), and in nineteen cases out of twenty he was right.

"Perhaps Mr. Townsend is the twentieth case," said Mrs. Almond.

"Perhaps he is, though he doesn't look to me at all like a twentieth case. But I will give him the benefit of the doubt, and, to make sure, I will go and talk with Mrs. Montgomery. She will almost certainly tell me I have done right; but it is just possible that she will prove to me that I have made the greatest mistake of my life. If she does, I will beg Mr. Townsend's pardon. You needn't invite her to meet me, as you kindly proposed; I will write her a frank letter, telling her how matters stand, and asking leave to come and see her."

"I am afraid the frankness will be chiefly on your side. The poor little woman will stand up for her brother, whatever he may be."

"Whatever he may be! I doubt that. People are not always so fond of their brothers."

"Ah," said Mrs. Almond, "when it's a question of thirty thousand a year coming into a family—"

"If she stands up for him on account of the money, she will be a humbug. If she is a humbug, I shall see it. If I see it, I won't waste time with her."

"She is not a humbug—she is an exemplary woman. She will not wish to play her brother a trick simply because he is selfish."

"If she is worth talking to, she will sooner play him a trick than that he should play Catherine one. Has she seen Catherine, by-the-way—does she know her?"

"Not to my knowledge. Mr. Townsend can have had no particular interest in bringing them together."

"If she is an exemplary woman, no. But we shall see to what extent she answers your description."

"I shall be curious to hear her description of you," said Mrs. Almond, with a laugh. "And, meanwhile, how is Catherine taking it?"

"As she takes everything—as a matter of course."

"Doesn't she make a noise? Hasn't she made a scene?"

"She is not scenic."

"I thought a lovelorn maiden was always scenic."

"A ridiculous widow is more so. Lavinia has made me a speech; she thinks me very arbitrary."

"She has a talent for being in the wrong," said Mrs. Almond. "But I am very sorry for Catherine, all the same."

"So am I. But she will get over it."

"You believe she will give him up?"

"I count upon it. She has such an admiration for her father."

"Oh, we know all about that. But it only makes me pity her the more. It makes her dilemma the more painful, and the effort of choosing between you and her lover almost impossible."

"If she can't choose, all the better."

"Yes; but he will stand there entreating her to choose, and Lavinia will pull on that side."

"I am glad she is not on my side; she is capable of ruining an excellent cause. The day Lavinia gets into your boat it capsizes. But she had better be careful," said the Doctor. "I will have no treason in my house."

"I suspect she will be careful; for she is at bottom very much afraid of you."

"They are both afraid of me, harmless as I am," the Doctor answered. "And it is on that that I build—on the salutary terror I inspire."

XIV

He wrote his frank letter to Mrs. Montgomery, who punctually answered it, mentioning an hour at which he might present himself in the Second Avenue. She lived in a neat little house of red brick, which had been freshly painted, with the edges of the bricks very sharply marked out in white. It has now disappeared, with its companions, to make room for a row of structures more majestic. There were green shutters upon the windows without slats, but pierced with little holes, arranged in groups; and before the house was a diminutive "yard," ornamented with a bush of mysterious character, and surrounded by a low wooden paling, painted in the same green as the shutters. The place looked like a magnified baby-house, and might have been taken down from a shelf in a toy-shop. Doctor Sloper, when he went to call, said to himself, as he glanced at the objects I have enumerated, that Mrs. Montgomery was evidently a thrifty and self-respecting little person—the modest proportions of her dwelling seemed to indicate that she was of small stature—who took a virtuous satisfaction in keeping herself tidy, and had resolved that, since she might not be splendid, she would at least be immaculate. She received him in a little parlor, which was precisely the parlor he had expected: a small unspeckled bower, ornamented with a desultory foliage of tissue-paper, and with clusters of glass drops, amidst which—to carry out the analogy—the temperature of the leafy season was maintained by means of a cast-iron stove, emitting a dry blue flame, and smelling strongly of varnish. The walls were embellished with engravings swathed in pink gauze, and the tables ornamented with volumes of extracts from the poets, usually bound in black cloth stamped with florid designs in jaundiced gilt. The Doctor had time to take cognizance of these details; for Mrs. Montgomery, whose conduct he pronounced under the circumstances inexcusable, kept him waiting some ten minutes before she appeared. At last, however, she rustled in, smoothing down a stiff poplin dress, with a little frightened flush in a gracefully rounded cheek.

She was a small, plump, fair woman, with a bright, clear eye, and an extraordinary air of neatness and briskness. But these qualities were evidently combined with an unaffected humility, and the Doctor gave her his esteem as soon as he had looked at her. A brave little person, with lively perceptions, and yet a disbelief in her own talent for social, as distinguished from practical, affairs—this was his rapid mental *résumé* of Mrs. Montgomery; who, as he saw, was flattered by what she regarded as the honor of his visit. Mrs. Montgomery, in her little red house in the Second Avenue, was a person for whom Doctor Sloper was one of the great men—one of the fine gentlemen of New York; and while she fixed her agitated eyes upon him, while she clasped her mittened hands together in her glossy poplin lap, she had the appearance of saying to herself that he quite answered her idea of what a distinguished guest would naturally be. She apologized for being late; but he interrupted her.

"It doesn't matter," he said; "for while I sat here I had time to think over what I wish to say to you, and to make up my mind how to begin."

"Oh, do begin!" murmured Mrs. Montgomery.

"It is not so easy," said the Doctor, smiling. "You will have gathered from my letter that I wish to ask you a few questions, and you may not find it very comfortable to answer them."

"Yes; I have thought what I should say. It is not very easy."

"But you must understand my situation—my state of

mind. Your brother wishes to marry my daughter, and I wish to find out what sort of a young man he is. A good way to do so seemed to be to come and ask you, which I have proceeded to do."

Mrs. Montgomery evidently took the situation very seriously; she was in a state of extreme moral concentration. She kept her pretty eyes, which were illumined by a sort of brilliant modesty, attached to his own countenance, and evidently paid the most earnest attention to each of his words. Her expression indicated that she thought his idea of coming to see her a very superior conception, but that she was really afraid to have opinions on strange subjects.

"I am extremely glad to see you," she said, in a tone which seemed to admit, at the same time, that this had nothing to do with the question.

The Doctor took advantage of this admission. "I didn't come to see you for your pleasure; I came to make you say disagreeable things—and you can't like that. What sort of a gentleman is your brother?"

Mrs. Montgomery's illuminated gaze grew vague, and began to wander. She smiled a little, and for some time made no answer, so that the Doctor at last became impatient. And her answer, when it came, was not satisfactory. "It is difficult to talk about one's brother."

"Not when one is fond of him, and when one has plenty of good to say."

"Yes, even then, when a good deal depends on it," said Mrs. Montgomery.

"Nothing depends on it for you."

"I mean for—for—" and she hesitated.

"For your brother himself. I see."

"I mean for Miss Sloper," said Mrs. Montgomery.

The Doctor liked this; it had the accent of sincerity. "Exactly; that's the point. If my poor girl should marry your brother, everything—as regards her happiness—would depend on his being a good fellow. She is the best creature in the world, and she could never do him a grain of injury. He, on the other hand, if he should not be all that we desire, might make her very miserable. That is why I want you to throw some light upon his character, you know. Of course, you are not bound to do it. My daughter, whom you have never seen, is nothing to you; and I, possibly, am only an indiscreet and impertinent old man. It is perfectly open to you to tell me that my visit is in very bad taste, and that I had better go about my business. But I don't think you will do this; because I think we shall interest you—my poor girl and I. I am sure that if you were to see Catherine she would interest you very much. I don't mean because she is interesting in the usual sense of the word, but because you would feel sorry for her. She is so soft, so simple-minded, she would be such an easy victim! A bad husband would have remarkable facilities for making her miserable; for she would have neither the intelligence nor the resolution to get the better of him, and yet she would have an exaggerated power of suffering. I see," added the Doctor, with his most insinuating, his most professional laugh, "you are already interested."

"I have been interested from the moment he told me he was engaged," said Mrs. Montgomery.

"Ah! he says that—he calls it an engagement?"

"Oh, he has told me you didn't like it."

"Did he tell you that I don't like *him?*"

"Yes, he told me that too. I said I couldn't help it," added Mrs. Montgomery.

"Of course you can't. But what you can do is to tell me I am right—to give me an attestation, as it were." And the Doctor accompanied this remark with another professional smile.

Mrs. Montgomery, however, smiled not at all; it was obvious that she could not take the humorous view of his appeal. "That is a good deal to ask," she said, at last.

"There can be no doubt of that; and I must, in conscience, remind you of the advantages a young man marrying my daughter would enjoy. She has an income of ten thousand dollars in her own right, left her by her mother; if she marries a husband I approve, she will come into almost twice as much more at my death."

Mrs. Montgomery listened in great earnestness to this splendid financial statement; she had never heard thousands of dollars so familiarly talked about. She flushed a little with excitement. "Your daughter will be immensely rich," she said, softly.

"Precisely—that's the bother of it."

"And if Morris should marry her, he—he—" And she hesitated, timidly.

"He would be master of all that money? By no means. He would be master of the ten thousand a year that she has from her mother; but I should leave every penny of my own fortune, earned in the laborious exercise of my profession, to my nephews and nieces."

Mrs. Montgomery dropped her eyes at this, and sat for some time gazing at the straw matting which covered her floor.

"I suppose it seems to you," said the Doctor, laughing, "that in so doing I should play your brother a very shabby trick."

"Not at all. That is too much money to get possession of so easily by marrying. I don't think it would be right."

"It's right to get all one can. But in this case your brother wouldn't be able. If Catherine marries without my consent, she doesn't get a penny from my own pocket."

"Is that certain?" asked Mrs. Montgomery, looking up.

"As certain as that I sit here."

"Even if she should pine away?"

"Even if she should pine to a shadow, which isn't probable."

"Does Morris know this?"

"I shall be most happy to inform him," the Doctor exclaimed.

Mrs. Montgomery resumed her meditations; and her visitor, who was prepared to give time to the affair, asked himself whether, in spite of her little conscientious air, she was not playing into her brother's hands. At the same time he was half ashamed of the ordeal to which he had subjected her, and was touched by the gentleness with which she bore it. "If she were a humbug," he said, "she would get angry, unless she be very deep indeed. It is not probable that she is as deep as that."

"What makes you dislike Morris so much?" she presently asked, emerging from her reflections.

"I don't dislike him in the least as a friend, as a companion. He seems to me a charming fellow, and I should think he would be excellent company. I dislike him exclusively as a son-in-law. If the only office of a son-in-law were to dine at the paternal table, I should set a high value upon your brother: he dines capitally. But that is a small part of his function, which, in general, is to be a protector and care-taker of my child, who is singularly ill-adapted to take care of herself. It is there that he doesn't satisfy me. I confess I have nothing but my impression to go by; but I am in the habit of trusting my impression. Of course you are at liberty to contradict it flat. He strikes me as selfish and shallow."

Mrs. Montgomery's eyes expanded a little, and the Doctor fancied he saw the light of admiration in them. "I wonder you have discovered he is selfish," she exclaimed.

"Do you think he hides it so well?"

"Very well indeed," said Mrs. Montgomery. "And I think we are all rather selfish," she added, quickly.

"I think so too; but I have seen people hide it better than he. You see I am helped by a habit I have of dividing people into classes, into types. I may easily be mistaken about your brother as an individual, but his type is written on his whole person."

"He is very good-looking," said Mrs. Montgomery.

The Doctor eyed her a moment. "You women are all the same! But the type to which your brother belongs was made to be the ruin of you, and you were made to be its handmaids and victims. The sign of the type in question is the determination—sometimes terrible in its quiet intensity—to accept nothing of life but its pleasures, and to secure these pleasures chiefly by the aid of your complaisant sex. Young men of this class never do anything for themselves that they can get other people to do for them, and it is the infatuation, the devotion, the superstition of others that keeps them going. These others, in ninety-nine cases out of a hundred, are women. What our young friends chiefly insist upon is that some one else shall suffer for them; and women do that sort of thing, as you must know, wonderfully well." The Doctor paused a moment, and then he added, abruptly, "You have suffered immensely for your brother!"

This exclamation was abrupt, as I say, but it was also perfectly calculated. The Doctor had been rather disappointed at not finding his compact and comfortable little hostess surrounded in a more visible degree by the ravages of Morris Townsend's immorality; but he had said to himself that this was not because the young man had spared her, but because she had contrived to plaster up her wounds. They were aching there behind the varnished stove, the festooned engravings, beneath her own neat little poplin bosom; and if he could only touch the tender spot, she would make a movement that would betray her. The words I have just quoted were an attempt to put his finger suddenly upon the place, and they had some of the success that he looked for. The tears sprung for a moment to Mrs. Montgomery's eyes, and she indulged in a proud little jerk of the head.

"I don't know how you have found that out!" she exclaimed.

"By a philosophic trick—by what they call induction. You know you have always your option of contradicting me. But kindly answer me a question: Don't you give your brother money? I think you ought to answer that."

"Yes, I have given him money," said Mrs. Montgomery.

"And you have not had much to give him?"

She was silent a moment. "If you ask me for a confession of poverty, that is easily made. I am very poor."

"One would never suppose it from your—your charming house," said the Doctor. "I learned from my sister that your income was moderate, and your family numerous."

"I have five children," Mrs. Montgomery observed; "but I am happy to say I can bring them up decently."

"Of course you can—accomplished and devoted as you are. But your brother has counted them over, I suppose?"

"Counted them over?"

"He knows there are five, I mean. He tells me it is he that brings them up."

Mrs. Montgomery stared a moment, and then quickly—"Oh yes; he teaches them—Spanish."

The Doctor laughed out. "That must take a great deal off your hands! Your brother also knows, of course, that you have very little money?"

"I have often told him so," Mrs. Montgomery exclaimed, more unreservedly than she had yet spoken. She was apparently taking some comfort in the Doctor's clairvoyance.

"Which means that you have often occasion to, and that he often sponges on you. Excuse the crudity of my language; I simply express a fact. I don't ask you how much of your money he has had, it is none of my business. I have ascertained what I suspected—what I wished." And the Doctor got up, gently smoothing his hat. "Your brother lives on you," he said, as he stood there.

Mrs. Montgomery quickly rose from her chair, following her visitor's movements with a look of fascination. But then, with a certain inconsequence—"I have never complained of him," she said.

"You needn't protest—you have not betrayed him. But I advise you not to give him any more money."

"Don't you see it is in my interest that he should marry

a rich person?" she asked. "If, as you say, he lives on me, I can only wish to get rid of him; and to put obstacles in the way of his marrying is to increase my own difficulties."

"I wish very much you would come to me with your difficulties," said the Doctor. "Certainly, if I throw him back on your hands, the least I can do is to help you to bear the burden. If you will allow me to say so, then, I shall take the liberty of placing in your hands, for the present, a certain fund for your brother's support."

Mrs. Montgomery stared; she evidently thought he was jesting; but she presently saw that he was not, and the complication of her feelings became painful. "It seems to me that I ought to be very much offended with you," she murmured.

"Because I have offered you money? That's a superstition," said the Doctor. "You must let me come and see you again, and we will talk about these things. I suppose that some of your children are girls?"

"I have two little girls," said Mrs. Montgomery.

"Well, when they grow up, and begin to think of taking husbands, you will see how anxious you will be about the moral character of these husbands. Then you will understand this visit of mine."

"Ah, you are not to believe that Morris's moral character is bad."

The Doctor looked at her a little, with folded arms. "There is something I should greatly like, as a moral satisfaction. I should like to hear you say, 'He is abominably selfish.'"

The words came out with the grave distinctness of his voice, and they seemed for an instant to create, to poor Mrs. Montgomery's troubled vision, a material image. She gazed at it an instant, and then she turned away. "You distress me, sir!" she exclaimed. "He is, after all, my brother; and his talents, his talents—" On these last words her voice quavered, and before he knew it she had burst into tears.

"His talents are first-rate," said the Doctor. "We must find the proper field for them." And he assured her most respectfully of his regret at having so greatly discomposed her. "It's all for my poor Catherine," he went on. "You must know her, and you will see."

Mrs. Montgomery brushed away her tears, and blushed at having shed them. "I should like to know your daughter," she answered; and then, in an instant—"Don't let her marry him!"

Doctor Sloper went away with the words gently humming in his ears—"Don't let her marry him!" They gave him the moral satisfaction of which he had just spoken, and their value was the greater that they had evidently cost a pang to poor little Mrs. Montgomery's family pride.

XV

He had been puzzled by the way that Catherine carried herself; her attitude at this sentimental crisis seemed to him unnaturally passive. She had not spoken to him again after that scene in the library, the day before his interview with Morris; and a week had elapsed without making any change in her manner. There was nothing in it that appealed for pity, and he was even a little disappointed at her not giving him an opportunity to make up for his harshness by some manifestation of liberality which should operate as a compensation. He thought a little of offering to take her for a tour in Europe; but he was determined to do this only in case she should seem mutely to reproach him. He had an idea that she would display a talent for mute reproaches, and he was surprised at not finding himself exposed to these silent batteries. She said nothing, either tacitly or explicitly, and as she was never very talkative, there was now no especial eloquence in her reserve. And poor Catherine was not sulky—a style of behavior for which she had too little histrionic talent—she was simply very patient. Of course she was thinking over her situation, and she was apparently doing so in a deliberate and unimpassioned manner, with a view of making the best of it.

"She will do as I have bidden her," said the Doctor; and he made the further reflection that his daughter was not a woman of a great spirit.

I know not whether he had hoped for a little more resistance for the sake of a little more entertainment; but he said to himself, as he had said before, that though it might have its momentary alarms, paternity was, after all, not an exciting vocation.

Catherine meanwhile had made a discovery of a very different sort; it had become vivid to her that there was a great excitement in trying to be a good daughter. She had an entirely new feeling, which may be described as a state of expectant suspense about her own actions. She watched herself as she would have watched another person, and wondered what she would do. It was as if this other person, who was both herself and not herself, had suddenly sprung into being, inspiring her with a natural curiosity as to the performance of untested functions.

"I am glad I have such a good daughter," said her father, kissing her, after the lapse of several days.

"I am trying to be good," she answered, turning away, with a conscience not altogether clear.

"If there is anything you would like to say to me, you know you must not hesitate. You needn't feel obliged to be so quiet. I shouldn't care that Mr. Townsend should be a frequent topic of conversation, but whenever you have anything particular to say about him I shall be very glad to hear it."

"Thank you," said Catherine; "I have nothing particular at present."

He never asked her whether she had seen Morris again, because he was sure that if this had been the case she would tell him. She had, in fact, not seen him; she had only written him a long letter. The letter, at least, was long for her; and, it may be added, that it was long for Morris; it consisted of five pages, in a remarkably neat and handsome hand. Catherine's handwriting was beautiful, and she was even a little proud of it: she was extremely fond of copying, and possessed volumes of extracts which testified to this accomplishment; volumes which she had exhibited one day to her lover, when the bliss of feeling that she was important in his eyes was exceptionally keen. She told Morris, in writing, that her father had expressed the wish that she should not see him again, and that she begged he would not come to the house until she should have "made up her mind." Morris replied with a passionate epistle, in which he asked to what, in Heaven's name, she wished to make up her mind. Had not her mind been made up two weeks before, and could it be possible that she entertained the idea of throwing him off? Did she mean to break down at the very beginning of their ordeal, after all the promises of fidelity she had both given and extracted? And he gave an account of his own interview with her father—an account not identical at all points with that offered in these pages. "He was terribly violent," Morris wrote, "but you know my self-control. I have need of it all when I remember that I have it in my power to break in upon your cruel captivity." Catherine sent him, in answer to this, a note of three lines. "I am in great trouble; do not doubt of my affection, but let me wait a little and think." The idea of a struggle with her father, of setting up her will against his own, was heavy on her soul, and it kept her quiet, as a great physical weight keeps us motionless. It never entered into her mind to throw her lover off; but from the first she tried to assure herself that there would be a peaceful way out of their difficulty. The assurance was vague, for it contained no element of positive conviction that her father would change his mind. She only had an idea that if she should be very good, the situation would in some mysterious manner improve. To be good she must be patient, outwardly submissive, abstain from judging her father too harshly, and from committing any act of open defiance. He was perhaps right, after all, to think as he did; by which Catherine meant not in the least that his judgment of Morris's motives in seeking to marry her was perhaps a just one, but that it was probably natural and proper that conscientious parents should be suspicious and even unjust. There were probably people in the world as bad as her father supposed Morris to be, and if there were the slightest chance of Morris being one of these sinister persons, the Doctor was right in taking it into account. Of course he could not know what she knew—how the purest love and truth were seated in the young man's eyes; but Heaven, in its time, might appoint a way of bringing him to such knowledge. Catherine expected a good deal of Heaven, and referred to the skies the initiative, as the French say, in dealing with her dilemma. She could not imagine herself imparting any kind of knowledge to her father; there was something superior even in his injustice, and absolute in his mistakes. But she could at least be good, and if she were only good enough, Heaven would invent some way of reconciling all things—the dignity of her father's errors and the sweetness of her own confidence, the strict performance of her filial duties, and the enjoyment of Morris Townsend's affection.

Poor Catherine would have been glad to regard Mrs. Penniman as an illuminating agent, a part which this lady herself, indeed, was but imperfectly prepared to play. Mrs. Penniman took too much satisfaction in the sentimental shadows of this little drama to have, for the moment, any great interest in dissipating them. She wished the plot to thicken, and the advice that she gave her niece tended, in her own imagination, to produce this result. It was rather incoherent counsel, and from one day to another it contradicted itself; but it was pervaded by an earnest desire that Catherine should do something striking. "You must *act,* my dear; in your situation the great thing is to act," said Mrs. Penniman, who found her niece altogether beneath her opportunities. Mrs. Penniman's real hope was that the girl would make a secret marriage, at which she should officiate as bride'swoman or duenna. She had a vision of this ceremony being performed in some subterranean chapel; subterranean chapels in New York were not frequent, but Mrs. Penniman's imagination was not chilled by trifles; and of the guilty couple—she liked to think of poor Catherine and her suitor as the guilty couple

—being shuffled away in a fast-whirling vehicle to some obscure lodging in the suburbs, where she would pay them (in a thick veil) clandestine visits; where they would endure a period of romantic privation; and when ultimately, after she should have been their earthly providence, their intercessor, their advocate, and their medium of communication with the world, they would be reconciled to her brother in an artistic tableau, in which she herself should be somehow the central figure. She hesitated as yet to recommend this course to Catherine, but she attempted to draw an attractive picture of it to Morris Townsend. She was in daily communication with the young man, whom she kept informed by letters of the state of affairs in Washington Square. As he had been banished, as she said, from the house, she no longer saw him; but she ended by writing to him that she longed for an interview. This interview could take place only on neutral ground, and she bethought herself greatly before selecting a place of meeting. She had an inclination for Greenwood Cemetery, but she gave it up as too distant; she could not absent herself for so long, as she said, without exciting suspicion. Then she thought of the Battery, but that was rather cold and windy, besides one's being exposed to intrusion from the Irish emigrants who at this point alight, with large appetites, in the New World; and at last she fixed upon an oyster saloon in the Seventh Avenue, kept by a negro—an establishment of which she knew nothing save that she had noticed it in passing. She made an appointment with Morris Townsend to meet him there, and she went to the tryst at dusk, enveloped in an impenetrable veil. He kept her waiting for half an hour—he had almost the whole width of the city to traverse—but she liked to wait, it seemed to intensify the situation. She ordered a cup of tea, which proved excessively bad, and this gave her a sense that she was suffering in a romantic cause. When Morris at last arrived, they sat together for half an hour in the duskiest corner of the back shop; and it is hardly too much to say that this was the happiest half-hour that Mrs. Penniman had known for years. The situation was really thrilling, and it scarcely seemed to her a false note when her companion asked for an oyster stew, and proceeded to consume it before her eyes. Morris, indeed, needed all the satisfaction that stewed oysters could give him, for it may be intimated to the reader that he regarded Mrs. Penniman in the light of a fifth wheel to his coach. He was in a state of irritation natural to a gentleman of fine parts who had been snubbed in a benevolent attempt to confer a distinction upon a young woman of inferior characteristics, and the insinuating sympathy of this somewhat desiccated matron appeared to offer him no practical relief. He thought her a humbug, and he judged of humbugs with a good deal of confidence. He had listened and made himself agreeable to her at first, in order to get a footing in Washington Square; and at present he needed all his self-command to be decently civil. It would have gratified him to tell her that she was a fantastic old woman, and that he would like to put her into an omnibus and send her home. We know, however, that Morris possessed the virtue of self-control, and he had moreover the constant habit of seeking to be agreeable; so that, although Mrs. Penniman's demeanor only exasperated his already unquiet nerves, he listened to her with a sombre deference in which she found much to admire.

XVI

THEY HAD of course immediately spoken of Catherine. "Did she send me a message, or—or anything?" Morris asked. He appeared to think that she might have sent him a trinket or a lock of her hair.

Mrs. Penniman was slightly embarrassed, for she had not told her niece of her intended expedition. "Not exactly a message," she said; "I didn't ask her for one, because I was afraid to—to excite her."

"I am afraid she is not very excitable." And Morris gave a smile of some bitterness.

"She is better than that—she is steadfast, she is true."

"Do you think she will hold fast, then?"

"To the death!"

"Oh, I hope it won't come to that," said Morris.

"We must be prepared for the worst, and that is what I wish to speak to you about."

"What do you call the worst?"

"Well," said Mrs. Penniman, "my brother's hard, intellectual nature."

"Oh, the devil!"

"He is impervious to pity," Mrs. Penniman added, by way of explanation.

"Do you mean that he won't come round?"

"He will never be vanquished by argument. I have studied him. He will be vanquished only by the accomplished fact."

"The accomplished fact?"

"He will come round afterward," said Mrs. Penniman, with extreme significance. "He cares for nothing but facts—he must be met by facts."

"Well," rejoined Morris, "it is a fact that I wish to marry his daughter. I met him with that the other day, but he was not at all vanquished."

Mrs. Penniman was silent a little, and her smile beneath the shadow of her capacious bonnet, on the edge of which her black veil was arranged curtain-wise, fixed itself upon Morris's face with a still more tender brilliancy. "Marry Catherine first, and meet him afterward!" she exclaimed.

"Do you recommend that?" asked the young man, frowning heavily.

She was a little frightened, but she went on with considerable boldness. "That is the way I see it: a private marriage—a private marriage." She repeated the phrase because she liked it.

"Do you mean that I should carry Catherine off? What do they call it—elope with her?"

"It is not a crime when you are driven to it," said Mrs. Penniman. "My husband, as I have told you, was a distinguished clergyman—one of the most eloquent men of his day. He once married a young couple that had fled from the house of the young lady's father; he was so interested in their story. He had no hesitation, and everything came out beautifully. The father was afterward reconciled, and thought everything of the young man. Mr. Penniman married them in the evening, about seven o'clock. The church was so dark you could scarcely see, and Mr. Penniman was intensely agitated—he was so sympathetic. I don't believe he could have done it again."

"Unfortunately, Catherine and I have not Mr. Penniman to marry us," said Morris.

"No, but you have me!" rejoined Mrs. Penniman, expressively. "I can't perform the ceremony, but I can help you; I can watch!"

"The woman's an idiot!" thought Morris; but he was obliged to say something different. It was not, however, materially more civil. "Was it in order to tell me this that you requested I would meet you here?"

Mrs. Penniman had been conscious of a certain vagueness in her errand, and of not being able to offer him any very tangible reward for his long walk. "I thought perhaps you would like to see one who is so near to Catherine," she observed, with considerable majesty; "and also," she added, "that you would value an opportunity of sending her something."

Morris extended his empty hands with a melancholy smile. "I am greatly obliged to you, but I have nothing to send."

"Haven't you a *word?*" asked his companion, with her suggestive smile coming back.

Morris frowned again. "Tell her to hold fast," he said, rather curtly.

"That is a good word—a noble word: it will make her happy for many days. She is very touching, very brave," Mrs. Penniman went on, arranging her mantle and preparing to depart. While she was so engaged she had an inspiration; she found the phrase that she could boldly offer as a vindication of the step she had taken. "If you marry Catherine at all risks," she said, "you will give my brother a proof of your being what he pretends to doubt."

"What he pretends to doubt?"

"Don't you know what that is?" Mrs. Penniman asked, almost playfully.

"It does not concern me to know," said Morris, grandly.

"Of course it makes you angry."

"I despise it," Morris declared.

"Ah, you know what it is, then?" said Mrs. Penniman, shaking her finger at him. "He pretends that you like—you like the money."

Morris hesitated a moment; and then, as if he spoke advisedly, "I *do* like the money!"

"Ah, but not—but not as he means it. You don't like it more than Catherine?"

He leaned his elbows on the table and buried his head in his hands. "You torture me!" he murmured. And, indeed, this was almost the effect of the poor lady's too importunate interest in his situation.

But she insisted in making her point. "If you marry her in spite of him, he will take for granted that you expect nothing of him, and are prepared to do without it; and so he will see that you are disinterested."

Morris raised his head a little, following this argument. "And what shall I gain by that?"

"Why, that he will see that he has been wrong in thinking that you wished to get his money."

"And seeing that I wish he would go to the deuce with it, he will leave it to a hospital. Is that what you mean?" asked Morris.

"No, I don't mean that; though that would be very grand," Mrs. Penniman quickly added. "I mean that, having done you such an injustice, he will think it his duty, at the end, to make some amends."

Morris shook his head, though it must be confessed he was a little struck with this idea. "Do you think he is so sentimental?"

"He is not sentimental," said Mrs. Penniman; "but, to be perfectly fair to him, I think he has, in his own narrow way, a certain sense of duty."

There passed through Morris Townsend's mind a rapid wonder as to what he might, even under a remote contingency, be indebted to from the action of this principle in Doctor Sloper's breast, and the inquiry exhausted itself in his sense of the ludicrous. "Your brother has no duties to me," he said presently, "and I none to him."

"Ah, but he has duties to Catherine."

"Yes; but you see, on that principle Catherine has duties to him as well."

Mrs. Penniman got up with a melancholy sigh, as if she thought him very unimaginative. "She has always performed them faithfully; and now do you think she has no duties to *you?*" Mrs. Penniman always, even in conversation, italicized her personal pronouns.

"It would sound harsh to say so. I am so grateful for her love," Morris added.

"I will tell her you said that. And now, remember that if you need me I am there." And Mrs. Penniman, who could think of nothing more to say, nodded vaguely in the direction of Washington Square.

Morris looked some moments at the sanded floor of the shop; he seemed to be disposed to linger a moment. At last, looking up with a certain abruptness, "It is your belief that if she marries me he will cut her off?" he asked.

Mrs. Penniman stared a little, and smiled. "Why, I have explained to you what I think would happen—that in the end it would be the best thing to do."

"You mean that, whatever she does, in the long run she will get the money?"

"It doesn't depend upon her, but upon you. Venture to appear as disinterested as you are," said Mrs. Penniman, ingeniously. Morris dropped his eyes on the sanded floor again, pondering this, and she pursued: "Mr. Penniman and I had nothing, and we were very happy. Catherine, moreover, has her mother's fortune, which, at the time my sister-in-law married, was considered a very handsome one."

"Oh, don't speak of that!" said Morris; and indeed it was quite superfluous, for he had contemplated the fact in all its lights.

"Austin married a wife with money—why shouldn't you?"

"Ah! but your brother was a doctor," Morris objected.

"Well, all young men can't be doctors."

"I should think it an extremely loathsome profession," said Morris, with an air of intellectual independence; then, in a moment, he went on rather inconsequently, "Do you suppose there is a will already made in Catherine's favor?"

"I suppose so—even doctors must die; and perhaps a little in mine," Mrs. Penniman frankly added.

"And you believe he would certainly change it—as regards Catherine?"

"Yes; and then change it back again."

"Ah, but one can't depend on that," said Morris.

"Do you want to *depend* on it?" Mrs. Penniman asked.

Morris blushed a little. "Well, I am certainly afraid of being the cause of an injury to Catherine."

"Ah! you must not be afraid. Be afraid of nothing, and everything will go well."

And then Mrs. Penniman paid for her cup of tea, and Morris paid for his oyster stew, and they went out together into the dimly-lighted wilderness of the Seventh Avenue. The dusk had closed in completely, and the street lamps were separated by wide intervals of a pavement in which cavities and fissures played a disproportionate part. An omnibus, emblazoned with strange pictures, went tumbling over the dislocated cobble-stones.

"How will you go home?" Morris asked, following this vehicle with an interested eye. Mrs. Penniman had taken his arm.

She hesitated a moment. "I think this manner would be pleasant," she said; and she continued to let him feel the value of his support.

So he walked with her through the devious ways of the west side of the town, and through the bustle of gathering nightfall in populous streets, to the quiet precinct of Washington Square. They lingered a moment at the foot of Doctor Sloper's white marble steps, above which a spotless white door, adorned with a glittering silver plate, seemed to figure for Morris the closed portal of happiness; and then Mrs. Penniman's companion rested a melancholy eye upon a lighted window in the upper part of the house.

"That is my room—my dear little room!" Mrs. Penniman remarked.

Morris started. "Then I needn't come walking round the Square to gaze at it."

"That's as you please. But Catherine's is behind; two noble windows on the second floor. I think you can see them from the other street."

"I don't want to see them, ma'am." And Morris turned his back to the house.

"I will tell her you have been *here,* at any rate," said Mrs. Penniman, pointing to the spot where they stood; "and I will give her your message—that she is to hold fast."

"Oh yes; of course. You know I write her all that."

"It seems to say more when it is spoken. And remember, if you need me, that I am *there,*" and Mrs. Penniman glanced at the third floor.

On this they separated, and Morris, left to himself, stood looking at the house a moment; after which he turned away, and took a gloomy walk round the Square, on the opposite side, close to the wooden fence. Then he came back, and paused for a minute in front of Doctor Sloper's dwelling. His eyes travelled over it; they even rested on the ruddy windows of Mrs. Penniman's apartment. He thought it a devilish comfortable house.

XVII

Mrs. Penniman told Catherine that evening—the two ladies were sitting in the back parlor—that she had had an interview with Morris Townsend; and on receiving this news the girl started with a sense of pain. She felt angry for the moment; it was almost the first time she had ever felt angry. It seemed to her that her aunt was meddlesome; and from this came a vague apprehension that she would spoil something.

"I don't see why you should have seen him. I don't think it was right," Catherine said.

"I was so sorry for him—it seemed to me some one ought to see him."

"No one but I," said Catherine, who felt as if she were making the most presumptuous speech of her life, and yet at the same time had an instinct that she was right in doing so.

"But you wouldn't, my dear," Aunt Lavinia rejoined; "and I didn't know what might have become of him."

"I have not seen him because my father has forbidden it," Catherine said, very simply.

There was a simplicity in this, indeed, which fairly vexed Mrs. Penniman. "If your father forbade you to go to sleep, I suppose you would keep awake!" she commented.

Catherine looked at her. "I don't understand you. You seem to me very strange."

"Well, my dear, you will understand me some day!" And Mrs. Penniman, who was reading the evening paper, which she perused daily from the first line to the last, resumed her occupation. She wrapped herself in silence; she was determined Catherine should ask her for an account of her interview with Morris. But Catherine was silent for so long that she almost lost patience; and she was on the point of remarking to her that she was very heartless, when the girl at last spoke.

"What did he say?" she asked.

"He said he is ready to marry you any day, in spite of everything."

Catherine made no answer to this, and Mrs. Penniman almost lost patience again; owing to which she at last volunteered the information that Morris looked very handsome, but terribly haggard.

"Did he seem sad?" asked her niece.

"He was dark under the eyes," said Mrs. Penniman. "So different from when I first saw him; though I am not sure that if I had seen him in this condition the first time, I should not have been even more struck with him. There is something brilliant in his very misery."

This was, to Catherine's sense, a vivid picture, and though she disapproved, she felt herself gazing at it. "Where did you see him?" she asked, presently.

"In—in the Bowery; at a confectioner's," said Mrs. Penniman, who had a general idea that she ought to dissemble a little.

"Whereabouts is the place?" Catherine inquired, after another pause.

"Do you wish to go there, my dear?" said her aunt.

"Oh no." And Catherine got up from her seat and went to the fire, where she stood looking awhile at the glowing coals.

"Why are you so dry, Catherine?" Mrs. Penniman said at last.

"So dry?"

"So cold—so irresponsive."

The girl turned very quickly. "Did *he* say that?"

Mrs. Penniman hesitated a moment. "I will tell you what he said. He said he feared only one thing—that you would be afraid."

"Afraid of what?"

"Afraid of your father."

Catherine turned back to the fire again, and then, after a pause, she said, "I *am* afraid of my father."

Mrs. Penniman got quickly up from her chair and approached her niece. "Do you mean to give him up, then?"

Catherine for some time never moved; she kept her eyes on the coals. At last she raised her head and looked at her aunt. "Why do you push me so?" she asked.

"I don't push you. When have I spoken to you before?"

"It seems to me that you have spoken to me several times."

"I am afraid it is necessary, then, Catherine," said Mrs. Penniman, with a good deal of solemnity. "I am afraid you don't feel the importance"—she paused a little; Catherine was looking at her—"the importance of not disappointing that gallant young heart!" And Mrs. Penniman went back to her chair by the lamp, and, with a little jerk, picked up the evening paper again.

Catherine stood there before the fire, with her hands behind her, looking at her aunt, to whom it seemed that the girl had never had just this dark fixedness in her gaze. "I don't think you understand or that you know me," she said.

"If I don't, it is not wonderful; you trust me so little."

Catherine made no attempt to deny this charge, and for some time more nothing was said. But Mrs. Penniman's imagination was restless, and the evening paper failed on this occasion to enchain it.

"If you succumb to the dread of your father's wrath," she said, "I don't know what will become of us."

"Did *he* tell you to say these things to me?"

"He told me to use my influence."

"You must be mistaken," said Catherine. "He trusts me."

"I hope he may never repent of it!" And Mrs. Penniman gave a little sharp slap to her newspaper. She knew not what to make of her niece, who had suddenly become stern and contradictious.

This tendency on Catherine's part was presently even more apparent. "You had much better not make any more appointments with Mr. Townsend," she said. "I don't think it is right."

Mrs. Penniman rose with considerable majesty. "My poor child, are you jealous of me?" she inquired.

"Oh, Aunt Lavinia!" murmured Catherine, blushing.

"I don't think it is your place to teach me what is right."

On this point Catherine made no concession. "It can't be right to deceive."

"I certainly have not deceived *you!*"

"Yes; but I promised my father—"

"I have no doubt you promised your father. But I have promised him nothing."

Catherine had to admit this, and she did so in silence. "I don't believe Mr. Townsend himself likes it," she said, at last.

"Doesn't like meeting me?"

"Not in secret."

"It was not in secret; the place was full of people."

"But it was a secret place—away off in the Bowery."

Mrs. Penniman flinched a little. "Gentlemen enjoy such things," she remarked, presently. "I know what gentlemen like."

"My father wouldn't like it, if he knew."

"Pray, do you propose to inform him?" Mrs. Penniman inquired.

"No, Aunt Lavinia. But please don't do it again."

"If I do it again you will inform him—is that what you mean? I do not share your dread of my brother; I have always known how to defend my own position. But I shall certainly never again take any step on your behalf; you are much too thankless. I knew you were not a spontaneous nature, but I believed you were firm, and I told your father that he would find you so. I am disappointed, but your father will not be." And with this Mrs. Penniman offered her niece a brief good-night, and withdrew to her own apartment.

XVIII

Catherine sat alone by the parlor fire—sat there for more than an hour, lost in her meditations. Her aunt seemed to her aggressive and foolish; and to see it so clearly—to judge Mrs. Penniman so positively—made her feel old and grave. She did not resent the imputation of weakness; it made no impression on her, for she had not the sense of weakness, and she was not hurt at not being appreciated. She had an immense respect for her father, and she felt that to displease him would be a misdemeanor analogous to an act of profanity in a great temple: but her purpose had slowly ripened, and she believed that her prayers had purified it of its violence. The evening advanced, and the lamp burnt dim without her noticing it; her eyes were fixed upon her terrible plan. She knew her father was in his study—that he had been there all the evening; from time to time she expected to hear him move. She thought he would perhaps come, as he sometimes came, into the parlor. At last the clock struck eleven, and the house was wrapped in silence; the servants had gone to bed. Catherine got up and went slowly to the door of the library, where she waited a moment, motionless. Then she knocked, and then she waited again. Her father had answered her, but she had not the courage to turn the latch. What she had said to her aunt was true enough—she was afraid of him; and in saying that she had no sense of weakness, she meant that she was not afraid of herself. She heard him move within, and he came and opened the door for her.

"What is the matter?" asked the Doctor. "You are standing there like a ghost!"

She went into the room, but it was some time before she

contrived to say what she had come to say. Her father, who was in his dressing-gown and slippers, had been busy at his writing-table, and after looking at her for some moments, and waiting for her to speak, he went and seated himself at his papers again. His back was turned to her—she began to hear the scratching of his pen. She remained near the door, with her heart thumping beneath her bodice; and she was very glad that his back was turned, for it seemed to her that she could more easily address herself to this portion of his person than to his face. At last she began, watching it while she spoke:

"You told me that if I should have anything more to say about Mr. Townsend you would be glad to listen to it."

"Exactly, my dear," said the Doctor, not turning round, but stopping his pen.

Catherine wished it would go on, but she herself continued: "I thought I would tell you that I have not seen him again, but that I should like to do so."

"To bid him good-bye?" asked the Doctor.

The girl hesitated a moment. "He is not going away."

The Doctor wheeled slowly round in his chair, with a smile that seemed to accuse her of an epigram; but extremes meet, and Catherine had not intended one. "It is not to bid him good-bye, then?" her father said.

"No, father, not that; at least not forever. I have not seen him again, but I should like to see him," Catherine repeated.

The Doctor slowly rubbed his underlip with the feather of his quill.

"Have you written to him?"

"Yes, four times."

"You have not dismissed him, then. Once would have done that."

"No," said Catherine; "I have asked him—asked him to wait."

Her father sat looking at her, and she was afraid he was

going to break out into wrath, his eyes were so fine and cold.

"You are a dear, faithful child," he said, at last. "Come here to your father." And he got up, holding out his hands toward her.

The words were a surprise, and they gave her an exquisite joy. She went to him, and he put his arm round her tenderly, soothingly; and then he kissed her. After this he said,

"Do you wish to make me very happy?"

"I should like to—but I am afraid I can't," Catherine answered.

"You can if you will. It all depends on your will."

"Is it to give him up?" said Catherine.

"Yes, it is to give him up."

And he held her still, with the same tenderness, looking into her face and resting his eyes on her averted eyes. There was a long silence; she wished he would release her.

"You are happier than I, father," she said, at last.

"I have no doubt you are unhappy just now. But it is better to be unhappy for three months and get over it, than for many years and never get over it."

"Yes, if that were so," said Catherine.

"It would be so; I am sure of that." She answered nothing, and he went on: "Have you no faith in my wisdom, in my tenderness, in my solicitude for your future?"

"Oh, father!" murmured the girl.

"Don't you suppose that I know something of men—their vices, their follies, their falsities?"

She detached herself, and turned upon him. "He is not vicious—he is not false!"

Her father kept looking at her with his sharp, pure eye. "You make nothing of my judgment, then?"

"I can't believe that!"

"I don't ask you to believe it, but to take it on trust."

Catherine was far from saying to herself that this was

an ingenious sophism; but she met the appeal none the less squarely. "What has he done—what do you know?"

"He has never done anything—he is a selfish idler."

"Oh, father, don't abuse him!" she exclaimed, pleadingly.

"I don't mean to abuse him; it would be a great mistake. You may do as you choose," he added, turning away.

"I may see him again?"

"Just as you choose."

"Will you forgive me?"

"By no means."

"It will only be for once."

"I don't know what you mean by once. You must either give him up or continue the acquaintance."

"I wish to explain—to tell him to wait."

"To wait for what?"

"Till you know him better—till you consent."

"Don't tell him any such nonsense as that. I know him well enough, and I shall never consent."

"But we can wait a long time," said poor Catherine, in a tone which was meant to express the humblest conciliation, but which had upon her father's nerves the effect of an iteration not characterized by tact.

The Doctor answered however, quietly enough: "Of course; you can wait till I die, if you like."

Catherine gave a cry of natural horror.

"Your engagement will have one delightful effect upon you; it will make you extremely impatient for that event."

Catherine stood staring, and the Doctor enjoyed the point he had made. It came to Catherine with the force—or rather with the vague impressiveness—of a logical axiom which it was not in her province to controvert; and yet, though it was a scientific truth, she felt wholly unable to accept it.

"I would rather not marry, if that were true," she said.

"Give me a proof of it, then; for it is beyond a question

that by engaging yourself to Morris Townsend you simply wait for my death."

She turned away, feeling sick and faint; and the Doctor went on: "And if you wait for it with impatience, judge, if you please, what *his* eagerness will be."

Catherine turned it over—her father's words had such an authority for her that her very thoughts were capable of obeying him. There was a dreadful ugliness in it, which seemed to glare at her through the interposing medium of her own feebler reason. Suddenly, however, she had an inspiration—she almost knew it to be an inspiration.

"If I don't marry before your death, I will not after," she said.

To her father, it must be admitted, this seemed only another epigram; and as obstinacy, in unaccomplished minds, does not usually select such a mode of expression, he was the more surprised at this wanton play of a fixed idea.

"Do you mean that for an impertinence?" he inquired; an inquiry of which, as he made it, he quite perceived the grossness.

"An impertinence? Oh, father, what terrible things you say!"

"If you don't wait for my death, you might as well marry immediately; there is nothing else to wait for."

For some time Catherine made no answer; but finally she said,

"I think Morris—little by little—might persuade you."

"I shall never let him speak to me again. I dislike him too much."

Catherine gave a long, low sigh; she tried to stifle it, for she had made up her mind that it was wrong to make a parade of her trouble, and to endeavor to act upon her father by the meretricious aid of emotion. Indeed, she even thought it wrong—in the sense of being inconsiderate—to attempt to act upon his feelings at all; her part was to effect some gentle, gradual change in his intellectual perception of poor Morris's character. But the means of effecting such a change were at present shrouded in mystery, and she felt miserably helpless and hopeless. She had exhausted all arguments, all replies. Her father might have pitied her, and in fact he did so; but he was sure he was right.

"There is one thing you can tell Mr. Townsend when you see him again," he said, "that if you marry without my consent, I don't leave you a farthing of money. That will interest him more than anything else you can tell him."

"That would be very right," Catherine answered. "I ought not in that case to have a farthing of your money."

"My dear child," the Doctor observed, laughing, "your simplicity is touching. Make that remark, in that tone, and with that expression of countenance, to Mr. Townsend, and take a note of his answer. It won't be polite—it will express irritation; and I shall be glad of that, as it will put me in the right; unless, indeed—which is perfectly possible—you should like him the better for being rude to you."

"He will never be rude to me," said Catherine, gently.

"Tell him what I say, all the same."

She looked at her father, and her quiet eyes filled with tears.

"I think I will see him, then," she murmured, in her timid voice.

"Exactly as you choose." And he went to the door and opened it for her to go out. The movement gave her a terrible sense of his turning her off.

"It will be only once, for the present," she added, lingering a moment.

"Exactly as you choose," he repeated, standing there with his hand on the door. "I have told you what I think. If you see him, you will be an ungrateful, cruel child; you will have given your old father the greatest pain of his life."

This was more than the poor girl could bear; her tears overflowed, and she moved toward her grimly consistent parent with a pitiful cry. Her hands were raised in supplication, but he sternly evaded this appeal. Instead of letting her sob out her misery on his shoulder, he simply took her by the arm and directed her course across the threshold, closing the door gently but firmly behind her. After he had done so, he remained listening. For a long time there was no sound; he knew that she was standing outside. He was sorry for her, as I have said; but he was so sure he was right. At last he heard her move away, and then her footstep creaked faintly upon the stairs.

The Doctor took several turns round his study, with his hands in his pockets, and a thin sparkle, possibly of irritation, but partly also of something like humor, in his eye. "By Jove," he said to himself, "I believe she will stick—I believe she will stick!" And this idea of Catherine "sticking" appeared to have a comical side, and to offer a prospect of entertainment. He determined, as he said to himself, to see it out.

XIX

It was for reasons connected with this determination that on the morrow he sought a few words of private conversation with Mrs. Penniman. He sent for her to the library, and he there informed her that he hoped very much that, as regarded this affair of Catherine's, she would mind her *p's* and *q's*.

"I don't know what you mean by such an expression," said his sister. "You speak as if I were learning the alphabet."

"The alphabet of common-sense is something you will never learn," the Doctor permitted himself to respond.

"Have you called me here to insult me?" Mrs. Penniman inquired.

"Not at all. Simply to advise you. You have taken up young Townsend; that's your own affair. I have nothing to do with your sentiments, your fancies, your affections, your delusions; but what I request of you is that you will keep these things to yourself. I have explained my views to Catherine; she understands them perfectly, and anything that she does further in the way of encouraging Mr. Townsend's attentions will be in deliberate opposition to my wishes. Anything that you should do in the way of giving her aid and comfort will be—permit me the expression—distinctly treasonable. You know high-treason is a capital offence: take care how you incur the penalty."

Mrs. Penniman threw back her head, with a certain expansion of the eye which she occasionally practised. "It seems to me that you talk like a great autocrat."

"I talk like my daughter's father."

"Not like your sister's brother," cried Lavinia.

"My dear Lavinia," said the Doctor. "I sometimes wonder whether I *am* your brother, we are so extremely different. In spite of differences, however, we can, at a pinch, understand each other; and that is the essential thing just now. Walk straight with regard to Mr. Townsend; that's all I ask. It is highly probable you have been corresponding with him for the last three weeks—perhaps even seeing him. I don't ask you—you needn't tell me." He had a moral conviction that she would contrive to tell a fib about the matter, which it would disgust him to listen to. "Whatever you have done, stop doing it; that's all I wish."

"Don't you wish also by chance to murder your child?" Mrs. Penniman inquired.

"On the contrary, I wish to make her live and be happy."

"You will kill her: she passed a dreadful night."

"She won't die of one dreadful night, nor of a dozen. Remember that I am a distinguished physician."

Mrs. Penniman hesitated a moment; then she risked her retort. "Your being a distinguished physician has not prevented you from already losing *two members* of your family."

She had risked it, but her brother gave her such a terribly incisive look—a look so like a surgeon's lancet—that she was frightened at her courage. And he answered her, in words that corresponded to the look, "It may not prevent me, either, from losing the society of still another."

Mrs. Penniman took herself off with whatever air of depreciated merit was at her command, and repaired to Catherine's room, where the poor girl was closeted. She knew all about her dreadful night, for the two had met again, the evening before, after Catherine left her father. Mrs. Penniman was on the landing of the second floor when her niece came upstairs; it was not remarkable that a person of so much subtlety should have discovered that Catherine had been shut up with the Doctor. It was still less remarkable that she should have felt an extreme curiosity to learn the result of this interview, and that this sentiment, combined with her great amiability and generosity, should have prompted her to regret the sharp words lately exchanged between her niece and herself. As the unhappy girl came into sight in the dusky corridor, she made a lively demonstration of sympathy. Catherine's bursting heart was equally oblivious; she only knew that her aunt was taking her into her arms. Mrs. Penniman drew her into Catherine's own room, and the two women sat there together far into the small hours, the younger one with her head on the other's lap, sobbing, and sobbing at first in a soundless, stifled manner, and then at last perfectly still. It gratified Mrs. Penniman to be able to feel conscientiously that this scene virtually removed the interdict which Catherine had placed upon her indulging in further communion with Morris Townsend. She was not gratified, however, when, in coming back to her niece's room before breakfast, she found that Catherine had risen and was preparing herself for this meal.

"You should not go to breakfast," she said; "you are not well enough, after your fearful night."

"Yes, I am very well, and I am only afraid of being late."

"I can't understand you," Mrs. Penniman cried. "You should stay in bed for three days."

"Oh, I could never do that," said Catherine, to whom this idea presented no attractions.

Mrs. Penniman was in despair; and she noted, with extreme annoyance, that the trace of the night's tears had completely vanished from Catherine's eyes. She had a most impracticable physique. "What effect do you expect to have upon your father," her aunt demanded, "if you come plumping down, without a vestige of any sort of feeling, as if nothing in the world had happened?"

"He would not like me to lie in bed," said Catherine, simply.

"All the more reason for your doing it. How else do you expect to move him?"

Catherine thought a little. "I don't know how; but not

in that way. I wish to be just as usual." And she finished dressing—and, according to her aunt's expression, went plumping down into the paternal presence. She was really too modest for consistent pathos.

And yet it was perfectly true that she had had a dreadful night. Even after Mrs. Penniman left her she had had no sleep; she lay staring at the uncomforting gloom, with her eyes and ears filled with the movement with which her father had turned her out of his room, and of the words in which he had told her that she was a heartless daughter. Her heart was breaking; she had heart enough for that. At moments it seemed to her that she believed him, and that to do what she was doing a girl must indeed be bad. She *was* bad; but she couldn't help it. She would try to appear good, even if her heart were perverted; and from time to time she had a fancy that she might accomplish something by ingenious concessions to form, though she should persist in caring for Morris. Catherine's ingenuities were indefinite, and we are not called upon to expose their hollowness. The best of them, perhaps, showed itself in that freshness of aspect which was so discouraging to Mrs. Penniman, who was amazed at the absence of haggardness in a young woman who for a whole night had lain quivering beneath a father's curse. Poor Catherine was conscious of her freshness; it gave her a feeling about the future which rather added to the weight upon her mind. It seemed a proof that she was strong and solid and dense, and would live to a great age—longer than might be generally convenient; and this idea was depressing, for it appeared to saddle her with a pretension the more, just when the cultivation of any pretension was inconsistent with her doing right. She wrote that day to Morris Townsend, requesting him to come and see her on the morrow; using very few words, and explaining nothing. She would explain everything face to face.

XX

On the morrow, in the afternoon, she heard his voice at the door, and his step in the hall. She received him in the big, bright front parlor, and she instructed the servant that, if any one should call, she was particularly engaged. She was not afraid of her father's coming in, for at that hour he was always driving about town. When Morris stood there before her, the first thing that she was conscious of was that he was even more beautiful to look at than fond recollection had painted him; the next was that he had pressed her in his arms. When she was free again it appeared to her that she had now indeed thrown herself into the gulf of defiance, and even, for an instant, that she had been married to him.

He told her that she had been very cruel, and had made him very unhappy; and Catherine felt acutely the difficulty of her destiny, which forced her to give pain in such opposite quarters. But she wished that, instead of reproaches, however tender, he would give her help; he was certainly wise enough and clever enough to invent some issue from their troubles. She expressed this belief, and Morris received the assurance as if he thought it natural; but he interrogated at first—as was natural too—rather than committed himself to marking out a course.

"You should not have made me wait so long," he said. "I don't know how I have been living; every hour seemed like years. You should have decided sooner."

"Decided?" Catherine asked.

"Decided whether you would keep me or give me up."

"Oh, Morris," she cried, with a long, tender murmur, "I never thought of giving you up!"

"What, then, were you waiting for?" The young man was ardently logical.

"I thought my father might—might—" and she hesitated.

"Might see how unhappy you were?"

"Oh no. But that he might look at it differently."

"And now you have sent for me to tell me that at last he does so. Is that it?"

This hypothetical optimism gave the poor girl a pang. "No, Morris," she said, solemnly, "he looks at it still in the same way."

"Then why have you sent for me?"

"Because I wanted to see you," cried Catherine, piteously.

"That's an excellent reason, surely. But did you want to look at me only? Have you nothing to tell me?"

His beautiful persuasive eyes were fixed upon her face, and she wondered what answer would be noble enough to make to such a gaze as that. For a moment her own eyes took it in, and then—"I *did* want to look at you," she said, gently. But after this speech, most inconsistently, she hid her face.

Morris watched her for a moment attentively. "Will you marry me to-morrow?" he asked, suddenly.

"To-morrow?"

"Next week, then—any time within a month?"

"Isn't it better to wait?" said Catherine.

"To wait for what?"

She hardly knew for what; but this tremendous leap alarmed her. "Till we have thought about it a little more."

He shook his head sadly and reproachfully. "I thought you had been thinking about it these three weeks. Do you want to turn it over in your mind for five years? You have given me more than time enough. My poor girl," he added, in a moment, "you are not sincere."

Catherine colored from brow to chin, and her eyes filled with tears. "Oh, how can you say that?" she murmured.

"Why, you must take me or leave me," said Morris, very reasonably. "You can't please your father and me both; you must choose between us."

"I have chosen you," she said, passionately.

"Then marry me next week!"

She stood gazing at him. "Isn't there any other way?"

"None that I know of for arriving at the same result. If there is, I should be happy to hear of it."

Catherine could think of nothing of the kind, and Morris's luminosity seemed almost pitiless. The only thing she could think of was that her father might, after all, come round; and she articulated, with an awkward sense of her helplessness in doing so, a wish that this miracle might happen.

"Do you think it is in the least degree likely?" Morris asked.

"It would be, if he could only know you."

"He can know me if he will. What is to prevent it?"

"His ideas, his reasons," said Catherine. "They are so—so terribly strong." She trembled with the recollection of them yet.

"Strong!" cried Morris. "I would rather you should think them weak."

"Oh, nothing about my father is weak," said the girl.

Morris turned away, walking to the window, where he stood looking out. "You are terribly afraid of him," he remarked at last.

She felt no impulse to deny it, because she had no shame in it; for, if it was no honor to herself, at least it was an honor to him. "I suppose I must be," she said, simply.

"Then you don't love me—not as I love you. If you fear your father more than you love me, then your love is not what I hoped it was."

"Ah, my friend!" she said, going to him.

"Do *I* fear anything?" he demanded, turning round on her. "For your sake what am I not ready to face?"

"You are noble—you are brave!" she answered, stopping short at a distance that was almost respectful.

"Small good it does me, if you are so timid."

"I don't think I am—*really*," said Catherine.

"I don't know what you mean by 'really.' It is really enough to make us miserable."

"I should be strong enough to wait—to wait a long time."

"And suppose after a long time your father should hate me worse than ever?"

"He wouldn't—he couldn't."

"He would be touched by my fidelity; is that what you mean? If he is so easily touched, then why should you be afraid of him?"

This was much to the point, and Catherine was struck by it. "I will try not to be," she said. And she stood there submissively, the image, in advance, of a dutiful and responsible wife. This image could not fail to recommend itself to Morris Townsend, and he continued to give proof of the high estimation in which he held her. It could only have been at the prompting of such a sentiment that he presently mentioned to her that the course recommended by Mrs. Penniman was an immediate union, regardless of consequences.

"Yes, Aunt Penniman would like that," Catherine said, simply, and yet with a certain shrewdness. It must, however, have been in pure simplicity, and from motives quite untouched by sarcasm, that a few moments after she went on to say to Morris that her father had given her a message for him. It was quite on her conscience to deliver this message, and had the mission been ten times more painful, she would have as scrupulously performed it. "He told me to tell you—to tell you very distinctly, and directly from himself—that if I marry without his consent, I shall not inherit a penny of his fortune. He made a great point of this. He seemed to think—he seemed to think—"

Morris flushed, as any young man of spirit might have flushed at an imputation of baseness. "What did he seem to think?"

"That it would make a difference."

"It *will* make a difference—in many things. We shall be by many thousands of dollars the poorer; and that is a great difference. But it will make none in my affection."

"We shall not want the money," said Catherine; "for you know I have a good deal myself."

"Yes, my dear girl, I know you have something. And he can't touch that."

"He would never," said Catherine. "My mother left it to me."

Morris was silent awhile. "He was very positive about this, was he?" he asked at last. "He thought such a message would annoy me terribly, and make me throw off the mask, eh?"

"I don't know what he thought," said Catherine, sadly.

"Please tell him that I care for his message as much as for that!" and Morris snapped his fingers sonorously.

"I don't think I could tell him that."

"Do you know you sometimes disappoint me," said Morris.

"I should think I might. I disappoint every one—father and Aunt Penniman."

"Well, it doesn't matter with me, because I am fonder of you than they are."

"Yes, Morris," said the girl, with her imagination—what there was of it—swimming in this happy truth, which seemed, after all, invidious to no one.

"Is it your belief that he will stick to it—stick to it forever—to this idea of disinheriting you?—that your goodness and patience will never wear out his cruelty?"

"The trouble is that if I marry you he will think I am not good. He will think that a proof."

"Ah, then he will never forgive you!"

This idea, sharply expressed by Morris's handsome lips,

renewed for a moment to the poor girl's temporarily pacified conscience all its dreadful vividness. "Oh, you must love me very much!" she cried.

"There is no doubt of that, my dear," her lover rejoined. "You don't like that word 'disinherited,'" he added, in a moment.

"It isn't the money; it is that he should—that he should feel so."

"I suppose it seems to you a kind of curse?" said Morris. "It must be very dismal. But don't you think," he went on, presently, "that if you were to try to be very clever, and to set rightly about it, you might in the end conjure it away? Don't you think," he continued further, in a tone of sympathetic speculation, "that a really clever woman, in your place, might bring him round at last? Don't you think—"

Here, suddenly, Morris was interrupted; these ingenious inquiries had not reached Catherine's ears. The terrible word disinheritance, with all its impressive moral reprobation, was still ringing there—seemed, indeed, to gather force as it lingered. The mortal chill of her situation struck more deeply into her childlike heart, and she was overwhelmed by a feeling of loneliness and danger. But her refuge was there, close to her, and she put out her hands to grasp it. "Ah, Morris," she said, with a shudder, "I will marry you as soon as you please!" and she surrendered herself, leaning her head on his shoulder.

"My dear good girl!" he exclaimed, looking down at his prize. And then he looked up again, rather vaguely, with parted lips and lifted eyebrows.

XXI

Doctor Sloper very soon imparted his conviction to Mrs. Almond in the same terms in which he had announced it to himself. "She's going to stick, by Jove! she's going to stick."

"Do you mean that she is going to marry him?" Mrs. Almond inquired.

"I don't know that; but she is not going to break down. She is going to drag out the engagement, in the hope of making me relent."

"And shall you not relent?"

"Shall a geometrical proposition relent? I am not so superficial."

"Doesn't geometry treat of surfaces?" asked Mrs. Almond, who, as we know, was clever, smiling.

"Yes, but it treats of them profoundly. Catherine and her young man are my surfaces; I have taken their measure."

"You speak as if it surprised you."

"It is immense; there will be a great deal to observe."

"You are shockingly cold-blooded!" said Mrs. Almond.

"I need to be, with all this hot blood about me. Young Townsend, indeed, is cool; I must allow him that merit."

"I can't judge him," Mrs. Almond answered; "but I am not at all surprised at Catherine."

"I confess I am a little; she must have been so deucedly divided and bothered."

"Say it amuses you outright. I don't see why it should be such a joke that your daughter adores you."

"It is the point where the adoration stops that I find it interesting to fix."

"It stops where the other sentiment begins."

"Not at all; that would be simple enough. The two things are extremely mixed up, and the mixture is extremely odd. It will produce some third element, and that's what I'm waiting to see. I wait with suspense—with positive excitement; and that is a sort of emotion that I didn't suppose Catherine would ever provide for me. I am really very much obliged to her."

"She will cling," said Mrs. Almond; "she will certainly cling."

"Yes, as I say, she will stick."

"Cling is prettier. That's what those very simple natures always do, and nothing could be simpler than Catherine. She doesn't take many impressions; but when she takes one, she keeps it. She is like a copper kettle that receives a dent: you may polish up the kettle, but you can't efface the mark."

"We must try and polish up Catherine," said the Doctor. "I will take her to Europe!"

"She won't forget him in Europe."

"He will forget her, then."

Mrs. Almond looked grave. "Should you really like that?"

"Extremely," said the Doctor.

Mrs. Penniman, meanwhile, lost little time in putting her self again in communication with Morris Townsend. She requested him to favor her with another interview, but she did not on this occasion select an oyster saloon as the scene of their meeting. She proposed that he should join her at the door of a certain church after service on Sunday afternoon; and she was careful not to appoint the place of worship which she usually visited, and where, as she said, the congregation would have spied upon her. She picked out a less elegant resort, and on issuing from its portal at the hour she had fixed she saw the young man standing apart. She offered him no recognition until she had crossed the street, and he had followed her to some distance. Here, with a smile, "excuse my apparent want of cordiality," she said. "You know what to believe about that. Prudence before everything." And on his asking her in what direction they should walk, "Where we shall be least observed," she murmured.

Morris was not in high good-humor, and his response to this speech was not particularly gallant. "I don't flatter myself we shall be much observed anywhere." Then he turned recklessly toward the centre of the town. "I hope you have come to tell me that he has knocked under," he went on.

"I am afraid I am not altogether a harbinger of good; and yet, too, I am to a certain extent a messenger of peace. I have been thinking a great deal, Mr. Townsend," said Mrs. Penniman.

"You think too much."

"I suppose I do; but I can't help it, my mind is so terribly active. When I give myself, I give myself. I pay the penalty in my headaches, my famous headaches—a perfect circlet of pain! But I carry it as a queen carries her crown. Would you believe that I have one now? I wouldn't, however, have missed our rendezvous for anything. I have something very important to tell you."

"Well, let's have it," said Morris.

"I was perhaps a little headlong the other day in advising you to marry immediately. I have been thinking it over, and now I see it just a little differently."

"You seem to have a great many different ways of seeing the same object."

"Their number is infinite!" said Mrs. Penniman, in a tone which seemed to suggest that this convenient faculty was one of her brightest attributes.

"I recommend you to take one way, and stick to it," Morris replied.

"Ah, but it isn't easy to choose. My imagination is never quiet, never satisfied. It makes me a bad adviser, perhaps, but it makes me a capital friend."

"A capital friend who gives bad advice!" said Morris.

"Not intentionally—and who hurries off, at every risk, to make the most humble excuses."

"Well, what do you advise me now?"

"To be very patient; to watch and wait."

"And is that bad advice or good?"

"That is not for me to say," Mrs. Penniman rejoined, with some dignity. "I only claim it is sincere."

"And will you come to me next week and recommend something different and equally sincere?"

"I may come to you next week, and tell you that I am in the streets."

"In the streets?"

"I have had a terrible scene with my brother, and he threatens, if anything happens, to turn me out of the house. You know I am a poor woman."

Morris had a speculative idea that she had a little property; but he naturally did not press this.

"I should be very sorry to see you suffer martyrdom for me," he said. "But you make your brother out a regular Turk."

Mrs. Penniman hesitated a little.

"I certainly do not regard Austin as an orthodox Christian."

"And am I to wait till he is converted?"

"Wait at any rate till he is less violent. Bide your time, Mr. Townsend; remember the prize is great."

Morris walked along some time in silence, tapping the railings and gate-posts very sharply with his stick.

"You certainly are devilish inconsistent!" he broke out at last. "I have already got Catherine to consent to a private marriage."

Mrs. Penniman was indeed inconsistent, for at this news she gave a little jump of gratification.

"Oh, when and where?" she cried. And then she stopped short.

Morris was a little vague about this.

"That isn't fixed; but she consents. It's deuced awkward now to back out."

Mrs. Penniman, as I say, had stopped short; and she stood there with her eyes fixed brilliantly on her companion.

"Mr. Townsend," she proceeded, "shall I tell you something. Catherine loves you so much that you may do anything."

This declaration was slightly ambiguous, and Morris opened his eyes.

"I am happy to hear it. But what do you mean by 'anything'?"

"You may postpone—you may change about; she won't think the worse of you."

Morris stood there still, with his raised eyebrows; then he said, simply and rather dryly, "Ah!" After this he remarked to Mrs. Penniman that if she walked so slowly she would attract notice, and he succeeded, after a fashion, in hurrying her back to the domicile of which her tenure had become so insecure.

XXII

He had slightly misrepresented the matter in saying that Catherine had consented to take the great step. We left her just now declaring that she would burn her ships behind her; but Morris, after having elicited this declaration, had become conscious of good reasons for not taking it up. He avoided, gracefully enough, fixing a day, though he left her under the impression that he had his eye on one. Catherine may have had her difficulties; but those of her circumspect suitor are also worthy of consideration. The prize was certainly great; but it was only to be won by striking the happy mean between precipitancy and caution. It would be all very well to take one's jump and trust to Providence; Providence was more especially on the side of clever people, and clever people were known by an indisposition to risk their bones.

The ultimate reward of a union with a young woman who was both unattractive and impoverished ought to be connected with immediate disadvantages by some very palpable chain. Between the fear of losing Catherine and her possible fortune altogether, and the fear of taking her too soon and finding this possible fortune as void of actuality as a collection of emptied bottles, it was not comfortable for Morris Townsend to choose—a fact that should be remembered by readers disposed to judge harshly of a young man who may have struck them as making but an indifferently successful use of fine natural parts. He had not forgotten that in any event Catherine had her own ten thousand a year; he had devoted an abundance of meditation to this circumstance. But with his fine parts he rated himself high, and he had a perfectly definite appreciation of his value, which seemed to him inadequately represented by the sum I have mentioned. At the same time he reminded himself that this sum was considerable, that everything is relative, and that if a modest income is less desirable than a large one, the complete absence of revenue is nowhere accounted an advantage.

These reflections gave him plenty of occupation, and made it necessary that he should trim his sail. Doctor Sloper's opposition was the unknown quantity in the problem he had to work out. The natural way to work it out was by marrying Catherine; but in mathematics there are many short cuts, and Morris was not without a hope that he should yet discover one. When Catherine took him at his word, and consented to renounce the attempt to mollify her father, he drew back skilfully enough, as I have said, and kept the wedding-day still an open question. Her faith in his sincerity was so complete that she was incapable of suspecting that he was playing with her; her trouble just now was of another kind. The poor girl had an admirable sense of honor, and from the moment she had brought herself to the point of violating her father's wish, it seemed to her that she had no right to enjoy his protection. It was on her conscience that she ought to live under his roof only so long as she conformed to his wisdom. There was a great deal of glory in such a position, but poor Catherine felt that she had forfeited her claim to it. She had cast her lot with a young man against whom he had solemnly warned her, and broken the contract under which he provided her with a happy home. She could not give up the young man, so she must leave the home; and the sooner the object of her preference offered her another, the sooner her situation would lose its awkward twist. This was close reasoning; but it was commingled with an infinite amount of merely instinctive penitence. Catherine's days, at this time, were dismal, and the weight of some of her hours was almost more than she could bear. Her father never looked at her, never spoke to her. He knew perfectly what he was about, and this was part of a plan. She looked at him as much as she dared (for she was afraid of seeming to offer herself to his observation), and she pitied him for the sorrow she had brought upon him. She held up her head and busied her hands, and went about her daily occupations; and when the state of things in Washington Square seemed intolerable, she closed her eyes and indulged herself with an intellectual vision of the man for whose sake she had broken a sacred law.

Mrs. Penniman, of the three persons in Washington Square, had much the most of the manner that belongs to a great crisis. If Catherine was quiet, she was quietly quiet, as I may say, and her pathetic effects, which there was no one to notice, were entirely unstudied and unintended. If the Doctor was stiff and dry, and absolutely indifferent to the presence of his companions, it was so lightly, neatly, easily done, that you would have had to know him well to discover that, on the whole, he rather enjoyed having to be so disagreeable. But Mrs. Penniman was elaborately reserved and significantly silent; there was a richer rustle in the very deliberate movements to which she confined herself, and when she occasionally spoke, in connection with some very trivial event, she had the air of meaning something deeper than what she said. Between Catherine and her father nothing had passed since the evening she went to speak to him in his study. She had something to say to him—it seemed to her she ought to say it—but she kept it back for fear of irritating him. He also had something to say to her; but he was determined not to speak first. He was interested, as we know, in seeing how, if she were left to herself, she would "stick." At last she told him she had seen Morris Townsend again, and that their relations remained quite the same.

"I think we shall marry—before very long. And probably, meanwhile, I shall see him rather often; about once a week—not more."

The Doctor looked at her coldly from head to foot, as if

she had been a stranger. It was the first time his eyes had rested on her for a week, which was fortunate, if that was to be their expression. "Why not three times a day?" he asked. "What prevents your meeting as often as you choose?"

She turned away a moment; there were tears in her eyes. Then she said, "It is better once a week."

"I don't see how it is better. It is as bad as it can be. If you flatter yourself that I care for little modifications of that sort, you are very much mistaken. It is as wrong of you to see him once a week as it would be to see him all day long. Not that it matters to me, however."

Catherine tried to follow these words, but they seemed to lead toward a vague horror from which she recoiled. "I think we shall marry pretty soon," she repeated, at last.

Her father gave her his dreadful look again, as if she were some one else. "Why do you tell me that? It's no concern of mine."

"Oh, father," she broke out, "don't you care, even if you do feel so?"

"Not a button. Once you marry, it's quite the same to me when, or where, or why you do it; and if you think to compound for your folly by hoisting your fly in this way, you may spare yourself the trouble."

With this he turned away. But the next day he spoke to her of his own accord, and his manner was somewhat changed. "Shall you be married within the next four or five months?" he asked.

"I don't know, father," said Catherine. "It is not very easy for us to make up our minds."

"Put it off, then, for six months, and in the meantime I will take you to Europe. I should like you very much to go."

It gave her such delight, after his words of the day before, to hear that he should "like" her to do something, and that he still had in his heart any of the tenderness of preference, that she gave a little exclamation of joy. But then she became conscious that Morris was not included in this proposal, and that—as regards really going—she would greatly prefer to remain at home with him. But she blushed none the less more comfortably than she had done of late. "It would be delightful to go to Europe," she remarked, with a sense that the idea was not original, and that her tone was not all it might be.

"Very well, then, we will go. Pack up your clothes."

"I had better tell Mr. Townsend," said Catherine.

Her father fixed his cold eyes upon her. "If you mean that you had better ask his leave, all that remains to me is to hope he will give it."

The girl was sharply touched by the pathetic ring of the words; it was the most calculated, the most dramatic little speech the Doctor had ever uttered. She felt that it was a great thing for her, under the circumstances, to have this fine opportunity of showing him her respect; and yet there was something else that she felt as well, and that she presently expressed. "I sometimes think that if I do what you dislike so much, I ought not to stay with you."

"To stay with me?"

"If I live with you, I ought to obey you."

"If that's your theory, it's certainly mine," said the Doctor, with a dry laugh.

"But if I don't obey you, I ought not to live with you—to enjoy your kindness and protection."

This striking argument gave the Doctor a sudden sense of having underestimated his daughter; it seemed even more than worthy of a young woman who had revealed the quality of unaggressive obstinacy. But it displeased him—displeased him deeply, and he signified as much. "That idea is in very bad taste," he said. "Did you get it from Mr. Townsend?"

"Oh no; it's my own," said Catherine, eagerly.

"Keep it to yourself, then," her father answered, more than ever determined she should go to Europe.

XXIII

If Morris Townsend was not to be included in this journey, no more was Mrs. Penniman, who would have been thankful for an invitation, but who (to do her justice) bore her disappointment in a perfectly lady-like manner. "I should enjoy seeing the works of Raphael and the ruins—the ruins of the Pantheon," she said to Mrs. Almond; "but, on the other hand, I shall not be sorry to be alone and at peace for the next few months in Washington Square. I want rest; I have been through so much in the last four months." Mrs. Almond thought it rather cruel that her brother should not take poor Lavinia abroad; but she easily understood that, if the purpose of his expedition was to make Catherine forget her lover, it was not in his interest to give his daughter this young man's best friend as a companion. "If Lavinia had not been so foolish, she might visit the ruins of the Pantheon," she said to herself; and she continued to regret her sister's folly, even though the latter assured her that she had often heard the relics in question most satisfactorily described by Mr. Penniman. Mrs. Penniman was perfectly aware that her brother's motive in undertaking a foreign tour was to lay a trap for Catherine's constancy; and she imparted this conviction very frankly to her niece.

"He thinks it will make you forget Morris," she said (she always called the young man "Morris" now): "out of sight, out of mind, you know. He thinks that all the things you will see over there will drive him out of your thoughts."

Catherine looked greatly alarmed. "If he thinks that, I ought to tell him beforehand."

Mrs. Penniman shook her head. "Tell him afterward, my dear—after he has had all the trouble and expense. That's the way to serve him." And she added, in a softer key, that it must be delightful to think of those who love us among the ruins of the Pantheon.

Her father's displeasure had cost the girl, as we know, a great deal of deep-welling sorrow—sorrow of the purest and most generous kind, without a touch of resentment or rancor; but for the first time, after he had dismissed with such contemptuous brevity her apology for being a charge upon him, there was a spark of anger in her grief. She had felt his contempt; it had scorched her; that speech about her bad taste had made her ears burn for three days. During this period she was less considerate; she had an idea—a rather vague one, but it was agreeable to her sense of injury—that now she was absolved from penance, and might do what she chose. She chose to write to Morris Townsend to meet her in the Square and take her to walk about the town. If she were going to Europe out of respect to her father, she might at least give herself this satisfaction. She felt in every way at present more free and more resolute; there was a force that urged her. Now at last, completely and unreservedly, her passion possessed her.

Morris met her at last, and they took a long walk. She told him immediately what had happened; that her father wished to take her away—it would be for six months—to Europe; she would do absolutely what Morris should think best. She hoped inexpressibly that he would think it best she should stay at home. It was some time before he said what he thought; he asked, as they walked along, a great many questions. There was one that especially struck her; it seemed so incongruous.

"Should you like to see all those celebrated things over there?"

"Oh no, Morris!" said Catherine, quite deprecatingly.

"Gracious Heaven, what a dull woman!" Morris exclaimed to himself.

"He thinks I will forget you," said Catherine; "that all these things will drive you out of my mind."

"Well, my dear, perhaps they will."

"Please don't say that," Catherine answered, gently, as they walked along. "Poor father will be disappointed."

Morris gave a little laugh. "Yes, I verily believe that your poor father will be disappointed. But you will have seen Europe," he added, humorously. "What a take-in!"

"I don't care for seeing Europe," Catherine said.

"You ought to care, my dear; and it may mollify your father."

Catherine, conscious of her obstinacy, expected little of this, and could not rid herself of the idea that in going abroad and yet remaining firm, she should play her father a trick. "Don't you think it would be a kind of deception?" she asked.

"Doesn't he want to deceive you?" cried Morris. "It will serve him right. I really think you had better go."

"And not be married for so long?"

"Be married when you come back. You can buy your wedding-clothes in Paris." And then Morris, with great kindness of tone, explained his view of the matter. It would be a good thing that she should go; it would put them completely in the right. It would show they were reasonable, and willing to wait. Once they were so sure of each other, they could afford to wait—what had they to fear? If there was a particle of chance that her father would be favorably affected by her going, that ought to settle it; for, after all, Morris was very unwilling to be the cause of her being disinherited. It was not for himself, it was for her and for her children. He was willing to wait for her; it would be hard, but he could do it. And over there, among beautiful scenes and noble monuments, perhaps the old gentleman would be softened; such things were supposed to exert a humanizing influence. He might be touched by her gentleness, her patience, her willingness to make any sacrifice but *that* one; and if she should appeal to him some day, in some celebrated spot—in Italy, say, in the evening; in Venice, in a gondola, by moonlight—if she should be a little clever about it, and touch the right chord, perhaps he would fold her in his arms, and tell her that he forgave her. Catherine was immensely struck with this conception of the affair, which seemed eminently worthy of her lover's brilliant intellect, though she viewed it askance in so far as it depended upon her own powers of execution. The idea of being "clever" in a gondola by moonlight appeared to her to involve elements of which her grasp was not active. But it was settled between them that she should tell her father that she was ready to follow him obediently anywhere, making the mental reservation that she loved Morris Townsend more than ever.

She informed the Doctor she was ready to embark, and he made rapid arrangements for this event. Catherine had many farewells to make, but with only two of them are we actively concerned. Mrs. Penniman took a discriminating view of her niece's journey; it seemed to her very proper that Mr. Townsend's destined bride should wish to embellish her mind by a foreign tour.

"You leave him in good hands," she said, pressing her lips to Catherine's forehead. (She was very fond of kissing people's foreheads; it was an involuntary expression of sympathy with the intellectual part.) "I shall see him often; I shall feel like one of the vestals of old tending the sacred flame."

"You behave beautifully about not going with us," Catherine answered, not presuming to examine this analogy.

"It is my pride that keeps me up," said Mrs. Penniman, tapping the body of her dress, which always gave forth a sort of metallic ring.

Catherine's parting with her lover was short, and few words were exchanged.

"Shall I find you just the same when I come back?" she

asked; though the question was not the fruit of scepticism.

"The same—only more so," said Morris, smiling.

It does not enter into our scheme to narrate in detail Doctor Sloper's proceedings in the Eastern hemisphere. He made the grand tour of Europe, travelled in considerable splendor, and (as was to have been expected in a man of his high cultivation) found so much in art and antiquity to interest him, that he remained abroad, not for six months, but for twelve. Mrs. Penniman, in Washington Square, accommodated herself to his absence. She enjoyed her uncontested dominion in the empty house, and flattered herself that she made it more attractive to their friends than when her brother was at home. To Morris Townsend, at least, it would have appeared that she made it singularly attractive. He was altogether her most frequent visitor, and Mrs. Penniman was very fond of asking him to tea. He had his chair—a very easy one—at the fireside in the back parlor (when the great mahogany sliding doors, with silver knobs and hinges, which divided this apartment from its more formal neighbor, were closed), and he used to smoke cigars in the Doctor's study, where he often spent an hour in turning over the curious collections of its absent proprietor. He thought Mrs. Penniman a goose, as we know; but he was no goose himself, and, as a young man of luxurious tastes and scanty resources, he found the house a perfect castle of indolence. It became for him a club with a single member. Mrs. Penniman saw much less of her sister than while the Doctor was at home; for Mrs. Almond had felt moved to tell her that she disapproved of her relations with Mr. Townsend. She had no business to be so friendly to a young man of whom their brother thought so meanly, and Mrs. Almond was surprised at her levity in foisting a most deplorable engagement upon Catherine.

"Deplorable!" cried Lavinia. "He will make her a lovely husband."

"I don't believe in lovely husbands," said Mrs. Almond;

"I only believe in good ones. If he marries her, and she comes into Austin's money, they may get on. He will be an idle, amiable, selfish, and, doubtless, tolerably good-natured fellow. But if she doesn't get the money, and he finds himself tied to her, Heaven have mercy on her! He will have none. He will hate her for his disappointment, and take his revenge; he will be pitiless and cruel. Woe betide poor Catherine! I recommend you to talk a little with his sister; it's a pity Catherine can't marry *her!*"

Mrs. Penniman had no appetite whatever for conversation with Mrs. Montgomery, whose acquaintance she made no trouble to cultivate; and the effect of this alarming forecast of her niece's destiny was to make her think it indeed a thousand pities that Mr. Townsend's generous nature should be embittered. Bright enjoyment was his natural element, and how could he be comfortable if there should prove to be nothing to enjoy? It became a fixed idea with Mrs. Penniman that he should yet enjoy her brother's fortune, on which she had acuteness enough to perceive that her own claim was small.

"If he doesn't leave it to Catherine, it certainly won't be to leave it to me," she said.

XXIV

THE DOCTOR, during the first six months he was abroad, never spoke to his daughter of their little difference, partly on system, and partly because he had a great many other things to think about. It was idle to attempt to ascertain the state of her affections without direct inquiry, because if she had not had an expressive manner among the familiar influences of home, she failed to gather animation from the mountains of Switzerland or the monuments of Italy. She was always her father's docile and reasonable associate—going through their sight-seeing in deferential silence, never complaining of fatigue, always ready to start at the hour he had appointed overnight, making no foolish criticisms, and indulging in no refinements of appreciation. "She is about as intelligent as the bundle of shawls," the Doctor said, her main superiority being that, while the bundle of shawls sometimes got lost, or tumbled out of the carriage, Catherine was always at her post, and had a firm and ample seat. But her father had expected this, and he was not constrained to set down her intellectual limitations as a tourist to sentimental depression; she had completely divested herself of the characteristics of a victim, and during the whole time that they were abroad she never uttered an audible sigh. He supposed she was in correspondence with Morris Townsend, but he held his peace about it, for he never saw the young man's letters, and Catherine's own missives were always given to the courier to post. She heard from her lover with considerable regularity, but his letters came enclosed in Mrs. Penniman's; so that, whenever the Doctor handed her a packet addressed in his sister's hand, he was an involuntary instrument of the passion he condemned. Catherine made this reflection, and six months earlier she would have felt bound to give him warning; but now she deemed herself absolved. There was a sore spot in her heart that his own words had made when once she spoke to him as she thought honor prompted; she would try and please him as far as she could, but she would never speak that way again. She read her lover's letters in secret.

One day, at the end of the summer, the two travellers found themselves in a lonely valley of the Alps. They were crossing one of the passes, and on the long ascent they had got out of the carriage and had wandered much in advance. After awhile the Doctor descried a foot-path which, leading through a transverse valley, would bring them out, as he justly supposed, at a much higher point of the ascent. They followed this devious way, and finally lost the path; the valley proved very wild and rough, and their walk became rather a scramble. They were good walkers, however, and they took their adventure easily; from time to time they stopped, that Catherine might rest; and then she sat upon a stone and looked about her at the hard-featured rocks and the glowing sky. It was late in the afternoon, in the last of August; night was coming on, and as they had reached a great elevation, the air was cold and sharp. In the west there was a great suffusion of cold red light, which made the sides of the little valley look only the more rugged and dusky. During one of their pauses her father left her and wandered away to some high place, at a distance, to get a view. He was out of sight; she sat there alone in the stillness, which was just touched by the vague murmur somewhere of a mountain brook. She thought of Morris Townsend, and the place was so desolate and lonely that he seemed very far away. Her father remained absent a long time; she began to wonder what had become of him. But at last he reappeared, coming toward her in the clear twilight, and she got up to go on. He made no motion to proceed, however, but came close to her, as if he had something to say. He stopped in front of her, and stood looking at her with eyes that had kept the light of the flushing snow-summits on which they had just been fixed. Then, abruptly, in a low tone, he asked her an unexpected question,

"Have you given him up?"

The question was unexpected, but Catherine was only superficially unprepared.

"No, father," she answered.

He looked at her again for some moments without speaking.

"Does he write to you?" he asked.

"Yes, about twice a month."

The Doctor looked up and down the valley, swinging his stick; then he said to her, in the same low tone,

"I am very angry."

She wondered what he meant—whether he wished to frighten her. If he did, the place was well chosen: this hard, melancholy dell, abandoned by the summer light, made her feel her loneliness. She looked around her, and her heart grew cold; for a moment her fear was great. But she could think of nothing to say, save to murmur, gently, "I am sorry."

"You try my patience," her father went on, "and you ought to know what I am. I am not a very good man. Though I am very smooth externally, at bottom I am very passionate; and I assure you I can be very hard."

She could not think why he told her these things. Had he brought her there on purpose, and was it part of a plan? What was the plan? Catherine asked herself. Was it to startle her suddenly into a retraction—to take an advantage of her by dread? Dread of what? The place was ugly and lonely, but the place could do her no harm. There was a kind of still intensity about her father which made him dangerous, but Catherine hardly went so far as to say to herself that it might be part of his plan to fasten his hand—the neat, fine, supple hand of a distinguished physician—in her throat. Nevertheless, she receded a step. "I am sure you can be anything you please," she said; and it was her simple belief.

"I am very angry," he replied, more sharply.

"Why has it taken you so suddenly?"

"It has not taken me suddenly. I have been raging inwardly for the last six months. But just now this seemed a good place to flare out. It's so quiet, and we are alone."

"Yes, it's very quiet," said Catherine, vaguely looking about her. "Won't you come back to the carriage?"

"In a moment. Do you mean that in all this time you have not yielded an inch?"

"I would if I could, father; but I can't."

The Doctor looked round him too. "Should you like to be left in such a place as this, to starve?"

"What do you mean?" cried the girl.

"That will be your fate—that's how he will leave you."

He would not touch her, but he had touched Morris. The warmth came back to her heart. "That is not true, father," she broke out, "and you ought not to say it. It is not right, and it's not true."

He shook his head slowly. "No, it's not right, because you won't believe it. But it *is* true. Come back to the carriage."

He turned away, and she followed him; he went faster, and was presently much in advance. But from time to time he stopped, without turning round, to let her keep up with him, and she made her way forward with difficulty, her heart beating with the excitement of having for the first time spoken to him in violence. By this time it had grown almost dark, and she ended by losing sight of him. But she kept her course, and after a little, the valley making a sudden turn, she gained the road, where the carriage stood waiting. In it sat her father, rigid and silent; in silence, too, she took her place beside him.

It seemed to her, later, in looking back upon all this,

that for days afterward not a word had been exchanged between them. The scene had been a strange one, but it had not permanently affected her feeling toward her father, for it was natural, after all, that he should occasionally make a scene of some kind, and he had let her alone for six months. The strangest part of it was that he had said he was not a good man; Catherine wondered a good deal what he had meant by that. The statement failed to appeal to her credence, and it was not grateful to any resentment that she entertained. Even in the utmost bitterness that she might feel, it would give her no satisfaction to think him less complete. Such a saying as that was a part of his great subtlety—men so clever as he might say anything and mean anything; and as to his being hard, that surely, in a man, was a virtue.

He let her alone for six months more—six months during which she accommodated herself without a protest to the extension of their tour. But he spoke again at the end of this time: it was at the very last, the night before they embarked for New York, in the hotel at Liverpool. They had been dining together in a great, dim, musty sitting-room; and then the cloth had been removed, and the Doctor walked slowly up and down. Catherine at last took her candle to go to bed, but her father motioned her to stay.

"What do you mean to do when you get home?" he asked, while she stood there with her candle in her hand.

"Do you mean about Mr. Townsend?"

"About Mr. Townsend."

"We shall probably marry."

The Doctor took several turns again while she waited. "Do you hear from him as much as ever?"

"Yes, twice a month," said Catherine, promptly.

"And does he always talk about marriage?"

"Oh yes; that is, he talks about other things too, but he always says something about that."

"I am glad to hear he varies his subjects; his letters might otherwise be monotonous."

"He writes beautifully," said Catherine, who was very glad of a chance to say it.

"They always write beautifully. However, in a given case that doesn't diminish the merit. So, as soon as you arrive, you are going off with him?"

This seemed a rather gross way of putting it, and something that there was of dignity in Catherine resented it. "I cannot tell you till we arrive," she said.

"That's reasonable enough," her father answered. "That's all I ask of you—that you *do* tell me, that you give me definite notice. When a poor man is to lose his only child, he likes to have an inkling of it beforehand."

"Oh, father! you will not lose me," Catherine said, spilling her candle wax.

"Three days before will do," he went on, "if you are in a position to be positive then. He ought to be very thankful to me, do you know. I have done a mighty good thing for him in taking you abroad; your value is twice as great, with all the knowledge and taste that you have acquired. A year ago, you were perhaps a little limited—a little rustic; but now you have seen everything, and appreciated everything, and you will be a most entertaining companion. We have fattened the sheep for him before he kills it." Catherine turned away, and stood staring at the blank door. "Go to bed," said her father; "and as we don't go abroad till noon, you may sleep late. We shall probably have a most uncomfortable voyage."

XXV

THE VOYAGE was indeed uncomfortable, and Catherine, on arriving in New York, had not the compensation of "going off," in her father's phrase, with Morris Townsend. She saw him, however, the day after she landed; and in the meantime he formed a natural subject of conversation between our heroine and her Aunt Lavinia, with whom, the night she disembarked, the girl was closeted for a long time before either lady retired to rest.

"I have seen a great deal of him," said Mrs. Penniman. "He is not very easy to know. I suppose you think you know him; but you don't, my dear. You will some day; but it will only be after you have lived with him. I may almost say *I* have lived with him," Mrs. Penniman proceeded, while Catherine stared. "I think I know him now; I have had such remarkable opportunities. You will have the same—or, rather, you will have better"; and Aunt Lavinia smiled. "Then you will see what I mean. It's a wonderful character, full of passion and energy, and just as true."

Catherine listened with a mixture of interest and apprehension. Aunt Lavinia was intensely sympathetic, and Catherine, for the past year, while she wandered through foreign galleries and churches, and rolled over the smoothness of posting roads, nursing the thoughts that never passed her lips, had often longed for the company of some intelligent person of her own sex. To tell her story to some kind woman—at moments it seemed to her that this would give her comfort, and she had more than once been on the point of taking the landlady, or the nice young person from the dress maker's, into her confidence. If a woman had been near her, she would on certain occasions have treated such a companion to a fit of weeping; and she had an apprehension that, on her return, this would form her response to Aunt Lavinia's first embrace. In fact, however, the two ladies had met, in Washington Square, without tears; and when they found themselves alone together a certain dryness fell upon the girl's emotion. It came over her with a greater force that Mrs. Penniman had enjoyed a whole year of her lover's society, and it was not a pleasure to her to hear her aunt explain and interpret the young man, speaking of him as if her own knowledge of him were supreme. It was not that Catherine was jealous; but her sense of Mrs. Penniman's innocent falsity, which had lain dormant, began to haunt her again, and she was glad that she was safely at home. With this, however, it was a blessing to be able to talk of Morris, to sound his name, to be with a person who was not unjust to him.

"You have been very kind to him," said Catherine. "He has written me that, often. I shall never forget that, Aunt Lavinia."

"I have done what I could; it has been very little. To let him come and talk to me, and give him his cup of tea—that was all. Your Aunt Almond thought it was too much, and used to scold me terribly; but she promised me, at least, not to betray me."

"To betray you?"

"Not to tell your father. He used to sit in your father's study," said Mrs. Penniman, with a little laugh.

Catherine was silent a moment. This idea was disagreeable to her, and she was reminded again, with pain, of her aunt's secretive habits. Morris, the reader may be informed, had had the tact not to tell her that he sat in her father's study. He had known her but for a few months, and her aunt had known her for fifteen years; and yet he would not have made the mistake of thinking that Catherine would see the joke of the thing. "I am sorry you made him go into father's room," she said, after awhile.

"I didn't send him; he went himself. He liked to look at the books, and at all those things in the glass cases. He knows all about them; he knows all about everything."

Catherine was silent again; then, "I wish he had found some employment," she said.

"He has found some employment. It's beautiful news, and he told me to tell you as soon as you arrive. He has gone into partnership with a commission merchant. It was all settled, quite suddenly, a week ago."

This seemed to Catherine indeed beautiful news; it had a fine prosperous air. "Oh, I'm so glad!" she said; and now, for a moment, she was disposed to throw herself on Aunt Lavinia's neck.

"It's much better than being under some one; and he has never been used to that," Mrs. Penniman went on. "He is just as good as his partner—they are perfectly equal. You see how right he was to wait. I should like to know what your father can say now! They have got an office in Duane Street, and little printed cards; he brought me one to show me. I have got it in my room, and you shall see it to-morrow. That's what he said to me the last time he was here—'You see how right I was to wait.' He has got other people under him instead of being a subordinate. He could never be a subordinate; I have often told him I could never think of him in that way."

Catherine assented to this proposition, and was very happy to know that Morris was his own master; but she was deprived of the satisfaction of thinking that she might communicate this news in triumph to her father. Her father would care equally little whether Morris were established in business or transported for life. Her trunks had been brought into her room, and further reference to her lover was for a short time suspended, while she opened them and displayed to her aunt some of the spoils of foreign travel. These were rich and abundant; and Catherine had brought home a present to every one—to every one save Morris, to whom she had brought simply her undiverted heart. To Mrs. Penniman she had been lavishly generous, and Aunt Lavinia spent half an hour in unfolding and folding again, with little ejaculations of gratitude and taste. She marched about for some time in a splendid cashmere shawl, which Catherine had begged her to accept, settling it on her shoulders, and twisting down her head to see how low the point descended behind.

"I shall regard it only as a loan," she said. "I will leave it to you again when I die; or, rather," she added, kissing her niece again, "I will leave it to your first-born little girl." And draped in her shawl, she stood there smiling.

"You had better wait till she comes," said Catherine.

"I don't like the way you say that," Mrs. Penniman rejoined, in a moment. "Catherine, are you changed?"

"No; I am the same."

"You have not swerved a line?"

"I am exactly the same," Catherine repeated, wishing her aunt were a little less sympathetic.

"Well, I am glad"; and Mrs. Penniman surveyed her cashmere in the glass. Then, "How is your father?" she asked, in a moment, with her eyes on her niece. "Your letters were so meagre—I could never tell."

"Father is very well."

"Ah, you know what I mean," said Mrs. Penniman, with a dignity to which the cashmere gave a richer effect. "Is he still implacable?"

"Oh yes!"

"Quite unchanged?"

"He is, if possible, more firm."

Mrs. Penniman took off her great shawl, and slowly folded it up. "That is very bad. You had no success with your little project."

"What little project?"

"Morris told me all about it. The idea of turning the tables on him, in Europe; of watching him, when he was agreeably impressed by some celebrated sight—he pretends to be so artistic, you know—and then just pleading with him and bringing him round."

"I never tried it. It was Morris's idea; but if he had been with us in Europe, he would have seen that father was never impressed in that way. He *is* artistic—tremendously artistic; but the more celebrated places we visited, and the more he admired them, the less use it would have been to plead with him. They seemed only to make him more determined—more terrible," said poor Catherine. "I shall never bring him round, and I expect nothing now."

"Well, I must say," Mrs. Penniman answered, "I never supposed you were going to give it up."

"I have given it up. I don't care now."

"You have grown very brave," said Mrs. Penniman, with a short laugh. "I didn't advise you to sacrifice your property."

"Yes, I am braver than I was. You asked me if I had changed; I have changed in that way. Oh," the girl went on, "I have changed very much. And it isn't my property. If *he* doesn't care for it, why should I?"

Mrs. Penniman hesitated. "Perhaps he does care for it."

"He cares for it for my sake, because he doesn't want to injure me. But he will know—he knows already—how little he need be afraid about that. Besides," said Catherine, "I have got plenty of money of my own. We shall be very well off; and now hasn't he got his business? I am delighted about that business." She went on talking, showing a good deal of excitement as she proceeded. Her aunt had never seen her with just this manner, and Mrs. Penniman, observing her, set it down to foreign travel, which had made her more positive, more mature. She thought also that Catherine had improved in appearance; she looked rather handsome. Mrs. Penniman wondered whether Morris Townsend would be struck with that. While she was engaged in this speculation, Catherine broke out, with a certain sharpness, "Why are you so contradictory, Aunt Penniman? You seem to think one thing at one time, and another at another. A year ago, before I went away, you wished me not to mind about displeasing father, and now you seem to recommend me to take another line. You change about so."

This attack was unexpected, for Mrs. Penniman was not used, in any discussion, to seeing the war carried into her own country—possibly because the enemy generally had doubts of finding subsistence there. To her own consciousness, the flowery fields of her reason had rarely been ravaged by a hostile force. It was perhaps on this account that in defending them she was majestic rather than agile.

"I don't know what you accuse me of, save of being too deeply interested in your happiness. It is the first time I have been told I am capricious. That fault is not what I am usually reproached with."

"You were angry last year that I wouldn't marry immediately, and now you talk about my winning my father over. You told me it would serve him right if he should take me to Europe for nothing. Well, he has taken me for nothing, and you ought to be satisfied. Nothing is changed—nothing but my feeling about father. I don't mind nearly so much now. I have been as good as I could, but he doesn't care. Now I don't care either. I don't know whether I have grown bad; perhaps I have. But I don't care for that. I have come home to be married—that's all I know. That ought to please you, unless you have taken up some new idea; you are so strange. You may do as you please, but you must never speak to me again about pleading with father. I shall never plead with him for anything; that is all over. He has put me off. I am come home to be married."

This was a more authoritative speech than she had ever heard on her niece's lips, and Mrs. Penniman was proportionately startled. She was, indeed, a little awe-struck, and the force of the girl's emotion and resolution left her nothing to reply. She was easily frightened, and she always carried off her discomfiture by a concession—a concession which was often accompanied, as in the present case, by a little nervous laugh.

XXVI

If she had disturbed her niece's temper—she began from this moment forward to talk a good deal about Catherine's temper, an article which up to that time had never been mentioned in connection with our heroine—Catherine had opportunity on the morrow to recover her serenity. Mrs. Penniman had given her a message from Morris Townsend to the effect that he would come and welcome her home on the day after her arrival. He came in the afternoon; but, as may be imagined, he was not on this occasion made free of Doctor Sloper's study. He had been coming and going, for the past year, so comfortably and irresponsibly, that he had a certain sense of being wronged by finding himself reminded that he must now limit his horizon to the front parlor, which was Catherine's particular province.

"I am very glad you have come back," he said; "it makes me very happy to see you again." And he looked at her, smiling, from head to foot, though it did not appear afterward that he agreed with Mrs. Penniman (who, womanlike, went more into details) in thinking her embellished.

To Catherine he appeared resplendent; it was some time before she could believe again that this beautiful young man was her own exclusive property. They had a great deal of characteristic lovers' talk—a soft exchange of inquiries and assurances. In these matters Morris had an excellent grace, which flung a picturesque interest even over the account of his début in the commission business—a subject as to which his companion earnestly questioned him. From time to time he got up from the sofa where they sat together, and walked about the room; after which he came back, smiling and passing his hand through his hair.

He was unquiet, as was natural in a young man who has just been reunited to a long-absent mistress, and Catherine made the reflection that she had never seen him so excited. It gave her pleasure, somehow, to note this fact. He asked her questions about her travels, to some of which she was unable to reply, for she had forgotten the names of places and the order of her father's journey. But for the moment she was so happy, so lifted up by the belief that her troubles at last were over, that she forgot to be ashamed of her meagre answers. It seemed to her now that she could marry him without the remnant of a scruple, or a single tremor save those that belonged to joy. Without waiting for him to ask, she told him that her father had come back in exactly the same state of mind—that he had not yielded an inch.

"We must not expect it now," she said, "and we must do without it."

Morris sat looking and smiling. "My poor, dear girl!" he exclaimed.

"You mustn't pity me," said Catherine. "I don't mind it now: I am used to it."

Morris continued to smile, and then he got up and walked about again. "You had better let me try him."

"Try to bring him over? You would only make him worse," Catherine answered, resolutely.

"You say that because I managed it so badly before. But I should manage it differently now. I am much wiser; I have had a year to think of it. I have more tact."

"Is that what you have been thinking of for a year?"

"Much of the time. You see, the idea sticks in my crop. I don't like to be beaten."

"How are you beaten if we marry?"

"Of course I am not beaten on the main issue; but I am, don't you see? on all the rest of it—on the question of my reputation, of my relations with your father, of my relations with my own children, if we should have any."

"We shall have enough for our children; we shall have

enough for everything. Don't you expect to succeed in business?"

"Brilliantly, and we shall certainly be very comfortable. But it isn't of the mere material comfort I speak; it is of the moral comfort," said Morris—"of the intellectual satisfaction."

"I have great moral comfort now," Catherine declared, very simply.

"Of course you have. But with me it is different. I have staked my pride on proving to your father that he is wrong, and now that I am at the head of a flourishing business, I can deal with him as an equal. I have a capital plan—do let me go at him!"

He stood before her with his bright face, his jaunty air, his hands in his pockets; and she got up, with her eyes resting on his own. "Please don't, Morris; please don't," she said; and there was a certain mild, sad firmness in her tone which he heard for the first time. "We must ask no favors of him—we must ask nothing more. He won't relent, and nothing good will come of it. I know it now—I have a very good reason."

"And pray what is your reason?"

She hesitated to bring it out, but at last it came. "He is not very fond of me."

"Oh, bother!" cried Morris, angrily.

"I wouldn't say such a thing without being sure. I saw it, I felt it, in England, just before he came away. He talked to me one night—the last night—and then it came over me. You can tell when a person feels that way. I wouldn't accuse him if he hadn't made me feel that way. I don't accuse him; I just tell you that that's how it is. He can't help it; we can't govern our affections. Do I govern mine? Mightn't he say that to me? It's because he is so fond of my mother, whom we lost so long ago. She was beautiful, and very, very brilliant; he is always thinking of her. I am not at all like her; Aunt Penniman has told me that. Of course it isn't my fault; but neither is it his fault. All I mean is, it's true; and it's a stronger reason for his never being reconciled than simply his dislike for you."

" 'Simply?' " cried Morris, with a laugh. "I am much obliged for that."

"I don't mind about his disliking you now; I mind everything less. I feel differently; I feel separated from my father."

"Upon my word," said Morris, "you are a queer family."

"Don't say that—don't say anything unkind," the girl entreated. "You must be very kind to me now, because, Morris, because"—and she hesitated a moment—"because I have done a great deal for you."

"Oh, I know that, my dear."

She had spoken up to this moment without vehemence or outward sign of emotion, gently, reasoningly, only trying to explain. But her emotion had been ineffectually smothered, and it betrayed itself at last in the trembling of her voice. "It is a great thing to be separated like that from your father, when you have worshipped him before. It has made me very unhappy; or it would have made me so if I didn't love you. You can tell when a person speaks to you as if—as if—"

"As if what?"

"As if they despised you!" said Catherine, passionately. "He spoke that way the night before we sailed. It wasn't much, but it was enough, and I thought of it on the voyage all the time. Then I made up my mind. I will never ask him for anything again, or expect anything from him. It would not be natural now. We must be very happy together, and we must not seem to depend upon his forgiveness. And, Morris, Morris, you must never despise me!"

This was an easy promise to make, and Morris made it with fine effect. But for the moment he undertook nothing more onerous.

XXVII

THE DOCTOR, of course, on his return, had a good deal of talk with his sisters. He was at no great pains to narrate his travels or to communicate his impressions of distant lands to Mrs. Penniman, upon whom he contented himself with bestowing a memento of his enviable experience in the shape of a velvet gown. But he conversed with her at some length about matters nearer home, and lost no time in assuring her that he was still an inflexible father.

"I have no doubt you have seen a great deal of Mr. Townsend, and done your best to console him for Catherine's absence," he said. "I don't ask you, and you needn't deny it. I wouldn't put the question to you for the world, and expose you to the inconvenience of having to—a—excogitate an answer. No one has betrayed you, and there has been no spy upon your proceedings. Elizabeth has told no tales, and has never mentioned you except to praise your good looks and good spirits. The thing is simply an inference of my own—an induction, as the philosophers say. It seems to me likely that you would have offered an asylum to an interesting sufferer. Mr. Townsend has been a good deal in the house; there is something in the house that tells me so. We doctors, you know, end by acquiring fine perceptions, and it is impressed upon my sensorium that he has sat in these chairs, in a very easy attitude, and warmed himself at that fire. I don't grudge him the comfort of it; it is the only one he will ever enjoy at my expense. It seems likely, indeed, that I shall be able to economize at his own. I don't know what you may have said to him, or what you may say hereafter; but I should like you to know that if you have encouraged him to believe that he will gain anything by hanging on, or that I have budged a hair's-breadth from the position I took up a year ago, you have played him a trick for which he may exact reparation. I'm not sure that he may not bring a suit against you. Of course you have done it conscientiously; you have made yourself believe that I can be tired out. This is the most baseless hallucination that ever visited the brain of a genial optimist. I am not in the least tired; I am as fresh as when I started; I am good for fifty years yet. Catherine appears not to have budged an inch either; she is equally fresh; so we are about where we were before. This, however, you know as well as I. What I wish is simply to give you notice of my own state of mind. Take it to heart, dear Lavinia. Beware of the just resentment of a deluded fortune-hunter!"

"I can't say I expected it," said Mrs. Penniman. "And I had a sort of foolish hope that you would come home without that odious ironical tone with which you treat the most sacred subjects."

"Don't undervalue irony; it is often of great use. It is not, however, always necessary, and I will show you how gracefully I can lay it aside I should like to know whether you think Morris Townsend will hang on?"

"I will answer you with your own weapons," said Mrs. Penniman. "You had better wait and see."

"Do you call such a speech as that one of my own weapons? I never said anything so rough."

"He will hang on long enough to make you very uncomfortable, then."

"My dear Lavinia," exclaimed the Doctor, "do you call that irony? I call it pugilism."

Mrs. Penniman, however, in spite of her pugilism, was a good deal frightened, and she took counsel of her fears. Her brother meanwhile took counsel, with many reservations, of Mrs. Almond, to whom he was no less generous than to Lavinia, and a good deal more communicative.

"I suppose she has had him there all the while," he said.

"I must look into the state of my wine. You needn't mind telling me now; I have already said all I mean to say to her on the subject."

"I believe he was in the house a good deal," Mrs. Almond answered. "But you must admit that your leaving Lavinia quite alone was a great change for her, and that it was natural she should want some society."

"I do admit that, and that is why I shall make no row about the wine; I shall set it down as compensation to Lavinia. She is capable of telling me that she drank it all herself. Think of the inconceivable bad taste, in the circumstances, of that fellow making free with the house—or coming there at all! If that doesn't describe him, he is indescribable."

"His plan is to get what he can. Lavinia will have supported him for a year," said Mrs. Almond. "It's so much gained."

"She will have to support him for the rest of his life, then," cried the Doctor; "but without wine, as they say at the *tables d'hôte.*"

"Catherine tells me he has set up a business, and is making a great deal of money."

The Doctor stared. "She has not told me that—and Lavinia didn't deign. Ah!" he cried, "Catherine has given me up. Not that it matters, for all that the business amounts to."

"She has not given up Mr. Townsend," said Mrs. Almond; "I saw that in the first half-minute. She has come home exactly the same."

"Exactly the same; not a grain more intelligent. She didn't notice a stick or a stone all the while we were away—not a picture nor a view, not a statue nor a cathedral."

"How could she notice? She had other things to think of; they are never for an instant out of her mind. She touches me very much."

"She would touch me if she didn't irritate me. That's the effect she has upon me now. I have tried everything upon her; I really have been quite merciless. But it is of no use whatever; she is absolutely *glued*. I have passed, in consequence, into the exasperated stage. At first I had a good deal of a certain genial curiosity about it; I wanted to see if she really would stick. But, good Lord, one's curiosity is satisfied! I see she is capable of it, and now she can let go."

"She will never let go," said Mrs. Almond.

"Take care, or you will exasperate me too. If she doesn't let go, she will be shaken off—sent tumbling into the dust. That's a nice position for my daughter. She can't see that if you are going to be pushed, you had better jump. And then she will complain of her bruises."

"She will never complain," said Mrs. Almond.

"That I shall object to even more. But the deuce will be that I can't prevent anything."

"If she is to have a fall," said Mrs. Almond, with a gentle laugh, "we must spread as many carpets as we can." And she carried out this idea by showing a great deal of motherly kindness to the girl.

Mrs. Penniman immediately wrote to Morris Townsend. The intimacy between these two was by this time consummate, but I must content myself with noting but a few of its features. Mrs. Penniman's own share in it was a singular sentiment, which might have been misinterpreted, but which in itself was not discreditable to the poor lady. It was a romantic interest in this attractive and unfortunate young man, and yet it was not such an interest as Catherine might have been jealous of. Mrs. Penniman had not a particle of jealousy of her niece. For herself, she felt as if she were Morris's mother or sister—a mother or sister of an emotional temperament—and she had an absorbing desire to make him comfortable and happy. She had striven to do so during the year that her brother left her an open field, and her efforts had been attended with the success that has been pointed out. She had never had a child of her own, and Catherine, whom she had done her best to invest with the importance that would naturally belong to a youthful

Penniman, had only partly rewarded her zeal. Catherine, as an object of affection and solicitude, had never had that picturesque charm which (as it seemed to her) would have been a natural attribute of her own progeny. Even the maternal passion in Mrs. Penniman would have been romantic and factitious, and Catherine was not constituted to inspire a romantic passion. Mrs. Penniman was as fond of her as ever, but she had grown to feel that with Catherine she lacked opportunity. Sentimentally speaking, therefore, she had (though she had not disinherited her niece) adopted Morris Townsend, who gave her opportunity in abundance. She would have been very happy to have a handsome and tyrannical son, and would have taken an extreme interest in his love affairs. This was the light in which she had come to regard Morris, who had conciliated her at first, and made his impression by his delicate and calculated deference—a sort of exhibition to which Mrs. Penniman was particularly sensitive. He had largely abated his deference afterward, for he economized his resources, but the impression was made, and the young man's very brutality came to have a sort of filial value. If Mrs. Penniman had had a son, she would probably have been afraid of him, and at this stage of our narrative she was certainly afraid of Morris Townsend. This was one of the results of his domestication in Washington Square. He took his ease with her—as, for that matter, he would certainly have done with his own mother.

XXVIII

THE LETTER was a word of warning; it informed him that the Doctor had come home more impracticable than ever. She might have reflected that Catherine would supply him with all the information he needed on this point; but we know that Mrs. Penniman's reflections were rarely just; and, moreover, she felt that it was not for her to depend on what Catherine might do. She was to do her duty, quite irrespective of Catherine. I have said that her young friend took his ease with her, and it is an illustration of the fact that he made no answer to her letter. He took note of it amply; but he lighted his cigar with it, and he waited, in tranquil confidence that he should receive another. "His state of mind really freezes my blood," Mrs. Penniman had written, alluding to her brother; and it would have seemed that upon this statement she could hardly improve. Nevertheless, she wrote again, expressing herself with the aid of a different figure. "His hatred of you burns with a lurid flame—the flame that never dies," she wrote. "But it doesn't light up the darkness of your future. If my affection could do so, all the years of your life would be an eternal sunshine. I can extract nothing from C.; she is so terribly secretive, like her father. She seems to expect to be married very soon, and has evidently made preparations in Europe—quantities of clothing, ten pairs of shoes, etc. My dear friend, you cannot set up in married life simply with a few pairs of shoes, can you? Tell me what you think of this. I am intensely anxious to see you, I have so much to say. I miss you dreadfully; the house seems so empty without you. What is the news down town? Is the business extending?—that dear little business: I think it's so brave of you! Couldn't I come to your office?—just for three minutes? I might pass for a customer—is that what you call them? I might come in to buy something—some shares or some railroad things. *Tell me what you think of this plan.* I would carry a little reticule, like a woman of the people."

In spite of the suggestion about the reticule, Morris appeared to think poorly of the plan, for he gave Mrs. Penniman no encouragement whatever to visit his office, which he had already represented to her as a place peculiarly and unnaturally difficult to find. But as she persisted in desiring an interview—up to the last, after months of intimate colloquy, she called these meetings "interviews"—he agreed that they should take a walk together, and was even kind enough to leave his office for this purpose during the hours at which business might have been supposed to be liveliest. It was no surprise to him, when they met at a street corner, in a region of empty lots and undeveloped pavements (Mrs. Penniman being attired as much as possible like a "woman of the people"), to find that, in spite of her urgency, what she chiefly had to convey to him was the assurance of her sympathy. Of such assurances, however, he had already a voluminous collection, and it would not have been worth his while to forsake a fruitful avocation merely to hear Mrs. Penniman say, for the thousandth time, that she had made his cause her own. Morris had something of his own to say. It was not an easy thing to bring out, and while he turned it over, the difficulty made him acrimonious.

"Oh yes, I know perfectly that he combines the properties of a lump of ice and a red-hot coal," he observed. "Catherine has made it thoroughly clear, and you have told me so till I am sick of it. You needn't tell me again; I am perfectly satisfied. He will never give us a penny; I regard that as mathematically proved."

Mrs. Penniman at this point had an inspiration.

"Couldn't you bring a lawsuit against him?" She wondered that this simple expedient had never occurred to her before.

"I will bring a lawsuit against *you,*" said Morris, "if you ask me any more such aggravating questions. A man should know when he is beaten," he added, in a moment. "I must give her up!"

Mrs. Penniman received this declaration in silence, though it made her heart beat a little. It found her by no means unprepared, for she had accustomed herself to the thought that, if Morris should decidedly not be able to get her brother's money, it would not do for him to marry Catherine without it. "It would not do," was a vague way of putting the thing; but Mrs. Penniman's natural affection completed the idea, which, though it had not as yet been so crudely expressed between them as in the form that Morris had just given it, had nevertheless been implied so often, in certain easy intervals of talk, as he sat stretching his legs in the Doctor's well-stuffed arm-chairs, that she had grown first to regard it with an emotion which she flattered herself was philosophic, and then to have a secret tenderness for it. The fact that she kept her tenderness secret proves, of course, that she was ashamed of it; but she managed to blink her shame by reminding herself that she was, after all, the official protector of her niece's marriage. Her logic would scarcely have passed muster with the Doctor. In the first place, Morris *must* get the money, and she would help him to it. In the second, it was plain it would never come to him, and it would be a grievous pity he should marry without it—a young man who might so easily find something better. After her brother had delivered himself, on his return from Europe, of that incisive little address that has been quoted, Morris's cause seemed so hopeless that Mrs. Penniman fixed her attention exclusively upon the latter branch of her argument. If Morris had been her son, she would certainly have sacrificed Catherine to a superior conception of his future; and to be ready to do so, as the case stood, was therefore even a finer degree of devotion. Nevertheless, it checked her breath a little to have the sacrificial knife, as it were, suddenly thrust into her hand.

Morris walked along a moment, and then he repeated, harshly,

"I must give her up!"

"I think I understand you," said Mrs. Penniman, gently.

"I certainly say it distinctly enough—brutally and vulgarly enough."

He was ashamed of himself, and his shame was uncomfortable; and as he was extremely intolerant of discomfort, he felt vicious and cruel. He wanted to abuse somebody, and he began, cautiously—for he was always cautious—with himself.

"Couldn't you take her down a little?" he asked.

"Take her down?"

"Prepare her—try and ease me off."

Mrs. Penniman stopped, looking at him very solemnly.

"My poor Morris, do you know how much she loves you?"

"No, I don't. I don't want to know. I have always tried to keep from knowing. It would be too painful."

"She will suffer much," said Mrs. Penniman.

"You must console her. If you are as good a friend to me as you pretend to be, you will manage it."

Mrs. Penniman shook her head sadly.

"You talk of my 'pretending' to like you; but I can't pretend to hate you. I can only tell her I think very highly of you; and how will that console her for losing you?"

"The Doctor will help you. He will be delighted at the thing being broken off; and as he is a knowing fellow, he will invent something to comfort her."

"He will invent a new torture," cried Mrs. Penniman. "Heaven deliver her from her father's comfort! It will consist of his crowing over her, and saying, 'I always told you so!' "

Morris colored a most uncomfortable red.

"If you don't console her any better than you console

me, you certainly won't be of much use. It's a damned disagreeable necessity; I feel it extremely, and you ought to make it easy for me."

"I will be your friend for life," Mrs. Penniman declared.

"Be my friend *now!*" and Morris walked on.

She went with him; she was almost trembling.

"Should you like me to tell her?" she asked.

"You mustn't tell her, but you can—you can—" And he hesitated, trying to think what Mrs. Penniman could do. "You can explain to her why it is. It's because I can't bring myself to step in between her and her father—to give him the pretext he grasps at so eagerly (it's a hideous sight!) for depriving her of her rights."

Mrs. Penniman felt with remarkable promptitude the charm of this formula.

"That's so like you," she said; "it's so finely felt."

Morris gave his stick an angry swing.

"Oh damnation!" he exclaimed, perversely.

Mrs. Penniman, however, was not discouraged.

"It may turn out better than you think Catherine is, after all, so very peculiar." And she thought she might take it upon herself to assure him that, whatever happened, the girl would be very quiet—she wouldn't make a noise. They extended their walk, and while they proceeded Mrs. Penniman took upon herself other things besides, and ended by having assumed a considerable burden; Morris being ready enough, as may be imagined, to put everything off upon her. But he was not for a single instant the dupe of her blundering alacrity; he knew that of what she promised she was competent to perform but an insignificant fraction, and the more she professed her willingness to serve him, the greater fool he thought her.

"What will you do if you don't marry her?" she ventured to inquire in the course of this conversation.

"Something brilliant," said Morris. "Shouldn't you like me to do something brilliant?"

The idea gave Mrs. Penniman exceeding pleasure.

"I shall feel sadly taken in if you don't."

"I shall have to, to make up for this. This isn't at all brilliant, you know."

Mrs. Penniman mused a little, as if there might be some way of making out that it was; but she had to give up the attempt, and, to carry off the awkwardness of failure, she risked a new inquiry.

"Do you mean—do you mean another marriage?"

Morris greeted this question with a reflection which was hardly the less impudent from being inaudible. "Surely women are more crude than men!" And then he answered, audibly,

"Never in the world!"

Mrs. Penniman felt disappointed and snubbed, and she relieved herself in a little vaguely sarcastic cry. He was certainly perverse.

"I give her up, not for another woman, but for a wider career," Morris announced.

This was very grand; but still Mrs. Penniman, who felt that she had exposed herself, was faintly rancorous.

"Do you mean never to come to see her again?" she asked, with some sharpness.

"Oh no, I shall come again; but what is the use of dragging it out? I have been four times since she came back, and it's terribly awkward work. I can't keep it up indefinitely; she oughtn't to expect that, you know. A woman should never keep a man dangling," he added, finely.

"Ah, but you must have your last parting!" urged his companion, in whose imagination the idea of last partings occupied a place inferior in dignity only to that of first meetings.

XXIX

HE CAME again, without managing the last parting; and again and again, without finding that Mrs. Penniman had as yet done much to pave the path of retreat with flowers. It was devilish awkward, as he said, and he felt a lively animosity for Catherine's aunt, who, as he had now quite formed the habit of saying to himself, had dragged him into the mess, and was bound in common charity to get him out of it. Mrs. Penniman, to tell the truth, had, in the seclusion of her own apartment—and, I may add, amid the suggestiveness of Catherine's, which wore in those days the appearance of that of a young lady laying out her *trousseau*—Mrs. Penniman had measured her responsibilities, and taken fright at their magnitude. The task of preparing Catherine and easing off Morris presented difficulties which increased in the execution, and even led the impulsive Lavinia to ask herself whether the modification of the young man's original project had been conceived in a happy spirit. A brilliant future, a wider career, a conscience exempt from the reproach of interference between a young lady and her natural rights—these excellent things might be too troublesomely purchased. From Catherine herself Mrs Penniman received no assistance whatever; the poor girl was apparently without suspicion of her danger. She looked at her lover with eyes of undiminished trust, and though she had less confidence in her aunt than in a young man with whom she had exchanged so many tender vows, she gave her no handle for explaining or confessing. Mrs. Penniman, faltering and wavering, declared Catherine was very stupid, put off the great scene, as she would have called it, from day to day, and wandered about, very uncomfortably, with her unexploded bomb in her hands. Morris's own scenes were very small ones just now; but even these were beyond his strength. He made his visits as brief as possible, and, while he sat with his mistress, found terribly little to talk about. She was waiting for him, in vulgar parlance, to name the day; and so long as he was unprepared to be explicit on this point, it seemed a mockery to pretend to talk about matters more abstract. She had no airs and no arts; she never attempted to disguise her expectancy. She was waiting on his good pleasure, and would wait modestly and patiently; his hanging back at this supreme time might appear strange, but of course he must have a good reason for it. Catherine would have made a wife of the gentle, old-fashioned pattern—regarding reasons as favors and windfalls, but no more expecting one every day than she would have expected a bouquet of camellias. During the period of her engagement, however, a young lady even of the most slender pretensions counts upon more bouquets than at other times; and there was a want of perfume in the air at this moment which at last excited the girl's alarm.

"Are you sick?" she asked of Morris. "You seem so restless, and you look pale."

"I am not at all well," said Morris; and it occurred to him that, if he could only make her pity him enough, he might get off.

"I am afraid you are overworked; you oughtn't to work so much."

"I must do that." And then he added, with a sort of calculated brutality, "I don't want to owe you everything."

"Ah, how can you say that?"

"I am too proud," said Morris.

"Yes—you are too proud."

"Well, you must take me as I am," he went on; "you can never change me."

"I don't want to change you," she said, gently; "I will take you as you are." And she stood looking at him.

"You know people talk tremendously about a man's marrying a rich girl," Morris remarked. "It's excessively disagreeable."

"But I am not rich," said Catherine.

"You are rich enough to make me talked about."

"Of course you are talked about. It's an honor."

"It's an honor I could easily dispense with."

She was on the point of asking him whether it was not a compensation for this annoyance that the poor girl who had the misfortune to bring it upon him loved him so dearly and believed in him so truly; but she hesitated, thinking that this would perhaps seem an exacting speech, and while she hesitated, he suddenly left her.

The next time he came, however, she brought it out, and she told him again that he was too proud. He repeated that he couldn't change, and this time she felt the impulse to say that with a little effort he might change.

Sometimes he thought that if he could only make a quarrel with her it might help him; but the question was how to quarrel with a young woman who had such treasures of concession. "I suppose you think the effort is all on your side," he broke out. "Don't you believe that I have my own effort to make?"

"It's all yours now," she said; "my effort is finished and done with."

"Well, mine is not."

"We must bear things together," said Catherine. "That's what we ought to do."

Morris attempted a natural smile. "There are some things which we can't very well bear together—for instance, separation."

"Why do you speak of separation?"

"Ah! you don't like it; I knew you wouldn't."

"Where are you going, Morris?" she suddenly asked.

He fixed his eye on her a moment, and for a part of that moment she was afraid of it. "Will you promise not to make a scene?"

"A scene!—do I make scenes?"

"All women do!" said Morris, with the tone of large experience.

"I don't. Where are you going?"

"If I should say I was going away on business, should you think it very strange?"

She wondered a moment, gazing at him. "Yes—no. Not if you will take me with you."

"Take you with me—on business?"

"What is your business? Your business is to be with me."

"I don't earn my living with you," said Morris. "Or rather," he cried, with a sudden inspiration, "that's just what I do—or what the world says I do!"

This ought perhaps to have been a great stroke, but it miscarried. "Where are you going?" Catherine simply repeated.

"To New Orleans—about buying some cotton."

"I am perfectly willing to go to New Orleans," Catherine said.

"Do you suppose I would take you to a nest of yellow-fever?" cried Morris. "Do you suppose I would expose you at such a time as this?"

"If there is yellow-fever, why should you go? Morris, you must not go."

"It is to make six thousand dollars," said Morris. "Do you grudge me that satisfaction?"

"We have no need of six thousand dollars. You think too much about money."

"You can afford to say that. This is a great chance; we heard of it last night." And he explained to her in what the chance consisted; and told her a long story, going over more than once several of the details, about the remarkable stroke of business which he and his partner had planned between them.

But Catherine's imagination, for reasons best known to herself, absolutely refused to be fired. "If you can go to New Orleans, I can go," she said. "Why shouldn't you catch yellow-fever quite as easily as I? I am every bit as strong as you, and not in the least afraid of any fever. When we were in Europe we were in very unhealthy places; my father used to make me take some pills. I never caught anything, and I never was nervous. What will be the use of six thousand dollars if you die of a fever? When persons are going to be married they oughtn't to think so much about business. You shouldn't think about cotton; you should think about me. You can go to New Orleans some other time—there will always be plenty of cotton. It isn't the moment to choose: we have waited too long already." She spoke more forcibly and volubly than he had ever heard her, and she held his arm in her two hands.

"You said you wouldn't make a scene," cried Morris. "I call this a scene."

"It's you that are making it. I have never asked you anything before. We have waited too long already." And it was a comfort to her to think that she had hitherto asked so little; it seemed to make her right to insist the greater now.

Morris bethought himself a little. "Very well, then; we won't talk about it any more. I will transact my business by letter." And he began to smooth his hat, as if to take leave.

"You won't go?" and she stood looking up at him.

He could not give up his idea of provoking a quarrel; it was so much the simplest way. He bent his eyes on her upturned face with the darkest frown he could achieve. "You are not discreet; you mustn't bully me."

But, as usual, she conceded everything. "No, I am not discreet; I know I am too pressing. But isn't it natural? It is only for a moment."

"In a moment you may do a great deal of harm. Try and be calmer the next time I come."

"When will you come?"

"Do you want to make conditions?" Morris asked. "I will come next Saturday."

"Come to-morrow," Catherine begged; "I want you to come to-morrow. I will be very quiet," she added; and her agitation had by this time become so great that the assurance was not unbecoming. A sudden fear had come over her; it was like the solid conjunction of a dozen disembodied doubts, and her imagination, at a single bound, had traversed an enormous distance. All her being, for the moment, was centred in the wish to keep him in the room.

Morris bent his head and kissed her forehead. "When you are quiet, you are perfection," he said; "but when you are violent, you are not in character."

It was Catherine's wish that there should be no violence about her save the beating of her heart, which she could not help; and she went on, as gently as possible, "Will you promise to come to-morrow?"

"I said Saturday!" Morris answered, smiling. He tried a frown at one moment, a smile at another; he was at his wit's end.

"Yes, Saturday too," she answered, trying to smile. "But to-morrow first." He was going to the door, and she went with him quickly. She leaned her shoulder against it; it seemed to her that she would do anything to keep him.

"If I am prevented from coming to-morrow, you will say I have deceived you," he said.

"How can you be prevented? You can come if you will."

"I am a busy man—I am not a dangler!" cried Morris, sternly.

His voice was so hard and unnatural that, with a helpless look at him, she turned away; and then he quickly laid his hand on the door-knob. He felt as if he were absolutely running away from her. But in an instant she was close to him again, and murmuring in a tone none the less penetrating for being low, "Morris, you are going to leave me."

"Yes, for a little while."

"For how long?"

"Till you are reasonable again."

"I shall never be reasonable, in that way." And she tried to keep him longer; it was almost a struggle. "Think of what I have done!" she broke out. "Morris, I have given up everything."

"You shall have everything back."

"You wouldn't say that if you didn't mean something. What is it?—what has happened?—what have I done?—what has changed you?"

"I will write to you—that is better," Morris stammered.

"Ah, you won't come back!" she cried, bursting into tears.

"Dear Catherine," he said, "don't believe that. I promise you that you shall see me again." And he managed to get away, and to close the door behind him.

XXX

It was almost the last outbreak of passion of her life; at least, she never indulged in another that the world knew anything about. But this one was long and terrible; she flung herself on the sofa and gave herself up to her grief. She hardly knew what had happened; ostensibly she had only had a difference with her lover, as other girls had had before, and the thing was not only not a rupture, but she was under no obligation to regard it even as a menace. Nevertheless, she felt a wound, even if he had not dealt it; it seemed to her that a mask had suddenly fallen from his face. He had wished to get away from her; he had been angry and cruel, and said strange things, with strange looks. She was smothered and stunned; she buried her head in the cushions, sobbing and talking to herself. But at last she raised herself, with the fear that either her father or Mrs. Penniman would come in; and then she sat there, staring before her, while the room grew darker. She said to herself that perhaps he would come back to tell her he had not meant what he said; and she listened for his ring at the door, trying to believe that this was probable. A long time passed, but Morris remained absent; the shadows gathered; the evening settled down on the meagre elegance of the light, clear-colored room; the fire went out. When it had grown dark, Catherine went to the window and looked out; she stood there for half an hour, on the mere chance that he would come up the steps. At last she turned away, for she saw her father come in. He had seen her at the window looking out, and he stopped a moment at the bottom of the white steps, and gravely, with an air of exaggerated courtesy, lifted his hat to her. The gesture was so incongruous to the condition she was in, this stately tribute of respect to a poor girl despised and forsaken was so out of place, that the thing gave her a kind of horror, and she hurried away to her room. It seemed to her that she had given Morris up.

She had to show herself half an hour later, and she was sustained at table by the immensity of her desire that her father should not perceive that anything had happened. This was a great help to her afterward, and it served her (though never as much as she supposed) from the first. On this occasion Doctor Sloper was rather talkative. He told a great many stories about a wonderful poodle that he had seen at the house of an old lady whom he visited professionally. Catherine not only tried to appear to listen to the anecdotes of the poodle, but she endeavored to interest herself in them, so as not to think of her scene with Morris. That perhaps was an hallucination; he was mistaken, she was jealous; people didn't change like that from one day to another. Then she knew that she had had doubts before—strange suspicions, that were at once vague and acute—and that he had been different ever since her return from Europe: whereupon she tried again to listen to her father, who told a story so remarkably well. Afterward she went straight to her own room; it was beyond her strength to undertake to spend the evening with her aunt. All the evening, alone, she questioned herself. Her trouble was terrible; but was it a thing of her imagination, engendered by an extravagant sensibility, or did it represent a clear-cut reality, and had the worst that was possible actually come to pass? Mrs. Penniman, with a degree of tact that was as unusual as it was commendable, took the line of leaving her alone. The truth is, that her suspicions having been aroused, she indulged a desire, natural to a timid person, that the explosion should be localized. So long as the air still vibrated she kept out of the way.

She passed and repassed Catherine's door several times in the course of the evening, as if she expected to hear a plaintive moan behind it. But the room remained perfectly still; and accordingly, the last thing before retiring to her own couch, she applied for admittance. Catherine was sitting up, and had a book that she pretended to be reading. She had no wish to go to bed, for she had no expectation of sleeping. After Mrs. Penniman had left her she sat up half the night, and she offered her visitor no inducement to remain. Her aunt came stealing in very gently, and approached her with great solemnity.

"I am afraid you are in trouble, my dear. Can I do anything to help you?"

"I am not in any trouble whatever, and do not need any help," said Catherine, fibbing roundly, and proving thereby that not only our faults, but our most involuntary misfortunes, tend to corrupt our morals.

"Has nothing happened to you?"

"Nothing whatever."

"Are you very sure, dear?"

"Perfectly sure."

"And can I really do nothing for you?"

"Nothing, aunt, but kindly leave me alone," said Catherine.

Mrs. Penniman, though she had been afraid of too warm a welcome before, was now disappointed at so cold a one; and in relating afterward, as she did to many persons, and with considerable variations of detail, the history of the termination of her niece's engagement, she was usually careful to mention that the young lady, on a certain occasion, had "hustled" her out of the room. It was characteristic of Mrs. Penniman that she related this fact, not in the least out of malignity to Catherine, whom she very sufficiently pitied, but simply from a natural disposition to embellish any subject that she touched.

Catherine, as I have said, sat up half the night, as if she still expected to hear Morris Townsend ring at the door. On the morrow this expectation was less unreasonable; but it was not gratified by the reappearance of the young man. Neither had he written; there was not a word of explanation or reassurance. Fortunately for Catherine, she could take refuge from her excitement, which had now become intense, in her determination that her father should see nothing of it. How well she deceived her father we shall have occasion to learn; but her innocent arts were of little avail before a person of the rare perspicacity of Mrs. Penniman. This lady easily saw that she was agitated, and if there was any agitation going forward, Mrs. Penniman was not a person to forfeit her natural share in it. She returned to the charge the next evening, and requested her niece to confide in her—to unburden her heart. Perhaps she should be able to explain certain things that now seemed dark, and that she knew more about than Catherine supposed. If Catherine had been frigid the night before, to-day she was haughty.

"You are completely mistaken, and I have not the least idea what you mean. I don't know what you are trying to fasten on me, and I have never had less need of any one's explanations in my life."

In this way the girl delivered herself, and from hour to hour kept her aunt at bay. From hour to hour Mrs. Penniman's curiosity grew. She would have given her little finger to know what Morris had said and done, what tone he had taken, what pretext he had found. She wrote to him, naturally, to request an interview; but she received, as naturally, no answer to her petition. Morris was not in a writing mood; for Catherine had addressed him two short notes which met with no acknowledgment. These notes were so brief that I may give them entire. "Won't you give me some sign that you didn't mean to be so cruel as you seemed on Tuesday?"—that was the first; the other was a little longer. "If I was unreasonable or suspicious on Tuesday—if I annoyed you or troubled you in any way—I beg your forgiveness, and I promise never again to be so foolish. I am punished enough, and I don't understand. Dear Morris, you are killing me!" These notes were despatched on the Friday and Saturday; but Saturday and Sunday passed without bringing the poor girl the satisfaction she desired. Her punishment accumulated; she continued to bear it, however, with a good deal of superficial fortitude. On Saturday morning, the Doctor, who had been watching in silence, spoke to his sister Lavinia.

"The thing has happened—the scoundrel has backed out!"

"Never!" cried Mrs. Penniman, who had bethought herself what she should say to Catherine, but was not provided with a line of defence against her brother, so that indignant negation was the only weapon in her hands.

"He has begged for a reprieve, then, if you like that better!"

"It seems to make you very happy that your daughter's affections have been trifled with."

"It does," said the Doctor; "for I had foretold it! It's a great pleasure to be in the right."

"Your pleasures make one shudder!" his sister exclaimed.

Catherine went rigidly through her usual occupations; that is, up to the point of going with her aunt to church on Sunday morning. She generally went to afternoon service as well; but on this occasion her courage faltered, and she begged of Mrs. Penniman to go without her.

"I am sure you have a secret," said Mrs. Penniman, with great significance, looking at her rather grimly.

"If I have, I shall keep it!" Catherine answered, turning away.

Mrs. Penniman started for church; but before she had arrived, she stopped and turned back, and before twenty minutes had elapsed she re-entered the house, looked into the empty parlors, and then went up-stairs and knocked at Catherine's door. She got no answer; Catherine was not in her room, and Mrs. Penniman presently ascertained that she was not in the house. "She has gone to him! she has fled!" Lavinia cried, clasping her hands with admiration and envy. But she soon perceived that Catherine had taken nothing with her—all her personal property in her room was intact—and then she jumped at the hypothesis that the girl had gone forth, not in tenderness, but in resentment. "She has followed him to his own door! she has burst upon him in his own apartment!" It was in these terms that Mrs. Penniman depicted to herself her niece's errand, which, viewed in this light, gratified her sense of the picturesque only a shade less strongly than the idea of a clandestine marriage. To visit one's lover, with tears and reproaches, at his own residence, was an image so agreeable to Mrs. Pennniman's mind that she felt a sort of æsthetic disappointment at its lacking, in this case, the harmonious accompaniments of darkness and storm. A quiet Sunday afternoon appeared an inadequate setting for it; and, indeed, Mrs. Penniman was quite out of humor with the conditions of the time, which passed very slowly as she sat in the front parlor, in her bonnet and her cashmere shawl, awaiting Catherine's return.

This event at last took place. She saw her—at the window—mount the steps, and she went to await her in the hall, where she pounced upon her as soon as she had entered the house, and drew her into the parlor, closing the door with solemnity. Catherine was flushed, and her eye was bright. Mrs. Penniman hardly knew what to think.

"May I venture to ask where you have been?" she demanded.

"I have been to take a walk," said Catherine. "I thought you had gone to church."

"I did go to church; but the service was shorter than usual. And pray where did you walk?"

"I don't know!" said Catherine.

"Your ignorance is most extraordinary! Dear Catherine, you can trust me."

"What am I to trust you with?"

"With your secret—your sorrow."

"I have *no* sorrow!" said Catherine, fiercely.

"My poor child," Mrs. Penniman insisted, "you can't deceive me. I know everything. I have been requested to—a—to converse with you."

"I don't want to converse!"

"It will relieve you. Don't you know Shakspeare's lines?—'The grief that does not speak!' My dear girl, it is better as it is!"

"What is better?" Catherine asked.

She was really too perverse. A certain amount of perversity was to be allowed for in a young lady whose lover had thrown her over; but not such an amount as would prove inconvenient to his apologists. "That you should be reasonable," said Mrs. Penniman, with some sternness; "that you should take counsel of worldly prudence, and submit to practical considerations; that you should agree to—a—separate."

Catherine had been ice up to this moment, but at this word she flamed up. "Separate? What do you know about our separating?"

Mrs. Penniman shook her head with a sadness in which there was almost a sense of injury. "Your pride is my pride, and your susceptibilities are mine. I see your side perfectly, but I also—" and she smiled with melancholy suggestiveness—"I also see the situation as a whole!"

This suggestiveness was lost upon Catherine, who repeated her violent inquiry. "Why do you talk about separation; what do you know about it?"

"We must study resignation," said Mrs. Penniman, hesitating, but sententious at a venture.

"Resignation to what?"

"To a change of—of our plans."

"My plans have not changed!" said Catherine, with a little laugh.

"Ah, but Mr. Townsend's have," her aunt answered, very gently.

"What do you mean?"

There was an imperious brevity in the tone of this in

quiry, against which Mrs. Penniman felt bound to protest; the information with which she had undertaken to supply her niece was after all a favor. She had tried sharpness, and she had tried sternness; but neither would do; she was shocked at the girl's obstinacy. "Ah well," she said, "if he hasn't told you! . . ." and she turned away.

Catherine watched her a moment in silence; then she hurried after her, stopping her before she reached the door. "Told me what? What do you mean? What are you hinting at and threatening me with?"

"Isn't it broken off?" asked Mrs. Penniman.

"My engagement? Not in the least!"

"I beg your pardon in that case. I have spoken too soon!"

"Too soon? Soon or late," Catherine broke out, "you speak foolishly and cruelly!"

"What has happened between you then?" asked her aunt, struck by the sincerity of this cry; "for something certainly has happened."

"Nothing has happened but that I love him more and more!"

Mrs. Penniman was silent an instant. "I suppose that's the reason you went to see him this afternoon."

Catherine flushed as if she had been struck. "Yes, I did go to see him! But that's my own business."

"Very well, then; we won't talk about it." And Mrs. Penniman moved toward the door again; but she was stopped by a sudden imploring cry from the girl.

"Aunt Lavinia, *where* has he gone?"

"Ah, you admit then that he has gone away! Didn't they know at his house?"

"They said he had left town. I asked no more questions; I was ashamed," said Catherine, simply enough.

"You needn't have taken so compromising a step if you had had a little more confidence in me," Mrs. Penniman observed, with a good deal of grandeur.

"Is it to New Orleans?" Catherine went on, irrelevantly.

It was the first time Mrs. Penniman had heard of New Orleans in this connection; but she was averse to letting Catherine know that she was in the dark. She attempted to strike an illumination from the instructions she had received from Morris. "My dear Catherine," she said, "when a separation has been agreed upon, the farther he goes away the better."

"Agreed upon? Has he agreed upon it with you?" A consummate sense of her aunt's meddlesome folly had come over her during the last five minutes, and she was sickened at the thought that Mrs. Penniman had been let loose, as it were, upon her happiness.

"He certainly has sometimes advised with me," said Mrs. Penniman.

"Is it you, then, that has changed him and made him so unnatural?" Catherine cried. "Is it you that have worked on him and taken him from me? He doesn't belong to you, and I don't see how you have anything to do with what is between us! Is it you that have made this plot, and told him to leave me? How could you be so wicked, so cruel? What have I ever done to you? Why can't you leave me alone? I was afraid you would spoil everything; for you *do* spoil everything you touch! I was afraid of you all the time we were abroad; I had no rest when I thought that you were always talking to him." Catherine went on with growing vehemence, pouring out, in her bitterness and in the clairvoyance of her passion (which suddenly, jumping all processes, made her judge her aunt finally and without appeal), the uneasiness which had lain for so many months upon her heart.

Mrs. Penniman was scared and bewildered; she saw no prospect of introducing her little account of the purity of Morris's motives. "You are a most ungrateful girl!" she cried. "Do you scold me for talking with him? I'm sure we never talked of anything but you!"

"Yes; and that was the way you worried him; you made him tired of my very name! I wish you had never spoken of me to him; I never asked your help!"

"I am sure if it hadn't been for me he would never have come to the house, and you would never have known that he thought of you," Mrs. Penniman rejoined, with a good deal of justice.

"I wish he never had come to the house, and that I never had known it! That's better than this," said poor Catherine.

"You are a very ungrateful girl," Aunt Lavinia repeated.

Catherine's outbreak of anger and the sense of wrong gave her, while they lasted, the satisfaction that comes from all assertion of force; they hurried her along, and there is always a sort of pleasure in cleaving the air. But at bottom she hated to be violent, and she was conscious of no aptitude for organized resentment. She calmed herself with a great effort, but with great rapidity, and walked about the room a few moments, trying to say to herself that her aunt had meant everything for the best. She did not succeed in saying it with much conviction, but after a little she was able to speak quietly enough.

"I am not ungrateful, but I am very unhappy. It's hard to be grateful for that," she said. "Will you please tell me where he is?"

"I haven't the least idea; I am not in secret correspondence with him!" And Mrs. Penniman wished, indeed, that she were, so that she might let him know how Catherine abused her, after all she had done.

"Was it a plan of his, then, to break off—?" By this time Catherine had become completely quiet.

Mrs. Penniman began again to have a glimpse of her chance for explaining. "He shrunk—he shrunk," she said; "he lacked courage, but it was the courage to injure you! He couldn't bear to bring down on you your father's curse."

Catherine listened to this with her eyes fixed upon her

aunt, and continued to gaze at her for some time afterward. "Did he tell you to say that?"

"He told me to say many things—all so delicate, so discriminating; and he told me to tell you he hoped you wouldn't despise him."

"I don't," said Catherine; and then she added, "And will he stay away forever?"

"Oh, forever is a long time. Your father, perhaps, won't live forever."

"Perhaps not."

"I am sure you appreciate—you understand—even though your heart bleeds," said Mrs. Penniman. "You doubtless think him too scrupulous. So do I, but I respect his scruples. What he asks of you is that you should do the same."

Catherine was still gazing at her aunt, but she spoke at last as if she had not heard or not understood her. "It has been a regular plan, then. He has broken it off deliberately; he has given me up."

"For the present, dear Catherine; he has put it off, only."

"He has left me alone," Catherine went on.

"Haven't you *me?*" asked Mrs. Penniman, with some solemnity.

Catherine shook her head slowly. "I don't believe it!" and she left the room.

XXXI

Though she had forced herself to be calm, she preferred practising this virtue in private, and she forbore to show herself at tea—a repast which, on Sundays, at six o'clock, took the place of dinner. Doctor Sloper and his sister sat face to face, but Mrs. Penniman never met her brother's eye. Late in the evening she went with him, but without Catherine, to their sister Almond's, where, between the two ladies, Catherine's unhappy situation was discussed with a frankness that was conditioned by a good deal of mysterious reticence on Mrs. Penniman's part.

"I am delighted he is not to marry her," said Mrs. Almond, "but he ought to be horsewhipped all the same."

Mrs. Penniman, who was shocked at her sister's coarseness, replied that he had been actuated by the noblest of motives—the desire not to impoverish Catherine.

"I am very happy that Catherine is not to be impoverished—but I hope he may never have a penny too much! And what does the poor girl say to *you?*" Mrs. Almond asked.

"She says I have a genius for consolation," said Mrs. Penniman.

This was the account of the matter that she gave to her sister, and it was perhaps with the consciousness of genius that, on her return that evening to Washington Square, she again presented herself for admittance at Catherine's door. Catherine came and opened it; she was apparently very quiet.

"I only want to give you a little word of advice," she said. "If your father asks you, say that everything is going on."

Catherine stood there, with her hand on the knob, looking at her aunt, but not asking her to come in. "Do you think he will ask me?"

"I am sure he will. He asked me just now, on our way home from your Aunt Elizabeth's. I explained the whole thing to your Aunt Elizabeth. I said to your father I knew nothing about it."

"Do you think he will ask me, when he sees—when he sees—?" But here Catherine stopped.

"The more he sees, the more disagreeable he will be," said her aunt.

"He shall see as little as possible!" Catherine declared.

"Tell him you are to be married."

"So I am," said Catherine, softly; and she closed the door upon her aunt.

She could not have said this two days later—for instance, on Tuesday, when she at last received a letter from Morris Townsend. It was an epistle of considerable length, measuring five large square pages, and written at Philadelphia. It was an explanatory document, and it explained a great many things, chief among which were the considerations that had led the writer to take advantage of an urgent "professional" absence to try and banish from his mind the image of one whose path he had crossed only to scatter it with ruins. He ventured to expect but partial success in this attempt, but he could promise her that, whatever his failure, he would never again interpose between her generous heart and her brilliant prospects and filial duties. He closed with an intimation that his professional pursuits might compel him to travel for some months, and with the hope that when they should each have accommodated themselves to what was sternly involved in their respective positions—even should this result not be reached for years—they should meet as friends, as fellow-sufferers, as innocent but philosophic victims of a great social law. That her life should be peaceful and happy was the dearest wish of him who ventured still to subscribe himself her most obedient servant. The letter was beautifully written, and Catherine, who kept it for many years after this, was able, when her sense of the bitterness of its meaning and the hollowness of its tone had grown less acute, to admire its grace of expression. At present, for a long time after she received it, all she had to help her was the determination, daily more rigid, to make no appeal to the compassion of her father.

He suffered a week to elapse, and then one day, in the morning, at an hour at which she rarely saw him, he strolled into the back parlor. He had watched his time, and he found her alone. She was sitting with some work, and he came and stood in front of her. He was going out; he had on his hat, and was drawing on his gloves.

"It doesn't seem to me that you are treating me just now with all the consideration I deserve," he said in a moment.

"I don't know what I have done," Catherine answered, with her eyes on her work.

"You have apparently quite banished from your mind the request I made you at Liverpool before we sailed—the request that you would notify me in advance before leaving my house."

"I have not left your house," said Catherine.

"But you intend to leave it, and, by what you gave me to understand, your departure must be impending. In fact, though you are still here in body, you are already absent in spirit. Your mind has taken up its residence with your prospective husband, and you might quite as well be lodged under the conjugal roof for all the benefit we get from your society."

"I will try and be more cheerful," said Catherine.

"You certainly ought to be cheerful; you ask a great deal if you are not. To the pleasure of marrying a charming young man you add that of having your own way; you strike me as a very lucky young lady!"

Catherine got up; she was suffocating. But she folded

her work deliberately and correctly, bending her burning face upon it. Her father stood where he had planted himself; she hoped he would go, but he smoothed and buttoned his gloves, and then he rested his hands upon his hips.

"It would be a convenience to me to know when I may expect to have an empty house," he went on. "When you go, your aunt marches."

She looked at him at last, with a long, silent gaze, which, in spite of her pride and her resolution, uttered part of the appeal she had tried not to make. Her father's cold gray eye sounded her own, and he insisted on his point.

"Is it to-morrow? Is it next week, or the week after?"

"I shall not go away!" said Catherine.

The Doctor raised his eyebrows. "Has he backed out?"

"I have broken off my engagement."

"Broken it off?"

"I have asked him to leave New York, and he has gone away for a long time."

The Doctor was both puzzled and disappointed, but he solved his perplexity by saying to himself that his daughter simply misrepresented—justifiably, if one would, but nevertheless, misrepresented—the facts; and he eased off his disappointment, which was that of a man losing a chance for a little triumph that he had rather counted on, by a few words that he uttered aloud.

"How does he take his dismissal?"

"I don't know!" said Catherine, less ingeniously than she had hitherto spoken.

"You mean you don't care? You are rather cruel, after encouraging him and playing with him for so long!"

The Doctor had his revenge, after all.

XXXII

OUR STORY has hitherto moved with very short steps, but as it approaches its termination it must take a long stride. As time went on, it might have appeared to the Doctor that his daughter's account of her rupture with Morris Townsend, mere bravado as he had deemed it, was in some degree justified by the sequel. Morris remained as rigidly and unremittingly absent as if he had died of a broken heart, and Catherine had apparently buried the memory of this fruitless episode as deep as if it had terminated by her own choice. We know that she had been deeply and incurably wounded, but the Doctor had no means of knowing it. He was certainly curious about it, and would have given a good deal to discover the exact truth; but it was his punishment that he never knew—his punishment, I mean, for the abuse of sarcasm in his relations with his daughter. There was a good deal of effective sarcasm in her keeping him in the dark, and the rest of the world conspired with her, in this sense to be sarcastic. Mrs. Penniman told him nothing, partly because he never questioned her—he made too light of Mrs. Penniman for that—and partly because she flattered herself that a tormenting reserve, and a serene profession of ignorance, would avenge her for his theory that she had meddled in the matter. He went two or three times to see Mrs. Montgomery, but Mrs. Montgomery had nothing to impart. She simply knew that her brother's engagement was broken off; and now that Miss Sloper was out of danger, she preferred not to bear witness in any way against Morris. She had done so before—however unwillingly—because she was sorry for Miss Sloper; but she was not sorry for Miss

Sloper now—not at all sorry. Morris had told her nothing about his relations with Miss Sloper at the time, and he had told her nothing since. He was always away, and he very seldom wrote to her; she believed he had gone to California. Mrs. Almond had, in her sister's phrase, "taken up" Catherine violently since the recent catastrophe; but, though the girl was very grateful to her for her kindness, she revealed no secrets, and the good lady could give the Doctor no satisfaction. Even, however, had she been able to narrate to him the private history of his daughter's unhappy love affair, it would have given her a certain comfort to leave him in ignorance; for Mrs. Almond was at this time not altogether in sympathy with her brother. She had guessed for herself that Catherine had been cruelly jilted—she knew nothing from Mrs. Penniman, for Mrs. Penniman had not ventured to lay the famous explanation of Morris's motives before Mrs. Almond, though she had thought it good enough for Catherine—and she pronounced her brother too consistently indifferent to what the poor creature must have suffered and must still be suffering. Doctor Sloper had his theory, and he rarely altered his theories. The marriage would have been an abominable one, and the girl had had a blessed escape. She was not to be pitied for that, and to pretend to condole with her would have been to make concessions to the idea that she had ever had a right to think of Morris.

"I put my foot on this idea from the first, and I keep it there now," said the Doctor. "I don't see anything cruel in that; one can't keep it there too long." To this Mrs. Almond more than once replied that, if Catherine had got rid of her incongruous lover, she deserved the credit of it, and that to bring herself to her father's enlightened view of the matter must have cost her an effort that he was bound to appreciate.

"I am by no means sure she has got rid of him," the Doctor said. "There is not the smallest probability that, after having been as obstinate as a mule for two years, she suddenly became amenable to reason. It is infinitely more probable that he got rid of her."

"All the more reason you should be gentle with her."

"I *am* gentle with her. But I can't do the pathetic; I can't pump up tears, to look graceful, over the most fortunate thing that ever happened to her."

"You have no sympathy," said Mrs. Almond; "that was never your strong point. You have only to look at her to see that, right or wrong, and whether the rupture came from herself or from him, her poor little heart is grievously bruised."

"Handling bruises, and even dropping tears on them, doesn't make them any better! My business is to see she gets no more knocks, and that I shall carefully attend to. But I don't at all recognize your description of Catherine. She doesn't strike me in the least as a young woman going about in search of a moral poultice. In fact, she seems to me much better than while the fellow was hanging about. She is perfectly comfortable and blooming; she eats and sleeps, takes her usual exercise, and overloads herself, as usual, with finery. She is always knitting some purse or embroidering some handkerchief, and it seems to me she turns these articles out about as fast as ever. She hasn't much to say; but when had she anything to say? She had her little dance, and now she is sitting down to rest. I suspect that, on the whole, she enjoys it."

"She enjoys it as people enjoy getting rid of a leg that has been crushed. The state of mind after amputation is doubtless one of comparative repose."

"If your leg is a metaphor for young Townsend, I can assure you he has never been crushed. Crushed? Not he! He is alive and perfectly intact; and that's why I am not satisfied."

"Should you have liked to kill him?" asked Mrs. Almond.

"Yes, very much. I think it is quite possible that it is all a blind."

"A blind?"

"An arrangement between them. *Il fait le mort,* as they say in France; but he is looking out of the corner of his eye. You can depend upon it, he has not burnt his ships; he has kept one to come back in. When I am dead, he will set sail again, and then she will marry him."

"It is interesting to know that you accuse your only daughter of being the vilest of hypocrites," said Mrs. Almond.

"I don't see what difference her being my only daughter makes. It is better to accuse one than a dozen. But I don't accuse any one. There is not the smallest hypocrisy about Catherine, and I deny that she even pretends to be miserable."

The Doctor's idea that the thing was a "blind" had its intermissions and revivals; but it may be said, on the whole, to have increased as he grew older; together with his impressions of Catherine's blooming and comfortable condition. Naturally, if he had not found grounds for viewing her as a lovelorn maiden during the year or two that followed her great trouble, he found none at a time when she had completely recovered her self-possession. He was obliged to recognize the fact that, if the two young people were waiting for him to get out of the way, they were at least waiting very patiently. He had heard from time to time that Morris was in New York; but he never remained there long, and, to the best of the Doctor's belief, had no communication with Catherine. He was sure they never met, and he had reason to suspect that Morris never wrote to her. After the letter that has been mentioned, she heard from him twice again, at considerable intervals; but on none of these occasions did she write herself. On the other hand, as the Doctor observed, she averted herself rigidly from the idea of marrying other people. Her opportunities for doing so were not numerous, but they occurred often enough to test her disposition. She refused a wid ower, a man with a genial temperament, a handsome for tune, and three little girls (he had heard that she was very fond of children, and he pointed to his own with some confidence); and she turned a deaf ear to the solicitations of a clever young lawyer, who, with the prospect of a great practice, and the reputation of a most agreeable man, had had the shrewdness, when he came to look about him for a wife, to believe that she would suit him better than several younger and prettier girls. Mr. Macalister, the widower, had desired to make a marriage of reason, and had chosen Catherine for what he supposed to be her latent matronly qualities; but John Ludlow, who was a year the girl's junior, and spoken of always as a young man who might have his "pick," was seriously in love with her. Catherine, however, would never look at him; she made it plain to him that she thought he came to see her too often. He afterward consoled himself, and married a very different person, little Miss Sturtevant, whose attractions were obvious to the dullest comprehension. Catherine, at the time of these events, had left her thirtieth year well behind her, and had quite taken her place as an old maid. Her father would have preferred she should marry, and he once told her that he hoped she would not be too fastidious. "I should like to see you an honest man's wife before I die," he said. This was after John Ludlow had been compelled to give it up, though the Doctor had advised him to persevere. The Doctor exercised no further pressure, and had the credit of not "worrying" at all over his daughter's singleness; in fact, he worried rather more than appeared, and there were considerable periods during which he felt sure that Morris Townsend was hidden behind some door. "If he is not, why doesn't she marry?" he asked himself. "Limited as her intelligence may be, she must understand perfectly well that she is made to do the usual thing." Catherine, however, became an admirable old maid. She formed habits, regulated her days upon a system of her own, interested herself in charitable institutions, asylums, hospitals, and aid societies; and went generally, with an even and noiseless step, about the rigid business of her life. This life had, however, a secret history as well as a public one—if I may talk of the public history of a mature and diffident spinster for whom publicity had always a combination of terrors. From her own point of view the great facts of her career were that Morris Townsend had trifled with her affection, and that her father had broken its spring. Nothing could ever alter these facts; they were always there, like her name, her age, her plain face. Nothing could ever undo the wrong or cure the pain that Morris had inflicted on her, and nothing could ever make her feel toward her father as she felt in her younger years. There was something dead in her life, and her duty was to try and fill the void. Catherine recognized this duty to the utmost; she had a great disapproval of brooding and moping. She had, of course, no faculty for quenching memory in dissipation; but she mingled freely in the usual gaieties of the town, and she became at last an inevitable figure at all respectable entertainments. She was greatly liked, and as time went on she grew to be a sort of kindly maiden-aunt to the younger portion of society. Young girls were apt to confide to her their love affairs (which they never did to Mrs. Penniman), and young men to be fond of her without knowing why. She developed a few harmless eccentricities; her habits, once formed, were rather stiffly maintained; her opinions, on all moral and social matters, were extremely conservative; and before she was forty she was regarded as an old-fashioned person, and an authority on customs that had passed away. Mrs. Penniman, in comparison, was quite a girlish figure; she grew younger as she advanced in life. She lost none of her relish for beauty and mystery, but she had little opportunity to exercise it. With Catherine's later wooers she failed to establish relations as intimate as those which had given her so many interesting hours in the society of Morris Townsend. These gentlemen had an indefinable mistrust of her good offices, and they never talked to her about Catherine's charms. Her ringlets, her buckles and bangles glistened more brightly with each succeeding year, and she remained quite the same officious and imaginative Mrs. Penniman, and the odd mixture of impetuosity and circumspection, that we have hitherto known. As regards one point, however, her circumspection prevailed, and she must be given due credit for it. For upward of seventeen years she never mentioned Morris Townsend's name to her niece. Catherine was grateful to her, but this consistent silence, so little in accord with her aunt's character, gave her a certain alarm, and she could never wholly rid herself of a suspicion that Mrs. Penniman sometimes had news of him.

XXXIII

LITTLE BY LITTLE Doctor Sloper had retired from his profession; he visited only those patients in whose symptoms he recognized a certain originality. He went again to Europe, and remained two years; Catherine went with him, and on this occasion Mrs. Penniman was of the party. Europe apparently had few surprises for Mrs. Penniman, who frequently remarked, in the most romantic sites, "You know I am very familiar with all this." It should be added that such remarks were usually not addressed to her brother, or yet to her niece, but to fellow-tourists who happened to be at hand, or even to the cicerone or the goatherd in the foreground.

One day, after his return from Europe, the Doctor said something to his daughter that made her start—it seemed to come from so far out of the past.

"I should like you to promise me something before I die."

"Why do you talk about your dying?" she asked.

"Because I am sixty-eight years old."

"I hope you will live a long time," said Catherine.

"I hope I shall! But some day I shall take a bad cold, and then it will not matter much what any one hopes. That will be the manner of my exit, and when it takes place, remember I told you so. Promise me not to marry Morris Townsend after I am gone."

This was what made Catherine start, as I have said; but her start was a silent one, and for some moments she said nothing. "Why do you speak of him?" she asked at last.

"You challenge everything I say. I speak of him because he's a topic, like any other. He's to be seen, like anyone else, and he is still looking for a wife—having had one and got rid of her, I don't know by what means. He has lately been in New York, and at your cousin Marian's house; your aunt Elizabeth saw him there."

"They neither of them told me," said Catherine.

"That's their merit; it's not yours. He has grown fat and bald, and he has not made his fortune. But I can't trust those facts alone to steel your heart against him, and that's why I ask you to promise."

"Fat and bald"; these words presented a strange image to Catherine's mind, out of which the memory of the most beautiful young man in the world had never faded. "I don't think you understand," she said. "I very seldom think of Mr. Townsend."

"It will be very easy for you to go on, then. Promise me, after my death, to do the same."

Again, for some moments, Catherine was silent; her father's request deeply amazed her; it opened an old wound, and made it ache afresh. "I don't think I can promise that," she answered.

"It would be a great satisfaction," said her father.

"You don't understand. I can't promise that."

The Doctor was silent a minute. "I ask you for a particular reason. I am altering my will."

This reason failed to strike Catherine; and indeed she scarcely understood it. All her feelings were merged in the sense that he was trying to treat her as he had treated her years before. She had suffered from it then; and now all her experience, all her acquired tranquillity and rigidity protested. She had been so humble in her youth that she could now afford to have a little pride, and there was something in this request, and in her father's thinking himself so free to make it, that seemed an injury to her dignity. Poor Catherine's dignity was not aggressive; it never sat in state; but if you pushed far enough you could find it. Her father had pushed very far.

"I can't promise," she simply repeated.

"You are very obstinate," said the Doctor.

"I don't think you understand."

"Please explain, then."

"I can't explain," said Catherine; "and I can't promise."

"Upon my word," her father exclaimed, "I had no idea how obstinate you are!"

She knew herself that she was obstinate, and it gave her a certain joy. She was now a middle-aged woman.

About a year after this, the accident that the Doctor had spoken of occurred: he took a violent cold. Driving out to Bloomingdale one April day to see a patient of unsound mind, who was confined in a private asylum for the insane, and whose family greatly desired a medical opinion from an eminent source, he was caught in a spring shower, and being in a buggy, without a hood, he found himself soaked to the skin. He came home with an ominous chill, and on the morrow he was seriously ill. "It is congestion of the lungs," he said to Catherine; "I shall need very good nursing. It will make no difference, for I shall not recover; but I wish everything to be done, to the smallest detail, as if I should. I hate an ill-conducted sick-room, and you will be so good as to nurse me, on the hypothesis that I shall get well." He told her which of his fellow-physicians to send for, and gave her a multitude of minute directions; it was quite on the optimistic hypothesis that she nursed him. But he had never been wrong in his life, and he was not wrong now. He was touching his seventieth year, and though he had a very well-tempered constitution, his hold upon life had lost its firmness. He died after three weeks' illness, during which Mrs. Penniman, as well as his daughter, had been assiduous at his bedside.

On his will being opened, after a decent interval, it was found to consist of two portions. The first of these dated from ten years back, and consisted of a series of dispositions by which he left the great mass of his property to his daughter, with becoming legacies to his two sisters. The second was a codicil, of recent origin, maintaining the annuities to Mrs Penniman and Mrs. Almond, but reducing Catherine's share to a fifth of what he had first bequeathed her. "She is amply provided for from her mother's side," the document ran, "never having spent more than a fraction of her income from this source; so that her fortune is already more than sufficient to attract those unscrupulous adventurers whom she has given me reason to believe that she persists in regarding as an interesting class." The large remainder of his property, therefore, Doctor Sloper had divided into seven unequal parts, which he left, as endowments, to as many different hospitals and schools of medicine in various cities of the Union.

To Mrs. Penniman it seemed monstrous that a man should play such tricks with other people's money; for after his death, of course, as she said, it was other people's. "Of course, you will immediately break the will," she remarked to Catherine.

"Oh no," Catherine answered, "I like it very much. Only I wish it had been expressed a little differently!"

XXXIV

It was her habit to remain in town very late in the summer; she preferred the house in Washington Square to any other habitation whatever, and it was under protest that she used to go to the sea-side for the month of August. At the sea she spent her month at an hotel. The year that her father died she intermitted this custom altogether, not thinking it consistent with deep mourning; and the year after that she put off her departure till so late that the middle of August found her still in the heated solitude of Washington Square. Mrs. Penniman, who was fond of a change, was usually eager for a visit to the country; but this year she appeared quite content with such rural impressions as she could gather at the parlor-window from the ailanthus-trees behind the wooden paling. The peculiar fragrance of this vegetation used to diffuse itself in the evening air, and Mrs. Penniman, on the warm nights of July, often sat at the open window and inhaled it. This was a happy moment for Mrs. Penniman; after the death of her brother she felt more free to obey her impulses. A vague oppression had disappeared from her life, and she enjoyed a sense of freedom of which she had not been conscious since the memorable time, so long ago, when the Doctor went abroad with Catherine and left her at home to entertain Morris Townsend. The year that had elapsed since her brother's death reminded her of that happy time, because, although Catherine, in growing older, had become a person to be reckoned with, yet her society was a very different thing, as Mrs. Penniman said, from that of a tank of cold water. The elder lady hardly knew what use to make of this larger margin of her life; she sat and looked at it very much as she had often sat, with her poised needle in her hand, before her tapestry-frame. She had a confident hope, however, that her rich impulses, her talent for embroidery, would still find their application, and this confidence was justified before many months had elapsed.

Catherine continued to live in her father's house, in spite of its being represented to her that a maiden lady of quiet habits might find a more convenient abode in one of the smaller dwellings, with brown stone fronts, which had at this time begun to adorn the transverse thoroughfares in the upper part of the town. She liked the earlier structure—it had begun by this time to be called an "old" house—and proposed to herself to end her days in it. If it was too large for a pair of unpretending gentlewomen, this was better than the opposite fault; for Catherine had no desire to find herself in closer quarters with her aunt. She expected to spend the rest of her life in Washington Square, and to enjoy Mrs. Penniman's society for the whole of this period; as she had a conviction that, long as she might live, her aunt would live at least as long, and always retain her brilliancy and activity. Mrs. Penniman suggested to her the idea of a rich vitality.

On one of those warm evenings in July of which mention has been made, the two ladies sat together at an open window, looking out on the quiet Square. It was too hot for lighted lamps, for reading, or for work; it might have appeared too hot even for conversation, Mrs. Penniman having long been speechless. She sat forward in the window, half on the balcony, humming a little song. Catherine was within the room, in a low rocking-chair, dressed in white, and slowly using a large palmetto fan. It was in this way, at this season, that the aunt and niece, after they had had tea, habitually spent their evenings.

"Catherine," said Mrs. Penniman at last, "I am going to say something that will surprise you."

"Pray do," Catherine answered; "I like surprises. And it is so quiet now."

"Well, then, I have seen Morris Townsend."

If Catherine was surprised, she checked the expression of it; she gave neither a start nor an exclamation. She remained, indeed, for some moments intensely still, and this may very well have been a symptom of emotion. "I hope he was well," she said at last.

"I don't know; he is a great deal changed. He would like very much to see you."

"I would rather not see him," said Catherine, quickly.

"I was afraid you would say that. But you don't seem surprised!"

"I am—very much."

"I met him at Marian's," said Mrs. Penniman. "He goes to Marian's, and they are so afraid you will meet him there. It's my belief that that's why he goes. He wants so much to see you." Catherine made no response to this, and Mrs. Penniman went on. "I didn't know him at first, he is so remarkably changed; but he knew me in a minute. He says I am not in the least changed. You know how polite he always was. He was coming away when I came, and we walked a little distance together. He is still very handsome, only of course he looks older, and he is not so—so animated as he used to be. There was a touch of sadness about him; but there was a touch of sadness about him before, especially when he went away. I am afraid he has not been very successful—that he has never got thoroughly established I don't suppose he is sufficiently plodding, and that, after all, is what succeeds in this world." Mrs. Penniman had not mentioned Morris Townsend's name to her niece for upwards of the fifth of a century; but now that she had broken the spell, she seemed to wish to make up for lost time, as if there had been a sort of exhilaration in hearing herself talk of him. She proceeded, however, with considerable caution, pausing occasionally to let Catherine give some sign. Catherine gave no other sign than to stop the rocking of her chair and the swaying of her fan; she sat motionless and silent. "It was on Tuesday last," said Mrs.

Penniman, "and I have been hesitating ever since about telling you. I didn't know how you might like it. At last I thought that it was so long ago that you would probably not have any particular feeling. I saw him again after meeting him at Marian's. I met him in the street, and he went a few steps with me. The first thing he said was about you; he asked ever so many questions. Marian didn't want me to speak to you; she didn't want you to know that they receive him. I told him I was sure that after all these years you couldn't have any feeling about that; you couldn't grudge him the hospitality of his own cousin's house. I said you would be bitter indeed if you did that. Marian has the most extraordinary ideas about what happened between you; she seems to think he behaved in some very unusual manner. I took the liberty of reminding her of the real facts, and placing the story in its true light. *He* has no bitterness, Catherine, I can assure you; and he might be excused for it, for things have not gone well with him. He has been all over the world, and tried to establish himself everywhere; but his evil star was against him. It is most interesting to hear him talk of his evil star. Everything failed; everything but his—you know, you remember—his proud, high spirit. I believe he married some lady somewhere in Europe. You know they marry in such a peculiar matter-of-course way in Europe; a marriage of reason they call it. She died soon afterward; as he said to me, she only flitted across his life. He has not been in New York for ten years; he came back a few days ago. The first thing he did was to ask me about you. He had heard you had never married; he seemed very much interested about that. He said you had been the real romance of his life."

Catherine had suffered her companion to proceed from point to point, and pause to pause, without interrupting her; she fixed her eyes on the ground and listened. But the last phrase I have quoted was followed by a pause of peculiar significance, and then, at last, Catherine spoke. It will be observed that before doing so she had received a good deal of information about Morris Townsend. "Please say no more; please don't follow up that subject."

"Doesn't it interest you?" asked Mrs. Penniman, with a certain timorous archness.

"It pains me," said Catherine.

"I was afraid you would say that. But don't you think you could get used to it? He wants so much to see you."

"Please don't, Aunt Lavinia," said Catherine, getting up from her seat. She moved quickly away, and went to the other window, which stood open to the balcony; and here, in the embrasure, concealed from her aunt by the white curtains, she remained a long time, looking out into the warm darkness. She had had a great shock; it was as if the gulf of the past had suddenly opened, and a spectral figure had risen out of it. There were some things she believed she had got over, some feelings that she had thought of as dead; but apparently there was a certain vitality in them still. Mrs. Penniman had made them stir themselves. It was but a momentary agitation, Catherine said to herself; it would presently pass away. She was trembling, and her heart was beating so that she could feel it; but this also would subside. Then suddenly, while she waited for a return of her calmness, she burst into tears. But her tears flowed very silently, so that Mrs. Penniman had no observation of them. It was perhaps, however, because Mrs. Penniman suspected them that she said no more that evening about Morris Townsend.

XXXV

HER REFRESHED attention to this gentleman had not those limits of which Catherine desired, for herself, to be conscious; it lasted long enough to enable her to wait another week before speaking of him again. It was under the same circumstances that she once more attacked the subject. She had been sitting with her niece in the evening; only on this occasion, as the night was not so warm, the lamp had been lighted, and Catherine had placed herself near it with a morsel of fancy-work. Mrs. Penniman went and sat alone for half an hour on the balcony; then she came in, moving vaguely about the room. At last she sank into a seat near Catherine, with clasped hands, and a little look of excitement.

"Shall you be angry if I speak to you again about *him?*" she asked.

Catherine looked up at her quietly. "Who is *he?*"

"He whom you once loved."

"I shall not be angry, but I shall not like it."

"He sent you a message," said Mrs. Penniman. "I promised him to deliver it, and I must keep my promise."

In all these years Catherine had had time to forget how little she had to thank her aunt for in the season of her misery; she had long ago forgiven Mrs. Penniman for taking too much upon herself. But for a moment this attitude of interposition and disinterestedness, this carrying of messages and redeeming of promises, brought back the sense that her companion was a dangerous woman. She had said she would not be angry; but for an instant she felt sore. "I don't care what you do with your promise!" she answered.

Mrs. Penniman, however, with her high conception of the sanctity of pledges, carried her point. "I have gone too far to retreat," she said, though precisely what this meant she was not at pains to explain. "Mr. Townsend wishes most particularly to see you, Catherine; he believes that if you knew how much, and why, he wishes it, you would consent to do so."

"There can be no reason," said Catherine; "no good reason."

"His happiness depends upon it. Is not that a good reason?" asked Mrs. Penniman, impressively.

"Not for me. My happiness does not."

"I think you will be happier after you have seen him. He is going away again—going to resume his wanderings. It is a very lonely, restless, joyless life. Before he goes he wishes to speak to you; it is a fixed idea with him—he is always thinking of it. He has something very important to say to you. He believes that you never understood him—that you never judged him rightly, and the belief has always weighed upon him terribly. He wishes to justify himself; he believes that in a very few words he could do so. He wishes to meet you as a friend."

Catherine listened to this wonderful speech without pausing in her work; she had now had several days to accustom herself to think of Morris Townsend again as an actuality. When it was over she said simply, "Please say to Mr. Townsend that I wish he would leave me alone."

She had hardly spoken when a sharp, firm ring at the door vibrated through the summer night. Catherine looked up at the clock; it marked a quarter past nine—a very late hour for visitors, especially in the empty condition of the town. Mrs. Penniman at the same moment gave a little start, and then Catherine's eyes turned quickly to her aunt. They met Mrs. Penniman's, and sounded them for a moment sharply. Mrs. Penniman was blushing; her look was a conscious one; it seemed to confess something.

Catherine guessed its meaning, and rose quickly from her chair.

"Aunt Penniman," she said, in a tone that scared her companion, "have you taken the *liberty* . . . ?"

"My dearest Catherine," stammered Mrs. Penniman, "just wait till you see him!"

Catherine had frightened her aunt, but she was also frightened herself; she was on the point of rushing to give orders to the servant, who was passing to the door, to admit no one; but the fear of meeting her visitor checked her.

"Mr. Morris Townsend."

This was what she heard, vaguely but recognizably, articulated by the domestic, while she hesitated. She had her back turned to the door of the parlor, and for some moments she kept it turned, feeling that he had come in. He had not spoken, however, and at last she faced about. Then she saw a gentleman standing in the middle of the room, from which her aunt had discreetly retired.

She would never have known him. He was forty-five years old, and his figure was not that of the straight, slim young man she remembered. But it was a very fine presence, and a fair and lustrous beard, spreading itself upon a well-presented chest, contributed to its effect. After a moment Catherine recognized the upper half of the face, which, though her visitor's clustering locks had grown thin, was still remarkably handsome. He stood in a deeply deferential attitude, with his eyes on her face. "I have ventured—I have ventured"; he said, and then he paused, looking about him, as if he expected her to ask him to sit down. It was the old voice; but it had not the old charm. Catherine, for a minute, was conscious of a distinct determination not to invite him to take a seat. Why had he come? It was wrong for him to come. Morris was embarrassed, but Catherine gave him no help. It was not that she was glad of his embarrassment; on the contrary, it excited all her own liabilities of this kind, and gave her great pain. But how could she welcome him when she felt so vividly that he ought not to have come? "I wanted so much—I was determined," Morris went on. But he stopped again; it was not easy. Catherine still said nothing, and he may well have recalled with apprehension her ancient faculty of silence. She continued to look at him, however, and as she did so she made the strangest observation. It seemed to be he, and yet not he; it was the man who had been everything, and yet this person was nothing. How long ago it was—how old she had grown—how much she had lived! She had lived on something that was connected with *him,* and she had consumed it in doing so. This person did not look unhappy. He was fair and well-preserved, perfectly dressed, mature and complete. As Catherine looked at him, the story of his life defined itself in his eyes; he had made himself comfortable, and he had never been caught. But even while her perception opened itself to this, she had no desire to catch him; his presence was painful to her, and she only wished he would go.

"Will you not sit down?" he asked.

"I think we had better not," said Catherine.

"I offend you by coming?" He was very grave; he spoke in a tone of the richest respect.

"I don't think you ought to have come."

"Did not Mrs. Penniman tell you—did she not give you my message?"

"She told me something, but I did not understand."

"I wish you would let *me* tell you—let me speak for myself."

"I don't think it is necessary," said Catherine.

"Not for you, perhaps, but for me. It would be a great satisfaction—and I have not many." He seemed to be coming nearer; Catherine turned away. "Can we not be friends again?" he asked.

"We are not enemies," said Catherine. "I have none but friendly feelings to you."

"Ah, I wonder whether you know the happiness it gives me to hear you say that!" Catherine uttered no intimation that she measured the influence of her words; and he presently went on, "You have not changed—the years have passed happily for you."

"They have passed very quietly," said Catherine.

"They have left no marks; you are admirably young." This time he succeeded in coming nearer—he was close to her; she saw his glossy perfumed beard, and his eyes above it looking strange and hard. It was very different from his old—from his young—face. If she had first seen him this way she would not have liked him. It seemed to her that he was smiling, or trying to smile. "Catherine," he said, lowering his voice, "I have never ceased to think of you."

"Please don't say these things," she answered.

"Do you hate me?"

"Oh no," said Catherine.

Something in her tone discouraged him, but in a moment he recovered himself. "Have you still some kindness for me, then?"

"I don't know why you have come here to ask me such things!" Catherine exclaimed.

"Because for many years it has been the desire of my life that we should be friends again."

"That is impossible."

"Why so? Not if you will allow it."

"I will not allow it," said Catherine.

He looked at her again in silence. "I see; my presence troubles you and pains you. I will go away; but you must give me leave to come again."

"Please don't come again," she said.

"Never?—never?"

She made a great effort; she wished to say something that would make it impossible he should ever again cross her threshold. "It is wrong of you. There is no propriety in it—no reason for it."

"Ah, dearest lady, you do me injustice!" cried Morris Townsend. "We have only waited, and now we are free."

"You treated me badly," said Catherine.

"Not if you think of it rightly. You had your quiet life with your father—which was just what I could not make up my mind to rob you of."

"Yes; I had that."

Morris felt it to be a considerable damage to his cause that he could not add that she had had something more besides; for it is needless to say that he had learned the contents of Doctor Sloper's will. He was, nevertheless, not at a loss. "There are worse fates than that!" he exclaimed, with expression; and he might have been supposed to refer to his own unprotected situation. Then he added, with a deeper tenderness, "Catherine, have you never forgiven me?"

"I forgave you years ago, but it is useless for us to attempt to be friends."

"Not if we forget the past. We have still a future, thank God!"

"I can't forget—I don't forget," said Catherine. "You treated me too badly. I felt it very much; I felt it for years." And then she went on, with her wish to show him that he must not come to her this way, "I can't begin again—I can't take it up. Everything is dead and buried. It was too serious; it made a great change in my life. I never expected to see you here."

"Ah, you are angry!" cried Morris, who wished immensely that he could extort some flash of passion from her calmness. In that case he might hope.

"No, I am not angry. Anger does not last that way for years. But there are other things. Impressions last, when they have been strong. But I can't talk."

Morris stood stroking his beard, with a clouded eye. "Why have you never married?" he asked, abruptly. "You have had opportunities."

"I didn't wish to marry."

"Yes, you are rich, you are free; you had nothing to gain."

"I had nothing to gain," said Catherine.

Morris looked vaguely round him, and gave a deep sigh. "Well, I was in hopes that we might still have been friends."

"I meant to tell you, by my aunt, in answer to your message—if you had waited for an answer—that it was unnecessary for you to come in that hope."

"Good-bye, then," said Morris. "Excuse my indiscretion."

He bowed, and she turned away—standing there, averted, with her eyes on the ground, for some moments after she had heard him close the door of the room.

In the hall he found Mrs. Penniman, fluttered and eager; she appeared to have been hovering there under the irreconcilable promptings of her curiosity and her dignity.

"That was a precious plan of yours!" said Morris, clapping on his hat.

"Is she so hard?" asked Mrs. Penniman.

"She doesn't care a button for me—with her confounded little dry manner."

"Was it very dry?" pursued Mrs. Penniman, with solicitude.

Morris took no notice of her question; he stood musing an instant, with his hat on. "But why the deuce, then, would she never marry?"

"Yes—why indeed?" sighed Mrs. Penniman. And then, as if from a sense of the inadequacy of this explanation, "But you will not despair—you will come back?"

"Come back? Damnation!" And Morris Townsend strode out of the house, leaving Mrs. Penniman staring.

Catherine, meanwhile, in the parlor, picking up her morsel of fancy-work, had seated herself with it again—for life, as it were.

PASSAGE ON *WASHINGTON SQUARE* FROM JAMES'S NOTEBOOKS

February 21st, 1879: Mrs. Kemble told me last evening the history of her brother H.'s engagement to Miss T. H.K. was a young ensign in a marching regiment, very handsome ('beautiful') said Mrs. K., but very luxurious and selfish, and without a penny to his name. Miss T. was a dull, plain, common-place girl, only daughter of the Master of King's Coll., Cambridge, who had a handsome private fortune (£4000 a year). She was very much in love with H.K., and was of that slow, sober, dutiful nature that an impression once made upon her, was made for ever. Her father disapproved strongly (and justly) of the engagement and informed her that if she married young K. he would not leave her a penny of his money. It was only in her money that H. was interested; he wanted a rich wife who would enable him to live at his ease and pursue his pleasures. Miss T. was in much tribulation and she asked Mrs. K. what she would advise her to do—Henry K. having taken the ground that if she would hold on and marry him the old Doctor would after a while relent and they should get the money. (It was in this belief that he was holding on to her.) Mrs. K. advised the young girl by *no means* to marry her brother. 'If your father does relent and you are well off, he will make you a kindly enough husband, so long as all goes well. But if he should not, and you were to be poor, your lot would be miserable. *Then* my brother would be a very uncomfortable companion—*then* he would visit upon you his disappointment and discontent.' Miss T. reflected a while; and then, as she was much in love with

<him>, she determined to disobey her father and take the consequences. Meanwhile H.K., however, had come to the conclusion that the father's forgiveness was not to be counted upon—that his attitude was very firm and that if they should marry, he would never see the money. *Then* all his effort was to disentangle himself. He went off, shook himself free of the engagement, let the girl go. She was deeply wounded—they separated. Some few years elapsed—her father died and she came into his fortune. She never received the addresses of another man—she always cared in secret for Henry K.—but she was determined to remain unmarried. K. lived about the world in different military stations, and at last, at the end of 10 years (or more), came back to England—still a handsome, selfish, impecunious soldier. One of his other sisters (Mrs. S.) then attempted to bring on the engagement again—knowing that Miss T. still cared for him. She tried to make Mrs. K. join her in this undertaking, but the latter refused, saying that it was an ignoble speculation and that her brother had forfeited every claim to being thought well of by Miss T. But K. again, on his own responsibility, paid his addresses to Miss T. She refused him—it was too late. And yet, said Mrs. K., she cared for him—and she would have married no other man. But H.K.'s selfishness had over-reached itself and this was the retribution of time.

EDITOR'S NOTE

The notebook entry alone survives to give us the genesis of *Washington Square*. No preface was written for the book by James, since he excluded this short novel from the highly selective New York Edition, from which he excluded also all his other novels and nearly all his tales which had the American scene for their setting. We can speculate that the reason for this was that he wanted the New York Edition to represent only Henry James the "cosmopolitan" rather than the American novelist. Another reason was that he considered *Washington Square* too slight a work, one of a group of three short "potboilers" written hastily in the late 1870's when "Daisy Miller" created a demand by editors for more of his fiction. James wrote *Confidence* for *Scribner's, The Europeans* for the *Atlantic Monthly* and *Washington Square* for *Harper's* where it was serialized with illustrations by George Du Maurier in 1880.

Frances Anne Kemble, the actress, who was 69 when Henry James got the anecdote from her which is given in his note, was to be for the rest of her life a close friend of the novelist. He spoke of her as having a "deep, rich, human nature" and it was his habit regularly to forsake many bright firesides in Victorian London to spend quiet evenings at Mrs. Kemble's home, listening to her memories of other days and her penetrating comments on the life of her time. The great actress had lived intensely and fully on both sides of the Atlantic in an age when women were not supposed to have careers or to move independently in the world. James's tribute to her, written just after her death in 1893, in his *Essays in London,* is a deeply felt and vivid portrait. The notebook entry shows how James's imagination, playing over a theme in an English setting, could refine and translate it into the Washington Square of his own childhood.

THE ASPERN PAPERS

1888

I

I HAD TAKEN Mrs. Prest into my confidence; without her in truth I should have made but little advance, for the fruitful idea in the whole business dropped from her friendly lips. It was she who found the short cut and loosed the Gordian knot. It is not supposed easy for women to rise to the large free view of anything, anything to be done; but they sometimes throw off a bold conception—such as a man wouldn't have risen to—with singular serenity. "Simply make them take you in on the footing of a lodger"—I don't think that unaided I should have risen to that. I was beating about the bush, trying to be ingenious, wondering by what combination of arts I might become an acquaintance, when she offered this happy suggestion that the way to become an acquaintance was first to become an intimate. Her actual knowledge of the Misses Bordereau was scarcely larger than mine, and indeed I had brought with me from England some definite facts that were new to her. Their name had been mixed up ages before with one of the greatest names of the century, and they now lived obscurely in Venice, lived on very small means, unvisited, unapproachable, in a sequestered and dilapidated old palace: this was the substance of my friend's impression of them. She herself had been established in Venice some fifteen years and had done a great deal of good there; but the circle of her benevolence had never embraced the two shy, mysterious and, as was somehow supposed, scarcely respectable Americans—they were believed to have lost in their long exile all national quality, besides being as their name implied of some remoter French affiliation—who asked no favours and desired no attention. In the early years of her residence she had made an attempt to see them, but this had been successful only as regards the little one, as Mrs. Prest called the niece; though in fact I afterwards found her the bigger of the two in inches. She had heard Miss Bordereau was ill and had a suspicion she was in want, and had gone to the house to offer aid, so that if there were suffering, American suffering in particular, she shouldn't have it on her conscience. The "little one" had received her in the great cold tarnished Venetian *sala,* the central hall of the house, paved with marble and roofed with dim cross-beams, and hadn't even asked her to sit down. This was not encouraging for me, who wished to sit so fast, and I remarked as much to Mrs. Prest. She replied, however, with profundity "Ah, but there's all the difference: I went to confer a favour and you'll go to ask one. If they're proud you'll be on the right side." And she offered to show me their house to begin with—to row me thither in her gondola. I let her know I had already been to look at it half a dozen times; but I accepted her invitation, for it charmed me to hover about the place. I had made my way to it the day after my arrival in Venice—it had been described to me in advance by the friend in England to whom I owed definite information as to their possession of the papers—laying siege to it with my eyes while I considered my plan of campaign. Jeffrey Aspern had never been in it that I knew of, but some note of his voice seemed to abide there by a roundabout implication and in a "dying fall."

Mrs. Prest knew nothing about the papers, but was interested in my curiosity, as always in the joys and sorrows of her friends. As we went, however, in her gondola, gliding there under the sociable hood with the bright Venetian picture framed on either side by the moveable window, I saw how my eagerness amused her and that she found my interest in my possible spoil a fine case of monomania. "One would think you expected from it the answer to the riddle of the universe," she said; and I denied the impeachment only by replying that if I had to choose between that precious solution and a bundle of Jeffrey Aspern's letters I knew indeed which would appear to me the greater boon. She pretended to make light of his genius and I took no pains to defend him. One doesn't defend one's god: one's god is in himself a defence. Besides, today, after his long comparative obscuration, he hangs high in the heaven of our literature for all the world to see; he's a part of the light by which we walk. The most I said was that he was no doubt not a woman's poet: to which she rejoined aptly enough that he had been at least Miss Bordereau's. The strange thing had been for me to discover in England that she was still alive: it was as if I had been told Mrs. Siddons was, or Queen Caroline, or the famous Lady Hamilton, for it seemed to me that she belonged to a generation as extinct. "Why she must be tremendously old—at least a hundred," I had said; but on coming to consider dates I saw it not strictly involved that she should have far exceeded the common span. None the less she was of venerable age and her relations with Jeffrey Aspern had occurred in her early womanhood. "That's her excuse," said Mrs. Prest half sententiously and yet also somewhat as if she were ashamed of making a speech so little in the real tone of Venice. As if a woman needed an excuse for having loved the divine poet! He had been not only one of the most brilliant minds of his day—and in those years, when the century was young, there were, as every one knows, many—but one of the most genial men and one of the handsomest.

The niece, according to Mrs. Prest, was of minor antiquity, and the conjecture was risked that she was only a grand-niece. This was possible; I had nothing but my share in the very limited knowledge of my English fellow-worshipper John Cumnor, who had never seen the couple. The world, as I say, had recognised Jeffrey Aspern, but Cumnor and I had recognised him most. The multitude to-day flocked to his temple, but of that temple he and I regarded ourselves as the appointed ministers. We held, justly, as I think, that we had done more for his memory than any one else, and had done it simply by opening lights into his life. He had nothing to fear from us because he had nothing to fear from the truth, which alone at such a distance of time we could be interested in establishing. His early death had been the only dark spot, as it were, on his fame, unless the papers in Miss Bordereau's hands should perversely bring out others. There had been an impression about 1825 that he had "treated her badly," just as there had been an impression that he had "served," as the London populace says, several other ladies in the same masterful way. Each of these cases Cumnor and I had been able to investigate, and we had never failed to acquit him conscientiously of any grossness. I judged him perhaps more indulgently than my friend; certainly, at any rate, it appeared to me that no man could have walked straighter in the given circumstances. These had been almost always difficult and dangerous. Half the women of his time, to speak liberally, had flung themselves at his head, and while the fury raged—the more that it was very catching—accidents, some of them grave, had not failed to occur. He was not a woman's poet, as I had said to Mrs. Prest, in the modern phase of his reputation; but the situation had been different when the man's own voice was mingled with his song. That voice, by every testimony, was one of the most charming ever heard. "Orpheus and the Mænads!" had been of course my foreseen judgement when first I turned over his correspondence. Almost all the Mænads were unreasonable and many of them unbearable, it struck me that he had been kinder and more considerate than in his place—if I could imagine myself in any such box—I should have found the trick of.

It was certainly strange beyond all strangeness, and I shall not take up space with attempting to explain it, that whereas among all these other relations and in these other directions of research we had to deal with phantoms and dust, the mere echoes of echoes, the one living source of information that had lingered on into our time had been unheeded by us. Every one of Aspern's contemporaries had, according to our belief, passed away; we had not been able to look into a single pair of eyes into which his had looked or to feel a transmitted contact in any aged hand that his had touched. Most dead of all did poor Miss Bordereau appear, and yet she alone had survived. We exhausted in the course of months our wonder that we had not found her out sooner, and the substance of our explanation was that she had kept so quiet. The poor lady on the whole had had reason for doing so. But it was a revelation to us that self-effacement on such a scale had been possible in the latter half of the nineteenth century—the age of newspapers and telegrams and photographs and interviewers. She had taken no great trouble for it either—hadn't hidden herself away in an undiscoverable hole, had boldly settled down in a city of exhibition. The one apparent secret of her safety had been that Venice contained so many much greater curiosities. And then accident had somehow favoured her, as was shown for example in the fact that Mrs. Prest had never happened to name her to me, though I had spent three weeks in Venice—under her nose, as it were—five years before. My friend indeed had not named her much to any one; she appeared almost to have forgotten the fact of her continuance. Of course Mrs. Prest hadn't the nerves of an editor. It was meanwhile no explanation of the old woman's having eluded us to say that she lived abroad, for our researches had again and again taken us—not only by correspondence but by personal enquiry—to France, to Germany, to Italy, in which countries, not counting his important stay in England, so many of the too few years of Aspern's career had been spent. We were glad to think at least that in all our promulgations—some people now consider I believe that we have overdone them—we had only touched in passing and in the most discreet manner on Miss Bordereau's connexion. Oddly enough, even if we had had the material—and we had often wondered what could have become of it—this would have been the most difficult episode to handle.

The gondola stopped, the old palace was there; it was a house of the class which in Venice carries even in extreme dilapidation the dignified name. "How charming! It's gray and pink!" my companion exclaimed; and that is the most comprehensive description of it. It was not particularly old, only two or three centuries; and it had an air not so much of decay as of quiet discouragement, as if it had rather missed its career. But its wide front, with a stone balcony from end to end of the *piano nobile* or most important floor, was architectural enough, with the aid of various pilasters and arches; and the stucco with which in the intervals it had long ago been endued was rosy in the April afternoon. It overlooked a clean melancholy rather lonely canal, which had a narrow *riva* or convenient footway on either side. "I don't know why—there are no brick gables," said Mrs. Prest, "but this corner has seemed to me before more Dutch than Italian, more like Amsterdam than like Venice. It's eccentrically neat, for reasons of its own; and though you may pass on foot scarcely any one ever thinks of doing so. It's as negative—considering *where* it is—as a Protestant Sunday. Perhaps the people are afraid of the Misses Bordereau. I dare say they have the reputation of witches."

I forget what answer I made to this—I was given up to two other reflexions. The first of these was that if the old lady lived in such a big and imposing house she couldn't be in any sort of misery and therefore wouldn't be tempted by a chance to let a couple of rooms. I expressed this fear to Mrs. Prest, who gave me a very straight answer. "If she didn't live in a big house how could it be a question of her having rooms to spare? If she were not amply lodged you'd lack ground to approach her. Besides, a big house here, and especially in this *quartier perdu,* proves nothing at all: it's perfectly consistent with a state of penury. Dilapidated old palazzi, if you'll go out of the way for them, are to be had for five shillings a year. And as for the people who live in them—no, until you've explored Venice socially as much as I have, you can form no idea of their domestic desolation. They live on nothing, for they've nothing to live on." The other idea that had come into my head was connected with a high blank wall which appeared to confine an expanse of ground on one side of the house. Blank I call it, but it was figured over with the patches that please a painter, repaired breaches, crumblings of plaster, extrusions of brick that had turned pink with time; while a few thin trees, with the poles of certain rickety trellises, were visible over the top. The place was a garden and apparently attached to the house. I suddenly felt that so attached it gave me my pretext.

I sat looking out on all this with Mrs. Prest (it was covered with the golden glow of Venice) from the shade of our *felze,* and she asked me if I would go in then, while she waited for me, or come back another time. At first I couldn't decide—it was doubtless very weak of me. I wanted still to think I *might* get a footing, and was afraid to meet failure, for it would leave me, as I remarked to my companion, without another arrow for my bow. "Why not another?" she enquired as I sat there hesitating and thinking it over; and she wished to know why even now and before taking the trouble of becoming an inmate—which might be wretchedly uncomfortable after all, even if it succeeded—I hadn't the resource of simply offering them a sum of money down. In that way I might get what I wanted without bad nights.

"Dearest lady," I exclaimed, "excuse the impatience of my tone when I suggest that you must have forgotten the very fact—surely I communicated it to you—which threw me on your ingenuity. The old woman won't have her relics and tokens so much as spoken of; they're personal, delicate, intimate, and she hasn't the feelings of the day, God bless her! If I should sound that note first I should certainly spoil the game. I can arrive at my spoils only by putting her off her guard, and I can put her off her guard only by ingratiating diplomatic arts. Hypocrisy, duplicity are my only chance. I'm sorry for it, but there's no baseness I wouldn't commit for Jeffrey Aspern's sake. First I must take tea with her—then tackle the main job." And I told over what had happened to John Cumnor on his respectfully writing to her. No notice whatever had been taken of his first letter, and the second had been answered very sharply, in six lines, by the niece. "Miss Bordereau requested her to say that she couldn't imagine what he meant by troubling them. They had none of Mr. Aspern's 'literary remains,' and if they *had* had wouldn't have dreamed of showing them to any one on any account whatever. She couldn't imagine what he was talking about and begged he would let her alone." I certainly didn't want to be met that way.

"Well," said Mrs. Prest after a moment and all provokingly, "perhaps they really haven't anything. If they deny it flat how are you sure?"

"John Cumnor's sure, and it would take me long to tell you how his conviction, or his very strong presumption—strong enough to stand against the old lady's not unnatural fib—has built itself up. Besides, he makes much of the internal evidence of the niece's letter."

"The internal evidence?"

"Her calling him 'Mr. Aspern.'"

"I don't see what that proves."

"It proves familiarity, and familiarity implies the possession of mementoes, of tangible objects. I can't tell you how that 'Mr.' affects me—how it bridges over the gulf of time and brings our hero near to me—nor what an edge it gives to my desire to see Juliana. You don't say 'Mr.' Shakespeare."

"Would I, any more, if I had a box full of his letters?"

"Yes, if he had been your lover and some one wanted them!" And I added that John Cumnor was so convinced, and so all the more convinced by Miss Bordereau's tone, that he would have come himself to Venice on the undertaking were it not for the obstacle of his having, for any confidence, to disprove his identity with the person who had written to them, which the old ladies would be sure to suspect in spite of dissimulation and a change of name. If they were to ask him point-blank if he were not their snubbed correspondent it would be too awkward for him to lie; whereas I was fortunately not tied in that way. I was a fresh hand—I could protest without lying.

"But you'll have to take a false name," said Mrs. Prest. "Juliana lives out of the world as much as it is possible to live, but she has none the less probably heard of Mr. Aspern's editors. She perhaps possesses what you've published."

"I've thought of that," I returned; and I drew out of my pocketbook a visiting card neatly engraved with a well-chosen *nom de guerre*.

"You're very extravagant—it adds to your immorality. You might have done it in pencil or ink," said my companion.

"This looks more genuine."

"Certainly you've the courage of your curiosity. But it will be awkward about your letters; they won't come to you in that mask."

"My banker will take them in and I shall go every day to get them. It will give me a little walk."

"Shall you depend all on that?" asked Mrs. Prest. "Aren't you coming to see me?"

"Oh you'll have left Venice for the hot months long before there are any results. I'm prepared to roast all summer—as well as through the long hereafter perhaps you'll say! Meanwhile John Cumnor will bombard me with letters addressed, in my feigned name, to the care of the padrona."

"She'll recognise his hand," my companion suggested.

"On the envelope he can disguise it."

"Well, you're a precious pair! Doesn't it occur to you that even if you're able to say you're not Mr. Cumnor in person they may still suspect you of being his emissary?"

"Certainly, and I see only one way to parry that."

"And what may that be?"

I hesitated a moment. "To make love to the niece."

"Ah," cried my friend, "wait till you see her!"

II

"I MUST WORK the garden—I must work the garden," I said to myself five minutes later and while I waited, upstairs, in the long, dusky sala, where the bare scagliola floor gleamed vaguely in a chink of the closed shutters. The place was impressive, yet looked somehow cold and cautious. Mrs. Prest had floated away, giving me a rendezvous at the end of half an hour by some neighbouring water-steps; and I had been let into the house, after pulling the rusty bell-wire, by a small red-headed and white-faced maid-servant, who was very young and not ugly and wore clicking pattens and a shawl in the fashion of a hood. She had not contented herself with opening the door from above by the usual arrangement of a creaking pulley, though she had looked down at me first from an upper window, dropping the cautious challenge which in Italy precedes the act of admission. I was irritated as a general thing by this survival of mediæval manners, though as so fond, if yet so special, an antiquarian I suppose I ought to have liked it; but, with my resolve to be genial from the threshold at any price, I took my false card out of my pocket and held it up to her, smiling as if it were a magic token. It had the effect of one indeed, for it brought her, as I say, all the way down. I begged her to hand it to her mistress, having first written on it in Italian the words: "Could you very kindly see a gentleman, a travelling American, for a moment?" The little maid wasn't hostile—even that was perhaps something gained. She coloured, she smiled and looked both frightened and pleased. I could see that my arrival was a great affair, that visits in such a house were rare and that she was a person who would have liked a bustling place. When she pushed forward the heavy door behind me I felt my foot in the citadel and promised myself ever so firmly to keep it there. She pattered across the damp stony lower hall and I followed her up the high staircase—stonier still, as it seemed—without an invitation. I think she had meant I should wait for her below, but such was not my idea, and I took up my station in the sala. She flitted, at the far end of it, into impenetrable regions, and I looked at the place with my heart beating as I had known it to do in dentists' parlours. It had a gloomy grandeur, but owed its character almost all to its noble shape and to the fine architectural doors, as high as those of grand frontages, which, leading into the various rooms, repeated themselves on either side at intervals. They were surmounted with old faded painted escutcheons, and here and there in the spaces between them hung brown pictures, which I noted as speciously bad, in battered and tarnished frames that were yet more desirable than the canvases themselves. With the exception of several straw-bottomed chairs that kept their backs to the wall the grand obscure vista contained little else to minister to effect. It was evidently never used save as a passage, and scantly even as that. I may add that by the time the door through which the maid-servant had escaped opened again my eyes had grown used to the want of light.

I hadn't meanwhile meant by my private ejaculation that I must myself cultivate the soil of the tangled enclosure which lay beneath the windows, but the lady who came toward me from the distance over the hard shining floor might have supposed as much from the way in which, as I went rapidly to meet her, I exclaimed, taking care to speak Italian: "The garden, the garden—do me the pleasure to tell me if it's yours!"

She stopped short, looking at me with wonder; and then, "Nothing here is mine," she answered in English, coldly and sadly.

"Oh you're English; how delightful!" I ingenuously cried. "But surely the garden belongs to the house?"

"Yes, but the house doesn't belong to me." She was a long lean pale person, habited apparently in a dull-coloured dressing-gown, and she spoke very simply and mildly. She didn't ask me to sit down, any more than years before—if she were the niece—she had asked Mrs. Prest, and we stood face to face in the empty pompous hall.

"Well then, would you kindly tell me to whom I must address myself? I'm afraid you will think me horribly intrusive, but you know I *must* have a garden—upon my honour I must!"

Her face was not young, but it was candid; it was not fresh, but it was clear. She had large eyes which were not bright, and a great deal of hair which was not "dressed," and long fine hands which were—possibly—not clean. She clasped these members almost convulsively as, with a confused alarmed look, she broke out: "Oh don't take it away from us; we like it ourselves!"

"You have the use of it then?"

"Oh yes. If it wasn't for that—!" And she gave a wan vague smile.

"Isn't it a luxury, precisely? That's why, intending to be in Venice some weeks, possibly all summer, and having some literary work, some reading and writing to do, so that I must be quiet and yet if possible a great deal in the open air—that's why I've felt a garden to be really indispensable. I appeal to your own experience," I went on with as sociable a smile as I could risk. "Now can't I look at yours?"

"I don't know, I don't understand," the poor woman murmured, planted there and letting her weak wonder deal—helplessly enough, as I felt—with my strangeness.

"I mean only from one of those windows—such grand ones as you have here—if you'll let me open the shutters." And I walked toward the back of the house. When I had advanced halfway I stopped and waited as in the belief she would accompany me. I had been of necessity quite abrupt, but I strove at the same time to give her the impression of extreme courtesy. "I've looked at furnished rooms all over the place, and it seems impossible to find any with a garden attached. Naturally in a place like Venice gardens are rare. It's absurd if you like, for a man, but I can't live without flowers."

"There are none to speak of down there." She came nearer, as if, though she mistrusted me, I had drawn her by an invisible thread. I went on again, and she continued as she followed me: "We've a few, but they're very common. It costs too much to cultivate them; one has to have a man."

"Why shouldn't I be the man?" I asked. "I'll work without wages; or rather I'll put in a gardener. You shall have the sweetest flowers in Venice."

She protested against this with a small quaver of sound that might have been at the same time a gush of rapture for my free sketch. Then she gasped: "We don't know you—we don't know you."

"You know me as much as I know you, or rather much more, because you know my name. And if you're English I'm almost a countryman."

"We're not English," said my companion, watching me in practical submission while I threw open the shutters of one of the divisions of the wide high window.

"You speak the language so beautifully: might I ask what you are?" Seen from above the garden was in truth shabby, yet I felt at a glance that it had great capabilities. She made no rejoinder, she was so lost in her blankness and gentleness, and I exclaimed, "You don't mean to say you're also by chance American?"

"I don't know. We used to be."

"Used to be? Surely you haven't changed?"

"It's so many years ago. We don't seem to be anything now."

"So many years that you've been living here? Well, I

don't wonder at that; it's a grand old house. I suppose you all use the garden," I went on, "but I assure you I shouldn't be in your way. I'd be very quiet and stay quite in one corner."

"We all use it?" she repeated after me vaguely, not coming close to the window but looking at my shoes. She appeared to think me capable of throwing her out.

"I mean all your family—as many as you are."

"There's only one other than me. She's very old. She never goes down."

I feel again my thrill at this close identification of Juliana; in spite of which, however, I kept my head. "Only one other in all this great house!" I feigned to be not only amazed but almost scandalized. "Dear lady, you must have space then to spare!"

"To spare?" she repeated—almost as for the rich unwonted joy to her of spoken words.

"Why you surely don't live (two quiet women—I see *you* are quiet, at any rate) in fifty rooms!" Then with a burst of hope and cheer I put the question straight: "Couldn't you for a good rent *let* me two or three? That would set me up!"

I had now struck the note that translated my purpose, and I needn't reproduce the whole of the tune I played. I ended by making my entertainer believe me an undesigning person, though of course I didn't even attempt to persuade her I was not an eccentric one. I repeated that I had studies to pursue; that I wanted quiet; that I delighted in a garden and had vainly sought one up and down the city; that I would undertake that before another month was over the dear old house should be smothered in flowers. I think it was the flowers that won my suit, for I afterwards found that Miss Tina—for such the name of this high tremulous spinster proved somewhat incongruously to be—had an insatiable appetite for them. When I speak of my suit as won I mean that before I left her she had promised me she would refer the question to her aunt.

I invited information as to who her aunt might be and she answered "Why Miss Bordereau!" with an air of surprise, as if I might have been expected to know. There were contradictions like this in Miss Tina which, as I observed later, contributed to make her rather pleasingly incalculable and interesting. It was the study of the two ladies to live so that the world shouldn't talk of them or touch them, and yet they had never altogether accepted the idea that it didn't hear of them. In Miss Tina at any rate a grateful susceptibility to human contact had not died out, and contact of a limited order there would be if I should come to live in the house.

"We've never done anything of the sort; we've never had a lodger or any kind of inmate." So much as this she made a point of saying to me. "We're very poor, we live very badly—almost on nothing. The rooms are very bare—those you might take; they've nothing at all in them. I don't know how you'd sleep, how you'd eat."

"With your permission I could easily put in a bed and a few tables and chairs. *C'est la moindre des choses* and the affair of an hour or two. I know a little man from whom I can hire for a trifle what I should so briefly want, what I should use; my gondolier can bring the things round in his boat. Of course in this great house you must have a second kitchen, and my servant who's a wonderfully handy fellow"—this personage was an evocation of the moment—"can easily cook me a chop there. My tastes and habits are of the simplest; I live on flowers!" And then I ventured to add that if they were very poor it was all the more reason they should let their rooms. They were bad economists—I had never heard of such a waste of material.

I saw in a moment my good lady had never before been spoken to in any such fashion—with a humorous firmness that didn't exclude sympathy, that was quite founded on it. She might easily have told me that my sympathy was impertinent, but this by good fortune didn't occur to her. I left her with the understanding that she would submit the question to her aunt and that I might come back the next day for their decision.

"The aunt will refuse; she'll think the whole proceeding very *louche!*" Mrs. Prest declared shortly after this, when I had resumed my place in her gondola. She had put the idea into my head and now—so littlc are women to be counted on—she appeared to take a despondent view of it. Her pessimism provoked me and I pretended to have the best hopes; I went so far as to boast of a distinct prevision of success. Upon this Mrs. Prest broke out, "Oh I see what's in your head! You fancy you've made such an impression in five minutes that she's dying for you to come and can be depended on to bring the old one round. If you do get in you'll count it as a triumph."

I did count it as a triumph, but only for the commentator—in the last analysis—not for the man, who had not the tradition of personal conquest. When I went back on the morrow the little maid-servant conducted me straight through the long sala—it opened there as before in large perspective and was lighter now, which I thought a good omen—into the apartment from which the recipient of my former visit had emerged on that occasion. It was a spacious shabby parlour with a fine old painted ceiling under which a strange figure sat alone at one of the windows. They come back to me now almost with the palpitation they caused, the successive states marking my consciousness that as the door of the room closed behind me I was really face to face with the Juliana of some of Aspern's most exquisite and most renowned lyrics. I grew used to her afterwards, though never completely; but as she sat there before me my heart beat as fast as if the miracle of resurrection had taken place for my benefit. Her presence seemed somehow to contain and express his own, and I felt nearer to him at that first moment of seeing her than I ever had been before or ever have been since. Yes, I remembr my emotions in their order, even including a curious little tremor that took me when I saw the niece not to be there.

With her, the day before, I had become sufficiently familiar, but it almost exceeded my courage—much as I had longed for the event—to be left alone with so terrible a relic as the aunt. She was too strange, too literally resurgent. Then came a check from the perception that we weren't really face to face, inasmuch as she had over her eyes a horrible green shade which served for her almost as a mask. I believed for the instant that she had put it on expressly, so that from underneath it she might take me all in without my getting at herself. At the same time it created a presumption of some ghastly death's head lurking behind it. The divine Juliana as a grinning skull—the vision hung there until it passed. Then it came to me that she *was* tremendously old—so old that death might take her at any moment, before I should have time to compass my end. The next thought was a correction to that; it lighted up the situation. She would die next week, she would die to-morrow—then I could pounce on her possessions and ransack her drawers. Meanwhile she sat there neither moving nor speaking. She was very small and shrunken, bent forward with her hands in her lap. She was dressed in black and her head was wrapped in a piece of old black lace which showed no hair.

My emotion keeping me silent she spoke first, and the remark she made was exactly the most unexpected.

III

"OUR HOUSE is very far from the centre, but the little canal is very *comme il faut.*"

"It's the sweetest corner of Venice and I can imagine nothing more charming," I hastened to reply. The old lady's voice was very thin and weak, but it had an agreeable, cultivated murmur and there was wonder in the thought that that individual note had been in Jeffrey Aspern's ear.

"Please to sit down there. I hear very well," she said quietly, as if perhaps I had been shouting; and the chair she pointed to was at a certain distance. I took possession of it, assuring her I was perfectly aware of my intrusion and of my not having been properly introduced, and that I could but throw myself on her indulgence. Perhaps the other lady, the one I had had the honour of seeing the day before, would have explained to her about the garden. That was literally what had given me courage to take a step so unconventional. I had fallen in love at sight with the whole place—she herself was probably so used to it that she didn't know the impression it was capable of making on a stranger—and I had felt it really a case to risk something. Was her own kindness in receiving me a sign that I was not wholly out in my calculation? It would make me extremely happy to think so. I could give her my word of honour that I was a most respectable inoffensive person and that as a co-tenant of the palace, so to speak, they would be barely conscious of my existence. I would conform to any regulations, any restrictions, if they would only let me enjoy the garden. Moreover I should be delighted to give her references, guarantees; they would be of the very best, both in Venice and in England, as well as in America.

She listened to me in perfect stillness and I felt her look at me with great penetration, though I could see only the lower part of her bleached and shrivelled face. Independently of the refining process of old age it had a delicacy which once must have been great. She had been very fair, she had had a wonderful complexion. She was silent a little after I had ceased speaking; then she began: "If you're so fond of a garden why don't you go to *terra firma,* where there are so many far better than this?"

"Oh it's the combination!" I answered, smiling; and then with rather a flight of fancy; "It's the idea of a garden in the middle of the sea."

"This isn't the middle of the sea; you can't so much as see the water."

I stared a moment, wondering if she wished to convict me of fraud. "Can't see the water? Why, dear madam, I can come up to the very gate in my boat."

She appeared inconsequent, for she said vaguely in reply to this: "Yes, if you've got a boat. I haven't any; it's many years since I have been in one of the *gondole.*" She uttered these words as if they designed a curious far-away craft known to her only by hearsay.

"Let me assure you of the pleasure with which I would put mine at your service!" I returned. I had scarcely said this however before I became aware that the speech was in questionable taste and might also do me the injury of making me appear too eager, too possessed of a hidden motive. But the old woman remained impenetrable and her attitude worried me by suggesting that she had a fuller vision of me than I had of her. She gave me no thanks for my somewhat extravagant offer, but remarked that the lady I had seen the day before was her niece; she would presently come in. She had asked her to stay away a little on purpose—had had her reasons for seeing me first alone. She relapsed into silence and I turned over the fact of these unmentioned reasons and the question of what might come yet; also that of whether I might venture on some judicious remark in praise of her companion. I went so far as to say I should be delighted to see our absent friend again: she had been so very patient with me, considering how odd she must have thought me—a declaration which drew from Miss Bordereau another of her whimsical speeches.

"She has very good manners; I bred her up myself!" I was on the point of saying that that accounted for the easy grace of the niece, but I arrested myself in time, and the next moment the old woman went on: "I don't care who you may be—I don't want to know; it signifies very little to-day." This had all the air of being a formula of dismissal, as if her next words would be that I might take myself off now that she had had the amusement of looking on the face of such a monster of indiscretion. Therefore I was all the more surprised when she added in her soft venerable quaver: "You may have as many rooms as you like—if you'll pay me a good deal of money."

I hesitated but an instant, long enough to measure what she meant in particular by this condition. First it struck me that she must have really a large sum in her mind; then I reasoned quickly that her idea of a large sum would probably not correspond to my own. My deliberation, I think, was not so visible as to diminish the promptitude with which I replied: "I will pay with pleasure and of course in advance whatever you may think it proper to ask me."

"Well then, a thousand francs a month," she said instantly, while her baffling green shade continued to cover her attitude.

The figure, as they say, was startling and my logic had been at fault. The sum she had mentioned was, by the Venetian measure of such matters, exceedingly large; there was many an old palace in an out-of-the-way corner that I might on such terms have enjoyed the whole of by the year. But so far as my resources allowed I was prepared to spend money, and my decision was quickly taken. I would pay her with a smiling face what she asked, but in that case I would make it up by getting hold of my "spoils" for nothing. Moreover if she had asked five times as much I should have risen to the occasion, so odious would it have seemed to me to stand chaffering with Aspern's Juliana. It was queer enough to have a question of money with her at all. I assured her that her views perfectly met my own and that on the morrow I should have the pleasure of putting three months' rent into her hand. She received this announcement with apparent complacency and with no discoverable sense that after all it would become her to say that I ought to see the rooms first. This didn't occur to her, and indeed her serenity was mainly what I wanted. Our little agreement was just concluded when the door opened and the younger lady appeared on the threshold. As soon as Miss Bordereau saw her niece she cried out almost gaily: "He'll give three thousand—three thousand to-morrow!"

Miss Tina stood still, her patient eyes turning from one of us to the other; then she brought out, scarcely above her breath: "Do you mean francs?"

"Did you mean francs or dollars?" the old woman asked of me at this.

"I think francs were what you said," I sturdily smiled.

"That's very good," said Miss Tina, as if she had felt how over-reaching her own question might have looked.

"What do *you* know? You're ignorant," Miss Bordereau remarked; not with acerbity but with a strange soft coldness.

"Yes, of money—certainly of money!" Miss Tina hastened to concede.

"I'm sure you've your own fine branches of knowledge," I took the liberty of saying genially. There was something painful to me, somehow, in the turn the conversation had taken, in the discussion of dollars and francs.

"She had a very good education when she was young.

I looked into that myself," said Miss Bordereau. Then she added: "But she has learned nothing since."

"I have always been with *you,*" Miss Tina rejoined very mildly, and of a certainty with no intention of an epigram.

"Yes, but for that—!" her aunt declared with more satirical force. She evidently meant that but for this her niece would never have got on at all; the point of the observation however being lost on Miss Tina, though she blushed at hearing her history revealed to a stranger. Miss Bordereau went on, addressing herself to me: "And what time will you come to-morrow with the money?"

"The sooner the better. If it suits you I'll come at noon."

"I am always here, but I have my hours," said the old woman as if her convenience were not to be taken for granted.

"You mean the times when you receive?"

"I never receive. But I'll see you at noon when you come with the money."

"Very good, I shall be punctual." To which I added: "May I shake hands with you on our contract?" I thought there ought to be some little form; it would make me really feel easier, for I was sure there would be no other. Besides, though Miss Bordereau couldn't to-day be called personally attractive and there was something even in her wasted antiquity that bade one stand at one's distance, I felt an irresistible desire to hold in my own for a moment the hand Jeffrey Aspern had pressed.

For a minute she made no answer, and I saw that my proposal failed to meet with her approbation. She indulged in no movement of withdrawal, which I half expected; she only said coldly: "I belong to a time when that was not the custom."

I felt rather snubbed but I exclaimed good-humouredly to Miss Tina, "Oh you'll do as well!" I shook hands with her while she assented with a small flutter. "Yes, yes, to show it's all arranged!"

"Shall you bring the money in gold?" Miss Bordereau demanded as I was turning to the door.

I looked at her a moment. "Aren't you a little afraid, after all, of keeping such a sum as that in the house?" It was not that I was annoyed at her avidity, but was truly struck with the disparity between such a treasure and such scanty means of guarding it.

"Whom should I be afraid of if I'm not afraid of you?" she asked with her shrunken grimness.

"Ah well," I laughed, "I shall be in point of fact a protector and I'll bring gold if you prefer."

"Thank you," the old woman returned with dignity and with an inclination of her head which evidently signified my dismissal. I passed out of the room, thinking how hard it would be to circumvent her. As I stood in the sala again I saw that Miss Tina had followed me, and I supposed that as her aunt had neglected to suggest I should take a look at my quarters it was her purpose to repair the omission. But she made no such overture; she only stood there with a dim, though not a languid smile, and with an effect of irresponsible incompetent youth almost comically at variance with the faded facts of her person. She was not infirm, like her aunt, but she struck me as more deeply futile, because her inefficiency was inward, which was not the case with Miss Bordereau's. I waited to see if she would offer to show me the rest of the house but I didn't precipitate the question, inasmuch as my plan was from this moment to spend as much of my time as possible in her society. A minute indeed elapsed before I committed myself.

"I've had better fortune than I hoped. It was very kind of her to see me. Perhaps you said a good word for me."

"It was the idea of the money," said Miss Tina.

"And did you suggest that?"

"I told her you'd perhaps pay largely."

"What made you think that?"

"I told her I thought you were rich."

"And what put that into your head?"

"I don't know; the way you talked."

"Dear me, I must talk differently now," I returned. "I'm sorry to say it's not the case."

"Well," said Miss Tina, "I think that in Venice the *forestieri* in general often give a great deal for something that after all isn't much." She appeared to make this remark with a comforting intention, to wish to remind me that if I had been extravagant I wasn't foolishly singular. We walked together along the sala, and as I took its magnificent measure I said that I was afraid it wouldn't form a part of my *quartiere.* Were my rooms by chance to be among those that opened into it? "Not if you go above—to the second floor," she answered as if she had rather taken for granted I would know my proper place.

"And I infer that that's where your aunt would like me to be."

"She said your apartments ought to be very distinct."

"That certainly would be best." And I listened with respect while she told me that above I should be free to take whatever I might like; that there was another staircase, but only from the floor on which we stood, and that to pass from it to the garden-level or to come up to my lodging I should have in effect to cross the great hall. This was an immense point gained; I foresaw that it would constitute my whole leverage in my relations with the two ladies. When I asked Miss Tina how I was to manage at present to find my way up she replied with an access of that sociable shyness which constantly marked her manner:

"Perhaps you can't. I don't see—unless I should go with you." She evidently hadn't thought of this before.

We ascended to the upper floor and visited a long succession of empty rooms. The best of them looked over the garden; some of the others had above the opposite rough-tiled house-tops a view of the blue lagoon. They were all dusty and even a little disfigured with long neglect, but I saw that by spending a few hundred francs I should be able to make three or four of them habitable enough. My experiment was turning out costly, yet now that I had all but taken possession I ceased to allow this to trouble me. I mentioned to my companion a few of the things I should put in, but she replied rather more precipitately than usual that I might do exactly what I liked: she seemed to wish to notify me that the Misses Bordereau would take none but the most veiled interest in my proceedings. I guessed that her aunt had instructed her to adopt this tone, and I may as well say now that I came afterwards to distinguish perfectly (as I believed) between the speeches she made on her own responsibility and those the old woman imposed upon her. She took no notice of the unswept condition of the rooms and indulged neither in explanations nor in apologies. I said to myself that this was a sign Juliana and her niece—disenchanting idea!—were untidy persons with a low Italian standard; but I afterwards recognised that a lodger who had forced an entrance had no *locus standi* as a critic. We looked out of a good many windows, for there was nothing within the rooms to look at, and still I wanted to linger. I asked her what several different objects in the prospect might be, but in no case did she appear to know. She was evidently not familiar with the view—it was as if she had not looked at it for years—and I presently saw that she was too preoccupied with something else to pretend to care for it. Suddenly she said—the remark was not suggested:

"I don't know whether it will make any difference to you, but the money is for me."

"The money—?"

"The money you're going to bring."

"Why you'll make me wish to stay here two or three years!" I spoke as benevolently as possible, though it had begun to act on my nerves that these women so associated with Aspern should so constantly bring the pecuniary question back.

"That would be very good for me," she answered almost gaily.

"You put me on my honour!"

She looked as if she failed to understand this, but went on: "She wants me to have more. She thinks she's going to die."

"Ah not soon I hope!" I cried with genuine feeling. I had perfectly considered the possibility of her destroying her documents on the day she should feel her end at hand. I believed that she would cling to them till then, and I was as convinced of her reading Aspern's letters over every night or at least pressing them to her withered lips. I would have given a good deal for some view of those solemnities. I asked Miss Tina if her venerable relative were seriously ill, and she replied that she was only very tired—she had lived so extraordinarily long. That was what she said herself—she wanted to die for a change. Besides, all her friends had been dead for ages; either they ought to have remained or she ought to have gone. That was another thing her aunt often said: she was not at all resigned—resigned, that is, to life.

"But people don't die when they like, do they?" Miss Tina inquired. I took the liberty of asking why, if there was actually enough money to maintain both of them, there would not be more than enough in case of her being left alone. She considered this difficult problem a moment and then said: "Oh well, you know, she takes care of me. She thinks that when I'm alone I shall be a great fool and shan't know how to manage."

"I should have supposed rather that you took care of *her*. I'm afraid she's very proud."

"Why, have you discovered that already?" Miss Tina cried with a dimness of glad surprise.

"I was shut up with her there for a considerable time and she struck me, she interested me extremely. It didn't take me long to make my discovery. She won't have much to say to me while I'm here."

"No, I don't think she will," my companion averred.

"Do you suppose she has some suspicion of me?"

Miss Tina's honest eyes gave me no sign I had touched a mark. "I shouldn't think so—letting you in after all so easily."

"You call it easily? She has covered her risk," I said. "But where is it one could take an advantage of her?"

"I oughtn't to tell you if I knew, ought I?" And Miss Tina added, before I had time to reply to this, smiling dolefully: "Do you think we've any weak points?"

"That's exactly what I'm asking. You'd only have to mention them for me to respect them religiously."

She looked at me hereupon with that air of timid but candid and even gratified curiosity with which she had confronted me from the first; after which she said: "There's nothing to tell. We're terribly quiet. I don't know how the days pass. We've no life."

"I wish I might think I should bring you a little."

"Oh we know what we want," she went on. "It's all right."

There were twenty things I desired to ask her: how in the world they did live; whether they had any friends or visitors, any relations in America or in other countries. But I judged such probings premature; I must leave it to a later chance. "Well, don't *you* be proud," I contented myself with saying. "Don't hide from me altogether."

"Oh I must stay with my aunt," she returned without looking at me. And at the same moment, abruptly, without any ceremony of parting, she quitted me and disappeared, leaving me to make my own way downstairs. I stayed a while longer, wandering about the bright desert—the sun was pouring in—of the old house, thinking the situation over on the spot. Not even the pattering little *serva* came to look after me, and I reflected that after all this treatment showed confidence.

IV

PERHAPS it did, but all the same, six weeks later, towards the middle of June, the moment when Mrs. Prest undertook her annual migration, I had made no measurable advance. I was obliged to confess to her that I had no results to speak of. My first step had been unexpectedly rapid, but there was no appearance it would be followed by a second. I was a thousand miles from taking tea with my hostesses—that privilege of which, as I reminded my good friend, we both had had a vision. She reproached me with lacking boldness and I answered that even to be bold you must have an opportunity: you may push on through a breach, but you can't batter down a dead wall. She returned that the breach I had already made was big enough to admit an army and accused me of wasting precious hours in whimpering in her salon when I ought to have been carrying on the struggle in the field. It is true that I went to see her very often—all on the theory that it would console me (I freely expressed my discouragement) for my want of success on my own premises. But I began to feel that it didn't console me to be perpetually chaffed for my scruples, especially since I was really so vigilant; and I was rather glad when my ironic friend closed her house for the summer. She had expected to gather amusement from the drama of my intercourse with the Misses Bordereau, and was disappointed that the intercourse, and consequently the drama, had not come off. "They'll lead you on to your ruin," she said before she left Venice. "They'll get all your money without showing you a scrap." I think I settled down to my business with more concentration after her departure.

It was a fact that up to that time I had not, save on a single brief occasion, had even a moment's contact with my queer hostesses. The exception had occurred when I carried them according to my promise the terrible three thousand francs. Then I found Miss Tina awaiting me in the hall, and she took the money from my hand with a promptitude that prevented my seeing her aunt. The old lady had promised to receive me, yet apparently thought nothing of breaking that vow. The money was contained in a bag of chamois leather, of respectable dimensions, which my banker had given me, and Miss Tina had to make a big fist to receive it. This she did with extreme solemnity though I tried to treat the affair a little as a joke. It was in no jocular strain, yet it was with a clearness akin to a brightness that she enquired, weighing the money in her two palms: "Don't you think it's too much?" To which I replied that this would depend on the amount of pleasure I should get for it. Hereupon she turned away from me quickly, as she had done the day before, murmuring in a tone different from any she had used hitherto: "Oh pleasure, pleasure—there's no pleasure in this house!"

After that, for a long time, I never saw her, and I wondered the common chances of the day shouldn't have helped us to meet. It could only be evident that she was immensely on her guard against them; and in addition to this the house was so big that for each other we were lost in it. I used to look out for her hopefully as I crossed the sala in my comings and goings, but I was not rewarded with a glimpse of the tail of her dress. It was as if she never peeped out of her aunt's apartment. I used to wonder what she did there week after week and year after year. I had never met so stiff a policy of seclusion; it was more than keeping quiet—it was like hunted creatures feigning death. The two ladies appeared to have no visitors whatever and no sort of contact with the world. I judged at least that people couldn't have come to the house and that Miss Tina couldn't have gone out without my catching some view of it. I did what I disliked myself for doing—considering it but as once in a way: I questioned my servant about their habits and let him infer that I should be interested in any information he might glean. But he gleaned amazingly little for a knowing Venetian: it must be added that where there is a perpetual fast there are very few crumbs on the floor. His ability in other ways was sufficient, if not quite all I had attributed to him on the occasion of my first interview with Miss Tina. He had helped my gondolier to bring me round a boatload of furniture; and when these articles had been carried to the top of the palace and distributed according to our associated wisdom he organized my household with such dignity as answered to its being composed exclusively of himself. He made me in short as comfortable as I could be with my indifferent prospects. I should have been glad if he had fallen in love with Miss Bordereau's maid or, failing this, had taken her in aversion; either event might have brought about some catastrophe, and a catastrophe might have led to some parley. It was my idea that she would have been sociable, and I myself on various occasions saw her flit to and fro on domestic errands, so that I was sure she was accessible. But I tasted of no gossip from that fountain, and I afterwards learned that Pasquale's affections were fixed upon an object that made him heedless of other women. This was a young lady with a powdered face, a yellow cotton gown and much leisure, who used often to come to see him. She practised, at her convenience, the art of a stringer of beads—these ornaments are made in Venice to profusion; she had her pocket full of them and I used to find them on the floor of my apartment—and kept an eye on the possible rival in the house. It was not for me of course to make the domestics tattle, and I never said a word to Miss Bordereau's cook.

It struck me as a proof of the old woman's resolve to have nothing to do with me that she should never have sent me a receipt for my three months' rent. For some days I looked out for it and then, when I had given it up, wasted a good deal of time in wondering what her reason had been for neglecting so indispensable and familiar a form. At first I was tempted to send her a reminder; after which I put by the idea—against my judgement as to what was right in the particular case—on the general ground of wishing to keep quiet. If Miss Bordereau suspected me of ulterior aims she would suspect me less if I should be businesslike, and yet I consented not to be. It was possible she intended her omission as an impertinence, a visible irony, to show how she could overreach people who attempted to overreach her. On that hypothesis it was well to let her see that one didn't notice her little tricks. The real reading of the matter, I afterwards gathered, was simply the poor lady's desire to emphasise the fact that I was in the enjoyment of a favour as rigidly limited as it had been liberally bestowed. She had given me part of her house, but she wouldn't add to that so much as a morsel of paper with her name on it. Let me say that even at first this didn't make me too miserable, for the whole situation had the charm of its oddity. I foresaw that I should have a summer after my own literary heart, and the sense of playing with my opportunity was much greater after all than any sense of being played with. There could be no Venetian business without patience, and since I adored the place I was much more in the spirit of it for having laid in a large provision. That spirit kept me perpetual company and seemed to look out at me from the revived immortal face—in which all his genius shone—of the great poet who was my prompter. I had invoked him and he had come; he hovered before me half the time; it was as if his bright ghost had returned to earth to assure me he regarded the affair as his own no less than as mine and that we should see it fraternally and fondly to a conclusion. It was as if he had said: "Poor dear, be easy with her; she has some natural prejudices; only give her time.

Strange as it may appear to you she was very attractive in 1820. Meanwhile aren't we in Venice together, and what better place is there for the meeting of dear friends? See how it glows with the advancing summer; how the sky and the sea and the rosy air and the marble of the palaces all shimmer and melt together." My eccentric private errand became a part of the general romance and the general glory—I felt even a mystic companionship, a moral fraternity with all those who in the past had been in the service of art. They had worked for beauty, for a devotion; and what else was I doing? That element was in everything that Jeffrey Aspern had written, and I was only bringing it to light.

I lingered in the sala when I went to and fro; I used to watch—as long as I thought decent—the door that led to Miss Bordereau's part of the house. A person observing me might have supposed I was trying to cast a spell on it or attempting some odd experiment in hypnotism. But I was only praying it might open or thinking what treasure probably lurked behind it. I hold it singular, as I look back, that I should never have doubted for a moment that the sacred relics were there; never have failed to know the joy of being beneath the same roof with them. After all they were under my hand—they had not escaped me yet; and they made my life continuous, in a fashion, with the illustrious life they had touched at the other end. I lost myself in this satisfaction to the point of assuming—in my quiet extravagance—that poor Miss Tina also went back, and still went back, as I used to phrase it. She did indeed, the gentle spinster, but not quite so far as Jeffrey Aspern, who was simple hearsay to her quite as he was to me. Only she had lived for years with Juliana, she had seen and handled all mementoes and—even though she was stupid—some esoteric knowledge had rubbed off on her. That was what the old woman represented—esoteric knowledge; and this was the idea with which my critical heart used to thrill. It literally beat faster often, of an evening when I had been out, as I stopped with my candle in the re-echoing hall on my way up to bed. It was as if at such a moment as that, in the stillness and after the long contradiction of the day, Miss Bordereau's secrets were in the air, the wonder of her survival more vivid. These were the acute impressions. I had them in another form, with more of a certain shade of reciprocity, during the hours I sat in the garden looking up over the top of my book at the closed windows of my hostess. In these windows no sign of life ever appeared; it was as if, for fear of my catching a glimpse of them, the two ladies passed their days in the dark. But this only emphasised their having matters to conceal; which was what I had wished to prove. Their motionless shutters became as expressive as eyes consciously closed, and I took comfort in the probability that, though invisible themselves, they kept me in view between the lashes.

I made a point of spending as much time as possible in the garden, to justify the picture I had originally given of my horticultural passion. And I not only spent time, but (hang it! as I said) spent precious money. As soon as I had got my rooms arranged and could give the question proper thought I surveyed the place with a clever expert and made terms for having it put in order. I was sorry to do this, for personally I liked it better as it was, with its weeds and its wild rich tangle, its sweet characteristic Venetian shabbiness. I had to be consistent, to keep my promise that I would smother the house in flowers. Moreover I clung to the fond fancy that by flowers I should make my way—I should succeed by big nosegays. I would batter the old women with lilies—I would bombard their citadel with roses. Their door would have to yield to the pressure when a mound of fragrance should be heaped against it. The place in truth had been brutally neglected. The Venetian capacity for dawdling is of the largest, and for a good many days unlimited litter was all my gardener had to show for his ministrations. There was a great digging of holes and carting about of earth, and after a while I grew so impatient that I had thoughts of sending for my "results" to the nearest stand. But I felt sure my friends would see through the chinks of their shutters where such tribute *couldn't* have been gathered, and might so make up their minds against my veracity. I possessed my soul and finally, though the delay was long, perceived some appearances of bloom. This encouraged me and I waited serenely enough till they multiplied. Meanwhile the real summer days arrived and began to pass, and as I look back upon them they seem to me almost the happiest of my life. I took more and more care to be in the garden whenever it was not too hot. I had an arbour arranged and a low table and an armchair put into it; and I carried out books and portfolios—I had always some business of writing in hand—and worked and waited and mused and hoped, while the golden hours elapsed and the plants drank in the light and the inscrutable old palace turned pale and then, as the day waned, began to recover and flush and my papers rustled in the wandering breeze of the Adriatic.

Considering how little satisfaction I got from it at first it is wonderful I shouldn't have grown more tired of trying to guess what mystic rites of ennui the Misses Bordereau celebrated in their darkened rooms; whether this had always been the tenor of their life and how in previous years they had escaped elbowing their neighbours. It was supposable they had then had other habits, forms and resources; that they must once have been young or at least middle-aged. There was no end to the questions it was possible to ask about them and no end to the answers it was not possible to frame. I had known many of my country-people in Europe and was familiar with the strange ways they were liable to take up there; but the Misses Bordereau formed altogether a new type of the American absentee. Indeed it was clear the American name had ceased to have any application to them—I had seen this in the ten minutes I spent in the old woman's room. You could never have said whence they came from the appearance of either of them; wherever it was they had long ago shed and unlearned all native marks and notes. There was nothing in them one recognised or fitted, and, putting the question of speech aside, they might have been Norwegians or Spaniards. Miss Bordereau, after all, had been in Europe nearly three-quarters of a century; it appeared by some verses addressed to her by Aspern on the occasion of his own second absence from America—verses of which Cumnor and I had after infinite conjecture established solidly enough the date—that she was even then, as a girl of twenty, on the foreign side of the sea. There was a profession in the poem—I hope not just for the phrase—that he had come back for her sake. We had no real light on her circumstances at that moment, any more than we had upon her origin, which we believed to be of the sort usually spoken of as modest. Cumnor had a theory that she had been a governess in some family in which the poet visited and that, in consequence of her position, there was from the first something unavowed, or rather something quite clandestine, in their relations. I on the other hand had hatched a little romance according to which she was the daughter of an artist, a painter or a sculptor, who had left the Western world, when the century was fresh, to study in the ancient schools. It was essential to my hypothesis that this amiable man should have lost his wife, should have been poor and unsuccessful and should have had a second daughter of a disposition quite different from Juliana's. It was also indispensable that he should have been accompanied to Europe by these young ladies and should have established himself there for the remainder of a struggling saddened life. There was a further implication that Miss Bordereau had had in her youth a perverse and reckless, albeit a generous and fascinating character, and that she had braved some wondrous chances. By what passions had she been ravaged, by what adventures and sufferings had she been blanched, what store of memories had she laid away for the monotonous future?

I asked myself these things as I sat spinning theories about her in my arbour and the bees droned in the flowers. It was incontestable that, whether for right or for wrong, most readers of certain of Aspern's poems (poems not as ambiguous as the sonnets—scarcely more divine, I think—of Shakespeare) had taken for granted that Juliana had not always adhered to the steep footway of renunciation. There hovered about her name a perfume of impenitent passion, an intimation that she had not been exactly as the respectable young person in general. Was this a sign that her singer had betrayed her, had given her away, as we say nowadays, to posterity? Certain it is that it would have been difficult to put one's finger on the passage in which her fair fame suffered injury. Moreover was not any fame fair enough that was so sure of duration and was associated with works immortal through their beauty? It was a part of my idea that the young lady had had a foreign lover—and say an unedifying tragical rupture—before her meeting with Jeffrey Aspern. She had lived with her father and sister in a queer old-fashioned expatriated artistic Bohemia of the days when the æsthetic was only the academic and the painters who knew the best models for *contadina* and *pifferaro* wore peaked hats and long hair. It was a society less awake than the coteries of to-day—in its ignorance of the wonderful chances, the opportunities of the early bird, with which its path was strewn—to tatters of old stuff and fragments of old crockery; so that Miss Bordereau appeared not to have picked up or have inherited many objects of importance. There was no enviable *bric-à-brac,* with its provoking legend of cheapness, in the room in which I had seen her. Such a fact as that suggested bareness, but none the less it worked happily into the sentimental interest I had always taken in the early movements of my countrymen as visitors to Europe. When Americans went abroad in 1820 there was something romantic, almost heroic in it, as compared with the perpetual ferryings of the present hour, the hour at which photography and other conveniences have annihilated surprise. Miss Bordereau had sailed with her family on a tossing brig in the days of long voyages and sharp differences; she had had her emotions on the top of yellow diligences, passed the night at inns where she dreamed of travellers' tales, and was most struck, on reaching the Eternal City, with the elegance of Roman pearls and scarfs and mosaic brooches. There was something touching to me in all that, and my imagination frequently went back to the period. If Miss Bordereau carried it there of course Jeffrey Aspern had at other times done so with greater force. It was a much more important fact, if one was looking at his genius critically, that he had lived in the days before the general transfusion. It had happened to me to regret that he had known Europe at all; I should have liked to see what he could have written without that experience, by which he had incontestably been enriched. But as his fate had ruled otherwise I went with him—I tried to judge how the general old order would have struck him. It was not only there, however, I watched him; the relations he had entertained with the special new had even a livelier interest. His own country after all had had most of his life, and his muse, as they said at that time, was essentially American. That was originally what I had prized him for; that at a period when our native land was nude and crude and provincial, when the famous "atmosphere" it is supposed to lack was not even missed, when literature was lonely there and art and form almost impossible, he had found means to live and write like one of the first; to be free and general and not at all afraid; to feel, understand and express everything.

V

I WAS seldom at home in the evening, for when I attempted to occupy myself in my apartments the lamplight brought in a swarm of noxious insects, and it was too hot for closed windows. Accordingly I spent the late hours either on the water—the moonlights of Venice are famous—or in the splendid square which serves as a vast forecourt to the strange old church of Saint Mark. I sat in front of Florian's café eating ices, listening to music, talking with acquaintances: the traveller will remember how the immense cluster of tables and little chairs stretches like a promontory into the smooth lake of the Piazza. The whole place, of a summer's evening, under the stars and with all the lamps, all the voices and light footsteps on marble—the only sounds of the immense arcade that encloses it—is an open-air saloon dedicated to cooling drinks and to a still finer degustation, that of the splendid impressions received during the day. When I didn't prefer to keep mine to myself there was always a stray tourist, disencumbered of his Bädeker, to discuss them with, or some domesticated painter rejoicing in the return of the season of strong effects. The great basilica, with its low domes and bristling embroideries, the mystery of its mosaic and sculpture, looked ghostly in the tempered gloom, and the sea-breeze passed between the twin columns of the Piazzetta, the lintels of a door no longer guarded, as gently as if a rich curtain swayed there. I used sometimes on these occasions to think of the Misses Bordereau and of the pity of their being shut up in apartments which in the Venetian July even Venetian vastness couldn't relieve of some stuffiness. Their life seemed miles away from the life of the Piazza, and no doubt it was really too late to make the austere Juliana change her habits. But poor Miss Tina would have enjoyed one of Florian's ices, I was sure; sometimes I even had thoughts of carrying one home to her. Fortunately my patience bore fruit and I was not obliged to do anything so ridiculous.

One evening about the middle of July I came in earlier than usual—I forgot what chance had led to this—and instead of going up to my quarters made my way into the garden. The temperature was very high; it was such a night as one would gladly have spent in the open air, and I was in no hurry to go to bed. I had floated home in my gondola, listening to the slow splash of the oar in the dark narrow canals, and now the only thought that occupied me was that it would be good to recline at one's length in the fragrant darkness on a garden bench. The odour of the canal was doubtless at the bottom of that aspiration, and the breath of the garden, as I entered it, gave consistency to my purpose. It was delicious—just such an air as must have trembled with Romeo's vows when he stood among the thick flowers and raised his arms to his mistress's balcony. I looked at the windows of the palace to see if by chance the example of Verona—Verona being not far off—had been followed; but everything was dim, as usual, and everything was still. Juliana might on the summer nights of her youth have murmured down from open windows at Jeffrey Aspern, but Miss Tina was not a poet's mistress any more than I was a poet. This however didn't prevent my gratification from being great as I became aware on reaching the end of the garden that my younger padrona was seated in one of the bowers. At first I made out but an indistinct figure, not in the least counting on such an overture from one of my hostesses; it even occurred to me that some enamoured maidservant had stolen in to keep a tryst with her sweetheart. I was going to turn away, not to frighten her, when the figure rose to its height and I recognised Miss Bordereau's niece. I must do myself the justice that I didn't wish to frighten her either, and much as I had longed for some such accident I should have been capable of retreating. It was as if I had laid a trap for her by coming home earlier than usual and by adding to that oddity my invasion of the garden. As she rose she spoke to me, and then I guessed that perhaps, secure in my almost inveterate absence, it was her nightly practice to take a lonely airing. There was no trap in truth, because I had had no suspicion. At first I took the words she uttered for an impatience of my arrival; but as she repeated them—I hadn't caught them clearly—I had the surprise of hearing her say: "Oh dear, I'm so glad you've come!" She and her aunt had in common the property of unexpected speeches. She came out of the arbour almost as if to throw herself in my arms.

I hasten to add that I escaped this ordeal and that she didn't even then shake hands with me. It was an ease to her to see me and presently she told me why—because she was nervous when out-of-doors at night alone. The plants and shrubs looked so strange in the dark, and there were all sorts of queer sounds—she couldn't tell what they were—like the noises of animals. She stood close to me, looking about her with an air of greater security but without any demonstration of interest in me as an individual. Then I felt how little nocturnal prowlings could have been her habit, and I was also reminded—I had been afflicted by the same in talking with her before I took possession—that it was impossible to allow too much for her simplicity.

"You speak as if you were lost in the backwoods," I cheeringly laughed. "How you manage to keep out of this charming place when you've only three steps to take to get into it is more than I've yet been able to discover. You hide away amazingly so long as I'm on the premises, I know; but I had a hope you peeped out a little at other times. You and your poor aunt are worse off than Carmelite nuns in their cells. Should you mind telling me how you exist without air, without exercise, without any sort of human contact? I don't see how you carry on the common business of life."

She looked at me as if I had spoken a strange tongue, and her answer was so little of one that I felt it make for irritation. "We go to bed very early—earlier than you'd believe." I was on the point of saying that this only deepened the mystery, but she gave me some relief by adding: "Before you came we weren't so private. But I've never been out at night."

"Never in these fragrant alleys, blooming here under your nose?"

"Ah," said Miss Tina, "they were never nice till now!" There was a finer sense in this and a flattering comparison, so that it seemed to me I had gained some advantage. As I might follow that further by establishing a good grievance I asked her why, since she thought my garden nice, she had never thanked me in any way for the flowers I had been sending up in such quantities for the previous three weeks. I had not been discouraged—there had been, as she would have observed, a daily armful; but I had been brought up in the common forms and a word of recognition now and then would have touched me in the right place.

"Why I didn't know they were for me!"

"They were for both of you. Why should I make a difference?"

Miss Tina reflected as if she might be thinking of a reason for that, but she failed to produce one. Instead of this she asked abruptly: "Why in the world do you want so much to know us?"

"I ought after all to make a difference," I replied. "That question's your aunt's; it isn't yours. You wouldn't ask it if you hadn't been put up to it."

"She didn't tell me to ask you," Miss Tina replied without confusion. She was indeed the oddest mixture of shyness and straightness.

"Well, she has often wondered about it herself and expressed her wonder to you. She has insisted on it, so that she has put the idea into your head that I'm insufferably pushing. Upon my word I think I've been very discreet. And how completely your aunt must have lost every tradition of sociability, to see anything out of the way in the idea that respectable intelligent people, living as we do under the same roof, should occasionally exchange a remark! What could be more natural? We are of the same country and have at least some of the same tastes, since, like you, I'm intensely fond of Venice."

My friend seemed incapable of grasping more than one clause in any proposition, and she now spoke quickly, eagerly, as if she were answering my whole speech: "I'm not in the least fond of Venice. I should like to go far away!"

"Has she always kept you back so?" I went on, to show her I could be as irrelevant as herself.

"She told me to come out to-night; she has told me very often," said Miss Tina. "It is I who wouldn't come. I don't like to leave her."

"Is she too weak, is she really failing?" I demanded, with more emotion, I think, that I meant to betray. I measured this by the way her eyes rested on me in the darkness. It embarrassed me a little, and to turn the matter off I continued genially: "Do let us sit down together comfortably somewhere—while you tell me all about her."

Miss Tina made no resistance to this. We found a bench less secluded, less confidential, as it were, than the one in the arbour; and we were still sitting there when I heard midnight ring out from those clear bells of Venice which vibrate with a solemnity of their own over the lagoon and hold the air so much more than the chimes of other places. We were together more than an hour and our interview gave, as it struck me, a great lift to my undertaking. Miss Tina accepted the situation without a protest, she had avoided me for three months, yet now she treated me almost as if these three months had made me an old friend. If I had chosen I might have gathered from this that though she had avoided me she had given a good deal of consideration to doing so. She paid no attention to the flight of time—never worried at my keeping her so long away from her aunt. She talked freely, answering questions and asking them and not even taking advantage of certain longish pauses by which they were naturally broken to say she thought she had better go in. It was almost as if she were waiting for something—something I might say to her—and intended to give me my opportunity. I was the more struck by this as she told me how much less well her aunt had been for a good many days, and in a way that was rather new. She was markedly weaker; at moments she showed no strength at all; yet more than ever before she wished to be left alone. That was why she had told her to come out—not even to remain in her own room, which was alongside; she pronounced poor Miss Tina "a worry, a bore and a source of aggravation." She sat still for hours together, as if for long sleep; she had always done that, musing and dozing; but at such times formerly she gave, in breaks, some small sign of life, of interest, liking her companion to be near her with her work. This sad personage confided to me that at present her aunt was so motionless as to create the fear she was dead; moreover she scarce ate or drank—one couldn't see what she lived on. The great thing was that she still on most days got up; the serious job was to dress her, to wheel her out of her bedroom. She clung to as many of her old habits as possible and had always, little company as they had received for years, made a point of sitting in the great parlour.

I scarce knew what to think of all this—of Miss Tina's sudden conversion to sociability and of the strange fact that the more the old woman appeared to decline to her end the less she should desire to be looked after. The story hung indifferently together, and I even asked myself if it mightn't be a trap laid for me, the result of a design to make me show my hand. I couldn't have told why my companions (as they could only by courtesy be called) should have this purpose—why they should try to trip up so lucrative a lodger. But at any hazard I kept on my guard, so that Miss Tina shouldn't have occasion again to ask me what I might really be "up to." Poor woman, before we parted for the night my mind was at rest as to what *she* might be. She was up to nothing at all.

She told me more about their affairs than I had hoped; there was no need to be prying, for it evidently drew her out simply to feel me listen and care. She ceased wondering why I *should,* and at last while describing the brilliant life they had led years before, she almost chattered. It was Miss Tina who judged it brilliant; she said that when they first came to live in Venice, years and years back—I found her essentially vague about dates and the order in which events had occurred—there was never a week they hadn't some visitor or didn't make some pleasant *passeggio* in the town. They had seen all the curiosities; they had even been to the Lido in a boat—she spoke as if I might think there was a way on foot; they had had a collation there, brought in three baskets and spread out on the grass. I asked her what people they had known and she said Oh very nice ones—the Cavaliere Bombicci and the Contessa Altemura, with whom they had had a great friendship! Also English people—the Churtons and the Goldies and Mrs. Stock-Stock, whom they had loved dearly; she was dead and gone, poor dear. That was the case with most of their kind circle—this expression was Miss Tina's own; though a few were left, which was a wonder considering how they had neglected them. She mentioned the names of two or three Venetian old women; of a certain doctor, very clever, who was so attentive—he came as a friend, he had really given up practice; of the *avvocato* Pochintesta, who wrote beautiful poems and had addressed one to her aunt. These people came to see them without fail every year, usually at the *capo d'anno,* and of old her aunt used to make them some little present—her aunt and she together: small things that she, Miss Tina, turned out with her own hand, paper lamp-shades, or mats for the decanters of wine at dinner, or those woollen things that in cold weather are worn on the wrists. The last few years there hadn't been many presents; she couldn't think what to make and her aunt had lost interest and never suggested. But the people came all the same; if the good Venetians liked you once they liked you for ever.

There was affecting matter enough in the good faith of this sketch of former social glories; the picnic at the Lido had remained vivid through the ages and poor Miss Tina evidently was of the impression that she had had a dashing youth. She had in fact had a glimpse of the Venetian world in its gossiping home-keeping parsimonious professional walks; for I noted for the first time how nearly she had acquired by contact the trick of the familiar soft-sounding almost infantile prattle of the place. I judged her to have imbibed this invertebrate dialect from the natural way the names of things and people—mostly purely local—rose to her lips. If she knew little of what they represented she knew still less of anything else. Her aunt had drawn in—the failure of interest in the table-mats and lamp-shades was a sign of that—and she hadn't been able to mingle in society or to entertain it alone; so that her range of reminiscence struck one as an old world altogether. Her tone, hadn't it been so decent, would have seemed to carry one back to the queer rococo Venice of Goldoni and Casanova. I found myself mistakenly think of her too as one of Jeffrey Aspern's contemporaries; this came from her having so little in common with my own. It was possible, I indeed reasoned, that she hadn't even heard of him; it might very well be that Juliana had forborne to lift for innocent eyes the veil that covered the temple of her glory. In this case she perhaps wouldn't know of the existence of the papers, and I welcomed that presumption—it made me feel more safe with her—till I remembered we had believed the letter of disavowal received by Cumnor to be in the handwriting of the niece. If it had been dictated to her she had of course to know what it was about; though the effect of it withal was to repudiate the idea of any connexion with the poet. I held it probable at all events that Miss Tina hadn't read a word of his poetry. Moreover if, with her companion, she had always escaped invasion and research, there was little occasion for her having got it into her head that people were "after" the letters. People had not been after them, for people hadn't heard of them. Cumnor's fruitless feeler would have been a solitary accident.

When midnight sounded Miss Tina got up; but she stopped at the door of the house only after she had wandered two or three times with me round the garden. "When shall I see you again?" I asked before she went in; to which she replied with promptness that she should like to come out the next night. She added, however, that she shouldn't come—she was so far from doing everything she liked.

"You might do a few things *I* like," I quite sincerely sighed.

"Oh you—I don't believe you!" she murmured at this, facing me with her simple solemnity.

"Why don't you believe me?"

"Because I don't understand you."

"That's just the sort of occasion to have faith." I couldn't say more, though I should have liked to, as I saw I only mystified her; for I had no wish to have it on my conscience that I might pass for having made love to her. Nothing less should I have seemed to do had I continued to beg a lady to "believe in me" in an Italian garden on a midsummer night. There was some merit in my scruples, for Miss Tina lingered and lingered: I made out in her conviction that she shouldn't really soon come down again and the wish therefore to protract the present. She insisted too on making the talk between us personal to ourselves; and altogether her behaviour was such as would have been possible only to a perfectly artless and a considerably witless woman.

"I shall like the flowers better now that I know them also meant for me."

"How could you have doubted it? If you'll tell me the kind you like best I'll send a double lot."

"Oh I like them all best!" Then she went on familiarly: "Shall you study—shall you read and write—when you go up to your rooms?"

"I don't do that at night—at this season. The lamplight brings in the animals."

"You might have known that when you came."

"I did know it!"

"And in winter do you work at night?"

"I read a good deal, but I don't often write." She listened as if these details had a rare interest, and suddenly a temptation quite at odds with all the prudence I had been teaching myself glimmered at me in her plain mild face. Ah yes, she was safe and I could make her safer! It seemed to me from one moment to another than I couldn't wait longer—that I really must take a sounding. So I went on: "In general before I go to sleep (very often in bed; it's a bad habit, but I confess to it) I read some great poet. In nine cases out of ten it's a volume of Jeffrey Aspern."

I watched her well as I pronounced that name, but I saw nothing wonderful. Why should I indeed? Wasn't Jeffrey Aspern the property of the human race?

"Oh *we* read him—we *have* read him," she quietly replied.

"He's my poet of poets—I know him almost by heart."

For an instant Miss Tina hesitated; then her sociability was too much for her. "Oh by heart—that's nothing;" and, though dimly, she quite lighted. "My aunt used to know him—to know him"—she paused an instant and I wondered what she was going to say—"to know him as a visitor."

"As a visitor?" I guarded my tone.

"He used to call on her and take her out."

I continued to stare. "My dear lady, he died a hundred years ago!"

"Well," she said amusingly, "my aunt's a hundred and fifty."

"Mercy on us!" I cried; "why didn't you tell me before? I should like so to ask her about him."

"She wouldn't care for that—she wouldn't tell you," Miss Tina returned.

"I don't care what she cares for! She *must* tell me—it's not a chance to be lost."

"Oh you should have come twenty years ago. Then she still talked about him."

"And what did she say?" I eagerly asked.

"I don't know—that he liked her immensely."

"And she—didn't she like *him?*"

"She said he was a god." Miss Tina gave me this information flatly, without expression; her tone might have made it a piece of trivial gossip. But it stirred me deeply as she dropped the words into the summer night; their sound might have been the light rustle of an old unfolded love-letter.

"Fancy, fancy!" I murmured. And then, "Tell me this, please—has she got a portrait of him? They're distressingly rare."

"A portrait? I don't know," said Miss Tina; and now there was discomfiture in her face. "Well, good-night!" she added; and she turned into the house.

I accompanied her into the wide dusky stone-paved passage that corresponded on the ground floor with our grand sala. It opened at one end into the garden, at the other upon the canal, and was lighted now only by the small lamp always left for me to take up as I went to bed.

An extinguished candle which Miss Tina apparently had brought down with her stood on the same table with it. "Good-night, good-night!" I replied, keeping beside her as she went to get her light. "Surely you'd know, shouldn't you, if she had one?"

"If she had what?" the poor lady asked, looking at me queerly over the flame of her candle.

"A portrait of the god. I don't know what I wouldn't give to see it."

"I don't know what she has got. She keeps her things locked up." And Miss Tina went away toward the staircase with the sense evidently of having said too much.

I let her go—I wished not to frighten her—and I contented myself with remarking that Miss Bordereau wouldn't have locked up such a glorious possession as that: a thing a person would be proud of and hang up in a prominent place on the parlour-wall. Therefore of course she hadn't any portrait. Miss Tina made no direct answer to this and, candle in hand, with her back to me, mounted two or three degrees. Then she stopped short and turned round, looking at me across the dusky space.

"Do you write—do you write?" There was a shake in her voice—she could scarcely bring it out.

"Do I write? Oh don't speak of my writing on the same day with Aspern's!"

"Do you write about *him*—do you pry into his life?"

"Ah that's your aunt's question; it can't be yours!" I said in a tone of slightly wounded sensibility.

"All the more reason then that you should answer it. Do you, please?"

I thought I had allowed for the falsehoods I should have to tell, but I found that in fact when it came to the point I hadn't. Besides, now that I had an opening there was a kind of relief in being frank. Lastly—it was perhaps fanciful, even fatuous—I guessed that Miss Tina personally wouldn't in the last resort be less my friend. So after a moment's hesitation I answered: "Yes, I've written about him and I'm looking for more material. In heaven's name have you got any?"

"Santo Dio!" she exclaimed without heeding my question; and she hurried upstairs and out of sight. I might count upon her in the last resort, but for the present she was visibly alarmed. The proof of it was that she began to hide again, so that for a fortnight I kept missing her. I found my patience ebbing and after four or five days of this I told the gardener to stop the "floral tributes."

VI

One afternoon, at last, however, as I came down from my quarters to go out, I found her in the sala: it was our first encounter on that ground since I had come to the house. She put on no air of being there by accident; there was an ignorance of such arts in her honest angular diffidence. That I might be quite sure she was waiting for me she mentioned it at once, but telling me with it that Miss Bordereau wished to see me: she would take me into the room at that moment if I had time. If I had been late for a love-tryst I would have stayed for this, and I quickly signified that I should be delighted to wait on my benefactress. "She wants to talk with you—to know you," Miss Tina said, smiling as if she herself appreciated that idea; and she led me to the door of her aunt's apartment. I stopped her a moment before she had opened it, looking at her with some curiosity. I told her that this was a great satisfaction to me and a great honour; but all the same I should like to ask what had made Miss Bordereau so markedly and suddenly change. It had been only the other day that she wouldn't suffer me near her. Miss Tina was not embarrassed by my question; she had as many little unexpected serenities, plausibilities almost, as if she told fibs, but the odd part of them was that they had on the contrary their source in her truthfulness. "Oh my aunt varies," she answered; "it's so terribly dull—I suppose she's tired."

"But you told me she wanted more and more to be alone."

Poor Miss Tina coloured as if she found me too pushing. "Well, if you don't believe she wants to see you, I haven't invented it! I think people often are capricious when they're very old."

"That's perfectly true. I only wanted to be clear as to whether you've repeated to her what I told you the other night."

"What you told me?"

"About Jeffrey Aspern—that I'm looking for materials."

"If I had told her do you think she'd have sent for you?"

"That's exactly what I want to know. If she wants to keep him to herself she might have sent for me to tell me so."

"She won't speak of him," said Miss Tina. Then as she opened the door she added in a lower tone: "I told her nothing."

The old woman was sitting in the same place in which I had seen her last, in the same position, with the same mystifying bandage over her eyes. Her welcome was to turn her almost invisible face to me and show me that while she sat silent she saw me clearly. I made no motion to shake hands with her; I now felt too well that this was out of place for ever. It had been sufficiently enjoined on me that she was too sacred for trivial modernisms—too venerable to touch. There was something so grim in her aspect—it was partly the accident of her green shade—as I stood there to be measured, that I ceased on the spot to doubt her suspecting me, though I didn't in the least myself suspect that Miss Tina hadn't just spoken the truth. She hadn't betrayed me, but the old woman's brooding instinct had served her; she had turned me over and over in the long still hours and had guessed. The worst of it was that she looked terribly like an old woman who at a pinch would, even like Sardanapalus, burn her treasure. Miss Tina pushed a chair forward, saying to me: "This will be a good place for you to sit." As I took possession of it I asked after Miss Bordereau's health; expressed the hope that in spite of the very hot weather it was satisfactory. She answered that it was good enough—good enough; that it was a great thing to be alive.

"Oh as to that, it depends upon what you compare it with!" I returned with a laugh.

"I don't compare—I don't compare. If I did that I should have given everything up long ago."

I liked to take this for a subtle allusion to the rapture she had known in the society of Jeffrey Aspern—though it was true that such an allusion would have accorded ill with the wish I imputed to her to keep him buried in her soul. What it accorded with was my constant conviction that no human being had ever had a happier social gift than his, and what it seemed to convey was that nothing in the world was worth speaking of if one pretended to speak of that. But one didn't pretend! Miss Tina sat down beside her aunt, looking as if she had reason to believe some wonderful talk would come off between us.

"It's about the beautiful flowers," said the old lady; "you sent us so many—I ought to have thanked you for them before. But I don't write letters and I receive company but at long intervals."

She hadn't thanked me while the flowers continued to come, but she departed from her custom so far as to send for me as soon as she began to fear they wouldn't come any more. I noted this; I remembered what an acquisitive propensity she had shown when it was a question of extracting gold from me, and I privately rejoiced at the happy thought I had had in suspending my tribute. She had missed it and was willing to make a concession to bring it back. At the first sign of this concession I could only go to meet her. "I'm afraid you haven't had many, of late, but they shall begin again immediately—to-morrow, to-night."

"Oh do send us some to-night!" Miss Tina cried as if it were a great affair.

"What else should you do with them? It isn't a manly

taste to make a bower of your room," the old woman remarked.

"I don't make a bower of my room, but I'm exceedingly fond of growing flowers, of watching their ways. There's nothing unmanly in that: it has been the amusement of philosophers, of statesmen in retirement; even I think of great captains."

"I suppose you know you can sell them—those you don't use," Miss Bordereau went on. "I dare say they wouldn't give you much for them; still, you could make a bargain."

"Oh I've never in my life made a bargain, as you ought pretty well to have gathered. My gardener disposes of them and I ask no questions."

"I'd ask a few, I can promise you!" said Miss Bordereau; and it was so I first heard the strange sound of her laugh, which was as if the faint "walking" ghost of her old-time tone had suddenly cut a caper. I couldn't get used to the idea that this vision of pecuniary profit was most what drew out the divine Juliana.

"Come into the garden yourself and pick them; come as often as you like; come every day. The flowers are all for you," I pursued, addressing Miss Tina and carrying off this veracious statement by treating it as an innocent joke. "I can't imagine why she doesn't come down," I added for Miss Bordereau's benefit.

"You must make her come; you must come up and fetch her," the old woman said to my stupefaction. "That odd thing you've made in the corner will do very well for her to sit in."

The allusion to the most elaborate of my shady coverts, a sketchy "summer-house," was irreverent; it confirmed the impression I had already received that there was a flicker of impertinence in Miss Bordereau's talk, a vague echo of the boldness or the archness of her adventurous youth and which had somehow automatically outlived passions and faculties. None the less I asked: "Wouldn't it be possible for you to come down there yourself? Wouldn't it do you good to sit there in the shade and the sweet air?"

"Oh sir, when I move out of this it won't be to sit in the air, and I'm afraid that any that may be stirring around me won't be particularly sweet! It will be a very dark shade indeed. But that won't be just yet," Miss Bordereau continued cannily, as if to correct any hopes this free glance at the last receptable of her mortality might lead me to entertain. "I've sat here many a day and have had enough of arbours in my time. But I'm not afraid to wait till I'm called."

Miss Tina had expected, as I felt, rare conversation, but perhaps she found it less gracious on her aunt's side—considering I had been sent for with a civil intention—than she had hoped. As to give the position a turn that would put our companion in a light more favourable she said to me: "Didn't I tell you the other night that she had sent me out? You see I can do what I like!"

"Do you pity her—do you teach her to pity herself?" Miss Bordereau demanded, before I had time to answer this appeal. "She has a much easier life than I had at her age."

"You must remember it has been quite open to me," I said, "to think you rather inhuman."

"Inhuman? That's what the poets used to call the women a hundred years ago. Don't try that; you won't do as well as they!" Juliana went on. "There's no more poetry in the world—that *I* know of at least. But I won't bandy words with you," she said, and I well remember the old-fashioned artificial sound she gave the speech. "You make me talk, talk, talk! It isn't good for me at all." I got up at this and told her I would take no more of her time; but she detained me to put a question, "Do you remember, the day I saw you about the rooms, that you offered us the use of your gondola?" And when I assented promptly, struck again with her disposition to make a "good thing" of my being there and wondering what she now had in her eye, she produced: "Why don't you take that girl out in it and show her the place?"

"Oh dear aunt, what do you want to do with me?" cried the "girl" with a piteous quaver. "I know all about the place!"

"Well then go with him and explain!" said Miss Bordereau, who gave an effect of cruelty to her implacable power of retort. This showed her as a sarcastic profane cynical old woman. "Haven't we heard that there have been all sorts of changes in all these years? You ought to see them, and at your age—I don't mean because you're so young—you ought to take the chances that come. You're old enough, my dear, and this gentleman won't hurt you. He'll show you the famous sunsets, if they still go on—*do* they go on? The sun set for me so long ago. But that's not a reason. Besides, I shall never miss you; you think you're too important. Take her to the Piazza; it used to be very pretty," Miss Bordereau continued, addressing herself to me. "What have they done with the funny old church? I hope it hasn't tumbled down. Let her look at the shops; she may take some money, she may buy what she likes."

Poor Miss Tina had got up, discountenanced and helpless, and as we stood there before her aunt it would certainly have struck a spectator of the scene that our venerable friend was making rare sport of us. Miss Tina protested in a confusion of exclamations and murmurs; but I lost no time in saying that if she would do me the honour to accept the hospitality of my boat I would engage she really shouldn't be bored. Or if she didn't want so much of my company, the boat itself, with the gondolier, was at her service; he was a capital oar and she might have every confidence. Miss Tina, without definitely answering this speech, looked away from me and out of the window, quite as if about to weep, and I remarked that once we had Miss Bordereau's approval we could easily come to an understanding. We would take an hour, whichever she liked, one of the very next days. As I made my obeisance to the old lady I asked her if she would kindly permit me to see her again.

For a moment she kept me; then she said: "Is it very necessary to your happiness?"

"It diverts me more than I can say."

"You're wonderfully civil. Don't you know it almost kills *me?*"

"How can I believe that when I see you more animated, more brilliant than when I came in?"

"That's very true, aunt," said Miss Tina. "I think it does you good."

"Isn't it touching, the solicitude we each have that the other shall enjoy herself?" sneered Miss Bordereau. "If you think me brilliant to-day you don't know what you are talking about; you've never seen an agreeable woman. What do you people know about good society?" she cried; but before I could tell her, "Don't try to pay me a compliment; I've been spoiled," she went on. "My door's shut, but you may sometimes knock."

With this she dismissed me and I left the room. The latch closed behind me, but Miss Tina, contrary to my hope, had remained within. I passed slowly across the hall and before taking my way downstairs waited a little. My hope was answered; after a minute my conductress followed me. "That's a delightful idea about the Piazza," I said. "When will you go—to-night, to-morrow?"

She had been disconcerted, as I have mentioned, but I had already perceived, and I was to observe again, that when Miss Tina was embarrassed she didn't—as most women would have in like case—turn away, floundering and hedging, but came closer, as it were, with a deprecating, a clinging appeal to be spared, to be protected. Her attitude was a constant prayer for aid and explanation, and yet no woman in the world could have been less of a comedian. From the moment you were kind to her she depended on you absolutely; her self-consciousness dropped and she took the greatest intimacy, the innocent intimacy that was all she could conceive, for granted. She didn't know, she now declared, what possessed her aunt, who had changed so quickly, who had got some idea. I replied that she must catch the idea and let me have it: we would go and take an ice together at Florian's and she should report while we listened to the band.

"Oh it will take me a long time to be able to 'report'!" she said rather ruefully; and she could promise me this satisfaction neither for that night nor for the next. I was patient now, however, for I felt I had only to wait; and in fact at the end of the week, one lovely evening after dinner, she stepped into my gondola, to which in honour of the occasion I had attached a second oar.

We swept in the course of five minutes into the Grand Canal; whereupon she uttered a murmur of ecstasy as fresh as if she had been a tourist just arrived. She had forgotten the splendor of the great water-way on a clear summer evening, and how the sense of floating between marble palaces and reflected lights disposed the mind to freedom and ease. We floated long and far, and though my friend gave no high-pitched voice to her glee I was sure of her full surrender. She was more than pleased, she was transported; the whole thing was an immense liberation. The gondola moved with slow strokes, to give her time to enjoy it, and she listened to the plash of the oars, which grew louder and more musically liquid as we passed into narrow canals, as if it were a revelation of Venice. When I asked her how long it was since she had thus floated, she answered: "Oh I don't know; a long time—not since my aunt began to be ill." This was not the only show of her extreme vagueness about the previous years and the line marking off the period of Miss Bordereau's eminence. I was not at liberty to keep her out long, but we took a considerable *giro* before going to the Piazza. I asked her no questions, holding off by design from her life at home and the things I wanted to know; I poured, rather, treasures of information about the objects before and around us into her ears, describing also Florence and Rome, discoursing on the charms and advantages of travel. She reclined, receptive, on the deep leather cushions, turned her eyes conscientiously to everything I noted and never mentioned to me till some time afterwards that she might be supposed to know Florence better than I, as she had lived there for years with her kinswoman. At last she said with the shy impatience of a child: "Are we not really going to the Piazza? That's what I want to see!" I immediately gave the order that we should go straight, after which we sat silent with the expectation of arrival. As some time still passed, however, she broke out of her own movement: "I've found out what's the matter with my aunt: she's afraid you'll go!"

I quite gasped. "What has put that into her head?"

"She has had an idea you've not been happy. That's why she is different now."

"You mean she wants to make me happier?"

"Well, she wants you not to go. She wants you to stay."

"I suppose you mean on account of the rent," I remarked candidly.

Miss Tina's candour but profited. "Yes, you know; so that I shall have more."

"How much does she want you to have?" I asked with all the gaiety I now felt. "She ought to fix the sum, so that I may stay till it's made up."

"Oh that wouldn't please me," said Miss Tina. "It would be unheard of, your taking that trouble."

"But suppose I should have my own reasons for staying in Venice?"

"Then it would be better for you to stay in some other house."

"And what would your aunt say to that?"

"She wouldn't like it at all. But I should think you'd do well to give up your reasons and go away altogether."

"Dear Miss Tina," I said, "it's not so easy to give up my reasons!"

She made no immediate answer to this, but after a moment broke out afresh: "I think I know what your reasons are!"

"I dare say, because the other night I almost told you how I wished you'd help me to make them good."

"I can't do that without being false to my aunt."

"What do you mean by being false to her?"

"Why she would never consent to what you want. She has been asked, she has been written to. It makes her fearfully angry."

"Then she *has* papers of value?" I precipitately cried.

"Oh she has everything!" sighed Miss Tina, with a curious weariness, a sudden lapse into gloom.

These words caused all my pulses to throb, for I regarded them as precious evidence. I felt them too deeply to speak, and in the interval the gondola approached the Piazzetta. After we had disembarked I asked my companion if she would rather walk round the square or go and sit before the great café; to which she replied that she would do whichever I liked best—I must only remember again how little time she had. I assured her there was plenty to do both, and we made the circuit of the long arcades. Her spirits revived at the sight of the bright shop-windows, and she lingered and stopped, admiring or disapproving of their contents, asking me what I thought of things, theorizing about prices. My attention wandered from her; her words of a while before "Oh she has everything!" echoed so in my consciousness. We sat down at last in the crowded circle at Florian's, finding an unoccupied table among those that were ranged in the square. It was a splendid night and all the world out-of-doors; Miss Tina couldn't have wished the elements more auspicious for her return to society. I saw she felt it all even more than she told, but her impressions were well-nigh too many for her. She had forgotten the attraction of the world and was learning that she had for the best years of her life been rather mercilessly cheated of it. This didn't make her angry; but as she took in the charming scene her face had, in spite of its smile of appreciation, the flush of a wounded surprise. She didn't speak, sunk in the sense of opportunities, for ever lost, that ought to have been easy; and this gave me a chance to say to her: "Did you mean a while ago that your aunt has a plan of keeping me on by admitting me occasionally to her presence?"

"She thinks it will make a difference with you if you sometimes see her. She wants you so much to stay that she's willing to make that concession."

"And what good does she consider I think it will do me to see her?"

"I don't know; it must be interesting," said Miss Tina simply. "You told her you found it so."

"So I did; but every one doesn't think that."

"No, of course not, or more people would try."

"Well, if she's capable of making that reflexion she's capable also of making this further one," I went on: "that I must have a particular reason for not doing as others do, in spite of the interest she offers—for not leaving her alone." Miss Tina looked as if she failed to grasp this rather complicated proposition; so I continued: "If you've not told her what I said to you the other night may she not at least have guessed it?"

"I don't know—she's very suspicious."

"But she hasn't been made so by indiscreet curiosity, by persecution?"

"No, no; it isn't that," said Miss Tina, turning on me a troubled face. "I don't know how to say it; it's on account of something—ages ago, before I was born—in her life."

"Something? What sort of thing?"—and I asked it as if I could have no idea.

"Oh she has never told me." And I was sure my friend spoke the truth.

Her extreme limpidity was almost provoking, and I felt

for the moment that she would have been more satisfactory if she had been less ingenuous. "Do you suppose it's something to which Jeffrey Aspern's letters and papers—I mean the things in her possession—have reference?"

"I dare say it is!" my companion exclaimed as if this were a very happy suggestion. "I've never looked at any of those things."

"None of them? Then how do you know what they are?"

"I don't," said Miss Tina placidly. "I've never had them in my hands. But I've seen them when she has had them out."

"Does she have them out often?"

"Not now, but she used to. She's very fond of them."

"In spite of their being compromising?"

"Compromising?" Miss Tina repeated as if vague as to what that meant. I felt almost as one who corrupts the innocence of youth.

"I allude to their containing painful memories."

"Oh I don't think anything's painful."

"You mean there's nothing to affect her reputation?"

An odder look even than usual came at this into the face of Miss Bordereau's niece—a confession, it seemed, of helplessness, an appeal to me to deal fairly, generously with her. I had brought her to the Piazza, placed her among charming influences, paid her an attention she appreciated, and now I appeared to show it all as a bribe—a bribe to make her turn in some way against her aunt. She was of a yielding nature and capable of doing almost anything to please a person markedly kind to her; but the greatest kindness of all would be not to presume too much on this. It was strange enough, as I afterwards thought, that she had not the least air of resenting my want of consideration for her aunt's character, which would have been in the worst possible taste if anything less vital—from my point of view—had been at stake. I don't think she really measured it. "Do you mean she ever did something bad?" she asked in a moment.

"Heaven forbid I should say so, and it's none of my business. Besides, if she did," I agreeably put it, "that was in other ages, in another world. But why shouldn't she destroy her papers?"

"Oh she loves them too much."

"Even now, when she may be near her end?"

"Perhaps when she's sure of that she will."

"Well, Miss Tina," I said, "that's just what I should like you to prevent."

"How can I prevent it?"

"Couldn't you get them away from her?"

"And give them to you?"

This put the case, superficially, with sharp irony, but I was sure of her not intending that. "Oh I mean that you might let me see them and look them over. It isn't for myself, or that I should want them at any cost to any one else. It's simply that they would be of such immense interest to the public, such immeasurable importance as a contribution to Jeffrey Aspern's history."

She listened to me in her usual way, as if I abounded in matters she had never heard of, and I felt almost as base as the reporter of a newspaper who forces his way into a house of mourning. This was marked when she presently said: "There was a gentleman who some time ago wrote to her in very much those words. He also wanted her papers."

"And did she answer him?" I asked, rather ashamed of not having my friend's rectitude.

"Only when he had written two or three times. He made her very angry."

"And what did she say?"

"She said he was a devil," Miss Tina replied categorically.

"She used that expression in her letter?"

"Oh no; she said it to me. She made me write to him."

"And what did you say?"

"I told him there were no papers at all."

"Ah poor gentleman!" I groaned.

"I knew there were, but I wrote what she bade me."

"Of course you had to do that. But I hope I shan't pass for a devil."

"It will depend upon what you ask me to do for you," my companion smiled.

"Oh if there's a chance of *your* thinking so my affair's in a bad way! I shan't ask you to steal for me, nor even to fib—for you *can't* fib, unless on paper. But the principal thing is this—to prevent her destroying the papers."

"Why I've no control of her," said Miss Tina. "It's she who controls me."

"But she doesn't control her own arms and legs, does she? The way she would naturally destroy her letters would be to burn them. Now she can't burn them without fire, and she can't get fire unless you give it to her."

"I've always done everything she has asked," my poor friend pleaded. "Besides, there's Olimpia."

I was on the point of saying that Olimpia was probably corruptible, but I thought it best not to sound that note. So I simply put it that this frail creature might perhaps be managed.

"Every one can be managed by my aunt," said Miss Tina. And then she remembered that her holiday was over; she must go home.

I laid my hand on her arm, across the table, to stay her a moment. "What I want of you is a general promise to help me."

"Oh how *can* I, how *can* I?" she asked, wondering and troubled. She was half-surprised, half-frightened at my attaching that importance to her, at my calling on her for action.

"This is the main thing: to watch our friend carefully and warn me in time, before she commits that dreadful sacrilege."

"I can't watch her when she makes me go out."

"That's very true."

"And when you do too."

"Mercy on us—do you think she'll have done anything to-night?"

"I don't know. She's very cunning."

"Are you trying to frighten me?" I asked.

I felt this question sufficiently answered when my companion murmured in a musing, almost envious way: "Oh but she loves them—she loves them!"

This reflexion, repeated with such emphasis, gave me great comfort; but to obtain more of that balm I said: "If she shouldn't intend to destroy the objects we speak of before her death she'll probably have made some disposition by will."

"By will?"

"Hasn't she made a will for your benefit?"

"Ah she has so little to leave. That's why she likes money," said Miss Tina.

"Might I ask, since we're really talking things over, what you and she live on?"

"On some money that comes from America, from a gentleman—I think a lawyer—in New York. He sends it every quarter. It isn't much!"

"And won't she have disposed of that?"

My companion hesitated—I saw she was blushing. "I believe it's mine," she said; and the look and tone which accompanied these words betrayed so the absence of the habit of thinking of herself that I almost thought her charming. The next instant she added: "But she had in an *avvocato* here once, ever so long ago. And some people came and signed something."

"They were probably witnesses. And you weren't asked to sign? Well then," I argued, rapidly and hopefully, "it's because you're the legatee. She must have left all her documents to you!"

"If she has it's with very strict conditions," Miss Tina responded, rising quickly, while the movement gave the words a small character of decision. They seemed to imply that the bequest would be accompanied with a proviso that the articles bequeathed should remain concealed from every inquisitive eye, and that I was very much mistaken if I thought her the person to depart from an injunction so absolute.

"Oh of course you'll have to abide by the terms," I said; and she uttered nothing to mitigate the rigour of this conclusion. None the less, later on, just before we disembarked at her own door after a return which had taken place almost in silence, she said to me abruptly: "I'll do what I can to help you." I was grateful for this—it was very well so far as it went; but it didn't keep me from remembering that night in a worried waking hour that I now had her word for it to re-enforce my own impression that the old woman was full of craft.

VII

THE FEAR of what this side of her character might have led her to do made me nervous for days afterwards. I waited for an intimation from Miss Tina; I almost read it as her duty to keep me informed, to let me know definitely whether or no Miss Bordereau had sacrificed her treasures. But as she gave no sign I lost patience and determined to put the case to the very touch of my own senses. I sent late one afternoon to ask if I might pay the ladies a visit, and my servant came back with surprising news. Miss Bordereau could be approached without the least difficulty; she had been moved out into the sala and was sitting by the window that overlooked the garden. I descended and found this picture correct; the old lady had been wheeled forth into the world and had a certain air, which came mainly perhaps from some brighter element in her dress, of being prepared again to have converse with it. It had not yet, however, begun to flock about her; she was perfectly alone and, though the door leading to her own quarters stood open, I had at first no glimpse of Miss Tina. The window at which she sat had the afternoon shade and, one of the shutters having been pushed back, she could see the pleasant garden, where the summer sun had by this time dried up too many of the plants—she could see the yellow light and the long shadows.

"Have you come to tell me you'll take the rooms for six months more?" she asked as I approached her, startling me by something coarse in her cupidity almost as much as if she hadn't already given me a specimen of it. Juliana's desire to make our acquaintance lucrative had been, as I have sufficiently indicated, a false note in my image of the woman who had inspired a great poet with immortal lines; but I may say here definitely that I after all recognised large allowance to be made for her. It was I who had kindled the unholy flame; it was I who had put into her head that she had the means of making money. She appeared never to have thought of that; she had been living wastefully for years, in a house five times too big for her, on a footing that I could explain only by the presumption that, excessive as it was, the space she enjoyed cost her next to nothing and that, small as were her revenues, they left her, for Venice, an appreciable margin. I had descended on her one day and taught her to calculate, and my almost extravagant comedy on the subject of the garden had presented me irresistibly in the light of a victim. Like all persons who achieve the miracle of changing their point of view late in life, she had been intensely converted; she had seized my hint with a desperate tremulous clutch.

I invited myself to go and get one of the chairs that stood, at a distance, against the wall—she had given herself no concern as to whether I should sit or stand; and while I placed it near her I began gaily: "Oh dear madam, what an imagination you have, what an intellectual sweep! I'm a poor devil of a man of letters who lives from day to day. How can I take palaces by the year? My existence is precarious. I don't know whether six months hence I shall have bread to put in my mouth. I've treated myself for once; it has been an immense luxury. But when it comes to going on——!"

"Are your rooms too dear? If they are you can have more for the same money," Juliana responded. "We can arrange, we can *combinare,* as they say here."

"Well yes, since you ask me, they're too dear, much too dear," I said. "Evidently you suppose me richer than I am."

She looked at me as from the mouth of her cave. "If you write books don't you sell them?"

"Do you mean don't people buy them? A little, a very

little—not so much as I could wish. Writing books, unless one be a great genius—and even then!—is the last road to fortune. I think there's no more money to be made by good letters."

"Perhaps you don't choose nice subjects. What do you write about?" Miss Bordereau implacably pursued.

"About the books of other people. I'm a critic, a commentator, an historian, in a small way." I wondered what she was coming to.

"And what other people now?"

"Oh better ones than myself: the great writers mainly—the great philosophers and poets of the past; those who are dead and gone and can't, poor darlings, speak for themselves."

"And what do you say about them?"

"I say they sometimes attached themselves to very clever women!" I replied as for pleasantness. I had measured, as I thought, my risk, but as my words fell upon the air they were to strike me as imprudent. However, I had launched them and I wasn't sorry, for perhaps after all the old woman would be willing to treat. It seemed tolerably obvious that she knew my secret; why therefore drag the process out? But she didn't take what I had said as a confession; she only asked:

"Do you think it's right to rake up the past?"

"I don't feel that I know what you mean by raking it up. How can we get at it unless we dig a little? The present has such a rough way of treading it down."

"Oh I like the past, but I don't like critics," my hostess declared with her hard complacency.

"Neither do I, but I like their discoveries."

"Aren't they mostly lies?"

"The lies are what they sometimes discover," I said, smiling at the quiet impertinence of this. "They often lay bare the truth."

"The truth is God's, it isn't man's; we had better leave it alone. Who can judge of it?—who can say?"

"We're terribly in the dark, I know," I admitted; "but if we give up trying what becomes of all the fine things? What becomes of the work I just mentioned, that of the great philosophers and poets? It's all vain words if there's nothing to measure it by."

"You talk as if you were a tailor," said Miss Bordereau whimsically; and then she added quickly and in a different manner: "This house is very fine; the proportions are magnificent. To-day I wanted to look at this part again. I made them bring me out here. When your man came just now to learn if I would see you I was on the point of sending for you to ask if you didn't mean to go on. I wanted to judge what I'm letting you have. This sala is very grand," she pursued like an auctioneer, moving a little, as I guessed, her invisible eyes. "I don't believe you often have lived in such a house, eh?"

"I can't often afford to!" I said.

"Well then how much will you give me for six months?"

I was on the point of exclaiming—and the air of excruciation in my face would have denoted a moral fact—"Don't, Juliana; for *his* sake, don't!" But I controlled myself and asked less passionately: "Why should I remain so long as that?"

"I thought you liked it," said Miss Bordereau with her shrivelled dignity.

"So I thought I should."

For a moment she said nothing more, and I left my own words to suggest to her what they might. I half-expected her to say, coldly enough, that if I had been disappointed we needn't continue the discussion, and this in spite of the fact that I believed her now to have in her mind—however it had come there—what would have told her that my disappointment was natural. But to my extreme surprise she ended by observing: "If you don't think we've treated you well enough perhaps we can discover some way of treating you better." This speech was somehow so incongruous that it made me laugh again, and I excused myself by saying that she talked as if I were a sulky boy pouting in the corner and having to be "brought round." I hadn't a grain of complaint to make; and could anything have exceeded Miss Tina's graciousness in accompanying me a few nights before to the Piazza? At this the old woman went on: "Well, you brought it on yourself!" And then in a different tone: "She's a very fine girl." I assented cordially to this proposition, and she expressed the hope that I did so not merely to be obliging, but that I really liked her. Meanwhile I wondered still more what Miss Bordereau was coming to. "Except for me, to-day," she said, "she hasn't a relation in the world." Did she by describing her niece as amiable and unencumbered wish to represent her as a *parti?*

It was perfectly true that I couldn't afford to go on with my rooms at a fancy price and that I had already devoted to my undertaking almost all the hard cash I had set apart for it. My patience and my time were by no means exhausted, but I should be able to draw upon them only on a more usual Venetian basis. I was willing to pay the precious personage with whom my pecuniary dealings were such a discord twice as much as any other *padrona di casa* would have asked, but I wasn't willing to pay her twenty times as much. I told her so plainly, and my plainness appeared to have some success, for she exclaimed: "Very good; you've done what I asked—you've made an offer!"

"Yes, but not for half a year. Only by the month."

"Oh I must think of that then." She seemed disappointed that I wouldn't tie myself to a period, and I guessed that she wished both to secure me and to discourage me; to say severely: "Do you dream that you can get off with less than six months? Do you dream that even by the end of that time you'll be appreciably nearer your victory?" What was most in my mind was that she had a fancy to play me the trick of making me engage myself when in fact she had sacrificed her treasure. There was a moment when my suspense on this point was so acute that I all but broke out with the question, and what kept it back was but an instinctive recoil—lest it should be a mistake—from the last violence of self-exposure. She was such a subtle old witch that one could never tell where one stood with her. You may imagine whether it cleared up the puzzle when, just after she had said she would think of my proposal and without any formal transition, she drew out of her pocket with an embarrassed hand a small object wrapped in crumpled white paper. She held it there a moment and then resumed: "Do you know much about curiosities?"

"About curiosities?"

"About antiquities, the old gimcracks that people pay so much for to-day. Do you know the kind of price they bring?"

I thought I saw what was coming, but I said ingenuously: "Do you want to buy something?"

"No, I want to sell. What would an amateur give me for that?" She unfolded the white paper and made a motion for me to take from her a small oval portrait. I possessed myself of it with fingers of which I could only hope that they didn't betray the intensity of their clutch, and she added: "I would part with it only for a good price."

At the first glance I recognized Jeffrey Aspern, and was well aware that I flushed with the act. As she was watching me however I had the consistency to exclaim: "What a striking face! Do tell me who it is."

"He's an old friend of mine, a very distinguished man in his day. He gave it me himself, but I'm afraid to mention his name, lest you never should have heard of him, critic and historian as you are. I know the world goes fast and one generation forgets another. He was all the fashion when I was young."

She was perhaps amazed at my assurance, but I was surprised at hers; at her having the energy, in her state of health and at her time of life, to wish to sport with me to that tune simply for her private entertainment—the humour to test me and practise on me and befool me. This at least was the interpretation that I put upon her production of the relic, for I couldn't believe she really desired to sell it or cared for any information I might give her. What she wished was to dangle it before my eyes and put a prohibitive price on it. "The face comes back to me, it torments me," I said, turning the object this way and that and looking at it very critically. It was a careful but not a supreme work of art, larger than the ordinary miniature and representing a young man with a remarkably handsome face, in a high-collared green coat and a buff waistcoat. I felt in the little work a virtue of likeness and judged it to have been painted when the model was about twenty-five. There are, as all the world knows, three other portraits of the poet in existence, but none of so early a date as this elegant image. "I've never seen the original, clearly a man of a past age, but I've seen other reproductions of this face," I went on. "You expressed doubt of this generation's having heard of the gentleman, but he strikes me for all the world as a celebrity. Now who is he? I can't put my finger on him—I can't give him a label. Wasn't he a writer? Surely he's a poet." I was determined that it should be she, not I, who should first pronounce Jeffrey Aspern's name.

My resolution was taken in ignorance of Miss Bordereau's extremely resolute character, and her lips never formed in my hearing the syllables that meant so much for her. She neglected to answer my question, but raised her hand to take back the picture, using a gesture which though impotent was in a high degree peremptory. "It's only a person who should know for himself that would give me my price," she said with a certain dryness.

"Oh then you have a price?" I didn't restore the charming thing; not from any vindictive purpose, but because I instinctively clung to it. We looked at each other hard while I retained it.

"I know the least I would take. What it occurred to me to ask you about is the most I shall be able to get."

She made a movement, drawing herself together as if, in a spasm of dread at having lost her prize she had been impelled to the immense effort of rising to snatch it from me. I instantly placed it in her hand again, saying as I did so: "I should like to have it myself, but with your ideas it would be quite beyond my mark."

She turned the small oval plate over in her lap, with its face down, and I heard her catch her breath as after a strain or an escape. This however did not prevent her saying in a moment: "You'd buy a likeness of a person you don't know by an artist who has no reputation?"

"The artist may have no reputation, but that thing's wonderfully well painted," I replied, to give myself a reason.

"It's lucky you thought of saying that, because the painter was my father."

"That makes the picture indeed precious!" I returned with gaiety; and I may add that a part of my cheer came from this proof I had been right in my theory of Miss Bordereau's origin. Aspern had of course met the young lady on his going to her father's studio as a sitter. I observed to Miss Bordereau that if she would entrust me with her property for twenty-four hours I should be happy to take advice on it; but she made no other reply than to slip it in silence into her pocket. This convinced me still more that she had no sincere intention of selling it during her lifetime, though she may have desired to satisfy herself as to the sum her niece, should she leave it to her, might expect eventually to obtain for it. "Well, at any rate, I hope you won't offer it without giving me notice," I said as she remained irresponsive. "Remember me as a possible purchaser."

"I should want your money first!" she returned with unexpected rudeness; and then, as if she bethought herself that I might well complain of such a tone and wished to turn the matter off, asked abruptly what I talked about with her niece when I went out with her that way of an evening.

"You speak as if we had set up the habit," I replied. "Certainly I should be very glad if it were to become our pleasant custom. But in that case I should feel a still greater scruple at betraying a lady's confidence."

"Her confidence? Has my niece confidence?"

"Here she is—she can tell you herself," I said; for Miss Tina now appeared on the threshold of the old woman's parlour. "Have you confidence, Miss Tina? Your aunt wants very much to know."

"Not in her, not in her!" the younger lady declared, shaking her head with a dolefulness that was neither jocular nor affected. "I don't know what to do with her; she has fits of horrid imprudence. She's so easily tired—and yet she has begun to roam, to drag herself about the house." And she looked down at her yoke-fellow of long years with a vacancy of wonder, as if all their contact and custom hadn't made her perversities, on occasion, any more easy to follow.

"I know what I'm about. I'm not losing my mind. I dare say you'd like to think so," said Miss Bordereau with a crudity of cynicism.

"I don't suppose you came out here yourself. Miss Tina must have had to lend you a hand," I interposed for conciliation.

"Oh she insisted we should push her; and when she insists!" said Miss Tina, in the same tone of apprehension; as if there were no knowing what service she disapproved of her aunt might force her next to render.

"I've always got most things done I wanted, thank God! The peope I've lived with have humoured me," the old woman continued, speaking out of the white ashes of her vanity.

I took it pleasantly up. "I suppose you mean they've obeyed you."

"Well, whatever it is—when they like one."

"It's just because I like you that I want to resist," said Miss Tina with a nervous laugh.

"Oh I suspect you'll bring Miss Bordereau upstairs next to pay me a visit," I went on; to which the old lady replied:

"Oh no; I can keep an eye on you from here!"

"You're very tired; you'll certainly be ill to-night!" cried Miss Tina.

"Nonsense, dear; I feel better at this moment than I've done for a month. To-morrow I shall come out again. I want to be where I can see this clever gentleman."

"Shouldn't you perhaps see me better in your sitting-room?" I asked.

"Don't you mean shouldn't you have a better chance at *me?*" she returned, fixing me a moment with her green shade.

"Ah I haven't that anywhere! I look at you but don't see you."

"You agitate her dreadfully—and that's not good," said Miss Tina, giving me a reproachful deterrent headshake.

"I want to watch you—I want to watch you!" Miss Bordereau went on.

"Well then let us spend as much of our time together as possible—I don't care where. That will give you every facility."

"Oh I've seen you enough for to-day. I'm satisfied. Now I'll go home," Juliana said. Miss Tina laid her hands on the back of the wheeled chair and began to push, but I begged her to let me take her place. "Oh yes, you may move me this way—you shan't in any other!" the old woman cried as she felt herself propelled firmly and easily over the smooth hard floor. Before we reached the door of her own apartment she bade me stop, and she took a long last look up and down the noble sala. "Oh it's a prodigious house!" she murmured; after which I pushed her forward. When we had entered the parlour Miss Tina let me know she should now be able to manage, and at the same moment the little red-haired *donna* came to meet her mistress. Miss Tina's idea was evidently to get her aunt immediately back to bed. I confess that in spite of this urgency

I was guilty of the indiscretion of lingering; it held me there to feel myself so close to the objects I coveted—which would be probably put away somewhere in the faded unsociable room. The place had indeed a bareness that suggested no hidden values; there were neither dusky nooks nor curtained corners, neither massive cabinets nor chests with iron bands. Moreover it was possible, it was perhaps even likely, that the old lady had consigned her relics to her bedroom, to some battered box that was shoved under the bed, to the drawer of some lame dressing-table, where they would be in the range of vision by the dim night-lamp. None the less I turned an eye on every article of furniture, on every conceivable cover for a hoard, and noticed that there were half a dozen things with drawers, and in particular a tall old secretary with brass ornaments of the style of the Empire—a receptacle somewhat infirm but still capable of keeping rare secrets. I don't know why this article so engaged me, small purpose as I had of breaking into it; but I stared at it so hard that Miss Tina noticed me and changed colour. Her doing this made me think I was right and that, wherever they might have been before, the Aspern papers at that moment languished behind the peevish little lock of the secretary. It was hard to turn my attention from the dull mahogany front when I reflected that a plain panel divided me from the goal of my hopes; but I gathered up my slightly scattered prudence and with an effort took leave of my hostess. To make the effort graceful I said to her that I should certainly bring her an opinion about the little picture.

"The little picture?" Miss Tina asked in surprise.

"What do *you* know about it, my dear?" the old woman demanded. "You needn't mind. I've fixed my price."

"And what may that be?"

"A thousand pounds."

"Oh Lord!" cried poor Miss Tina irrepressibly.

"Is that what she talks to you about?" said Miss Bordereau

"Imagine your aunt's wanting to know!" I had to separate from my younger friend with only those words, though I should have liked immensely to add: "For heaven's sake meet me to-night in the garden!"

VIII

As IT TURNED out the precaution had not been needed, for three hours later, just as I had finished my dinner, Miss Tina appeared, unannounced, in the open doorway of the room in which my simple repasts were served. I remember well that I felt no surprise at seeing her; which is not a proof of my not believing in her timidity. It was immense, but in a case in which there was a particular reason for boldness it never would have prevented her from running up to my floor. I saw that she was now quite full of a particular reason; it threw her forward—made her seize me, as I rose to meet her, by the arm.

"My aunt's very ill; I think she's dying!"

"Never in the world," I answered bitterly. "Don't you be afraid!"

"Do go for a doctor—do, do! Olimpia's gone for the one we always have, but she doesn't come back; I don't know what has happened to her. I told her that if he wasn't at home she was to follow him where he had gone; but apparently she's following him all over Venice. I don't know what to do—she looks so as if she were sinking."

"May I see her, may I judge?" I asked. "Of course I shall be delighted to bring some one; but hadn't we better send my man instead, so that I may stay with you?"

Miss Tina assented to this and I dispatched my servant for the best doctor in the neighbourhood. I hurried downstairs with her, and on the way she told me that an hour after I quitted them in the afternoon Miss Bordereau had had an attack of "oppression," a terrible difficulty in breathing. This had subsided, but had left her so exhausted that she didn't come up: she seemed all spent and gone.

I repeated that she wasn't gone, that she wouldn't go yet; whereupon Miss Tina gave me a sharper sidelong glance than she had ever favoured me withal and said: "Really, what do you mean? I suppose you don't accuse her of making-believe!" I forget what reply I made to this, but I fear that in my heart I thought the old woman capable of any weird manœuvre. Miss Tina wanted to know what I had done to her; her aunt had told her I had made her so angry. I declared I had done nothing whatever—I had been exceedingly careful; to which my companion rejoined that our friend had assured her she had had a scene with me—a scene that had upset her. I answered with some resentment that the scene had been of *her* making—that I couldn't think what she was angry with me for unless for not seeing my way to give a thousand pounds for the portrait of Jeffrey Aspern. "And did she show you that? Oh gracious—oh deary me!" groaned Miss Tina, who seemed to feel the situation pass out of her control and the elements of her fate thicken round her. I answered her I'd give anything to possess it, yet that I had no thousand pounds; but I stopped when we came to the door of Miss Bordereau's room. I had an immense curiosity to pass it, but I thought it my duty to represent to Miss Tina that if I made the invalid angry she ought perhaps to be spared the sight of me. "The sight of you? Do you think she can *see?*" my companion demanded, almost with indignation. I did think so but forbore to say it, and I softly followed my conductress.

I remember that what I said to her as I stood for a moment beside the old woman's bed was: "Does she never show you her eyes then? Have you never seen them?" Miss Bordereau had been divested of her green shade, but—it was not my fortune to behold Juliana in her nightcap—the upper half of her face was covered by the fall of a piece of dingy lacelike muslin, a sort of extemporised hood which, wound round her head, descended to the end of her nose, leaving nothing visible but her white withered cheeks and puckered mouth, closed tightly and, as it were, consciously. Miss Tina gave me a glance of surprise, evidently not seeing a reason for my impatience. "You mean she always wears something? She does it to preserve them."

"Because they're so fine?"

"Oh to-day, to-day!" And Miss Tina shook her head speaking very low. "But they used to be magnificent!"

"Yes indeed—we've Aspern's word for that." And as I looked again at the old woman's wrappings I could imagine her not having wished to allow any supposition that the great poet had overdone it. But I didn't waste my time in considering Juliana, in whom the appearance of respiration was so slight as to suggest that no human attention could ever help her more. I turned my eyes once more all over the room, rummaging with them the closets, the chests of drawers, the tables. Miss Tina at once noted their direction and read, I think, what was in them; but she didn't answer it, turning away restlessly, anxiously, so that I felt rebuked, with reason, for an appetite well-nigh indecent in the presence of our dying companion. All the same I took another view, endeavouring to pick out mentally the receptacle to try first, for a person who should wish to put his hand on Miss Bordereau's papers directly after her death. The place was a dire confusion; it looked like the dressing-room of an old actress. There were clothes hanging over chairs, odd-looking shabby bundles here and there, and various pasteboard boxes piled together, battered, bulging and discoloured, which might have been fifty years old. Miss Tina after a moment noticed the direction of my eyes again, and, as if she guessed how I judged such appearances—forgetting I had no business to judge them at all—said, perhaps to defend herself from the imputation of complicity in the disorder:

"She likes it this way; we can't move things. There are old bandboxes she has had most of her life." Then she added, half-taking pity on my real thought: "Those things were *there*." And she pointed to a small low trunk which stood under a sofa that just allowed room for it. It struck me as a queer superannuated coffer, of painted wood, with elaborate handles and shrivelled straps and with the colour—it had last been endued with a coat of light green—much rubbed off. It evidentlty had travelled with Juliana in the olden time—in the days of her adventures, which it had shared. It would have made a strange figure arriving at a modern hotel.

"*Were* there—they aren't now?" I asked, startled by Miss Tina's implication.

She was going to answer, but at that moment the doctor came in—the doctor whom the little maid had been sent to fetch and whom she had at last overtaken. My servant, going on his own errand, had met her with her companion in tow, and in the sociable Venetian spirit, retracing his steps with them, had also come up to the threshold of the padrona's room, where I saw him peep over the doctor's shoulder. I motioned him away the more instantly that the sight of his prying face reminded me how little I myself had to do there—an admonition confirmed by the sharp way the little doctor eyed me, his air of taking me for a rival who had the field before him. He was a short fat brisk gentleman who wore the tall hat of his profession and seemed to look at everything but his patient. He kept me still in range, as if it struck him I too should be better for a dose, so that I bowed to him and left him with the women, going down to smoke a cigar in the garden. I was nervous; I couldn't go further; I couldn't leave the place. I don't know exactly what I thought might happen, but I felt it important to be there. I wandered about the alleys—the warm night had come on—smoking cigar after cigar and studying the light in Miss Bordereau's windows. They were open now, I could see; the situation was different. Sometimes the light moved, but not quickly; it didn't suggest the hurry of a crisis. Was the old woman dying or was she already dead? Had the doctor said that there was nothing to be done at her tremendous age but to let her quietly pass away? or had he simply announced with a look a little more conventional that the end of the end had come? Were the other two women just going and coming over the offices that follow in such a case? It made me uneasy not to be nearer, as if I thought the doctor himself might carry away the papers with him. I bit my cigar hard while it assailed me again that perhaps there were now no papers to carry!

I wandered about an hour and more. I looked out for Miss Tina at one of the windows, having a vague idea that she might come there to give me some sign. Wouldn't she see the red tip of my cigar in the dark and feel sure I was hanging on to know what the doctor had said? I'm afraid it's a proof of the grossness of my anxieties that I should have taken in some degree for granted at such an hour, in the midst of the greatest change that could fall on her, poor Miss Tina's having also a free mind for them. My servant came down and spoke to me; he knew nothing save that the doctor had gone after a visit of half an hour. If he had stayed half an hour then Miss Bordereau was still alive: it couldn't have taken so long to attest her decease. I sent the man out of the house; there were moments when the sense of his curiosity annoyed me, and this was one of them. *He* had been watching my cigar-tip from an upper window, if Miss Tina hadn't; he couldn't know what I was after and I couldn't tell him, though I suspected in him fantastic private theories about me which he thought fine and which, had I more exactly known them, I should have thought offensive.

I went upstairs at last, but I mounted no higher than the sala. The door of Miss Bordereau's apartment was open, showing from the parlour the dimness of a poor candle. I went toward it with a light tread, and at the same moment Miss Tina appeared and stood looking at me as I approached. "She's better, she's better," she said even before I had asked. "The doctor has given her something; she woke up, came back to life while he was there. He says there's no immediate danger."

"No immediate danger? Surely he thinks her condition serious!"

"Yes, because she had been excited. That affects her dreadfully."

"It will do so again then, because she works herself up. She did so this afternoon."

"Yes, she mustn't come out any more," said Miss Tina with one of her lapses into a deeper detachment.

"What's the use of making such a remark as that," I permitted myself to ask, "if you begin to rattle her about again the first time she bids you?"

"I won't—I won't do it any more."

"You must learn to resist her," I went on.

"Oh yes, I shall; I shall do so better if you tell me it's right."

"You mustn't do it for me—you must do it for yourself. It all comes back to you, if you're scared and upset."

"Well, I'm not upset now," said Miss Tina placidly enough. "She's very quiet."

"Is she conscious again—does she speak?"

"No, she doesn't speak, but she takes my hand. She holds it fast."

"Yes," I returned, "I can see what force she still has by the way she grabbed that picture this afternoon. But if she holds you fast how comes it that you're here?"

Miss Tina waited a little; though her face was in deep shadow—she had her back to the light in the parlour and I had put down my own candle far off, near the door of the sala—I thought I saw her smile ingenuously. "I came on purpose—I had heard your step."

"Why I came on tiptoe, as soundlessly as possible."

"Well, I had heard you," said Miss Tina.

"And is your aunt alone now?"

"Oh no—Olimpia sits there."

On my side I debated. "Shall we then pass in there?" And I nodded at the parlour; I wanted more and more to be on the spot.

"We can't talk there—she'll hear us."

I was on the point of replying that in that case we'd sit silent, but I felt too much this wouldn't do, there was something I desired so immensely to ask her. Thus I hinted we might walk a little in the sala, keeping more at the other end, where we shouldn't disturb our friend. Miss Tina assented unconditionally; the doctor was coming again, she said, and she would be there to meet him at the door. We strolled through the fine superfluous hall, where on the marble floor—particularly as at first we said nothing—our footsteps were more audible than I had expected. When we reached the other end—the wide window, inveterately closed, connecting with the balcony that overhung the canal—I submitted that we had best remain there, as she would see the doctor arrive the sooner. I opened the window and we passed out on the balcony. The air of the canal seemed even heavier, hotter than that of the sala. The place was hushed and void; the quiet neighborhood had gone to sleep. A lamp, here and there, over the narrow black water, glimmered in double; the voice of a man going homeward singing, his jacket on his shoulder and his hat on his ear, came to us from a distance. This didn't prevent the scene from being very *comme il faut,* as Miss Bordereau had called it the first time I saw her. Presently a gondola passed along the canal with its slow rhythmical plash, and as we listened we watched it in silence. It didn't stop, it didn't carry the doctor; and after it had gone on I said to Miss Tina:

"And where are they now—the things that were in the trunk?"

"In the trunk?"

"That green box you pointed out to me in her room. You said her papers had been there; you seemed to mean she had transferred them."

"Oh yes; they're not in the trunk," said Miss Tina.

"May I ask if you've looked?"

"Yes, I've looked—for you."

"How for me, dear Miss Tina? Do you mean you'd have given them to me if you had found them?"—and I fairly trembled with the question.

She delayed to reply and I waited. Suddenly she broke out: "I don't know what I'd do—what I wouldn't!"

"Would you look again—somewhere else?"

She had spoken with a strange unexpected emotion, and she went on in the same tone: "I can't—I can't—while she lies there. It isn't decent."

"No, it isn't decent," I replied gravely. "Let the poor lady rest in peace." And the words, on my lips, were not hypocritical, for I felt reprimanded and shamed.

Miss Tina added in a moment, as if she had guessed this and were sorry for me, but at the same time wished to explain that I did push her, or at least harp on the chord, too much: "I can't deceive her that way. I can't deceive her—perhaps on her deathbed."

"Heaven forbid I should ask you, though I've been guilty myself!"

"You've been guilty?"

"I've sailed under false colours." I felt now I must make a clean breast of it, must tell her I had given her an invented name on account of my fear her aunt would have heard of me and so refuse to take me in. I explained this as well as that I had really been a party to the letter addressed them by John Cumnor months before.

She listened with great attention, almost in fact gaping for wonder, and when I had made my confession she said: "Then your real name—what is it?" She repeated it over twice when I had told her, accompanying it with the exclamation "Gracious, gracious!" Then she added: "I like your own best."

"So do I,"—and I felt my laugh rueful. "Ouf! it's a relief to get rid of the other."

"So it was a regular plot—a kind of conspiracy?"

"Oh a conspiracy—we were only two," I replied, leaving out of course Mrs. Prest.

She considered; I thought she was perhaps going to pronounce us very base. But this was not her way, and she remarked after a moment, as in candid impartial contemplation: "How much you must want them!"

"Oh I do, passionately!" I grinned, I fear to admit. And this chance made me go on, forgetting my compunction of a moment before. "How can she possibly have changed their place herself? How can she walk? How can she arrive at that sort of muscular exertion? How can she lift and carry things?"

"Oh when one wants and when one has so much will!" said Miss Tina as if she had thought over my question already herself and had simply had no choice but that answer—the idea that in the dead of night, or at some moment when the coast was clear, the old woman had been capable of a miraculous effort.

"Have you questioned Olimpia? Hasn't she helped her—hasn't she done it for her?" I asked; to which my friend replied promptly and positively that their servant had had nothing to do with the matter, though without admitting definitely that she had spoken to her. It was as if she were a little shy, a little ashamed now, of letting me see how much she had entered into my uneasiness and had me on her mind. Suddenly she said to me without any immediate relevance:

"I rather feel you a new person, you know, now that you've a new name."

"It isn't a new one; it's a very good old one, thank fortune!"

She looked at me a moment. "Well, I do like it better."

"Oh if you didn't I would almost go on with the other!"

"Would you really?"

I laughed again, but I returned for all answer: "Of course if she can rummage about that way she can perfectly have burnt them."

"You must wait—you must wait," Miss Tina mournfully moralised; and her tone ministered little to my patience, for it seemed after all to accept that wretched possibility. I would teach myself to wait, I declared nevertheless; because in the first place I couldn't do otherwise and in the second I had her promise, given me the other night, that she would help me.

"Of course if the papers are gone that's no use," she said; not as if she wished to recede, but only to be conscientious.

"Naturally. But if you could only find out!" I groaned, quivering again.

"I thought you promised you'd wait."

"Oh you mean wait even for that?"

"For what then?"

"Ah, nothing," I answered rather foolishly, being ashamed to tell her what had been implied in my acceptance of delay—the idea that she would perhaps do more for me than merely find out.

I know not if she guessed this; at all events she seemed to bethink herself of some propriety of showing me more rigour. "I didn't promise to deceive, did I? I don't think I did."

"It doesn't much matter whether you did or not, for you couldn't!"

Nothing is more possible than that she wouldn't have contested this even hadn't she been diverted by our seeing the doctor's gondola shoot into the little canal and approach the house. I noted that he came as fast as if he believed our proprietress still in danger. We looked down at him while he disembarked and then went back into the sala to meet him. When he came up, however, I naturally left Miss Tina to go off with him alone, only asking her leave to come back later for news.

I went out of the house and walked far, as far as the Piazza, where my restlessness declined to quit me. I was unable to sit down; it was very late now though there were people still at the little tables in front of the cafés: I could but uneasily revolve, and I did so half a dozen times. The only comfort, none the less, was in my having told Miss

Tina who I really was. At last I took my way home again, getting gradually and all but inextricably lost, as I did whenever I went out in Venice: so that it was considerably past midnight when I reached my door. The sala, upstairs, was as dark as usual and my lamp as I crossed it found nothing satisfactory to show me. I was disappointed, for I had notified Miss Tina that I would come back for a report, and I thought she might have left a light there as a sign. The door of the ladies' apartment was closed; which seemed a hint that my faltering friend had gone to bed in impatience of waiting for me. I stood in the middle of the place, considering, hoping she would hear me and perhaps peep out, saying to myself too that she would never go to bed with her aunt in a state so critical; she would sit up and watch—she would be in a chair, in her dressing-gown. I went nearer the door; I stopped there and listened. I heard nothing at all and at last I tapped gently. No answer came and after another minute I turned the handle. There was no light in the room; this ought to have prevented my entrance, but it had no such effect. If I have frankly stated the importunities, the indelicacies, of which my desire to possess myself of Jeffrey Aspern's papers had made me capable I needn't shrink, it seems to me, from confessing this last indiscretion. I regard it as the worst thing I did, yet there were extenuating circumstances. I was deeply though doubtless not disinterestedly anxious for more news of Juliana, and Miss Tina had accepted from me, as it were, a rendezvous which it might have been a point of honour with me to keep. It may be objected that her leaving the place dark was a positive sign that she released me, and to this I can only reply that I wished not to be released.

The door to Miss Bordereau's room was open and I could see beyond it the faintness of a taper. There was no sound—my footstep caused no one to stir. I came further into the room; I lingered there lamp in hand. I wanted to give Miss Tina a chance to come to me if, as I couldn't doubt, she were still with her aunt. I made no noise to call her; I only waited to see if she wouldn't notice my light. She didn't, and I explained this—I found afterwards I was right—by the idea that she had fallen asleep. If she had fallen asleep her aunt was not on her mind, and my explanation ought to have led me to go out as I had come. I must repeat again that it didn't, for I found myself at the same moment given up to something else. I had no definite purpose, no bad intention, but felt myself held to the spot by an acute, though absurd, sense of opportunity. Opportunity for what I couldn't have said, inasmuch as it wasn't in my mind that I might proceed to thievery. Even had this tempted me I was confronted with the evident fact that Miss Bordereau didn't leave her secretary, her cupboard and the drawers of her tables gaping. I had no keys, no tools and no ambition to smash her furniture. None the less it came to me that I was now, perhaps alone, unmolested, at the hour of freedom and safety, nearer to the source of my hopes than I had ever been. I held up my lamp, let the light play on the different objects as if it could tell me something. Still there came no movement from the other room. If Miss Tina was sleeping she was sleeping sound. Was she doing so—generous creature—on purpose to leave me the field? Did she know I was there and was she just keeping quiet to see what I would do—what I *could* do? Yet might I, when it came to that? She herself knew even better than I how little.

I stopped in front of the secretary, gaping at it vainly and no doubt grotesquely; for what had it to say to me after all? In the first place it was locked, and in the second it almost surely contained nothing in which I was interested. Ten to one the papers had been destroyed, and even if they hadn't the keen old woman wouldn't have put them in such a place as that after removing them from the green trunk—wouldn't have transferred them, with the idea of their safety on her brain, from the better hiding-place to the worse. The secretary was more conspicuous, more exposed in a room in which she could no longer mount guard. It opened with a key, but there was a small brass handle, like a button as well; I saw this as I played my lamp over it. I did something more, for the climax of my crisis; I caught a glimpse of the possibility that Miss Tina wished me really to understand. If she didn't so wish me, if she wished me to keep away, why hadn't she locked the door of communication between the sitting-room and the sala? That would have been a definite sign that I was to leave them alone. If I didn't leave them alone she meant me to come for a purpose—a purpose now represented by the super-subtle inference that to oblige me she had unlocked the secretary. She hadn't left the key, but the lid would probably move if I touched the button. This possibility pressed me hard and I bent very close to judge. I didn't propose to do anything, not even—not in the least—to let down the lid; I only wanted to test my theory, to see if the cover *would* move. I touched the button with my hand—a mere touch would tell me; and as I did so—it is embarrassing for me to relate it—I looked over my shoulder. It was a chance, an instinct, for I had really heard nothing. I almost let my luminary drop and certainly I stepped back, straightening myself up at what I saw. Juliana stood there in her nightdress, by the doorway of her room, watching me; her hands were raised, she had lifted the everlasting curtain that covered half her face, and for the first, the last, the only time I beheld her extraordinary eyes. They glared at me; they were like the sudden drench, for a caught burglar, of a flood of gaslight; they made me horribly ashamed. I never shall forget her strange little bent white tottering figure, with its lifted head, her attitude, her expression; neither shall I forget the tone in which as I turned, looking at her, she hissed out passionately, furiously:

"Ah you publishing scoundrel!"

I can't now say what I stammered to excuse myself, to

explain; but I went toward her to tell her I meant no harm. She waved me off with her old hands, retreating before me in horror; and the next thing I knew she had fallen back with a quick spasm, as if death had descended on her, into Miss Tina's arms.

IX

I LEFT Venice the next morning, directly on learning that my hostess had not succumbed, as I feared at the moment, to the shock I had given her—the shock I may also say she had given me. How in the world could I have supposed her capable of getting out of bed by herself? I failed to see Miss Tina before going; I only saw the *donna,* whom I entrusted with a note for her younger mistress. In this note I mentioned that I should be absent but a few days. I went to Treviso, to Bassano, to Castelfranco; I took walks and drives and looked at musty old churches with ill-lighted pictures; I spent hours seated smoking at the doors of cafés, where there were flies and yellow curtains, on the shady side of sleepy little squares. In spite of these pastimes, which were mechanical and perfunctory, I scantly enjoyed my travels: I had had to gulp down a bitter draught and couldn't get rid of the taste. It had been devilish awkward, as the young men say, to be found by Juliana in the dead of night examining the attachment of her bureau; and it had not been less so to have to believe for a good many hours after that it was highly probable I had killed her. My humiliation galled me, but I had to make the best of it, had, in writing to Miss Tina to minimise it, as well as account for the posture in which I had been discovered. As she gave me no word of answer I couldn't know what impression I made on her. It rankled for me that I had been called a publishing scoundrel, since certainly I did publish and no less certainly hadn't been very delicate. There was a moment when I stood convinced that the only way to purge my dishonour was to take myself straight away on the instant; to sacrifice my hopes and relieve the two poor women for ever of the oppression of my intercourse. Then I reflected that I had better try a short absence first, for I must already have had a sense (unexpressed and dim) that in disappearing completely it wouldn't be merely my own hopes I should condemn to extinction. It would perhaps answer if I kept dark long enough to give the elder lady time to believe herself rid of me. That she would wish to be rid of me after this—if I wasn't rid of her—was now not to be doubted: that midnight monstrosity would have cured her of the disposition to put up with my company for the sake of my dollars. I said to myself that after all I couldn't abandon Miss Tina, and I continued to say this even while I noted that she quite ignored my earnest request—I had given her two or three addresses, at little towns, *poste restante*—for some sign of her actual state. I would have made my servant write me news but that he was unable to manage a pen. Couldn't I measure the scorn of Miss Tina's silence—little disdainful as she had ever been? Really the soreness pressed; yet if I had scruples about going back I had others about not doing so, and I wanted to put myself on a better footing. The end of it was that I did return to Venice on the twelfth day; and as my gondola gently bumped against our palace steps a fine palpitation of suspense showed me the violence my absence had done me.

I had faced about so abruptly that I hadn't even telegraphed to my servant. He was therefore not at the station to meet me, but he poked out his head from an upper window when I reached the house. "They have put her into earth, *quella vecchia,*" he said to me in the lower hall while he shouldered my valise; and he grinned and almost winked as if he knew I should be pleased with his news.

"She's dead!" I cried, giving him a very different look.

"So it appears, since they've buried her."

"It's all over then? When was the funeral?"

"The other yesterday. But a funeral you could scarcely call it, signore: *roba da niente—un piccolo passeggio brutto* of two gondolas. Poveretta!" the man continued, referring apparently to Miss Tina. His conception of funerals was that they were mainly to amuse the living.

I wanted to know about Miss Tina, how she might be and generally where; but I asked him no more questions till we had got upstairs. Now that the fact had met me I took a bad view of it, especially of the idea that poor Miss Tina had had to manage by herself after the end. What did she know about arrangements, about the steps to take in such a case? Poveretta indeed! I could only hope the doctor had given her support and that she hadn't been neglected by the old friends of whom she had told me, the little band of the faithful whose fidelity consisted in coming to the house once a year. I elicited from my servant that two old ladies and an old gentleman had in fact rallied round Miss Tina and had supported her—they had come for her in a gondola of their own—during the journey to the cemetery, the little red-walled island of tombs which lies to the north of the town and on the way to Murano. It appeared from these signs that the Misses Bordereau were Catholics, a discovery I had never made, as the old woman couldn't go to church and her niece, so far as I perceived, either didn't, or went only to early mass in the parish before I was stirring. Certainly even the priests respected their seclusion; I had never caught the whisk of the curato's skirt. That evening, an hour later, I sent my servant down with five words on a card to ask if Miss Tina would see me for a few moments. She was not in the house, where he had sought her, he told me when he came back, but in the garden walking about to refresh herself and picking the flowers quite as if they belonged to her. He had found her there and she would be happy to see me.

I went down and passed half an hour with poor Miss Tina. She had always had a look of musty mourning, as if she were wearing out old robes of sorrow that wouldn't come to an end; and in this particular she made no different show. But she clearly had been crying, crying a great deal—simply, satisfyingly, refreshingly, with a primitive retarded sense of solitude and violence. But she had none of the airs or graces of grief, and I was almost surprised to see her stand there in the first dusk with her hands full of admirable roses and smile at me with reddened eyes. Her white face, in the frame of her mantilla, looked longer, leaner than usual. I hadn't doubted her being irreconcilably disgusted with me, her considering I ought to have been on the spot to advise her, to help her; and, though I believed there was no rancour in her composition and no great conviction of the importance of her affairs, I had prepared myself for a change in her manner, for some air of injury and estrangement, which should say to my conscience: "Well, you're a nice person to have professed things!" But historic truth compels me to declare that this poor lady's dull face ceased to be dull, almost ceased to be plain, as she turned it gladly to her late aunt's lodger. That touched him extremely and he thought it simplified his situation until he found it didn't. I was as kind to her that evening as I knew how to be, and I walked about the garden with her as long as seemed good. There was no explanation of any sort between us; I didn't ask her why she hadn't answered my letter. Still less did I repeat what I had said to her in that communication; if she chose to let me suppose she had forgotten the position in which Miss Bordereau had surprised me and the effect of the discovery on the old woman, I was quite willing to take it that way: I was grateful to her for not treating me as if I had killed her aunt.

We strolled and strolled, though really not much passed between us save the recognition of her bereavement, conveyed in my manner and in the expression she had of depending on me now, since I let her see I still took an interest in her. Miss Tina's was no breast for the pride or the pretense of independence; she didn't in the least suggest that she knew at present what would become of her. I forbore to press on that question, however, for I certainly was not prepared to say that I would take charge of her. I was cautious; not ignobly, I think, for I felt her knowledge of life to be so small that in her unsophisticated vision there would be no reason why—since I seemed to pity her—I shouldn't somehow look after her. She told me how her aunt had died, very peacefully at the last, and how everything had been done afterwards by the care of her good friends—fortunately, thanks to me, she said, smiling, there was money in the house. She repeated that when once the "nice" Italians like you they are your friends for life, and when we had gone into this she asked me about my *giro,* my impressions, my adventures, the places I had seen. I told her what I could, making it up partly, I'm afraid, as in my disconcerted state I had taken little in; and after she had heard me she exclaimed, quite as if she had forgotten her aunt and her sorrow, "Dear, dear, how much I should like to do such things—to take an amusing little journey!" It came over me for the moment that I ought to propose some enterprise, say I would accompany her anywhere she liked; and I remarked at any rate that a pleasant excursion—to give her a change—might be managed; we would think of it, talk it over. I spoke never a word of the Aspern documents, asked no question as to what she had ascertained or what had otherwise happened with regard to them before Juliana's death. It wasn't that I wasn't on pins and needles to know, but that I thought it more decent not to show greed again so soon after the catastrophe. I hoped she herself would say something, but she never glanced that way, and I thought this natural at the time. Later on, however, that night, it occurred to me that her silence was matter for suspicion; since if she had talked of my movements, of anything so detached as the Giorgione at Castelfranco, she might have alluded to what she could easily remember was in my mind. It was not to be supposed that the emotion produced by her aunt's death had blotted out the recollection that I was interested in that lady's relics, and I fidgeted afterwards as it came to me that her reticence might very possibly just mean that no relics survived. We separated in the garden—it was she who said she must go in; now that she was alone on the *piano nobile* I felt that (judged at any rate by Venetian ideas) I was on rather a different footing in regard to the invasion of it. As I shook hands with her for good-night I asked her if she had some general plan, had thought over what she had best do. "Oh yes, oh yes, but I haven't settled anything yet," she replied quite cheerfully. Was her cheerfulness explained by the impression that I would settle for her?

I was glad the next morning that we had neglected practical questions, as this gave me a pretext for seeing her again immediately. There was a practical enough question now to be touched on. I owed it to her to let her know formally that of course I didn't expect her to keep me on as a lodger, as also to show some interest in her own tenure, what she might have on her hands in the way of a lease. But I was not destined, as befell, to converse with her for more than an instant on either of these points. I sent her no message; I simply went down to the sala and walked to and fro there. I knew she would come out; she would promptly see me accessible. Somehow I preferred not to be shut up with her; gardens and big halls seemed better places to talk. It was a splendid morning, with something in the air that told of the waning of the long Venetian summer; a freshness from the sea that stirred the flowers in the garden and made a pleasant draught in the house, less shuttered and darkened now than when the old woman was alive. It was the beginning of autumn, of the end of the golden months. With this it was the end of my experiment—or would be in the course of half an hour, when I should really have learned that my dream had been reduced to ashes. After that there would be nothing left for me but to go to the station; for seriously—and as it struck me in the morning light—I couldn't linger there to act as guardian to a piece of middle-aged female helplessness. If she hadn't saved the papers wherein should I be indebted to her? I think I winced a little as I asked myself how much, if she *had* saved them, I should have to recognise and, as it were, reward such a courtesy. Mightn't that service after all saddle me with a guardianship? If this idea didn't make me more uncomfortable as I walked up and down it was because I was convinced I had nothing to look to. If the old woman hadn't destroyed everything before she pounced on me in the parlour she had done so the next day.

It took Miss Tina rather longer than I had expected to act on my calculation; but when at last she came out she looked at me without surprise. I mentioned I had been waiting for her and she asked why I hadn't let her know. I was glad a few hours later on that I had checked myself before remarking that a friendly intuition might have told her: it turned to comfort for me that I hadn't played even to that mild extent on her sensibility. What I did say was virtually the truth—that I was too nervous, since I expected her now to settle my fate.

"Your fate?" said Miss Tina, giving me a queer look; and as she spoke I noticed a rare change in her. Yes, she was other than she had been the evening before—less natural and less easy. She had been crying the day before and was not crying now, yet she struck me as less confident. It was as if something had happened to her during the night, or at least as if she had thought of something that troubled her—something in particular that affected her relations with me, made them more embarrassing and more complicated. Had she simply begun to feel that her aunt's not being there now altered my position?

"I mean about our papers. *Are* there any? You must know now."

"Yes, there are a great many; more than I supposed." I was struck with the way her voice trembled as she told me this.

"Do you mean you've got them in there—and that I may see them?"

"I don't think you can see them," said Miss Tina, with an extraordinary expression of entreaty in her eyes, as if the dearest hope she had in the world now was that I wouldn't take them from her. But how could she expect me to make such a sacrifice as that after all that had passed between us? What had I come back to Venice for but to see them, to take them? My joy at learning they were still in existence was such that if the poor woman had gone down on her knees to beseech me never to mention them again I would have treated the proceeding as a bad joke. "I've got them but I can't show them," she lamentably added.

"Not even to me? Ah Miss Tina!" I broke into a tone of infinite remonstrance and reproach.

She coloured and the tears came back to her eyes; I measured the anguish it cost her to take such a stand which a dreadful sense of duty had imposed on her. It made me quite sick to find myself confronted with that particular obstacle; all the more that it seemed to me I had been distinctly encouraged to leave it out of account. I quite held Miss Tina to have assured me that if she had no greater hindrance than that——! "You don't mean to say you made her a death-bed promise? It was precisely against your doing anything of that sort that I thought I was safe. Oh I would rather she had burnt the papers outright than have to reckon with such a treachery as that."

"No, it isn't a promise," said Miss Tina.

"Pray what is it then?"

She hung fire, but finally said: "She tried to burn them, but I prevented it. She had hid them in her bed."

"In her bed—?"

"Between the mattresses. That's where she put them when she took them out of the trunk. I can't understand how she did it, because Olimpia didn't help her. She tells me so and I believe her. My aunt only told her afterwards, so that she shouldn't undo the bed—anything but the sheets. So it was very badly made," added Miss Tina simply.

"I should think so! And how did she try to burn them?"

"She didn't try much; she was too weak those last days. But she told me—she charged me. Oh it was terrible! She couldn't speak after that night. She could only make signs."

"And what did you do?"

"I took them away. I locked them up."

"In the secretary?"

"Yes, in the secretary," said Miss Tina, reddening again.

"Did you tell her you'd burn them?"

"No, I didn't—on purpose."

"On purpose to gratify me?"

"Yes, only for that."

"And what good will you have done me if after all you won't show them?"

"Oh none. I know that—I know that," she dismally sounded.

"And did she believe you had destroyed them?"

"I don't know what she believed at the last. I couldn't tell—she was too far gone."

"Then if there was no promise and no assurance I can't see what ties you."

"Oh she hated it so—she hated it so! She was so jealous. But here's the portrait—you may have that," the poor woman announced, taking the little picture, wrapped up in the same manner in which her aunt had wrapped it, out of her pocket.

"I may have it—do you mean you give it to me?" I gasped as it passed into my hand.

"Oh yes."

"But it's worth money—a large sum."

"Well!" said Miss Tina, still with her strange look.

I didn't know what to make of it, for it could scarcely mean that she wanted to bargain like her aunt. She spoke as for making me a present. "I can't take it from you as a gift," I said, "and yet I can't afford to pay you for it according to the idea Miss Bordereau had of its value. She rated it at a thousand pounds."

"Couldn't we sell it?" my friend threw off.

"God forbid! I prefer the picture to the money."

"Well then keep it."

"You're very generous."

"So are you."

"I don't know why you should think so," I returned; and this was true enough, for the good creature appeared to have in her mind some rich reference that I didn't in the least seize.

"Well, you've made a great difference for me," she said.

I looked at Jeffrey Aspern's face in the little picture, partly in order not to look at that of my companion, which had begun to trouble me, even to frighten me a little—it had taken so very odd, so strained and unnatural a cast. I made no answer to this last declaration; I but privately consulted Jeffrey Aspern's delightful eyes with my own—they were so young and brilliant yet so wise and so deep; I asked him what on earth was the matter with Miss Tina. He seemed to smile at me with mild mockery; he might have been amused at my case. I had got into a pickle for him—as if he needed it! He was unsatisfactory for the only moment since I had known him. Nevertheless, now that I held the little picture in my hand I felt it would be a precious possession. "Is this a bribe to make me give up the papers?" I presently and all perversely asked. "Much as I value this, you know, if I were to be obliged to choose the papers are what I should prefer. Ah but ever so much!"

"How can you choose—how can you choose?" Miss Tina returned slowly and woefully.

"I see! Of course there's nothing to be said if you regard the interdiction that rules on you as quite insurmountable. In this case it must seem to you that to part with them would be an impiety of the worst kind, a simple sacrilege!"

She shook her head, only lost in the queerness of her

case. "You'd understand if you had known her. I'm afraid," she quavered suddenly—"I'm afraid! She was terrible when she was angry."

"Yes, I saw something of that, that night. She was terrible. Then I saw her eyes. Lord, they were fine!"

"I see them—they stare at me in the dark!" said Miss Tina.

"You've grown nervous with all you've been through."

"Oh yes, very—very!"

"You mustn't mind; that will pass away," I said kindly. Then I added resignedly, for it really seemed to me that I must accept the situation: "Well, so it is, and it can't be helped. I must renounce." My friend, at this, with her eyes on me, gave a low soft moan, and I went on: "I only wish to goodness she had destroyed them; then there would be nothing more to say. And I can't understand why, with her ideas, she didn't."

"Oh she lived on them!" said Miss Tina.

"You can imagine whether that makes me want less to see them," I returned not quite so desperately. "But don't let me stand here as if I had it in my soul to tempt you to anything base. Naturally, you understand, I give up my rooms. I leave Venice immediately." And I took up my hat, which I had placed on a chair. We were still rather awkwardly on our feet in the middle of the sala. She had left the door of the apartments open behind her, but had not led me that way.

A strange spasm came into her face as she saw me take my hat. "Immediately—do you mean to-day?" The tone of the words was tragic—they were a cry of desolation.

"Oh no; not so long as I can be of the least service to you."

"Well, just a day or two more—just two or three days," she panted. Then controlling herself she added in another manner: "She wanted to say something to me—the last day—something very particular. But she couldn't."

"Something very particular?"

"Something more about the papers."

"And did you guess—have you any idea?"

"No, I've tried to think—but I don't know. I've thought all kinds of things."

"As for instance?"

"Well, that if you were a relation it would be different."

I wondered. "If I were a relation—?"

"If you weren't a stranger. Then it would be the same for you as for me. Anything that's mine would be yours, and you could do what you like. I shouldn't be able to prevent you—and you'd have no responsibility."

She brought out this droll explanation with a nervous rush and as if speaking words got by heart. They gave me an impression of a subtlety which at first I failed to follow. But after a moment her face helped me to see further, and then the queerest of light came to me. It was embarrassing, and I bent my head over Jeffrey Aspern's portrait. What an odd expression was in his face! "Get out of it as you can, my dear fellow!" I put the picture into the pocket of my coat and said to Miss Tina: "Yes, I'll sell it for you. I shan't get a thousand pounds by any means, but I shall get something good."

She looked at me through pitiful tears, but seemed to try to smile as she returned: "We can divide the money."

"No, no, it shall be all yours." Then I went on: "I think I know what your poor aunt wanted to say. She wanted to give directions that the papers should be buried with her."

Miss Tina appeared to weigh this suggestion; after which she answered with striking decision, "Oh no, she wouldn't have thought that safe!"

"It seems to me nothing could be safer."

"She had an idea that when people want to publish they're capable—!" And she paused, very red.

"Of violating a tomb? Mercy on us, what must she have thought of me!"

"She wasn't just, she wasn't generous!" my companion cried with sudden passion.

The light that had come into my mind a moment before spread further. "Ah don't say that, for we *are* a dreadful race." Then I pursued: "If she left a will that may give you some idea."

"I've found nothing of the sort—she destroyed it. She was very fond of me," Miss Tina added with an effect of extreme inconsequence. "She wanted me to be happy. And if any person should be kind to me—she wanted to speak of that."

I was almost awestricken by the astuteness with which the good lady found herself inspired, transparent astuteness as it was and stitching, as the phrase is, with white thread. "Depend upon it she didn't want to make any provision that would be agreeable to *me*."

"No, not to you, but quite to me. She knew I should like it if you could carry out your idea. Not because she cared for you, but because she did think of me," Miss Tina went on with her unexpected persuasive volubility. "You could see the things—you could use them." She stopped, seeing I grasped the sense of her conditional—stopped long enough for me to give some sign that I didn't give. She must have been conscious, however, that though my face showed the greatest embarrassment ever painted on a human countenance it was not set as a stone, it was also full of compassion. It was a comfort to me a long time afterwards to consider that she couldn't have seen in me the smallest symptom of disrespect. "I don't know what to do; I'm too tormented, I'm too ashamed!" she continued with vehemence. Then turning away from me and burying her face in her hands she burst into a flood of tears. If she didn't know what to do it may be imagined whether I knew better. I stood there dumb, matching her while her sobs resounded in the great empty hall. In a moment she was up at me again with her streaming eyes. "I'd give you everything, and she'd understand, where she is—she'd forgive me!"

"Ah Miss Tina—ah Miss Tina." I stammered for all

reply. I didn't know what to do, as I say, but at a venture I made a wild vague movement in consequence of which I found myself at the door. I remember standing there and saying, "It wouldn't do, it wouldn't do!"—saying it pensively, awkwardly, grotesquely, while I looked away to the opposite end of the sala as at something very interesting. The next thing I remembered is that I was downstairs and out of the house. My gondola was there and my gondolier, reclining on the cushions, sprang up as soon as he saw me. I jumped in and to his usual *"Dove commanda?"* replied, in a tone that made him stare: "Anywhere, anywhere; out into the lagoon!"

He rowed me away and I sat there prostrate, groaning softly to myself, my hat pulled over my brow. What in the name of the preposterous did she mean if she didn't mean to offer me her hand? That was the price—that was the price! And did she think I wanted it, poor deluded infatuated extravagant lady? My gondolier, behind me, must have seen my ears red as I wondered, motionless there under the fluttering *tenda* with my hidden face, noticing nothing as we passed—wondered whether her delusion, her infatuation had been my own reckless work. Did she think I had made love to her even to get the papers? I hadn't, I hadn't; I repeated that over to myself for an hour, for two hours, till I was wearied if not convinced. I don't know where, on the lagoon, my gondolier took me; we floated aimlessly and with slow rare strokes. At last I became conscious that we were near the Lido, far up, on the right hand, as you turn your back to Venice, and I made him put me ashore. I wanted to walk, to move, to shed some of my bewilderment. I crossed the narrow strip and got to the sea-beach—I took my way toward Malamocco. But presently I flung myself down again on the warm sand, in the breeze, on the coarse dry grass. It took it out of me to think I had been so much at fault, that I had unwittingly but nonetheless deplorably trifled. But I hadn't given her cause—distinctly I hadn't. I had said to Mrs. Prest that I would make love to her; but it had been a joke without consequences and I had never said it to my victim. I had been as kind as possible because I really liked her; but since when had that become a crime where a woman of such an age and such an appearance was concerned? I am far from remembering clearly the succession of events and feelings during this long day of confusion, which I spent entirely in wandering about, without going home, until late at night; it only comes back to me that there were moments when I pacified my conscience and others when I lashed it into pain. I didn't laugh all day—that I do recollect; the case, however it might have struck others, seemed to me so little amusing. I should have been better employed perhaps in taking in the comic side of it. At any rate, whether I had given cause or not, there was no doubt whatever that I couldn't pay the price. I couldn't accept the proposal. I couldn't, for a bundle of tattered papers, marry a ridiculous pathetic provincial old woman. It was a proof of how little she supposed the idea would come to me that she should have decided to suggest it herself in that practical argumentative heroic way—with the timidity, however, so much more striking than the boldness, that her reasons appeared to come first and her feelings afterward.

As the day went on I grew to wish I had never heard of Aspern's relics, and I cursed the extravagant curiosity that had put John Cumnor on the scent of them. We had more than enough material without them, and my predicament was the just punishment of that most fatal of human follies, our not having known when to stop. It was very well to say it was no predicament, that the way out was simple, that I had only to leave Venice by the first train in the morning, after addressing Miss Tina a note which should be placed in her hand as soon as I got clear of the house; for it was strong proof of my quandary that when I tried to make up the note to my taste in advance—I would put it on paper as soon as I got home, before going to bed—I couldn't think of anything but "How can I thank you for the rare confidence you've placed in me?" That would never do; it sounded exactly as if an acceptance were to follow. Of course I might get off without writing at all, but that would be brutal, and my idea was still to exclude brutal solutions. As my confusion cooled I lost myself in wonder at the importance I had attached to Juliana's crumpled scraps; the thought of them became odious to me and I was as vexed with the old witch for the superstition that had prevented her from destroying them as I was with myself for having already spent more money than I could afford in attempting to control their fate. I forget what I did, where I went after leaving the Lido, and at what hour or with what recovery of composure I made my way back to my boat. I only know that in the afternoon, when the air was aglow with the sunset, I was standing before the church of Saints John and Paul and looking up at the small square-jawed face of Bartolommeo Colleoni, the terrible *condottiere* who sits so sturdily astride of his huge bronze horse on the high pedestal on which Venetian gratitude maintains him. The statue is incomparable, the finest of all mounted figures, unless that of Marcus Aurelius, who rides benignant before the Roman Capitol, be finer: but I was not thinking of that; I only found myself staring at the triumphant captain as if he had had an oracle on his lips. The western light shines into all his grimness at that hour and makes it wonderfully personal. But he continued to look far over my head, at the red immersion of another day—he had seen so many go down into the lagoon through the centuries—and if he were thinking of battles and stratagems they were of a different quality from any I had to tell him of. He couldn't direct me what to do, gaze up at him as I might. Was it before this or after that I wandered about for an hour in the small canals, to the continued stupefaction of my gondolier, who had never seen me so restless and yet so void of a purpose and could extract from me no order but "Go anywhere—everywhere—all over the place?" He reminded me that I had not lunched and expressed therefore respectfully the hope that I would dine earlier. He had had long periods of leisure during the day, when I had left the boat and rambled, so that I was not obliged to consider him, and I told him that till the morrow, for reasons, I should touch no meat. It was an effect of poor Miss Tina's proposal, not altogether auspicious, that I had quite lost my appetite. I don't know why it happened that on this occasion I was more than ever struck with that queer air of sociability, of cousinship and family life, which makes up half the expression of Venice. Without streets and vehicles, the uproar of wheels, the brutality of horses, and with its little winding ways where people crowd together, where voices sound as in the corridors of a house, where the human step circulates as if it skirted the angles of furniture and shoes never wear out, the place has the character of an immense collective apartment, in which Piazza San Marco is the most ornamented corner and palaces and churches, for the rest, play the part of great divans of repose, tables of entertainment, expanses of decoration. And somehow the splendid common domicile, familiar domestic and resonant, also resembles a theatre with its actors clicking over bridges and, in straggling processions, tripping along fondamentas. As you sit in your gondola the footways that in certain parts edge the canals assume to the eye the importance of a stage, meeting it at the same angle, and the Venetian figures, moving to and fro against the battered scenery of their little houses of comedy, strike you as members of an endless dramatic troupe.

I went to bed that night very tired and without being able to compose an address to Miss Tina. Was this failure the reason why I became conscious the next morning as soon as I awoke of a determination to see the poor lady again the first moment she would receive me? That had something to do with it, but what had still more was the fact that during my sleep the oddest revulsion had taken place in my spirit. I found myself aware of this almost as soon as I opened my eyes: it made me jump out of my bed with the movement of a man who remembers that he has left the house-door ajar or a candle burning under a shelf. Was I still in time to save my goods? That question was in my heart; for what had now come to pass was that in the unconscious cerebration of sleep I had swung back to a passionate appreciation of Juliana's treasure. The pieces composing it were now more precious than ever and a positive ferocity had come into my need to acquire them. The condition Miss Tina had attached to that act no longer appeared an obstacle worth thinking of, and for an hour this morning my repentant imagination brushed it aside. It was absurd I should be able to invent nothing; absurd to renounce so easily and turn away helpless from the idea that the only way to become possessed was to unite myself to her for life. I mightn't unite myself, yet I might still have what she had. I must add that by the time I sent down to ask if she would see me I had invented no alternative, though in fact I drew out my dressing in the interest of my wit. This failure was humiliating, yet what could the alternative be? Miss Tina sent back word I might come; and as I descended the stairs and crossed the sala to her door—this time she received me in her aunt's forlorn parlour—I hoped she wouldn't think my announcement was to be "favourable." She certainly would have understood my recoil of the day before.

As soon as I came into the room I saw that she had done so, but I also saw something which had not been in my forecast. Poor Miss Tina's sense of her failure had produced a rare alteration in her, but I had been too full of stratagems and spoils to think of that. Now I took it in; I can scarcely tell how it startled me. She stood in the middle of the room with a face of mildness bent upon me, and her look of forgiveness, of absolution, made her angelic. It beautified her: she was younger; she was not a ridiculous old woman. This trick of her expression, this magic of her spirit, transfigured her, and while I still noted it I heard a whisper somewhere in the depths of my conscience: "Why not, after all—why not?" It seemed to me I *could* pay the price. Still more distinctly however than the whisper I heard Miss Tina's own voice. I was so struck with the different effect she made on me that at first I wasn't clearly aware of what she was saying; then I recognised she had bade me good-bye—she said something about hoping I should be very happy.

"Good-bye—good-bye?" I repeated with an inflection interrogative and probably foolish.

I saw she didn't feel the interrogation, she only heard the words; she had strung herself up to accepting our separation and they fell upon her ear as a proof. "Are you going to-day?" she asked. "But it doesn't matter, for whenever you go I shall not see you again. I don't want to." And she smiled strangely, with an infinite gentleness. She had never doubted my having left her the day before in horror. How *could* she, since I hadn't come back before night to contradict, even as a simple form, even as an act of common humanity, such an idea? And now she had the force of soul—Miss Tina with force of soul was a new conception—to smile at me in her abjection.

"What shall you do—where shall you go?" I asked.

"Oh I don't know. I've done the great thing. I've destroyed the papers."

"Destroyed them?" I wailed.

"Yes; what was I to keep them for? I burnt them last night, one by one, in the kitchen."

"One by one?" I coldly echoed it.

"It took a long time—there were so many." The room seemed to go round me as she said this and a real darkness for a moment descended on my eyes. When it passed, Miss Tina was there still, but the transfiguration was over and she had changed back to a plain dingy elderly person. It was in this character she spoke as she said "I can't stay with you longer, I can't;" and it was in this character she turned her back upon me, as I had turned mine upon her twenty-four hours before, and moved to the door of her room. Here she did what I hadn't done when I quitted her—she paused long enough to give me one look. I have never forgotten it and I sometimes still suffer from it, though it was not resentful. No, there was no resentment, nothing hard or vindictive in poor Miss Tina; for when, later, I sent her, as the price of the portrait of Jeffrey Aspern, a larger sum of money than I had hoped to be able to gather for her, writing to her that I had sold the picture, she kept it with thanks; she never sent it back. I wrote her that I had sold the picture, but I admitted to Mrs. Prest at the time—I met this other friend in London that autumn—that it hangs above my writing-table. When I look at it I can scarcely bear my loss—I mean of the precious papers.

PASSAGE ON *THE ASPERN PAPERS* FROM JAMES'S NOTEBOOKS

Florence, January 12th, 1887. Hamilton (V.L.'s brother) told me a curious thing of Capt. Silsbee—the Boston art-critic and Shelley-worshipper; that is of a curious adventure of his. Miss Claremont,[1] Byron's *ci-devant* mistress (the mother of Allegra) was living, until lately, here in Florence, at a great age, 80 or thereabouts, and with her lived her niece, a younger Miss Claremont—of about 50. Silsbee knew that they had interesting papers—letters of Shelley's and Byron's—he had known it for a long time and cherished the idea of getting hold of them. To this end he laid the plan of going to lodge with the Misses Claremont—hoping that the old lady in view of her great age and failing condition would die while he was there, so that he might then put his hand upon the documents, which she hugged close in life. He carried out this scheme —and things *se passèrent* as he had expected. The old woman *did* die—and then he approached the younger one —the old maid of 50—on the subject of his desires. Her answer was—'I will give you all the letters if you marry me!' H. says that Silsbee *court encore.* Certainly there is a little subject there: the picture of the two faded, queer, poor and discredited old English women—living on into a strange generation, in their musty corner of a foreign town—with these illustrious letters their most precious possession. Then the plot of the Shelley fanatic—his watchings and waitings—the way he *couvers*[2] the treasure. The

[1] Clairmont is the usual form of the name, and the one used by James in his preface to *The Aspern Papers.*

[2] Here James uses the infinitive of a French verb—*couver*—and adds an English termination.

denouement needn't be the one related of poor Silsbee; and at any rate the general situation is in itself a subject and a picture. It strikes me much. The interest would be in some price that the man has to pay—that the old woman—or the survivor—sets upon the papers. His hesitations—his struggle—for he really would give almost anything.—The Countess Gamba came in while I was there: her husband is a nephew of the Guiccioli—and it was *à propos* of their having a lot of Byron's letters of which they are rather illiberal and dangerous guardians, that H. told me the above. They won't show them or publish any of them—and the Countess was very angry once on H.'s representing to her that it was her duty—especially to the English public!—to let them at least be seen. *Elle se fiche bien* of the English public. She says the letters—addressed in Italian to the Guiccioli—are discreditable to Byron; and H. elicited from her that she had *burned* one of them!

JAMES'S PREFACE TO *THE ASPERN PAPERS*

1908

I NOT only recover with ease, but I delight to recall, the first impulse given to the idea of "The Aspern Papers." It is at the same time true that my present mention of it may perhaps too effectually dispose of any complacent claim to my having "found" the situation. Not that I quite know indeed what situations the seeking fabulist does "find"; he seeks them enough assuredly, but his discoveries are, like those of the navigator, the chemist, the biologist, scarce more than alert recognitions. He *comes upon* the interesting thing as Columbus came upon the isle of San Salvador, because he had moved in the right direction for it—also because he knew, with the encounter, what "making land" then and there represented. Nature had so placed it, to profit—if as profit we may measure the matter!—by his fine unrest, just as history, "literary history" we in this connection call it, had in an out-of-the-way corner of the great garden of life thrown off a curious flower that I was to feel worth gathering as soon as I saw it. I got wind of my positive fact, I followed the scent. It was in Florence years ago; which is precisely, of the whole matter, what I like most to remember. The air of the old-time Italy invests it, a mixture that on the faintest invitation I rejoice again to inhale—and this in spite of the mere cold renewal, ever, of the infirm side of that felicity, the sense, in the whole element, of things too numerous, too deep, too obscure, too strange, or even simply too beautiful, for any ease of intellectual relation. One must pay one's self largely with words, I think, one must induce almost any "Italian subject" *to make believe* it gives up its secret, in order to keep at all on working—or call them perhaps rather playing—terms with the general impression. We entertain it thus, the impression, by the aid of a merciful convention which resembles the fashion of our intercourse with Iberians or Orientals whose form of courtesy places everything they have at our disposal. We thank them and call upon them, but without acting on their professions. The offer has been too large and our assurance is too small; we peep at most into two or three of the chambers of their hospitality, with the rest of the case stretching beyond our ken and escaping our penetration. The pious fiction suffices; we have entered, we have seen, we are charmed. So, right and left, in Italy—before the great historic complexity at least—penetration fails; we scratch at the extensive surface, we meet the perfunctory smile, we hang about in the golden air. But we exaggerate our gathered values only if we are eminently witless. It is fortunately the exhibition in all the world before which, as admirers, we can most remain superficial without feeling silly.

All of which I note, however, perhaps with too scant relevance to the inexhaustible charm of Roman and Florentine memories. Off the ground, at a distance, our fond indifference to being "silly" grows fonder still; the working convention, as I have called it—the convention of the real revelations and surrenders on one side and the real immersions and appreciations on the other—has not only nothing to keep it down, but every glimpse of contrast, every pang of exile and every nostalgic twinge to keep it up. These latter haunting presences in fact, let me note, almost reduce at first to a mere blurred, sad, scarcely consolable vision this present revisiting, re-appropriating impulse. There are parts of one's past, evidently, that bask consentingly and serenely enough in the light of other days—which is but the intensity of thought; and there are other parts that take it as with agitation and pain, a troubled consciousness that heaves as with the disorder of drinking it deeply in. So it is at any rate, fairly in too thick and rich a retrospect, that I see my old Venice of "The Aspern Papers," that I see the still earlier one of Jeffrey Aspern himself, and that I see even the comparatively recent Florence that was to drop into my ear the solicitation of these things. I would fain "lay it on" thick for the very love of them—that at least I may profess; and, with the ground of this desire frankly admitted, something that somehow makes, in the whole story, for a romantic harmony. I have had occasion in the course of these remarks to define my sense of the romantic, and am glad to encounter again here an instance of that virtue as I understand it. I shall presently say why this small case so ranges itself, but must first refer more exactly to the thrill of appreciation it was immediately to excite in me. I saw it somehow at the very first blush as romantic—for the use, of course I mean, I should certainly have had to make of it—that Jane Clairmont, the half-sister of Mary

Godwin, Shelley's second wife and for a while the intimate friend of Byron and the mother of his daughter Allegra, should have been living on in Florence, where she had long lived, up to our own day, and that in fact, had I happened to hear of her but a little sooner, I might have seen her in the flesh. The question of whether I should have wished to do so was another matter—the question of whether I shouldn't have preferred to keep her preciously unseen, to run no risk, in other words, by too rude a choice, of depreciating that romance-value which, as I say, it was instantly inevitable to attach (through association above all, with another signal circumstance) to her long survival.

I had luckily not had to deal with the difficult option; difficult in such a case by reason of that odd law which somehow always makes the minimum of valid suggestion serve the man of imagination better than the maximum. The historian, essentially, wants more documents than he can really use; the dramatist only wants more liberties than he can really take. Nothing, fortunately, however, had, as the case stood, depended on my delicacy; I might have "looked up" Miss Clairmont in previous years had I been earlier informed—the silence about her seemed full of the "irony of fate"; but I felt myself more concerned with the mere strong fact of her having testified for the reality and the closeness of our relation to the past than with any question of the particular sort of person I might have flattered myself I "found." I had certainly at the very least been saved the undue simplicity of pretending to read meanings into things absolutely sealed and beyond test or proof—to tap a fount of waters that couldn't possibly not have run dry. The thrill of learning that she had "overlapped," and by so much, and the wonder of my having doubtless at several earlier seasons passed again and again, all unknowing, the door of her house, where she sat above, within call and in her habit as she lived, these things gave me all I wanted; I seem to remember in fact that my more or less immediately recognising that I positively oughtn't

—"for anything to come of it"—to have wanted more. I saw, quickly, how something might come of it *thus;* whereas a fine instinct told me that the effect of a nearer view of the case (the case of the overlapping) would probably have had to be quite differently calculable. It was really with another item of knowledge, however, that I measured the mistake I should have made in waking up sooner to the question of opportunity. That item consisted of the action taken on the premises by a person who *had* waked up in time, and the legend of whose consequent adventure, as a few spoken words put it before me, at once kindled a flame. This gentleman, an American of long ago, an ardent Shelleyite, a singularly marked figure and himself in the highest degree a subject for a free sketch—I had known him a little, but there is not a reflected glint of him in "The Aspern Papers"—was named to me as having made interest with Miss Clairmont to be accepted as a lodger on the calculation that she would have Shelley documents for which, in the possibly not remote event of her death, he would thus enjoy priority of chance to treat with her representatives. He had at any rate, according to the legend, become, on earnest Shelley grounds, her yearning, though also her highly diplomatic, *pensionnaire*—but without gathering, as was to befall, the fruit of his design.

Legend here dropped to another key; it remained in a manner interesting, but became to my ear a trifle coarse, or at least rather vague and obscure. It mentioned a younger female relative of the ancient woman as a person who, for a queer climax, had had to be dealt with; it flickered so for a moment and then, as a light, to my great relief, quite went out. It had flickered indeed but at the best —yet had flickered enough to give me my "facts," bare facts of intimation; which, scant handful though they were, were more distinct and more numerous than I mostly *like* facts: like them, that is, as we say of an etcher's progressive subject, in an early "state." Nine tenths of the artist's interest in them is that of what he shall add to them and how he shall turn them. Mine, however, in the connexion I speak of, had fortunately got away from me, and quite of their own movement, in time not to crush me. So it was, at all events, that my imagination preserved power to react under the mere essential charm—that, I mean, of a final scene of the rich dim Shelley drama played out in the very theatre of our own "modernity." This was the beauty that appealed to me; there had been, so to speak, a forward continuity, from the actual man, the divine poet, on; and the curious, the ingenious, the admirable thing would be to throw it backward again, to compress—squeezing it hard! —the connexion that had drawn itself out, and convert so the stretched relation into a value of nearness on our own part. In short I saw my chance as admirable, and one reason, when the direction is right, may serve as well as fifty; but if I "took over," as I say, everything that was of the essence, I stayed my hand for the rest. The Italian side of the legend closely clung; if only because the so possible terms of my Juliana's life in the Italy of other days could make conceivable for her the fortunate privacy, the long uninvaded and uninterviewed state on which I represent her situation as founded. Yes, a surviving unexploited unparagraphed Juliana was up to a quarter of a century since still supposeable—as much so as any such buried treasure, any such grave unprofaned, would defy probability now. And then the case had the air of the past just in the degree in which that air, I confess, most appeals to me—when the region over which it hangs is far enough away without being too far.

I delight in a palpable imaginable *visitable* past—in the nearer distances and the clearer mysteries, the marks and signs of a world we may reach over to as by making a long arm we grasp an object at the other end of our own table. The table is the one, the common expanse, and where we lean, so stretching, we find it firm and continuous. That, to my imagination, is the past fragrant of all, or of almost all, the poetry of the thing outlived and lost and gone, and yet in which the precious element of closeness, telling so of connexions but tasting so of differences, remains appreciable. With more moves back the element of the appreciable shrinks—just as the charm of looking over a garden-wall into another garden breaks down when successions of walls appear. The other gardens, those still beyond, may be there, but even by use of our longest ladder we are baffled and bewildered—the view is mainly a view of barriers. The one partition makes the place we have wondered about *other,* both richly and recogniseably so; but who shall pretend to impute an effect of composition to the twenty? We are divided of course between liking to feel the past strange and liking to feel it familiar; the difficulty is, for intensity, to catch it at the moment when the scales of the balance hang with the right evenness. I say for intensity, for we may profit by them in other aspects enough if we are content to measure or to feel loosely. It would take me too far, however, to tell why the particular afternoon light that I thus call intense rests clearer to my sense on the Byronic age, as I conveniently name it, than on periods more protected by the "dignity" of history. With the times beyond, intrinsically more "strange," the tender grace, for the backward vision, has faded, the afternoon darkened; for any time nearer to us the special effect hasn't begun. So there, to put the matter crudely, is the appeal I fondly recognise, an appeal residing doubtless more in the "special effect," in some deep associational force, than in a virtue more intrinsic. I am afraid I must add, since I allow myself so much to fantasticate, that the impulse had more than once taken me to project the Byronic age and the afternoon light across the great sea, to see in short whether association would carry so far and what the young century might pass for on that side of the modern world where it was not only itself so irremediably youngest, but was bound up with youth in everything else. There was a refinement of curiosity in this imputation of a golden strangeness to

American social facts—though I cannot pretend, I fear, that there was any greater wisdom.

Since what it had come to then was, harmlessly enough, cultivating a sense of the past under that close protection, it was natural, it was fond and filial, to wonder if a few of the distilled drops mightn't be gathered from some vision of, say, "old" New York. Would that human congeries, to aid obligingly in the production of a fable, be conceivable as "taking" the afternoon light with the right happy slant?—or could a recogniseable reflexion of the Byronic age, in other words, be picked up on the banks of the Hudson? (Only just there, beyond the great sea, if anywhere: in no other connexion would the question so much as raise its head. I admit that Jeffrey Aspern isn't even feebly localised, but I *thought* New York as I projected him.) It was "amusing," in any case, always, to try experiments; and the experiment for the right *transposition* of my Juliana would be to fit her out with an immortalising poet as transposed as herself. Delicacy had demanded, I felt, that my appropriation of the Florentine legend should purge it, first of all, of references too obvious; so that, to begin with, I shifted the scene of the adventure. Juliana, as I saw her, was thinkable only in Byronic and more or less immediately post-Byronic Italy; but there were conditions in which she was ideally arrangeable, as happened, especially in respect to the later time and the long undetected survival; there being absolutely no refinement of the mouldy rococo, in human or whatever other form, that you may not disembark at the dislocated water-steps of almost any decayed monument of Venetian greatness in auspicious quest of. It was a question, in fine, of covering one's tracks—though with no great elaboration I am bound to admit; and I felt I couldn't cover mine more than in postulating a comparative American Byron to match an American Miss Clairmont—she as absolute as she would. I scarce know whether best to say for this device to-day that it cost me little or that it cost me much; it was "cheap" or expensive according to the degree of verisimilitude artfully obtained. If that degree appears *nil* the "art," such as it was, is wasted, and my remembrance of the contention, on the part of a highly critical friend who at that time and later on often had my ear, that it had been simply foredoomed to be wasted, puts before me the passage in the private history of "The Aspern Papers," that I now find, I confess, most interesting. I comfort myself for the needful brevity of a present glance at it by the sense that the general question involved, under criticism, can't but come up for us again at higher pressure.

My friend's argument bore then—at the time and afterward—on my vicious practice, as he maintained, of postulating for the purpose of my fable celebrities who not only *hadn't* existed in the conditions I imputed to them, but who for the most part (and in no case more markedly than in that of Jeffrey Aspern) couldn't possibly have done so. The stricture was to apply itself to a whole group of short fictions in which I had, with whatever ingenuity, assigned to several so-called eminent figures positions absolutely unthinkable in our actual encompassing air, an air definitely unfavourable to certain forms of eminence. It was vicious, my critic contended, to flourish forth on one's page "great people," public persons, who shouldn't more or less square with our quite definite and calculable array of such notabilities; and by this rule I was heavily incriminated. The rule demanded that the "public person" portrayed should be at least of the tradition, of the general complexion, of the face-value, exactly, of some past or present producible counterfoil. Mere private figures, under one's hand, might correspond with nobody, it being of their essence to be but narrowly known; the represented state of being conspicuous, on the other hand, involved before anything else a recognition—and none of my eminent folk were recogniseable. It was all very well for instance to have put one's self at such pains for Miriam Rooth in "The Tragic Muse"; but *there* was misapplied zeal, there a case of pitiful waste, crying aloud to be denounced. Miriam is offered not as a young person passing unnoticed by her age—like the Biddy Dormers and Julia Dallows, say, of the same book, but as a high rarity, a time-figure of the scope inevitably attended by other commemorations. Where on earth would be then Miriam's inscribed "counterfoil," and in what conditions of the contemporary English theatre, in what conditions of criticism, of appreciation, under what conceivable Anglo-Saxon star, might we take an artistic value of this order either for produced or for recognised? We are, as a "public," chalk-marked by nothing, more unmistakeably, than by the truth that we know nothing of such values—any more than, as my friend was to impress on me, we are susceptible of consciousness of such others (these in the sphere of literary eminence) as my Neil Paraday in "The Death of the Lion," as my Hugh Vereker in "The Figure in the Carpet," as my Ralph Limbert, above all, in "The Next Time," as sundry unprecedented and unmatched heroes and martyrs of the artistic ideal, in short, elsewhere exemplified in my pages. We shall come to these objects of animadversion in another hour, when I shall have no difficulty in producing the defence I found for them—since, obviously, I hadn't cast them into the world *all* naked and ashamed; and I deal for the moment but with the stigma in general as Jeffrey Aspern carries it.

The charge being that I foist upon our early American annals a distinguished presence for which they yield me absolutely no warrant—"Where, within them, gracious heaven, were we to look for so much as an approach to the social elements of habitat and climate of birds of that note and plumage?"—I find his link with reality then just in the tone of the picture wrought round him. What was that tone but exactly, but exquisitely, calculated, the harmless hocus-pocus under cover of which we might suppose him to have existed? This tone is the tone, artistically speaking of "amusement," the current floating that precious influence home quite as one of those high tides watched by the smugglers of old might, in case of their boat's being boarded, be trusted to wash far up the strand the cask of foreign liquor expertly committed to it. If through our lean prime Western period no dim and charming ghost of an adventurous lyric genius might by a stretch of fancy flit, if the time was really too hard to "take," in the light form proposed, the elegant reflexion, then so much the worse for the time—it was all one could say! The retort to that of course was that such a plea represented no "link" with reality—which was what was under discussion—but only a link, and flimsy enough too, with the deepest depths of the artificial: the restrictive truth exactly contended for, which may embody my critic's last word rather of course than my own. My own, so far as I shall pretend in that especial connexion to report it, was that one's warrant, in such a case, hangs essentially on the question of whether or no the false element imputed would have borne that test of further development which so exposes the wrong and so consecrates the right. My last word was, heaven forgive me, that, occasion favouring, I could have perfectly "worked out" Jeffrey Aspern. The boast remains indeed to be verified when we shall arrive at the other challenged cases.

EDITOR'S NOTE

Henry James wrote *The Aspern Papers* swiftly in Venice during the summer of 1887 and sent it off promptly to Thomas Bailey Aldrich, editor of the *Atlantic Monthly,* confident that he had written a little masterpiece. He was deeply irritated when the magazine delayed publication, and it was to this he was alluding when, in a letter to William Dean Howells in January of 1888, he complained that editors kept back his tales "as if they were ashamed of them" and expressed the hope that "some day, all my buried prose will kick off its various tombstones at once." This phrase has been interpreted as a prediction of the James "revival." It was actually an explicit allusion to the editorial lethargy James was encountering at a time when he was highly productive and had a large number of short tales and *nouvelles* outstanding in the magazines, but unpublished by them. *The Aspern Papers* finally came out in the March-May 1888 *Atlantic* and time has confirmed Henry James's judgment of the tale.

The allusion to "Hamilton (V.L's brother)" in the notebook entry is clearly to Eugene Lee-Hamilton, the half brother of the writer Vernon Lee both of whom lived in Florence for many years.

The Aspern Papers shows Henry James's particular attitude toward the past. Early in his career he decided he would never write about a past too far removed from his own day. He felt that writers—unless they created panoramic historical novels like Walter Scott's—were guilty of "humbug" when they evoked historical scenes out of old books and old documents. It is significant that in his unfinished novel, *The Sense of the Past,* in which James wanted to deal with another era, he did so only by showing it through the eyes of someone from the present—which is the only way the past can ever be really seen. And the past he chose for this novel was indeed a *visitable* one—the 1820's, that is when his own father was a boy.

It has generally been assumed that Juliana Bordereau, the ancient mistress of Jeffrey Aspern and possessor of the Aspern papers, as created by James, was modelled on Jane Clairmont. James, however, never saw Miss Clairmont, and in his preface amuses himself with the thought that he *might* have looked her up had he known she had lived into his own time. John Singer Sargent, who was born in Florence, remembered seeing her once when he was 13 and he may have described her to James. The novelist, however, needed no description to portray an aged woman—he had for years cultivated elderly females, Mme. Mohl in Paris, Mrs. Procter, Fanny Kemble. He considered them "windows on the past." But there is good reason for believing that if Juliana Bordereau was inspired by Jane Clairmont in the drama of the Shelley relics, someone else sat for the portrait.

Miss Bordereau is minutely described in *The Aspern Papers,* not at her first appearance but by stages. The Aspern enthusiast sees her as a "strange figure . . . too strange, literally resurgent." He cannot see her eyes; they are covered by a "horrible green shade." We get a glimpse of an old woman "very small and shrunken, bent forward with her hands in her lap. She was dressed in black and her head was wrapped in a piece of old black lace which showed no hair." We see her eyes only once, in the dramatic moment when the "publishing scoundrel" is caught red-handed seeking to rifle the desk. Juliana, white-haired and withered "had lifted the ever-lasting curtain that covered half her face, and for the first, the last, the only time, I beheld her extraordinary eyes. They glared at me; they were like a sudden drench, for a caught burglar, of a flood of gaslight; they made me horribly ashamed. I never shall forget her strange little bent white tottering figure, with its lifted head. . . ."

In *A Small Boy and Others* (New York 1913) Henry James sketches for us in two luminous pages the elder sister of his mother's grandmother as he remembered her in advanced age, from his boyhood years. The sketch is one of a series of brilliant family portraits to be found in the book. Great-Aunt Wyckoff is remembered by Henry (he is writing at 70) as an "image of living antiquity . . . that I was never to see surpassed" which is what Juliana was—in fact she is humorously described in the tale at one point as being 150. James saw the Great-Aunt always enthroned, like Juliana, "hooded and draped and tucked in," giving brief orders like some divinity. Was she, the Small Boy wondered, really, as she seemed, so tremendously old? And the old man, writing this reminiscence, mused that "It was the Past that one touched in her, the American past of preponderant unutterable queerness. . . ." It is this remark which forges the main link between the hooded Great-Aunt Wyckoff and the green-shaded Juliana, for in creating the latter James explained in his preface "I delight in a palpable imaginable *visitable* past . . . the marks and signs of a world we may reach over to as by making a long arm we grasp an object at the other end of our own table." The *visitable* Past was "the poetry of the thing outlived and lost and gone."

Henry James, in his own life, had found the most vivid "*visitable* Past" in the New York of the 1850's between his sixth and twelfth years. It was this past which he drew on for *Washington Square* and we are not surprised therefore when we find him explaining, a few lines after his definition of the near-Past, that, in writing *The Aspern Papers,* "I thought New York . . . it was natural, it was fond and filial, to wonder if a few of the distilled drops mightn't be gathered from some vision of, say, 'old' New York . . . could a recognizable reflection of the Byronic age, in other words, be picked upon on the banks of the Hudson?" He could find no Shelley and no Byron in early America, but he could validly predicate a romantic poet. It is this fact, this invoking of America while dreaming an old Venetian story, which adds a confirmatory touch to our speculation. That Great-Aunt Wyckoff, an old lady, should resemble Juliana, an old lady, is understandable; that in dealing with old ladies Henry James should invoke the Past, with a capital "P," follows logically. But that he "thought New York" while projecting Jeffrey Aspern would mean that he would think of the one "image of living antiquity" that he was "never to see surpassed," and who might have been, in other circumstances, a Jane Clairmont or a Juliana. The Small Boy, in Manhattan of the mid-century, had reached over, making his little arm as long as possible and caught the old lady out of the 18th century with her "large face in which the odd blackness of eyebrow and of a couple of other touches suggested the conventional marks of a painted image . . . so rich and strange is the pleasure of finding the past—the Past above all—answered for to one's touch, this being our only way to be sure of it."

And the greater writer, at the height of his power, almost half a century later, by the same stroke recovered Jane Clairmont-Juliana Bordereau from the 18th century—postulating "a comparative American Byron" in Aspern to match "an American Miss Clairmont." In America, in James's experience, only Great-Aunt Wyckoff was "ancient" enough, and sufficiently out of a distant yet visitable past, to resemble Juliana.

THE PUPIL

1892

I

THE POOR young man hesitated and procrastinated: it cost him such an effort to broach the subject of terms, to speak of money to a person who spoke only of feelings and, as it were, of the aristocracy. Yet he was unwilling to take leave, treating his engagement as settled, without some more conventional glance in that direction than he could find an opening for in the manner of the large affable lady who sat there drawing a pair of soiled *gants de Suède* through a fat jewelled hand and, at once pressing and gliding, repeated over and over everything but the thing he would have liked to hear. He would have liked to hear the figure of his salary; but just as he was nervously about to sound that note the little boy came back—the little boy Mrs. Moreen had sent out of the room to fetch her fan. He came back without the fan, only with the casual observation that he couldn't find it. As he dropped this cynical confession he looked straight and hard at the candidate for the honour of taking his education in hand. This personage reflected somewhat grimly that the first thing he should have to teach his little charge would be to appear to address himself to his mother when he spoke to her—especially not to make her such an improper answer as that.

When Mrs. Moreen bethought herself of this pretext for

getting rid of their companion Pemberton supposed it was precisely to approach the delicate subject of his remuneration. But it had been only to say some things about her son that it was better a boy of eleven shouldn't catch. They were extravagantly to his advantage save when she lowered her voice to sigh, tapping her left side familiarly, "And all overclouded by *this,* you know; all at the mercy of a weakness—!" Pemberton gathered that the weakness was in the region of the heart. He had known the poor child was not robust: this was the basis on which he had been invited to treat, through an English lady, an Oxford acquaintance, then at Nice, who happened to know both his needs and those of the amiable American family looking out for something really superior in the way of a resident tutor.

The young man's impression of his prospective pupil, who had come into the room as if to see for himself the moment Pemberton was admitted, was not quite the soft solicitation the visitor had taken for granted. Morgan Moreen was somehow sickly without being "delicate," and that he looked intelligent—it is true Pemberton would have enjoyed his being stupid—only added to the suggestion that, as with his big mouth and big ears he really couldn't be called pretty, he might too utterly fail to please. Pemberton was modest, was even timid; and the chance that his small scholar would prove cleverer than himself had quite figured, to his anxiety, among the dangers of an untried experiment. He reflected, however, that these were risks one had to run when one accepted a position, as it was called, in a private family; when as yet one's university honours had, pecuniarily speaking, remained barren. At any rate when Mrs. Moreen got up as to intimate that, since it was understood he would enter upon his duties within the week she would let him off now, he succeeded, in spite of the presence of the child, in squeezing out a phrase about the rate of payment. It was not the fault of the conscious smile which seemed a reference to the lady's expensive identity, it was not the fault of this demonstration, which had, in a sort, both vagueness and point, if the allusion didn't sound rather vulgar. This was exactly because she became still more gracious to reply: "Oh I can assure you that all that will be quite regular."

Pemberton only wondered, while he took up his hat, what "all that" was to amount to—people had such different ideas. Mrs. Moreen's words, however, seemed to commit the family to a pledge definite enough to elicit from the child a strange little comment in the shape of the mocking foreign ejaculation "Oh la-la!"

Pemberton, in some confusion, glanced at him as he walked slowly to the window with his back turned, his hands in his pockets and the air in his elderly shoulders of a boy who didn't play. The young man wondered if he should be able to teach him to play, though his mother had said it would never do and that this was why school was impossible. Mrs. Moreen exhibited no discomfiture; she only continued blandly: "Mr. Moreen will be delighted to meet your wishes. As I told you, he has been called to London for a week. As soon as he comes back you shall have it out with him."

This was so frank and friendly that the young man could only reply, laughing as his hostess laughed: "Oh I don't imagine we shall have much of a battle."

"They'll give you anything you like," the boy remarked unexpectedly, returning from the window. "We don't mind what anything costs—we live awfully well."

"My darling, you're too quaint!" his mother exclaimed, putting out to caress him a practised but ineffectual hand. He slipped out of it, but looked with intelligent innocent eyes at Pemberton, who had already had time to notice that from one moment to the other his small satiric face seemed to change its time of life. At this moment it was infantine, yet it appeared also to be under the influence of curious intuitions and knowledges. Pemberton rather disliked precocity and was disappointed to find gleams of it in a disciple not yet in his teens. Nevertheless he divined on the spot that Morgan wouldn't prove a bore. He would prove on the contrary a source of agitation. This idea held the young man, in spite of a certain repulsion.

"You pompous little person! We're not extravagant!" Mrs. Moreen gaily protested, making another unsuccessful attempt to draw the boy to her side. "You must know what to expect," she went on to Pemberton.

"The less you expect the better!" her companion interposed. "But we *are* people of fashion."

"Only so far as *you* make us so!" Mrs. Moreen tenderly mocked. "Well then, on Friday—don't tell me you're superstitious—and mind you don't fail us. Then you'll see us all. I'm so sorry the girls are out. I guess you'll like the girls. And, you know, I've another son, quite different from this one."

"He tries to imitate me," Morgan said to their friend.

"He tries? Why he's twenty years old!" cried Mrs. Moreen.

"You're very witty," Pemberton remarked to the child—a proposition his mother echoed with enthusiasm, declaring Morgan's sallies to be the delight of the house.

The boy paid no heed to this; he only enquired abruptly of the visitor, who was surprised afterwards that he hadn't struck him as offensively forward: "Do you *want* very much to come?"

"Can you doubt it after such a description of what I shall hear?" Pemberton replied. Yet he didn't want to come at all; he was coming because he had to go somewhere, thanks to the collapse of his fortune at the end of a year abroad spent on the system of putting his scant patrimony into a single full wave of experience. He had had his full wave but couldn't pay the score at his inn. Moreover he had caught in the boy's eyes the glimpse of a far-off appeal.

"Well, I'll do the best I can for you," said Morgan; with which he turned away again. He passed out of one of the long windows; Pemberton saw him go and lean on the parapet of the terrace. He remained there while the young man took leave of his mother, who, on Pemberton's looking as if he expected a farewell from him, interposed with: "Leave him, leave him; he's so strange!" Pemberton supposed her to fear something he might say. "He's a genius—you'll love him," she added. "He's much the most interesting person in the family." And before he could invent some civility to oppose to this she wound up with: "But we're all good, you know!"

"He's a genius—you'll love him!" were words that recurred to our aspirant before the Friday, suggesting among many things that geniuses were not invariably loveable. However, it was all the better if there was an element that would make tutorship absorbing: he had perhaps taken too much for granted it would only disgust him. As he left the villa after his interview he looked up at the balcony and saw the child leaning over it. "We shall have great larks!" he called up.

Morgan hung fire a moment and then gaily returned: "By the time you come back I shall have thought of something witty!"

This made Pemberton say to himself "After all he's rather nice."

II

On the Friday he saw them all, as Mrs. Moreen had promised, for her husband had come back and the girls and the other son were at home. Mr. Moreen had a white moustache, a confiding manner and, in his buttonhole, the ribbon of a foreign order—bestowed, as Pemberton eventually learned, for services. For what services he never clearly ascertained: this was a point—one of a larger number—that Mr. Moreen's manner never confided. What it emphatically did confide was that he was even more a man of the world than you might first make out. Ulick, the firstborn, was in visible training for the same profession—under the disadvantage as yet, however, of a buttonhole but feebly floral and a moustache with no pretensions to type. The girls had hair and figures and manners and small fat feet, but had never been out alone. As for Mrs. Moreen, Pemberton saw on a nearer view that her elegance was intermittent and her parts didn't always match. Her husband, as she had promised, met with enthusiasm Pemberton's ideas in regard to a salary. The young man had endeavoured to keep these stammerings modest, and Mr. Moreen made it no secret that *he* found them wanting in "style." He further mentioned that he aspired to be intimate with his children, to be their best friend, and that he was always looking out for them. That was what he went off for, to London and other places—to look out; and this vigilance was the theory of life, as well as the real occupation, of the whole family. They all looked out, for they were very frank on the subject of its being necessary. They desired it to be understood that they were earnest people, and also that their fortune, though quite adequate for earnest people, required the most careful administration. Mr. Moreen, as the parent bird, sought sustenance for the nest. Ulick invoked support mainly at the club, where Pemberton guessed that it was usually served on green cloth. The girls used to do up their hair and their frocks themselves, and our young man felt appealed to to be glad, in regard to Morgan's education, that, though it must naturally be of the best, it didn't cost too much. After a little he *was* glad, forgetting at times his own needs in the interest inspired by the child's character and culture and the pleasure of making easy terms for him.

During the first weeks of their acquaintance Morgan had been as puzzling as a page in an unknown language—altogether different from the obvious little Anglo-Saxons who had misrepresented childhood to Pemberton. Indeed the whole mystic volume in which the boy had been amateurishly bound demanded some practice in translation. Today, after a considerable interval, there is something phantasmagoric, like a prismatic reflexion or a serial novel, in Pemberton's memory of the queerness of the Moreens. If it were not for a few tangible tokens—a lock of Morgan's hair cut by his own hand, and the half-dozen letters received from him when they were disjoined—the whole episode and the figures peopling it would seem too inconsequent for anything but dreamland. Their supreme quaintness was their success—as it appeared to him for a while at the time; since he had never seen a family so brilliantly equipped for failure. Wasn't it success to have kept him so hatefully long? Wasn't it success to have drawn him in that first morning at déjeuner, the Friday he came—it was enough to *make* one superstitious—so that he utterly committed himself, and this not by calculation or on a signal, but from a happy instinct which made them, like a band of gipsies, work so neatly together? They amused him as much as if they had really been a band of gipsies. He was still young and had not seen much of the world—his English years had been properly arid; therefore the reversed conventions of the Moreens—for they had *their* desperate properties—struck him as topsy-turvy. He had encountered nothing like them at Oxford; still less had any such note been struck to his younger American ear during the four years at Yale in which he had richly supposed himself to be reacting against a Puritan strain. The reaction of the Moreens, at any rate, went ever so much further. He had thought himself very sharp that first day in hitting them all off in his mind with the "cosmopolite" label. Later it seemed feeble and colourless—confessedly helplessly provisional.

He yet when he first applied it felt a glow of joy—for an instructor he was still empirical—rise from the apprehension that living with them would really be to see life. Their sociable strangeness was an imitation of that—their chatter of tongues, their gaiety and good humour, their infinite dawdling (they were always getting themselves up, but it took for ever, and Pemberton had once found Mr. Moreen shaving in the drawing-room), their French, their Italian and, cropping up in the foreign fluencies, their cold tough slices of American. They lived on maccaroni and coffee—they had these articles prepared in perfection—but they knew recipes for a hundred other dishes. They overflowed with music and song, were always humming and catching each other up, and had a sort of professional acquaintance with Continental cities. They talked of "good places" as if they had been pickpockets or strolling players. They had at Nice a villa, a carriage, a piano and a banjo, and they went to official parties. They were a perfect calendar of the "days" of their friends, which Pemberton knew them, when they were indisposed, to get out of bed to go to, and which made the week larger than life when Mrs. Moreen talked of them with Paula and Amy. Their initiations gave their new inmate at first an almost dazzling sense of culture. Mrs. Moreen had translated something at some former period—an author whom it made Pemberton feel *borné* never to have heard of. They could imitate Venetian and sing Neapolitan, and when they wanted to say something very particular communicated with each other in an ingenious dialect of their own, an elastic spoken cipher which Pemberton at first took for some *patois* of one of their countries, but which he "caught on to" as he would not have grasped provincial development of Spanish or German.

"It's the family language—Ultramoreen," Morgan explained to him drolly enough; but the boy rarely condescended to use it himself, though he dealt in colloquial Latin as if he had been a little prelate.

Among all the "days" with which Mrs. Moreen's memory was taxed she managed to squeeze in one of her own, which her friends sometimes forgot. But the house drew a frequented air from the number of fine people who were freely named there and from several mysterious men with foreign titles and English clothes whom Morgan called the Princes and who, on sofas with the girls, talked French very loud—though sometimes with some oddity of accent—as if to show they were saying nothing improper. Pemberton wondered how the Princes could ever propose in that tone and so publicly: he took for granted cynically that this was what was desired of them. Then he recognised that even for the chance of such an advantage Mrs. Moreen would never allow Paula and Amy to receive alone. These young ladies were not at all timid, but it was just the safeguards that made them so candidly free. It was a houseful of Bohemians who wanted tremendously to be Philistines.

In one respect, however, certainly, they achieved no rigour—they were wonderfully amiable and ecstatic about Morgan. It was a genuine tenderness, an artless admiration, equally strong in each. They even praised his beauty, which was small, and were as afraid of him as if they felt him of finer clay. They spoke of him as a little angel and a prodigy—they touched on his want of health with long, vague faces. Pemberton feared at first an extravagance that might make him hate the boy, but before this happened he had become extravagant himself. Later, when he had grown rather to hate the others, it was a bribe to patience for him that they were at any rate nice about Morgan, going on tiptoe if they fancied he was showing symptoms, and even giving up somebody's "day" to procure him a pleasure. Mixed with this too was the oddest wish to make him independent, as if they had felt themselves not good enough for him. They passed him over to the new members of their circle very much as if wishing to force some charity of adoption on so free an agent and get rid of their own charge. They were delighted when they saw Morgan take so to his kind playfellow, and could think of no higher praise for the young man. It was strange how they contrived to reconcile the appearance, and indeed the essential fact, of adoring the child with their eagerness to wash their hands of him. Did they want to get rid of him before he should find them out? Pemberton was finding them out month by month. The boy's fond family, however this might be, turned their backs with exaggerated delicacy, as if to avoid the reproach of interfering. Seeing in time how little he had in common with them—it was by *them* he first observed it; they proclaimed it with complete humility—his companion was moved to speculate on the mysteries of transmission, the far jumps of heredity. Where his detachment from most of the things they represented had come from was more than an observer could say—it certainly had burrowed under two or three generations.

As for Pemberton's own estimate of his pupil, it was a good while before he got the point of view, so little had he been prepared for it by the smug young barbarians to whom the tradition of tutorship, as hitherto revealed to him, had been adjusted. Morgan was scrappy and surprising, deficient in many properties supposed common to the *genus* and abounding in others that were the portion only of the supernaturally clever. One day his friend made a great stride: it cleared up the question to perceive that Morgan *was* supernaturally clever and that, though the formula was temporarily meagre, this would be the only assumption on which one could successfully deal with him.

He had the general quality of a child for whom life had not been simplified by school, a kind of homebred sensibility which might have been bad for himself but was charming for others, and a whole range of refinement and perception—little musical vibrations as taking as picked-up airs—begotten by wandering about Europe at the tail of his migratory tribe. This might not have been an education to recommend in advance, but its results with so special a subject were as appreciable as the marks on a piece of fine porcelain. There was at the same time in him a small strain of stoicism, doubtless the fruit of having had to begin early to bear pain, which counted for pluck and made it of less consequence that he might have been thought at school rather a polyglot little beast. Pemberton indeed quickly found himself rejoicing that school was out of the question: in any million of boys it was probably good for all but one, and Morgan was that millionth. It would have made him comparative and superior—it might have made him really require kicking. Pemberton would try to be school himself—a bigger seminary than five hundred grazing donkeys, so that, winning no prizes, the boy would remain unconscious and irresponsible and amusing—amusing, because, though life was already intense in his childish nature, freshness still made there a strong draught for jokes. It turned out that even in the still air of Morgan's various disabilities jokes flourished greatly. He was a pale lean acute undeveloped little cosmopolite, who liked intellectual gymnastics and who also, as regards the behaviour of mankind, had noticed more things than you might suppose, but who nevertheless had his proper playroom of superstitions, where he smashed a dozen toys a day.

III

At Nice once, toward evening, as the pair rested in the open air after a walk, and looked over the sea at the pink western lights, he said suddenly to his comrade: "Do you like it, you know—being with us all in this intimate way?"

"My dear fellow, why should I stay if I didn't?"

"How do I know you'll stay? I'm almost sure you won't, very long."

"I hope you don't mean to dismiss me," said Pemberton.

Morgan debated, looking at the sunset. "I think if I did right I ought to."

"Well, I know I'm supposed to instruct you in virtue; but in that case don't do right."

"You're very young—fortunately," Morgan went on, turning to him again.

"Oh yes, compared with you!"

"Therefore it won't matter so much if you do lose a lot of time."

"That's the way to look at it," said Pemberton accommodatingly.

They were silent a minute; after which the boy asked: "Do you like my father and my mother very much?"

"Dear me, yes. Charming people."

Morgan received this with another silence; then unexpectedly, familiarly, but at the same time affectionately, he remarked: "You're a jolly old humbug!"

For a particular reason the words made our young man change colour. The boy noticed in an instant that he had turned red, whereupon he turned red himself and pupil and master exchanged a longish glance in which there was a consciousness of many more things than are usually touched upon, even tacitly, in such a relation. It produced for Pemberton an embarrassment; it raised in a shadowy form a question—this was the first glimpse of it—destined to play a singular and, as he imagined, owing to the altogether peculiar conditions, an unprecedented part in his intercourse with his little companion. Later, when he found himself talking with the youngster in a way in which few youngsters could ever have been talked with, he thought of that clumsy moment on the bench at Nice as the dawn of an understanding that had broadened. What had added to the clumsiness then was that he thought it his duty to declare to Morgan that he might abuse him, Pemberton, as much as he liked, but must never abuse his parents. To this Morgan had the easy retort that he hadn't dreamed of abusing them; which appeared to be true: it put Pemberton in the wrong.

"Then why am I a humbug for saying *I* think them charming?" the young man asked, conscious of a certain rashness.

"Well—they're not your parents."

"They love you better than anything in the world—never forget that," said Pemberton.

"Is that why you like them so much?"

"They're very kind to me," Pemberton replied evasively.

"You *are* a humbug!" laughed Morgan, passing an arm into his tutor's. He leaned against him looking off at the sea again and swinging his long thin legs.

"Don't kick my shins," said Pemberton while he reflected "Hang it, I can't complain of them to the child!"

"There's another reason too," Morgan went on, keeping his legs still.

"Another reason for what?"

"Besides their not being your parents."

"I don't understand you," said Pemberton.

"Well, you will before long. All right!"

He did understand fully before long, but he made a

fight even with himself before he confessed it. He thought it the oddest thing to have a struggle with the child about. He wondered he didn't hate the hope of the Moreens for bringing the struggle on. But by the time it began any such sentiment for that scion was closed to him. Morgan was a special case, and to know him was to accept him on his own odd terms. Pemberton had spent his aversion to special cases before arriving at knowledge. When at last he did arrive his quandary was great. Against every interest he had attached himself. They would have to meet things together. Before they went home that evening at Nice the boy had said, clinging to his arm:

"Well, at any rate you'll hang on to the last."

"To the last?"

"Till you're fairly beaten."

"*You* ought to be fairly beaten!" cried the young man, drawing him closer.

IV

A YEAR after he had come to live with them Mr. and Mrs. Moreen suddenly gave up the villa at Nice. Pemberton had got used to suddenness, having seen it practised on a considerable scale during two jerky little tours—one in Switzerland the first summer, and the other late in the winter, when they all ran down to Florence and then, at the end of ten days, liking it much less than they had intended, straggled back in mysterious depression. They had returned to Nice "for ever," as they said; but this didn't prevent their squeezing, one rainy muggy May night, into a second-class railway-carriage—you could never tell by which class they would travel—where Pemberton helped them to stow away a wonderful collection of bundles and bags. The explanation of this manœuvre was that they had determined to spend the summer "in some bracing place"; but in Paris they dropped into a small furnished apartment—a fourth floor in a third-rate avenue, where there was a smell on the staircase and the *portier* was hateful—and passed the next four months in blank indigence.

The better part of this baffled sojourn was for the preceptor and his pupil, who, visiting the Invalides and Notre Dame, the Conciergerie and all the museums, took a hundred remunerative rambles. They learned to know their Paris, which was useful, for they came back another year for a longer stay, the general character of which in Pemberton's memory to-day mixes pitiably and confusedly with that of the first. He sees Morgan's shabby knickerbockers —the everlasting pair that didn't match his blouse and that as he grew longer could only grow faded. He remembers the particular holes in his three or four pair of coloured stockings.

Morgan was dear to his mother, but he never was better dressed than was absolutely necessary—partly, no doubt, by his own fault, for he was as indifferent to his appearance as a German philosopher. "My dear fellow, you *are* coming to pieces," Pemberton would say to him in sceptical remonstrance; to which the child would reply, looking at him serenely up and down: "My dear fellow, so are you! I don't want to cast you in the shade." Pemberton could have no rejoinder for this—the assertion so closely represented the fact. If however the deficiencies of his own wardrobe were a chapter by themselves he didn't like his little charge to look too poor. Later he used to say "Well, if we're poor, why, after all, shouldn't we look it?" and he consoled himself with thinking there was something rather elderly and gentlemanly in Morgan's disrepair—it differed from the untidiness of the urchin who plays and spoils his things. He could trace perfectly the degrees by which, in proportion as her little son confined himself to his tutor for society, Mrs. Moreen shrewdly forbore to renew his garments. She did nothing that didn't show, neglected him because he escaped notice, and then, as he illustrated this clever policy, discouraged at home his public appearances. Her position was logical enough—those members of her family who did show had to be showy.

During this period and several others Pemberton was quite aware of how he and his comrade might strike people; wandering languidly through the Jardin des Plantes as if they had nowhere to go, sitting on the winter days in the galleries of the Louvre, so splendidly ironical to the homeless, as if for the advantage of the *calorifère*. They joked about it sometimes: it was the sort of joke that was perfectly within the boy's compass. They figured themselves as part of the vast vague hand-to-mouth multitude of the enormous city and pretended they were proud of their position in it—it showed them "such a lot of life" and made them conscious of a democratic brotherhood. If Pemberton couldn't feel a sympathy in destitution with his small companion—for after all Morgan's fond parents would never have let him really suffer—the boy would at least feel it with him, so it came to the same thing. He used sometimes to wonder what people would think they were—to fancy they were looked askance at, as if it might be a suspected case of kidnapping. Morgan wouldn't be taken for a young patrician with a preceptor—he wasn't smart enough; though he might pass for his companion's sickly little brother. Now and then he had a five-franc piece, and except once, when they bought a couple of lovely neckties, one of which he made Pemberton accept, they laid it out scientifically in old books. This was sure to be a great day, always spent on the quays, in a rummage of the dusty boxes that garnish the parapets. Such occasions helped them to live, for their books ran low very soon after the beginning of their acquaintance. Pemberton had a good many in England, but he was obliged to write to a friend and ask him kindly to get some fellow to give him something for them.

If they had to relinquish that summer the advantage of the bracing climate the young man couldn't but suspect this failure of the cup when at their very lips to have been the effect of a rude jostle of his own. This had represented his first blow-out, as he called it, with his patrons; his first successful attempt—though there was little other success about it—to bring them to a consideration of his impossible position. As the ostensible eve of a costly journey the moment had struck him as favourable to an earnest protest, the presentation of an ultimatum. Ridiculous as it sounded, he had never yet been able to compass an uninterrupted private interview with the elder pair or with either of them singly. They were always flanked by their elder children, and poor Pemberton usually had his own little charge at his side. He was conscious of its being a house in which the surface of one's delicacy got rather smudged; nevertheless he had preserved the bloom of his scruple against announcing to Mr. and Mrs. Moreen with publicity that he shouldn't be able to go on longer without a little money. He was still simple enough to suppose Ulick and Paula and Amy might not know that since his arrival he had only had a hundred and forty francs; and he was magnanimous enough to wish not to compromise their parents in their eyes. Mr. Moreen now listened to him, as he listened to every one and to every thing, like a man of the world, and seemed to appeal to him—though not of course too grossly—to try and be a little more of one himself. Pemberton recognised in fact the importance of the character—from the advantage it gave Mr. Moreen. He was not even confused or embarrassed, whereas the young man in his service was more so than there was any reason for. Neither was he surprised—at least any more than a gentleman had to be who freely confessed himself a little shocked—though not perhaps strictly at Pemberton.

"We must go into this, mustn't we, dear?" he said to his wife. He assured his young friend that the matter should have his very best attention; and he melted into space as elusively as if, at the door, he were taking an inevitable but deprecatory precedence. When, the next moment, Pemberton found himself alone with Mrs. Moreen it was to hear her say "I see, I see"—stroking the roundness of her chin and looking as if she were only hesitating between a dozen easy remedies. If they didn't make their push Mr. Moreen could at least disappear for several days. During his absence his wife took up the subject again spontaneously, but her contribution to it was merely that she had thought all the while they were getting on so beautifully. Pemberton's reply to this revelation was that unless they immediately put down something on account he would leave them on the spot and for ever. He knew she would wonder how he would get away, and for a moment expected her to enquire. She didn't, for which he was almost grateful to her, so little was he in a position to tell.

"You won't, you *know* you won't—you're too interested," she said. "You *are* interested, you know you are, you dear kind man!" She laughed with almost condemnatory archness, as if it were a reproach—though she wouldn't insist; and flirted a soiled pocket-handkerchief at him.

Pemberton's mind was fully made up to take his step the following week. This would give him time to get an answer to a letter he had dispatched to England. If he did in the event nothing of the sort—that is if he stayed another year and then went away only for three months—it was not merely because before the answer to his letter came (most unsatisfactory when it did arrive) Mr. Moreen generously counted out to him, and again with the sacrifice to "form" of a marked man of the world, three hundred francs in elegant ringing gold. He was irritated to find that Mrs. Moreen was right, that he couldn't at the pinch bear to leave the child. This stood out clearer for the very reason that, the night of his desperate appeal to his patrons, he had seen fully for the first time where he was. Wasn't it another proof of the success with which those patrons practised their arts that they had managed to avert for so long the illuminating flash? It descended on our friend with a breadth of effect which perhaps would have struck a spectator as comical, after he had returned to his little servile room, which looked into a close court where a bare dirty opposite wall took, with the sound of shrill clatter, the reflexion of lighted back windows. He had simply given himself away to a band of adventurers. The idea, the word itself, wore a romantic horror for him—he had always lived on such safe lines. Later it assumed a more interesting, almost a soothing, sense: it pointed a moral, and Pemberton could enjoy a moral. The Moreens were adventurers not merely because they didn't pay their debts, because they lived on society, but because their whole view of life, dim and confused and instinctive, like that of clever colour-blind animals, was speculative and rapacious and mean. Oh they were "respectable," and that only made them more *immondes!* The young man's analysis, while he brooded, put it at last very simply—they were adventurers because they were toadies and snobs. That was the completest account of them—it was the law of their being. Even when this truth became vivid to their ingenious inmate he remained unconscious of how much his mind had been prepared for it by the extraordinary little boy who had now become such a complication in his life. Much less could he then calculate on the information he was still to owe the extraordinary little boy.

V

But it was during the ensuing time that the real problem came up—the problem of how far it was excusable to discuss the turpitude of parents with a child of twelve, of thirteen, of fourteen. Absolutely inexcusable and quite impossible it of course at first appeared; and indeed the question didn't press for some time after Pemberton had received his three hundred francs. They produced a temporary lull, a relief from the sharpest pressure. The young man frugally amended his wardrobe and even had a few francs in his pocket. He thought the Moreens looked at him as if he were almost too smart, as if they ought to take care not to spoil him. If Mr. Moreen hadn't been such a man of the world he would perhaps have spoken of the freedom of such neckties on the part of a subordinate. But Mr. Moreen was always enough a man of the world to let things pass—he had certainly shown that. It was singular how Pemberton guessed that Morgan, though saying nothing about it, knew something had happened. But three hundred francs, especially when one owed money, couldn't last for ever; and when the treasure was gone—the boy knew when it had failed—Morgan did break ground. The party had returned to Nice at the beginning of the winter, but not to the charming villa. They went to an hotel, where they stayed three months, and then moved to another establishment, explaining that they had left the first because, after waiting and waiting, they couldn't get the rooms they wanted. These apartments, the rooms they wanted, were generally very splendid; but fortunately they never *could* get them—fortunately, I mean, for Pemberton, who reflected always that if they had got them there would have been a still scanter educational fund. What Morgan said at last was said suddenly, irrelevantly, when the moment came, in the middle of a lesson, and consisted of the apparently unfeeling words: "You ought to *filer,* you know—you really ought."

Pemberton stared. He had learnt enough French slang from Morgan to know that to *filer* meant to cut sticks. "Ah my dear fellow, don't turn me off!"

Morgan pulled a Greek lexicon toward him—he used a Greek-German—to look out a word, instead of asking it of Pemberton. "You can't go on like this, you know."

"Like what, my boy?"

"You know they don't pay you up," said Morgan, blushing and turning his leaves.

"Don't pay me?" Pemberton stared again and feigned amazement. "What on earth put that into your head?"

"It has been there a long time," the boy replied rummaging his book.

Pemberton was silent, then he went on: "I say, what are you hunting for? They pay me beautifully."

"I'm hunting for the Greek for awful whopper," Morgan dropped.

"Find that rather for gross impertinence and disabuse your mind. What do I want of money?"

"Oh that's another question!"

Pemberton wavered—he was drawn in different ways. The severely correct thing would have been to tell the boy that such a matter was none of his business and bid him go on with his lines. But they were really too intimate for that; it was not the way he was in the habit of treating him; there had been no reason it should be. On the other hand Morgan had quite lighted on the truth—he really shouldn't be able to keep it up much longer; therefore why not let him know one's real motive for forsaking him? At the same time it wasn't decent to abuse to one's pupil the family of one's pupil; it was better to misrepresent than to do that. So in reply to his comrade's last exclamation he just declared, to dismiss the subject, that he had received several payments.

"I say—I say!" the boy ejaculated, laughing.

"That's all right," Pemberton insisted. "Give me your written rendering."

Morgan pushed a copybook across the table, and he began to read the page, but with something running in his head that made it no sense. Looking up after a minute or two he found the child's eyes fixed on him and felt in them something strange. Then Morgan said: "I'm not afraid of the stern reality."

"I haven't yet seen the thing you *are* afraid of—I'll do you that justice!"

This came out with a jump—it was perfectly true—and evidently gave Morgan pleasure. "I've thought of it a long time," he presently resumed.

"Well, don't think of it any more."

The boy appeared to comply, and they had a comfortable and even an amusing hour. They had a theory that they were very thorough, and yet they seemed always to be in the amusing part of lessons, the intervals between the dull dark tunnels, where there were waysides and jolly views. Yet the morning was brought to a violent end by Morgan's suddenly leaning his arms on the table, burying his head in them and bursting into tears: at which Pemberton was the more startled that, as it then came over him, it was the first time he had ever seen the boy cry and that the impression was consequently quite awful.

The next day, after much thought, he took a decision and, believing it to be just, immediately acted on it. He cornered Mr. and Mrs. Moreen again and let them know that if on the spot they didn't pay him all they owed him he wouldn't only leave their house but would tell Morgan exactly what had brought him to it.

"Oh you *haven't* told him?" cried Mrs. Moreen with a pacifying hand on her well-dressed bosom.

"Without warning you? For what do you take me?" the young man returned.

Mr. and Mrs. Moreen looked at each other; he could see that they appreciated, as tending to their security, his superstition of delicacy, and yet that there was a certain alarm in their relief. "My dear fellow," Mr. Moreen demanded, "what use *can* you have, leading the quiet life we all do, for such a lot of money?"—a question to which Pemberton made no answer, occupied as he was in noting that what passed in the mind of his patrons was something like: "Oh then, if we've felt that the child, dear little angel, has judged us and how he regards us, and we haven't been betrayed, he must have guessed—and in short it's *general!*" an inference that rather stirred up Mr. and Mrs. Moreen, as Pemberton had desired it should. At the same time, if he had supposed his threat would do something towards bringing them round, he was disappointed to find them taking for granted—how vulgar their perception *had* been!—that he had already given them away. There was a mystic uneasiness in their parental breasts, and that had been the inferior sense of it. None the less, however, his threat did touch them; for if they had escaped it was only to meet a new danger. Mr. Moreen appealed to him, on every precedent, as a man of the world; but his wife had recourse, for the first time since his domestication with them, to a fine *hauteur,* reminding him that a devoted mother, with her child, had arts that protected her against gross misrepresentation.

"I should misrepresent you grossly if I accused you of common honesty!" our friend replied; but as he closed the door behind him sharply, thinking he had not done himself much good, while Mr. Moreen lighted another cigarette, he heard his hostess shout after him more touchingly:

"Oh you do, you *do,* put the knife to one's throat!"

The next morning, very early, she came to his room. He recognised her knock, but had no hope she brought him money; as to which he was wrong, for she had fifty francs in her hand. She squeezed forward in her dressing-gown, and he received her in his own, between his bath-tub and his bed. He had been tolerably schooled by this time to the "foreign ways" of his hosts. Mrs. Moreen was ardent, and when she was ardent she didn't care what she did; so she now sat down on his bed, his clothes being on the chairs, and, in her preoccupation, forgot, as she glanced round, to be ashamed of giving him such a horrid room. What Mrs. Moreen's ardour now bore upon was the design of persuading him that in the first place she was very good-natured to bring him fifty francs, and that in the second, if he would only see it, he was really too absurd to expect to be *paid*. Wasn't he paid enough without perpetual money—wasn't he paid by the comfortable luxurious home he enjoyed with them all, without a care, an anxiety, a solitary want? Wasn't he sure of his position, and wasn't that everything to a young man like him, quite unknown, with singularly little to show, the ground of whose exorbitant pretensions it had never been easy to discover? Wasn't he paid above all by the sweet relation he had established with Morgan—quite ideal as from master to pupil—and by the simple privilege of knowing and living with so amazingly gifted a child; than whom really (and she meant literally what she said) there was no better company in Europe? Mrs. Moreen herself took to appealing to him as a man of the world; she said "Voyons, mon cher," and "My dear man, look here now"; and urged him to be reasonable, putting it before him that it was truly a chance for him. She spoke as if, according as he *should* be reasonable, he would prove himself worthy to be her son's tutor and of the extraordinary confidence they had placed in him.

After all, Pemberton reflected, it was only a difference of theory and the theory didn't matter much. They had hitherto gone on that of remunerated, as now they would go on that of gratuitous, service; but why should they have so many words about it? Mrs. Moreen at all events continued to be convincing; sitting there with her fifty francs she talked and reiterated as women reiterate, and bored and irritated him, while he leaned against the wall with his hands in the pockets of his wrapper, drawing it together round his legs and looking over the head of his visitor at the grey negations of his window. She wound up with saying: "You see I bring you a definite proposal."

"A definite proposal?"

"To make our relations regular, as it were—to put them on a comfortable footing."

"I see—it's a system," said Pemberton. "A kind of organised blackmail."

Mrs. Moreen bounded up, which was exactly what he wanted. "What do you mean by that?"

"You practise on one's fears—one's fears about the child if one should go away."

"And pray what would happen to him in that event?" she demanded with majesty.

"Why he'd be alone with *you.*"

"And pray with whom *should* a child be but with those whom he loves most?"

"If you think that, why don't you dismiss me?"

"Do you pretend he loves you more than he loves *us?*" cried Mrs. Moreen.

"I think he ought to. I make sacrifices for him. Though I've heard of those *you* make I don't see them."

Mrs. Moreen stared a moment; then with emotion she grasped her inmate's hand. "*Will* you make it—the sacrifice?"

He burst out laughing. "I'll see. I'll do what I can. I'll stay a little longer. Your calculation's just—I *do* hate intensely to give him up; I'm fond of him and he thoroughly interests me, in spite of the inconvenience I suffer. You know my situation perfectly. I haven't a penny in the world and, occupied as you see me with Morgan, am unable to earn money."

Mrs. Moreen tapped her undressed arm with her folded bank-note. "Can't you write articles? Can't you translate as *I* do?"

"I don't know about translating; it's wretchedly paid."

"I'm glad to earn what I can," said Mrs. Moreen with prodigious virtue.

"You ought to tell me who you do it for." Pemberton paused a moment, and she said nothing; so he added: "I've tried to turn off some little sketches, but the magazines won't have them—they're declined with thanks."

"You see then you're not such a phœnix," his visitor pointedly smiled—"to pretend to abilities you're sacrificing for our sake."

"I haven't time to do things properly," he ruefully went on. Then as it came over him that he was almost abjectly good-natured to give these explanations he added: "If I stay on longer it must be on one condition—that Morgan shall know distinctly on what footing I am."

Mrs. Moreen demurred. "Surely you don't want to show off to a child?"

"To show *you* off, do you mean?"

Again she cast about, but this time it was to produce a still finer flower. "And *you* talk of blackmail!"

"You can easily prevent it," said Pemberton.

"And *you* talk of practising on fears!" she bravely pushed on.

"Yes, there's no doubt I'm a great scoundrel."

His patroness met his eyes—it was clear she was in straits. Then she thrust out her money at him. "Mr. Moreen desired me to give you this on account."

"I'm much obliged to Mr. Moreen, but we *have* no account."

"You won't take it?"

"That leaves me more free," said Pemberton.

"To poison my darling's mind?" groaned Mrs. Moreen.

"Oh your darling's mind—!" the young man laughed.

She fixed him a moment, and he thought she was going

of break out tormentedly, pleadingly: "For God's sake, tell me what *is* in it!" But she checked this impulse—another was stronger. She pocketed the money—the crudity of the alternative was comical—and swept out of the room with the desperate concession: "You may tell him any horror you like!"

VI

A COUPLE of days after this, during which he had failed to profit by so free a permission, he had been for a quarter of an hour walking with his charge in silence when the boy became sociable again with the remark: "I'll tell you how I know it; I know it through Zénobie."

"Zénobie? Who in the world is *she?*"

"A nurse I used to have—ever so many years ago. A charming woman. I liked her awfully, and she liked me."

"There's no accounting for tastes. What is it you know through her?"

"Why what their idea is. She went away because they didn't fork out. She did like me awfully, and she stayed two years. She told me all about it—that at last she could never get her wages. As soon as they saw how much she liked me they stopped giving her anything. They thought she'd stay for nothing—just *because,* don't you know?" And Morgan had a queer little conscious lucid look. "She did stay ever so long—as long as she could. She was only a poor girl. She used to send money to her mother. At last she couldn't afford it any longer, and went away in a fearful rage one night—I mean of course in a rage against *them.* She cried over me tremendously, she hugged me nearly to death. She told me all about it," the boy repeated. "She told me it was their idea. So I guessed, ever so long ago, that they have had the same idea with you."

"Zénobie was very sharp," said Pemberton. "And she made you so."

"Oh that wasn't Zénobie; that was nature. And experience!" Morgan laughed.

"Well, Zénobie was a part of your experience."

"Certainly I was a part of hers, poor dear!" the boy wisely sighed. "And I'm part of yours."

"A very important part. But I don't see how you know I've been treated like Zénobie."

"Do you take me for the biggest dunce you've known?" Morgan asked. "Haven't I been conscious of what we've been through together?"

"What we've been through?"

"Our privations—our dark days."

"Oh our days have been bright enough."

Morgan went on in silence for a moment. Then he said: "My dear chap, you're a hero!"

"Well, you're another!" Pemberton retorted.

"No I'm not, but I ain't a baby. I won't stand it any longer. You must get some occupation that pays. I'm ashamed, I'm ashamed!" quavered the boy with a ring of passion, like some high silver note from a small cathedral chorister, that deeply touched his friend.

"We ought to go off and live somewhere together," the young man said.

"I'll go like a shot if you'll take me."

"I'd get some work that would keep us both afloat," Pemberton continued.

"So would I. Why shouldn't *I* work? I ain't such a beastly little muff as *that* comes to."

"The difficulty is that your parents wouldn't hear of it. They'd never part with you; they worship the ground you tread on. Don't you see the proof of it?" Pemberton developed. "They don't dislike me; they wish me no harm; they're very amiable people; but they're perfectly ready to expose me to any awkwardness in life for your sake."

The silence in which Morgan received his fond sophistry struck Pemberton somehow as expressive. After a moment the child repeated: "You *are* a hero!" Then he added: "They leave me with you altogether. You've all the responsibility. They put me off on you from morning till night. Why then should they object to my taking up with you completely? I'd help you."

"They're not particularly keen about my being helped, and they delight in thinking of you as *theirs*. They're tremendously proud of you."

"I'm not proud of *them*. But you know that," Morgan returned.

"Except for the little matter we speak of they're charming people," said Pemberton, not taking up the point made for his intelligence, but wondering greatly at the boy's own, and especially at this fresh reminder of something he had been conscious of from the first—the strangest thing in his friend's large little composition, a temper, a sensibility, even a private ideal, which made him as privately disown the stuff his people were made of. Morgan had in secret a small loftiness which made him acute about betrayed meanness; as well as a critical sense for the manners immediately surrounding him that was quite without precedent in a juvenile nature, especially when one noted that it had not made this nature "old-fashioned," as the word is of children—quaint or wizened or offensive. It was as if he had been a little gentleman and had paid the penalty by discovering that he was the only such person in his family. This comparison didn't make him vain, but it could make him melancholy and a trifle austere. While Pemberton guessed at these dim young things, shadows of shadows, he was partly drawn on and partly checked, as for a scruple, by the charm of attempting to sound the little cool shallows that were so quickly growing deeper. When he tried to figure to himself the morning twilight of childhood, so as to deal with it safely, he saw it was never fixed, never arrested, that ignorance, at the instant he touched it, was already flushing faintly into knowledge, that there was nothing that at a given moment you could say an intelligent child didn't know. It seemed to him that he himself knew too much to imagine Morgan's simplicity and too little to disembroil his tangle.

The boy paid no heed to his last remark; he only went on: "I'd have spoken to them about their idea, as I call it, long ago, if I hadn't been sure what they'd say."

"And what would they say?"

"Just what they said about what poor Zénobie told me—that it was a horrid dreadful story, that they had paid her every penny they owed her."

"Well, perhaps they had," said Pemberton.

"Perhaps they've paid you!"

"Let us pretend they have, and *n'en parlons plus.*"

"They accused her of lying and cheating"—Morgan stuck to historic truth. "That's why I don't want to speak to them."

"Lest they should accuse me too?" To this Morgan made no answer, and his companion, looking down at him—the boy turned away his eyes, which had filled—saw that he couldn't have trusted himself to utter. "You're right. Don't worry them," Pemberton pursued. "Except for that, they *are* charming people."

"Except for *their* lying and *their* cheating?"

"I say—I say!" cried Pemberton, imitating a little tone of the lad's which was itself an imitation.

"We must be frank, at the last; we *must* come to an understanding," said Morgan with the importance of the small boy who lets himself think he is arranging great affairs—almost playing at shipwreck or at Indians. "I know all about everything."

"I dare say your father has his reasons," Pemberton replied, but too vaguely, as he was aware.

"For lying and cheating?"

"For saving and managing and turning his means to the best account. He has plenty to do with his money. You're an expensive family."

"Yes, I'm very expensive," Morgan concurred in a manner that made his preceptor burst out laughing.

"He's saving for *you,*" said Pemberton. "They think of you in everything they do."

"He might, while he's about it, save a little—" The boy paused, and his friend waited to hear what. Then Morgan brought out oddly: "A little reputation."

"Oh there's plenty of that. That's all right!"

"Enough of it for the people they know, no doubt. The people they know are awful."

"Do you mean the princes? We mustn't abuse the princes."

"Why not? They haven't married Paula—they haven't married Amy. They only clean out Ulick."

"You *do* know everything!" Pemberton declared.

"No I don't after all. I don't know what they live on, or how they live, or *why* they live! What have they got and how did they get it? Are they rich, are they poor, or have they a *modeste aisance?* Why are they always chiveying me about—living one year like ambassadors and the next like paupers? Who are they, anyway, and what are they? I've thought of all that—I've thought of a lot of things. They're so beastly worldly. That's what I hate most—oh I've *seen* it! All they care about is to make an appearance and to pass for something or other. What the dickens do they want to pass for? What *do* they, Mr. Pemberton?"

"You pause for a reply," said Pemberton, treating the question as a joke, yet wondering too and greatly struck with his mate's intense if imperfect vision. "I haven't the least idea."

"And what good does it do? Haven't I seen the way people treat them—the 'nice' people, the ones they want to know? They'll take anything from them—they'll lie down and be trampled on. The nice ones hate that—they just sicken them. You're the only really nice person we know."

"Are you sure? They don't lie down for me!"

"Well, you shan't lie down for them. You've got to go—that's what you've got to do," said Morgan.

"And what will become of you?"

"Oh I'm growing up. I shall get off before long. I'll see you later."

"You had better let me finish you," Pemberton urged, lending himself to the child's strange superiority.

Morgan stopped in their walk, looking up at him. He had to look up much less than a couple of years before—he had grown, in his loose leanness, so long and high. "Finish me?" he echoed.

"There are such a lot of jolly things we can do together yet. I want to turn you out—I want you to do me credit."

Morgan continued to look at him. "To give you credit—do you mean?"

"My dear fellow, you're too clever to live."

"That's just what I'm afraid you think. No, no; it isn't fair—I can't endure it. We'll separate next week. The sooner it's over the sooner to sleep."

"If I hear of anything—any other chance—I promise to go," Pemberton said.

Morgan consented to consider this. "But you'll be honest," he demanded; "you won't pretend you haven't heard?"

"I'm much more likely to pretend I have."

"But what can you hear of, this way, stuck in a hole with us? You ought to be on the spot, to go to England—you ought to go to America."

"One would think you were *my* tutor!" said Pemberton.

Morgan walked on and after a little had begun again: "Well, now that you know I know and that we look at the facts and keep nothing back—it's much more comfortable, isn't it?"

"My dear boy, it's so amusing, so interesting, that it will surely be quite impossible for me to forego such hours as these."

This made Morgan stop once more. "You *do* keep something back. Oh you're not straight—*I* am!"

"How am I not straight?"

"Oh you've got your idea!"

"My idea?"

"Why that I probably shan't make old—make older—bones, and that you can stick it out till I'm removed."

"You *are* too clever to live!" Pemberton repeated.

"I call it a mean idea," Morgan pursued. "But I shall punish you by the way I hang on."

"Look out or I'll poison you!" Pemberton laughed.

"I'm stronger and better every year. Haven't you noticed that there hasn't been a doctor near me since you came?"

"I'm your doctor," said the young man, taking his arm and drawing him tenderly on again.

Morgan proceeded and after a few steps gave a sigh of mingled weariness and relief. "Ah now that we look at the facts it's all right!"

VII

They looked at the facts a good deal after this; and one of the first consequences of their doing so was that Pemberton stuck it out, in his friend's parlance, for the purpose. Morgan made the facts so vivid and so droll, and at the same time so bald and so ugly, that there was fascination in talking them over with him, just as there would have been heartlessness in leaving him alone with them. Now that the pair had such perceptions in common it was useless for them to pretend they didn't judge such people; but the very judgement and the exchange of perceptions created another tie. Morgan had never been so interesting as now that he himself was made plainer by the side light of these confidences. What came out in it most was the small fine passion of his pride. He had plenty of that, Pemberton felt—so much that one might perhaps wisely wish for it some early bruises. He would have liked his people to have a spirit and had waked up to the sense of their perpetually eating humble-pie. His mother would consume any amount, and his father would consume even more than his mother. He had a theory that Ulick had wriggled out of an "affair" at Nice: there had once been a flurry at home, a regular panic, after which they all went to bed and took medicine, not to be accounted for on any other supposition. Morgan had a romantic imagination, fed by poetry and history, and he would have liked those who "bore his name"—as he used to say to Pemberton with the humour that made his queer delicacies manly—to carry themselves with an air. But their one idea was to get in with people who didn't want them and to take snubs as if they were honourable scars. Why people didn't want them more he didn't know—that was people's own affair; after all they weren't superficially repulsive, they were a hundred times cleverer than most of the dreary grandees, the "poor swells" they rushed about Europe to catch up with. "After all they *are* amusing—they are!" he used to pronounce with the wisdom of the ages. To which Pemberton always replied: "Amusing—the great Moreen troupe? Why they're altogether delightful; and if it weren't for the hitch that you and I (feeble performers!) make in the *ensemble* they'd carry everything before them."

What the boy couldn't get over was the fact that this particular blight seemed, in a tradition of self-respect, so undeserved and so arbitrary. No doubt people had a right to take the line they liked; but why should *his* people have liked the line of pushing and toadying and lying and cheating? What had their forefathers—all decent folk, so far as he knew—done to them, or what had *he* done to them? Who had poisoned their blood with the fifth-rate social ideal, the fixed idea of making smart acquaintances and getting into the *monde chic,* especially when it was foredoomed to failure and exposure? They showed so what they were after; that was what made the people they wanted not want *them.* And never a wince for dignity, never a throb of shame at looking each other in the face, never any independence or resentment or disgust. If his father or his brother would only knock some one down once or twice a year! Clever as they were they never guessed the impression they made. They were good-natured, yes—as good-natured as Jews at the doors of clothing-shops! But was that the model one wanted one's family to follow? Morgan had dim memories of an old grandfather, the maternal, in New York, whom he had been taken across the ocean at the age of five to see: a gentleman with a high neck-cloth and a good deal of pronunciation, who wore a dress-coat in the morning, which made one wonder what he wore in the evening, and had or was supposed to have, "property" and something to do with the Bible Society. It couldn't have been but that *he* was a good type. Pemberton himself remembered Mrs. Clancy, a widowed sister of Mr. Moreen's, who was as irritating as a moral tale and had paid a fortnight's visit to the family at Nice shortly after he came to live with them. She was "pure and refined," as Amy said over the banjo, and had the air of not knowing what they meant when they talked, and of keeping something rather important back. Pemberton judged that what she kept back was an approval of many of their ways; therefore it was to be supposed that she too was of a good type, and that Mr. and Mrs. Moreen and Ulick and Paula and Amy might easily have been of a better one if they would.

But that they wouldn't was more and more perceptible from day to day. They continued to "chivey," as Morgan called it, and in due time became aware of a variety of reasons for proceeding to Venice. They mentioned a great many of them—they were always strikingly frank and had the brightest friendly chatter, at the late foreign breakfast in especial, before the ladies had made up their faces, when they leaned their arms on the table, had something to follow the *demi-tasse,* and, in the heat of familiar discussion as to what they "really ought" to do, fell inevitably into the languages in which they could *tutoyer.* Even Pemberton liked them then; he could endure even Ulick when he heard him give his little flat voice for the "sweet sea-city." That was what made him have a sneaking kindness for them—that they were so out of the workaday world and kept him so out of it. The summer had waned when, with cries of ecstasy, they all passed out on the balcony that overhung the Grand Canal. The sunsets then were splendid and the Dorringtons had arrived. The Dorringtons were the only reason they hadn't talked of at breakfast; but the reasons they didn't talk of at breakfast always came out in the end. The Dorringtons on the other hand came out very little; or else when they did they stayed—as was natural—for hours, during which periods Mrs. Moreen and the girls sometimes called at their hotel (to see if they had returned) as many as three times running. The gondola was for the ladies, as in Venice too there were "days," which Mrs. Moreen knew in their order an hour after she arrived. She immediately took one herself, to which the Dorringtons never came, though on a certain occasion when Pemberton and his pupil were together at Saint Mark's—where, taking the best walks they had ever had and haunting a hundred churches, they spent a great deal of time—they saw the old lord turn up with Mr. Moreen and Ulick, who showed him the dim basilica as if it belonged to them. Pemberton noted how much less, among its curiosities, Lord Dorrington carried himself as a man of the world; wondering too whether, for such services, his companions took a fee from him. The autumn at any rate waned, the Dorringtons departed, and Lord Verschoyle, the eldest son, had proposed neither for Amy nor for Paula.

One sad November day, while the wind roared round the old palace and the rain lashed the lagoon, Pemberton, for exercise and even somewhat for warmth—the Moreens were horribly frugal about fires; it was a cause of suffering to their inmate—walked up and down the big bare *sala* with his pupil. The scagliola floor was cold, the high battered casements shook in the storm, and the stately decay of the place was unrelieved by a particle of furniture. Pemberton's spirits were low, and it came over him that the fortune of the Moreens was now even lower. A blast of desolation, a portent of disgrace and disaster, seemed to draw through the comfortless hall. Mr. Moreen and Ulick were in the Piazza, looking out for something, strolling drearily, in mackintoshes, under the arcades; but still, in spite of mackintoshes, unmistakeable men of the world. Paula and Amy were in bed—it might have been thought they were staying there to keep warm. Pemberton looked askance at the boy at his side, to see to what extent he was conscious of these dark omens. But Morgan, luckily for him, was now mainly conscious of growing taller and stronger and indeed of being in his fifteenth year. This fact was intensely interesting to him and the basis of a private theory—which, however, he had imparted to his tutor—that in a little while he should stand on his own feet. He considered that the situation would change—that in short he should be "finished," grown up, producible in the world of affairs and ready to prove himself of sterling ability. Sharply as he was capable at times of analysing, as he called it, his life, there were happy hours when he remained, as he also called it—and as the name, really, of their right ideal—"jolly" superficial; the proof of which was his fundamental assumption that he should presently go to Oxford, to Pemberton's college, and aided and abetted by Pemberton, do the most wonderful things. It depressed the young man to see how little in such a project he took account of ways and means: in other connexions he mostly kept to the measure. Pemberton tried to imagine the Moreens at Oxford and fortunately failed; yet unless they were to adopt it as a residence there would be no *modus vivendi* for Morgan. How could he live without an allowance, and where was the allowance to come from? He, Pemberton, might live on Morgan; but how could Morgan live on *him?* What was to become of him anyhow? Somehow the fact that he was a big boy now, with better prospects of health, made the question of his future more difficult. So long as he was markedly frail the great consideration he inspired seemed enough of an answer to it. But at the bottom of Pemberton's heart was the recognition of his probably being strong enough to live and not yet strong enough to struggle or to thrive. Morgan himself at any rate was in the first flush of the rosiest consciousness of adolescence, so that the beating of the tempest seemed to him after all but the voice of life and the challenge of fate. He had on his shabby little overcoat, with the collar up, but was enjoying his walk.

It was interrupted at last by the appearance of his mother at the end of the *sala*. She beckoned him to come to her, and while Pemberton saw him, complaisant, pass down the long vista and over the damp false marble, he wondered what was in the air. Mrs. Moreen said a word to the boy and made him go into the room she had quitted. Then, having closed the door after him, she directed her steps swiftly to Pemberton. There *was* something in the air, but his wildest flight of fancy wouldn't have suggested what it proved to be. She signified that she had made a pretext to get Morgan out of the way, and then she enquired—without hesitation—if the young man could favour her with the loan of three louis. While, before bursting into a laugh, he stared at her with surprise, she declared that she was awfully pressed for the money; she was desperate for it—it would save her life.

"Dear lady, *c'est trop fort!*" Pemberton laughed in the manner and with the borrowed grace of idiom that marked the best colloquial, the best anecdotic, moments of his friends themselves. "Where in the world do you suppose I should get three louis, *du train dont vous allez?*"

"I thought you worked—wrote things. Don't they pay you?"

"Not a penny."

"Are you such a fool as to work for nothing?"

"You ought surely to know that."

Mrs. Moreen stared, then she coloured a little. Pemberton saw she had quite forgotten the terms—if "terms" they could be called—that he had ended by accepting from herself; they had burdened her memory as little as her conscience. "Oh yes, I see what you mean—you've been very nice about that; but why drag it in so often?" She had been perfectly urbane with him ever since the rough scene of explanation in his room the morning he made her accept *his* "terms"—the necessity of his making his case known to Morgan. She had felt no resentment after seeing there was no danger Morgan would take the matter up with her. Indeed, attributing this immunity to the good taste of his influence with the boy, she had once said to Pemberton "My dear fellow, it's an immense comfort you're a gentleman." She repeated this in substance now. "Of course you're a gentleman—that's a bother the less!" Pemberton reminded her that he had not "dragged in" anything that wasn't already in as much as his foot was in his shoe; and she also repeated her prayer that, somewhere and somehow, he would find her sixty francs. He took the liberty of hinting that if he could find them it wouldn't be to lend them to *her*—as to which he consciously did himself injustice, knowing that if he had them he would certainly put them at her disposal. He accused himself, at bottom and not unveraciously, of a fantastic, a demoralised sympathy with her. If misery made strange bed-fellows it also made strange sympathies. It was moreover a part of the abasement of living with such people that one had to make vulgar retorts, quite out of one's own tradition of good manners. "Morgan, Morgan, to what pass have I come for you?" he groaned while Mrs. Moreen floated voluminously down the *sala* again to liberate the boy, wailing as she went that everything was too odious.

Before their young friend was liberated there came a thump at the door communicating with the staircase, followed by the apparition of a dripping youth who poked in his head. Pemberton recognised him as the bearer of a telegram and recognised the telegram as addressed to himself. Morgan came back as, after glancing at the signature—that of a relative in London—he was reading the words: "Found jolly job for you, engagement to coach opulent youth on own terms. Come at once." The answer happily was paid and the messenger waited. Morgan, who had drawn near, waited too and looked hard at Pemberton; and Pemberton, after a moment, having met his look, handed him the telegram. It was really by wise looks—they knew each other so well now—that, while the telegraph-boy, in his waterproof cape, made a great puddle on the floor, the thing was settled between them. Pemberton wrote the answer with a pencil against the frescoed wall, and the messenger departed. When he had gone the young man explained himself.

"I'll make a tremendous charge; I'll earn a lot of money in a short time, and we'll live on it."

"Well, I hope the opulent youth will be a dismal dunce—he probably will," Morgan parenthesised—"and keep you a long time a-hammering of it in."

"Of course the longer he keeps me the more we shall have for our old age."

"But suppose *they* don't pay you!" Morgan awfully suggested.

"Oh there are not two such—!" But Pemberton pulled up; he had been on the point of using too invidious a term. Instead of this he said "Two such fatalities."

Morgan flushed—the tears came to his eyes. *"Dites toujours* two such rascally crews!" Then in a different tone he added: "Happy opulent youth!"

"Not if he's a dismal dunce."

"Oh they're happier then. But you can't have everything, can you?" the boy smiled.

Pemberton held him fast, hands on his shoulders—he had never loved him so. "What will become of *you,* what will you do?" He thought of Mrs. Moreen, desperate for sixty francs.

"I shall become an *homme fait."* And then as if he recognised all the bearings of Pemberton's allusion: "I shall get on with them better when you're not here."

"Ah don't say that—it sounds as if I set you against them!"

"You do—the sight of you. It's all right; you know what I mean. I shall be beautiful. I'll take their affairs in hand; I'll marry my sisters."

"You'll marry yourself!" joked Pemberton; as high, rather tense pleasantry would evidently be the right, or the safest, tone for their separation.

It was, however, not purely in this strain that Morgan suddenly asked: "But I say—how will you get to your jolly job? You'll have to telegraph to the opulent youth for money to come on."

Pemberton bethought himself. "They won't like that, will they?"

"Oh look out for them!"

Then Pemberton brought out his remedy. "I'll go to the American Consul; I'll borrow some money of him—just for the few days, on the strength of the telegram."

Morgan was hilarious. "Show him the telegram—then collar the money and stay!"

Pemberton entered into the joke sufficiently to reply that for Morgan he was really capable of that; but the boy, growing more serious, and to prove he hadn't meant what he said, not only hurried him off to the Consulate—since he was to start that evening, as he had wired to his friend—but made sure of their affair by going with him. They splashed through the tortuous perforations and over the humpbacked bridges, and they passed through the Piazza, where they saw Mr. Moreen and Ulick go into a jeweller's shop. The Consul proved accommodating—Pemberton said it wasn't the letter, but Morgan's grand air—and on their way back they went into Saint Mark's for a hushed ten minutes. Later they took up and kept up the fun of it to the very end; and it seemed to Pemberton a part of that fun that Mrs. Moreen, who was very angry when he had announced her his intention, should charge him, grotesquely and vulgarly and in reference to the loan she had vainly endeavoured to effect, with bolting lest they should "get something out" of him. On the other hand he had to do Mr. Moreen and Ulick the justice to recognise that when on coming in *they* heard the cruel news they took it like perfect men of the world.

VIII

WHEN he got at work with the opulent youth, who was to be taken in hand for Balliol, he found himself unable to say if this aspirant had really such poor parts or if the appearance were only begotten of his own long association with an intensely living little mind. From Morgan he heard half a dozen times: the boy wrote charming young letters, a patchwork of tongues, with indulgent postscripts in the family Volapuk and, in little squares and rounds and crannies of the text, the drollest illustrations—letters that he was divided between the impulse to show his present charge as a vain, a wasted incentive, and the sense of something in them that publicity would profane. The opulent youth went up in due course and failed to pass; but it seemed to add to the presumption that brilliancy was not expected of him all at once that his parents, condoning the lapse, which they good-naturedly treated as little as possible as if it were Pemberton's, should have sounded the rally again, begged the young coach to renew the siege.

The young coach was now in a position to lend Mrs. Moreen three louis, and he sent her a post-office order even for a larger amount. In return for his favour he received a frantic scribbled line from her: "Implore you to come back instantly—Morgan dreadfully ill." They were on the rebound, once more in Paris—often as Pemberton had seen them depressed he had never seen them crushed—and communication was therefore rapid. He wrote to the boy to ascertain the state of his health, but awaited the answer in vain. He accordingly, after three days, took an abrupt leave of the opulent youth and, crossing the Channel, alighted at the small hotel, in the quarter of the Champs Élysées, of which Mrs. Moreen had given him the address. A deep if dumb dissatisfaction with this lady and her companions bore him company: they couldn't be vulgarly honest, but they could live at hotels, in velvety *entresols,* amid a smell of burnt pastilles, surrounded by the most expensive city in Eruope. When he had left them in Venice it was with an irrepressible suspicion that something was going to happen; but the only thing that could have taken place was again their masterly retreat. "How is he? where is he?" he asked of Mrs. Moreen; but before she could speak these questions were answered by the pressure round his neck of a pair of arms, in shrunken sleeves, which still were perfectly capable of an effusive young foreign squeeze.

"Dreadfully ill—I don't see it!" the young man cried. And then to Morgan: "Why on earth didn't you relieve me? Why didn't you answer my letter?"

Mrs. Moreen declared that when she wrote he was very bad, and Pemberton learned at the same time from the boy that he had answered every letter he had received. This led to the clear inference that Pemberton's note had been kept from him so that the game to be practised should not be interfered with. Mrs. Moreen was prepared to see the fact exposed, as Pemberton saw the moment he faced her that she was prepared for a good many other things. She was prepared above all to maintain that she had acted from a sense of duty, that she was enchanted she had got him over, whatever they might say, and that it was useless of him to pretend he didn't know in all his bones that his place at such a time was with Morgan. He had taken the boy away from them and now had no right to abandon him. He had created for himself the gravest responsibilities and must at least abide by what he had done.

"Taken him away from you?" Pemberton exclaimed indignantly.

"Do it—do it for pity's sake; that's just what I want. I can't stand *this*—and such scenes. They're awful frauds—poor dears!" These words broke from Morgan, who had intermitted his embrace, in a key which made Pemberton turn quickly to him and see that he had suddenly seated himself, was breathing in great pain and was very pale.

"*Now* do you say he's not in a state, my precious pet?" shouted his mother, dropping on her knees before him with clasped hands, but touching him no more than if he had been a gilded idol. "It will pass—it's only for an instant; but don't say such dreadful things!"

"I'm all right—all right," Morgan panted to Pemberton, whom he sat looking up at with a strange smile, his hands resting on either side of the sofa.

"Now do you pretend I've been dishonest, that I've deceived?" Mrs. Moreen flashed at Pemberton as she got up.

"It isn't *he* says it, it's I!" the boy returned, apparently easier but sinking back against the wall; while his restored friend, who had sat down beside him, took his hand and bent over him.

"Darling child, one does what one can; there are so many things to consider," urged Mrs. Moreen. "It's his *place*—his only place. You see *you* think it is now."

"Take me away—take me away," Morgan went on, smiling to Pemberton with his white face.

"Where shall I take you, and how—oh *how*, my boy?" the young man stammered, thinking of the rude way in which his friends in London held that, for his convenience, with no assurance of prompt return, he had thrown them over; of the just resentment with which they would already have called in a successor, and of the scant help to finding fresh employment that resided for him in the grossness of his having failed to pass his pupil.

"Oh we'll settle that. You used to talk about it," said Morgan. "If we can only go all the rest's a detail."

"Talk about it as much as you like, but don't think you can attempt it. Mr. Moreen would never consent—it would be so *very* hand-to-mouth," Pemberton's hostess beautifully explained to him. Then to Morgan she made it clearer: "It would destroy our peace, it would break our hearts. Now that he's back it will be all the same again. You'll have your life, your work and your freedom, and we'll all be happy as we used to be. You'll bloom and grow perfectly well, and we won't have any more silly experiments, will we? They're too absurd. It's Mr. Pemberton's place—every one in his place. You in yours, your papa in his, me in mine—*n'est-ce pas, chéri?* We'll all forget how foolish we've been and have lovely times."

She continued to talk and to surge vaguely about the little draped stuffy salon while Pemberton sat with the boy, whose colour gradually came back; and she mixed up her reasons, hinting that there were going to be changes, that the other children might scatter (who knew?—Paula had her ideas) and that then it might be fancied how much the poor old parent-birds would want the little nestling. Morgan looked at Pemberton, who wouldn't let him move; and Pemberton knew exactly how he felt at hearing himself called a little nestling. He admitted that he had had one or two bad days, but he protested afresh against the wrong of his mother's having made them the ground of an appeal to poor Pemberton. Poor Pemberton could laugh now, apart from the comicality of Mrs. Moreen's mustering so much philosophy for her defence—she seemed to shake it out of her agitated petticoats, which knocked over the light gilt chairs—so little did their young companion, *marked*, unmistakeably marked at the best, strike him as qualified to repudiate any advantage.

He himself was in for it at any rate. He should have Morgan on his hands again indefinitely; though indeed he saw the lad had a private theory to produce which would be intended to smooth this down. He was obliged to him for it in advance; but the suggested amendment didn't keep his heart rather from sinking, any more than it prevented him from accepting the prospect on the spot, with some confidence moreover that he should do even better if he could have a little supper. Mrs. Moreen threw out more hints about the changes that were to be looked for, but she was such a mixture of smiles and shudders—she confessed she was very nervous—that he couldn't tell if she were in high feather or only in hysterics. If the family was really at last going to pieces why shouldn't she recognise the necessity of pitching Morgan into some sort of lifeboat? This presumption was fostered by the fact that they were established in luxurious quarters in the capital of pleasure; that was exactly where they naturally *would* be established in view of going to pieces. Moreover didn't she mention that Mr. Moreen and the others were enjoying themselves at the opera with Mr. Granger, and wasn't *that* also precisely where one would look for them on the eve of a smash? Pemberton gathered that Mr. Granger was a rich vacant American—a big bill with a flourishy heading and no items; so that one of Paula's "ideas" was probably that this time she hadn't missed fire—by which straight shot indeed she would have shattered the general cohesion. And if the cohesion was to crumble what would become of poor Pemberton? He felt quite enough bound up with them to figure to his alarm as a dislodged block in the edifice.

It was Morgan who eventually asked if no supper had been ordered for him; sitting with him below, later, at the dim delayed meal, in the presence of a great deal of corded green plush, a plate of ornamental biscuit and an aloofness marked on the part of the waiter. Mr. Moreen had explained that they had been obliged to secure a room for the visitor out of the house; and Morgan's consolation—he offered it while Pemberton reflected on the nastiness of luke-warm sauces—proved to be, largely, that this circumstance would facilitate their escape. He talked of their escape—recurring to it often afterwards—as if they were making up a "boy's book" together. But he likewise expressed his sense that there was something in the air, that the Moreens couldn't keep it up much longer. In point of fact, as Pemberton was to see, they kept it up for five or six months. All the while, however, Morgan's contention was designed to cheer him. Mr. Moreen and Ulick, whom he had met the day after his return, accepted that return like perfect men of the world. If Paula and Amy treated it even with less formality an allowance was to be made for them, inasmuch as Mr. Granger hadn't come to the opera after all. He had only placed his box at their service, with a bouquet for each of the party; there was even one apiece, embittering the thought of his profusion, for Mr. Moreen and Ulick. "They're all like that," was Morgan's comment; "at the very last, just when we think we've landed them they're back in the deep sea!"

Morgan's comments in these days were more and more free; they even included a large recognition of the extraordinary tenderness with which he had been treated while Pemberton was away. Oh yes, they couldn't do enough to be nice to him, to show him they had him on their mind and make up for his loss. That was just what made the whole thing so sad and caused him to rejoice after all in Pemberton's return—he had to keep thinking of their affection less, had less sense of obligation. Pemberton laughed out at this last reason, and Morgan blushed and said "Well, dash it, you know what I mean." Pemberton knew perfectly what he meant; but there were a good many things that—dash it too!—it didn't make any clearer. This episode of his second sojourn in Paris stretched itself out wearily, with their resumed readings and wanderings and maunderings, their potterings on the quays, their hauntings of the museums, their occasional lingerings in the Palais Royal when the first sharp weather came on and there was a comfort in warm emanations, before Chevet's wonderful succulent window. Morgan wanted to hear all about the opulent youth—he took an immense interest in him. Some of the details of his opulence—Pemberton could spare him none of them—evidently fed the boy's appreciation of all his friend had given up to come back to him;

but in addition to the greater reciprocity established by that heroism he had always his little brooding theory, in which there was a frivolous gaiety too, that their long probation was drawing to a close. Morgan's conviction that the Moreens couldn't go on much longer kept pace with their unexpended impetus with which, from month to month, they did go on. Three weeks after Pemberton had rejoined them they went on to another hotel, a dingier one than the first; but Morgan rejoiced that his tutor had at least still not sacrificed the advantage of a room outside. He clung to the romantic utility of this when the day, or rather the night, should arrive for their escape.

For the first time, in this complicated connexion, our friend felt his collar gall him. It was, as he had said to Mrs. Moreen in Venice, *trop fort*—everything was *trop fort*. He could neither really throw off his blighting burden nor find in it the benefit of a pacified conscience or of a rewarded affection. He had spent all the money accruing to him in England, and he saw his youth going and that he was getting nothing back for it. It was all very well of Morgan to count it for reparation that he should now settle on him permanently—there was an irritating flaw in such a view. He saw what the boy had in his mind; the conception that as his friend had had the generosity to come back he must show his gratitude by giving him his life. But the poor friend didn't desire the gift—what could he do with Morgan's dreadful little life? Of course at the same time that Pemberton was irritated he remembered the reason, which was very honourable to Morgan and which dwelt simply in his making one so forget that he was no more than a patched urchin. If one dealt with him on a different basis one's misadventures were one's own fault. So Pemberton waited in a queer confusion of yearning and alarm for the catastrophe which was held to hang over the house of Moreen, of which he certainly at moments felt the symptoms brush his cheek and as to which he wondered much in what form it would find its liveliest effect.

Perhaps it would take the form of sudden dispersal—a frightened *sauve qui peut,* a scuttling into selfish corners. Certainly they were less elastic than of yore; they were evidently looking for something they didn't find. The Dorringtons hadn't re-appeared, the princes had scattered; wasn't that the beginning of the end? Mrs. Moreen had lost her reckoning of the famous "days"; her social calendar was blurred—it had turned its face to the wall. Pemberton suspected that the great, the cruel discomfiture had been the unspeakable behaviour of Mr. Granger, who seemed not to know what he wanted, or, what was much worse, what *they* wanted. He kept sending flowers, as if to bestrew the path of his retreat, which was never the path of a return. Flowers were all very well, but—Pemberton could complete the proposition. It was now positively conspicuous that in the long run the Moreens were a social failure; so that the young man was almost grateful the run had not been short. Mr. Moreen indeed was still occasionally able to get away on business and, what was more surprising, was likewise able to get back. Ulick had no club, but you couldn't have discovered it from his appearance, which was as much as ever that of a person looking at life from the window of such an institution; therefore Pemberton was doubly surprised at an answer he once heard him make his mother in the desperate tone of a man familiar with the worst privations. Her question Pemberton had not quite caught; it appeared to be an appeal for a suggestion as to whom they might get to take Amy. "Let the Devil take her!" Ulick snapped; so that Pemberton could see that they had not only lost their amiability but had ceased to believe in themselves. He could also see that if Mrs. Moreen was trying to get people to take her children she might be regarded as closing the hatches for the storm. But Morgan would be the last she would part with.

One winter afternoon—it was a Sunday—he and the boy walked far together in the Bois de Boulogne. The evening was so splendid, the cold lemon-coloured sunset so clear, the stream of carriages and pedestrians so amusing and the fascination of Paris so great, that they stayed out later than usual and became aware that they should have to hurry home to arrive in time for dinner. They hurried accordingly, arm-in-arm, good-humoured and hungry, agreeing that there was nothing like Paris after all and that after everything too that had come and gone they were not yet sated with innocent pleasures. When they reached the hotel they found that, though scandalously late, they were in time for all the dinner they were likely to sit down to. Confusion reigned in the apartments of the Moreens—very shabby ones this time, but the best in the house—and before the interrupted service of the table, with objects displaced almost as if there had been a scuffle and a great wine-stain from an overturned bottle, Pemberton couldn't blink the fact that there had been a scene of the last proprietary firmness. The storm had come—they were all seeking refuge. The hatches were down, Paula and Amy were invisible—they had never tried the most casual art upon Pemberton, but he felt they had enough of an eye to him not to wish to meet him as young ladies whose frocks had been confiscated—and Ulick appeared to have jumped overboard. The host and his staff, in a word, had ceased to "go on" at the pace of their guests, and the air of embarrassed detention, thanks to a pile of gaping trunks in the passage, was strangely commingled with the air of indignant withdrawal.

When Morgan took all this in—and he took it in very quickly—he coloured to the roots of his hair. He had walked from his infancy among difficulties and dangers, but he had never seen a public exposure. Pemberton noticed in a second glance at him that the tears had rushed into his eyes and that they were tears of a new and untasted bitterness. He wondered an instant, for the boy's sake, whether he might successfully pretend not to understand. Not successfully, he felt, as Mr. and Mrs. Moreen, dinnerless by their extinguished hearth, rose before him in their little dishonoured salon, casting about with glassy eyes for the nearest port in such a storm. They were not prostrate but were horribly white, and Mrs. Moreen had evidently been crying. Pemberton quickly learned however that her grief was not for the loss of her dinner, much as she usually enjoyed it, but the fruit of a blow that struck even deeper, as she made all haste to explain. He would see for himself, so far as that went, how the great change had come, the dreadful bolt had fallen, and how they would now all have to turn themselves about. Therefore cruel as it was to them to part with their darling she must look to him to carry a little further the influence he had so fortunately acquired with the boy—to induce his young charge to follow him into some modest retreat. They depended on him—that was the fact—to take their delightful child temporarily under his protection: it would leave Mr. Moreen and herself so much more free to give the proper attention (too little, alas! had been given) to the readjustment of their affairs.

"We trust you—we feel we *can,*" said Mrs. Moreen, slowly rubbing her plump white hands and looking with compunction hard at Morgan, whose chin, not to take liberties, her husband stroked with a tentative paternal forefinger.

"Oh yes—we feel that we *can*. We trust Mr. Pemberton fully, Morgan," Mr. Moreen pursued.

Pemberton wondered again if he might pretend not to understand; but everything good gave way to the intensity of Morgan's understanding. "Do you mean he may take me to live with him for ever and ever?" cried the boy. "May take me away, away, anywhere he likes?"

"For ever and ever? *Comme vous-y-allez!*" Mr. Moreen laughed indulgently. "For as long as Mr. Pemberton may be so good."

"We've struggled, we've suffered," his wife went on; "but you've made him so your own that we've already been through the worst of the sacrifice."

Morgan had turned away from his father—he stood looking at Pemberton with a light in his face. His sense of shame for their common humiliated state had dropped; the case had another side—the thing was to clutch at *that.* He had a moment of boyish joy, scarcely mitigated by the reflexion that with this unexpected consecration of his hope—too sudden and too violent; the turn taken was away from a *good* boy's book—the "escape" was left on their hands. The boyish joy was there an instant, and Pemberton was almost scared at the rush of gratitude and affection that broke through his first abasement. When he stammered "My dear fellow, what do you say to *that?*" how could one not say something enthusiastic? But there was more need for courage at something else that immediately followed and that made the lad sit down quickly on the nearest chair. He had turned quite livid and had raised his hand to his left side. They were all three looking at him, but Mrs. Moreen suddenly bounded forward. "Ah his darling little heart!" she broke out; and this time, on her knees before him and without respect for the idol, she caught him ardently in her arms. "You walked him too far, you hurried him too fast!" she hurled over her shoulder at Pemberton. Her son made no protest, and the next instant, still holding him, she sprang up with her face convulsed and with the terrified cry "Help, help! he's going, he's gone!" Pemberton saw with equal horror, by Morgan's own stricken face, that he was beyond their wildest recall. He pulled him half out of his mother's hands, and for a moment, while they held him together, they looked all their dismay into each other's eyes. "He couldn't stand it with his weak organ," said Pemberton—"the shock, the whole scene, the violent emotion."

"But I thought he *wanted* to go to you!" wailed Mrs. Moreen.

"I *told* you he didn't, my dear," her husband made answer. Mr. Moreen was trembling all over and was in his way as deeply affected as his wife. But after the very first he took his bereavement as a man of the world.

JAMES'S PREFACE TO *THE PUPIL*

1908

I PASS BY, for the moment, the second of these compositions, finding in the third, which again deals with the experience of a very young person, a connexion more immediate; and this even at the risk of seeming to undermine my remark of a few pages back as to the comparative sensibility of the sexes. My urchin of "The Pupil" (1891) has sensibility in abundance, it would seem—and yet preserves in spite of it, I judge, his strong little male quality. But there are fifty things to say here; which indeed rush upon me within my present close limits in such a cloud as to demand much clearance. This is perhaps indeed but the aftersense of the assault made on my mind, as I perfectly recall, by every aspect of the original vision, which struck me as abounding in aspects. It lives again for me, this vision, as it first alighted; though the inimitable prime flutter, the air as of an ineffable sign made by the immediate beat of the wings of the poised figure of fancy that has just settled, is one of those guarantees of value that can never be recaptured. The sign has been made to the seer only—it is *his* queer affair; of which any report to others, not as yet involved, has but the same effect of flatness as attends, amid a group gathered under the canopy of night, any stray allusion to a shooting star. The miracle, since miracle it seems, is all for the candid exclaimer. The miracle for the author of "The Pupil," at any rate, was when, years ago, one summer day, in a very hot Italian railway-carriage, which stopped and dawdled everywhere, favouring conversation, a friend with whom I shared it, a doctor of medicine who had come from a far country to settle in

Florence, happened to speak to me of a wonderful American family, an odd adventurous, extravagant band, of high but rather unauthenticated pretensions, the most interesting member of which was a small boy, acute and precocious, afflicted with a heart of weak action, but beautifully intelligent, who saw their prowling precarious life exactly as it was, and measured and judged it, and measured and judged *them,* all round, ever so quaintly; presenting himself in short as an extraordinary little person. Here was more than enough for a summer's day even in old Italy—here was a thumping windfall. No process and no steps intervened: I *saw,* on the spot, little Morgan Moreen, I saw all the rest of the Moreens; I felt, to the last delicacy, the nature of my young friend's relation with them (he had become at once my young friend) and, by the same stroke, to its uttermost fine throb, the subjection to *him* of the beguiled, bewildered, defrauded, unremunerated, yet after all richly repaid youth who would to a certainty, under stress of compassion, embark with the tribe on tutorship, and whose edifying connexion with it would be my leading document.

This must serve as my account of the origin of "The Pupil": it will commend itself, I feel, to all imaginative and projective persons who have had—and what imaginative and projective person hasn't?—any like experience of the suddenly-determined *absolute* of perception. The whole cluster of items forming the image is on these occasions born at once; the parts are not pieced together, they conspire and interdepend; but what it really comes to, no doubt, is that at a simple touch an old latent and dormant impression, a buried germ, implanted by experience and then forgotten, flashes to the surface as a fish, with a single "squirm," rises to the baited hook, and there meets instantly the vivifying ray. I remember at all events having no doubt of anything or anyone here; the vision kept to the end its ease and its charm; it worked itself out with confidence. These are minor matters when the question is of minor results; yet almost any assured and downright imaginative act is—granted the sort of record in which I here indulge—worth fondly commemorating. One cherishes, after the fact, any proved case of the independent life of the imagination; above all if by that faculty one has been appointed mainly to live. We are then *never* detached from the question of what it may out of simple charity do for us. Besides which, in relation to the poor Moreens, innumerable notes, as I have intimated, all equally urging their relevance, press here to the front. The general adventure of the little composition itself—for singular things were to happen to it, though among such importunities not the most worth noting now—would be, occasion favouring, a thing to live over; moving as one did, roundabout it, in I scarce know what thick and coloured air of slightly tarnished anecdote, of dim association, of casual confused romance; a compound defying analysis, but truly, for the social chronicler, any student in especial of the copious "cosmopolite" legend, a boundless and tangled, but highly explorable, garden. Why, somehow—these were the intensifying questions—did one see the Moreens, whom I place at Nice, at Venice, in Paris, as of the special essence of the little old miscellaneous cosmopolite Florence, the Florence of other, of irrecoverable years, the restless yet withal so convenient scene of a society that has passed away for ever with all its faded ghosts and fragile relics; immaterial presences that have quite ceased to revisit (trust an old romancer's, an old pious observer's fine sense to have made sure of it!) walks and prospects once sacred and shaded, but now laid bare, gaping wide, despoiled of their past and unfriendly to any appreciation of it?—through which the unconscious Barbarians troop with the regularity and passivity of "supplies," or other promiscuous goods, prepaid and forwarded.

They had nothing to do, the dear Moreens, with this dreadful period, any more than I, as occupied and charmed with them, was humiliatingly subject to it; we were, all together, of a better romantic age and faith; we referred ourselves, with our highest complacency, to the classic years of the great Americano-European legend; the years of limited communication, of monstrous and unattenuated contrast, of prodigious and unrecorded adventure. The comparatively brief but infinitely rich "cycle" of romance embedded in the earlier, the very early American reactions and returns (mediæval in the sense of being, at most, of the mid-century), what does it resemble today but a gold-mine overgrown and smothered, dislocated, and no longer workable?—all for want of the right indications for sounding, the right implements for digging, doubtless even of the right workmen, those with the right tradition and "feeling" for the job. The most extraordinary things appear to have happened, during that golden age, in the "old" countries—in Asia and Africa as well as in Europe—to the candid children of the West, things admirably incongruous and incredible; but no story of all the list was to find its just interpreter, and nothing is now more probable than that every key to interpretation has been lost. The modern reporter's big brushes, attached to broom-handles that match the height of his sky-scrapers, would sadly besmear the fine parchment of our missing record. We were to lose, clearly, at any rate, a vast body of precious anecdotes, a long gallery of wonderful portraits, an array of the oddest possible figures in the oddest possible attitudes. The Moreens were of the family then of the great unstudied precursors—poor and shabby members, no doubt; dim and superseded types. I must add indeed that, such as they were, or as they may at present incoherently appear, I don't pretend really to have "done" them; all I have given in "The Pupil" is little Morgan's troubled vision of them as reflected in the vision, also troubled enough, of his devoted friend. The manner of the thing may thus illustrate the author's incorrigible taste for gradations and superpositions of effect; his love, when it is a question of a picture, of anything that makes for proportion and perspective, that contributes to a view of *all* the dimensions. Addicted to seeing "through"—one thing through another, accordingly, and still other things through *that*—he takes, too greedily perhaps, on any errand, as many things as possible by the way. It is after this fashion that he incurs the stigma of labouring uncannily for a certain fullness of truth—truth diffused, distributed and, as it were, atmospheric.

EDITOR'S NOTE

No notebook entry has been found for "The Pupil" but it is almost certain that the "doctor of medicine who had come from a far country to settle in Florence" was Dr. W. W. Baldwin, an American physician who settled in the Italian city and for many years had a flourishing practice there. Both Henry James and his philosopher-brother, William, were friends of Baldwin and during visits to England he served as consultant in the treatment of Henry's invalid sister, Alice, during her last illness.

James paid two visits to Baldwin in Italy, in the spring of 1890, and described him to friends as "a charming and glowing little man." In July of that year he went on a little tour with Baldwin of certain "romantic and untrodden Tuscany corners" and it was doubtless during this trip that he got the story of "The Pupil." He wrote it late that same summer and sent it in October to the *Atlantic Monthly* whose new editor, Horace E. Scudder, rejected it, probably fearing that the picture of a mendacious American family would not appeal to *Atlantic* readers. An unpublished letter to Scudder expresses Henry James's "shock of a perfectly honest surprise." He had no trouble in placing the tale in England, where it appeared in *Longman's* in April 1891. In a second letter to Scudder, James said he "could not see that it was a performance that the *Atlantic* ought to have declined—nor banish from my mind the reflection that the responsibility, in any case, as regards the readers of the magazine, the public, should, when it's a question of an old and honourable reputation, be left with the author himself. The editor, under such circumstances, may fairly leave it to him—and I should not have shrunk from any account the readers might have held me to." [1]

[1] I am indebted to Mr. Donald Brien, owner of the Scudder correspondence, for permission to quote from it here.

Posterity has confirmed James's judgment of his story rather than Scudder's. The little hint given by Dr. Baldwin appealed to James for many reasons. He could paint a wandering American family in Europe with ease; in his own childhood he had experienced the casual, uncertain vaguenesses and uncertainties to which Morgan Moreen is exposed, and while James's parents in no way resembled the shoddy parents of Morgan, James knew what it was like to drift from place to place, and to be left in the hands of tutors and governesses. He knew too what anxieties economic uncertainty could provoke in children, remembering vividly the American depression of 1856-57 which caused the James family to beat a hasty retreat from a luxurious apartment in Paris to a modest domicile in Boulogne-sur-mer. Out of this personal past, Henry James's imagination wove this tender tale of a sensitive boy and his tutor, the first of a series of stories about children adrift in the world amid indifferent adults—and adults who by their indifference or neglect, or by meddling, made life a nightmare for the young. One has only to read *What Maisie Knew, The Other House* and *The Turn of the Screw* to see how this theme grew on James's hands during the 1890's.

THE BEAST IN THE JUNGLE

1903

I

WHAT determined the speech that startled him in the course of their encounter scarcely matters, being probably but some words spoken by himself quite without intention —spoken as they lingered and slowly moved together after their renewal of acquaintance. He had been conveyed by friends an hour or two before to the house at which she was staying; the party of visitors at the other house, of whom he was one, and thanks to whom it was his theory, as always, that he was lost in the crowd, had been invited over to luncheon. There had been after luncheon much dispersal, all in the interest of the original motive, a view of Weatherend itself and the fine things, intrinsic features, pictures, heirlooms, treasures of all the arts, that made the place almost famous; and the great rooms were so numerous that guests could wander at their will, hang back from the principal group and in cases where they took such matters with the last seriousness give themselves up to mysterious appreciations and measurements. There were persons to be observed, singly or in couples, bending toward objects in out-of-the-way corners with their hands on their knees and their heads nodding quite as with the emphasis of an excited sense of smell. When they were two they either mingled their sounds of ecstasy or melted into silences of even deeper import, so that there were aspects of the occasion that gave it for Marcher much the air of the "look round," previous to a sale highly advertised, that excites or quenches, as may be, the dream of acquisition. The dream of acquisition at Weatherend would have had to be wild indeed, and John Marcher found himself, among such suggestions, disconcerted almost equally by the presence of those who knew too much and by that of those who knew nothing. The great rooms caused so much poetry and history to press upon him that he needed some straying apart to feel in a proper relation with them, though this impulse was not, as happened, like the gloating of some of his companions, to be compared to the movements of a dog sniffing a cupboard. It had an issue promptly enough in a direction that was not to have been calculated.

It led, briefly, in the course of the October afternoon, to his closer meeting with May Bartram, whose face, a reminder, yet not quite a remembrance, as they sat much separated at a very long table, had begun merely by troubling him rather pleasantly. It affected him as the sequel of something of which he had lost the beginning. He knew it, and for the time quite welcomed it, as a continuation, but didn't know what it continued, which was an interest or an amusement the greater as he was also somehow aware—yet without a direct sign from her—that the young woman herself hadn't lost the thread. She hadn't lost it, but she wouldn't give it back to him, he saw, without some putting forth of his hand for it; and he not only saw that, but saw several things more, things odd enough in the light of the fact at the moment some accident of grouping brought them face to face he was still merely fumbling with the idea that any contact between them in the past would have had no importance. If it had had no importance he scarcely knew why his actual impression of her should so seem to have so much; the answer to which, however, was that in such a life as they all appeared to be leading for the moment one could but take things as they came. He was satisfied, without in the least being able to say why, that this young lady might roughly have ranked in the house as a poor relation; satisfied also that she was not there on a brief visit, but was more or less a part of the establishment—almost a working, a remunerated part. Didn't she enjoy at periods a protection that she paid for by helping, among other services, to show the place and explain it, deal with the tiresome people, answer questions about the dates of the building, the styles of the furniture, the authorship of the pictures, the favourite haunts of the ghost? It wasn't that she looked as if you could have given her shillings—it was impossible to look less so. Yet when she finally drifted toward him, distinctly handsome, though ever so much older—older than when he had seen her before—it might have been as an effect of her guessing that he had, within the couple of hours, devoted more imagination to her than to all the others put together, and had thereby penetrated to a kind of truth that the others were too stupid for. She *was* there on harder terms than any one; she was there as a consequence of things suffered, one way and another, in the interval of years; and she remembered him very much as she was remembered—only a good deal better.

By the time they at last thus came to speech they were alone in one of the rooms—remarkable for a fine portrait over the chimney-place—out of which their friends had passed, and the charm of it was that even before they had spoken they had practically arranged with each other to stay behind for talk. The charm, happily, was in other things too—partly in there being scarce a spot at Weatherend without something to stay behind for. It was in the way the autumn day looked into the high windows as it waned; the way the red light, breaking at the close from under a low sombre sky, reached out in a long shaft and played over old wainscots, old tapestry, old gold, old colour. It was most of all perhaps in the way she came to him as if, since she had been turned on to deal with the simpler sort, he might, should he choose to keep the whole thing down, just take her mild attention for a part of her general business. As soon as he heard her voice, however, the gap was filled up and the missing link supplied; the slight irony he divined in her attitude lost its advantage. He almost jumped at it to get there before her. "I met you years and years ago in Rome. I remember all about it." She confessed to disappointment—she had been so sure he didn't; and to prove how well he did he began to pour forth the particular recollections that popped up as he called for them. Her face and her voice, all at his service now, worked the miracle—the impression operating like the torch of a lamplighter who touches into flame, one by one, a long row of gas-jets. Marcher flattered himself the illumination was brilliant, yet he was really still more pleased on her showing him, with amusement, that in his haste to make everything right he had got most things rather wrong. It hadn't been at Rome—it had been at Naples; and it hadn't been eight years before—it had been more nearly ten. She hadn't been, either, with her uncle and aunt, but with her mother and her brother; in addition to which it was not with the Pembles *he* had been, but with the Boyers, coming down in their company from Rome—a point on which she insisted, a little to his confusion, and as to which she had her evidence in hand. The Boyers she had known, but didn't know the Pembles, though she had heard of them, and it was the people he was with who had made them acquainted. The incident of the thunderstorm that had raged round them with such violence as to drive them for refuge into an excavation—this incident had not occurred at the Palace of the Cæsars, but at Pompeii, on an occasion when they had been present there at an important find.

He accepted her amendments, he enjoyed her corrections, though the moral of them was, she pointed out, that he *really* didn't remember the least thing about her; and he only felt it as a drawback that when all was made strictly historic there didn't appear much of anything left. They lingered together still, she neglecting her office—for from the moment he was so clever she had no proper right to him—and both neglecting the house, just waiting as to see if a memory or two more wouldn't again breathe on them. It hadn't taken them many minutes, after all, to put down on the table, like the cards of a pack, those that constituted their respective hands; only what came out was that the pack was unfortunately not perfect—that the past, invoked, invited, encouraged, could give them, naturally, no more than it had. It had made them anciently meet—her at twenty, him at twenty-five; but nothing was so strange, they seemed to say to each other, as that, while so occupied, it hadn't done a little more for them. They looked at each other as with the feeling of an occasion missed; the present would have been so much better if the other, in the far distance, in the foreign land, hadn't been so stupidly meagre. There weren't apparently, all counted, more than a dozen little old things that had succeeded in coming to pass between them; trivialities of youth, simplicities of freshness, stupidities of ignorance, small possible germs, but too deeply buried—too deeply (didn't it seem?) to sprout after so many years. Marcher could only feel he ought to have rendered her some service—saved her from a capsized boat in the Bay or at least recovered her dressing-bag, filched from her cab in the streets of Naples by a lazzarone with a stiletto. Or it would have been nice if he could have been taken with fever all alone at his hotel, and she could have come to look after him, to write to his people, to drive him out in convalescence. *Then* they would be in possession of the something or other that their actual show seemed to lack. It yet somehow presented itself, this show, as too good to be spoiled; so that they were reduced for a few minutes more to wondering a little helplessly why—since they seemed to know a certain number of the same people—their reunion had been so long averted. They didn't use that name for it, but their delay from minute to minute to join the others was a kind of confession that they didn't quite want it to be a failure. Their attempted supposition of reasons for their not having met but showed how little they knew of each other. There came in fact a moment when Marcher felt a positive pang. It was vain to pretend she was an old friend, for all the communities were wanting, in spite of which it was as an old friend that he saw she would have suited him. He had new ones enough—was surrounded with them for instance on the stage of the other house; as a new one he probably wouldn't have so much as noticed her. He would have liked to invent something, get her to make believe with him that some passage of a romantic or critical kind *had* originally occurred. He was really almost reaching out in imagination—as against time—for something that would do, and saying to himself that if it didn't come this sketch of a fresh start would show for quite awkwardly bungled. They would separate, and now for no second or no third chance. They would have tried and not succeeded. Then it was, just at the turn, as he afterwards made it out to himself, that, everything else failing, she herself decided to take up the case and, as it were, save the situation. He felt as soon as she spoke that she had been consciously keeping back what she said and hoping to get on without it; a scruple in her that immensely touched him when, by the end of three or four minutes more, he was able to measure it. What she brought out, at any rate, quite cleared the air and supplied the link—the link it was so odd he should frivolously have managed to lose.

"You know you told me something I've never forgotten and that again and again has made me think of you since; it was that tremendously hot day when we went to Sorrento, across the bay, for the breeze. What I allude to was what you said to me, on the way back, as we sat under the awning of the boat enjoying the cool. Have you forgotten?"

He had forgotten and was even more surprised than ashamed. But the great thing was that he saw in this no vulgar reminder of any "sweet" speech. The vanity of women had long memories, but she was making no claim on him of a compliment or a mistake. With another woman, a totally different one, he might have feared the recall possibly even of some imbecile "offer." So, in having to say that he had indeed forgotten, he was conscious rather of a loss than of a gain; he already saw an interest in the matter of her mention. "I try to think—but I give it up. Yet I remember the Sorrento day."

"I'm not very sure you do," May Bartram after a moment said; "and I'm not very sure I ought to want you to. It's dreadful to bring a person back at any time to what he was ten years before. If you've lived away from it," she smiled, "so much the better."

"Ah if *you* haven't why should I?" he asked.

"Lived away, you mean, from what I myself was?"

"From what *I* was. I was of course an ass," Marcher went on; "but I would rather know from you just the sort of ass I was than—from the moment you have something in your mind—not know anything."

Still, however, she hesitated. "But if you've completely ceased to be that sort—?"

"Why I can then all the more bear to know. Besides, perhaps I haven't."

"Perhaps. Yet if you haven't," she added, "I should suppose you'd remember. Not indeed that *I* in the least connect with my impression the invidious name you use. If I had only thought you foolish," she explained, "the thing I speak of wouldn't so have remained with me. It was about yourself." She waited as if it might come to him; but as, only meeting her eyes in wonder, he gave no sign, she burnt her ships. "Has it ever happened?"

Then it was that, while he continued to stare, a light broke for him and the blood slowly came to his face, which began to burn with recognition. "Do you mean I told you—?" But he faltered, lest what came to him shouldn't be right, lest he should only give himself away.

"It was something about yourself that it was natural one shouldn't forget—that is if one remembered you at all. That's why I ask you," she smiled, "if the thing you then spoke of has ever come to pass?"

Oh then he saw, but he was lost in wonder and found himself embarrassed. This, he also saw, made her sorry for him, as if her allusion had been a mistake. It took him but a moment, however, to feel it hadn't been, much as it had been a surprise. After the first little shock of it her knowledge on the contrary began, even if rather strangely, to taste sweet to him. She was the only other person in the world then who would have it, and she had had it all these years, while the fact of his having so breathed his secret had unaccountably faded from him. No wonder they couldn't have met as if nothing had happened. "I judge," he finally said, "that I know what you mean. Only I had strangely enough lost any sense of having taken you so far into my confidence."

"Is it because you've taken so many others as well?"

"I've taken nobody. Not a creature since then."

"So that I'm the only person who knows?"

"The only person in the world."

"Well," she quickly replied, "I myself have never spoken. I've never, never repeated of you what you told me." She looked at him so that he perfectly believed her. Their eyes met over it in such a way that he was without a doubt. "And I never will."

She spoke with an earnestness that, as if almost excessive, put him at ease about her possible derision. Somehow the whole question was a new luxury to him—that is from the moment she was in possession. If she didn't take the sarcastic view she clearly took the sympathetic, and that was what he had had, in all the long time, from no one whomsoever. What he felt was that he couldn't at present have begun to tell her, and yet could profit perhaps exquisitely by the accident of having done so of old. "Please don't then. We're just right as it is."

"Oh I am," she laughed, "if you are!" To which she added: "Then you do still feel in the same way?"

It was impossible he shouldn't take to himself that she was really interested, though it all kept coming as perfect surprise. He had thought of himself so long as abominably alone, and lo he wasn't alone a bit. He hadn't been, it appeared, for an hour—since those moments on the Sorrento boat. It was *she* who had been, he seemed to see as he looked at her—she who had been made so by the graceless fact of his lapse of fidelity. To tell her what he had told her—what had it been but to ask something of her? something that she had given, in her charity, without his having, by a remembrance, by a return of the spirit, failing another encounter, so much as thanked her. What he had asked of her had been simply at first not to laugh at him. She had beautifully not done so for ten years, and she was not doing so now. So he had endless gratitude to make up. Only for that he must see just how he had figured to her. "What, exactly, was the account I gave—?"

"Of the way you did feel? Well, it was very simple. You said you had had from your earliest time, as the deepest thing within you, the sense of being kept for something rare and strange, possibly prodigious and terrible, that was sooner or later to happen to you, that you had in your bones the foreboding and the conviction of, and that would perhaps overwhelm you."

"Do you call that very simple?" John Marcher asked.

She thought a moment. "It was perhaps because I seemed, as you spoke, to understand it."

"You do understand it?" he eagerly asked.

Again she kept her kind eyes on him. "You still have the belief?"

"Oh!" he exclaimed helplessly. There was too much to say.

"Whatever it's to be," she clearly made out, "it hasn't yet come."

He shook his head in complete surrender now. "It hasn't yet come. Only, you know, it isn't anything I'm to *do,* to achieve in the world, to be distinguished or admired for. I'm not such an ass as *that.* It would be much better, no doubt, if I were."

"It's to be something you're merely to suffer?"

"Well, say to wait for—to have to meet, to face, to see suddenly break out in my life; possibly destroying all further consciousness, possibly annihilating me; possibly, on the other hand, only altering everything, striking at the root of all my world and leaving me to the consequences, however they shape themselves."

She took this in, but the light in her eyes continued for him not to be that of mockery. "Isn't what you describe perhaps but the expectation—or at any rate the sense of danger, familiar to so many people—of falling in love?"

John Marcher wondered. "Did you ask me that before?"

"No—I wasn't so free-and-easy then. But it's what strikes me now."

"Of course," he said after a moment, "it strikes you. Of course it strikes *me.* Of course what's in store for me may be no more than that. The only thing is," he went on, "that I think if it had been that I should by this time know."

"Do you mean because you've *been* in love?" And then as he but looked at her in silence: "You've been in love, and it hasn't meant such a cataclysm, hasn't proved the great affair?"

"Here I am, you see. It hasn't been overwhelming."

"Then it hasn't been love," said May Bartram.

"Well, I at least thought it was. I took it for that—I've taken it till now. It was agreeable, it was delightful, it was miserable," he explained. "But it wasn't strange. It wasn't what *my* affair's to be."

"You want something all to yourself—something that nobody else knows or *has* known?"

"It isn't a question of what I 'want'—God knows I don't want anything. It's only a question of the apprehension that haunts me—that I live with day by day."

He said this so lucidly and consistently that he could see it further impose itself. If she hadn't been interested before she'd have been interested now. "Is it a sense of coming violence?"

Evidently now too again he liked to talk of it. "I don't think of it as—when it does come—necessarily violent. I only think of it as natural and as of course above all unmistakeable. I think of it simply as *the* thing. *The* thing will of itself appear natural."

"Then how will it appear strange?"

Marcher bethought himself. "It won't—to *me*."

"To whom then?"

"Well," he replied, smiling at last, "say to you."

"Oh then I'm to be present?"

"Why you *are* present—since you know."

"I see." She turned it over. "But I mean at the catastrophe."

At this, for a minute, their lightness gave way to their gravity; it was as if the long look they exchanged held them together. "It will only depend on yourself—if you'll watch with me."

"Are you afraid?" she asked.

"Don't leave me *now*," he went on.

"Are you afraid?" she repeated.

"Do you think me simply out of my mind?" he pursued instead of answering. "Do I merely strike you as a harmless lunatic?"

"No," said May Bartram. "I understand you. I believe you."

"You mean you feel how my obsession—poor old thing!—may correspond to some possible reality?"

"To some possible reality."

"Then you *will* watch with me?"

She hesitated, then for the third time put her question. "Are you afraid?"

"Did I tell you I was—at Naples?"

"No, you said nothing about it."

"Then I don't know. And I should *like* to know," said John Marcher. "You'll tell me yourself whether you think so. If you'll watch with me you'll see."

"Very good then." They had been moving by this time across the room, and at the door, before passing out, they paused as for the full wind-up of their understanding. "I'll watch with you," said May Bartram.

II

THE FACT that she "knew"—knew and yet neither chaffed him nor betrayed him—had in a short time begun to constitute between them a goodly bond, which became more marked when, within the year that followed their afternoon at Weatherend, the opportunities for meeting multiplied. The event that thus promoted these occasions was the death of the ancient lady her great-aunt, under whose wing, since losing her mother, she had to such an extent found shelter, and who, though but the widowed mother of the new successor to the property, had succeeded—thanks to a high tone and a high temper—in not forfeiting the supreme position at the great house. The deposition of this personage arrived but with her death, which, followed by many changes, made in particular a difference for the young woman in whom Marcher's expert attention had recognised from the first a dependent with a pride that might ache though it didn't bristle. Nothing for a long time had made him easier than the thought that the aching must have been much soothed by Miss Bartram's now finding herself able to set up a small home in London. She had acquired property, to an amount that made that luxury just possible, under her aunt's extremely complicated will, and when the whole matter began to be straightened out, which indeed took time, she let him know that the happy issue was at last in view. He had seen her again before that day, both because she had more than once accompanied the ancient lady to town and because he had paid another visit to the friends who so conveniently made of Weatherend one of the charms of their own hospitality. These friends had taken him back there; he had achieved there again with Miss Bartram some quiet detachment; and he had in London succeeded in persuading her to more than one brief absence from her aunt. They went together, on these latter occasions, to the National Gallery and the South Kensington Museum, where, among vivid reminders, they talked of Italy at large—not now attempting to recover, as at first, the taste of their youth and their ignorance. That recovery, the first day at Weatherend, had served its purpose well, had given them quite enough; so that they were, to Marcher's sense, no longer hovering about the headwaters of their stream, but had felt their boat pushed sharply off and down the current.

They were literally afloat together; for our gentleman this was marked, quite as marked as that the fortunate cause of it was just the buried treasure of her knowledge. He had with his own hands dug up this little hoard, brought to light—that is to within reach of the dim day constituted by their discretions and privacies—the object of value the hiding-place of which he had, after putting it into the ground himself, so strangely, so long forgotten. The rare luck of his having again just stumbled on the spot made him indifferent to any other question; he would doubtless have devoted more time to the odd accident of his lapse of memory if he hadn't been moved to devote so much to the sweetness, the comfort, as he felt, for the future, that this accident itself had helped to keep fresh. It had never entered into his plan that any one should "know," and mainly for the reason that it wasn't in him to tell any one. That would have been impossible, for nothing but the amusement of a cold world would have waited on it. Since, however, a mysterious fate had opened his mouth betimes, in spite of him, he would count that a compensation and profit by it to the utmost. That the right person *should* know tempered the asperity of his secret more even than his shyness had permitted him to imagine; and May Bartram was clearly right, because—well, because there she was. Her knowledge simply settled it; he would have been sure enough by this time had she been wrong. There was that in his situation, no doubt, that disposed him too much to see her as a mere confidant, taking all her light for him from the fact—the fact only—of her interest in his predicament; from her mercy, sympathy, seriousness, her consent not to regard him as the funniest of the funny. Aware, in fine, that her price for him was just in her giving him this constant sense of his being admirably spared, he was careful to remember that she had also a life of her own, with things that might happen to *her,* things that in friendship one should likewise take account of. Something fairly remarkable came to pass with him, for that matter, in this connexion—something represented by a certain passage of his consciousness, in the suddenest way, from one extreme to the other.

He had thought himself, so long as nobody knew, the most disinterested person in the world, carrying his concentrated burden, his perpetual suspense, ever so quietly, holding his tongue about it, giving others no glimpse of it nor of its effect upon his life, asking of them no allowance and only making on his side all those that were asked. He hadn't disturbed people with the queerness of their having to know a haunted man, though he had had moments of rather special temptation on hearing them say they were forsooth "unsettled." If they were as unsettled as he was—he who had never been settled for an hour in his life—they would know what it meant. Yet it wasn't, all the same, for him to make them, and he listened to them civilly enough. This was why he had such good—though possibly such rather colourless—manners; this was why, above all, he could regard himself, in a greedy world, as decently—as in fact perhaps even a little sublimely—unselfish. Our point is accordingly that he valued this character quite sufficiently to measure his present danger of letting it lapse, against which he promised himself to be much on his guard. He was quite ready, none the less, to be selfish just a little, since surely no more charming occasion for it had come to him. "Just a little," in a word, was just as much as Miss Bartram, taking one day with another, would let him. He never would be in the least coercive, and would keep well before him the lines on which consideration for her—the very highest—ought to proceed. He would thoroughly establish the heads under which her affairs, her requirements, her peculiarities—he went so far as to give them the latitude of that name—would come into their intercourse. All this naturally was a sign of how much he took the intercourse itself for granted. There was nothing more to be done about *that.* It simply existed; had sprung into being with her first penetrating question to him in the autumn light there at Weatherend. The real form it should have taken on the basis that stood out large was the form of their marrying. But the devil in this was that the very basis itself put marrying out of the question. His conviction, his apprehension, his obsession, in short, wasn't a privilege he could invite a woman to share; and that consequence of it was precisely what was the matter with him. Something or other lay in wait for him, amid the twists and the turns of the months and the years, like a crouching beast in the jungle. It signified little whether the crouching beast were destined to slay him or to be slain. The definite point was the inevitable spring of the creature; and the definite lesson from that was that a man of feeling didn't cause himself to be accompanied by a lady on a tiger-hunt. Such was the image under which he had ended by figuring his life.

They had at first, none the less, in the scattered hours spent together, made no allusion to that view of it; which was a sign he was handsomely alert to give that he didn't expect, that he in fact didn't care, always to be talking about it. Such a feature in one's outlook was really like a hump on one's back. The difference it made every minute of the day existed quite independently of discussion. One discussed of course *like* a hunchback, for there was always, if nothing else, the hunchback face. That remained, and she was watching him; but people watched best, as a general thing, in silence, so that such would be predominantly the manner of their vigil. Yet he didn't want, at the same time, to be tense and solemn; tense and solemn was what he imagined he too much showed for with other people. The thing to be, with the one person who knew, was easy and natural—to make the reference rather than be seeming to avoid it, to avoid it rather than be seeming to make it, and to keep it, in any case, familiar, facetious even, rather than pedantic and portentous. Some such consideration as the latter was doubtless in his mind for instance when he wrote pleasantly to Miss Bartram that perhaps the great thing he had so long felt as in the lap of the gods was no more than this circumstance, which touched him so nearly, of her acquiring a house in London. It was the first allusion they had yet again made, needing any other hitherto so little; but when she replied, after having given him the news, that she was by no means satisfied with such a trifle as the climax to so special a suspense, she almost set him wondering if she hadn't even a larger conception of singularity for him than he had for himself. He was at all events destined to become aware little by little, as time went by, that she was all the while looking at his life, judging it, measuring it, in the light of the thing she knew, which grew to be at last, with the consecration of the years, never mentioned between them save as "the real truth" about him. That had always been his own form of reference to it, but she adopted the form so quietly that, looking back at the end of a period, he knew there was no moment at which it was traceable that she had, as he might say, got inside his idea, or exchanged the attitude of beautifully indulging for that of still more beautifully believing him.

It was always open to him to accuse her of seeing him but as the most harmless of maniacs, and this, in the long run—since it covered so much ground—was his easiest description of their friendship. He had a screw loose for her, but she liked him in spite of it and was practically, against the rest of the world, his kind wise keeper, unremunerated but fairly amused and, in the absence of other near ties, not disreputably occupied. The rest of the world of course thought him queer, but she, she only, knew how, and above all why, queer; which was precisely what enabled her to dispose the concealing veil in the right folds. She took his gaiety from him—since it had to pass with them for gaiety—as she took everything else; but she certainly so far justified by her unerring touch his finer sense of the degree to which he had ended by convincing her. *She* at least never spoke of the secret of his life except as "the real truth about you," and she had in fact a wonderful way of making it seem, as such, the secret of her own life too. That was in fine how he so constantly felt her as allowing for him; he couldn't on the whole call it anything else. He allowed himself, but she, exactly, allowed still more; partly because, better placed for a sight of the matter, she traced his unhappy perversion through reaches of its course into which he could scarce follow it. He knew how he felt, but, besides knowing that, she knew how he *looked* as well; he knew each of the things of importance he was insidiously kept from doing, but she could add up the amount they made, understand how much, with a lighter weight on his spirit, he might have done, and thereby established how, clever as he was, he fell short. Above all she was in the secret of the difference between the forms he went through—those of his little office under Government, those of caring for his modest patrimony, for his library, for his garden in the country, for the people in London whose invitations he accepted and repaid—and the detachment that reigned beneath them and that made of all behaviour, all that could in the least be called behaviour, a long act of dissimulation. What it had come to was that he wore a mask painted with the social simper, out of the eyeholes of which there looked eyes of an expression not in the least matching the other features. This the stupid world, even after years, had never more than half-discovered. It was only May Bartram who had, and she achieved, by an art indescribable, the feat of at once—or perhaps it was only alternately—meeting the eyes from in front and mingling her own vision, as from over his shoulder, with their peep through the apertures.

So while they grew older together she did watch with him, and so she let this association give shape and colour to her own existence. Beneath *her* forms as well detachment had learned to sit, and behaviour had become for her, in the social sense, a false account of herself. There was but one account of her that would have been true all the while and that she could give straight to nobody, least of all to John Marcher. Her whole attitude was a virtual statement, but the perception of that only seemed called to take its place for him as one of the many things necessarily crowded out of his consciousness. If she had moreover, like himself, to make sacrifices to their real truth, it was to be granted that her compensation might have affected her as more prompt and more natural. They had long periods, in this London time, during which, when they were together, a stranger might have listened to them without in the least pricking up his ears; on the other hand the real truth was equally liable at any moment to rise to the surface, and the auditor would then have wondered indeed what they were talking about. They had from an early hour made up their mind that society was, luckily, unintelligent, and the margin allowed them by this had fairly become one of their commonplaces. Yet there were still moments when the situation turned almost fresh—usually under the effect of some expression drawn from herself. Her expressions doubtless repeated themselves, but her intervals were generous. "What saves us, you know, is that we answer so completely to so usual an appearance: that of the man and woman whose friendship has become such a daily habit—or almost—as to be at last indispensable." That for instance was a remark she had frequently enough had occasion to make, though she had given it at different times different developments. What we are especially concerned with is the turn it happened to take from her one afternoon when he had come to see her in honour of her birthday. This anniversary had fallen on a Sunday, at a season of thick fog and general outward gloom; but he had brought her his customary offering, having known her now long enough to have established a hundred small traditions. It was one of his proofs to himself, the present he made her on her birthday, that he hadn't sunk into real selfishness. It was mostly nothing more than a small trinket, but it was always fine of its kind, and he was regularly careful to pay for it more than he thought he could afford. "Our habit saves you at least, don't you see? because it makes you, after all, for the vulgar, indistinguishable from other men. What's the most inveterate mark of men in general? Why the capacity to spend endless time with dull women—to spend it I won't say without being bored, but without minding that they are, without being driven off at a tangent by it; which comes to the same thing. I'm your dull woman, a part of the daily bread for which you pray at church. That covers your tracks more than anything."

"And what covers yours?" asked Marcher, whom his dull woman could mostly to this extent amuse. "I see of course what you mean by your saving me, in this way and that, so far as other people are concerned—I've seen it all along. Only what is it that saves *you?* I often think, you know, of that."

She looked as if she sometimes thought of that too, but rather in a different way. "Where other people, you mean, are concerned?"

"Well, you're really so in with me, you know—as a sort of result of my being so in with yourself. I mean of my having such an immense regard for you, being so tremendously mindful of all you've done for me. I sometimes ask myself if it's quite fair. Fair I mean to have so involved and—since one may say it—interested you. I almost feel as if you hadn't really had time to do anything else."

"Anything else but be interested?" she asked. "Ah what else does one ever want to be? If I've been 'watching' with you, as we long ago agreed I was to do, watching's always in itself an absorption."

"Oh certainly," John Marcher said, "if you hadn't had your curiosity—! Only doesn't it sometimes come to you as time goes on that your curiosity isn't being particularly repaid?"

May Bartram had a pause. "Do you ask that, by any chance, because you feel at all that yours isn't? I mean because you have to wait so long."

Oh he understood what she meant! "For the thing to happen that never does happen? For the beast to jump out? No, I'm just where I was about it. It isn't a matter as to which I can *choose,* I can decide for a change. It isn't one as to which there *can* be a change. It's in the lap of the gods. One's in the hands of one's law—there one is. As to the form the law will take, the way it will operate, that's its own affair."

"Yes," Miss Bartram replied; "of course one's fate's coming, of course it *has* come in its own form and its own way, all the while. Only, you know, the form and the way in your case were to have been—well, something so exceptional and, as one may say, so particularly *your* own."

Something in this made him look at her with suspicion. "You say 'were to *have* been,' as if in your heart you had begun to doubt."

"Oh!" she vaguely protested.

"As if you believed," he went on, "that nothing will now take place."

She shook her head slowly but rather inscrutably. "You're far from my thought."

He continued to look at her. "What then is the matter with you?"

"Well," she said after another wait, "the matter with me is simply that I'm more sure than ever my curiosity, as you call it, will be but too well repaid."

They were frankly grave now; he had got up from his seat, had turned once more about the little drawing-room to which, year after year, he brought his inevitable topic; in which he had, as he might have said, tasted their intimate community with every sauce, where every object was as familiar to him as the things of his own house and the very carpets were worn with his fitful walk very much as the desks in old counting-houses are worn by the elbows of generations of clerks. The generations of his nervous moods had been at work there, and the place was the written history of his whole middle life. Under the impression of what his friend had just said he knew himself, for some reason, more aware of these things; which made him, after a moment, stop again before her. "Is it possibly that you've grown afraid?"

"Afraid?" He thought, as she repeated the word, that his question had made her, a little, change colour; so that, lest he should have touched on a truth, he explained very kindly: "You remember that that was what you asked *me* long ago—that first day at Weatherend."

"Oh yes, and you told me you didn't know—that I was to see for myself. We've said little about it since, even in so long a time."

"Precisely," Marcher interposed—"quite as if it were too delicate a matter for us to make free with. Quite as if we might find, on pressure, that I *am* afraid. For then," he said, "we shouldn't, should we? quite know what to do."

She had for the time no answer to this question. "There have been days when I thought you were. Only, of course," she added, "there have been days when we have thought almost anything."

"Everything. Oh!" Marcher softly groaned as with a gasp, half-spent, at the face, more uncovered just then than it had been for a long while, of the imagination always with them. It had always had its incalculable moments of glaring out, quite as with the very eyes of the very Beast, and, used as he was to them, they could still draw from him the tribute of a sigh that rose from the depths of his being. All they had thought, first and last, rolled over him; the past seemed to have been reduced to mere barren speculation. This in fact was what the place had just struck him as so full of—the simplification of everything but the state of suspense. That remained only by seeming to hang in the void surrounding it. Even his original fear, if fear it had been, had lost itself in the desert. "I judge, however," he continued, "that you see I'm not afraid now."

"What I see, as I make it out, is that you've achieved something almost unprecedented in the way of getting used to danger. Living with it so long and so closely you've lost your sense of it; you know it's there, but you're indifferent, and you cease even, as of old, to have to whistle in the dark. Considering what the danger is," May Bartram wound up, "I'm bound to say I don't think your attitude could well be surpassed."

John Marcher faintly smiled. "It's heroic?"

"Certainly—call it that."

It was what he would have liked indeed to call it. "I *am* then a man of courage?"

"That's what you were to show me."

He still, however, wondered. "But doesn't the man of courage know what he's afraid of—or *not* afraid of? I don't know *that,* you see. I don't focus it. I can't name it. I only know I'm exposed."

"Yes, but exposed—how shall I say?—so directly. So intimately. That's surely enough."

"Enough to make you feel then—as what we may call the end and the upshot of our watch—that I'm not afraid?"

"You're not afraid. But it isn't," she said, "the end of our watch. That is it isn't the end of yours. You've everything still to see."

"Then why haven't you?" he asked. He had had, all along, to-day, the sense of her keeping something back, and he still had it. As this was his first impression of that it quite made a date. The case was the more marked as she didn't at first answer; which in turn made him go on. "You know something I don't." Then his voice, for that of a man of courage, trembled a little. "You know what's to happen." Her silence, with the face she showed, was almost a confession—it made him sure. "You know, and you're afraid to tell me. It's so bad that you're afraid I'll find out."

All this might be true, for she did look as if, unexpectedly to her, he had crossed some mystic line that she had secretly drawn round her. Yet she might, after all, not have worried; and the real climax was that he himself, at all events, needn't. "You'll never find out."

III

It was all to have made, none the less, as I have said, a date; which came out in the fact that again and again, even after long intervals, other things that passed between them wore in relation to this hour but the character of recalls and results. Its immediate effect had been indeed rather to lighten insistence—almost to provoke a reaction; as if their topic had dropped by its own weight and as if moreover, for that matter, Marcher had been visited by one of his occasional warnings against egotism. He had kept up, he felt, and very decently on the whole, his consciousness of the importance of not being selfish, and it was true that he had never sinned in that direction without promptly enough trying to press the scales the other way. He often repaired his fault, the season permitting, by inviting his friend to accompany him to the opera; and it not infrequently thus happened that, to show he didn't wish her to have but one sort of food for her mind, he was the cause of her appearing there with him a dozen nights in the month. It even happened that, seeing her home at such times, he occasionally went in with her to finish, as he called it, the evening, and, the better to make his point, sat down to the frugal but always careful little supper that awaited his pleasure. His point was made, he thought, by his not eternally insisting with her on himself; made for instance, at such hours, when it befell that, her piano at hand and each of them familiar with it, they went over passages of the opera together. It chanced to be on one of these occasions, however, that he reminded her of her not having answered a certain question he had put to her during the talk that had taken place between them on her last birthday. "What is it that saves *you?*"—saved her, he meant, from that appearance of variation from the usual human type. If he had practically escaped remark, as she pretended, by doing, in the most important particular, what most men do—find the answer to life in patching up an alliance of a sort with a woman no better than himself—how had she escaped it, and how could the alliance, such as it was, since they must suppose it had been more or less noticed, have failed to make her rather positively talked about?

"I never said," May Bartram replied, "that it hadn't made me a good deal talked about."

"Ah well then you're not 'saved.'"

"It hasn't been a question for me. If you've had your woman I've had," she said, "my man."

"And you mean that makes you all right?"

Oh it was always as if there were so much to say! "I don't know why it shouldn't make me—humanly, which is what we're speaking of—as right as it makes you."

"I see," Marcher returned. "'Humanly,' no doubt, as showing that you're living for something. Not, that is, just for me and my secret."

May Bartram smiled. "I don't pretend it exactly shows that I'm not living for you. It's my intimacy with you that's in question."

He laughed as he saw what she meant. "Yes, but since, as you say, I'm only, so far as people make out, ordinary, you're—aren't you?—no more than ordinary either. You help me to pass for a man like another. So if I *am,* as I understand you, you're not compromised. Is that it?"

She had another of her waits, but she spoke clearly enough. "That's it. It's all that concerns me—to help you to pass for a man like another."

He was careful to acknowledge the remark handsomely. "How kind, how beautiful, you are to me! How shall I ever repay you?"

She had her last grave pause, as if there might be a choice of ways. But she chose. "By going on as you are."

It was into this going on as he was that they relapsed, and really for so long a time that the day inevitably came for a further sounding of their depths. These depths, constantly bridged over by a structure firm enough in spite of its lightness and of its occasional oscillation in the somewhat vertiginous air, invited on occasion, in the interest of their nerves, a dropping of the plummet and a measurement of the abyss. A difference had been made moreover, once for all, by the fact that she had all the while not appeared to feel the need of rebutting his charge of an idea within her that she didn't dare to express—a charge uttered just before one of the fullest of their later discussions ended. It had come up for him then that she "knew" something and that what she knew was bad—too bad to tell him. When he had spoken of it as visibly so bad that she was afraid he might find it out, her reply had left the matter too equivocal to be let alone and yet, for Marcher's special sensibility, almost too formidable again to touch. He circled about it at a distance that alternately narrowed and widened and that still wasn't much affected by the consciousness in him that there was nothing she could "know," after all, any better than he did. She had no source of knowledge he hadn't equally—except of course that she might have finer nerves. That was what women had where they were interested; they made out things, where people were concerned, that the people often couldn't have made out for themselves. Their nerves, their sensibility, their imagination, were conductors and revealers, and the beauty of May Bartram was in particular that she had given herself so to his case. He felt in these days what, oddly enough, he had never felt before, the growth of a dread of losing her by some catastrophe—some catastrophe that yet wouldn't at all be *the* catastrophe: partly because she had almost of a sudden begun to strike him as more useful to him than ever yet, and partly by reason of an appearance of uncertainty in her health, coincident and equally new. It was characteristic of the inner detachment he had hitherto so successfully cultivated and to which our whole account of him is a reference, it was characteristic that his complications, such as they were, had never yet seemed so as at this crisis to thicken about him, even to the point of making him ask himself if he were, by any chance, of a truth, within sight or sound, within touch or reach, within the immediate jurisdiction, of the thing that waited.

When the day came, as come it had to, that his friend confessed to him her fear of a deep disorder in her blood, he felt somehow the shadow of a change and the chill of a shock. He immediately began to imagine aggravations and disasters, and above all to think of her peril as the direct menace for himself of personal privation. This indeed gave him one of those partial recoveries of equanimity that were agreeable to him—it showed him that what was still first in his mind was the loss she herself might suffer. "What if she should have to die before knowing, before seeing—?" It would have been brutal, in the early stages of her trouble, to put that question to her; but it had immediately sounded for him to his own concern, and the possibility was what most made him sorry for her. If she did "know," moreover, in the sense of her having had some—what should he think?—mystical irresistible light, this would make the matter not better, but worse, inasmuch as her original adoption of his own curiosity had quite become the basis of her life. She had been living to see what would *be* to be seen, and it would quite lacerate her to have to give up before the accomplishment of the vision. These reflexions, as I say, quickened his generosity; yet, make them as he might, he saw himself, with the lapse of the period, more and more disconcerted. It lapsed for him with a strange steady sweep, and the oddest oddity was that it gave him, independently of the threat of much inconvenience, almost the only positive surprise his career, if career it could be called, had yet offered him. She kept the house as she had never done; he had to go to her to see her—she could meet him nowhere now, though there was scarce a corner of their loved old London in which she hadn't in the past, at one time or another, done so; and he found her always seated by her fire in the deep old-fashioned chair she was less and less able to leave. He had been struck one day, after an absence exceeding his usual measure, with her suddenly looking much older to him than he had ever thought of her being; then he recognised that the suddenness was all on his side—he had just simply and suddenly noticed. She looked older because inevitably, after so many years, she *was* old, or almost; which was of course true in still greater measure of her companion. If she was old, or almost, John Marcher assuredly was, and yet it was her showing of the lesson, not his own, that brought the truth home to him. His surprises began here; when once they had begun they multiplied; they came rather with a rush: it was as if, in the oddest way in the world, they had all been kept back, sown in a thick cluster, for the late afternoon of life, the time at which for people in general the unexpected has died out.

One of them was that he should have caught himself—for he *had* so done—*really* wondering if the great accident would take form now as nothing more than his being condemned to see this charming woman, this admirable friend, pass away from him. He had never so unreservedly qualified her as while confronted in thought with such a possibility; in spite of which there was small doubt for him that as an answer to his long riddle the mere effacement of even so fine a feature of his situation would be an abject anticlimax. It would represent, as connected with his past attitude, a drop of dignity under the shadow of which his existence could only become the most grotesque of failures. He had been far from holding it a failure—long as he had waited for the appearance that was to make it a success. He had waited for quite another thing, not for such a thing as that. The breath of his good faith came short, however, as he recognised how long he had waited, or how long at least his companion had. That she, at all events, might be recorded as having waited in vain—this affected him sharply, and all the more because of his at first having done little more than amuse himself with the idea. It grew more grave as the gravity of her condition grew, and the state of mind it produced in him, which he himself ended by watching as if it had been some definite disfigurement of his outer person, may pass for another of his surprises. This conjoined itself still with another, the really stupefying consciousness of a question that he would have allowed to shape itself had he dared. What did everything mean—what, that is, did *she* mean, she and her vain waiting and her probable death and the soundless admonition of it all—unless that, at this time of day, it was simply, it was overwhelmingly too late? He had never at any stage of his queer consciousness admitted the whisper of such a correction; he had never till within these last few months been so false to his conviction as not to hold that what was to come to him had time, whether *he* struck himself as having it or not. That at last, at last, he certainly hadn't it, to speak of, or had it but in the scantiest measure—such, soon enough, as things went with him, became the inference with which his old obsession had to reckon: and this it was not helped to do by the more and more confirmed appearance that the great vagueness casting the long shadow in which he had lived had, to attest itself, almost no margin left. Since it was in Time that he was to have met his fate, so it was in Time that his fate was to have acted; and as he waked up to the sense of no longer being young, which was exactly the sense of being stale, just as that, in turn, was the sense of being weak, he waked up to another matter beside. It all hung together; they were subject, he and the great vagueness, to an equal and indivisible law. When the possibilities themselves had accordingly turned stale, when the secret of the gods had grown faint, had perhaps even quite evaporated, that, and that only, was failure. It wouldn't have been failure to be bankrupt, dishonoured, pilloried, hanged; it was failure not to be anything. And so, in the dark valley into which his path had taken its unlooked-for twist, he wondered not a little as he groped. He didn't care what awful crash might overtake him, with what ignominy or what monstrosity he might yet be associated—since he wasn't after all too utterly old to suffer—if it would only be decently proportionate to the posture he had kept, all his life, in the threatened presence of it. He had but one desire left—that he shouldn't have been "sold."

IV

THEN it was that, one afternoon, while the spring of the year was young and new she met all in her own way his frankest betrayal of these alarms. He had gone in late to see her, but evening hadn't settled and she was presented to him in that long fresh light of waning April days which affects us often with a sadness sharper than the greyest hours of autumn. The week had been warm, the spring was supposed to have begun early, and May Bartram sat, for the first time in the year, without a fire; a fact that, to Marcher's sense, gave the scene of which she formed part a smooth and ultimate look, an air of knowing, in its immaculate order and cold meaningless cheer, that it would never see a fire again. Her own aspect—he could scarce have said why—intensified this note. Almost as white as wax, with the marks and signs in her face as numerous and as fine as if they had been etched by a needle, with soft white draperies relieved by a faded green scarf on the delicate tone of which the years had further refined, she was the picture of a serene and exquisite but impenetrable sphinx, whose head, or indeed all whose person, might have been powdered with silver. She was a sphinx, yet with her white petals and green fronds she might have been a lily too—only an artificial lily, wonderfully imitated and constantly kept, without dust or stain, though not exempt from a slight droop and a complexity of faint creases, under some clear glass bell. The perfection of household care, of high polish and finish, always reigned in her rooms, but they now looked most as if everything had been wound up, tucked in, put away, so that she might sit with folded hands and with nothing more to do. She was "out of it," to Marcher's vision; her work was over; she communicated with him as across some gulf or from some island of rest that she had already reached, and it made him feel strangely abandoned. Was it—or rather wasn't it—that if for so long she had been watching with him the answer to their question must have swum into her ken and taken on its name, so that her occupation was verily gone? He had as much as charged her with this in saying to her, many months before, that she even then knew something she was keeping from him. It was a point he had never since ventured to press, vaguely fearing as he did that it might become a difference, perhaps a disagreement, between them. He had in this later time turned nervous, which was what he in all the other years had never been; and the oddity was that his nervousness should have waited till he had begun to doubt, should have held off so long as he was sure. There was something, it seemed to him, that the wrong word would bring down on his head, something that would so at least ease off his tension. But he wanted not to speak the wrong word; that would make everything ugly. He wanted the knowledge he lacked to drop on him, if drop it could, by its own august weight. If she was to forsake him it was surely for her to take leave. This was why he didn't directly ask her again what she knew; but it was also why, approaching the matter from another side, he said to her in the course of his visit: "What do you regard as the very worst that at this time of day *can* happen to me?"

He had asked her that in the past often enough; they had, with the odd irregular rhythm of their intensities and avoidances, exchanged ideas about it and then had seen the ideas washed away by cool intervals, washed like figures traced in sea-sand. It had ever been the mark of their talk that the oldest allusions in it required but a little dismissal and reaction to come out again, sounding for the hour as new. She could thus at present meet his enquiry quite freshly and patiently. "Oh yes, I've repeatedly thought, only it always seemed to me of old that I couldn't quite make up my mind. I thought of dreadful things, between which it was difficult to choose; and so must you have done."

"Rather! I feel now as if I had scarce done anything else. I appear to myself to have spent my life in thinking of nothing *but* dreadful things. A great many of them I've at different times named to you, but there were others I couldn't name."

"They were too, too dreadful?"

"Too, too dreadful—some of them."

She looked at him a minute, and there came to him as he met it an inconsequent sense that her eyes, when one got their full clearness, were still as beautiful as they had been in youth, only beautiful with a strange cold light—a light that somehow was a part of the effect, if it wasn't rather a part of the cause, of the pale hard sweetness of the season and the hour. "And yet," she said at last, "there are horrors we've mentioned."

It deepened the strangeness to see her, as such a figure in such a picture, talk of "horrors," but she was to do in a few minutes something stranger yet—though even of this he was to take the full measure but afterwards—and the note of it already trembled. It was, for the matter of that, one of the signs that her eyes were having again the high flicker of their prime. He had to admit, however, what she said. "Oh yes, there were times when we did go far." He caught himself in the act of speaking as if it all were over. Well, he wished it were; and the consummation depended for him clearly more and more on his friend.

But she had now a soft smile. "Oh far—!"

It was oddly ironic. "Do you mean you're prepared to go further?"

She was frail and ancient and charming as she continued to look at him, yet it was rather as if she had lost the thread. "Do you consider that we went far?"

"Why I thought it the point you were just making—that we *had* looked most things in the face."

"Including each other?" She still smiled. "But you're

quite right. We've had together great imaginations, often great fears; but some of them have been unspoken."

"Then the worst—we haven't faced that. I *could* face it, I believe, if I knew what you think it. I feel," he explained, "as if I had lost my power to conceive such things." And he wondered if he looked as blank as he sounded. "It's spent."

"Then why do you assume," she asked, "that mine isn't?"

"Because you've given me signs to the contrary. It isn't a question for you of conceiving, imagining, comparing. It isn't a question now of choosing." At last he came out with it. "You know something I don't. You've shown me that before."

These last words had affected her, he made out in a moment, exceedingly, and she spoke with firmness. "I've shown you, my dear, nothing."

He shook his head. "You can't hide it."

"Oh, oh!" May Bartram sounded over what she couldn't hide. It was almost a smothered groan.

"You admitted it months ago, when I spoke of it to you as of something you were afraid I should find out. Your answer was that I couldn't, that I wouldn't, and I don't pretend I have. But you had something therefore in mind, and I now see how it must have been, how it still is, the possibility that, of all possibilities, has settled itself for you as the worst. This," he went on, "is why I appeal to you. I'm only afraid of ignorance today—I'm not afraid of knowledge." And then as for a while she said nothing: "What makes me sure is that I see in your face and feel here, in this air and amid these appearances, that you're out of it. You've done. You've had your experience. You leave me to my fate."

Well, she listened, motionless and white in her chair, as on a decision to be made, so that her manner was fairly an avowal, though still, with a small fine inner stiffness, an imperfect surrender. "It *would* be the worst," she finally let herself say. "I mean the thing I've never said."

It hushed him a moment. "More monstrous than all the monstrosities we've named?"

"More monstrous. Isn't that what you sufficiently express," she asked, "in calling it the worst?"

Marcher thought. "Assuredly—if you mean, as I do, something that includes all the loss and all the shame that are thinkable."

"It would if it *should* happen," said May Bartram. "What we're speaking of, remember, is only my idea."

"It's your belief," Marcher returned. "That's enough for me. I feel your beliefs are right. Therefore if, having this one, you give me no more light on it, you abandon me."

"No, no!" she repeated. "I'm with you—don't you see?—still." And as to make it more vivid to him she rose from her chair—a movement she seldom risked in these days—and showed herself, all draped and all soft, in her fairness and slimness. "I haven't forsaken you."

It was really, in its effort against weakness, a generous assurance, and had the success of the impulse not, happily, been great, it would have touched him to pain more than to pleasure. But the cold charm in her eyes had spread, as she hovered before him, to all the rest of her person, so that it was for the minute almost a recovery of youth. He couldn't pity her for that; he could only take her as she showed—as capable even yet of helping him. It was as if, at the same time, her light might at any instant go out; wherefore he must make the most of it. There passed before him with intensity the three or four things he wanted most to know; but the question that came of itself to his lips really covered the others. "Then tell me if I shall consciously suffer."

She promptly shook her head. "Never!"

It confirmed the authority he imputed to her, and it produced on him an extraordinary effect. "Well, what's better than that? Do you call that the worst?"

"You think nothing is better?" she asked.

She seemed to mean something so special that he again

sharply wondered, though still with the dawn of a prospect of relief. "Why not, if one doesn't *know?*" After which, as their eyes, over his question, met in a silence, the dawn deepened and something to his purpose came prodigiously out of her very face. His own, as he took it in, suddenly flushed to the forehead, and he gasped with the force of a perception to which, on the instant, everything fitted. The sound of his gasp filled the air; then he became articulate. "I see—if I don't suffer!"

In her own look, however, was doubt. "You see what?"

"Why what you mean—what you've always meant."

She again shook her head. "What I mean isn't what I've always meant. It's different."

"It's something new?"

She hung back from it a little. "Something new. It's not what you think. I see what you think."

His divination drew breath then; only her correction might be wrong. "It isn't that I *am* a blockhead?" he asked between faintness and grimness. "It isn't that it's all a mistake?"

"A mistake?" she pityingly echoed. *That* possibility, for her, he saw, would be monstrous; and if she guaranteed him the immunity from pain it would accordingly not be what she had in mind. "Oh no," she declared; "it's nothing of that sort. You've been right."

Yet he couldn't help asking himself if she weren't, thus pressed, speaking but to save him. It seemed to him he should be most in a hole if his history should prove all a platitude. "Are you telling me the truth, so that I shan't have been a bigger idiot than I can bear to know? I *haven't* lived with a vain imagination, in the most besotted illusion? I haven't waited but to see the door shut in my face?"

She shook her head again. "However the case stands *that* isn't the truth. Whatever the reality, it *is* a reality. The door isn't shut. The door's open," said May Bartram.

"Then something's to come?"

She waited once again, always with her cold sweet eyes

on him. "It's never too late." She had, with her gliding step, diminished the distance between them, and she stood nearer to him, close to him, a minute, as if still charged with the unspoken. Her movement might have been for some finer emphasis of what she was at once hesitating and deciding to say. He had been standing by the chimney-piece, fireless and sparely adorned, a small perfect old French clock and two morsels of rosy Dresden constituting all its furniture; and her hand grasped the shelf while she kept him waiting, grasped it a little as for support and encouragement. She only kept him waiting, however; that is he only waited. It had become suddenly, from her movement and attitude, beautiful and vivid to him that she had something more to give him; her wasted face delicately shone with it—it glittered almost as with the white lustre of silver in her expression. She was right, incontestably, for what he saw in her face was the truth, and strangely, without consequence, while their talk of it as dreadful was still in the air, she appeared to present it as inordinately soft. This, prompting bewilderment, made him but gape the more gratefully for her revelation, so that they continued for some minutes silent, her face shining at him, her contact imponderably pressing, and his stare all kind but all expectant. The end, none the less, was that what he had expected failed to come to him. Something else took place instead, which seemed to consist at first in the mere closing of her eyes. She gave way at the same instant to a slow fine shudder, and though he remained staring—though he stared in fact but the harder—turned off and regained her chair. It was the end of what she had been intending, but it left him thinking only of that.

"Well, you don't say—?"

She had touched in her passage a bell near the chimney and had sunk back strangely pale. "I'm afraid I'm too ill."

"Too ill to tell me?" It sprang up sharp to him, and almost to his lips, the fear she might die without giving him light. He checked himself in time from so expressing his question, but she answered as if she had heard the words.

"Don't you know—now?"

"'Now'—?" She had spoken as if some difference had been made within the moment. But her maid, quickly obedient to her bell, was already with them. "I know nothing." And he was afterwards to say to himself that he must have spoken with odious impatience, such an impatience as to show that, supremely disconcerted, he washed his hands of the whole question.

"Oh!" said May Bartram.

"Are you in pain?" he asked as the woman went to her.

"No," said May Bartram.

Her maid, who had put an arm round her as if to take her to her room, fixed on him eyes that appealingly contradicted her; in spite of which, however, he showed once more his mystification. "What then has happened?"

She was once more, with her companion's help, on her feet, and, feeling withdrawal imposed on him, he had blankly found his hat and gloves and had reached the door. Yet he waited for her answer. "What *was* to," she said.

V

HE CAME BACK the next day, but she was then unable to see him, and as it was literally the first time this had occurred in the long stretch of their acquaintance he turned away, defeated and sore, almost angry—or feeling at least that such a break in their custom was really the beginning of the end—and wandered alone with his thoughts, especially with the one he was least able to keep down. She was dying and he would lose her; she was dying and his life would end. He stopped in the Park, into which he had passed, and stared before him at his recurrent doubt. Away from her the doubt pressed again; in her presence he had believed her, but as he felt his forlornness he threw himself into the explanation that, nearest at hand, had most of a miserable warmth for him and least of a cold torment. She had deceived him to save him—to put him off with something in which he should be able to rest. What could the thing that was to happen to him be, after all, but just this thing that had begun to happen? Her dying, her death, his consequent solitude—*that* was what he had figured as the Beast in the Jungle, that was what had been in the lap of the gods. He had had her word for it as he left her—what else on earth could she have meant? It wasn't a thing of a monstrous order; not a fate rare and distinguished; not a stroke of fortune that overwhelmed and immortalized; it had only the stamp of the common doom. But poor Marcher at this hour judged the common doom sufficient. It would serve his turn, and even as the consummation of infinite waiting he would bend his pride to accept it. He sat down on a bench in the twilight. He hadn't been a fool. Something had *been*, as she had said, to come. Before he rose indeed it had quite struck him that the final fact really matched with the long avenue through which he had had to reach it. As sharing his suspense and as giving herself all, giving her life, to bring it to an end, she had come with him every step of the way. He had lived by her aid, and to leave her behind would be cruelly, damnably to miss her. What could be more overwnelming than that?

Well, he was to know within the week, for though she kept him a while at bay, left him restless and wretched during a series of days on each of which he asked about her only again to have to turn away, she ended his trial by receiving him where she had always received him. Yet she had been brought out at some hazard into the presence of so many of the things that were, consciously, vainly, half their past, and there was scant service left in the gentleness of her mere desire, all too visible, to check his obsession and wind up his long trouble. That was clearly what she wanted, the one thing more for her own peace while she could still put out her hand. He was so affected by her state that, once seated by her chair, he was moved to let everything go; it was she herself therefore who brought him back, took up again, before she dismissed him, her last word of the other time. She showed how she wished to leave their business in order. "I'm not sure you understood. You've nothing to wait for more. It *has* come."

Oh how he looked at her! "Really?"

"Really."

"The thing that, as you said, *was* to?"

"The thing that we began in our youth to watch for."

Face to face with her once more he believed her; it was a claim to which he had so abjectly little to oppose. "You mean that it has come as a positive definite occurrence, with a name and a date?"

"Positive. Definite. I don't know about the 'name,' but oh with a date!"

He found himself again too helplessly at sea. "But come in the night—come and passed me by?"

May Bartram had her strange faint smile. "Oh no, it hasn't passed you by!"

"But if I haven't been aware of it and it hasn't touched me—?"

"Ah your not being aware of it"—and she seemed to hesitate an instant to deal with this—"your not being aware of it is the strangeness *in* the strangeness. It's the wonder *of* the wonder." She spoke as with the softness almost of a sick child, yet now at last, at the end of all, with the perfect straightness of a sibyl. She visibly knew that she knew, and the effect on him was of something co-ordinate, in its high character, with the law that had ruled him. It was the true voice of the law; so on her lips would the law itself have sounded. "It *has* touched you," she went on. "It has done its office. It has made you all its own."

"So utterly without my knowing it?"

"So utterly without your knowing it." His hand, as he leaned to her, was on the arm of her chair, and, dimly smiling always now, she placed her own on it. "It's enough if *I* know it."

"Oh!" he confusedly breathed, as she herself of late so often had done.

"What I long ago said is true. You'll never know now, and I think you ought to be content. You've *had* it," said May Bartram.

"But had what?"

"Why what was to have marked you out. The proof of your law. It has acted. I'm too glad," she then bravely added, "to have been able to see what it's *not*."

He continued to attach his eyes to her, and with the sense that it was all beyond him, and that *she* was too, he would still have sharply challenged her hadn't he so felt it an abuse of her weakness to do more than take devoutly what she gave him, take it hushed as to a revelation. If he did speak, it was out of the foreknowledge of his loneliness to come. "If you're glad of what it's 'not' it might then have been worse?"

She turned her eyes away, she looked straight before her; with which after a moment: "Well, you know our fears."

He wondered. "It's something then we never feared?"

On this slowly she turned to him. "Did we ever dream, with all our dreams, that we should sit and talk of it thus?"

He tried for a little to make out that they had; but it was as if their dreams, numberless enough, were in solution in some thick cold mist through which thought lost itself. "It might have been that we couldn't talk?"

"Well"—she did her best for him—"not from this side. This, you see," she said, "is the *other* side."

"I think," poor Marcher returned, "that all sides are the same to me." Then, however, as she gently shook her head in correction: "We mightn't, as it were, have got across—?"

"To where we are—no. We're *here*"—she made her weak emphasis.

"And much good does it do us!" was her friend's frank comment.

"It does us the good it can. It does us the good that *it* isn't here. It's past. It's behind," said May Bartram. "Before—" but her voice dropped.

He had got up, not to tire her, but it was hard to combat his yearning. She after all told him nothing but that his light had failed—which he knew well enough without her. "Before—?" he blankly echoed.

"Before, you see, it was always to *come*. That kept it present."

"Oh I don't care what comes now! Besides," Marcher added, "it seems to me I liked it better present, as you say, than I can like it absent with *your* absence."

"Oh mine!"—and her pale hands made light of it.

"With the absence of everything." He had a dreadful sense of standing there before her for—so far as anything but this proved, this bottomless drop was concerned—the last time of their life. It rested on him with a weight he felt he could scarce bear, and this weight it apparently was that still pressed out what remained in him of speakable protest. "I believe you; but I can't begin to pretend I understand. *Nothing,* for me, is past; nothing *will* pass till I pass myself, which I pray my stars may be as soon as possible. Say, however," he added, "that I've eaten my cake, as you contend, to the last crumb—how can the thing I've never felt at all be the thing I was marked out to feel?"

She met him perhaps less directly, but she met him unperturbed. "You take your 'feelings' for granted. You were to suffer your fate. That was not necessarily to know it."

"How in the world—when what is such knowledge but suffering?"

She looked up at him a while in silence. "No—you don't understand."

"I suffer," said John Marcher.

"Don't, don't!"

"How can I help at least *that?*"

"Don't!" May Bartram repeated.

She spoke it in a tone so special, in spite of her weakness, that he stared an instant—stared as if some light, hitherto hidden, had shimmered across his vision. Darkness again closed over it, but the gleam had already become for him an idea. "Because I haven't the right—?"

"Don't *know*—when you needn't," she mercifully urged. "You needn't—for we shouldn't."

"Shouldn't?" If he could but know what she meant!

"No—it's too much."

"Too much?" he still asked but, with a mystification that was the next moment of a sudden to give way. Her words, if they meant something, affected him in this light—the light also of her wasted face—as meaning *all,* and the sense of what knowledge had been for herself came over him with a rush which broke through into a question. "Is it of that then you're dying?"

She but watched him, gravely at first, as to see, with this, where he was, and she might have seen something or feared something that moved her sympathy. "I would live for you still—if I could." Her eyes closed for a little, as if, withdrawn into herself, she were for a last time trying. "But I can't!" she said as she raised them again to take leave of him.

She couldn't indeed, as but too promptly and sharply appeared, and he had no vision of her after this that was anything but darkness and doom. They had parted for ever in that strange talk; access to her chamber of pain, rigidly guarded, was almost wholly forbidden him; he was feeling now moreover, in the face of doctors, nurses, the two or three relatives attracted doubtless by the presumption of what she had to "leave," how few were the rights, as they were called in such cases, that he had to put forward, and how odd it might even seem that their intimacy shouldn't have given him more of them. The stupidest fourth cousin had more, even though she had been nothing in such a person's life. She had been a feature of features in *his,* for what else was it to have been so indispensable? Strange beyond saying were the ways of existence, baffling for him the anomaly of his lack, as he felt it to be, of producible claim. A woman might have been, as it were, everything to him, and it might yet present him in no connexion that any one seemed held to recognise. If this was the case in these closing weeks it was the case more sharply on the occasion of the last offices rendered, in the great grey London cemetery, to what had been mortal, to what had been precious, in his friend. The concourse at her grave was not numerous, but he saw himself treated as scarce more nearly concerned with it than if there had been a thousand others. He was in short from this moment face to face with the fact that he was to profit extraordinarily little by the interest May Bartram had taken in him. He couldn't quite have said what he expected, but he hadn't surely expected this approach to a double privation. Not only had her interest failed him, but he seemed to feel himself unattended—

and for a reason he couldn't seize—by the distinction, the dignity, the propriety, if nothing else, of the man markedly bereaved. It was as if in the view of society he had not *been* markedly bereaved, as if there still failed some sign or proof of it, and as if none the less his character could never be affirmed nor the deficiency ever made up. There were moments as the weeks went by when he would have liked, by some almost aggressive act, to take his stand on the intimacy of his loss, in order that it *might* be questioned and his retort, to the relief of his spirit, so recorded; but the moments of an irritation more helpless followed fast on these, the moments during which, turning things over with a good conscience but with a bare horizon, he found himself wondering if he oughtn't to have begun, so to speak, further back.

He found himself wondering indeed at many things, and this last speculation had others to keep it company. What could he have done, after all, in her lifetime, without giving them both, as it were, away? He couldn't have made known she was watching him, for that would have published the superstition of the Beast. This was what closed his mouth now—now that the Jungle had been threshed to vacancy and that the Beast had stolen away. It sounded too foolish and too flat; the difference for him in this particular, the extinction in his life of the element of suspense, was such as in fact to surprise him. He could scarce have said what the effect resembled; the abrupt cessation, the positive prohibition, of music perhaps, more than anything else, in some place all adjusted and all accustomed to sonority and to attention. If he could at any rate have conceived lifting the veil from his image at some moment of the past (what had he done, after all, if not lift it to *her*?) so to do this today, to talk to people at large of the Jungle cleared and confide to them that he now felt it as safe, would have been not only to see them listen as to a goodwife's tale, but really to hear himself tell one. What it presently came to in truth was that poor Marcher waded through his beaten grass, where no life stirred, where no breath sounded, where no evil eye seemed to gleam from a possible lair, very much as if vaguely looking for the Beast, and still more as if acutely missing it. He walked about in an existence that had grown strangely more spacious, and, stopping fitfully in places where the undergrowth of life struck him as closer, asked himself yearningly, wondered secretly and sorely, if it would have lurked here or there. It would have at all events *sprung;* what was at least complete was his belief in the truth itself of the assurance given him. The change from his old sense to his new was absolute and final: what was to happen *had* so absolutely and finally happened that he was as little able to know a fear for his future as to know a hope; so absent in short was any question of anything still to come. He was to live entirely with the other question, that of his unidentified past, that of his having to see his fortune impenetrably muffled and masked.

The torment of this vision became then his occupation; he couldn't perhaps have consented to live but for the possibility of guessing. She had told him, his friend, not to guess; she had forbidden him, so far as he might, to know, and she had even in a sort denied the power in him to learn: which were so many things, precisely, to deprive him of rest. It wasn't that he wanted, he argued for fairness, that anything past and done should repeat itself; it was only that he shouldn't, as an anticlimax, have been taken sleeping so sound as not to be able to win back by an effort of thought the lost stuff of consciousness. He declared to himself at moments that he would either win it back or have done with consciousness for ever; he made this idea his one motive in fine, made it so much his passion that none other, to compare with it, seemed ever to have touched him. The lost stuff of consciousness became thus for him as a strayed or stolen child to an unappeasable father; he hunted it up and down very much as if he were knocking at doors and enquiring of the police. This was the spirit in which, inevitably, he set himself to travel; he started on a journey that was to be as long as he could make it; it danced before him that, as the other side of the globe couldn't possibly have less to say to him, it might, by a possibility of suggestion, have more. Before he quitted London, however, he made a pilgrimage to May Bartram's grave, took his way to it through the endless avenues of the grim suburban metropolis, sought it out in the wilderness of tombs, and, though he had come but for the renewal of the act of farewell, found himself, when he had at last stood by it, beguiled into long intensities. He stood for an hour, powerless to turn away and yet powerless to penetrate the darkness of death; fixing with his eyes her inscribed name and date, beating his forehead against the fact of the secret they kept, drawing his breath, while he waited, as if some sense would in pity of him rise from the stones. He kneeled on the stones, however, in vain; they kept what they concealed; and if the face of the tomb did become a face for him it was because her two names became a pair of eyes that didn't know him. He gave them a last long look, but no palest light broke.

VI

HE STAYED away, after this, for a year; he visited the depths of Asia, spending himself on scenes of romantic interest. of superlative sanctity; but what was present to him everywhere was that for a man who had known what *he* had known the world was vulgar and vain. The state of mind in which he had lived for so many years shone out to him, in reflexion, as a light that coloured and refined, a light beside which the glow of the East was garish and cheap and thin. The terrible truth was that he had lost—with everything else—a distinction as well; the things he saw couldn't help being common when he had become common to look at them. He was simply now one of them himself—he was in the dust, without a peg for the sense of difference; and there were hours when, before the temples of gods and the sepulchres of kings, his spirit turned for nobleness of association to the barely discriminated slab in the London suburb. That had become for him, and more intensely with time and distance, his one witness of a past glory. It was all that was left to him for proof or pride, yet the past glories of Pharaohs were nothing to him as he thought of it. Small wonder then that he came back to it on the morrow of his return. He was drawn there this time as irresistibly as the other, yet with a confidence, almost, that was doubtless the effect of the many months that had elapsed. He had lived, in spite of himself, into his change of feeling, and in wandering over the earth had wandered, as might be said, from the circumference to the centre of his desert. He had settled to his safety and accepted perforce his extinction; figuring to himself, with some colour, in the likeness of certain little old men he remembered to have seen, of whom, all meagre and wizened as they might look, it was related that they had in their time fought twenty duels or been loved by ten princesses. They indeed had been wondrous for others while he was but wondrous for himself; which, however, was exactly the cause of his haste to renew the wonder by getting back, as he might put it, into his own presence. That had quickened his steps and checked his delay. If his visit was prompt it was because he had been separated so long from the part of himself that alone he now valued.

It's accordingly not false to say that he reached his goal with a certain elation and stood there again with a certain assurance. The creature beneath the sod *knew* of his rare experience, so that, strangely now, the place had lost for him its mere blankness of expression. It met him in mildness—not, as before, in mockery; it wore for him the air of conscious greeting that we find, after absence, in things that have closely belonged to us and which seem to confess of themselves to the connexion. The plot of ground, the graven tablet, the tended flowers affected him so as belonging to him that he resembled for the hour a contented landlord reviewing a piece of property. Whatever had happened—well, had happened. He had not come back this time with the vanity of that question, his former worrying "What, *what?*" now practically so spent. Yet he would none the less never again so cut himself off from the spot; he would come back to it every month, for if he did nothing else by its aid he at least held up his head. It thus grew for him, in the oddest way, a positive resource; he carried out his idea of periodical returns, which took their place at last among the most inveterate of his habits. What it all amounted to, oddly enough, was that in his finally so simplified world this garden of death gave him the few square feet of earth on which he could still most live. It was as if, being nothing anywhere else for any one, nothing even for himself, he were just everything here, and if not for a crowd of witnesses or indeed for any witness but John Marcher, then by clear right of the register that he could scan like an open page. The open page was the tomb of his friend, and *there* were the facts of the past, there the truth of his life, there the backward reaches in which he could lose himself. He did this from time to time with such effect that he seemed to wander through the old years with his hand in the arm of a companion who was, in the most extraordinary manner, his other, his younger self; and to wander, which was more extraordinary yet, round and round a third presence—not wandering she, but stationary, still, whose eyes, turning with his revolution, never ceased to follow him, and whose seat was his point, so to speak, of orientation. Thus in short he settled to live—feeding all on the sense that he once *had* lived, and dependent on it not alone for a support but for an identity.

It sufficed him in its way for months and the year elapsed; it would doubtless even have carried him further but for an accident, superficially slight, which moved him, quite in another direction, with a force beyond any of his impressions of Egypt or of India. It was a thing of the merest chance—the turn, as he afterwards felt, of a hair, though he was indeed to live to believe that if light hadn't come to him in this particular fashion it would still have come in another. He was to live to believe this, I say, though he was not to live, I may not less definitely mention, to do much else. We allow him at any rate the benefit of the conviction, struggling up for him at the end, that, whatever might have happened or not happened, he would have come round of himself to the light. The incident of an autumn day had put the match to the train laid from of old by his misery. With the light before him he knew that even of late his ache had only been smothered. It was strangely drugged, but it throbbed; at the touch it began to bleed. And the touch, in the event, was the face of a fellow mortal. This face, one grey afternoon when the leaves were thick in the alleys, looked into Marcher's own, at the cemetery, with an expression like the cut of a blade. He felt it, that is, so deep down that he winced at the steady thrust. The person who so mutely assaulted him was a figure he had noticed, on reaching his own goal, absorbed by a grave a short distance away, a grave apparently fresh, so that the emotion of the visitor would probably match it for frankness. This fact alone forbade further attention, though during the time he stayed he remained vaguely conscious of his neighbour, a middle-aged man apparently, in mourning, whose bowed back, among the clustered monuments and mortuary yews, was constantly presented. Marcher's theory that these were elements in contact with which he himself revived, had suffered, on this occasion, it may be granted, a marked, an excessive check. The autumn day was dire for him as none had recently been, and he rested with a heaviness he had not yet known on the low stone table that bore May Bartram's name. He rested without power to move, as if some spring in him, some spell vouchsafed, had suddenly been broken for ever. If he could have done that moment as he wanted he would simply have stretched himself on the slab that was ready to take him, treating it as a place prepared to receive his last sleep. What in all the wide world had he now to keep awake for? He stared before him with the question, and it was then that, as one of the cemetery walks passed near him, he caught the shock of the face.

His neighbour at the other grave had withdrawn, as he himself, with force enough in him, would have done by now, and was advancing along the path on his way to one of the gates. This brought him close, and his pace was slow, so that—and all the more as there was a kind of hunger in his look—the two men were for a minute directly confronted. Marcher knew him at once for one of the deeply stricken—a perception so sharp that nothing else in the picture comparatively lived, neither his dress, his age, nor his presumable character and class; nothing lived but the deep ravage of the features he showed. He *showed* them—that was the point; he was moved, as he passed, by some impulse that was either a signal for sympathy or, more possibly, a challenge to an opposed sorrow. He might already have been aware of our friend, might at some previous hour have noticed in him the smooth habit of the scene, with which the state of his own senses so scantly consorted, and might thereby have been stirred as by an overt discord. What Marcher was at all events conscious of was in the first place that the image of scarred passion presented to him was conscious too—of something that profaned the air; and in the second that, roused, startled, shocked, he was yet the next moment looking after it, as it went, with envy. The most extraordinary thing that had happened to him —though he had given that name to other matters as well —took place, after his immediate vague stare, as a consequence of this impression. The stranger passed, but the raw glare of his grief remained, making our friend wonder in pity what wrong, what wound it expressed, what injury not to be healed. What had the man *had,* to make him by the loss of it so bleed and yet live?

Something—and this reached him with a pang—that *he,* John Marcher, hadn't; the proof of which was precisely John Marcher's arid end. No passion had ever touched him, for this was what passion meant; he had survived and maundered and pined, but where had been *his* deep ravage? The extraordinary thing we speak of was the sudden rush of the result of this question. The sight that had just met his eyes named to him, as in letters of quick flame, something he had utterly, insanely missed, and what he had missed made these things a train of fire, made them mark themselves in an anguish of inward throbs. He had seen *outside* of his life, not learned it within, the way a woman was mourned when she had been loved for herself: such was the force of his conviction of the meaning of the stranger's face, which still flared for him as a smoky torch. It hadn't come to him, the knowledge, on the wings of experience; it had brushed him, jostled him, upset him, with the disrespect of chance, the insolence of accident. Now that the illumination had begun, however, it blazed to the zenith, and what he presently stood there gazing at was the sounded void of his life. He gazed, he drew breath, in pain; he turned in his dismay, and, turning, he had before him in sharper incision than ever the open page of his story. The name on the table smote him as the passage of his neighbour had done, and what it said to him, full in the face, was that *she* was what he had missed. This was the awful thought, the answer to all the past, the vision at the dread clearness of which he grew as cold as the stone beneath him. Everything fell together, confessed, explained, overwhelmed; leaving him most of all stupefied at the blindness he had cherished. The fate he had been marked for he had met with a vengeance—he had emptied the cup to the lees; he had been the man of his time, *the* man, to whom nothing on earth was to have happened. That was the rare stroke—that was his visitation. So he saw it, as we say, in pale horror, while the pieces fitted and fitted. So *she* had seen it while he didn't, and so she served at this hour to drive the truth home. It was the truth, vivid and monstrous, that all the while he had waited the wait was itself his portion. This the companion of his vigil had at a given moment made out, and she had then offered him the chance to baffle his doom. One's doom, however, was never baffled, and on the day she told him his own had come down she had seen him but stupidly stare at the escape she offered him.

The escape would have been to love her; then, *then* he would have lived. *She* had lived—who could say now with what passion?—since she had loved him for himself; whereas he had never thought of her (ah how it hugely glared at him!) but in the chill of his egotism and the light of her use. Her spoken words came back to him—the chain stretched and stretched. The Beast had lurked indeed, and the Beast, at its hour, had sprung; it had sprung in that twilight of the cold April when, pale, ill, wasted, but all beautiful, and perhaps even then recoverable, she had risen from her chair to stand before him and let him imaginably guess. It had sprung as he didn't guess; it had sprung as she hopelessly turned from him, and the mark, by the time he left her, had fallen where it *was* to fall. He had justified his fear and achieved his fate; he had failed, with the last exactitude, of all he was to fail of; and a moan now rose to his lips as he remembered she had prayed he mightn't know. This horror of waking—*this* was knowledge, knowledge under the breath of which the very tears in his eyes seemed to freeze. Through them, none the less, he tried to fix it and hold it; he kept it there before him so that he might feel the pain. That at least, belated and bitter, had something of the taste of life. But the bitterness suddenly sickened him, and it was as if, horribly, he saw, in the truth, in the cruelty of his image, what had been appointed and done. He saw the Jungle of his life and saw the lurking Beast; then, while he looked, perceived it, as by a stir of the air, rise, huge and hideous, for the leap that was to settle him. His eyes darkened—it was close; and, instinctively turning, in his hallucination, to avoid it, he flung himself, face down, on the tomb.

PASSAGES ON *THE BEAST IN THE JUNGLE* FROM JAMES'S NOTEBOOKS

I

February 5th, 1895. What is there in the idea of *Too late* —of some friendship or passion or bond—some affection long desired and waited for, that is formed too late?—I mean too late in life altogether. Isn't there something in the idea that 2 persons may meet (as if they had looked for each other for years) only in time to feel how much it might have meant for them if they had only met earlier? This is vague, nebulous—the mere hint of a hint. They but meet to part or to suffer—they meet when one is dying—'or something of that sort.' They may have been dimly conscious, in the past, of the possibility between them—been groping for each other in the darkness. It's love, it's friendship, it's mutual comprehension—it's whatever one will. They've heard of each other, perhaps—felt each other, been conscious, each, of some tug at the cord—some vibration of the other's heartstrings. It's a passion that *might* have been. I seem to be coinciding simply with the idea of the married person encountering the *real* mate, etc.; but that is not what I mean. Married or not—the marriage is a detail. Or rather, I fancy, there would have been no marriage conceivable for either. Haven't they waited—waited too long —till something else has happened? The only other 'something else' than marriage must have been, doubtless, the wasting of life. And the wasting of life is the implication of death. There may be the germ of a situation in this; but it obviously requires digging out. x x x x x

There comes back to me, *à propos* of it, and as vaguely and crookedly hooking itself on to it, somehow, that *concetto* that I have jotted down in another notebook—that of the little tragedy of the man who has renounced his ambition, the dream of his youth, his genius, talent, vocation—with all the honour and glory it might have brought him: sold it, bartered it, exchanged it for something very different and inferior, but mercenary and worldly. I've only to write these few words, however, to see that the 2 ideas have nothing to do with each other. They are different stories. What I fancied in this last mentioned was that this Dead Self of the poor man's lives for him still in some indirect way, in the sympathy, the fidelity (the relation of some kind) of another. I tried to give a hint in my former note, of what this vicarious self, as it were, might amount to. It will require returning to; and what I wanted not to let slip altogether was simply some reminder of the beauty, the little tragedy, attached perhaps to the situation of the man of genius who, in some accursed hour of his youth, has bartered away the fondest vision of that youth and lives ever afterwards in the shadow of the bitterness of the regret. My other little note contained the fancy of his *recovering* a little of the lost joy, of the Dead Self, in his intercourse with some person, some woman, who knows what that self was, in whom it still lives a little. This intercourse is his real life. But I think I said that there was a banality in that; that, practically, the little situation will have often enough been treated; and that therefore the thing could, probably, only take a form as the story, not of the man, but of the woman herself. It's *the woman's sense of what might <have been> in him* that arrives at the intensity. (The link of connection between the foregoing and this was simply my little feeling that they each dealt with might-have-beens.) *She is his Dead Self: he is alive in her and dead in himself*—that is something like the little formula I seemed to *entrevoir*. He himself, the man, must, *in* the tale, also materially die—die in the flesh as he had died long ago in the spirit, the *right* one. Then it is that his lost treasure revives most—no longer *contrarié* by his material existence, existence in his false self, his wrong one.— But I fear there isn't much in it: it would take a deuce of a deal of following up.

II

Lamb House, August 27th, 1901. Meanwhile there is something else—a very tiny *fantaisie* probably—in small notion that comes to me of a man haunted by the fear, more and more, throughout life, that *something will happen to him:*

he doesn't quite know what. His life *seems* safe and ordered, his liabilities and exposures (as a *result* of the fear) a good deal curtailed and cut down, so that the years go by and the stroke doesn't fall. Yet 'It *will* come, it will still come,' he finds himself believing—and indeed saying to some one, some second-consciousness in the anecdote. 'It will come before death; I shan't die without it.' Finally I think it must be *he* who sees—not the 2d consciousness. Mustn't indeed the '2d consciousness' be some woman, and it be she who *helps* him to see? She has always loved him—yes, *that,* for the story, 'pretty,' and he, saving, protecting, exempting his life (always, really, with and *for* the fear), has never known it. He likes her, talks to her, confides in her, sees her often —*la côtoie,* as to her hidden passion, but never guesses. She meanwhile, all the time, sees his life as it is. It is to her that he tells his fear—yes, she is the '2d consciousness.' At first she *feels,* herself, for him, his feeling of his fear, and is tender, reassuring, protective. Then she reads, as I say, his real case, and is, though unexpressedly, *lucid.* The years go by and *she sees the thing not happen.* At last one day they are somehow, some day, face to face over it, and then she speaks. 'It *has,* the great thing you've always lived in dread of, had the foreboding of—it *has* happened to you.' He wonders—when, how, what? 'What is it?—why, it is that *nothing* has happened!' Then, later on, I think, to keep up the prettiness, it must be that HE sees, that he understands. She has loved him always—and *that* might have happened. But it's too late—she's dead. That, I think, at least, he comes to later on, after an interval, after her death. She is dying, or ill, when she says it. He *then* DOESN'T understand, doesn't see—or so far, only, as to agree with her, ruefully, that that very well *may* be it: that nothing has happened. He goes back; she is gone; she is dead. *What* she has said to him has in a way, by its truth, created the need for her, made him want her, *positively* want her, more. But she is gone, he has lost her, and *then* he sees all she has meant. She has loved him. (*It must come for the*

READER *thus, at this moment.*) With his base safety and shrinkage he never knew. *That* was what might have happened, and what *has* happened is that it didn't.

JAMES'S PREFACE TO *THE BEAST IN THE JUNGLE*

1909

To DESIRE, amid these collocations, to place, so far as possible, like with like, was to invite "The Beast in the Jungle" to stand here next in order. As to the accidental determinant of which composition, once more—of comparatively recent date and destined, like its predecessor, first to see the light in a volume of miscellanies ("The Better Sort," 1903)—I remount the stream of time, all enquiringly, but to come back empty-handed. The subject of this elaborated fantasy—which, I must add, I hold a successful thing only as its motive may seem to the reader to stand out sharp—can't quite have belonged to the immemorial company of such solicitations; though in spite of this I meet it, in ten lines of an old note-book, but as a recorded conceit and an accomplished fact. Another poor sensitive gentleman, fit indeed to mate with Stransom of "The Altar"—my attested predilection for poor sensitive gentlemen almost embarrasses me as I march!—was to have been, after a strange fashion and from the threshold of his career, condemned to keep counting with the unreasoned prevision of some extraordinary fate; the conviction, lodged in his brain, part and parcel of his imagination from far back, that experience would be marked for him, and whether for good or for ill, by some rare distinction, some incalculable violence or unprecedented stroke. So I seemed to see him start in life—under the so mixed star of the extreme of apprehension and the extreme of confidence; all to the logical, the quite inevitable effect of the complication aforesaid: his having to wait and wait for the right recognition; none of the mere usual and normal human adventures, whether delights or disconcertments, appearing to conform to the great type of his fortune. So it is that he's depicted. No gathering appearance, no descried or interpreted promise or portent, affects his superstitious soul either as a damnation deep enough (if damnation be in question) for his appointed *quality* of consciousness, or as a translation into bliss sublime enough (on *that* hypothesis) to fill, in vulgar parlance, the bill. Therefore as each item of experience comes, with its possibilities, into view, he can but dismiss it under this sterilising habit of the failure to find it good enough and thence to appropriate it.

His one desire remains of course to meet his fate, or at least to divine it, to see it as intelligible, to learn it, in a word; but none of its harbingers, pretended or supposed, speak his ear in the true voice; they wait their moment at his door only to pass on unheeded, and the years ebb while he holds his breath and stays his hand and—from the dread not less of imputed pride than of imputed pusillanimity—stifles his distinguished secret. He perforce lets everything go—leaving all the while his general presumption disguised and his general abstention unexplained; since he's ridden by the idea of what things may lead to, since they mostly always lead to human communities, wider or intenser, of experience, and since, above all, in his uncertainty, he mustn't compromise others. Like the blinded seeker in the old-fashioned game he "burns," on occasion, as with the sense of the hidden thing near—only to deviate again however into the chill; the chill that indeed settles on him as the striking of his hour is deferred. His career thus resolves itself into a great negative adventure, my report of which presents, for its centre, the fine case that has caused him most tormentedly to "burn," and then most unprofitably to stray. He is afraid to recognise what he incidentally misses, since what his high belief amounts to is not that he shall have felt and vibrated less than any one else, but that he shall have felt and vibrated more; which no acknowledgement of the minor loss must conflict with. Such a course of existence naturally involves a climax—the final flash of the light under which he reads his lifelong riddle and sees his conviction proved. He has indeed been marked and indeed suffered his fortune—which is precisely to have been the man in the world to whom nothing whatever was to happen. My picture leaves him overwhelmed—at last he has understood; though in thus disengaging my treated theme for the reader's benefit I seem to acknowledge that this more detached witness may not successfully have done so. I certainly grant that any felt merit in the thing must all depend on the clearness and charm with which the subject just noted expresses itself.

EDITOR'S NOTE

The theme of "too late" first adumbrated in the note of February 5, 1895 was revived in the notebooks six years later in another form to give Henry James the subject for his masterpiece in the shorter form, "The Beast in the Jungle." This story was an offshoot of the novel *The Ambassadors,* which also has implicit in it the theme of "too late"; indeed, the story was written immediately after the completion of the novel. It was never serialized and went directly into a volume of tales, *The Better Sort,* which Henry James brought out in 1903. In the New York Edition James coupled "The Beast in the Jungle" with "The Altar of the Dead" as tales of the "quasi-supernatural" and incorporated them in the volume containing his ghost stories. In doing this he seems to have suggested that John Marcher is as haunted as any man who is visited by ghosts. Marcher's ghosts—the beasts in his private jungle—spring from his own mind.

In *The Ambassadors,* Lambert Strether, a middle-aged New Englander, arrives in Paris and wonders whether he hasn't returned to Europe too late. He is enjoined to "live all you can," by which James meant to "be aware all you can" and "to see all you can" into life. The degree of what this world held for Strether was represented by the degree of his ever-growing perceptions. And the reverse instance is that of John Marcher who perceives nothing. He is not aware. For him the terror of his unawareness, the fear of the unknown, is the "beast in the jungle." When it springs finally, it is "too late."

THE JOLLY CORNER

1909

I

"EVERY ONE asks me what I 'think' of everything," said Spencer Brydon; "and I make answer as I can—begging or dodging the question, putting them off with any nonsense. It wouldn't matter to any of them really," he went on, "for, even were it possible to meet in that stand-and-deliver way so silly a demand on so big a subject, my 'thoughts' would still be almost altogether about something that concerns only myself." He was talking to Miss Staverton, with whom for a couple of months now he had availed himself of every possible occasion to talk; this disposition and this resource, this comfort and support, as the situation in fact presented itself, having promptly enough taken the first place in the considerable array of rather unattenuated surprises attending his so strangely belated return to America. Everything was somehow a surprise; and that might be natural when one had so long and so consistently neglected everything, taken pains to give surprises so much margin for play. He had given them more than thirty years—thirty-three, to be exact; and they now seemed to him to have organised their performance quite on the scale of that licence. He had been twenty-three on leaving New York—he was fifty-six today: unless indeed he were to reckon as he had sometimes, since his repatriation, found himself feeling; in which case he would have lived longer than is often allotted to man. It would have taken a century, he repeatedly said to himself, and said also to Alice Staverton, it would have taken a longer absence and a more averted mind than those even of which he had been guilty, to pile up the differences, the newnesses, the queernesses, above all the bignesses, for the better or the worse, that at present assaulted his vision wherever he looked.

The great fact all the while however had been the incalculability; since he *had* supposed himself, from decade to decade, to be allowing, and in the most liberal and intelligent manner, for brilliancy of change. He actually saw that he had allowed for nothing; he missed what he would have been sure of finding, he found what he would never have imagined. Proportions and values were upside-down; the ugly things he had expected, the ugly things of his far away youth, when he had too promptly waked up to a sense of the ugly—these uncanny phenomena placed him rather, as it happened, under the charm; whereas the "swagger" things, the modern, the monstrous, the famous things, those he had more particularly, like thousands of ingenuous enquirers every year, come over to see, were exactly his sources of dismay. They were as so many set traps for displeasure, above all for reaction, of which his restless tread was constantly pressing the spring. It was interesting, doubtless, the whole show, but it would have been too disconcerting hadn't a certain finer truth saved the situation. He had distinctly not, in this steadier light, come over *all* for the monstrosities; he had come, not only in the last analysis but quite on the face of the act, under an impulse with which they had nothing to do. He had come—putting the thing pompously—to look at his "property," which he had thus for a third of a century not been within four thousand miles of; or, expressing it less sordidly, he had yielded to the humour of seeing again his house on the jolly corner, as he usually, and quite fondly, described it—the one in which he had first seen the light, in which various members of his family had lived and had died, in which the holidays of his over-schooled boyhood had been passed and the few social flowers of his chilled adolescence gathered, and which, alienated then for so long a period, had, through the successive deaths of his two brothers and the termination of old arrangements, come wholly into his hands. He was the owner of another, not quite so "good"—the jolly corner having been, from far back, superlatively extended and consecrated; and the value of the pair represented his main capital, with an income consisting, in these later years, of their respective rents which (thanks precisely to their original excellent type) had never been depressingly low. He could live in "Europe," as he had been in the habit of living, on the product of these flourishing New York leases, and all the better since, that of the second structure, the mere number in its long row, having within a twelvemonth fallen in, renovation at a high advance had proved beautifully possible.

These were items of property indeed, but he had found himself since his arrival distinguishing more than ever between them. The house within the street, two bristling blocks westward, was already in course of reconstruction as a tall mass of flats; he had acceded, some time before, to overtures for this conversion—in which, now that it was going forward, it had been not the least of his astonishments to find himself able, on the spot, and though without a previous ounce of such experience, to participate with a certain intelligence, almost with a certain authority. He had lived his life with his back so turned to such concerns and his face addressed to those of so different an order that he scarce knew what to make of this lively stir, in a compartment of his mind never yet penetrated, of a capacity for business and a sense for construction. These virtues, so common all round him now, had been dormant in his own organism—where it might be said of them perhaps that they had slept the sleep of the just. At present, in the splendid autumn weather—the autumn at least was a pure boon in the terrible place—he loafed about his "work" undeterred, secretly agitated; not in the least "minding" that the whole proposition, as they said, was vulgar and sordid, and ready to climb ladders, to walk the plank, to handle materials and look wise about them, to ask questions, in fine, and challenge explanations and really "go into" figures.

It amused, it verily quite charmed him; and, by the same stroke, it amused, and even more, Alice Staverton, though perhaps charming her perceptibly less. She wasn't however going to be better off for it, as *he* was—and so astonishingly much: nothing was now likely, he knew, ever to make her better off than she found herself, in the afternoon of life, as the delicately frugal possessor and tenant of the small house in Irving Place to which she had subtly managed to cling through her almost unbroken New York career. If he knew the way to it now better than to any other address among the dreadful multiplied numberings which seemed to him to reduce the whole place to some vast ledger-page, overgrown, fantastic, of ruled and criss-crossed lines and figures—if he had formed, for his consolation, that habit, it was really not a little because of the charm of his having encountered and recognised, in the vast wilderness of the wholesale, breaking through the mere gross generalisation of wealth and force and success, a small still scene where items and shades, all delicate things, kept the sharpness of the notes of a high voice perfectly trained, and where economy hung about like the scent of a garden. His old friend lived with one maid and herself dusted her relics and trimmed her lamps and polished her silver; she stood off, in the awful modern crush, when she could, but she sallied forth and did battle when the challenge was really to "spirit," the spirit she after all confessed to, proudly and a little shyly, as to that of the better time, that of *their* common, their quite far-away and antediluvian social period and order. She made use of the street-cars when need be, the terrible things that people scrambled for as the panic-stricken at sea scramble for the boats; she affronted, inscrutably, under stress, all the public concussions and ordeals; and yet, with that slim mystifying grace of her appearance, which defied you to say if she were a fair young woman who looked older through trouble, or a fine smooth older one who looked young through successful indifference; with her precious reference, above all, to memories and histories into which he could enter, she was as exquisite for him as some pale pressed flower (a rarity to begin with), and, failing other sweetnesses, she was a sufficient reward of his effort. They had communities of knowledge, "their" knowledge (this discriminating possessive was always on her lips) of presences of the other age, presences all over laid, in his case, by the experience of a man and the freedom of a wanderer, overlaid by pleasure, by infidelity, by passages of life that were strange and dim to her, just by "Europe" in short, but still unobscured, still exposed and cherished, under that pious visitation of the spirit from which she had never been diverted.

She had come with him one day to see how his "apartment-house" was rising; he had helped her over gaps and explained to her plans, and while they were there had happened to have, before her, a brief but lively discussion with the man in charge, the representative of the building-firm that had undertaken his work. He had found himself quite "standing-up" to this personage over a failure on the latter's part to observe some detail of one of their noted conditions, and had so lucidly urged his case that, besides ever so prettily flushing, at the time, for sympathy in his triumph, she had afterwards said to him (though to a slightly greater effect of irony) that he had clearly for too many years neglected a real gift. If he had but stayed at home he would have anticipated the inventor of the sky-scraper. If he had but stayed at home he would have discovered his genius in time really to start some new variety of awful architectural hare and run it till it burrowed in a gold-mine. He was to remember these words, while the weeks elapsed, for the small silver ring they had sounded over the queerest and deepest of his own lately most disguised and most muffled vibrations.

It had begun to be present to him after the first fortnight, it had broken out with the oddest abruptness, this particular wanton wonderment: it met him there—and this was the image under which he himself judged the matter, or at least, not a little, thrilled and flushed with it—very much as he might have been met by some strange figure, some unexpected occupant, at a turn of one of the dim passages of an empty house. The quaint analogy quite hauntingly remained with him, when he didn't indeed rather improve it by a still intenser form: that of his opening a door behind which he would have made sure of finding nothing, a door into a room shuttered and void, and yet so coming, with a great suppressed start, on some quite erect confronting presence, something planted in the middle of the place and facing him through the dusk. After that visit to the house in construction he walked with his companion to see the other and always so much the better one, which in the eastward direction formed one of the corners, the "jolly" one precisely, of the street now so generally dishonoured and disfigured in its westward reaches, and of the comparatively conservative Avenue. The Avenue still had pretensions, as Miss Staverton said, to decency; the old people had mostly gone, the old names were unknown, and here and there an old association seemed to stray, all vaguely, like some very aged person, out too late, whom you might meet and feel the impulse to watch or follow, in kindness, for safe restoration to shelter.

They went in together, our friends; he admitted himself with his key, as he kept no one there, he explained, preferring, for his reasons, to leave the place empty, under a simple arrangement with a good woman living in the neighbourhood and who came for a daily hour to open windows and dust and sweep. Spencer Brydon had his reasons and was growingly aware of them; they seemed to him better each time he was there, though he didn't name them all to his companion, any more than he told her as yet how often, how quite absurdly often, he himself came. He only let her see for the present, while they walked through the great blank rooms, that absolute vacancy reigned and that, from top to bottom, there was nothing but Mrs. Muldoon's broomstick, in a corner, to tempt the burglar. Mrs. Muldoon was then on the premises, and she loquaciously attended the visitors, preceding them from room to room and pushing back shutters and throwing up sashes—all to show them, as she remarked, how little there was to see. There was little indeed to see in the great gaunt shell where the main dispositions and the general apportionment of space, the style of an age of ampler allowances, had nevertheless for its master their honest pleading message, affecting him as some good old servant's, some lifelong retainer's appeal for a character, or even for a retiring-pension; yet it was also a remark of Mrs. Muldoon's that, glad as she was to oblige him by her noonday round, there was a request she greatly hoped he would never make of her. If he should wish her for any reason to come in after dark she would just tell him, if he "plased," that he must ask it of somebody else.

The fact that there was nothing to see didn't militate for the worthy woman against what one *might* see, and she put it frankly to Miss Staverton that no lady could be expected to like, could she? "craping up to thim top storeys in the ayvil hours." The gas and the electric light were off the house, and she fairly evoked a gruesome vision of her march through the great grey rooms—so many of them as there were too!—with her glimmering taper. Miss Staverton met her honest glare with a smile and the profession that she herself certainly would recoil from such an adventure. Spencer Brydon meanwhile held his peace—for the moment; the question of the "evil" hours in his old home had already become too grave for him. He had begun some time since to "crape," and he knew just why a packet of candles addressed to that pursuit had been stowed by his own hand, three weeks before, at the back of a drawer of the fine old sideboard that occupied, as a "fixture," the deep recess in the dining-room. Just now he laughed at his companions —quickly however changing the subject; for the reason that, in the first place, his laugh struck him even at that moment as starting the odd echo, the conscious human resonance (he scarce knew how to qualify it) that sounds made while he was there alone sent back to his ear or his fancy; and that, in the second, he imagined Alice Staverton for the instant on the point of asking him, with a divination, if he ever so prowled. There were divinations he was unprepared for, and he had at all events averted enquiry by the time Mrs. Muldoon had left them, passing on to other parts.

There was happily enough to say, on so consecrated a spot, that could be said freely and fairly; so that a whole train of declarations was precipitated by his friend's having herself broken out, after a yearning look round: "But I hope you don't mean they want you to pull *this* to pieces!" His answer came, promptly, with his re-awakened wrath: it was of course exactly what they wanted, and what they were "at" him for, daily, with the iteration of people who couldn't for their life understand a man's liability to decent feelings. He had found the place, just as it stood and beyond what he could express, an interest and a joy. There were values other than the beastly rent-values, and in short, in short—! But it was thus Miss Staverton took him up. "In short you're to make so good a thing of your sky-scraper that, living in luxury on *those* ill-gotten gains, you can afford for a while to be sentimental here!" Her smile had for him, with the words, the particular mild irony with which he found half her talk suffused; an irony without bitterness and that came, exactly, from her having so much imagination—not, like the cheap sarcasms with which one heard most people, about the world of "society," bid for the reputation of cleverness, from nobody's really having any. It was agreeable to him at this very moment to be sure that when he had answered, after a brief demur, "Well yes: so precisely, you may put it!" her imagination would still do him justice. He explained that even if never a dollar were to come to him from the other house he would nevertheless cherish this one; and he dwelt, further, while they lingered and wandered, on the fact of the stupefaction he was already exciting, the positive mystification he felt himself create.

He spoke of the value of all he read into it, into the mere sight of the walls, mere shapes of the rooms, mere sound of the floors, mere feel, in his hand, of the old silver-plated knobs of the several mahogany doors, which suggested the pressure of the palms of the dead; the seventy years of the past in fine that these things represented, the annals of nearly three generations, counting his grandfather's, the one that had ended there, and the impalpable ashes of his long-extinct youth, afloat in the very air like microscopic motes. She listened to everything; she was a woman who answered intimately but who utterly didn't chatter. She scattered abroad therefore no cloud of words; she could assent, she could agree, above all she could encourage, without doing that. Only at the last she went a little further than he had done himself. "And then how do you know? You may still, after all, want to live here." It rather indeed pulled him up, for it wasn't what he had been thinking, at least in her sense of the words. "You mean I may decide to stay on for the sake of it?"

"Well, *with* such a home—!" But, quite beautifully, she had too much tact to dot so monstrous an *i*, and it was precisely an illustration of the way she didn't rattle. How could any one—of any wit—insist on any one else's "wanting" to live in New York?

"Oh," he said, "I *might* have lived here (since I had my opportunity early in life); I might have put in here all these years. Then everything would have been different enough —and, I dare say, 'funny' enough. But that's another matter. And then the beauty of it—I mean of my perversity, of my refusal to agree to a 'deal'—is just in the total absence of a reason. Don't you see that if I had a reason about the matter at all it would *have* to be the other way, and would then be inevitably a reason of dollars? There are no reasons here *but* of dollars. Let us therefore have none whatever—not the ghost of one."

They were back in the hall then for departure, but from where they stood the vista was large, through an open door, into the great square main saloon, with its almost antique felicity of brave spaces between windows. Her eyes came back from that reach and met his own a moment. "Are you very sure the 'ghost' of one doesn't, much rather, serve—?"

He had a positive sense of turning pale. But it was as near as they were then to come. For he made answer, he believed, between a glare and a grin: "Oh ghosts—of course the place must swarm with them! I should be ashamed of it if it didn't. Poor Mrs. Muldoon's right, and it's why I haven't asked her to do more than look in."

Miss Staverton's gaze again lost itself, and things she didn't utter, it was clear, came and went in her mind. She might even for the minute, off there in the fine room, have imagined some element dimly gathering. Simplified like the death-mask of a handsome face, it perhaps produced for her just then an effect akin to the stir of an expression in the "set" commemorative plaster. Yet whatever her impression may have been she produced instead a vague platitude. "Well, if it were only furnished and lived in—!"

She appeared to imply that in case of its being still furnished he might have been a little less opposed to the idea of a return. But she passed straight into the vestibule, as if to leave her words behind her, and the next moment he had opened the house-door and was standing with her on the steps. He closed the door and, while he re-pocketed his key, looking up and down, they took in the comparatively harsh actuality of the Avenue, which reminded him of the assault of the outer light of the Desert on the traveller emerging from an Egyptian tomb. But he risked before they stepped into the street his gathered answer to her speech. "For me it *is* lived in. For me it *is* furnished." At which it was easy for her to sigh "Ah yes—!" all vaguely and discreetly; since his parents and his favourite sister, to say nothing of other kin, in numbers, had run their course and met their end there. That represented, within the walls, ineffaceable life.

It was a few days after this that, during an hour passed with her again, he had expressed his impatience of the too flattering curiosity—among the people he met—about his appreciation of New York. He had arrived at none at all that was socially producible, and as for that matter of his "thinking" (thinking the better or the worse of anything there) he was wholly taken up with one subject of thought. It was mere vain egoism, and it was moreover, if she liked, a morbid obsession. He found all things come back to the question of what he personally might have been, how he might have led his life and "turned out," if he had not so, at the outset, given it up. And confessing for the first time to the intensity within him of this absurd speculation—which but proved also, no doubt, the habit of too selfishly thinking—he affirmed the impotence there of any other source of interest, any other native appeal. "What would it have made of me, what would it have made of me? I keep for ever wondering, all idiotically; as if I could possibly know! I see what it has made of dozens of others, those I meet, and it positively aches within me, to the point of exasperation, that it would have made something of me as well. Only I can't make out *what,* and the worry of it, the small rage of curiosity never to be satisfied, brings back what I remember to have felt, once or twice, after judging best, for reasons, to burn some important letter unopened. I've been sorry, I've hated it—I've never known what was in the letter. You may of course say it's a trifle—!"

"I don't say it's a trifle," Miss Staverton gravely interrupted.

She was seated by her fire, and before her, on his feet and restless, he turned to and fro between this intensity of his idea and a fitful and unseeing inspection, through his single eye-glass, of the dear little old objects on her chimney-piece. Her interruption made him for an instant look at her harder. "I shouldn't care if you did!" he laughed, however; "and it's only a figure, at any rate, for the way I now feel. *Not* to have followed my perverse young course—and almost in the teeth of my father's curse, as I may say; not to have kept it up, so, 'over there,' from that day to this, without a doubt or a pang; not, above all, to have liked it, to have loved it, so much, loved it, no doubt, with such an abysmal conceit of my own preference: some variation from *that,* I say, must have produced some different effect for my life and for my 'form.' I should have stuck here—if it had been possible; and I was too young, at twenty-three, to judge, *pour deux sous,* whether it *were* possible. If I had waited I might have seen it was, and then I might have been, by staying here, something nearer to one of these types who have been hammered so hard and made so keen by their conditions. It isn't that I admire them so much—the question of any charm in them, or of any charm, beyond that of the rank money-passion, exerted by their conditions *for* them, has nothing to do with the matter: it's only a question of what fantastic, yet perfectly possible, development of my own nature I mayn't have missed. It comes over me that I had then a strange *alter ego* deep down somewhere within me, as the full-blown flower is in the small tight bud, and that I just took the course, I just transferred him to the climate, that blighted him for once and for ever."

"And you wonder about the flower," Miss Staverton said. "So do I, if you want to know; and so I've been wondering these several weeks. I believe in the flower," she continued, "I feel it would have been quite splendid, quite huge and monstrous."

"Monstrous above all!" her visitor echoed; "and I imagine, by the same stroke, quite hideous and offensive."

"You don't believe that," she returned; "if you did you

wouldn't wonder. You'd know, and that would be enough for you. What you feel—and what I feel *for* you—is that you'd have had power."

"You'd have liked me that way?" he asked.

She barely hung fire. "How should I not have liked you?"

"I see. You'd have liked me, have preferred me, a billionaire!"

"How should I not have liked you?" she simply again asked.

He stood before her still—her question kept him motionless. He took it in, so much there was of it; and indeed his not otherwise meeting it testified to that. "I know at least what I am," he simply went on; "the other side of the medal's clear enough. I've not been edifying—I believe I'm thought in a hundred quarters to have been barely decent. I've followed strange paths and worshipped strange gods; it must have come to you again and again—in fact you've admitted to me as much—that I was leading, at any time these thirty years, a selfish frivolous scandalous life. And you see what it has made of me."

She just waited, smiling at him. "You see what it has made of *me*."

"Oh you're a person whom nothing can have altered. You were born to be what you are, anywhere, anyway: you've the perfection nothing else could have blighted. And don't you see how, without my exile, I shouldn't have been waiting till now—?" But he pulled up for the strange pang.

"The great thing to see," she presently said, "seems to me to be that it has spoiled nothing. It hasn't spoiled your being here at last. It hasn't spoiled this. It hasn't spoiled your speaking—" She also however faltered.

He wondered at everything her controlled emotion might mean. "Do you believe then—too dreadfully!—that I *am* as good as I might ever have been?"

"Oh no! Far from it!" With which she got up from her chair and was nearer to him. "But I don't care," she smiled.

"You mean I'm good enough?"

She considered a little. "Will you believe it if I say so? I mean will you let that settle your question for you?" And then as if making out in his face that he drew back from this, that he had some idea which, however absurd, he couldn't yet bargain away: "Oh you don't care either—but very differently: you don't care for anything but yourself."

Spencer Brydon recognised it—it was in fact what he had absolutely professed. Yet he importantly qualified. "*He* isn't myself. He's the just so totally other person. But I do want to see him," he added. "And I can. And I shall."

Their eyes met for a minute while he guessed from something in hers that she divined his strange sense. But neither of them otherwise expressed it, and her apparent understanding, with no protesting shock, no easy derision, touched him more deeply than anything yet, constituting for his stifled perversity, on the spot, an element that was like breathable air. What she said however was unexpected. "Well, *I've* seen him."

"You—?"

"I've seen him in a dream."

"Oh a 'dream'—!" It let him down.

"But twice over," she continued. "I saw him as I see you now."

"You've dreamed the same dream—?"

"Twice over," she repeated. "The very same."

This did somehow a little speak to him, as it also gratified him. "You dream about me at that rate?"

"Ah about *him!*" she smiled.

His eyes again sounded her. "Then you know all about him." And as she said nothing more: "What's the wretch like?"

She hesitated, and it was as if he were pressing her so hard that, resisting for reasons of her own, she had to turn away. "I'll tell you some other time!"

II

IT WAS after this that there was most of a virtue for him, most of a cultivated charm, most of a preposterous secret thrill, in the particular form of surrender to his obsession and of address to what he more and more believed to be his privilege. It was what in these weeks he was living for—since he really felt life to begin but after Mrs. Muldoon had retired from the scene and, visiting the ample house from attic to cellar, making sure he was alone, he knew himself in safe possession and, as he tacitly expressed it, let himself go. He sometimes came twice in the twenty-four hours; the moments he liked best were those of gathering dusk, of the short autumn twilight; this was the time of which, again and again, he found himself hoping most. Then he could, as seemed to him, most intimately wander and wait, linger and listen, feel his fine attention, never in his life before so fine, on the pulse of the great vague place: he preferred the lampless hour and only wished he might have prolonged each day the deep crepuscular spell. Later—rarely much before midnight, but then for a considerable vigil—he watched with his glimmering light; moving slowly, holding it high, playing it far, rejoicing above all, as much as he might, in open vistas, reaches of communication between rooms and by passages; the long straight chance or show, as he would have called it, for the revelation he pretended to invite. It was practice he found he could perfectly "work" without exciting remark; no one was in the least the wiser for it; even Alice Staverton, who was moreover a well of discretion, didn't quite fully imagine.

He let himself in and let himself out with the assurance of calm proprietorship; and accident so far favoured him that, if a fat Avenue "officer" had happened on occasion to see him entering at eleven-thirty, he had never yet, to the best of his belief, been noticed as emerging at two. He walked there on the crisp November nights, arrived regularly at the evening's end; it was as easy to do this after dining out as to take his way to a club or to his hotel. When he left his club, if he hadn't been dining out, it was ostensibly to go to his hotel; and when he left his hotel, if he had spent a part of the evening there, it was ostensibly to go to his club. Everything was easy in fine; everything conspired and promoted: there was truly even in the strain of his experience something that glossed over, something that salved and simplified, all the rest of consciousness. He circulated, talked, renewed, loosely and pleasantly, old relations—met indeed, so far as he could, new expectations and seemed to make out on the whole that in spite of the career, of such different contacts, which he had spoken of to Miss Staverton as ministering so little, for those who might have watched it, to edification, he was positively rather liked than not. He was a dim secondary social success—and all with people who had truly not an idea of him. It was all mere surface sound, this murmur of their welcome, this popping of their corks—just as his gestures of response were the extravagant shadows, emphatic in proportion as they meant little, of some game of *ombres chinoises*. He projected himself all day, in thought, straight over the bristling line of hard unconscious heads and into the other, the real, the waiting life; the life that, as soon as he had heard behind him the click of his great house-door, began for him, on the jolly corner, as beguilingly as the slow opening bars of some rich music follows the tap of the conductor's wand.

He always caught the first effect of the steel point of his stick on the old marble of the hall pavement, large black-and-white squares that he remembered as the admiration of his childhood and that had then made in him, as he now saw, for the growth of an early conception of style. This effect was the dim reverberating tinkle as of some far-off bell hung who should say where?—in the depths of the house, of the past, of that mystical other world that might have flourished for him had he not, for weal or woe, abandoned it. On this impression he did ever the same thing; he put his stick noiselessly away in a corner—feeling the place once more in the likeness of some great glass bowl, all precious concave crystal, set delicately humming by the play of a moist finger round its edge. The concave crystal held, as it were, this mystical other world, and the indescribably fine murmur of its rim was the sigh there, the scarce audible pathetic wail to his strained ear, of all the old baffled forsworn possibilities. What he did therefore by this appeal of his hushed presence was to wake them into such measure of ghostly life as they might still enjoy. They were shy, all but unappeasably shy, but they weren't really sinister; at least they weren't as he had hitherto felt them—before they had taken the Form he so yearned to make them take, the Form he at moments saw himself in the light of fairly hunting on tiptoe, the points of his evening-shoes, from room to room and from storey to storey.

That was the essence of his vision—which was all rank folly, if one would, while he was out of the house and otherwise occupied, but which took on the last verisimilitude as soon as he was placed and posted. He knew what he meant and what he wanted; it was as clear as the figure on a cheque presented in demand for cash. His *alter ego* "walked" —that was the note of his image of him, while his image of his motive for his own odd pastime was the desire to waylay him and meet him. He roamed, slowly, warily, but all restlessly, he himself did—Mrs. Muldoon had been right, absolutely, with her figure of their "craping"; and the presence he watched for would roam restlessly too. But it would be as cautious and as shifty; the conviction of its probable, in fact its already quite sensible, quite audible evasion of pursuit grew for him from night to night, laying on him finally a rigour to which nothing in his life had been comparable. It had been the theory of many superficially-judging persons, he knew, that he was wasting that life in a surrender to sensations, but he had tasted of no pleasure so fine as his actual tension, had been introduced to no sport that demanded at once the patience and the nerve of this stalking of a creature more subtle, yet at bay perhaps more formidable, than any beast of the forest. The terms, the comparisons, the very practices of the chase positively came again into play; there were even moments when passages of his occasional experience as a sportsman, stirred memories, from his younger time, of moor and mountain and desert, revived for him—and to the increase of his keenness—by the tremendous force of analogy. He found himself at moments—once he had placed his single light on some mantel-shelf or in some recess—stepping back into shelter or shade, effacing himself behind a door or in an embrasure, as he had sought of old the vantage of rock and tree; he found himself holding his breath and living in the joy of the instant, the supreme suspense created by big game alone.

He wasn't afraid (though putting himself the question as he believed gentlemen on Bengal tiger-shoots or in close quarters with the great bear of the Rockies had been known to confess to having put it); and this indeed—since here at least he might be frank!—because of the impression, so intimate and so strange, that he himself produced as yet a dread, produced certainly a strain, beyond the liveliest he was likely to feel. They fell for him into categories, they fairly became familiar, the signs, for his own perception, of the alarm his presence and his vigilance created; though leaving him always to remark, portentously, on his probably having formed a relation, his probably enjoying a consciousness, unique in the experience of man. People enough, first and last, had been in terror of apparitions, but who had ever before so turned the tables and become himself, in the apparitional world, an incalculable terror? He might have found this sublime had he quite dared to think of it; but he didn't too much insist, truly, on that side of his privilege. With habit and repetition he gained to an extraordinary degree the power to penetrate the dusk of distances and the darkness of corners, to resolve back into their innocence the treacheries of uncertain light, the evil-looking forms taken in the gloom by mere shadows, by accidents of the air, by shifting effects of perspective; putting down his dim luminary he could still wander on without it, pass into other rooms and, only knowing it was there behind him in case of need, see his way about, visually project for his purpose a comparative clearness. It made him feel, this acquired faculty, like some monstrous stealthy cat; he wondered if he would have glared at these moments with large shining yellow eyes, and what it mightn't verily be, for the poor hard-pressed *alter ego,* to be confronted with such a type.

He liked however the open shutters; he opened everywhere those Mrs. Muldoon had closed, closing them as carefully afterwards, so that she shouldn't notice: he liked—oh this he did like, and above all in the upper rooms!—the sense of the hard silver of the autumn stars through the window-panes, and scarcely less the flare of the street-lamps below, the white electric lustre which it would have taken curtains to keep out. This was human actual social; this was of the world he had lived in, and he was more at his ease certainly for the countenance, coldly general and impersonal, that all the while and in spite of his detachment it seemed to give him. He had support of course mostly in the rooms at the wide front and the prolonged side; it failed him considerably in the central shades and the parts at the back. But if he sometimes, on his rounds, was glad of his optical reach, so none the less often the rear of the house affected him as the very jungle of his prey. The place was there more subdivided; a large "extension" in particular, where small rooms for servants had been multiplied, abounded in nooks and corners, in closets and passages, in the ramifications especially of an ample back staircase over which he leaned, many a time, to look far down—not deterred from his gravity even while aware that he might, for a spectator, have figured some solemn simpleton playing at hide-and-seek. Outside in fact he might himself make that ironic *rapprochement;* but within the walls, and in spite of the clear windows, his consistency was proof against the cynical light of New York.

It had belonged to that idea of the exasperated consciousness of his victim to become a real test for him; since he had quite put it to himself from the first that, oh distinctly! he could "cultivate" his whole perception. He had felt it as above all open to cultivation—which indeed was but another name for his manner of spending his time. He was bringing it on, bringing it to perfection, by practice; in consequence of which it had grown so fine that he was now aware of impressions, attestations of his general postulate, that couldn't have broken upon him at once. This was the case more specifically with a phenomenon at last quite frequent for him in the upper rooms, the recognition—absolutely unmistakeable, and by a turn dating from a particular hour, his resumption of his campaign after a diplomatic drop, a calculated absence of three nights—of his being definitely followed, tracked at a distance carefully taken and to the express end that he should the less confidently, less arrogantly, appear to himself merely to pursue. It worried, it finally quite broke him up, for it proved, of all the conceivable impressions, the one least suited to his book. He was kept in sight while remaining himself—as regards the essence of his position—sightless, and his only recourse then was in abrupt turns, rapid recoveries of ground. He wheeled about, retracing his steps, as if he might so catch in his face at least the stirred air of some other quick revolution. It was indeed true that his fully dislocalised thought of these manœuvres recalled to him Pantaloon, at the Christmas farce, buffeted and tricked from behind by ubiquitous Harlequin; but it left intact the influence of the conditions themselves each time he was re-exposed to them, so that in fact this association, had he suffered it to become constant, would on a certain side have but ministered to his intenser gravity. He had made, as I have said, to create on the premises the baseless sense of a reprieve, his three absences; and the result of the third was to confirm the after-effect of the second.

On his return, that night—the night succeeding his last intermission—he stood in the hall and looked up the staircase with a certainty more intimate than any he had yet known. "He's *there,* at the top, and waiting—not, as in general, falling back for disappearance. He's holding his ground, and it's the first time—which is a proof, isn't it? that something has happened for him." So Brydon argued with his hand on the banister and his foot on the lowest stair; in which position he felt as never before the air chilled by his logic. He himself turned cold in it, for he seemed of a sudden to know what now was involved. "Harder pressed?—yes, he takes it in, with its thus making clear to him that I've come, as they say, 'to stay.' He finally doesn't like and can't bear it, in the sense, I mean, that his wrath, his menaced interest, now balances with his dread. I've hunted him till he has 'turned': that, up there, is what has happened—he's the fanged or the antlered animal brought at last to bay." There came to him, as I say—but determined by an influence beyond my notation!—the acuteness of this certainty; under which however the next moment he had broken into a sweat that he would as little have consented to attribute to fear as he would have dared immediately to act upon it for enterprise. It marked none the less a prodigious thrill, a thrill that represented sudden dismay, no doubt, but also represented, and with the selfsame throb, the strangest, the most joyous, possibly the next minute almost the proudest, duplication of consciousness.

"He has been dodging, retreating, hiding, but now, worked up to anger, he'll fight!"—this intense impression made a single mouthful, as it were, of terror and applause. But what was wondrous was that the applause, for the felt fact, was so eager, since, if it was his other self he was running to earth, this ineffable identity was thus in the last resort not unworthy of him. It bristled there—somewhere near at hand, however unseen still—as the hunted thing, even as the trodden worm of the adage *must* at last bristle; and Brydon at this instant tasted probably of a sensation more complex than had ever before found itself consistent with sanity. It was as if it would have shamed him that a character so associated with his own should triumphantly succeed in just skulking, should to the end not risk the open, so that the drop of this danger was, on the spot, a great lift of the whole situation. Yet with another rare shift of the same subtlety he was already trying to measure by how much more he himself might now be in peril of fear; so rejoicing that he could, in another form, actively inspire that fear, and simultaneously quaking for the form in which he might passively know it.

The apprehension of knowing it must after a little have grown in him, and the strangest moment of his adventure perhaps, the most memorable or really most interesting, afterwards, of his crisis, was the lapse of certain instants of concentrated conscious *combat,* the sense of a need to hold on to something, even after the manner of a man slipping and slipping on some awful incline; the vivid impulse, above all, to move, to act, to charge, somehow and upon something —to show himself, in a word, that he wasn't afraid. The state of "holding-on" was thus the state to which he was momentarily reduced; if there had been anything, in the great vacancy, to seize, he would presently have been aware of having clutched it as he might under a shock at home have clutched the nearest chair-back. He had been surprised at any rate—of this he *was* aware—into something unprecedented since his original appropriation of the place; he had closed his eyes, held them tight, for a long minute, as with that instinct of dismay and that terror of vision. When he opened them the room, the other contiguous rooms, extraordinarily, seemed lighter—so light, almost, that at first he took the change for day. He stood firm, however that might be, just where he had paused; his resistance had helped him—it was as if there were something he had tided over. He knew after a little what this was—it had been in the imminent danger of flight. He had stiffened his will against going; without this he would have made for the stairs, and it seemed to him that, still with his eyes closed, he would have descended them, would have known how, straight and swiftly, to the bottom.

Well, as he had held out, here he was—still at the top, among the more intricate upper rooms and with the gauntlet of the others, of all the rest of the house, still to run when it should be his time to go. He would go at his time—only at his time: didn't he go every night very much at the same hour? He took out his watch—there was light for that: it was scarcely a quarter past one, and he had never withdrawn so soon. He reached his lodgings for the most part at two—with his walk of a quarter of an hour. He would wait for the last quarter—he wouldn't stir till then; and he kept his watch there with his eyes on it, reflecting while he held it that this deliberate wait, a wait with an effort, which he recognised, would serve perfectly for the attestation he desired to make. It would prove his courage—unless indeed the latter might most be proved by his budging at last from his place. What he mainly felt now was that, since he hadn't originally scuttled, he had his dignities—which had never in his life seemed so many—all to preserve and to carry aloft. This was before him in truth as a physical image, an image almost worthy of an age of greater romance. That remark indeed glimmered for him only to glow the next instant with a finer light; since what age of romance, after all, could have matched either the state of his mind or, "objectively," as they said, the wonder of his situation? The only difference would have been that, brandishing his dignities over his head as in a parchment scroll, he might then—that is in the heroic time—have proceeded downstairs with a drawn sword in his other grasp.

At present, really, the light he had set down on the mantel of the next room would have to figure his sword; which utensil, in the course of a minute, he had taken the requisite number of steps to possess himself of. The door between the rooms was open, and from the second another door opened to a third. These rooms, as he remembered, gave all three upon a common corridor as well, but there was a fourth, beyond them, without issue save through the preceding. To have moved, to have heard his step again, was appreciably a help; though even in recognising this he lingered once more a little by the chimney-piece on which his light had rested. When he next moved, just hesitating where to turn, he found himself considering a circumstance that, after his first and comparatively vague apprehension of it, produced in him the start that often attends some pang of recollection, the violent shock of having ceased happily to forget. He had come into sight of the door in which the brief chain of communication ended and which he now surveyed from the nearer threshold, the one not directly facing it. Placed at some distance to the left of this point, it would have admitted him to the last room of the four, the room without other approach or egress, had it not, to his intimate conviction, been closed *since* his former visitation, the matter probably of a quarter of an hour before. He stared with all his eyes at the wonder of the fact, arrested again where he stood and again holding his breath while he sounded its sense. Surely it had been *subsequently* closed—that is it had been on his previous passage indubitably open!

He took it full in the face that something had happened between—that he couldn't not have noticed before (by which he meant on his original tour of all the rooms that evening) that such a barrier had exceptionally presented itself. He had indeed since that moment undergone an agitation so extraordinary that it might have muddled for him any earlier view; and he tried to convince himself that he might perhaps then have gone into the room and, inadvertently, automatically, on coming out, have drawn the door after him. The difficulty was that this exactly was what he never did; it was against his whole policy, as he might have said, the essence of which was to keep vistas clear. He had them from the first, as he was well aware, quite on the brain: the strange apparition, at the far end of one of them, of his baffled "prey" (which had become by so sharp an irony so little the term now to apply!) was the form of success his imagination had most cherished, projecting into it always a refinement of beauty. He had known fifty times the start of perception that had afterwards dropped; had fifty times gasped to himself "There!" under some fond brief hallucination. The house, as the case stood, admirably lent itself; he might wonder at the taste, the native architecture of the particular time, which could rejoice so in the multiplication of doors—the opposite extreme to the modern, the actual almost complete proscription of them; but it had fairly contributed to provoke this obsession of the presence encountered telescopically, as he might say, focussed and studied in diminishing perspective and as by a rest for the elbow.

It was with these considerations that his present attention was charged—they perfectly availed to make what he saw portentous. He *couldn't,* by any lapse, have blocked that aperture; and if he hadn't, if it was unthinkable, why what else was clear but that there had been another agent? Another agent?—he had been catching, as he felt, a moment back, the very breath of him; but when had he been so close as in this simple, this logical, this completely personal act? It was so logical, that is, that one might have *taken* it for personal; yet for what did Brydon take it, he asked himself, while, softly panting, he felt his eyes almost leave their sockets. Ah this time at last they *were,* the two, the opposed projections of him, in presence; and this time, as much as one would, the question of danger loomed. With it rose, as not before, the question of courage—for what he knew the blank face of the door to say to him was "Show us how much you have!" It stared, it glared back at him with that challenge; it put to him the two alternatives: should he just push it open or not? Oh to have this consciousness was to *think*—and to think, Brydon knew, as he stood there, was, with the lapsing moments, not to have acted! Not to have acted—that was the misery and the pang—was even still not to act; was in fact *all* to feel the thing in another, in a new and terrible way. How long did he pause and how long did he debate? There was presently nothing to measure it; for his vibration had already changed—as just by the effect of its intensity. Shut up there, at bay, defiant, and with the prodigy of the thing palpably proveably *done,* thus giving notice like some stark signboard—under that accession of accent the situation itself had turned; and Brydon at last remarkably made up his mind on what it had turned to.

It had turned altogether to a different admonition; to a supreme hint, for him, of the value of Discretion! This slowly dawned, no doubt—for it could take its time; so perfectly, on his threshold, had he been stayed, so little as yet had he either advanced or retreated. It was the strangest of all things that now when, by his taking ten steps and applying his hand to a latch, or even his shoulder and his knee, if necessary, to a panel, all the hunger of his prime need might have been met, his high curiosity crowned, his unrest assuaged—it was amazing, but it was also exquisite and rare, that insistence should have, at a touch, quite dropped from him. Discretion—he jumped at that; and yet not, verily, at such a pitch, because it saved his nerves or his skin, but because, much more valuably, it saved the situation. When I say he "jumped" at it I feel the consonance of this term with the fact that—at the end indeed of I know not how long—he did move again, he crossed straight to the door. He wouldn't touch it—it seemed now that he might *if* he would: he would only just wait there a little, to show, to prove, that he wouldn't. He had thus another station, close to the thin partition by which revelation was denied him; but with his eyes bent and his hands held off in a mere intensity of stillness. He listened as if there had been something to hear, but this attitude, while it lasted, was his own communication. "If you won't then—good: I spare you and

I give up. You affect me as by the appeal positively for pity: you convince me that for reasons rigid and sublime—what do I know?—we both of us should have suffered. I respect them then, and, though moved and privileged as, I believe, it has never been given to man, I retire, I renounce—never, on my honour, to try again. So rest for ever—and let *me!*"

That, for Brydon was the deep sense of this last demonstration—solemn, measured, directed, as he felt it to be. He brought it to a close, he turned away; and now verily he knew how deeply he had been stirred. He retraced his steps, taking up his candle, burnt, he observed, well-nigh to the socket, and marking again, lighten it as he would, the distinctness of his footfall; after which, in a moment, he knew himself at the other side of the house. He did here what he had not yet done at these hours—he opened half a casement, one of those in the front, and let in the air of the night; a thing he would have taken at any time previous for a sharp rupture of his spell. His spell was broken now, and it didn't matter—broken by his concession and his surrender, which made it idle henceforth that he should ever come back. The empty street—its other life so marked even by the great lamplit vacancy—was within call, within touch; he stayed there as to be in it again, high above it though he was still perched; he watched as for some comforting common fact, some vulgar human note, the passage of a scavenger or a thief, some night-bird however base. He would have blessed that sign of life; he would have welcomed positively the slow approach of his friend the policeman, whom he had hitherto only sought to avoid, and was not sure that if the patrol had come into sight he mightn't have felt the impulse to get into relation with it, to hail it, on some pretext, from his fourth floor.

The pretext that wouldn't have been too silly or too compromising, the explanation that would have saved his dignity and kept his name, in such a case, out of the papers, was not definite to him: he was so occupied with the thought of recording his Discretion—as an effect of the vow he had just uttered to his intimate adversary—that the importance of this loomed large and something had overtaken all ironically his sense of proportion. If there had been a ladder applied to the front of the house, even one of the vertiginous perpendiculars employed by painters and roofers and sometimes left standing overnight, he would have managed somehow, astride of the window-sill, to compass by outstretched leg and arm that mode of descent. If there had been some such uncanny thing as he had found in his room at hotels, a workable fire-escape in the form of notched cable or a canvas shoot, he would have availed himself of it as a proof—well, of his present delicacy. He nursed that sentiment, as the question stood, a little in vain, and even—at the end of he scarce knew, once more, how long—found it, as by the action on his mind of the failure of response of the outer world, sinking back to vague anguish. It seemed to him he had waited an age for some stir of the great grim hush; the life of the town was itself under a spell—so unnaturally, up and down the whole prospect of known and rather ugly objects, the blankness and the silence lasted. Had they ever, he asked himself, the hard-faced houses, which had begun to look livid in the dim dawn, had they ever spoken so little to any need of his spirit? Great builded voids, great crowded stillnesses put on, often, in the heart of cities, for the small hours, a sort of sinister mask, and it was of this large collective negation that Brydon presently became conscious—all the more that the break of day was, almost incredibly, now at hand, proving to him what a night he had made of it.

He looked again at his watch, saw what had become of his time-values (he had taken hours for minutes—not, as in other tense situations, minutes for hours) and the strange air of the streets was but the weak, the sullen flush of a dawn in which everything was still locked up. His choked appeal from his own open window had been the sole note of life, and he could but break off at last as for a worse despair.

Yet while so deeply demoralised he was capable again of an impulse denoting—at least by his present measure—extraordinary resolution; of retracing his steps to the spot where he had turned cold with the extinction of his last pulse of doubt as to there being in the place another presence than his own. This required an effort strong enough to sicken him; but he had his reason, which over-mastered for the moment everything else. There was the whole of the rest of the house to traverse, and how should he screw himself to that if the door he had seen closed were at present open? He could hold to the idea that the closing had practically been for him an act of mercy, a chance offered him to descend, depart, get off the ground and never again profane it. This conception held together, it worked; but what it meant for him depended now clearly on the amount of forbearance his recent action, or rather his recent inaction, had engendered. The image of the "presence," whatever it was, waiting there for him to go—this image had not yet been so concrete for his nerves as when he stopped short of the point at which certainty would have come to him. For, with all his resolution, or more exactly with all his dread, he did stop short—he hung back from really seeing. The risk was too great and his fear too definite: it took at this moment an awful specific form.

He knew—yes, as he had never known anything—that, *should* he see the door open, it would all too abjectly be the end of him. It would mean that the agent of his shame—for his shame was the deep abjection—was once more at large and in general possession; and what glared him thus in the face was the act that this would determine for him. It would send him straight about to the window he had left open, and by that window, be long ladder and dangling rope as absent as they would, he saw himself uncontrollably insanely fatally take his way to the street. The hideous chance of this he at least could avert; but he could only avert it by recoiling in time from assurance. He had the whole house to deal with, this fact was still there; only he now knew that uncertainty alone could start him. He stole back from where he had checked himself—merely to do so was suddenly like safety—and, making blindly for the greater staircase, left gaping rooms and sounding passages behind. Here was the top of the stairs, with a fine large dim descent and three spacious landings to mark off. His instinct was all for mildness, but his feet were harsh on the floors, and, strangely, when he had in a couple of minutes become aware of this, it counted somehow for help. He couldn't have spoken, the tone of his voice would have scared him, and the common conceit or resource of "whistling in the dark" (whether literally or figuratively) have appeared basely vulgar; yet he liked none the less to hear himself go, and when he had reached his first landing—taking it all with no rush, but quite steadily—that stage of success drew from him a gasp of relief.

The house, withal, seemed immense, the scale of space again inordinate; the open rooms to no one of which his eyes deflected, gloomed in their shuttered state like mouths of caverns; only the high skylight that formed the crown of the deep well created for him a medium in which he could advance, but which might have been, for queerness of colour, some watery under-world. He tried to think of something noble, as that his property was really grand, a splendid possession; but this nobleness took the form too of the clear delight with which he was finally to sacrifice it. They might come in now, the builders, the destroyers—they might come as soon as they would. At the end of two flights he had dropped to another zone, and from the middle of the third, with only one more left, he recognised the influence of the lower windows, of half-drawn blinds, of the occasional gleam of street-lamps, of the glazed spaces of the vestibule. This was the bottom of the sea, which showed an illumination of its own and which he even saw paved—when at a given moment he drew up to sink a long look over the banisters—with the marble squares of his childhood. By that time indubitably he felt, as he might have said in a commoner cause, better; it had allowed him to stop and draw breath, and the ease increased with the sight of the old black-and-white slabs. But what he most felt was that now surely, with the element of impunity pulling him as by hard firm hands, the case was settled for what he might have seen above had he dared that last look. The closed door, blessedly remote now, was still closed—and he had only in short to reach that of the house.

He came down further, he crossed the passage forming the access to the last flight; and if here again he stopped an instant it was almost for the sharpness of the thrill of assured escape. It made him shut his eyes—which opened again to the straight slope of the remainder of the stairs. Here was impunity still, but impunity almost excessive; inasmuch as the side-lights and the high fan-tracery of the entrance were glimmering straight into the hall; an appearance produced, he the next instant saw, by the fact that the vestibule gaped wide, that the hinged halves of the inner door had been thrown far back. Out of that again the *question* sprang at him, making his eyes, as he felt, half-start from his head, as they had done, at the top of the house, before the sign of the other door. If he had left that one open, hadn't he left this one closed, and wasn't he now in *most* immediate presence of some inconceivable occult activity? It was as sharp, the question, as a knife in his side, but the answer hung fire still and seemed to lose itself in the vague darkness to which the thin admitted dawn, glimmering archwise over the whole outer door, made a semicircular margin, a cold silvery nimbus that seemed to play a little as he looked—to shift and expand and contract.

It was as if there had been something within it, protected by indistinctness and corresponding in extent with the opaque surface behind, the painted panels of the last barrier to his escape, of which the key was in his pocket. The indistinctness mocked him even while he stared, affected him as somehow shrouding or challenging certitude, so that after faltering an instant on his step he let himself go with the sense that here *was* at last something to meet, to touch, to take, to know—something all unnatural and dreadful, but to advance upon which was the condition for him either of liberation or of supreme defeat. The penumbra, dense and dark, was the virtual screen of a figure which stood in it as still as some image erect in a niche or as some black-vizored sentinel guarding a treasure. Brydon was to know afterwards, was to recall and make out, the particular thing he had believed during the rest of his descent. He saw, in its great grey glimmering margin, the central vagueness diminish, and he felt it to be taking the very form toward which, for so many days, the passion of his curiosity had yearned. It gloomed, it loomed, it was something, it was somebody, the prodigy of a personal presence.

Rigid and conscious, spectral yet human, a man of his own substance and stature waited there to measure himself with his power to dismay. This only could it be—this only till he recognised, with his advance, that what made the face dim was the pair of raised hands that covered it and in which, so far from being offered in defiance, it was buried as for dark deprecation. So Brydon, before him, took him in; with every fact of him now, in the higher light, hard and acute—his planted stillness, his vivid truth, his grizzled bent head and white masking hands, his queer actuality of evening-dress, of dangling double eye-glass, of gleaming silk lappet and white linen, of pearl button and gold watch-guard and polished shoe. No portrait by a great modern master could have presented him with more intensity, thrust him out of his frame with more art, as if there had been "treatment," of the consummate sort, in his every shade and salience. The revulsion, for our friend, had become, before he knew it, immense—this drop, in the act of apprehension, to the sense of his adversary's inscrutable manœuvre. That meaning at least, while he gaped, it offered him; for he could but gape at his other self in this other anguish, gape as a proof that *he,* standing there for the achieved, the enjoyed, the triumphant life, couldn't be faced in his triumph. Wasn't the proof in the splendid covering hands, strong and completely spread?—so spread and so intentional that, in spite of a special verity that surpassed every other, the fact that one of these hands had lost two fingers, which were reduced to stumps, as if accidentally shot away, the face was effectually guarded and saved.

"Saved," though, *would* it be?—Brydon breathed his wonder till the very impunity of his attitude and the very insistence of his eyes produced, as he felt, a sudden stir which showed the next instant as a deeper portent, while the head raised itself, the betrayal of a braver purpose. The hands, as he looked, began to move, to open; then, as if deciding in a flash, dropped from the face and left it uncovered and presented. Horror, with the sight, had leaped into Brydon's throat, gasping there in a sound he couldn't utter; for the bared identity was too hideous as *his,* and his glare was the passion of his protest. The face, *that* face, Spencer Brydon's?—he searched it still, but looking away from it in dismay and denial, falling straight from his height and sublimity. It was unknown, inconceivable, awful, disconnected from any possibility—! He had been "sold," he inwardly moaned, stalking such game as this: the presence before him was a presence, the horror within him a horror, but the waste of his nights had been only grotesque and the success of his adventure an irony. Such an identity fitted his at *no* point, made its alternative monstrous. A thousand times yes, as it came upon him nearer now—the face was the face of a stranger. It came upon him nearer now, quite as one of those expanding fantastic images projected by the magic lantern of childhood; for the stranger, whoever he might be, evil, odious, blatant, vulgar, had advanced as for aggression, and he knew himself give ground. Then harder pressed still, sick with the force of his shock, and falling back as under the hot breath and the roused passion of a life larger than his own, a rage of personality before which his own collapsed, he felt the whole vision turn to darkness and his very feet give way. His head went round; he was going; he had gone.

III

WHAT had next brought him back, clearly—though after how long?—was Mrs. Muldoon's voice, coming to him from quite near, from so near that he seemed presently to see her as kneeling on the ground before him while he lay looking up at her; himself not wholly on the ground, but half-raised and upheld—conscious, yes, of tenderness of support and, more particularly, of a head pillowed in extraordinary softness and faintly refreshing fragrance. He considered, he wondered, his wit but half at his service; then another face intervened, bending more directly over him, and he finally knew that Alice Staverton had made her lap an ample and perfect cushion to him, and that she had to this end seated herself on the lowest degree of the staircase, the rest of his long person remaining stretched on his old black-and-white slabs. They were cold, these marble squares of his youth; but *he* somehow was not, in this rich return of consciousness—the most wonderful hour, little by little, that he had ever known, leaving him, as it did, so gratefully, so abysmally passive, and yet as with a treasure of intelligence waiting all round him for quiet appropriation; dissolved, he might call it, in the air of the place and producing the golden glow of a late autumn afternoon. He had come back, yes—come back from further away than any man but himself had ever travelled; but it was strange how with this sense what he had come back *to* seemed really the great thing, and as if his prodigious journey had been all for the sake of it. Slowly but surely his consciousness grew, his vision of his state thus completing itself: he had been miraculously *carried* back—lifted and carefully borne as from where he had been picked up, the uttermost end of an interminable grey passage. Even with this he was suffered to rest, and what had now brought him to knowledge was the break in the long mild motion.

It had brought him to knowledge, to knowledge—yes, this was the beauty of his state; which came to resemble more and more that of a man who has gone to sleep on some news of a great inheritance, and then, after dreaming it away, after profaning it with matters strange to it, has waked up again to serenity of certitude and has only to lie and watch it grow. This was the drift of his patience—that he had only to let it shine on him. He must moreover, with intermissions, still have been lifted and borne; since why and how else should he have known himself, later on, with the afternoon glow intenser, no longer at the foot of his stairs—situated as these now seemed at that dark other end of his tunnel—but on a deep window-bench of his high saloon, over which had been spread, couch-fashion, a mantle of soft stuff lined with grey fur that was familiar to his eyes and that one of his hands kept fondly feeling as for its pledge of truth. Mrs. Muldoon's face had gone, but the other, the second he had recognised, hung over him in a way that showed how he was still propped and pillowed. He took it all in, and the more he took it the more it seemed to suffice: he was as much at peace as if he had had food and drink. It was the two women who had found him, on Mrs. Muldoon's having plied, at her usual hour, her latch-key —and on her having above all arrived while Miss Staverton still lingered near the house. She had been turning away, all anxiety, from worrying the vain bell-handle—her calculation having been of the hour of the good woman's visit; but the latter, blessedly, had come up while she was still there, and they had entered together. He had then lain, beyond the vestibule, very much as he was lying now —quite, that is, as he appeared to have fallen, but all so wondrously without bruise or gash; only in a depth of stupor. What he most took in, however, at present, with the steadier clearance, was that Alice Staverton had for a long unspeakable moment not doubted he was dead.

"It must have been that I *was.*" He made it out as she held him. "Yes—I can only have died. You brought me literally to life. Only," he wondered, his eyes rising to her, "only, in the name of all the benedictions, how?"

It took her but an instant to bend her face and kiss him, and something in the manner of it, and in the way her hands clasped and locked his head while he felt the cool charity and virtue of her lips, something in all this beatitude somehow answered everything. "And now I keep you," she said.

"Oh keep me, keep me!" he pleaded while her face still hung over him: in response to which it dropped again and stayed close, clingingly close. It was the seal of their situation—of which he tasted the impress for a long blissful moment in silence. But he came back. "Yet how did you know—?"

"I was uneasy. You were to have come, you remember—and you had sent no word."

"Yes, I remember—I was to have gone to you at one today." It caught on to their "old" life and relation—which were so near and so far. "I was still out there in my strange darkness—where was it, what was it? I must have stayed there so long." He could but wonder at the depth and the duration of his swoon.

"Since last night?" she asked with a shade of fear for her possible indiscretion.

"Since this morning—it must have been: the cold dim dawn of today. Where have I been," he vaguely wailed, "where have I been?" He felt her hold him close, and it was as if this helped him now to make in all security his mild moan. "What a long dark day!"

All in her tenderness she had waited a moment. "In the cold dim dawn?" she quavered.

But he had already gone on piecing together the parts

of the whole prodigy. "As I didn't turn up you came straight—?"

She barely cast about. "I went first to your hotel—where they told me of your absence. You had dined out last evening and hadn't been back since. But they appeared to know you had been at your club."

"So you had the idea of *this*—?"

"Of what?" she asked in a moment.

"Well—of what has happened."

"I believed at least you'd have been here. I've known, all along," she said, "that you've been coming."

" 'Known' it—?"

"Well, I've believed it. I said nothing to you after that talk we had a month ago—but I felt sure. I knew you *would,*" she declared.

"That I'd persist, you mean?"

"That you'd see him."

"Ah but I didn't!" cried Brydon with his long wail. "There's somebody—an awful beast; whom I brought, too horribly, to bay. But it's not me."

At this she bent over him again, and her eyes were in his eyes. "No—it's not you." And it was as if, while her face hovered, he might have made out in it, hadn't it been so near, some particular meaning blurred by a smile. "No, thank heaven," she repeated—"it's not you! Of course it wasn't to have been."

"Ah but it *was,*" he gently insisted. And he stared before him now as he had been staring for so many weeks. "I was to have known myself."

"You couldn't!" she returned consolingly. And then reverting, and as if to account further for what she had herself done, "But it wasn't only *that,* that you hadn't been at home," she went on. "I waited till the hour at which we had found Mrs. Muldoon that day of my going with you; and she arrived, as I've told you, while, failing to bring any one to the door, I lingered in my despair on the steps. After a little, if she hadn't come, by such a mercy, I should have found means to hunt her up. But it wasn't," said Alice Staverton, as if once more with her fine intention—"it wasn't only that."

His eyes, as he lay, turned back to her. "What more then?"

She met it, the wonder she had stirred. "In the cold dim dawn, you say? Well, in the cold dim dawn of this morning I too saw you."

"Saw *me*—?"

"Saw *him,*" said Alice Staverton. "It must have been at the same moment."

He lay an instant taking it in—as if he wished to be quite reasonable. "At the same moment?"

"Yes—in my dream again, the same one I've named to you. He came back to me. Then I knew it for a sign. He had come to you."

At this Brydon raised himself; he had to see her better. She helped him when she understood his movement, and he sat up, steadying himself beside her there on the window-bench and with his right hand grasping her left. *"He* didn't come to me."

"You came to yourself," she beautifully smiled.

"Ah I've come to myself now—thanks to you, dearest. But this brute, with his awful face—this brute's a black stranger. He's none of *me,* even as I *might* have been," Brydon sturdily declared.

But she kept the clearness that was like the breath of infallibility. "Isn't the whole point that you'd have been different?"

He almost scowled for it. "As different as *that*—?"

Her look again was more beautiful to him than the things of this world. "Haven't you exactly wanted to know *how* different? So this morning," she said, "you appeared to me."

"Like *him?*"

"A black stranger!"

"Then how did you know it was I?"

"Because, as I told you weeks ago, my mind, my imagination, had worked so over what you might, what you mightn't have been—to show you, you see, how I've thought of you. In the midst of that you came to me—that my wonder might be answered. So I knew," she went on; "and believed that, since the question held you too so fast, as you told me that day, you too would see for yourself. And when this morning I again saw I knew it would be because you had—and also then, from the first moment, because you somehow wanted me. *He* seemed to tell me of that. So why," she strangely smiled, "shouldn't I like him?"

It brought Spencer Brydon to his feet. "You 'like' that horror—?"

"I *could* have liked him. And to me," she said, "he was no horror. I had accepted him."

"'Accepted'—?" Brydon oddly sounded.

"Before, for the interest of his difference—yes. And as *I* didn't disown him, as *I* knew him—which you at last, confronted with him in his difference, so cruelly didn't, my dear—well, he must have been, you see, less dreadful to me. And it may have pleased him that I pitied him."

She was beside him on her feet, but still holding his hand—still with her arm supporting him. But though it all brought for him thus a dim light, "You 'pitied' him?" he grudgingly, resentfully asked.

"He has been unhappy; he has been ravaged," she said.

"And haven't I been unhappy? Am not I—you've only to look at me!—ravaged?"

"Ah I don't say I like him *better,*" she granted after a thought. "But he's grim, he's worn—and things have happened to him. He doesn't make shift, for sight, with your charming monocle."

"No"—it struck Brydon: "I couldn't have sported mine 'downtown.' They'd have guyed me there."

"His great convex pince-nez—I saw it, I recognised the kind—is for his poor ruined sight. And his poor right hand—!"

"Ah!" Brydon winced—whether for his proved identity

or for his lost fingers. Then, "He has a million a year," he lucidly added. "But he hasn't you."

"And he isn't—no, he isn't—*you!*" she murmured as he drew her to his breast.

EDITOR'S NOTE

In his prefaces to the New York Edition, Henry James devotes only a few lines to "The Jolly Corner" asserting that there was "more to say than my space allows." He did say, however, that "A very limited thing being on this occasion in question, I was moved to adopt as my motive an analysis of some one of the conceivably rarest and intensest grounds for an 'unnatural' anxiety, a *malaise* so incongruous and discordant, in the given prosaic prosperous conditions, as almost to be compromising." He spoke of the tale as a "finished fantasy."

There is no note in the notebooks devoted to the story. It is derived from James's long-planned and never-finished novel, *The Sense of the Past,* which was later dramatized as *Berkeley Square.* The idea of that ghostly novel was that a young man from the present walks into an old house in London and finds himself in another era. Gradually he begins to feel he is a prisoner of the past. His *malaise* consists of an over-riding anxiety that he may never get back to the present. The people in the past see him as a strange and threatening person who knows more than they do. He haunts them. They haunt him. The novel would have been James's supreme ghostly work: a work in which everyone is haunted.

From this plan he disengaged the idea of a New Yorker wandering into the house of his childhood after years abroad in search of his past. And this is the story of "The Jolly Corner." James had revisited New York after an absence of twenty years just before he wrote the tale. It too is a tale of the haunter and the haunted; but in this case it is a man haunted by himself, as he was and as he might have been. In a larger sense, it is the story of people who fear to face themselves.

THE ART OF FICTION
1888

I SHOULD not have affixed so comprehensive a title to these few remarks, necessarily wanting in any completeness upon a subject the full consideration of which would carry us far, did I not seem to discover a pretext for my temerity in the interesting pamphlet lately published under this name by Mr. Walter Besant. Mr. Besant's lecture at the Royal Institution—the original form of his pamphlet—appears to indicate that many persons are interested in the art of fiction, and are not indifferent to such remarks, as those who practise it may attempt to make about it. I am therefore anxious not to lose the benefit of this favourable association, and to edge in a few words under cover of the attention which Mr. Besant is sure to have excited. There is something very encouraging in his having put into form certain of his ideas on the mystery of story-telling.

It is a proof of life and curiosity—curiosity on the part of the brotherhood of novelists as well as on the part of their readers. Only a short time ago it might have been supposed that the English novel was not what the French call *discutable*. It had no air of having a theory, a conviction, a consciousness of itself behind it—of being the expression of an artistic faith, the result of choice and comparison. I do not say it was necessarily the worse tor that: it would take much more courage than I possess to intimate that the form of the novel as Dickens and Thackeray (for instance) saw it had any taint of incompleteness. It was, however, *naïf* (if I may help myself out with another French word); and evidently if it be destined to suffer in any way for having lost its *naïveté* it has now an idea of making sure of the corresponding advantages. During the period I have alluded to there was a comfortable, good-humoured feeling abroad that a novel is a novel, as a pudding is a pudding, and that our only business with it could be to swallow it. But within a year or two, for some reason or other, there have been signs of returning animation—the era of discussion would appear to have been to a certain extent opened. Art lives upon discussion, upon experiment, upon curiosity, upon variety of attempt, upon the exchange of views and the comparison of standpoints; and there is a presumption that those times when no one has anything particular to say about it, and has no reason to give for practice or preference, though they may be times of honour, are not times of development—are times, possibly even, a little of dullness. The successful application of any art is a delightful spectacle, but the theory too is interesting; and though there is a great deal of the latter without the former I suspect there has never been a genuine success that has not had a latent core of conviction. Discussion, suggestion, formulation, these things are fertilizing when they are frank and sincere. Mr. Besant has set an excellent example in saying what he thinks, for his part, about the way in which fiction should be written, as well as about the way in which it should be published; for his view of the "art," carried on into an appendix, covers that too. Other labourers in the same field will doubtless take up the argument, they will give it the light of their experience, and the effect will surely be to make our interest in the novel a little more what it had for some time threatened to fail to be—a serious, active, inquiring interest, under protection of which this delightful study may, in moments of confidence, venture to say a little more what it thinks of itself.

It must take itself seriously for the public to take it so. The old superstition about fiction being "wicked" has doubtless died out in England; but the spirit of it lingers in a certain oblique regard directed toward any story which does not more or less admit that it is only a joke. Even the most jocular novel feels in some degree the weight of the proscription that was formerly directed against literary levity: the jocularity does not always succeed in passing for orthodoxy. It is still expected, though perhaps people are ashamed to say it, that a production which is after all only a "make-believe" (for what else is a "story"?) shall be in some degree apologetic—shall renounce the pretension of attempting really to represent life. This, of course, any sensible, wide-awake story declines to do, for it quickly perceives that the tolerance granted to it on such a condition is only an attempt to stifle it disguised in the form of generosity. The old evangelical hostility to the novel, which was as explicit as it was narrow, and which regarded it as little less favourable to our immortal part than a stage-play, was in reality far less insulting. The only reason for the existence of a novel is that it does attempt to represent life. When it relinquishes this attempt, the same attempt that we see on the canvas of the painter, it will have arrived at a very strange pass. It is not expected of the picture that it will make itself humble in order to be forgiven; and the analogy between the art of the painter and the art of the novelist is, so far as I am able to see, complete. Their inspiration is the same, their process (allowing for the different quality of the vehicle) is the same, their success is the same. They may learn from each other, they may explain and sustain each other. Their cause is the same, and the honour of one is the honour of another. The Mahometans think a picture an unholy thing, but it is a long time since any Christian did, and it is therefore the more odd that in the Christian mind the traces (dissimulated though they may be) of a suspicion of the sister art should linger to this day. The only effectual way to lay it to rest is to emphasize the analogy to which I just alluded—to insist on the fact that as the picture is reality, so the novel is history. That is the only general description (which does it justice) that we may give of the novel. But history also is allowed to represent life; it is not, any more than painting, expected to apologize. The subject-matter of fiction is stored up likewise in documents and records, and if it will not give itself away, as they say in California, it must speak with assurance, with the tone of the historian. Certain accomplished novelists have a habit of giving themselves away which must often bring tears to the eyes of people who take their fiction seriously. I was lately struck, in reading over many pages of Anthony Trollope, with his want of discretion in this particular. In a digression, a parenthesis or an aside, he concedes to the reader that he and this trusting friend are only "making believe." He admits that the events he narrates have not really happened, and that he can give his narrative any turn the reader may like best. Such a betrayal of a sacred office seems to me, I confess, a terrible crime; it is what I mean by the attitude of apology, and it shocks me every whit as much in Trollope as it would have shocked me in Gibbon or Macaulay. It implies that the novelist is less occupied in looking for the truth (the truth, of course I mean, that he assumes, the premises that we must grant him, whatever they may be) than the historian, and in doing so it deprives him at a stroke of all his standing-room. To represent and illustrate the past, the actions of men, is the task of either writer, and the only difference that I can see is, in proportion as he succeeds, to the honour of the novelist, consisting as it does in his having more difficulty in collecting his evidence, which is so far from being purely literary. It seems to me to give him a great character, the fact that he has at once so much in common with the philosopher and the painter; this double analogy is a magnificent heritage.

It is of all this evidently that Mr. Besant is full when he insists upon the fact that fiction is one of the *fine* arts, deserving in its turn of all the honours and emoluments that have hitherto been reserved for the successful profession of music, poetry, painting, architecture. It is impossible to insist too much on so important a truth, and the place that Mr. Besant demands for the work of the novelist may be represented, a trifle less abstractly, by saying that he demands not only that it shall be reputed artistic, but that it shall be reputed very artistic indeed. It is excellent that he should have struck this note, for his doing so indicates that there was need of it, that his proposition may be to many people a novelty. One rubs one's eyes at the thought; but the rest of Mr. Besant's essay confirms the revelation. I suspect in truth that it would be possible to confirm it still further, and that one would not be far wrong in saying that in addition to the people to whom it has never occurred that a novel ought to be artistic, there are a great many others who, if this principle were urged upon them, would be filled with an indefinable mistrust. They would find it difficult to explain their repugnance, but it would operate strongly to put them on their guard. "Art," in our Protestant communities, where so many things have got so strangely twisted about, is supposed in certain circles to have some vaguely injurious effect upon those who make it an important consideration, who let it weigh in the balance. It is assumed to be opposed in some mysterious manner to morality, to amusement, to instruction. When it is embodied in the work of the painter (the sculptor is another affair!) you know what it is: it stands there before you, in the honesty of pink and green and a gilt frame; you can see the worst of it at a glance, and you can be on your guard. But when it is introduced into literature it becomes more insidious—there is danger of its hurting you before you know it. Literature should be either instructive or amusing, and there is in many minds an impression that these artistic preoccupations, the search for form, contribute to neither end, interfere indeed with both. They are too frivolous to be edifying, and too serious to be diverting; and they are moreover priggish and paradoxical and superfluous. That, I think, represents the manner in which the latent thought of many people who read novels as an exercise in skipping would explain itself if it were to become articulate. They would argue, of course, that a novel ought to be "good," but they would interpret this term in a fashion of their own, which indeed would vary considerably from one critic to another. One would say that being good means representing virtuous and aspiring characters, placed in prominent positions; another would say that it depends on a "happy ending," on a distribution at the last of prizes, pensions, husbands, wives, babies, millions, appended paragraphs, and cheerful remarks. Another still would say that it means being full of incident and movement, so that we shall wish to jump ahead, to see who was the mysterious stranger, and if the stolen will was ever found, and shall not be distracted from this pleasure by any tiresome analysis or "description." But they would all agree that the "artistic" idea would spoil some of their fun. One would hold it accountable for all the description, another would see it revealed in the absence of sympathy. Its hostility to a happy ending would be evident, and it might even in some cases render any ending at all impossible. The "ending" of a novel is, for many persons, like that of a good dinner, a course of dessert and ices, and the artist in fiction is regarded as a sort of meddlesome doctor who forbids agreeable aftertastes. It is therefore true that this conception of Mr. Besant's of the novel as a superior form encounters not only a negative but a positive indifference. It matters little that as a work of art it should really be as little or as much of its essence to supply happy endings, sympathetic characters, and an objective tone, as if it were a work of mechanics: the association of ideas, however incongruous, might easily be too much for it if an eloquent voice were not sometimes raised to call attention to the fact that it is at once as free and as serious a branch of literature as any other.

Certainly this might sometimes be doubted in presence of the enormous number of works of fiction that appeal to the credulity of our generation, for it might easily seem that there could be no great character in a commodity so quickly and easily produced. It must be admitted that good novels are much compromised by bad ones, and that the field at large suffers discredit from overcrowding. I think, however, that this injury is only superficial, and that the superabundance of written fiction proves nothing against the principle itself. It has been vulgarized, like all other kinds of literature, like everything else to-day, and it has proved more than some kinds accessible to vulgarization. But there is as much difference as there ever was between a good novel and a bad one: the bad is swept with all the daubed canvases and spoiled marble into some unvisited limbo, or infinite rubbish-yard beneath the back-windows of the world, and the good subsists and emits its light and stimulates our desire for perfection. As I shall take the liberty of making but a single criticism of Mr. Besant, whose tone is so full of the love of his art, I may as well have done with it at once. He seems to me to mistake in attempting to say so definitely beforehand what sort of an affair the good novel will be. To indicate the danger of such an error as that has been the purpose of these few pages; to suggest that certain traditions on the subject, applied *a priori,* have already had much to answer for, and that the good health of an art which undertakes so immediately to reproduce life must demand that it be perfectly free. It lives upon exercise, and the very meaning of exercise is freedom. The only obligation to which in advance we may hold a novel, without incurring the accusation of being arbitrary, is that it be interesting. That general responsibility rests upon it, but it is the only one I can think of. The ways in which it is at liberty to accomplish this result (of interesting us) strike me as innumerable, and such as can only suffer from being marked out or fenced in by prescription. They are as various as the temperament of man, and they are successful in proportion as they reveal a particular mind, different from others. A novel is in its broadest definition a personal, a direct impression of life: that, to begin with, constitutes its value, which is greater or less according to the intensity of the impression. But there will be no intensity at all, and therefore no value, unless there is freedom to feel and say. The tracing of a line to be followed, of a tone to be taken, of a form to be filled out, is a limitation of that freedom and a suppression of the very thing that we are most curious about. The form, it seems to me, is to be appreciated after the fact: then the author's choice has been made, his standard has been indicated; then we can follow lines and directions and compare tones and resemblances. Then in a word we can enjoy one of the most charming of pleasures, we can estimate quality, we can apply the test of execution. The execution belongs to the author alone; it is what is most personal to him, and we measure him by that. The advantage, the luxury, as well as the torment and responsibility of the novelist, is that there is no limit to what he may attempt as an executant—no limit to his possible experiments, efforts, discoveries, successes. Here it is especially that he works, step by step, like his brother of the brush, of whom we may always say that he has painted his picture in a manner best known to himself. His manner is his secret, not necessarily a jealous one. He cannot disclose it as a general thing if he would; he would be at a loss to teach it to others. I say this with a due recollection of having insisted on the community of method of the artist who paints a picture and the artist who writes a novel. The painter *is* able to teach the rudiments of his practice, and it is possible, from the study of good work (granted the aptitude), both to learn how to paint and to learn how to write. Yet it remains true, without injury to the *rapprochement,* that the literary artist would be obliged to say to his pupil much more than the other, "Ah, well, you must do it as you can!" It is a question of degree, a matter of delicacy. If there are exact sciences, there are also exact arts, and the grammar of painting is so much more definite that it makes the difference.

I ought to add, however, that if Mr. Besant says at the

beginning of his essay that the "laws of fiction may be laid down and taught with as much precision and exactness as the laws of harmony, perspective, and proportion," he mitigates what might appear to be an extravagance by applying his remark to "general" laws, and by expressing most of these rules in a manner with which it would certainly be unaccommodating to disagree. That the novelist must write from his experience, that his "characters must be real and such as might be met with in actual life"; that "a young lady brought up in a quiet country village should avoid descriptions of garrison life," and "a writer whose friends and personal experiences belong to the lower middle-class should carefully avoid introducing his characters into society"; that one should enter one's notes in a common-place book; that one's figures should be clear in outline; that making them clear by some trick of speech or of carriage is a bad method, and "describing them at length" is a worse one; that English Fiction should have a "conscious moral purpose"; that "it is almost impossible to estimate too highly the value of careful workmanship—that is, of style"; that "the most important point of all is the story," that "the story is everything": these are principles with most of which it is surely impossible not to sympathize. That remark about the lower middle-class writer and his knowing his place is perhaps rather chilling; but for the rest I should find it difficult to dissent from any one of these recommendations. At the same time, I should find it difficult positively to assent to them, with the exception, perhaps, of the injunction as to entering one's notes in a common-place book. They scarcely seem to me to have the quality that Mr. Besant attributes to the rules of the novelist—the "precision and exactness" of "the laws of harmony, perspective, and proportion." They are suggestive, they are even inspiring, but they are not exact, though they are doubtless as much so as the case admits of: which is a proof of that liberty of interpretation for which I just contended. For the value of these different injunctions—so beautiful and so vague—is wholly in the meaning one attaches to them. The characters, the situation, which strike one as real will be those that touch and interest one most, but the measure of reality is very difficult to fix. The reality of Don Quixote or of Mr. Micawber is a very delicate shade; it is a reality so coloured by the author's vision that, vivid as it may be, one would hesitate to propose it as a model: one would expose one's self to some very embarrassing questions on the part of a pupil. It goes without saying that you will not write a good novel unless you possess the sense of reality; but it will be difficult to give you a recipe for calling that sense into being. Humanity is immense, and reality has a myriad forms; the most one can affirm is that some of the flowers of fiction have the odour of it, and others have not; as for telling you in advance how your nosegay should be composed, that is another affair. It is equally excellent and inconclusive to say that one must write from experience; to our suppositious aspirant such a declaration might savour of mockery. What kind of experience is intended, and where does it begin and end? Experience is never limited, and it is never complete; it is an immense sensibility, a kind of huge spider-web of the finest silken threads suspended in the chamber of consciousness, and catching every air-borne particle in its tissue. It is the very atmosphere of the mind; and when the mind is imaginative—much more when it happens to be that of a man of genius—it takes to itself the faintest hints of life, it converts the very pulses of the air into revelations. The young lady living in a village has only to be a damsel upon whom nothing is lost to make it quite unfair (as it seems to me) to declare to her that she shall have nothing to say about the military. Greater miracles have been seen than that, imagination assisting, she should speak the truth about some of these gentlemen. I remember an English novelist, a woman of genius, telling me that she was much commended for the impression she had managed to give in one of her tales of the nature and way of life of the French Protestant youth. She had been asked where she learned so much about this recondite being, she had been congratulated on her peculiar opportunities. These opportunities consisted in her having once, in Paris, as she ascended a staircase, passed an open door where, in the household of a *pasteur*, some of the young Protestants were seated at table round a finished meal. The glimpse made a picture; it lasted only a moment, but that moment was experience. She had got her direct personal impression, and she turned out her type. She knew what youth was, and what Protestantism; she also had the advantage of having seen what it was to be French, so that she converted these ideas into a concrete image and produced a reality. Above all, however, she was blessed with the faculty which when you give it an inch takes an ell, and which for the artist is a much greater source of strength than any accident of residence or of place in the social scale. The power to guess the unseen from the seen, to trace the implication of things, to judge the whole piece by the pattern, the condition of feeling life in general so completely that you are well on your way to knowing any particular corner of it—this cluster of gifts may almost be said to constitute experience, and they occur in country and in town, and in the most differing stages of education. If experience consists of impressions, it may be said that impressions *are* experience, just as (have we not seen it?) they are the very air we breathe. Therefore, if I should certainly say to a novice, "Write from experience and experience only," I should feel that this was rather a tantalizing monition if I were not careful immediately to add, "Try to be one of the people on whom nothing is lost!"

I am far from intending by this to minimize the importance of exactness—of truth of detail. One can speak best from one's own taste, and I may therefore venture to say that the air of reality (solidity of specification) seems to me to be the supreme virtue of a novel—the merit on which all its other merits (including that conscious moral purpose of which Mr. Besant speaks) helplessly and submissively depend. If it be not there they are all as nothing, and if these be there, they owe their effect to the success with which the author has produced the illusion of life. The cultivation of this success, the study of this exquisite process, form, to my taste, the beginning and the end of the art of the novelist. They are his inspiration, his despair, his reward, his torment, his delight. It is here in very truth that he competes with life; it is here that he competes with his brother the painter in *his* attempt to render the look of things, the look that conveys their meaning, to catch the colour, the relief, the expression, the surface, the substance of the human spectacle. It is in regard to this that Mr. Besant is well inspired when he bids him take notes. He cannot possibly take *too* many, he cannot possibly take enough. All life solicits him, and to "render" the simplest surface, to produce the most momentary illusion, is a very complicated business. His case would be easier, and the rule would be more exact, if Mr. Besant had been able to tell him what notes to take. But this, I fear, he can never learn in any manual; it is the business of his life. He has to take a great many in order to select a few, he has to work them up as he can, and even the guides and philosophers who might have most to say to him must leave him alone when it comes to the application of precepts, as we leave the painter in communion with his palette. That his characters "must be clear in outline," as Mr. Besant says—he feels that down to his boots; but how he shall make them so is a secret between his good angel and himself. It would be absurdly simple if he could be taught that a great deal of "description" would make them so, or that on the contrary the absence of description and the cultivation of dialogue, or the absence of dialogue and the multiplication of "incident," would rescue him from his difficulties. Nothing, for instance, is more possible than that he be of a turn of mind for which this odd, literal opposition of description and dialogue, incident and description, has little meaning and light. People often talk of these things as if they had a kind of internecine distinctness, instead of melting into each other at every breath, and being intimately associated parts of one general effort of expression. I cannot imagine composition existing in a series of blocks, nor conceive, in any novel worth discussing at all, of a passage of description that is not in its intention narrative, a passage of dialogue that is not in its intention descriptive, a touch of truth of any sort that does not partake of the nature of incident, or an incident that derives its interest from any other source than the general and only source of the success of a work of art—that of being illustrative. A novel is a living thing, all one and continuous, like any other organism, and in proportion as it lives will it be found, I think, that in each of the parts there is something of each of the other parts. The critic who over the close texture of a finished work shall pretend to trace a geography of items will mark some frontiers as artificial, I fear, as any that have been known to history. There is an old-fashioned distinction between the novel of character and the novel of incident which must have cost many a smile to the intending fabulist who was keen about his work. It appears to me as little to the point as the equally celebrated distinction between the novel and the romance—to answer as little to any reality. There are bad novels and good novels, as there are bad pictures and good pictures; but that is the only distinction in which I see any meaning, and I can as little imagine speaking of a novel of character as I can imagine speaking of a picture of character. When one says picture one says of character, when one says novel one says of incident, and the terms may be transposed at will. What is character but the determination of incident? What is incident but the illustration of character? What is either a picture or a novel that is *not* of character? What else do we seek in it and find in it? It is an incident for a woman to stand up with her hand resting on a table and look out at you in a certain way; or if it be not an incident I think it will be hard to say what it is. At the same time it is an expression of character. If you say you don't see it (character in *that—allons donc!*), this is exactly what the artist who has reasons of his own for thinking he *does* see it undertakes to show you. When a young man makes up his mind that he has not faith enough after all to enter the church as he intended, that is an incident, though you may not hurry to the end of the chapter to see whether perhaps he doesn't change once more. I do not say that these are extraordinary or startling incidents. I do not pretend to estimate the degree of interest proceeding from them, for this will depend upon the skill of the painter. It sounds almost puerile to say that some incidents are intrinsically much more important than others, and I need not take this precaution after having professed my sympathy for the major ones in remarking that the only classification of the novel that I can understand is into that which has life and that which has it not.

The novel and the romance, the novel of incident and that of character—these clumsy separations appear to me to have been made by critics and readers for their own convenience, and to help them out of some of their occasional queer predicaments, but to have little reality or interest for the producer, from whose point of view it is of course that we are attempting to consider the art of fiction. The case is the same with another shadowy category which Mr. Besant apparently is disposed to set up—that of the "modern English novel"; unless indeed it be that in this matter he has fallen into an accidental confusion of standpoints. It is not quite clear whether he intends the remarks in which he alludes to it to be didactic or historical. It is as difficult to suppose a person intending to write a modern English as to suppose him writing an ancient English novel: that is a label which begs the question. One writes the novel, one paints the picture, of one's language and of one's time, and calling it modern English will not, alas! make the difficult task any easier. No more, unfortunately, will calling this or that work of one's fellow-artist a romance—unless it be, of course, simply for the pleasantness of the thing, as for instance when Hawthorne gave this heading to his story of

Blithedale. The French, who have brought the theory of fiction to remarkable completeness, have but one name for the novel, and have not attempted smaller things in it, that I can see, for that. I can think of no obligation to which the "romancer" would not be held equally with the novelist; the standard of execution is equally high for each. Of course it is of execution that we are talking—that being the only point of a novel that is open to contention. This is perhaps too often lost sight of, only to produce interminable confusions and cross-purposes. We must grant the artist his subject, his idea, his *donnée:* our criticism is applied only to what he makes of it. Naturally I do not mean that we are bound to like it or find it interesting: in case we do not our course is perfectly simple—to let it alone. We may believe that of a certain idea even the most sincere novelist can make nothing at all, and the event may perfectly justify our belief; but the failure will have been a failure to execute, and it is in the execution that the fatal weakness is recorded. If we pretend to respect the artist at all, we must allow him his freedom of choice, in the face, in particular cases, of innumerable presumptions that the choice will not fructify. Art derives a considerable part of its beneficial exercise from flying in the face of presumptions, and some of the most interesting experiments of which it is capable are hidden in the bosom of common things. Gustave Flaubert has written a story about the devotion of a servant-girl to a parrot, and the production, highly-finished as it is, cannot on the whole be called a success. We are perfectly free to find it flat, but I think it might have been interesting; and I, for my part, am extremely glad he should have written it; it is a contribution to our knowledge of what can be done—or what cannot. Ivan Turgénieff has written a tale about a deaf and dumb serf and a lap-dog, and the thing is touching, loving, a little masterpiece. He struck the note of life where Gustave Flaubert missed it—he flew in the face of a presumption and achieved a victory.

Nothing, of course, will ever take the place of the good

old fashion of "liking" a work of art or not liking it: the most improved criticism will not abolish that primitive, that ultimate test. I mention this to guard myself from the accusation of intimating that the idea, the subject, of a novel or a picture, does not matter. It matters, to my sense, in the highest degree, and if I might put up a prayer it would be that artists should select none but the richest. Some, as I have already hastened to admit, are much more remunerative than others, and it would be a world happily arranged in which persons intending to treat them should be exempt from confusions and mistakes. This fortunate condition will arrive only, I fear, on the same day that critics become purged from error. Meanwhile, I repeat, we do not judge the artist with fairness unless we say to him,

"Oh, I grant you your starting-point, because if I did not I should seem to prescribe to you, and heaven forbid I should take that responsibility. If I pretend to tell you what you must not take, you will call upon me to tell you then what you must take; in which case I shall be prettily caught. Moreover, it isn't till I have accepted your data that I can begin to measure you. I have the standard, the pitch; I have no right to tamper with your flute and then criticize your music. Of course I may not care for your idea at all; I may think it silly, or stale, or unclean; in which case I wash my hands of you altogether. I may content myself with believing that you will not have succeeded in being interesting, but I shall, of course, not attempt to demonstrate it, and you will be as indifferent to me as I am to you. I needn't remind you that there are all sorts of tastes: who can know it better? Some people, for excellent reasons, don't like to read about carpenters; others, for reasons even better, don't like to read about courtesans. Many object to Americans. Others (I believe they are mainly editors and publishers) won't look at Italians. Some readers don't like quiet subjects; others don't like bustling ones. Some enjoy a complete illusion, others the consciousness of large concessions. They choose their novels accordingly, and if they don't care about your idea they won't, *a fortiori,* care about your treatment."

So that it comes back very quickly, as I have said, to the liking: in spite of M. Zola, who reasons less powerfully than he represents, and who will not reconcile himself to this absoluteness of taste, thinking that there are certain things that people ought to like, and that they can be made to like. I am quite at a loss to imagine anything (at any rate in this matter of fiction) that people *ought* to like or to dislike. Selection will be sure to take care of itself, for it has a constant motive behind it. That motive is simply experience. As people feel life, so they will feel the art that is most closely related to it. This closeness of relation is what we should never forget in talking of the effort of the novel. Many people speak of it as a factitious, artificial form, a product of ingenuity, the business of which is to alter and arrange the things that surround us, to translate them into conventional, traditional moulds. This, however, is a view of the matter which carries us but a very short way, condemns the art to an eternal repetition of a few familiar *clichés,* cuts short its development, and leads us straight up to a dead wall. Catching the very note and trick, the strange irregular rhythm of life, that is the attempt whose strenuous force keeps Fiction upon her feet. In proportion as in what she offers us we see life *without* rearrangement do we feel that we are touching the truth; in proportion as we see it *with* rearrangement do we feel that we are being put off with a substitute, a compromise and convention. It is not uncommon to hear an extraordinary assurance of remark in regard to this matter of rearranging, which is often spoken of as if it were the last word of art. Mr. Besant seems to me in danger of falling into the great error with his rather unguarded talk about "selection." Art is essentially selection, but it is a selection whose main care is to be typical, to be inclusive. For many people art means rose-coloured window-panes, and selection means picking a bouquet for Mrs. Grundy. They will tell you glibly that artistic considerations have nothing to do with the disagreeable, with the ugly; they will rattle off shallow commonplaces about the province of art and the limits of art till you are moved to some wonder in return as to the province and the limits of ignorance. It appears to me that no one can ever have made a seriously artistic attempt without becoming conscious of an immense increase—a kind of revelation—of freedom. One perceives in that case—by the light of a heavenly ray—that the province of art is all life, all feeling, all observation, all vision. As Mr. Besant so justly intimates, it is all experience. That is a sufficient answer to those who maintain that it must not touch the sad things of life, who stick into its divine unconscious bosom little prohibitory inscriptions on the end of sticks, such as we see in public gardens—"It is forbidden to walk on the grass; it is forbidden to touch the flowers; it is not allowed to introduce dogs or to remain after dark; it is requested to keep to the right." The young aspirant in the line of fiction whom we continue to imagine will do nothing without taste, for in that case his freedom would be of little use to him; but the first advantage of his taste will be to reveal to him the absurdity of the little sticks and tickets. If he have taste, I must add, of course he will have ingenuity, and my disrespectful reference to that quality just now was not meant to imply that it is useless in fiction. But it is only a secondary aid; the first is a capacity for receiving straight impressions.

Mr. Besant has some remarks on the question of "the story" which I shall not attempt to criticize, though they seem to me to contain a singular ambiguity, because I do not think I understand them. I cannot see what is meant by talking as if there were a part of a novel which is the story and part of it which for mystical reasons is not—unless indeed the distinction be made in a sense in which it is difficult to suppose that any one should attempt to convey anything. "The story," if it represents anything, represents the subject, the idea, the *donnée* of the novel; and there is surely no "school"—Mr. Besant speaks of a school—which urges that a novel should be all treatment and no subject. There must assuredly be something to treat; every school is intimately conscious of that. This sense of the story being the idea, the starting-point, of the novel, is the only one that I see in which it can be spoken of as something different from its organic whole; and since in proportion as the work is successful the idea permeates and penetrates it, informs and animates it, so that every word and every punctuation-point contribute directly to the expression, in that proportion do we lose our sense of the story being a blade which may be drawn more or less out of its sheath. The story and the novel, the idea and the form, are the needle and thread, and I never heard of a guild of tailors who recommended the use of the thread without the needle, or the needle without the thread. Mr. Besant is not the only critic who may be observed to have spoken as if there were certain things in life which constitute stories, and certain others which do not. I find the same odd implication in an entertaining article in the *Pall Mall Gazette,* devoted, as it happens, to Mr. Besant's lecture. "The story is the thing!" says this graceful writer, as if with a tone of opposition to some other idea. I should think it was, as every painter who, as the time for "sending in" his picture looms in the distance, finds himself still in quest of a subject—as every belated artist not fixed about his theme will heartily agree. There are some subjects which speak to us and others which do not, but he would be a clever man who should undertake to give a rule—an *index expurgatorius*—by which the story and the no-story should be known apart. It is impossible (to me at least) to imagine any such rule which shall not be altogether arbitrary. The writer in the *Pall Mall* opposes the delightful (as I suppose) novel of *Margot la Balafrée* to certain tales in which "Bostonian nymphs" appear to have "rejected English dukes for psychological reasons." I am not acquainted with the romance just designated, and can scarcely forgive the *Pall Mall* critic for not mentioning the name of the author, but the title appears to refer to a lady who may have received a scar in some heroic adventure. I am inconsolable at not being acquainted with this episode, but am utterly at a loss to see why it is a story when the rejection (or acceptance) of a duke is not, and why a reason, psychological or other, is not a subject when a cicatrix is. They are all particles of the multitudinous life with which the novel deals, and surely no dogma which pretends to make it lawful to touch the one and unlawful to touch the other will stand for a moment on its feet. It is the special picture that must stand or fall, according as it seem to possess truth or to lack it. Mr. Besant does not, to my sense, light up the subject by intimating that a story must, under penalty of not being a story, consist of "adventures." Why of adventures more than of green spectacles? He mentions a category of impossible things, and among them he places "fiction without adventure." Why without adventure, more than without matrimony, or celibacy, or parturition, or cholera, or hydropathy, or Jansenism? This seems to me to bring the novel back to the hapless little *rôle* of being an artificial, ingenious thing—bring it down from its large, free character of an immense and exquisite correspondence with life. And what *is* adventure, when it comes to that, and by what sign is the listening pupil to recognize it? It is an adventure—an immense one—for me to write this little article; and for a Bostonian nymph to reject an English duke is an adventure only less stirring, I should say, than for an English duke to be rejected by a Bostonian nymph. I see dramas within dramas in that, and innumerable points of view. A psychological reason is, to my imagination, an object adorably pictorial; to catch the tint of its complexion—I feel as if that idea might inspire one to Titianesque efforts. There are few things more exciting to me, in short, than a psychological reason, and yet, I protest, the novel seems to me the most magnificent form of art. I have just been reading, at the same time, the delightful story of *Treasure Island,* by Mr. Robert Louis Stevenson and, in a manner less consecutive, the last tale from M. Edmond de Goncourt, which is entitled *Chérie.* One of these works treats of murders, mysteries, islands of dreadful renown, hair-breadth escapes, miraculous coincidences and buried doubloons. The other treats of a little French girl who lived in a fine house in Paris, and died of wounded sensibility because no one would marry her. I call *Treasure Island* delightful, because it appears to me to have succeeded wonderfully in what it attempts; and I venture to bestow no epithet upon *Chérie,* which strikes me as having failed deplorably in what it attempts—that is in tracing the development of the moral consciousness of a child. But one of these productions strikes me as exactly as much of a novel as the other, and as having a "story" quite as much. The moral consciousness of a child is as much a part of life as the islands of the Spanish Main, and the one sort of geography seems to me to have those "surprises" of which Mr. Besant speaks quite as much as the other. For myself (since it comes back in the last resort, as I say, to the preference of the individual), the picture of the child's experience has the advantage that I can at successive steps (an immense luxury, near to the "sensual pleasure" of which Mr. Besant's critic in the *Pall Mall* speaks) say Yes or No, as it may be, to what the artist puts before me. I have been a child in fact, but I have been on a quest for a buried treasure only in supposition, and it is a simple accident that with M. de Goncourt I should have for the most part to say No. With George Eliot, when she painted that country with a far other intelligence, I always said Yes.

The most interesting part of Mr. Besant's lecture is unfortunately the briefest passage—his very cursory allusion to the "conscious moral purpose" of the novel. Here again it is not very clear whether he be recording a fact or laying down a principle; it is a great pity that in the latter case he should not have developed his idea. This branch of the subject is of immense importance, and Mr. Besant's few words point to considerations of the wildest reach, not to be lightly disposed of. He will have treated the art of fiction but superficially who is not prepared to go every inch of the way that these considerations will carry him. It is for this reason that at the beginning of these remarks I was careful to notify the reader that my reflections on so large a theme have no pretension to be exhaustive. Like Mr. Besant, I have left the question of the morality of the novel till the last, and at the last I find I have used up my space. It is a question surrounded with difficulties, as witness the very first that meets us, in the form of a definite question, on the threshold. Vagueness, in such a discussion, is fatal, and what is the meaning of your morality and your conscious moral purpose? Will you not define your terms and explain how (a novel being a picture) a picture can be either moral or immoral? You wish to paint a moral picture or carve a moral statue: will you not tell us how you would set about it? We are discussing the Art of Fiction; questions of art are questions (in the widest sense) of execution; questions of morality are quite another affair, and will you not let us see how it is that you find it so easy to mix them up? These things are so clear to Mr. Besant that he has deduced from them a law which he sees embodied in English Fiction, and which is "a truly admirable thing and a great cause for congratulation." It is a great cause for congratulation indeed when such thorny problems become as smooth as silk. I may add that in so far as Mr. Besant perceives that in point of fact English Fiction has addressed itself preponderantly to these delicate questions he will appear to many people to have made a vain discovery. They will have been positively struck, on the contrary, with the moral timidity of the usual English novelist; with his (or with her) aversion to face the difficulties with which on every side the treatment of reality bristles. He is apt to be extremely shy (whereas the picture that Mr. Besant draws is a picture of boldness), and the sign of his work, for the most part, is a cautious silence on certain subjects. In the English novel (by which of course

I mean the American as well), more than in any other, there is a traditional difference between that which people know and that which they agree to admit that they know, that which they see and that which they speak of, that which they feel to be a part of life and that which they allow to enter into literature. There is the great difference, in short, between what they talk of in conversation and what they talk of in print. The essence of moral energy is to survey the whole field, and I should directly reverse Mr. Besant's remark and say not that the English novel has a purpose, but that it has a diffidence. To what degree a purpose in a work of art is a source of corruption I shall not attempt to inquire; the one that seems to me least dangerous is the purpose of making a perfect work. As for our novel, I may say lastly on this score that as we find it in England to-day it strikes me as addressed in a large degree to "young people," and that this in itself constitutes a presumption that it will be rather shy. There are certain things which it is generally agreed not to discuss, not even to mention, before young people. That is very well, but the absence of discussion is not a symptom of the moral passion. The purpose of the English novel—"a truly admirable thing, and a great cause for congratulation"—strikes me therefore as rather negative.

There is one point at which the moral sense and the artistic sense lie very near together; that is in the light of the very obvious truth that the deepest quality of a work of art will always be the quality of the mind of the producer. In proportion as that intelligence is fine will the novel, the picture, the statue partake of the substance of beauty and truth. To be constituted of such elements is, to my vision, to have purpose enough. No good novel will ever proceed from a superficial mind; that seems to me an axiom which, for the artist in fiction, will cover all needful moral ground: if the youthful aspirant take it to heart it will illuminate for him many of the mysteries of "purpose." There are many other useful things that might be said to him, but I have come to the end of my article, and can only touch them as I pass.

The critic in the *Pall Mall Gazette,* whom I have already quoted, draws attention to the danger, in speaking of the art of fiction, of generalizing. The danger that he has in mind is rather, I imagine, that of particularizing, for there are some comprehensive remarks which, in addition to those embodied in Mr. Besant's suggestive lecture, might without fear of misleading him be addressed to the ingenuous student. I should remind him first of the magnificence of the form that is open to him, which offers to sight so few restrictions and such innumerable opportunities. The other arts, in comparison, appear confined and hampered; the various conditions under which they are exercised are so rigid and definite. But the only condition that I can think of attaching to the composition of the novel is, as I have already said, that it be sincere. This freedom is a splendid privilege, and the first lesson of the young novelist is to learn to be worthy of it.

"Enjoy it as it deserves [I should say to him]; take possession of it, explore it to its utmost extent, publish it, rejoice in it. All life belongs to you, and do not listen either to those who would shut you up into corners of it and tell you that it is only here and there that art inhabits, or to those who would persuade you that this heavenly messenger wings her way outside of life altogether, breathing a superfine air, and turning away her head from the truth of things. There is no impression of life, no manner of seeing it and feeling it, to which the plan of the novelist may not offer a place; you have only to remember that talents so dissimilar as those of Alexandre Dumas and Jane Austen, Charles Dickens and Gustave Flaubert have worked in this field with equal glory. Do not think too much about optimism and pessimism; try and catch the colour of life itself. In France to-day we see a prodigious effort (that of Émile Zola, to whose solid and serious work no explorer of the capacity of the novel can allude without respect), we see an extraordinary effort vitiated by a spirit of pessimism on a narrow basis. M. Zola is magnificent, but he strikes an English reader as ignorant; he has an air of working in the dark; if he had as much light as energy, his results would be of the highest value. As for the aberrations of a shallow optimism, the ground (of English fiction especially) is strewn with their brittle particles as with broken glass. If you must indulge in conclusions, let them have the taste of a wide knowledge. Remember that your first duty is to be as complete as possible—to make as perfect a work. Be generous and delicate and pursue the prize."

EDITOR'S NOTE

"The Art of Fiction" was published by Henry James in *Longman's* in September 1884 as a reply to a lecture delivered by Walter Besant, a minor Victorian novelist and historian, before the Royal Institution in London. Besant spoke on "Fiction as a Fine Art" and tried to set down a series of laws for novel-writing that Henry James found too rigid and too didactic. Besant's lecture, which inspired James, has long been forgotten; but the Jamesian essay remains as one of the finest statements ever made on the art of the novel. The debate did not end with this essay. Robert Louis Stevenson, a friend of James's, chimed in with "A Humble Remonstrance," a charming rejoinder in which he essentially agreed with James. He took issue, however, with the realistic school of writers, arguing that fiction must create an illusion of realism, since it cannot be life or imitate life, but is rather a representation of it.

